THE TROLL GARDEN
AND OTHER
SHORT STORIES

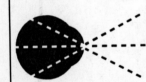

This Large Print Book carries the
Seal of Approval of N.A.V.H.

THE TROLL GARDEN
AND OTHER
SHORT STORIES

WILLA CATHER

KENNEBEC LARGE PRINT

A part of Gale, Cengage Learning

GALE
CENGAGE Learning

Detroit • New York • San Francisco • New Haven, Conn • Waterville, Maine • London

GALE
CENGAGE Learning™

Kennebec Large Print, a part of Gale, Cengage Learning.
Kennebec Large Print® Perennial Favorites Collection.
The text of this Large Print edition is unabridged.
Other aspects of the book may vary from the original edition.
Set in 16 pt. Plantin.

LIBRARY OF CONGRESS CATALOGING-IN-PUBLICATION DATA

Cather, Willa, 1873–1947.
  The troll garden, and other short stories / by Willa Cather.
    p. cm. — (Kennebec Large Print perennial favorites collection)
  ISBN-13: 978-1-4104-3389-3 (softcover)
  ISBN-10: 1-4104-3389-7 (softcover)
  1. Large type books. I. Title.
PS3505.A87T75 2011
813'.52—dc22   2010043184

Originally published in 1905 and is now in Public Domain in the United States.

Printed in the United States of America
  1 2 3 4 5   14 13 12 11 10

ED361

CONTENTS

THE TROLL GARDEN 7

Flavia and Her Artists 13
The Sculptor's Funeral 50
The Garden Lodge 70
"A Death in the Desert" 87
The Marriage of Phaedra 117
A Wagner Matinée 142
Paul's Case 154

OTHER SHORT STORIES 183

Coming, Aphrodite!. 185
The Diamond Mine 238
A Gold Slipper 286
Scandal 309
Alexander's Bridge 333
Peter 426
On the Divide 431
Eric Hermannson's Soul 450
The Sentimentality of
    William Tavener 482

5

The Namesake 490
The Echanted Bluff. 506
The Joy of Nelly Deane 519
The Bohemian Girl. 540
Consequences 599
The Bookkeeper's Wife 627
Ardessa 644
Her Boss 668

The Troll Garden

A FAIRY PALACE, WITH A FAIRY GARDEN; . . . . .
INSIDE THE TROLLS DWELL, ... WORKING AT
THEIR MAGIC FORGES, MAKING AND MAKING ALWAYS
THINGS RARE AND STRANGE.

CHARLES KINGSLEY

"We must not look at Goblin men,
We must not buy their fruits;
Who knows upon what soil they fed
Their hungry thirsty roots?"

GOBLIN MARKET.

To
Isabelle McClung

FLAVIA AND HER ARTISTS

As the train neared Tarrytown, Imogen Willard began to wonder why she had consented to be one of Flavia's house party at all. She had not felt enthusiastic about it since leaving the city, and was experiencing a prolonged ebb of purpose, a current of chilling indecision, under which she vainly sought for the motive which had induced her to accept Flavia's invitation.

Perhaps it was a vague curiosity to see Flavia's husband, who had been the magician of her childhood and the hero of innumerable Arabian fairy tales. Perhaps it was a desire to see M. Roux, whom Flavia had announced as the especial attraction of the occasion. Perhaps it was a wish to study that remarkable woman in her own setting.

Imogen admitted a mild curiosity concerning Flavia. She was in the habit of taking people rather seriously, but somehow found it impossible to take Flavia so, because of the very vehemence and insistence with which Flavia demanded it. Submerged in her studies, Imogen had, of late years, seen very little of Flavia; but Flavia, in her hurried visits to New York, between her excursions from studio to studio — her luncheons with this lady who had to play at a matinée, and her dinners with that singer who had an evening concert —

had seen enough of her friend's handsome daughter to conceive for her an inclination of such violence and assurance as only Flavia could afford. The fact that Imogen had shown rather marked capacity in certain esoteric lines of scholarship, and had decided to specialize in a well-sounding branch of philology at the Ecole des Chartes, had fairly placed her in that category of "interesting people" whom Flavia considered her natural affinities, and lawful prey.

When Imogen stepped upon the station platform she was immediately appropriated by her hostess, whose commanding figure and assurance of attire she had recognized from a distance. She was hurried into a high tilbury and Flavia, taking the driver's cushion beside her, gathered up the reins with an experienced hand.

"My dear girl," she remarked, as she turned the horses up the street, "I was afraid the train might be late. M. Roux insisted upon coming up by boat and did not arrive until after seven."

"To think of M. Roux's being in this part of the world at all, and subject to the vicissitudes of river boats! Why in the world did he come over?" queried Imogen with lively interest. "He is the sort of man who must dissolve and become a shadow outside of Paris."

"Oh, we have a houseful of the most interesting people," said Flavia, professionally. "We have actually managed to get Ivan Schemetzkin. He was ill in California at the close of his concert tour, you know, and he is recuperating with us, after his wearing journey from the coast. Then there is Jules Martel, the painter; Signor Donati, the tenor; Professor Schotte, who has dug up Assyria, you know; Restzhoff, the Russian chemist; Alcée Buisson, the philologist; Frank Wellington, the novelist; and Will Maidenwood, the editor of *Woman*. Then there is my second cousin, Jemima Broadwood, who made such a hit in Pinero's comedy last winter, and Frau Lichtenfeld. *Have* you read her?"

Imogen confessed her utter ignorance of Frau Lichtenfeld, and Flavia went on.

"Well, she is a most remarkable person; one of those advanced German women, a militant iconoclast, and this drive will not be long enough to permit of my telling you her history. Such a story! Her novels were the talk of all Germany when I was there last, and several of them have been suppressed — an honor in Germany, I understand. 'At Whose Door' has been translated. I am so unfortunate as not to read German."

"I'm all excitement at the prospect of meeting Miss Broadwood," said Imogen. "I've seen her in nearly everything she does. Her stage personality is delightful. She always reminds me of a nice, clean, pink-and-white boy who has just had his cold bath, and come down all aglow for a run before breakfast."

"Yes, but isn't it unfortunate that she will limit herself to those minor comedy parts that are so little appreciated in this country? One ought to be satisfied with nothing less than the best, ought one?" The peculiar, breathy tone in which Flavia always uttered that word "best," the most worn in her vocabulary, always jarred on Imogen and always made her obdurate.

"I don't at all agree with you," she said reservedly. "I thought every one admitted that the most remarkable thing about Miss Broadwood is her admirable sense of fitness, which is rare enough in her profession."

Flavia could not endure being contradicted; she always seemed to regard it in the light of a defeat, and usually colored unbecomingly. Now she changed the subject.

"Look, my dear," she cried, "there is Frau Lichtenfeld now, coming to meet us. Doesn't she look as if she had just escaped out of Valhalla? She is actually over six feet."

Imogen saw a woman of immense stature, in a very short skirt and a broad, flapping sun hat, striding down the hillside at a long, swinging gait. The refugee from Valhalla approached, panting. Her heavy, Teutonic features were scarlet from the rigor of her exercise, and her hair, under her flapping sun hat, was tightly befrizzled about her brow. She fixed her sharp little eyes upon Imogen and extended both her hands.

"So this is the little friend?" she cried, in a rolling baritone.

Imogen was quite as tall as her hostess; but everything, she reflected, is comparative. After the introduction Flavia apologized.

"I wish I could ask you to drive up with us, Frau Lichtenfeld."

"Ah, no!" cried the giantess, drooping her head in humorous caricature of a time-honored pose of the heroines of sentimental romances. "It has never been my fate to be fitted into corners. I have never known the sweet privileges of the tiny."

Laughing, Flavia started the ponies, and the colossal woman, standing in the middle of the dusty road, took off her wide hat and waved them a farewell which, in scope of gesture, recalled the salute of a plumed cavalier.

When they arrived at the house, Imogen looked

16

about her with keen curiosity, for this was veritably the work of Flavia's hands, the materialization of hopes long deferred. They passed directly into a large, square hall with a gallery on three sides, studio fashion. This opened at one end into a Dutch breakfast room, beyond which was the large dining room. At the other end of the hall was the music room. There was a smoking room, which one entered through the library behind the staircase. On the second floor there was the same general arrangement: a square hall, and, opening from it, the guest chambers, or, as Miss Broadwood termed them, the "cages."

When Imogen went to her room, the guests had begun to return from their various afternoon excursions. Boys were gliding through the halls with ice water, covered trays, and flowers, colliding with maids and valets who carried shoes and other articles of wearing apparel. Yet, all this was done in response to inaudible bells, on felt soles, and in hushed voices, so that there was very little confusion about it.

Flavia had at last built her house and hewn out her seven pillars; there could be no doubt, now, that the asylum for talent, the sanatorium of the arts, so long projected, was an accomplished fact. Her ambition had long ago outgrown the dimensions of her house on Prairie Avenue; besides, she had bitterly complained that in Chicago traditions were against her. Her project had been delayed by Arthur's doggedly standing out for the Michigan woods, but Flavia knew well enough that certain of the *aves rares* — "the best" — could not be lured so far away from the seaport, so she declared herself for the historic Hudson and knew no retreat. The establishing of a New York office had at length overthrown Arthur's last valid objection to quitting the lake country for three months of the year; and Arthur could be wearied into anything, as those who knew him knew.

Flavia's house was the mirror of her exultation; it was a temple to the gods of Victory, a sort of triumphal arch. In her earlier days she had swallowed experiences that would have unmanned one of less torrential enthusiasm or blind pertinacity. But, of late years, her determination had told; she saw less and less of those mysterious persons with mysterious obstacles in their path and mysterious grievances against the world, who had once frequented her house on Prairie Avenue. In the stead of this multitude of the unarrived, she had now the few, the select, "the best." Of all that band of indigent retainers who had once fed at her board like the suitors in the halls of Penelope, only Alcée Buisson still retained his right of entrée. He alone had remembered that ambition hath a knapsack at his back, wherein he puts alms to oblivion, and he alone had been considerate enough to do what Flavia had expected of him, and give his name a current value in the world. Then, as Miss Broadwood put it, "he was her first real one," — and Flavia, like Mohammed, could remember her first believer.

"The House of Song," as Miss Broadwood had called it, was the outcome of Flavia's more exalted strategies. A woman who made less a point of sympathizing with their delicate organisms, might have sought to plunge these phosphorescent pieces into the tepid bath of domestic life; but Flavia's discernment was deeper. This must be a refuge where the shrinking soul, the sensitive brain, should be unconstrained; where the caprice

18

of fancy should outweigh the civil code, if necessary. She considered that this much Arthur owed her; for she, in her turn, had made concessions. Flavia had, indeed, quite an equipment of epigrams to the effect that our century creates the iron genii which evolve its fairy tales: but the fact that her husband's name was annually painted upon some ten thousand threshing machines in reality contributed very little to her happiness.

Arthur Hamilton was born and had spent his boyhood in the West Indies, and physically he had never lost the brand of the tropics. His father, after inventing the machine which bore his name, had returned to the States to patent and manufacture it. After leaving college, Arthur had spent five years ranching in the West and traveling abroad. Upon his father's death he had returned to Chicago and, to the astonishment of all his friends, had taken up the business — without any demonstration of enthusiasm, but with quiet perseverance, marked ability, and amazing industry. Why or how a self-sufficient, rather ascetic man of thirty, indifferent in manner, wholly negative in all other personal relations, should have doggedly wooed and finally married Flavia Malcolm was a problem that had vexed older heads than Imogen's.

While Imogen was dressing she heard a knock at her door, and a young woman entered whom she at once recognized as Jemima Broadwood — "Jimmy" Broadwood she was called by people in her own profession. While there was something unmistakably professional in her frank *savoir-faire,* "Jimmy's" was one of those faces to which the rouge never seems to stick. Her eyes were keen and gray as a windy April sky, and so far from

19

having been seared by calcium lights, you might have fancied they had never looked on anything less bucolic than growing fields and country fairs. She wore her thick, brown hair short and parted at the side; and, rather than hinting at freakishness, this seemed admirably in keeping with her fresh, boyish countenance. She extended to Imogen a large, well-shaped hand which it was a pleasure to clasp.

"Ah! You are Miss Willard, and I see I need not introduce myself. Flavia said you were kind enough to express a wish to meet me, and I preferred to meet you alone. Do you mind if I smoke?"

"Why, certainly not," said Imogen, somewhat disconcerted and looking hurriedly about for matches.

"There, be calm, I'm always prepared," said Miss Broadwood, checking Imogen's flurry with a soothing gesture, and producing an oddly fashioned silver match-case from some mysterious recess in her dinner gown. She sat down in a deep chair, crossed her patent-leather Oxfords, and lit her cigarette. "This matchbox," she went on meditatively, "once belonged to a Prussian officer. He shot himself in his bathtub, and I bought it at the sale of his effects."

Imogen had not yet found any suitable reply to make to this rather irrelevant confidence, when Miss Broadwood turned to her cordially: "I'm awfully glad you've come, Miss Willard, though I've not quite decided why you did it. I wanted very much to meet you. Flavia gave me your thesis to read."

"Why, how funny!" ejaculated Imogen.

"On the contrary," remarked Miss Broadwood.

20

"I thought it decidedly lacked humor."

"I meant," stammered Imogen, beginning to feel very much like Alice in Wonderland, "I meant that I thought it rather strange Mrs. Hamilton should fancy you would be interested."

Miss Broadwood laughed heartily. "Now, don't let my rudeness frighten you. Really, I found it very interesting, and no end impressive. You see, most people in my profession are good for absolutely nothing else, and, therefore, they have a deep and abiding conviction that in some other line they might have shone. Strange to say, scholarship is the object of our envious and particular admiration. Anything in type impresses us greatly; that's why so many of us marry authors or newspapermen and lead miserable lives." Miss Broadwood saw that she had rather disconcerted Imogen, and blithely tacked in another direction. "You see," she went on, tossing aside her half-consumed cigarette, "some years ago Flavia would not have deemed me worthy to open the pages of your thesis — nor to be one of her house party of the chosen, for that matter. I've Pinero to thank for both pleasures. It all depends on the class of business I'm playing whether I'm in favor or not. Flavia is my second cousin, you know, so I can say whatever disagreeable things I choose with perfect good grace. I'm quite desperate for someone to laugh with, so I'm going to fasten myself upon you — for, of course, one can't expect any of these gypsy-dago people to see anything funny. I don't intend you shall lose the humor of the situation. What do you think of Flavia's infirmary for the arts, anyway?"

"Well, it's rather too soon for me to have any opinion at all," said Imogen, as she again turned to her dressing. "So far, you are the only one of the artists I've met."

"One of them?" echoed Miss Broadwood. "One of the *artists?* My offense may be rank, my dear, but I really don't deserve that. Come, now, whatever badges of my tribe I may bear upon me, just let me divest you of any notion that I take myself seriously."

Imogen turned from the mirror in blank astonishment and sat down on the arm of a chair, facing her visitor. "I can't fathom you at all, Miss Broadwood," she said frankly. "Why shouldn't you take yourself seriously? What's the use of beating about the bush? Surely you know that you are one of the few players on this side of the water who have at all the spirit of natural or ingenuous comedy?"

"Thank you, my dear. Now we are quite even about the thesis, aren't we? Oh, did you mean it? Well, you *are* a clever girl. But you see it doesn't do to permit oneself to look at it in that light. If we do, we always go to pieces and waste our substance astarring as the unhappy daughter of the Capulets. But there, I hear Flavia coming to take you down; and just remember I'm not one of them — the artists, I mean."

Flavia conducted Imogen and Miss Broadwood downstairs. As they reached the lower hall they heard voices from the music room, and dim figures were lurking in the shadows under the gallery, but their hostess led straight to the smoking room. The June evening was chilly, and a fire had been lighted in the fireplace. Through the deepening dusk, the firelight flickered upon the pipes and curious weapons on the wall and threw an orange glow over the Turkish hangings. One side of the smoking room was entirely of glass, separating it from the conservatory, which was flooded with white light from the electric bulbs. There was about the darkened room some suggestion of certain chambers in the Arabian Nights, opening on a court of palms. Perhaps it was partially this memory-evoking suggestion that caused Imogen to start so violently when she saw dimly, in a blur of shadow, the figure of a man, who sat smoking in a low, deep chair before the fire. He was long, and thin, and brown. His long, nerveless hands drooped from the arms of his chair. A brown mustache shaded his mouth, and his eyes were sleepy and apathetic. When Imogen entered he rose indolently and gave her his hand, his manner barely courteous.

"I am glad you arrived promptly, Miss Willard," he said with an indifferent drawl. "Flavia was afraid you might be late. You had a pleasant ride up, I hope?"

"Oh, very, thank you, Mr. Hamilton," she replied, feeling that he did not particularly care whether she replied at all.

Flavia explained that she had not yet had time to dress for dinner, as she had been attending to Mr. Will Maidenwood, who had become faint after hurting his finger in an obdurate window, and immediately excused herself. As she left, Hamilton turned to Miss Broadwood with a rather spiritless smile.

"Well, Jimmy," he remarked, "I brought up a piano box full of fireworks for the boys. How do you suppose we'll manage to keep them until the Fourth?"

"We can't, unless we steel ourselves to deny

23

there are any on the premises," said Miss Broadwood, seating herself on a low stool by Hamilton's chair and leaning back against the mantel. "Have you seen Helen, and has she told you the tragedy of the tooth?"

"She met me at the station, with her tooth wrapped up in tissue paper. I had tea with her an hour ago. Better sit down, Miss Willard;" he rose and pushed a chair toward Imogen, who was standing peering into the conservatory. "We are scheduled to dine at seven, but they seldom get around before eight."

By this time Imogen had made out that here the plural pronoun, third person, always referred to the artists. As Hamilton's manner did not spur one to cordial intercourse, and as his attention seemed directed to Miss Broadwood, insofar as it could be said to be directed to anyone, she sat down facing the conservatory and watched him, unable to decide in how far he was identical with the man who had first met Flavia Malcolm in her mother's house, twelve years ago. Did he at all remember having known her as a little girl, and why did his indifference hurt her so, after all these years? Had some remnant of her childish affection for him gone on living, somewhere down in the sealed caves of her consciousness, and had she really expected to find it possible to be fond of him again? Suddenly she saw a light in the man's sleepy eyes, an unmistakable expression of interest and pleasure that fairly startled her. She turned quickly in the direction of his glance, and saw Flavia, just entering, dressed for dinner and lit by the effulgence of her most radiant manner. Most people considered Flavia handsome, and there was no gainsaying that she carried her five-and-

24

thirty years splendidly. Her figure had never grown matronly, and her face was of the sort that does not show wear. Its blond tints were as fresh and enduring as enamel — and quite as hard. Its usual expression was one of tense, often strained, animation, which compressed her lips nervously. A perfect scream of animation, Miss Broadwood had called it, created and maintained by sheer, indomitable force of will. Flavia's appearance on any scene whatever made a ripple, caused a certain agitation and recognition, and, among impressionable people, a certain uneasiness. For all her sparkling assurance of manner, Flavia was certainly always ill at ease and, even more certainly, anxious. She seemed not convinced of the established order of material things, seemed always trying to conceal her feeling that walls might crumble, chasms open, or the fabric of her life fly to the winds in irretrievable entanglement. At least this was the impression Imogen got from that note in Flavia which was so manifestly false.

Hamilton's keen, quick, satisfied glance at his wife had recalled to Imogen all her inventory of speculations about them. She looked at him with compassionate surprise. As a child she had never permitted herself to believe that Hamilton cared at all for the woman who had taken him away from her; and since she had begun to think about them again, it had never occurred to her that anyone could become attached to Flavia in that deeply personal and exclusive sense. It seemed quite as irrational as trying to possess oneself of Broadway at noon.

When they went out to dinner Imogen realized the completeness of Flavia's triumph. They were people of one name, mostly, like kings; people whose names stirred the imagination like a romance or a melody. With the notable exception of M. Roux, Imogen had seen most of them before, either in concert halls or lecture rooms; but they looked noticeably older and dimmer than she remembered them.

Opposite her sat Schemetzkin, the Russian pianist, a short, corpulent man, with an apoplectic face and purplish skin, his thick, iron-gray hair tossed back from his forehead. Next to the German giantess sat the Italian tenor — the tiniest of men — pale, with soft, light hair, much in disorder, very red lips, and fingers yellowed by cigarettes. Frau Lichtenfeld shone in a gown of emerald green, fitting so closely as to enhance her natural floridness. However, to do the good lady justice, let her attire be never so modest, it gave an effect of barbaric splendor. At her left sat Herr Schotte, the Assyriologist, whose features were effectually concealed by the convergence of his hair and beard, and whose glasses were continually falling into his plate. This gentleman had removed more tons of earth in the course of his explorations than had any of his confreres, and his vigorous attack upon his food seemed to suggest the strenuous nature of his accustomed toil. His eyes were small and deeply set, and his forehead bulged fiercely above his eyes in a bony ridge. His heavy brows completed the leonine suggestion of his face. Even to Imogen, who knew something of his work and greatly respected it, he was entirely too reminiscent of the Stone Age to be altogether an agreeable dinner companion. He seemed, indeed, to have absorbed something of the savagery of those early types of life which he continually studied.

Frank Wellington, the young Kansas man who had been two years out of Harvard and had published three historical novels, sat next to Mr. Will Maidenwood, who was still pale from his recent sufferings and carried his hand bandaged. They took little part in the general conversation, but, like the lion and the unicorn, were always at it, discussing, every time they met, whether there were or were not passages in Mr. Wellington's works which should be eliminated, out of consideration for the Young Person. Wellington had fallen into the hands of a great American syndicate which most effectually befriended struggling authors whose struggles were in the right direction, and which had guaranteed to make him famous before he was thirty. Feeling the security of his position he stoutly defended those passages which jarred upon the sensitive nerves of the young editor of *Woman*. Maidenwood, in the smoothest of voices, urged the necessity of the author's recognizing certain restrictions at the outset, and Miss Broadwood, who joined the argument quite without invitation or encouragement, seconded him with pointed and malicious remarks which caused the young editor manifest discomfort. Restzhoff, the chemist, demanded the attention of the entire company for his exposition of his devices for manufacturing ice cream from vegetable oils and for administering drugs in bonbons.

Flavia, always noticeably restless at dinner, was somewhat apathetic toward the advocate of peptonized chocolate and was plainly concerned about the sudden departure of M. Roux, who had announced that it would be necessary for him to leave tomorrow. M. Emile Roux, who sat at Flavia's right, was a man in middle life and quite bald, clearly without personal vanity, though his publishers preferred to circulate only those of his portraits taken in his ambrosial youth. Imogen was considerably shocked at his unlikeness to the slender, black-stocked Rolla he had looked at twenty. He had declined into the florid, settled heaviness of indifference and approaching age. There was, however, a certain look of durability and solidity about him; the look of a man who has earned the right to be fat and bald, and even silent at dinner if he chooses.

Throughout the discussion between Wellington and Will Maidenwood, though they invited his participation, he remained silent, betraying no sign either of interest or contempt. Since his arrival he had directed most of his conversation to Hamilton, who had never read one of his twelve great novels. This perplexed and troubled Flavia. On the night of his arrival Jules Martel had enthusiastically declared, "There are schools and schools, manners and manners; but Roux is Roux, and Paris sets its watches by his clock." Flavia had already repeated this remark to Imogen. It haunted her, and each time she quoted it she was impressed anew.

Flavia shifted the conversation uneasily, evidently exasperated and excited by her repeated failures to draw the novelist out. "Monsieur Roux," she began abruptly, with her most animated smile, "I remember so well a statement I read some years ago in your 'Mes Etudes des Femmes' to the effect that you had never met a really intellectual woman. May I ask, without being impertinent, whether that assertion still represents your experience?"

28

"I meant, madam," said the novelist conservatively, "intellectual in a sense very special, as we say of men in whom the purely intellectual functions seem almost independent."

"And you still think a woman so constituted a mythical personage?" persisted Flavia, nodding her head encouragingly.

"*Une Meduse*, madam, who, if she were discovered, would transmute us all into stone," said the novelist, bowing gravely. "If she existed at all," he added deliberately, "it was my business to find her, and she has cost me many a vain pilgrimage. Like Rudel of Tripoli, I have crossed seas and penetrated deserts to seek her out. I have, indeed, encountered women of learning whose industry I have been compelled to respect; many who have possessed beauty and charm and perplexing cleverness; a few with remarkable information and a sort of fatal facility."

"And Mrs. Browning, George Eliot, and your own Mme. Dudevant?" queried Flavia with that fervid enthusiasm with which she could, on occasion, utter things simply incomprehensible for their banality — at her feats of this sort Miss Broadwood was wont to sit breathless with admiration.

"Madam, while the intellect was undeniably present in the performances of those women, it was only the stick of the rocket. Although this woman has eluded me I have studied her conditions and perturbances as astronomers conjecture the orbits of planets they have never seen. If she exists, she is probably neither an artist nor a woman with a mission, but an obscure personage, with imperative intellectual needs, who absorbs rather than produces."

Flavia, still nodding nervously, fixed a strained glance of interrogation upon M. Roux. "Then you think she would be a woman whose first necessity would be to know, whose instincts would be satisfied only with the best, who could draw from others; appreciative, merely?"

The novelist lifted his dull eyes to his interlocutress with an untranslatable smile and a slight inclination of his shoulders. "Exactly so; you are really remarkable, madam," he added, in a tone of cold astonishment.

After dinner the guests took their coffee in the music room, where Schemetzkin sat down at the piano to drum ragtime, and give his celebrated imitation of the boardingschool girl's execution of Chopin. He flatly refused to play anything more serious, and would practice only in the morning, when he had the music room to himself. Hamilton and M. Roux repaired to the smoking room to discuss the necessity of extending the tax on manufactured articles in France — one of those conversations which particularly exasperated Flavia.

After Schemetzkin had grimaced and tortured the keyboard with malicious vulgarities for half an hour, Signor Donati, to put an end to his torture, consented to sing, and Flavia and Imogen went to fetch Arthur to play his accompaniments. Hamilton rose with an annoyed look and placed his cigarette on the mantel. "Why yes, Flavia, I'll accompany him, provided he sings something with a melody, Italian arias or ballads, and provided the recital is not interminable."

"You will join us, M. Roux?"

"Thank you, but I have some letters to write," replied the novelist, bowing.

As Flavia had remarked to Imogen, "Arthur really played accompaniments remarkably well." To hear him recalled vividly the days of her childhood, when he always used to spend his business vacations at her mother's home in Maine. He had possessed for her that almost hypnotic influence which young men sometimes exert upon little girls. It was a sort of phantom love affair, subjective and fanciful, a precocity of instinct, like that tender and maternal concern which some little girls feel for their dolls. Yet this childish infatuation is capable of all the depressions and exaltations of love itself, it has its bitter jealousies, cruel disappointments, its exacting caprices.

Summer after summer she had awaited his coming and wept at his departure, indifferent to the gayer young men who had called her their sweetheart and laughed at everything she said. Although Hamilton never said so, she had been always quite sure that he was fond of her. When he pulled her up the river to hunt for fairy knolls shut about by low, hanging willows, he was often silent for an hour at a time, yet she never felt he was bored or was neglecting her. He would lie in the sand smoking, his eyes half-closed, watching her play, and she was always conscious that she was entertaining him. Sometimes he would take a copy of "Alice in Wonderland" in his pocket, and no one could read it as he could, laughing at her with his dark eyes, when anything amused him. No one else could laugh so, with just their eyes, and without moving a muscle of their face. Though he usually smiled at passages that seemed not at all funny to the child, she always laughed gleefully, because he was so seldom moved to mirth that any such demonstration delighted her and she took the credit of it entirely to herself. Her own inclination had been for serious stories, with sad endings, like the Little Mermaid, which he had once told her in an unguarded moment when she had a cold, and was put to bed early on her birthday night and cried because she could not have her party. But he highly disapproved of this preference, and had called it a morbid taste, and always shook his finger at her when she asked for the story. When she had been particularly good, or particularly neglected by other people, then he would sometimes melt and tell her the story, and never laugh at her if she enjoyed the "sad ending" even to tears. When Flavia had taken him away and he came no more, she wept inconsolably for the space of two weeks, and refused to learn her lessons. Then she found the story of the Little Mermaid herself, and forgot him.

Imogen had discovered at dinner that he could still smile at one secretly, out of his eyes, and that he had the old manner of outwardly seeming bored, but letting you know that he was not. She was intensely curious about his exact state of feeling toward his wife, and more curious still to catch a sense of his final adjustment to the conditions of life in general. This, she could not help feeling, she might get again — if she could have him alone for an hour, in some place where there was a little river and a sandy cove bordered by drooping willows, and a blue sky seen through white sycamore boughs.

That evening, before retiring, Flavia entered her husband's room, where he sat in his smoking jacket, in one of his favorite low chairs.

"I suppose it's a grave responsibility to bring an ardent, serious young thing like Imogen here among all these fascinating personages," she remarked reflectively. "But, after all, one can never tell. These grave, silent girls have their own charm, even for facile people."

"Oh, so that is your plan?" queried her husband dryly. "I was wondering why you got her up here. She doesn't seem to mix well with the faciles. At least, so it struck me."

Flavia paid no heed to this jeering remark, but repeated, "No, after all, it may not be a bad thing."

"Then do consign her to that shaken reed, the tenor," said her husband yawning. "I remember she used to have a taste for the pathetic."

"And then," remarked Flavia coquettishly, "after all, I owe her mother a return in kind. She was not afraid to trifle with destiny."

But Hamilton was asleep in his chair.

Next morning Imogen found only Miss Broad-wood in the breakfast room.

"Good morning, my dear girl, whatever are you doing up so early? They never breakfast before eleven. Most of them take their coffee in their room. Take this place by me."

Miss Broadwood looked particularly fresh and encouraging in her blue serge walking skirt, her open jacket displaying an expanse of stiff, white shirt bosom, dotted with some almost imperceptible figure, and a dark blue-and-white necktie, neatly knotted under her wide, rolling collar. She wore a white rosebud in the lapel of her coat, and decidedly she seemed more than ever like a nice, clean boy on his holiday. Imogen was just hoping that they would breakfast alone when Miss Broad-wood exclaimed, "Ah, there comes Arthur with the children. That's the reward of early rising in this house; you never get to see the youngsters at any other time."

Hamilton entered, followed by two dark, handsome little boys. The girl, who was very tiny, blonde like her mother, and exceedingly frail, he carried in his arms. The boys came up and said good morning with an ease and cheerfulness uncommon, even in well-bred children, but the little girl hid her face on her father's shoulder.

"She's a shy little lady," he explained as he put her gently down in her chair. "I'm afraid she's like her father; she can't seem to get used to meeting people. And you, Miss Willard, did you dream of the White Rabbit or the Little Mermaid?"

"Oh, I dreamed of them all! All the personages of that buried civilization," cried Imogen, delighted that his estranged manner of the night before had entirely vanished and feeling that, somehow, the old confidential relations had been restored during the night.

"Come, William," said Miss Broadwood, turning to the younger of the two boys, "and what did you dream about?"

"We dreamed," said William gravely — he was the more assertive of the two and always spoke for both — "we dreamed that there were fireworks hidden in the basement of the carriage house; lots and lots of fireworks."

His elder brother looked up at him with apprehensive astonishment, while Miss Broadwood hastily put her napkin to her lips and Hamilton dropped his eyes. "If little boys dream things, they are so apt not to come true," he reflected sadly. This shook even the redoubtable William, and he glanced nervously at his brother. "But do things vanish just because they have been dreamed?" he

34

objected.

"Generally that is the very best reason for their vanishing," said Arthur gravely.

"But, Father, people can't help what they dream," remonstrated Edward gently.

"Oh, come! You're making these children talk like a Maeterlinck dialogue," laughed Miss Broadwood.

Flavia presently entered, a book in her hand, and bade them all good morning. "Come, little people, which story shall it be this morning?" she asked winningly. Greatly excited, the children followed her into the garden. "She does then, sometimes," murmured Imogen as they left the breakfast room.

"Oh, yes, to be sure," said Miss Broadwood cheerfully. "She reads a story to them every morning in the most picturesque part of the garden. The mother of the Gracchi, you know. She does so long, she says, for the time when they will be intellectual companions for her. What do you say to a walk over the hills?"

As they left the house they met Frau Lichtenfeld and the bushy Herr Schotte — the professor cut an astonishing figure in golf stockings — returning from a walk and engaged in an animated conversation on the tendencies of German fiction.

"Aren't they the most attractive little children," exclaimed Imogen as they wound down the road toward the river.

"Yes, and you must not fail to tell Flavia that you think so. She will look at you in a sort of startled way and say, 'Yes, aren't they?' and maybe she will go off and hunt them up and have tea with them, to fully appreciate them. She is awfully afraid of missing anything good, is Flavia. The way those youngsters manage to conceal their guilty presence in the House of Song is a wonder."

"But don't any of the artist-folk fancy children?" asked Imogen.

"Yes, they just fancy them and no more. The chemist remarked the other day that children are like certain salts which need not be actualized because the formulae are quite sufficient for practical purposes. I don't see how even Flavia can endure to have that man about."

"I have always been rather curious to know what Arthur thinks of it all," remarked Imogen cautiously.

"Thinks of it!" ejaculated Miss Broadwood. "Why, my dear, what would any man think of having his house turned into an hotel, habited by freaks who discharge his servants, borrow his money, and insult his neighbors? This place is shunned like a lazaretto!"

"Well, then, why does he — why does he —" persisted Imogen.

"Bah!" interrupted Miss Broadwood impatiently, "why did he in the first place? That's the question."

"Marry her, you mean?" said Imogen coloring.

"Exactly so," said Miss Broadwood sharply, as she snapped the lid of her matchbox.

"I suppose that is a question rather beyond us, and certainly one which we cannot discuss," said Imogen. "But his toleration on this one point puzzles me, quite apart from other complications."

"Toleration? Why this point, as you call it, simply is Flavia. Who could conceive of her without it? I don't know where it's all going to end, I'm sure, and I'm equally sure that, if it were not for Arthur, I shouldn't care," declared Miss Broadwood,

36

drawing her shoulders together.

"But will it end at all, now?"

"Such an absurd state of things can't go on indefinitely. A man isn't going to see his wife make a guy of herself forever, is he? Chaos has already begun in the servants' quarters. There are six different languages spoken there now. You see, it's all on an entirely false basis. Flavia hasn't the slightest notion of what these people are really like, their good and their bad alike escape her. They, on the other hand, can't imagine what she is driving at. Now, Arthur is worse off than either faction; he is not in the fairy story in that he sees these people exactly as they are, *but* he is utterly unable to see Flavia as they see her. There you have the situation. Why can't he see her as we do? My dear, that has kept me awake o' nights. This man who has thought so much and lived so much, who is naturally a critic, really takes Flavia at very nearly her own estimate. But now I am entering upon a wilderness. From a brief acquaintance with her you can know nothing of the icy fastnesses of Flavia's self-esteem. It's like St. Peter's; you can't realize its magnitude at once. You have to grow into a sense of it by living under its shadow. It has perplexed even Emile Roux, that merciless dissector of egoism. She has puzzled him the more because he saw at a glance what some of them do not perceive at once, and what will be mercifully concealed from Arthur until the trump sounds; namely, that all Flavia's artists have done or ever will do means exactly as much to her as a symphony means to an oyster; that there is no bridge by which the significance of any work of art could be conveyed to her."

"Then, in the name of goodness, why does she

bother?" gasped Imogen. "She is pretty, wealthy, well-established; why should she bother?"

"That's what M. Roux has kept asking himself. I can't pretend to analyze it. She reads papers on the Literary Landmarks of Paris, the Loves of the Poets, and that sort of thing, to clubs out in Chicago. To Flavia it is more necessary to be called clever than to breathe. I would give a good deal to know that glum Frenchman's diagnosis. He has been watching her out of those fishy eyes of his as a biologist watches a hemisphereless frog."

For several days after M. Roux's departure Flavia gave an embarrassing share of her attention to Imogen. Embarrassing, because Imogen had the feeling of being energetically and futilely explored, she knew not for what. She felt herself under the globe of an air pump, expected to yield up something. When she confined the conversation to matters of general interest Flavia conveyed to her with some pique that her one endeavor in life had been to fit herself to converse with her friends upon those things which vitally interested them. "One has no right to accept their best from people unless one gives, isn't it so? I want to be able to give — !" she declared vaguely. Yet whenever Imogen strove to pay her tithes and plunged bravely into her plans for study next winter, Flavia grew absent-minded and interrupted her by amazing generalizations or by such embarrassing questions as, "And these grim studies really have charm for you; you are quite buried in them; they make other things seem light and ephemeral?"

"I rather feel as though I had got in here under false pretenses," Imogen confided to Miss Broadwood. "I'm sure I don't know what it is that she wants of me."

"Ah," chuckled Jemima, "you are not equal to these heart to heart talks with Flavia. You utterly fail to communicate to her the atmosphere of that untroubled joy in which you dwell. You must remember that she gets no feeling out of things herself, and she demands that you impart yours to her by some process of psychic transmission. I once met a blind girl, blind from birth, who could discuss the peculiarities of the Barbizon school with just Flavia's glibness and enthusiasm. Ordinarily Flavia knows how to get what she wants from people, and her memory is wonderful. One evening I heard her giving Frau Lichtenfeld some random impressions about Hedda Gabler which she extracted from me five years ago; giving them with an impassioned conviction of which I was never guilty. But I have known other people who could appropriate your stories and opinions; Flavia is infinitely more subtle than that; she can soak up the very thrash and drift of your daydreams, and take the very thrills off your back, as it were."

After some days of unsuccessful effort, Flavia withdrew herself, and Imogen found Hamilton ready to catch her when she was tossed afield. He seemed only to have been awaiting this crisis, and at once their old intimacy reestablished itself as a thing inevitable and beautifully prepared for. She convinced herself that she had not been mistaken in him, despite all the doubts that had come up in later years, and this renewal of faith set more than one question thumping in her brain. "How did he, how can he?" she kept repeating with a tinge of her childish resentment, "what right had he to waste anything so fine?"

39

■ ■ ■ ■

When Imogen and Arthur were returning from a walk before luncheon one morning about a week after M. Roux's departure, they noticed an absorbed group before one of the hall windows. Herr Schotte and Restzhoff sat on the window seat with a newspaper between them, while Wellington, Schemetzkin, and Will Maidenwood looked over their shoulders. They seemed intensely interested, Herr Schotte occasionally pounding his knees with his fists in ebullitions of barbaric glee. When Imogen entered the hall, however, the men were all sauntering toward the breakfast room and the paper was lying innocently on the divan. During luncheon the personnel of that window group were unwontedly animated and agreeable all save Schemetzkin, whose stare was blanker than ever, as though Roux's mantle of insulting indifference had fallen upon him, in addition to his own oblivious self-absorption. Will Maidenwood seemed embarrassed and annoyed; the chemist employed himself with making polite speeches to Hamilton. Flavia did not come down to lunch — and there was a malicious gleam under Herr Schotte's eyebrows. Frank Wellington announced nervously that an imperative letter from his protecting syndicate summoned him to the city.

After luncheon the men went to the golf links, and Imogen, at the first opportunity, possessed herself of the newspaper which had been left on the divan. One of the first things that caught her eye was an article headed "Roux on Tuft Hunters; The Advanced American Woman as He Sees Her;

Aggressive, Superficial, and Insincere." The entire interview was nothing more nor less than a satiric characterization of Flavia, aquiver with irritation and vitriolic malice. No one could mistake it; it was done with all his deftness of portraiture. Imogen had not finished the article when she heard a footstep, and clutching the paper she started precipitately toward the stairway as Arthur entered. He put out his hand, looking critically at her distressed face.

"Wait a moment, Miss Willard," he said peremptorily, "I want to see whether we can find what it was that so interested our friends this morning. Give me the paper, please."

Imogen grew quite white as he opened the journal. She reached forward and crumpled it with her hands. "Please don't, please don't," she pleaded; "it's something I don't want you to see. Oh, why will you? it's just something low and despicable that you can't notice."

Arthur had gently loosed her hands, and he pointed her to a chair. He lit a cigar and read the article through without comment. When he had finished it he walked to the fireplace, struck a match, and tossed the flaming journal between the brass andirons.

"You are right," he remarked as he came back, dusting his hands with his handkerchief. "It's quite impossible to comment. There are extremes of blackguardism for which we have no name. The only thing necessary is to see that Flavia gets no wind of this. This seems to be my cue to act; poor girl."

Imogen looked at him tearfully; she could only murmur, "Oh, why did you read it!"

Hamilton laughed spiritlessly. "Come, don't you

41

worry about it. You always took other people's troubles too seriously. When you were little and all the world was gay and everybody happy, you must needs get the Little Mermaid's troubles to grieve over. Come with me into the music room. You remember the musical setting I once made you for the Lay of the Jabberwock? I was trying it over the other night, long after you were in bed, and I decided it was quite as fine as the Erl-King music. How I wish I could give you some of the cake that Alice ate and make you a little girl again. Then, when you had got through the glass door into the little garden, you could call to me, perhaps, and tell me all the fine things that were going on there. What a pity it is that you ever grew up!" he added, laughing; and Imogen, too, was thinking just that.

At dinner that evening, Flavia, with fatal persistence, insisted upon turning the conversation to M. Roux. She had been reading one of his novels and had remembered anew that Paris set its watches by his clock. Imogen surmised that she was tortured by a feeling that she had not sufficiently appreciated him while she had had him. When she first mentioned his name she was answered only by the pall of silence that fell over the company. Then everyone began to talk at once, as though to correct a false position. They spoke of him with a fervid, defiant admiration, with the sort of hot praise that covers a double purpose. Imogen fancied she could see that they felt a kind of relief at what the man had done, even those who despised him for doing it; that they felt a spiteful hate against Flavia, as though she had tricked them, and a certain contempt for themselves that they had been beguiled. She was reminded of the fury of the crowd in the fairy tale, when once the child had called out that the king was in his night clothes. Surely these people knew no more about Flavia than they had known before, but the mere fact that the thing had been said altered the situation. Flavia, meanwhile, sat chattering amiably, pathetically unconscious of her nakedness.

Hamilton lounged, fingering the stem of his wineglass, gazing down the table at one face after another and studying the various degrees of self-consciousness they exhibited. Imogen's eyes followed his, fearfully. When a lull came in the spasmodic flow of conversation, Arthur, leaning back in his chair, remarked deliberately, "As for M. Roux, his very profession places him in that class of men whom society has never been able to accept unconditionally because it has never been able to assume that they have any ordered notion of taste. He and his ilk remain, with the mountebanks and snake charmers, people indispensable to our civilization, but wholly unreclaimed by it; people whom we receive, but whose invitations we do not accept."

Fortunately for Flavia, this mine was not exploded until just before the coffee was brought. Her laughter was pitiful to hear; it echoed through the silent room as in a vault, while she made some tremulously light remark about her husband's drollery, grim as a jest from the dying. No one responded and she sat nodding her head like a mechanical toy and smiling her white, set smile through her teeth, until Alcée Buisson and Frau Lichtenfeld came to her support.

After dinner the guests retired immediately to their rooms, and Imogen went upstairs on tiptoe, feeling the echo of breakage and the dust of crumbling in the air. She wondered whether Flavia's habitual note of uneasiness were not, in a manner, prophetic, and a sort of unconscious premonition, after all. She sat down to write a letter, but she found herself so nervous, her head so hot and her hands so cold, that she soon abandoned the effort, just as she was about to seek Miss Broadwood, Flavia entered and embraced her hysterically.

"My dearest girl," she began, "was there ever such an unfortunate and incomprehensible speech made before? Of course it is scarcely necessary to explain to you poor Arthur's lack of tact, and that he meant nothing. But they! Can they be expected to understand? He will feel wretchedly about it when he realizes what he has done, but in the meantime? And M. Roux, of all men! When we were so fortunate as to get him, and he made himself so unreservedly agreeable, and I fancied that, in his way, Arthur quite admired him. My dear, you have no idea what that speech has done. Schemetzkin and Herr Schotte have already sent me word that they must leave us tomorrow. Such a thing from a host!" Flavia paused, choked by tears of vexation and despair.

Imogen was thoroughly disconcerted; this was the first time she had ever seen Flavia betray any personal emotion which was indubitably genuine. She replied with what consolation she could. "Need they take it personally at all? It was a mere observation upon a class of people —"

"Which he knows nothing whatever about, and with whom he has no sympathy," interrupted Flavia. "Ah, my dear, you could not be *expected* to understand. You can't realize, knowing Arthur as

44

you do, his entire lack of any aesthetic sense whatever. He is absolutely *nil,* stone deaf and stark blind, on that side. He doesn't mean to be brutal, it is just the brutality of utter ignorance. They always feel it — they are so sensitive to unsympathetic influences, you know; they know it the moment they come into the house. I have spent my life apologizing for him and struggling to conceal it; but in spite of me, he wounds them; his very attitude, even in silence, offends them. Heavens! Do I not know? Is it not perpetually and forever wounding me? But there has never been anything so dreadful as this — never! If I could conceive of any possible motive, even!"

"But, surely, Mrs. Hamilton, it was, after all, a mere expression of opinion, such as we are any of us likely to venture upon any subject whatever. It was neither more personal nor more extravagant than many of M. Roux's remarks."

"But, Imogen, certainly M. Roux has the right. It is a part of his art, and that is altogether another matter. Oh, this is not the only instance!" continued Flavia passionately, "I've always had that narrow, bigoted prejudice to contend with. It has always held me back. But this — !"

"I think you mistake his attitude," replied Imogen, feeling a flush that made her ears tingle. "That is, I fancy he is more appreciative than he seems. A man can't be very demonstrative about those things — not if he is a real man. I should not think you would care much about saving the feelings of people who are too narrow to admit of any other point of view than their own." She stopped, finding herself in the impossible position of attempting to explain Hamilton to his wife; a task which, if once begun, would necessitate an

45

entire course of enlightenment which she doubted Flavia's ability to receive, and which she could offer only with very poor grace.

"That's just where it stings most" — here Flavia began pacing the floor — "it is just because they have all shown such tolerance and have treated Arthur with such unfailing consideration that I can find no reasonable pretext for his rancor. How can he fail to see the value of such friendships on the children's account, if for nothing else! What an advantage for them to grow up among such associations! Even though he cares nothing about these things himself he might realize that. Is there nothing I could say by way of explanation? To them, I mean? If someone were to explain to them how unfortunately limited he is in these things —"

"I'm afraid I cannot advise you," said Imogen decidedly, "but that, at least, seems to me impossible."

Flavia took her hand and glanced at her affectionately, nodding nervously. "Of course, dear girl, I can't ask you to be quite frank with me. Poor child, you are trembling and your hands are icy. Poor Arthur! But you must not judge him by this altogether; think how much he misses in life. What a cruel shock you've had. I'll send you some sherry. Good night, my dear."

When Flavia shut the door Imogen burst into a fit of nervous weeping.

Next morning she awoke after a troubled and restless night. At eight o'clock Miss Broadwood entered in a red and white striped bathrobe.

"Up, up, and see the great doom's image!" she cried, her eyes sparkling with excitement. "The hall is full of trunks, they are packing. What bolt

46

has fallen? It's you, *ma cherie,* you've brought Ulysses home again and the slaughter has begun!" she blew a cloud of smoke triumphantly from her lips and threw herself into a chair beside the bed.

Imogen, rising on her elbow, plunged excitedly into the story of the Roux interview, which Miss Broadwood heard with the keenest interest, frequently interrupting her with exclamations of delight. When Imogen reached the dramatic scene which terminated in the destruction of the newspaper, Miss Broadwood rose and took a turn about the room, violently switching the tasselled cords of her bathrobe.

"Stop a moment," she cried, "you mean to tell me that he had such a heaven-sent means to bring her to her senses and didn't use it — that he held such a weapon and threw it away?"

"Use it?" cried Imogen unsteadily. "Of course he didn't! He bared his back to the tormentor, signed himself over to punishment in that speech he made at dinner, which everyone understands but Flavia. She was here for an hour last night and disregarded every limit of taste in her maledictions."

"My dear!" cried Miss Broadwood, catching her hand in inordinate delight at the situation, "do you see what he has done? There'll be no end to it. Why he has sacrificed himself to spare the very vanity that devours him, put rancors in the vessels of his peace, and his eternal jewel given to the common enemy of man, to make them kings, the seed of Banquo kings! He is magnificent!"

"Isn't he always that?" cried Imogen hotly. "He's like a pillar of sanity and law in this house of shams and swollen vanities, where people stalk about with a sort of madhouse dignity, each one

47

fancying himself a king or a pope. If you could have heard that woman talk of him! Why, she thinks him stupid, bigoted, blinded by middle-class prejudices. She talked about his having no aesthetic sense and insisted that her artists had always shown him tolerance. I don't know why it should get on my nerves so, I'm sure, but her stupidity and assurance are enough to drive one to the brink of collapse."

"Yes, as opposed to his singular fineness, they are calculated to do just that," said Miss Broad-wood gravely, wisely ignoring Imogen's tears. "But what has been is nothing to what will be. Just wait until Flavia's black swans have flown! You ought not to try to stick it out; that would only make it harder for everyone. Suppose you let me telephone your mother to wire you to come home by the evening train?"

"Anything, rather than have her come at me like that again. It puts me in a perfectly impossible position, and he *is* so fine!"

"Of course it does," said Miss Broadwood sympathetically, "and there is no good to be got from facing it. I will stay because such things interest me, and Frau Lichtenfeld will stay because she has no money to get away, and Buisson will stay because he feels somewhat responsible. These complications are interesting enough to cold-blooded folk like myself who have an eye for the dramatic element, but they are distracting and demoralizing to young people with any serious purpose in life."

Miss Broadwood's counsel was all the more generous seeing that, for her, the most interesting element of this denouement would be eliminated by Imogen's departure. "If she goes now, she'll get over it," soliloquized Miss Broadwood. "If she stays, she'll be wrung for him and the hurt may go deep enough to last. I haven't the heart to see her spoiling things for herself." She telephoned Mrs. Willard and helped Imogen to pack. She even took it upon herself to break the news of Imogen's going to Arthur, who remarked, as he rolled a cigarette in his nerveless fingers:

"Right enough, too. What should she do here with old cynics like you and me, Jimmy? Seeing that she is brim full of dates and formulae and other positivisms, and is so girt about with illusions that she still casts a shadow in the sun. You've been very tender of her, haven't you? I've watched you. And to think it may all be gone when we see her next. 'The common fate of all things rare,' you know. What a good fellow you are, anyway, Jimmy," he added, putting his hands affectionately on her shoulders.

Arthur went with them to the station. Flavia was so prostrated by the concerted action of her guests that she was able to see Imogen only for a moment in her darkened sleeping chamber, where she kissed her hysterically, without lifting her head, bandaged in aromatic vinegar. On the way to the station both Arthur and Imogen threw the burden of keeping up appearances entirely upon Miss Broadwood, who blithely rose to the occasion. When Hamilton carried Imogen's bag into the car, Miss Broadwood detained her for a moment, whispering as she gave her a large, warm handclasp, "I'll come to see you when I get back to town; and, in the meantime, if you meet any of our artists, tell them you have left Caius Marius among the ruins of Carthage."

The Sculptor's Funeral

A group of the townspeople stood on the station siding of a little Kansas town, awaiting the coming of the night train, which was already twenty minutes overdue. The snow had fallen thick over everything; in the pale starlight the line of bluffs across the wide, white meadows south of the town made soft, smoke-colored curves against the clear sky. The men on the siding stood first on one foot and then on the other, their hands thrust deep into their trousers pockets, their overcoats open, their shoulders screwed up with the cold; and they glanced from time to time toward the southeast, where the railroad track wound along the river shore. They conversed in low tones and moved about restlessly, seeming uncertain as to what was expected of them. There was but one of the company who looked as though he knew exactly why he was there; and he kept conspicuously apart; walking to the far end of the platform, returning to the station door, then pacing up the track again, his chin sunk in the high collar of his overcoat, his burly shoulders drooping forward, his gait heavy and dogged. Presently he was approached by a tall, spare, grizzled man clad in a faded Grand Army suit, who shuffled out from the group and advanced with a certain deference,

50

craning his neck forward until his back made the angle of a jackknife three-quarters open.

"I reckon she's agoin' to be pretty late ag'in tonight, Jim," he remarked in a squeaky falsetto. "S'pose it's the snow?"

"I don't know," responded the other man with a shade of annoyance, speaking from out an astonishing cataract of red beard that grew fiercely and thickly in all directions.

The spare man shifted the quill toothpick he was chewing to the other side of his mouth. "It ain't likely that anybody from the East will come with the corpse, I s'pose," he went on reflectively.

"I don't know," responded the other, more curtly than before.

"It's too bad he didn't belong to some lodge or other. I like an order funeral myself. They seem more appropriate for people of some reputation," the spare man continued, with an ingratiating concession in his shrill voice, as he carefully placed his toothpick in his vest pocket. He always carried the flag at the G. A. R. funerals in the town.

The heavy man turned on his heel, without replying, and walked up the siding. The spare man shuffled back to the uneasy group. "Jim's ez full ez a tick, ez ushel," he commented commiseratingly.

Just then a distant whistle sounded, and there was a shuffling of feet on the platform. A number of lanky boys of all ages appeared as suddenly and slimily as eels wakened by the crack of thunder; some came from the waiting room, where they had been warming themselves by the red stove, or half-asleep on the slat benches; others uncoiled themselves from baggage trucks or slid out of express wagons. Two clambered down from the driver's seat of a hearse that stood backed up against the siding. They straightened their stooping shoulders and lifted their heads, and a flash of momentary animation kindled their dull eyes at that cold, vibrant scream, the world-wide call for men. It stirred them like the note of a trumpet; just as it had often stirred the man who was coming home tonight, in his boyhood.

The night express shot, red as a rocket, from out the eastward marsh lands and wound along the river shore under the long lines of shivering poplars that sentineled the meadows, the escaping steam hanging in gray masses against the pale sky and blotting out the Milky Way. In a moment the red glare from the headlight streamed up the snow-covered track before the siding and glittered on the wet, black rails. The burly man with the disheveled red beard walked swiftly up the platform toward the approaching train, uncovering his head as he went. The group of men behind him hesitated, glanced questioningly at one another, and awkwardly followed his example. The train stopped, and the crowd shuffled up to the express car just as the door was thrown open, the spare man in the G. A. B. suit thrusting his head forward with curiosity. The express messenger appeared in the doorway, accompanied by a young man in a long ulster and traveling cap.

"Are Mr. Merrick's friends here?" inquired the young man.

The group on the platform swayed and shuffled uneasily. Philip Phelps, the banker, responded with dignity: "We have come to take charge of the body. Mr. Merrick's father is very feeble and can't be about."

52

"Send the agent out here," growled the express messenger, "and tell the operator to lend a hand."

The coffin was got out of its rough box and down on the snowy platform. The townspeople drew back enough to make room for it and then formed a close semicircle about it, looking curiously at the palm leaf which lay across the black cover. No one said anything. The baggage man stood by his truck, waiting to get at the trunks. The engine panted heavily, and the fireman dodged in and out among the wheels with his yellow torch and long oilcan, snapping the spindle boxes. The young Bostonian, one of the dead sculptor's pupils who had come with the body, looked about him helplessly. He turned to the banker, the only one of that black, uneasy, stoop-shouldered group who seemed enough of an individual to be addressed.

"None of Mr. Merrick's brothers are here?" he asked uncertainly.

The man with the red heard for the first time stepped up and joined the group. "No, they have not come yet; the family is scattered. The body will be taken directly to the house." He stooped and took hold of one of the handles of the coffin.

"Take the long hill road up, Thompson — it will be easier on the horses," called the liveryman as the undertaker snapped the door of the hearse and prepared to mount to the driver's seat.

Laird, the red-bearded lawyer, turned again to the stranger: "We didn't know whether there would be anyone with him or not," he explained. "It's a long walk, so you'd better go up in the hack." He pointed to a single, battered conveyance, but the young man replied stiffly: "Thank you, but I think I will go up with the hearse. If

53

you don't object," turning to the undertaker, "I'll ride with you."

They clambered up over the wheels and drove off in the starlight tip the long, white hill toward the town. The lamps in the still village were shining from under the low, snow-burdened roofs; and beyond, on every side, the plains reached out into emptiness, peaceful and wide as the soft sky itself, and wrapped in a tangible, white silence.

When the hearse backed up to a wooden sidewalk before a naked, weatherbeaten frame house, the same composite, ill-defined group that had stood upon the station siding was huddled about the gate. The front yard was an icy swamp, and a couple of warped planks, extending from the sidewalk to the door, made a sort of rickety footbridge. The gate hung on one hinge and was opened wide with difficulty. Steavens, the young stranger, noticed that something black was tied to the knob of the front door.

The grating sound made by the casket, as it was drawn from the hearse, was answered by a scream from the house; the front door was wrenched open, and a tall, corpulent woman rushed out bareheaded into the snow and flung herself upon the coffin, shrieking: "My boy, my boy! And this is how you've come home to me!"

As Steavens turned away and closed his eyes with a shudder of unutterable repulsion, another woman, also tall, but flat and angular, dressed entirely in black, darted out of the house and caught Mrs. Merrick by the shoulders, crying sharply: "Come, come, Mother; you mustn't go on like this!" Her tone changed to one of obsequious solemnity as she turned to the banker: "The parlor is ready, Mr. Phelps."

The bearers carried the coffin along the narrow boards, while the undertaker ran ahead with the coffin-rests. They bore it into a large, unheated room that smelled of dampness and disuse and furniture polish, and set it down under a hanging lamp ornamented with jingling glass prisms and before a "Rogers group" of John Alden and Priscilla, wreathed with smilax. Henry Steavens stared about him with the sickening conviction that there had been some horrible mistake, and that he had somehow arrived at the wrong destination. He looked painfully about over the clover-green Brussels, the fat plush upholstery, among the hand-painted china plaques and panels, and vases, for some mark of identification, for something that might once conceivably have belonged to Harvey Merrick. It was not until he recognized his friend in the crayon portrait of a little boy in kilts and curls hanging above the piano that he felt willing to let any of these people approach the coffin.

"Take the lid off, Mr. Thompson; let me see my boy's face," wailed the elder woman between her sobs. This time Steavens looked fearfully, almost beseechingly into her face, red and swollen under its masses of strong, black, shiny hair. He flushed, dropped his eyes, and then, almost incredulously, looked again. There was a kind of power about her face — a kind of brutal handsomeness, even, but it was scarred and furrowed by violence, and so colored and coarsened by fiercer passions that grief seemed never to have laid a gentle finger there. The long nose was distended and knobbed at the end, and there were deep lines on either side of it; her heavy, black brows almost met across her forehead; her teeth were large and square and set far apart — teeth that could tear.

She filled the room; the men were obliterated, seemed tossed about like twigs in an angry water, and even Steavens felt himself being drawn into the whirlpool.

The daughter — the tall, rawboned woman in crêpe, with a mourning comb in her hair which curiously lengthened her long face sat stiffly upon the sofa, her hands, conspicuous for their large knuckles, folded in her lap, her mouth and eyes drawn down, solemnly awaiting the opening of the coffin. Near the door stood a mulatto woman, evidently a servant in the house, with a timid bearing and an emaciated face pitifully sad and gentle. She was weeping silently, the corner of her calico apron lifted to her eyes, occasionally suppressing a long, quivering sob. Steavens walked over and stood beside her.

Feeble steps were heard on the stairs, and an old man, tall and frail, odorous of pipe smoke, with shaggy, unkept gray hair and a dingy beard, tobacco stained about the mouth, entered uncertainly. He went slowly up to the coffin and stood, rolling a blue cotton handkerchief between his hands, seeming so pained and embarrassed by his wife's orgy of grief that he had no consciousness of anything else.

"There, there, Annie, dear, don't take on so," he quavered timidly, putting out a shaking hand and awkwardly patting her elbow. She turned with a cry and sank upon his shoulder with such violence that he tottered a little. He did not even glance toward the coffin, but continued to look at her with a dull, frightened, appealing expression, as a spaniel looks at the whip. His sunken cheeks slowly reddened and burned with miserable shame. When his wife rushed from the room her daughter strode after her with set lips. The servant stole up to the coffin, bent over it for a moment, and then slipped away to the kitchen, leaving Steavens, the lawyer, and the father to themselves. The old man stood trembling and looking down at his dead son's face. The sculptor's splendid head seemed even more noble in its rigid stillness than in life. The dark hair had crept down upon the wide forehead; the face seemed strangely long, but in it there was not that beautiful and chaste repose which we expect to find in the faces of the dead. The brows were so drawn that there were two deep lines above the beaked nose, and the chin was thrust forward defiantly. It was as though the strain of life had been so sharp and bitter that death could not at once wholly relax the tension and smooth the countenance into perfect peace — as though he were still guarding something precious and holy, which might even yet be wrested from him.

The old man's lips were working under his stained beard. He turned to the lawyer with timid deference: "Phelps and the rest are comin' back to set up with Harve, ain't they?" he asked. "Thank 'ee, Jim, thank 'ee." He brushed the hair back gently from his son's forehead. "He was a good boy, Jim; always a good boy. He was ez gentle ez a child and the kindest of 'em all — only we didn't none of us ever onderstand him." The tears trickled slowly down his beard and dropped upon the sculptor's coat.

"Martin, Martin. Oh, Martin! come here," his wife wailed from the top of the stairs. The old man started timorously: "Yes, Annie, I'm coming." He turned away, hesitated stood for a moment in miserable indecision; then he reached back and patted the dead man's hair softly, and stumbled from the room.

"Poor old man, I didn't think he had any tears left. Seems as if his eyes would have gone dry long ago. At his age nothing cuts very deep," remarked the lawyer.

Something in his tone made Steavens glance up. While the mother had been in the room the young man had scarcely seen anyone else; but now, from the moment he first glanced into Jim Laird's florid face and bloodshot eyes, he knew that he had found what he had been heartsick at not finding before — the feeling, the understanding, that must exist in someone, even here.

The man was red as his beard, with features swollen and blurred by dissipation, and a hot, blazing blue eye. His face was strained — that of a man who is controlling himself with difficulty — and he kept plucking at his beard with a sort of fierce resentment. Steavens, sitting by the window, watched him turn down the glaring lamp, still its jangling pendants with an angry gesture, and then stand with his hands locked behind him, staring down into the master's face. He could not help wondering what link there could have been between the porcelain vessel and so sooty a lump of potter's clay.

From the kitchen an uproar was sounding; when the dining-room door opened the import of it was clear. The mother was abusing the maid for having forgotten to make the dressing for the chicken salad which had been prepared for the watchers. Steavens had never heard anything in the least like it; it was injured, emotional, dramatic abuse, unique and masterly in its excruciating cruelty, as violent and unrestrained as had been her grief of twenty minutes before. With a shudder of disgust the lawyer went into the dining room and closed the door into the kitchen.

"Poor Roxy's getting it now," he remarked when he came back. "The Merricks took her out of the poorhouse years ago; and if her loyalty would let her, I guess the poor old thing could tell tales that would curdle your blood. She's the mulatto woman who was standing in here a while ago, with her apron to her eyes. The old woman is a fury; there never was anybody like her for demonstrative piety and ingenious cruelty. She made Harvey's life a hell for him when he lived at home; he was so sick ashamed of it. I never could see how he kept himself so sweet."

"He was wonderful," said Steavens slowly, "wonderful; but until tonight I have never known how wonderful."

"That is the true and eternal wonder of it, anyway; that it can come even from such a dung heap as this," the lawyer cried, with a sweeping gesture which seemed to indicate much more than the four walls within which they stood.

"I think I'll see whether I can get a little air. The room is so close I am beginning to feel rather faint," murmured Steavens, struggling with one of the windows. The sash was stuck, however, and would not yield, so he sat down dejectedly and began pulling at his collar. The lawyer came over, loosened the sash with one blow of his red fist, and sent the window up a few inches. Steavens thanked him, but the nausea which had been gradually climbing into his throat for the last half-hour left him with but one desire — a desperate feeling that he must get away from this place with what was left of Harvey Merrick. Oh, he comprehended well enough now the quiet bitterness of the smile that he had seen so often on his master's lips!

He remembered that once, when Merrick returned from a visit home, he brought with him a singularly feeling and suggestive bas-relief of a thin, faded old woman, sitting and sewing something pinned to her knee; while a full-lipped, full-blooded little urchin, his trousers held up by a single gallows, stood beside her, impatiently twitching her gown to call her attention to a butterfly he had caught. Steavens, impressed by the tender and delicate modeling of the thin, tired face, had asked him if it were his mother. He remembered the dull flush that had burned up in the sculptor's face.

The lawyer was sitting in a rocking chair beside the coffin, his head thrown back and his eyes closed. Steavens looked at him earnestly, puzzled at the line of the chin, and wondering why a man should conceal a feature of such distinction under that disfiguring shock of beard. Suddenly, as though he felt the young sculptor's keen glance, he opened his eyes.

"Was he always a good deal of an oyster?" he asked abruptly. "He was terribly shy as a boy."

"Yes, he was an oyster, since you put it so," rejoined Steavens. "Although he could be very fond of people, he always gave one the impression of being detached. He disliked violent emotion; he was reflective, and rather distrustful of himself — except, of course, as regarded his work. He was surefooted enough there. He distrusted men pretty thoroughly and women even more, yet somehow without believing ill of them. He was determined, indeed, to believe the best, but he seemed afraid to investigate."

"A burnt dog dreads the fire," said the lawyer grimly, and closed his eyes.

Steavens went on and on, reconstructing that whole miserable boyhood. All this raw, biting ugliness had been the portion of the man whose tastes were refined beyond the limits of the reasonable — whose mind was an exhaustless gallery of beautiful impressions, and so sensitive that the mere shadow of a poplar leaf flickering against a sunny wall would be etched and held there forever. Surely, if ever a man had the magic word in his fingertips, it was Merrick. Whatever he touched, he revealed its holiest secret; liberated it from enchantment and restored it to its pristine loveliness, like the Arabian prince who fought the enchantress spell for spell. Upon whatever he had come in contact with, he had left a beautiful record of the experience — a sort of ethereal signature; a scent, a sound, a color that was his own.

Steavens understood now the real tragedy of his master's life; neither love nor wine, as many had conjectured, but a blow which had fallen earlier and cut deeper than these could have done — a shame not his, and yet so unescapably his, to bide in his heart from his very boyhood. And without — the frontier warfare; the yearning of a boy, cast ashore upon a desert of newness and ugliness and sordidness, for all that is chastened and old, and noble with traditions.

At eleven o'clock the tall, flat woman in black crêpe entered, announced that the watchers were arriving, and asked them "to step into the dining room." As Steavens rose the lawyer said dryly: "You go on — it'll be a good experience for you, doubtless; as for me, I'm not equal to that crowd tonight; I've had twenty years of them."

As Steavens closed the door after him be glanced back at the lawyer, sitting by the coffin in the dim light, with his chin resting on his hand.

The same misty group that had stood before the door of the express car shuffled into the dining room. In the light of the kerosene lamp they separated and became individuals. The minister, a pale, feeble-looking man with white hair and blond chin-whiskers, took his seat beside a small side table and placed his Bible upon it. The Grand Army man sat down behind the stove and tilted his chair back comfortably against the wall, fishing his quill toothpick from his waistcoat pocket. The two bankers, Phelps and Elder, sat off in a corner behind the dinner table, where they could finish their discussion of the new usury law and its effect on chattel security loans. The real estate agent, an old man with a smiling, hypocritical face, soon joined them. The coal-and-lumber dealer and the cattle shipper sat on opposite sides of the hard coal-burner, their feet on the nickel-work. Steavens took a book from his pocket and began to read. The talk around him ranged through various topics of local interest while the house was quieting down. When it was clear that the members of the family were in bed the Grand Army man hitched his shoulders and, untangling his long legs, caught his heels on the rounds of his chair.

"S'pose there'll be a will, Phelps?" he queried in his weak falsetto.

The banker laughed disagreeably and began trimming his nails with a pearl-handled pocket-knife.

"There'll scarcely be any need for one, will there?" he queried in his turn.

The restless Grand Army man shifted his position again, getting his knees still nearer his chin. "Why, the ole man says Harve's done right well lately," he chirped.

The other banker spoke up. "I reckon he means by that Harve ain't asked him to mortgage any more farms lately, so as he could go on with his education."

"Seems like my mind don't reach back to a time when Harve wasn't bein' edycated," tittered the Grand Army man.

There was a general chuckle. The minister took out his handkerchief and blew his nose sonorously. Banker Phelps closed his knife with a snap. "It's too bad the old man's sons didn't turn out better," he remarked with reflective authority. "They never hung together. He spent money enough on Harve to stock a dozen cattle farms and he might as well have poured it into Sand Creek. If Harve had stayed at home and helped nurse what little they had, and gone into stock on the old man's bottom farm, they might all have been well fixed. But the old man had to trust everything to tenants and was cheated right and left."

"Harve never could have handled stock none," interposed the cattleman. "He hadn't it in him to be sharp. Do you remember when he bought Sander's mules for eight-year-olds, when everybody in town knew that Sander's father-in-law give 'em to his wife for a wedding present eighteen years before, an' they was full-grown mules then."

Everyone chuckled, and the Grand Army man rubbed his knees with a spasm of childish delight.

"Harve never was much account for anything

practical, and he shore was never fond of work," began the coal-and-lumber dealer. "I mind the last time he was home; the day he left, when the old man was out to the barn helpin' his hand hitch up to take Harve to the train, and Cal Moots was patchin' up the fence, Harve, he come out on the step and sings out, in his ladylike voice: 'Cal Moots, Cal Moots! please come cord my trunk.' "

"That's Harve for you," approved the Grand Army man gleefully. "I kin hear him howlin' yet when he was a big feller in long pants and his mother used to whale him with a rawhide in the barn for lettin' the cows git foundered in the cornfield when he was drivin' 'em home from pasture. He killed a cow of mine that-a-way onc't — a pure Jersey and the best milker I had, an' the ole man had to put up for her. Harve, he was watchin' the sun set acros't the marshes when the anamile got away; he argued that sunset was on-common fine."

"Where the old man made his mistake was in sending the boy East to school," said Phelps, stroking his goatee and speaking in a deliberate, judicial tone. "There was where he got his head full of traipsing to Paris and all such folly. What Harve needed, of all people, was a course in some first-class Kansas City business college."

The letters were swimming before Steavens's eyes. Was it possible that these men did not understand, that the palm on the coffin meant nothing to them? The very name of their town would have remained forever buried in the postal guide had it not been now and again mentioned in the world in connection with Harvey Merrick's. He remembered what his master had said to him on the day of his death, after the congestion of both lungs had shut off any probability of recovery, and the sculptor had asked his pupil to send his body home. "It's not a pleasant place to be lying while the world is moving and doing and bettering," he had said with a feeble smile, "but it rather seems as though we ought to go back to the place we came from in the end. The townspeople will come in for a look at me; and after they have had their say I shan't have much to fear from the judgment of God. The wings of the Victory, in there" — with a weak gesture toward his studio — "will not shelter me."

The cattleman took up the comment. "Forty's young for a Merrick to cash in; they usually hang on pretty well. Probably he helped it along with whisky."

"His mother's people were not long-lived, and Harvey never had a robust constitution," said the minister mildly. He would have liked to say more. He had been the boy's Sunday-school teacher, and had been fond of him; but he felt that he was not in a position to speak. His own sons had turned out badly, and it was not a year since one of them had made his last trip home in the express car, shot in a gambling house in the Black Hills.

"Nevertheless, there is no disputin' that Harve frequently looked upon the wine when it was red, also variegated, and it shore made an oncommon fool of him," moralized the cattleman.

Just then the door leading into the parlor rattled loudly, and everyone started involuntarily, looking relieved when only Jim Laird came out. His red face was convulsed with anger, and the Grand Army man ducked his head when he saw the spark in his blue, bloodshot eye. They were all afraid of Jim; he was a drunkard, but he could twist the

65

law to suit his client's needs as no other man in all western Kansas could do; and there were many who tried. The lawyer closed the door gently behind him, leaned back against it and folded his arms, cocking his head a little to one side. When he assumed this attitude in the courtroom, ears were always pricked up, as it usually foretold a flood of withering sarcasm.

"I've been with you gentlemen before," he began in a dry, even tone, "when you've sat by the coffins of boys born and raised in this town; and, if I remember rightly, you were never any too well satisfied when you checked them up. What's the matter, anyhow? Why is it that reputable young men are as scarce as millionaires in Sand City? It might almost seem to a stranger that there was some way something the matter with your progressive town. Why did Ruben Sayer, the brightest young lawyer you ever turned out, after he had come home from the university as straight as a die, take to drinking and forge a check and shoot himself? Why did Bill Merrit's son die of the shakes in a saloon in Omaha? Why was Mr. Thomas's son, here, shot in a gambling house? Why did young Adams burn his mill to beat the insurance companies and go to the pen?"

The lawyer paused and unfolded his arms, laying one clenched fist quietly on the table. "I'll tell you why. Because you drummed nothing but money and knavery into their ears from the time they wore knickerbockers; because you carped away at them as you've been carping here tonight, holding our friends Phelps and Elder up to them for their models, as our grandfathers held up George Washington and John Adams. But the boys, worse luck, were young and raw at the busi-

66

ness you put them to; and how could they match coppers with such artists as Phelps and Elder? You wanted them to be successful rascals; they were only unsuccessful ones — that's all the difference. There was only one boy ever raised in this borderland between ruffianism and civilization who didn't come to grief, and you hated Harvey Merrick more for winning out than you hated all the other boys who got under the wheels. Lord, Lord, how you did hate him! Phelps, here, is fond of saying that he could buy and sell us all out any time he's a mind to; but he knew Harve wouldn't have given a tinker's damn for his bank and all his cattle farms put together; and a lack of appreciation, that way, goes hard with Phelps.

"Old Nimrod, here, thinks Harve drank too much; and this from such as Nimrod and me!

"Brother Elder says Harve was too free with the old man's money — fell short in filial consideration, maybe. Well, we can all remember the very tone in which brother Elder swore his own father was a liar, in the county court; and we all know that the old man came out of that partnership with his son as bare as a sheared lamb. But maybe I'm getting personal, and I'd better be driving ahead at what I want to say."

The lawyer paused a moment, squared his heavy shoulders, and went on: "Harvey Merrick and I went to school together, back East. We were dead in earnest, and we wanted you all to be proud of us some day. We meant to be great men. Even I, and I haven't lost my sense of humor, gentlemen, I meant to be a great man. I came back here to practice, and I found you didn't in the least want me to be a great man. You wanted me to be a shrewd lawyer — oh, yes! Our veteran here wanted

67

me to get him an increase of pension, because he had dyspepsia; Phelps wanted a new county survey that would put the widow Wilson's little bottom farm inside his south line; Elder wanted to lend money at 5 per cent a month and get it collected; old Stark here wanted to wheedle old women up in Vermont into investing their annuities in real estate mortgages that are not worth the paper they are written on. Oh, you needed me hard enough, and you'll go on needing me; and that's why I'm not afraid to plug the truth home to you this once.

"Well, I came back here and became the damned shyster you wanted me to be. You pretend to have some sort of respect for me; and yet you'll stand up and throw mud at Harvey Merrick, whose soul you couldn't dirty and whose hands you couldn't tie. Oh, you're a discriminating lot of Christians! There have been times when the sight of Harvey's name in some Eastern paper has made me hang my head like a whipped dog; and, again, times when I liked to think of him off there in the world, away from all this hog wallow, doing his great work and climbing the big, clean upgrade he'd set for himself.

"And we? Now that we've fought and lied and sweated and stolen, and hated as only the disappointed strugglers in a bitter, dead little Western town know how to do, what have we got to show for it? Harvey Merrick wouldn't have given one sunset over your marshes for all you've got put together, and you know it. It's not for me to say why, in the inscrutable wisdom of God, a genius should ever have been called from this place of hatred and bitter waters; but I want this Boston man to know that the drivel he's been hearing

68

here tonight is the only tribute any truly great man could ever have from such a lot of sick, side-tracked, burnt-dog, land-poor sharks as the here-present financiers of Sand City — upon which town may God have mercy!"

The lawyer thrust out his hand to Steavens as he passed him, caught up his overcoat in the hall, and had left the house before the Grand Army man had had time to lift his ducked head and crane his long neck about at his fellows.

Next day Jim Laird was drunk and unable to attend the funeral services. Steavens called twice at his office, but was compelled to start East without seeing him. He had a presentiment that he would hear from him again, and left his address on the lawyer's table; but if Laird found it, he never acknowledged it. The thing in him that Harvey Merrick had loved must have gone underground with Harvey Merrick's coffin; for it never spoke again, and Jim got the cold he died of driving across the Colorado mountains to defend one of Phelps's sons, who had got into trouble out there by cutting government timber.

THE GARDEN LODGE

When Caroline Noble's friends learned that Raymond d'Esquerré was to spend a month at her place on the Sound before he sailed to fill his engagement for the London opera season, they considered it another striking instance of the perversity of things. That the month was May, and the most mild and florescent of all the blue-and-white Mays the middle coast had known in years, but added to their sense of wrong. D'Esquerré, they learned, was ensconced in the lodge in the apple orchard, just beyond Caroline's glorious garden, and report went that at almost any hour the sound of the tenor's voice and of Caroline's crashing accompaniment could be heard floating through the open windows, out among the snowy apple boughs. The Sound, steel-blue and dotted with white sails, was splendidly seen from the windows of the lodge. The garden to the left and the orchard to the right had never been so riotous with spring, and had burst into impassioned bloom, as if to accommodate Caroline, though she was certainly the last woman to whom the witchery of Freya could be attributed; the last woman, as her friends affirmed, to at all adequately appreciate and make the most of such a setting for the great tenor.

Of course, they admitted, Caroline was musical — well, she ought to be! — but in that, as in everything, she was paramountly cool-headed, slow of impulse, and disgustingly practical; in that, as in everything else, she had herself so provokingly well in hand. Of course, it would be she, always mistress of herself in any situation, she, who would never be lifted one inch from the ground by it, and who would go on superintending her gardeners and workmen as usual — it would be she who got him. Perhaps some of them suspected that this was exactly why she did get him, and it but nettled them the more.

Caroline's coolness, her capableness, her general success, especially exasperated people because they felt that, for the most part, she had made herself what she was; that she had cold-bloodedly set about complying with the demands of life and making her position comfortable and masterful. That was why, everyone said, she had married Howard Noble. Women who did not get through life so well as Caroline, who could not make such good terms either with fortune or their husbands, who did not find their health so unfailingly good, or hold their looks so well, or manage their children so easily, or give such distinction to all they did, were fond of stamping Caroline as a materialist, and called her hard.

The impression of cold calculation, of having a definite policy, which Caroline gave, was far from a false one; but there was this to be said for her — that there were extenuating circumstances which her friends could not know.

If Caroline held determinedly to the middle course, if she was apt to regard with distrust everything which inclined toward extravagance, it was not because she was unacquainted with other standards than her own, or had never seen another side of life. She had grown up in Brooklyn, in a shabby little house under the vacillating administration of her father, a music teacher who usually neglected his duties to write orchestral compositions for which the world seemed to have no especial need. His spirit was warped by bitter vindictiveness and puerile self-commiseration, and he spent his days in scorn of the labor that brought him bread and in pitiful devotion to the labor that brought him only disappointment, writing interminable scores which demanded of the orchestra everything under heaven except melody.

It was not a cheerful home for a girl to grow up in. The mother, who idolized her husband as the music lord of the future, was left to a lifelong battle with broom and dustpan, to neverending conciliatory overtures to the butcher and grocer, to the making of her own gowns and of Caroline's, and to the delicate task of mollifying Auguste's neglected pupils.

The son, Heinrich, a painter, Caroline's only brother, had inherited all his father's vindictive sensitiveness without his capacity for slavish application. His little studio on the third floor had been much frequented by young men as unsuccessful as himself, who met there to give themselves over to contemptuous derision of this or that artist whose industry and stupidity had won him recognition. Heinrich, when he worked at all, did newspaper sketches at twenty-five dollars a week. He was too indolent and vacillating to set himself seriously to his art, too irascible and poignantly self-conscious to make a living, too much addicted to lying late in bed, to the incontinent

72

reading of poetry, and to the use of chloral to be anything very positive except painful. At twenty-six he shot himself in a frenzy, and the whole wretched affair had effectually shattered his mother's health and brought on the decline of which she died. Caroline had been fond of him, but she felt a certain relief when he no longer wandered about the little house, commenting ironically upon its shabbiness, a Turkish cap on his head and a cigarette hanging from between his long, tremulous fingers.

After her mother's death Caroline assumed the management of that bankrupt establishment. The funeral expenses were unpaid, and Auguste's pupils had been frightened away by the shock of successive disasters and the general atmosphere of wretchedness that pervaded the house. Auguste himself was writing a symphonic poem, Icarus, dedicated to the memory of his son. Caroline was barely twenty when she was called upon to face this tangle of difficulties, but she reviewed the situation candidly. The house had served its time at the shrine of idealism; vague, distressing, unsatisfied yearnings had brought it low enough. Her mother, thirty years before, had eloped and left Germany with her music teacher, to give herself over to lifelong, drudging bondage at the kitchen range. Ever since Caroline could remember, the law in the house had been a sort of mystic worship of things distant, intangible and unattainable. The family had lived in successive ebullitions of generous enthusiasm, in talk of masters and masterpieces, only to come down to the cold facts in the case; to boiled mutton and to the necessity of turning the dining-room carpet. All these emotional pyrotechnics had ended in petty jealousies, in neglected duties, and in cowardly fear of the little grocer on the corner.

From her childhood she had hated it, that humiliating and uncertain existence, with its glib tongue and empty pockets, its poetic ideals and sordid realities, its indolence and poverty tricked out in paper roses. Even as a little girl, when vague dreams beset her, when she wanted to lie late in bed and commune with visions, or to leap and sing because the sooty little trees along the street were putting out their first pale leaves in the sunshine, she would clench her hands and go to help her mother sponge the spots from her father's waistcoat or press Heinrich's trousers. Her mother never permitted the slightest question concerning anything Auguste or Heinrich saw fit to do, but from the time Caroline could reason at all she could not help thinking that many things went wrong at home. She knew, for example, that her father's pupils ought not to be kept waiting half an hour while he discussed Schopenhauer with some bearded socialist over a dish of herrings and a spotted tablecloth. She knew that Heinrich ought not to give a dinner on Heine's birthday, when the laundress had not been paid for a month and when he frequently had to ask his mother for carfare. Certainly Caroline had served her apprenticeship to idealism and to all the embarrassing inconsistencies which it sometimes entails, and she decided to deny herself this diffuse, ineffectual answer to the sharp questions of life.

When she came into the control of herself and the house she refused to proceed any further with her musical education. Her father, who had intended to make a concert pianist of her, set this down as another item in his long list of disappointments and his grievances against the world. She was young and pretty, and she had worn turned gowns and soiled gloves and improvised hats all her life. She wanted the luxury of being like other people, of being honest from her hat to her boots, of having nothing to hide, not even in the matter of stockings, and she was willing to work for it. She rented a little studio away from that house of misfortune and began to give lessons. She managed well and was the sort of girl people liked to help. The bills were paid and Auguste went on composing, growing indignant only when she refused to insist that her pupils should study his compositions for the piano. She began to get engagements in New York to play accompaniments at song recitals. She dressed well, made herself agreeable, and gave herself a chance. She never permitted herself to look further than a step ahead, and set herself with all the strength of her will to see things as they are and meet them squarely in the broad day. There were two things she feared even more than poverty: the part of one that sets up an idol and the part of one that bows down and worships it.

When Caroline was twenty-four she married Howard Noble, then a widower of forty, who had been for ten years a power in Wall Street. Then, for the first time, she had paused to take breath. It took a substantialness as unquestionable as his; his money, his position, his energy, the big vigor of his robust person, to satisfy her that she was entirely safe. Then she relaxed a little, feeling that there was a barrier to be counted upon between her and that world of visions and quagmires and failure.

Caroline had been married for six years when

Raymond d'Esquerré came to stay with them. He came chiefly because Caroline was what she was; because he, too, felt occasionally the need of getting out of Klingsor's garden, of dropping down somewhere for a time near a quiet nature, a cool head, a strong hand. The hours he had spent in the garden lodge were hours of such concentrated study as, in his fevered life, he seldom got in anywhere. She had, as he told Noble, a fine appreciation of the seriousness of work.

One evening two weeks after d'Esquerré had sailed, Caroline was in the library giving her husband an account of the work she had laid out for the gardeners. She superintended the care of the grounds herself. Her garden, indeed, had become quite a part of her; a sort of beautiful adjunct, like gowns or jewels. It was a famous spot, and Noble was very proud of it.

"What do you think, Caroline, of having the garden lodge torn down and putting a new summer house there at the end of the arbor; a big rustic affair where you could have tea served in midsummer?" he asked.

"The lodge?" repeated Caroline looking at him quickly. "Why, that seems almost a shame, doesn't it, after d'Esquerré has used it?"

Noble put down his book with a smile of amusement.

"Are you going to be sentimental about it? Why, I'd sacrifice the whole place to see that come to pass. But I don't believe you could do it for an hour together."

"I don't believe so, either," said his wife, smiling.

Noble took up his book again and Caroline went into the music room to practice. She was not

76

ready to have the lodge torn down. She had gone there for a quiet hour every day during the two weeks since d'Esquerré had left them. It was the sheerest sentiment she had ever permitted herself. She was ashamed of it, but she was childishly unwilling to let it go.

Caroline went to bed soon after her husband, but she was not able to sleep. The night was close and warm, presaging storm. The wind had fallen, and the water slept, fixed and motionless as the sand. She rose and thrust her feet into slippers and, putting a dressing gown over her shoulders, opened the door of her husband's room; he was sleeping soundly. She went into the hall and down the stairs; then, leaving the house through a side door, stepped into the vine-covered arbor that led to the garden lodge. The scent of the June roses was heavy in the still air, and the stones that paved the path felt pleasantly cool through the thin soles of her slippers. Heat-lightning flashed continuously from the bank of clouds that had gathered over the sea, but the shore was flooded with moonlight and, beyond, the rim of the Sound lay smooth and shining. Caroline had the key of the lodge, and the door creaked as she opened it. She stepped into the long, low room radiant with the moonlight which streamed through the bow window and lay in a silvery pool along the waxed floor. Even that part of the room which lay in the shadow was vaguely illuminated; the piano, the tall candlesticks, the picture frames and white casts standing out as clearly in the half-light as did the sycamores and black poplars of the garden against the still, expectant night sky. Caroline sat down to think it all over. She had come here to do just that every day of the two weeks since d'Esquerré's departure, but, far from ever having reached a conclusion, she had succeeded only in losing her way in a maze of memories — sometimes bewilderingly confused, sometimes too acutely distinct — where there was neither path, nor clue, nor any hope of finality. She had, she realized, defeated a lifelong regimen; completely confounded herself by falling unaware and incontinently into that luxury of reverie which, even as a little girl, she had so determinedly denied herself, she had been developing with alarming celerity that part of one which sets up an idol and that part of one which bows down and worships it.

It was a mistake, she felt, ever to have asked d'Esquerré to come at all. She had an angry feeling that she had done it rather in self-defiance, to rid herself finally of that instinctive fear of him which had always troubled and perplexed her. She knew that she had reckoned with herself before he came; but she had been equal to so much that she had never really doubted she would be equal to this. She had come to believe, indeed, almost arrogantly in her own malleability and endurance; she had done so much with herself that she had come to think that there was nothing which she could not do; like swimmers, overbold, who reckon upon their strength and their power to hoard it, forgetting the ever-changing moods of their adversary, the sea.

And d'Esquerré was a man to reckon with. Caroline did not deceive herself now upon that score. She admitted it humbly enough, and since she had said good-by to him she had not been free for a moment from the sense of his formidable power. It formed the undercurrent of her consciousness; whatever she might be doing or thinking, it went on, involuntarily, like her breathing, sometimes welling up until suddenly she found herself suffocating. There was a moment of this tonight, and Caroline rose and stood shuddering, looking about her in the blue duskiness of the silent room. She had not been here at night before, and the spirit of the place seemed more troubled and insistent than ever it had in the quiet of the afternoons. Caroline brushed her hair back from her damp forehead and went over to the bow window. After raising it she sat down upon the low seat. Leaning her head against the sill, and loosening her nightgown at the throat, she half-closed her eyes and looked off into the troubled night, watching the play of the heat-lightning upon the massing clouds between the pointed tops of the poplars.

Yes, she knew, she knew well enough, of what absurdities this spell was woven; she mocked, even while she winced. His power, she knew, lay not so much in anything that he actually had — though he had so much — or in anything that he actually was, but in what he suggested, in what he seemed picturesque enough to have or be and that was just anything that one chose to believe or to desire. His appeal was all the more persuasive and alluring in that it was to the imagination alone, in that it was as indefinite and impersonal as those cults of idealism which so have their way with women. What he had was that, in his mere personality, he quickened and in a measure gratified that something without which — to women — life is no better than sawdust, and to the desire for which most of their mistakes and tragedies and astonishingly poor bargains are due.

D'Esquerré had become the center of a movement, and the Metropolitan had become the temple of a cult. When he could be induced to cross the Atlantic, the opera season in New York was successful; when he could not, the management lost money; so much everyone knew. It was understood, too, that his superb art had disproportionately little to do with his peculiar position. Women swayed the balance this way or that; the opera, the orchestra, even his own glorious art, achieved at such a cost, were but the accessories of himself; like the scenery and costumes and even the soprano, they all went to produce atmosphere, were the mere mechanics of the beautiful illusion.

Caroline understood all this; tonight was not the first time that she had put it to herself so. She had seen the same feeling in other people, watched for it in her friends, studied it in the house night after night when he sang, candidly putting herself among a thousand others.

D'Esquerré's arrival in the early winter was the signal for a feminine hegira toward New York. On the nights when he sang women flocked to the Metropolitan from mansions and hotels, from typewriter desks, schoolrooms, shops, and fitting rooms. They were of all conditions and complexions. Women of the world who accepted him knowingly as they sometimes took champagne for its agreeable effect; sisters of charity and overworked shopgirls, who received him devoutly; withered women who had taken doctorate degrees and who worshipped furtively through prism spectacles; business women and women of affairs, the Amazons who dwelt afar from men in the stony fastnesses of apartment houses. They all entered into the same romance; dreamed, in terms

80

as various as the hues of fantasy, the same dream; drew the same quick breath when he stepped upon the stage, and, at his exit, felt the same dull pain of shouldering the pack again.

There were the maimed, even; those who came on crutches, who were pitted by smallpox or grotesquely painted by cruel birth stains. These, too, entered with him into enchantment. Stout matrons became slender girls again; worn spinsters felt their cheeks flush with the tenderness of their lost youth. Young and old, however hideous, however fair, they yielded up their heat — whether quick or latent — sat hungering for the mystic bread wherewith he fed them at this eucharist of sentiment.

Sometimes, when the house was crowded from the orchestra to the last row of the gallery, when the air was charged with this ecstasy of fancy, he himself was the victim of the burning reflection of his power. They acted upon him in turn; he felt their fervent and despairing appeal to him; it stirred him as the spring drives the sap up into an old tree; he, too, burst into bloom. For the moment he, too, believed again, desired again, he knew not what, but something.

But it was not in these exalted moments that Caroline had learned to fear him most. It was in the quiet, tired reserve, the dullness, even, that kept him company between these outbursts that she found that exhausting drain upon her sympathies which was the very pith and substance of their alliance. It was the tacit admission of disappointment under all this glamour of success — the helplessness of the enchanter to at all enchant himself — that awoke in her an illogical, womanish desire to in some way compensate, to make it up to him.

She had observed drastically to herself that it was her eighteenth year he awoke in her — those hard years she had spent in turning gowns and placating tradesmen, and which she had never had time to live. After all, she reflected, it was better to allow one's self a little youth — to dance a little at the carnival and to live these things when they are natural and lovely, not to have them coming back on one and demanding arrears when they are humiliating and impossible. She went over tonight all the catalogue of her self-deprivations; recalled how, in the light of her father's example, she had even refused to humor her innocent taste for improvising at the piano; how, when she began to teach, after her mother's death, she had struck out one little indulgence after another, reducing her life to a relentless routine, unvarying as clockwork. It seemed to her that ever since d'Esquerré first came into the house she had been haunted by an imploring little girlish ghost that followed her about, wringing its hands and entreating for an hour of life.

The storm had held off unconscionably long; the air within the lodge was stifling, and without the garden waited, breathless. Everything seemed pervaded by a poignant distress; the hush of feverish, intolerable expectation. The still earth, the heavy flowers, even the growing darkness, breathed the exhaustion of protracted waiting. Caroline felt that she ought to go; that it was wrong to stay; that the hour and the place were as treacherous as her own reflections. She rose and began to pace the floor, stepping softly, as though in fear of awakening someone, her figure, in its thin drapery, diaphanously vague and white. Still unable to shake off the obsession of the intense stillness, she sat down at the piano and began to run over the first act of the *Walküre,* the last of his roles they had practiced together; playing listlessly and absently at first, but with gradually increasing seriousness. Perhaps it was the still heat of the summer night, perhaps it was the heavy odors from the garden that came in through the open windows; but as she played there grew and grew the feeling that he was there, beside her, standing in his accustomed place. In the duet at the end of the first act she heard him clearly: *"Thou art the Spring for which I sighed in Winter's cold embraces."* Once as he sang it, he had put his arm about her, his one hand under her heart, while with the other he took her right from the keyboard, holding her as he always held *Sieglinde* when he drew her toward the window. She had been wonderfully the mistress of herself at the time; neither repellent nor acquiescent. She remembered that she had rather exulted, then, in her self-control — which he had seemed to take for granted, though there was perhaps the whisper of a question from the hand under her heart. *"Thou art the Spring for which I sighed in Winter's cold embraces."* Caroline lifted her hands quickly from the keyboard, and she bowed her head in them, sobbing.

The storm broke and the rain beat in, spattering her nightdress until she rose and lowered the windows. She dropped upon the couch and began fighting over again the battles of other days, while the ghosts of the slain rose as from a sowing of dragon's teeth. The shadows of things, always so scorned and flouted, bore down upon her merciless and triumphant. It was not enough; this happy, useful, well-ordered life was not enough. It

83

did not satisfy, it was not even real. No, the other things, the shadows — they were the realities. Her father, poor Heinrich, even her mother, who had been able to sustain her poor romance and keep her little illusions amid the tasks of a scullion, were nearer happiness than she. Her sure foundation was but made ground, after all, and the people in Klingsor's garden were more fortunate, however barren the sands from which they conjured their paradise.

The lodge was still and silent; her fit of weeping over, Caroline made no sound, and within the room, as without in the garden, was the blackness of storm. Only now and then a flash of lightning showed a woman's slender figure rigid on the couch, her face buried in her hands.

Toward morning, when the occasional rumbling of thunder was heard no more and the beat of the raindrops upon the orchard leaves was steadier, she fell asleep and did not waken until the first red streaks of dawn shone through the twisted boughs of the apple trees. There was a moment between world and world, when, neither asleep nor awake, she felt her dream grow thin, melting away from her, felt the warmth under her heart growing cold. Something seemed to slip from the clinging hold of her arms, and she groaned protestingly through her parted lips, following it a little way with fluttering hands. Then her eyes opened wide and she sprang up and sat holding dizzily to the cushions of the couch, staring down at her bare, cold feet, at her laboring breast, rising and falling under her open nightdress.

The dream was gone, but the feverish reality of it still pervaded her and she held it as the vibrating string holds a tone. In the last hour the shadows had had their way with Caroline. They had shown her the nothingness of time and space, of system and discipline, of closed doors and broad waters. Shuddering, she thought of the Arabian fairy tale in which the genie brought the princess of China to the sleeping prince of Damascus and carried her through the air back to her palace at dawn. Caroline closed her eyes and dropped her elbows weakly upon her knees, her shoulders sinking together. The horror was that it had not come from without, but from within. The dream was no blind chance; it was the expression of something she had kept so close a prisoner that she had never seen it herself, it was the wail from the donjon deeps when the watch slept. Only as the outcome of such a night of sorcery could the thing have been loosed to straighten its limbs and measure itself with her; so heavy were the chains upon it, so many a fathom deep, it was crushed down into darkness. The fact that d'Esquerré happened to be on the other side of the world meant nothing; had he been here, beside her, it could scarcely have hurt her self-respect so much. As it was, she was without even the extenuation of an outer impulse, and she could scarcely have despised herself more had she come to him here in the night three weeks ago and thrown herself down upon the stone slab at the door there.

Caroline rose unsteadily and crept guiltily from the lodge and along the path under the arbor, terrified lest the servants should be stirring, trembling with the chill air, while the wet shrubbery, brushing against her, drenched her nightdress until it clung about her limbs.

At breakfast her husband looked across the table at her with concern. "It seems to me that you are looking rather fagged, Caroline. It was a beastly night to sleep. Why don't you go up to the mountains until this hot weather is over? By the way, were you in earnest about letting the lodge stand?"

Caroline laughed quietly. "No, I find I was not very serious. I haven't sentiment enough to forego a summer house. Will you tell Baker to come tomorrow to talk it over with me? If we are to have a house party, I should like to put him to work on it at once."

Noble gave her a glance, half-humorous, half-vexed. "Do you know I am rather disappointed?" he said. "I had almost hoped that, just for once, you know, you would be a little bit foolish."

"Not now that I've slept over it," replied Caroline, and they both rose from the table, laughing.

"A Death in the Desert"

Everett Hilgarde was conscious that the man in the seat across the aisle was looking at him intently. He was a large, florid man, wore a conspicuous diamond solitaire upon his third finger, and Everett judged him to be a traveling salesman of some sort. He had the air of an adaptable fellow who had been about the world and who could keep cool and clean under almost any circumstances.

The "High Line Flyer," as this train was derisively called among railroad men, was jerking along through the hot afternoon over the monotonous country between Holdridge and Cheyenne. Besides the blond man and himself the only occupants of the car were two dusty, bedraggled-looking girls who had been to the Exposition at Chicago, and who were earnestly discussing the cost of their first trip out of Colorado. The four uncomfortable passengers were covered with a sediment of fine, yellow dust which clung to their hair and eyebrows like gold powder. It blew up in clouds from the bleak, lifeless country through which they passed, until they were one color with the sagebrush and sandhills. The gray-and-yellow desert was varied only by occasional ruins of deserted towns, and the little red boxes of station houses, where the spindling trees and sickly vines in the bluegrass yards made little green reserves fenced off in that confusing wilderness of sand.

As the slanting rays of the sun beat in stronger and stronger through the car windows, the blond gentleman asked the ladies' permission to remove his coat, and sat in his lavender striped shirt sleeves, with a black silk handkerchief tucked carefully about his collar. He had seemed interested in Everett since they had boarded the train at Holdridge, and kept glancing at him curiously and then looking reflectively out of the window, as though he were trying to recall something. But wherever Everett went someone was almost sure to look at him with that curious interest, and it had ceased to embarrass or annoy him. Presently the stranger, seeming satisfied with his observation, leaned back in his seat, half-closed his eyes, and began softly to whistle the "Spring Song" from *Proserpine,* the cantata that a dozen years before had made its young composer famous in a night. Everett had heard that air on guitars in Old Mexico, on mandolins at college glees, on cottage organs in New England hamlets, and only two weeks ago he had heard it played on sleighbells at a variety theater in Denver. There was literally no way of escaping his brother's precocity. Adriance could live on the other side of the Atlantic, where his youthful indiscretions were forgotten in his mature achievements, but his brother had never been able to outrun *Proserpine,* and here he found it again in the Colorado sand hills. Not that Everett was exactly ashamed of *Proserpine;* only a man of genius could have written it, but it was the sort of thing that a man of genius outgrows as soon as he can.

Everett unbent a trifle and smiled at his neighbor across the aisle. Immediately the large man rose and, coming over, dropped into the seat facing Hilgarde, extending his card.

"Dusty ride, isn't it? I don't mind it myself; I'm used to it. Born and bred in de briar patch, like Br'er Rabbit. I've been trying to place you for a long time; I think I must have met you before."

"Thank you," said Everett, taking the card; "my name is Hilgarde. You've probably met my brother, Adriance; people often mistake me for him."

The traveling man brought his hand down upon his knee with such vehemence that the solitaire blazed.

"So I was right after all, and if you're not Adriance Hilgarde, you're his double. I thought I couldn't be mistaken. Seen him? Well, I guess! I never missed one of his recitals at the Auditorium, and he played the piano score of *Proserpine* through to us once at the Chicago Press Club. I used to be on the *Commercial* there before I began to travel for the publishing department of the concern. So you're Hilgarde's brother, and here I've run into you at the jumping-off place. Sounds like a newspaper yarn, doesn't it?"

The traveling man laughed and offered Everett a cigar, and plied him with questions on the only subject that people ever seemed to care to talk to Everett about. At length the salesman and the two girls alighted at a Colorado way station, and Everett went on to Cheyenne alone.

The train pulled into Cheyenne at nine o'clock, late by a matter of four hours or so; but no one seemed particularly concerned at its tardiness except the station agent, who grumbled at being kept in the office overtime on a summer night.

When Everett alighted from the train he walked down the platform and stopped at the track crossing, uncertain as to what direction he should take to reach a hotel. A phaeton stood near the crossing, and a woman held the reins. She was dressed in white, and her figure was clearly silhouetted against the cushions, though it was too dark to see her face. Everett had scarcely noticed her, when the switch engine came puffing up from the opposite direction, and the headlight threw a strong glare of light on his face. Suddenly the woman in the phaeton uttered a low cry and dropped the reins. Everett started forward and caught the horse's head, but the animal only lifted its ears and whisked its tail in impatient surprise. The woman sat perfectly still, her head sunk between her shoulders and her handkerchief pressed to her face. Another woman came out of the depot and hurried toward the phaeton, crying, "Katharine, dear, what is the matter?"

Everett hesitated a moment in painful embarrassment, then lifted his hat and passed on. He was accustomed to sudden recognitions in the most impossible places, especially by women, but this cry out of the night had shaken him.

While Everett was breakfasting the next morning, the headwaiter leaned over his chair to murmur that there was a gentleman waiting to see him in the parlor. Everett finished his coffee and went in the direction indicated, where he found his visitor restlessly pacing the floor. His whole manner betrayed a high degree of agitation, though his physique was not that of a man whose nerves lie near the surface. He was something below medium height, square-shouldered and solidly built. His thick, closely cut hair was beginning to show gray about the ears, and his bronzed face was heavily lined. His square brown hands were locked behind him, and he held his shoulders like a man conscious of responsibilities; yet, as he turned to greet Everett, there was an incongruous diffidence in his address.

"Good morning, Mr. Hilgarde," he said, extending his hand; "I found your name on the hotel register. My name is Gaylord. I'm afraid my sister startled you at the station last night, Mr. Hilgarde, and I've come around to apologize."

"Ah! The young lady in the phaeton? I'm sure I didn't know whether I had anything to do with her alarm or not. If I did, it is I who owe the apology."

The man colored a little under the dark brown of his face.

"Oh, it's nothing you could help, sir, I fully understand that. You see, my sister used to be a pupil of your brother's, and it seems you favor him; and when the switch engine threw a light on your face it startled her."

Everett wheeled about in his chair. "Oh! *Katharine* Gaylord! Is it possible! Now it's you who have given me a turn. Why, I used to know her when I was a boy. What on earth —"

"Is she doing here?" said Gaylord, grimly filling out the pause. "You've got at the heart of the matter. You knew my sister had been in bad health for a long time?"

"No, I had never heard a word of that. The last I knew of her she was singing in London. My brother and I correspond infrequently and seldom get beyond family matters. I am deeply sorry to hear this. There are more reasons why I am concerned than I can tell you."

The lines in Charley Gaylord's brow relaxed a little.

"What I'm trying to say, Mr. Hilgarde, is that she wants to see you. I hate to ask you, but she's so set on it. We live several miles out of town, but my rig's below, and I can take you out anytime you can go."

"I can go now, and it will give me real pleasure to do so," said Everett, quickly. "I'll get my hat and be with you in a moment."

When he came downstairs Everett found a cart at the door, and Charley Gaylord drew a long sigh of relief as he gathered up the reins and settled back into his own element.

"You see, I think I'd better tell you something about my sister before you see her, and I don't know just where to begin. She traveled in Europe with your brother and his wife, and sang at a lot of his concerts; but I don't know just how much you know about her."

"Very little, except that my brother always thought her the most gifted of his pupils, and that when I knew her she was very young and very beautiful and turned my head sadly for a while."

Everett saw that Gaylord's mind was quite engrossed by his grief. He was wrought up to the point where his reserve and sense of proportion had quite left him, and his trouble was the one vital thing in the world. "That's the whole thing," he went on, flicking his horses with the whip.

"She was a great woman, as you say, and she didn't come of a great family. She had to fight her own way from the first. She got to Chicago, and then to New York, and then to Europe, where she went up like lightning, and got a taste for it all; and now she's dying here like a rat in a hole, out of her own world, and she can't fall back into ours. We've grown apart, some way — miles and miles apart — and I'm afraid she's fearfully unhappy."

"It's a very tragic story that you are telling me, Gaylord," said Everett. They were well out into the country now, spinning along over the dusty plains of red grass, with the ragged-blue outline of the mountains before them.

"Tragic!" cried Gaylord, starting up in his seat, "my God, man, nobody will ever know how tragic. It's a tragedy I live with and eat with and sleep with, until I've lost my grip on everything. You see she had made a good bit of money, but she spent it all going to health resorts. It's her lungs, you know. I've got money enough to send her anywhere, but the doctors all say it's no use. She hasn't the ghost of a chance. It's just getting through the days now. I had no notion she was half so bad before she came to me. She just wrote that she was all run down. Now that she's here, I think she'd be happier anywhere under the sun, but she won't leave. She says it's easier to let go of life here, and that to go East would be dying twice. There was a time when I was a brakeman with a run out of Bird City, Iowa, and she was a little thing I could carry on my shoulder, when I could get her everything on earth she wanted, and she hadn't a wish my $80 a month didn't cover; and now, when I've got a little property together, I can't buy her a night's sleep!"

Everett saw that, whatever Charley Gaylord's present status in the world might be, he had brought the brakeman's heart up the ladder with him, and the brakeman's frank avowal of sentiment. Presently Gaylord went on:

"You can understand how she has outgrown her

family. We're all a pretty common sort, railroaders from away back. My father was a conductor. He died when we were kids. Maggie, my other sister, who lives with me, was a telegraph operator here while I was getting my grip on things. We had no education to speak of. I have to hire a stenographer because I can't spell straight — the Almighty couldn't teach me to spell. The things that make up life to Kate are all Greek to me, and there's scarcely a point where we touch any more, except in our recollections of the old times when we were all young and happy together, and Kate sang in a church choir in Bird City. But I believe, Mr. Hilgarde, that if she can see just one person like you, who knows about the things and people she's interested in, it will give her about the only comfort she can have now."

The reins slackened in Charley Gaylord's hand as they drew up before a showily painted house with many gables and a round tower. "Here we are," he said, turning to Everett, "and I guess we understand each other."

They were met at the door by a thin, colorless woman, whom Gaylord introduced as "my sister, Maggie." She asked her brother to show Mr. Hilgarde into the music room, where Katharine wished to see him alone.

When Everett entered the music room he gave a little start of surprise, feeling that he had stepped from the glaring Wyoming sunlight into some New York studio that he had always known. He wondered which it was of those countless studios, high up under the roofs, over banks and shops and wholesale houses, that this room resembled, and he looked incredulously out of the window at the

94

gray plain that ended in the great upheaval of the Rockies.

The haunting air of familiarity about the room perplexed him. Was it a copy of some particular studio he knew, or was it merely the studio atmosphere that seemed so individual and poignantly reminiscent here in Wyoming? He sat down in a reading chair and looked keenly about him. Suddenly his eye fell upon a large photograph of his brother above the piano. Then it all became clear to him: this was veritably his brother's room. If it were not an exact copy of one of the many studios that Adriance had fitted up in various parts of the world, wearying of them and leaving almost before the renovator's varnish had dried, it was at least in the same tone. In every detail Adriance's taste was so manifest that the room seemed to exhale his personality.

Among the photographs on the wall there was one of Katharine Gaylord, taken in the days when Everett had known her, and when the flash of her eye or the flutter of her skirt was enough to set his boyish heart in a tumult. Even now, he stood before the portrait with a certain degree of embarrassment. It was the face of a woman already old in her first youth, thoroughly sophisticated and a trifle hard, and it told of what her brother had called her fight. The camaraderie of her frank, confident eyes was qualified by the deep lines about her mouth and the curve of the lips, which was both sad and cynical. Certainly she had more good will than confidence toward the world, and the bravado of her smile could not conceal the shadow of an unrest that was almost discontent. The chief charm of the woman, as Everett had known her, lay in her superb figure and in her

95

eyes, which possessed a warm, lifegiving quality like the sunlight; eyes which glowed with a sort of perpetual *salutat* to the world. Her head, Everett remembered as peculiarly well-shaped and proudly poised. There had been always a little of the imperatrix about her, and her pose in the photograph revived all his old impressions of her unattachedness, of how absolutely and valiantly she stood alone.

Everett was still standing before the picture, his hands behind him and his head inclined, when he heard the door open. A very tall woman advanced toward him, holding out her hand. As she started to speak, she coughed slightly; then, laughing, said, in a low, rich voice, a trifle husky: "You see I make the traditional Camille entrance — with the cough. How good of you to come, Mr. Hilgarde."

Everett was acutely conscious that while addressing him she was not looking at him at all, and, as he assured her of his pleasure in coming, he was glad to have an opportunity to collect himself. He had not reckoned upon the ravages of a long illness. The long, loose folds of her white gown had been especially designed to conceal the sharp outlines of her emaciated body, but the stamp of her disease was there; simple and ugly and obtrusive, a pitiless fact that could not be disguised or evaded. The splendid shoulders were stooped, there was a swaying unevenness in her gait, her arms seemed disproportionately long, and her hands were transparently white and cold to the touch. The changes in her face were less obvious; the proud carriage of the head, the warm, clear eyes, even the delicate flush of color in her cheeks, all defiantly remained, though they were all in a lower key — older, sadder, softer.

She sat down upon the divan and began nervously to arrange the pillows. "I know I'm not an inspiring object to look upon, but you must be quite frank and sensible about that and get used to it at once, for we've no time to lose. And if I'm a trifle irritable you won't mind? — for I'm more than usually nervous."

"Don't bother with me this morning, if you are tired," urged Everett. "I can come quite as well tomorrow."

"Gracious, no!" she protested, with a flash of that quick, keen humor that he remembered as a part of her. "It's solitude that I'm tired to death of — solitude and the wrong kind of people. You see, the minister, not content with reading the prayers for the sick, called on me this morning. He happened to be riding by on his bicycle and felt it his duty to stop. Of course, he disapproves of my profession, and I think he takes it for granted that I have a dark past. The funniest feature of his conversation is that he is always excusing my own vocation to me — condoning it, you know — and trying to patch up my peace with my conscience by suggesting possible noble uses for what he kindly calls my talent."

Everett laughed. "Oh! I'm afraid I'm not the person to call after such a serious gentleman — I can't sustain the situation. At my best I don't reach higher than low comedy. Have you decided to which one of the noble uses you will devote yourself?"

Katharine lifted her hands in a gesture of renunciation and exclaimed: "I'm not equal to any of them, not even the least noble. I didn't study that method."

She laughed and went on nervously: "The

parson's not so bad. His English never offends me, and he has read Gibbon's *Decline and Fall,* all five volumes, and that's something. Then, he has been to New York, and that's a great deal. But how we are losing time! Do tell me about New York; Charley says you're just on from there. How does it look and taste and smell just now? I think a whiff of the Jersey ferry would be as flagons of cod-liver oil to me. Who conspicuously walks the Rialto now, and what does he or she wear? Are the trees still green in Madison Square, or have they grown brown and dusty? Does the chaste Diana on the Garden Theatre still keep her vestal vows through all the exasperating changes of weather? Who has your brother's old studio now, and what misguided aspirants practice their scales in the rookeries about Carnegie Hall? What do people go to see at the theaters, and what do they eat and drink there in the world nowadays? You see, I'm homesick for it all, from the Battery to Riverside. Oh, let me die in Harlem!" She was interrupted by a violent attack of coughing, and Everett, embarrassed by her discomfort, plunged into gossip about the professional people he had met in town during the summer and the musical outlook for the winter. He was diagraming with his pencil, on the back of an old envelope he found in his pocket, some new mechanical device to be used at the Metropolitan in the production of the *Rheingold,* when he became conscious that she was looking at him intently, and that he was talking to the four walls.

Katharine was lying back among the pillows, watching him through half-closed eyes, as a painter looks at a picture. He finished his explanation vaguely enough and put the envelope back in his pocket. As he did so she said, quietly: "How wonderfully like Adriance you are!" and he felt as though a crisis of some sort had been met and tided over.

He laughed, looking up at her with a touch of pride in his eyes that made them seem quite boyish. "Yes, isn't it absurd? It's almost as awkward as looking like Napoleon — but, after all, there are some advantages. It has made some of his friends like me, and I hope it will make you."

Katharine smiled and gave him a quick, meaning glance from under her lashes. "Oh, it did that long ago. What a haughty, reserved youth you were then, and how you used to stare at people and then blush and look cross if they paid you back in your own coin. Do you remember that night when you took me home from a rehearsal and scarcely spoke a word to me?"

"It was the silence of admiration," protested Everett, "very crude and boyish, but very sincere and not a little painful. Perhaps you suspected something of the sort? I remember you saw fit to be very grown-up and worldly."

"I believe I suspected a pose; the one that college boys usually affect with singers — 'an earthen vessel in love with a star,' you know. But it rather surprised me in you, for you must have seen a good deal of your brother's pupils. Or had you an omnivorous capacity, and elasticity that always met the occasion?"

"Don't ask a man to confess the follies of his youth," said Everett, smiling a little sadly; "I am sensitive about some of them even now. But I was not so sophisticated as you imagined. I saw my brother's pupils come and go, but that was about all. Sometimes I was called on to play accompaniments, or to fill out a vacancy at a rehearsal, or to order a carriage for an infuriated soprano who had thrown up her part. But they never spent any time on me, unless it was to notice the resemblance you speak of."

"Yes," observed Katharine, thoughtfully, "I noticed it then, too; but it has grown as you have grown older. That is rather strange, when you have lived such different lives. It's not merely an ordinary family likeness of feature, you know, but a sort of interchangeable individuality; the suggestion of the other man's personality in your face like an air transposed to another key. But I'm not attempting to define it; it's beyond me; something altogether unusual and a trifle — well, uncanny," she finished, laughing.

"I remember," Everett said seriously, twirling the pencil between his fingers and looking, as he sat with his head thrown back, out under the red window blind which was raised just a little, and as it swung back and forth in the wind revealed the glaring panorama of the desert — a blinding stretch of yellow, flat as the sea in dead calm, splotched here and there with deep purple shadows; and, beyond, the ragged-blue outline of the mountains and the peaks of snow, white as the white clouds — "I remember, when I was a little fellow I used to be very sensitive about it. I don't think it exactly displeased me, or that I would have had it otherwise if I could, but it seemed to me like a birthmark, or something not to be lightly spoken of. People were naturally always fonder of Ad than of me, and I used to feel the chill of reflected light pretty often. It came into even my relations with my mother. Ad went abroad to study when he was absurdly young, you know, and mother was all broken up over it. She did her whole duty by each of us, but it was sort of generally understood among us that she'd have made burnt offerings of us all for Ad any day. I was a little fellow then, and when she sat alone on the porch in the summer dusk she used sometimes to call me to her and turn my face up in the light that streamed out through the shutters and kiss me, and then I always knew she was thinking of Adriance."

"Poor little chap," said Katharine, and her tone was a trifle huskier than usual. "How fond people have always been of Adriance! Now tell me the latest news of him. I haven't heard, except through the press, for a year or more. He was in Algeria then, in the valley of the Chelif, riding horseback night and day in an Arabian costume, and in his usual enthusiastic fashion he had quite made up his mind to adopt the Mohammedan faith and become as nearly an Arab as possible. How many countries and faiths has he adopted, I wonder? Probably he was playing Arab to himself all the time. I remember he was a sixteenth-century duke in Florence once for weeks together."

"Oh, that's Adriance," chuckled Everett. "He is himself barely long enough to write checks and be measured for his clothes. I didn't hear from him while he was an Arab; I missed that."

"He was writing an Algerian suite for the piano then; it must be in the publisher's hands by this time. I have been too ill to answer his letter, and have lost touch with him."

Everett drew a letter from his pocket. "This came about a month ago. It's chiefly about his new opera, which is to be brought out in London next winter. Read it at your leisure."

"I think I shall keep it as a hostage, so that I may be sure you will come again. Now I want you to play for me. Whatever you like; but if there is anything new in the world, in mercy let me hear it. For nine months I have heard nothing but 'The Baggage Coach Ahead' and 'She Is My Baby's Mother.' "

He sat down at the piano, and Katharine sat near him, absorbed in his remarkable physical likeness to his brother and trying to discover in just what it consisted. She told herself that it was very much as though a sculptor's finished work had been rudely copied in wood. He was of a larger build than Adriance, and his shoulders were broad and heavy, while those of his brother were slender and rather girlish. His face was of the same oval mold, but it was gray and darkened about the mouth by continual shaving. His eyes were of the same inconstant April color, but they were reflective and rather dull; while Adriance's were always points of highlight, and always meaning another thing than the thing they meant yesterday. But it was hard to see why this earnest man should so continually suggest that lyric, youthful face that was as gay as his was grave. For Adriance, though he was ten years the elder, and though his hair was streaked with silver, had the face of a boy of twenty, so mobile that it told his thoughts before he could put them into words. A contralto, famous for the extravagance of her vocal methods and of her affections, had once said to him that the shepherd boys who sang in the Vale of Tempe must certainly have looked like young Hilgarde; and the comparison had been appropriated by a hundred shyer women who preferred to quote.

■ ■ ■ ■

As Everett sat smoking on the veranda of the Inter-Ocean House that night, he was a victim to random recollections. His infatuation for Katharine Gaylord, visionary as it was, had been the most serious of his boyish love affairs, and had long disturbed his bachelor dreams. He was painfully timid in everything relating to the emotions, and his hurt had withdrawn him from the society of women. The fact that it was all so done and dead and far behind him, and that the woman had lived her life out since then, gave him an oppressive sense of age and loss. He bethought himself of something he had read about "sitting by the hearth and remembering the faces of women without desire," and felt himself an octogenarian.

He remembered how bitter and morose he had grown during his stay at his brother's studio when Katharine Gaylord was working there, and how he had wounded Adriance on the night of his last concert in New York. He had sat there in the box while his brother and Katharine were called back again and again after the last number, watching the roses go up over the footlights until they were stacked half as high as the piano, brooding, in his sullen boy's heart, upon the pride those two felt in each other's work — spurring each other to their best and beautifully contending in song. The footlights had seemed a hard, glittering line drawn sharply between their life and his; a circle of flame set about those splendid children of genius. He walked back to his hotel alone and sat in his window staring out on Madison Square until long after midnight, resolving to beat no more at doors that he could never enter and realizing more keenly than ever before how far this glorious world of beautiful creations lay from the paths of men like himself. He told himself that he had in common with this woman only the baser uses of life.

Everett's week in Cheyenne stretched to three, and he saw no prospect of release except through the thing he dreaded. The bright, windy days of the Wyoming autumn passed swiftly. Letters and telegrams came urging him to hasten his trip to the coast, but he resolutely postponed his business engagements. The mornings he spent on one of Charley Gaylord's ponies, or fishing in the mountains, and in the evenings he sat in his room writing letters or reading. In the afternoon he was usually at his post of duty. Destiny, he reflected, seems to have very positive notions about the sort of parts we are fitted to play. The scene changes and the compensation varies, but in the end we usually find that we have played the same class of business from first to last. Everett had been a stopgap all his life. He remembered going through a looking glass labyrinth when he was a boy and trying gallery after gallery, only at every turn to bump his nose against his own face — which, indeed, was not his own, but his brother's. No matter what his mission, east or west, by land or sea, he was sure to find himself employed in his brother's business, one of the tributary lives which helped to swell the shining current of Adriance Hilgarde's. It was not the first time that his duty had been to comfort, as best he could, one of the broken things his brother's imperious speed had cast aside and forgotten. He made no attempt to analyze the situation or to state it in exact terms;

but he felt Katharine Gaylord's need for him, and he accepted it as a commission from his brother to help this woman to die. Day by day he felt her demands on him grow more imperious, her need for him grow more acute and positive; and day by day he felt that in his peculiar relation to her his own individuality played a smaller and smaller part. His power to minister to her comfort, he saw, lay solely in his link with his brother's life. He understood all that his physical resemblance meant to her. He knew that she sat by him always watching for some common trick of gesture, some familiar play of expression, some illusion of light and shadow, in which he should seem wholly Adriance. He knew that she lived upon this and that her disease fed upon it; that it sent shudders of remembrance through her and that in the exhaustion which followed this turmoil of her dying senses, she slept deep and sweet and dreamed of youth and art and days in a certain old Florentine garden, and not of bitterness and death.

The question which most perplexed him was, "How much shall I know? How much does she wish me to know?" A few days after his first meeting with Katharine Gaylord, he had cabled his brother to write her. He had merely said that she was mortally ill; he could depend on Adriance to say the right thing — that was a part of his gift. Adriance always said not only the right thing, but the opportune, graceful, exquisite thing. His phrases took the color of the moment and the then-present condition, so that they never savored of perfunctory compliment or frequent usage. He always caught the lyric essence of the moment, the poetic suggestion of every situation. Moreover, he usually did the right thing, the opportune, graceful, exquisite thing — except, when he did very cruel things — bent upon making people happy when their existence touched his, just as he insisted that his material environment should be beautiful; lavishing upon those near him all the warmth and radiance of his rich nature, all the homage of the poet and troubadour, and, when they were no longer near, forgetting — for that also was a part of Adriance's gift.

Three weeks after Everett had sent his cable, when he made his daily call at the gaily painted ranch house, he found Katharine laughing like a schoolgirl. "Have you ever thought," she said, as he entered the music room, "how much these seances of ours are like Heine's 'Florentine Nights,' except that I don't give you an opportunity to monopolize the conversation as Heine did?" She held his hand longer than usual, as she greeted him, and looked searchingly up into his face. "You are the kindest man living; the kindest," she added, softly.

Everett's gray face colored faintly as he drew his hand away, for he felt that this time she was looking at him and not at a whimsical caricature of his brother. "Why, what have I done now?" he asked, lamely. "I can't remember having sent you any stale candy or champagne since yesterday."

She drew a letter with a foreign postmark from between the leaves of a book and held it out, smiling. "You got him to write it. Don't say you didn't, for it came direct, you see, and the last address I gave him was a place in Florida. This deed shall be remembered of you when I am with the just in Paradise. But one thing you did not ask him to do, for you didn't know about it. He has sent me his latest work, the new sonata, the most ambitious thing he has ever done, and you are to play it for me directly, though it looks horribly intricate. But first for the letter; I think you would better read it aloud to me."

Everett sat down in a low chair facing the window seat in which she reclined with a barricade of pillows behind her. He opened the letter, his lashes half-veiling his kind eyes, and saw to his satisfaction that it was a long one — wonderfully tactful and tender, even for Adriance, who was tender with his valet and his stable boy, with his old gondolier and the beggar-women who prayed to the saints for him.

The letter was from Granada, written in the Alhambra, as he sat by the fountain of the Patio di Lindaraxa. The air was heavy, with the warm fragrance of the South and full of the sound of splashing, running water, as it had been in a certain old garden in Florence, long ago. The sky was one great turquoise, heated until it glowed. The wonderful Moorish arches threw graceful blue shadows all about him. He had sketched an outline of them on the margin of his notepaper. The subtleties of Arabic decoration had cast an unholy spell over him, and the brutal exaggerations of Gothic art were a bad dream, easily forgotten. The Alhambra itself had, from the first, seemed perfectly familiar to him, and he knew that he must have trod that court, sleek and brown and obsequious, centuries before Ferdinand rode into Andalusia. The letter was full of confidences about his work, and delicate allusions to their old happy days of study and comradeship, and of her own work, still so warmly remembered and appreciatively discussed everywhere he went.

As Everett folded the letter he felt that Adriance

had divined the thing needed and had risen to it in his own wonderful way. The letter was consistently egotistical and seemed to him even a trifle patronizing, yet it was just what she had wanted. A strong realization of his brother's charm and intensity and power came over him; he felt the breath of that whirlwind of flame in which Adriance passed, consuming all in his path, and himself even more resolutely than he consumed others. Then he looked down at this white, burnt-out brand that lay before him. "Like him, isn't it?" she said, quietly.

"I think I can scarcely answer his letter, but when you see him next you can do that for me. I want you to tell him many things for me, yet they can all be summed up in this: I want him to grow wholly into his best and greatest self, even at the cost of the dear boyishness that is half his charm to you and me. Do you understand me?"

"I know perfectly well what you mean," answered Everett, thoughtfully. "I have often felt so about him myself. And yet it's difficult to prescribe for those fellows; so little makes, so little mars."

Katharine raised herself upon her elbow, and her face flushed with feverish earnestness. "Ah, but it is the waste of himself that I mean; his lashing himself out on stupid and uncomprehending people until they take him at their own estimate. He can kindle marble, strike fire from putty, but is it worth what it costs him?"

"Come, come," expostulated Everett, alarmed at her excitement. "Where is the new sonata? Let him speak for himself."

He sat down at the piano and began playing the first movement, which was indeed the voice of Adriance, his proper speech. The sonata was the most ambitious work he had done up to that time and marked the transition from his purely lyric vein to a deeper and nobler style. Everett played intelligently and with that sympathetic comprehension which seems peculiar to a certain lovable class of men who never accomplish anything in particular. When he had finished he turned to Katharine.

"How he has grown!" she cried. "What the three last years have done for him! He used to write only the tragedies of passion; but this is the tragedy of the soul, the shadow coexistent with the soul. This is the tragedy of effort and failure, the thing Keats called hell. This is my tragedy, as I lie here spent by the racecourse, listening to the feet of the runners as they pass me. Ah, God! The swift feet of the runners!"

She turned her face away and covered it with her straining hands. Everett crossed over to her quickly and knelt beside her. In all the days he had known her she had never before, beyond an occasional ironical jest, given voice to the bitterness of her own defeat. Her courage had become a point of pride with him, and to see it going sickened him.

"Don't do it," he gasped. "I can't stand it, I really can't, I feel it too much. We mustn't speak of that; it's too tragic and too vast."

When she turned her face back to him there was a ghost of the old, brave, cynical smile on it, more bitter than the tears she could not shed. "No, I won't be so ungenerous; I will save that for the watches of the night when I have no better company. Now you may mix me another drink of some sort. Formerly, when it was not *if* I should ever sing Brunnhilde, but quite simply when I *should* sing Brunnhilde, I was always starving myself and thinking what I might drink and what I might not. But broken music boxes may drink whatsoever they list, and no one cares whether they lose their figure. Run over that theme at the beginning again. That, at least, is not new. It was running in his head when we were in Venice years ago, and he used to drum it on his glass at the dinner table. He had just begun to work it out when the late autumn came on, and the paleness of the Adriatic oppressed him, and he decided to go to Florence for the winter, and lost touch with the theme during his illness. Do you remember those frightful days? All the people who have loved him are not strong enough to save him from himself! When I got word from Florence that he had been ill I was in Nice filling a concert engagement. His wife was hurrying to him from Paris, but I reached him first. I arrived at dusk, in a terrific storm. They had taken an old palace there for the winter, and I found him in the library — a long, dark room full of old Latin books and heavy furniture and bronzes. He was sitting by a wood fire at one end of the room, looking, oh, so worn and pale! — as he always does when he is ill, you know. Ah, it is so good that you *do* know! Even his red smoking jacket lent no color to his face. His first words were not to tell me how ill he had been, but that that morning he had been well enough to put the last strokes to the score of his *Souvenirs d'Automne.* He was as I most like to remember him: so calm and happy and tired; not gay, as he usually is, but just contented and tired with that heavenly tiredness that comes after a good work done at last. Outside, the rain poured down in torrents, and the wind moaned for the

110

pain of all the world and sobbed in the branches of the shivering olives and about the walls of that desolated old palace. How that night comes back to me! There were no lights in the room, only the wood fire which glowed upon the hard features of the bronze Dante, like the reflection of purgatorial flames, and threw long black shadows about us; beyond us it scarcely penetrated the gloom at all, Adriance sat staring at the fire with the weariness of all his life in his eyes, and of all the other lives that must aspire and suffer to make up one such life as his. Somehow the wind with all its world-pain had got into the room, and the cold rain was in our eyes, and the wave came up in both of us at once — that awful, vague, universal pain, that cold fear of life and death and God and hope — and we were like two clinging together on a spar in midocean after the shipwreck of everything. Then we heard the front door open with a great gust of wind that shook even the walls, and the servants came running with lights, announcing that Madam had returned, *'and in the book we read no more that night.'*"

She gave the old line with a certain bitter humor, and with the hard, bright smile in which of old she had wrapped her weakness as in a glittering garment. That ironical smile, worn like a mask through so many years, had gradually changed even the lines of her face completely, and when she looked in the mirror she saw not herself, but the scathing critic, the amused observer and satirist of herself. Everett dropped his head upon his hand and sat looking at the rug. "How much you have cared!" he said.

"Ah, yes, I cared," she replied, closing her eyes with a long-drawn sigh of relief; and lying perfectly

111

still, she went on: "You can't imagine what a comfort it is to have you know how I cared, what a relief it is to be able to tell it to someone. I used to want to shriek it out to the world in the long nights when I could not sleep. It seemed to me that I could not die with it. It demanded some sort of expression. And now that you know, you would scarcely believe how much less sharp the anguish of it is."

Everett continued to look helplessly at the floor. "I was not sure how much you wanted me to know," he said.

"Oh, I intended you should know from the first time I looked into your face, when you came that day with Charley. I flatter myself that I have been able to conceal it when I chose, though I suppose women always think that. The more observing ones may have seen, but discerning people are usually discreet and often kind, for we usually bleed a little before we begin to discern. But I wanted you to know; you are so like him that it is almost like telling him himself. At least, I feel now that he will know some day, and then I will be quite sacred from his compassion, for we none of us dare pity the dead. Since it was what my life has chiefly meant, I should like him to know. On the whole I am not ashamed of it. I have fought a good fight."

"And has he never known at all?" asked Everett, in a thick voice.

"Oh! Never at all in the way that you mean. Of course, he is accustomed to looking into the eyes of women and finding love there; when he doesn't find it there he thinks he must have been guilty of some discourtesy and is miserable about it. He has a genuine fondness for everyone who is not stupid or gloomy, or old or preternaturally ugly. Granted youth and cheerfulness, and a moderate amount of wit and some tact, and Adriance will always be glad to see you coming around the corner. I shared with the rest; shared the smiles and the gallantries and the droll little sermons. It was quite like a Sunday-school picnic; we wore our best clothes and a smile and took our turns. It was his kindness that was hardest. I have pretty well used my life up at standing punishment."

"Don't; you'll make me hate him," groaned Everett.

Katharine laughed and began to play nervously with her fan. "It wasn't in the slightest degree his fault; that is the most grotesque part of it. Why, it had really begun before I ever met him. I fought my way to him, and I drank my doom greedily enough."

Everett rose and stood hesitating. "I think I must go. You ought to be quiet, and I don't think I can hear any more just now."

She put out her hand and took his playfully. "You've put in three weeks at this sort of thing, haven't you? Well, it may never be to your glory in this world, perhaps, but it's been the mercy of heaven to me, and it ought to square accounts for a much worse life than yours will ever be."

Everett knelt beside her, saying, brokenly: "I stayed because I wanted to be with you, that's all. I have never cared about other women since I met you in New York when I was a lad. You are a part of my destiny, and I could not leave you if I would."

She put her hands on his shoulders and shook her head. "No, no; don't tell me that. I have seen enough of tragedy, God knows. Don't show me

113

any more just as the curtain is going down. No, no, it was only a boy's fancy, and your divine pity and my utter pitiableness have recalled it for a moment. One does not love the dying, dear friend. If some fancy of that sort had been left over from boyhood, this would rid you of it, and that were well. Now go, and you will come again tomorrow, as long as there are tomorrows, will you not?" She took his hand with a smile that lifted the mask from her soul, that was both courage and despair, and full of infinite loyalty and tenderness, as she said softly:

"For ever and for ever, farewell, Cassius;
  If we do meet again, why, we shall smile;
  If not, why then, this parting was well made."

The courage in her eyes was like the clear light of a star to him as he went out.

On the night of Adriance Hilgarde's opening concert in Paris Everett sat by the bed in the ranch house in Wyoming, watching over the last battle that we have with the flesh before we are done with it and free of it forever. At times it seemed that the serene soul of her must have left already and found some refuge from the storm, and only the tenacious animal life were left to do battle with death. She labored under a delusion at once pitiful and merciful, thinking that she was in the Pullman on her way to New York, going back to her life and her work. When she aroused from her stupor it was only to ask the porter to waken her half an hour out of Jersey City, or to remonstrate with him about the delays and the roughness of the road. At midnight Everett and the nurse were left alone with her. Poor Charley Gaylord had lain

114

down on a couch outside the door. Everett sat looking at the sputtering night lamp until it made his eyes ache. His head dropped forward on the foot of the bed, and he sank into a heavy, distressful slumber. He was dreaming of Adriance's concert in Paris, and of Adriance, the troubadour, smiling and debonair, with his boyish face and the touch of silver gray in his hair. He heard the applause and he saw the roses going up over the footlights until they were stacked half as high as the piano, and the petals fell and scattered, making crimson splotches on the floor. Down this crimson pathway came Adriance with his youthful step, leading his prima donna by the hand; a dark woman this time, with Spanish eyes.

The nurse touched him on the shoulder; he started and awoke. She screened the lamp with her hand. Everett saw that Katharine was awake and conscious, and struggling a little. He lifted her gently on his arm and began to fan her. She laid her hands lightly on his hair and looked into his face with eyes that seemed never to have wept or doubted. "Ah, dear Adriance, dear, dear," she whispered.

Everett went to call her brother, but when they came back the madness of art was over for Katharine.

Two days later Everett was pacing the station siding, waiting for the westbound train. Charley Gaylord walked beside him, but the two men had nothing to say to each other. Everett's bags were piled on the truck, and his step was hurried and his eyes were full of impatience, as he gazed again and again up the track, watching for the train. Gaylord's impatience was not less than his own; these two, who had grown so close, had now become painful and impossible to each other, and longed for the wrench of farewell.

As the train pulled in Everett wrung Gaylord's hand among the crowd of alighting passengers. The people of a German opera company, en route to the coast, rushed by them in frantic haste to snatch their breakfast during the stop. Everett heard an exclamation in a broad German dialect, and a massive woman whose figure persistently escaped from her stays in the most improbable places rushed up to him, her blond hair disordered by the wind, and glowing with joyful surprise she caught his coat sleeve with her tightly gloved hands.

"Herr Gott, Adriance, *lieber Freund,"* she cried, emotionally.

Everett quickly withdrew his arm and lifted his hat, blushing. "Pardon me, madam, but I see that you have mistaken me for Adriance Hilgarde. I am his brother," he said quietly, and turning from the crestfallen singer, he hurried into the car.

THE MARRIAGE OF PHAEDRA

The sequence of events was such that MacMaster did not make his pilgrimage to Hugh Treffinger's studio until three years after that painter's death. MacMaster was himself a painter, an American of the Gallicized type, who spent his winters in New York, his summers in Paris, and no inconsiderable amount of time on the broad waters between. He had often contemplated stopping in London on one of his return trips in the late autumn, but he had always deferred leaving Paris until the prick of necessity drove him home by the quickest and shortest route.

Treffinger was a comparatively young man at the time of his death, and there had seemed no occasion for haste until haste was of no avail. Then, possibly, though there had been some correspondence between them, MacMaster felt certain qualms about meeting in the flesh a man who in the flesh was so diversely reported. His intercourse with Treffinger's work had been so deep and satisfying, so apart from other appreciations, that he rather dreaded a critical juncture of any sort. He had always felt himself singularly inept in personal relations, and in this case he had avoided the issue until it was no longer to be feared or hoped for. There still remained, however,

Treffinger's great unfinished picture, the *Marriage of Phaedra,* which had never left his studio, and of which MacMaster's friends had now and again brought report that it was the painter's most characteristic production.

The young man arrived in London in the evening, and the next morning went out to Kensington to find Treffinger's studio. It lay in one of the perplexing bystreets off Holland Road, and the number he found on a door set in a high garden wall, the top of which was covered with broken green glass and over which a budding lilac bush nodded. Treffinger's plate was still there, and a card requesting visitors to ring for the attendant. In response to MacMaster's ring, the door was opened by a cleanly built little man, clad in a shooting jacket and trousers that had been made for an ampler figure. He had a fresh complexion, eyes of that common uncertain shade of gray, and was closely shaven except for the incipient muttonchops on his ruddy cheeks. He bore himself in a manner strikingly capable, and there was a sort of trimness and alertness about him, despite the too-generous shoulders of his coat. In one hand he held a bulldog pipe, and in the other a copy of *Sporting Life.* While MacMaster was explaining the purpose of his call he noticed that the man surveyed him critically, though not impertinently. He was admitted into a little tank of a lodge made of whitewashed stone, the back door and windows opening upon a garden. A visitor's book and a pile of catalogues lay on a deal table, together with a bottle of ink and some rusty pens. The wall was ornamented with photographs and colored prints of racing favorites.

"The studio is h'only open to the public on Saturdays and Sundays," explained the man — he referred to himself as "Jymes" — "but of course we make exceptions in the case of pynters. Lydy Elling Treffinger 'erself is on the Continent, but Sir 'Ugh's orders was that pynters was to 'ave the run of the place." He selected a key from his pocket and threw open the door into the studio which, like the lodge, was built against the wall of the garden.

MacMaster entered a long, narrow room, built of smoothed planks, painted a light green; cold and damp even on that fine May morning. The room was utterly bare of furniture — unless a stepladder, a model throne, and a rack laden with large leather portfolios could be accounted such — and was windowless, without other openings than the door and the skylight, under which hung the unfinished picture itself. MacMaster had never seen so many of Treffinger's paintings together. He knew the painter had married a woman with money and had been able to keep such of his pictures as he wished. These, with all of his replicas and studies, he had left as a sort of common legacy to the younger men of the school he had originated.

As soon as he was left alone MacMaster sat down on the edge of the model throne before the unfinished picture. Here indeed was what he had come for; it rather paralyzed his receptivity for the moment, but gradually the thing found its way to him.

At one o'clock he was standing before the collection of studies done for *Boccaccio's Garden* when he heard a voice at his elbow.

"Pardon, sir, but I was just about to lock up and

119

go to lunch. Are you lookin' for the figure study of Boccaccio 'imself?" James queried respectfully. "Lydy Elling Treffinger give it to Mr. Rossiter to take down to Oxford for some lectures he's been agiving there."

"Did he never paint out his studies, then?" asked MacMaster with perplexity. "Here are two completed ones for this picture. Why did he keep them?"

"I don't know as I could say as to that, sir," replied James, smiling indulgently, "but that was 'is way. That is to say, 'e pynted out very frequent, but 'e always made two studies to stand; one in watercolors and one in oils, before 'e went at the final picture — to say nothink of all the pose studies 'e made in pencil before he begun on the composition proper at all. He was that particular. You see, 'e wasn't so keen for the final effect as for the proper pyntin' of 'is pictures. 'E used to say they ought to be well made, the same as any other h'article of trade. I can lay my 'and on the pose studies for you, sir." He rummaged in one of the portfolios and produced half a dozen drawings. "These three," he continued, "was discarded; these two was the pose he finally accepted; this one without alteration, as it were.

"That's in Paris, as I remember," James continued reflectively. "It went with the *Saint Cecilia* into the Baron H——'s collection. Could you tell me, sir, 'as 'e it still? I don't like to lose account of them, but some 'as changed 'ands since Sir 'Ugh's death."

"H——'s collection is still intact, I believe," replied MacMaster. "You were with Treffinger long?"

"From my boyhood, sir," replied James with

gravity. "I was a stable boy when 'e took me."

"You were his man, then?"

"That's it, sir. Nobody else ever done anything around the studio. I always mixed 'is colors and 'e taught me to do a share of the varnishin'; 'e said as 'ow there wasn't a 'ouse in England as could do it proper. You ayn't looked at the *Marriage* yet, sir?" he asked abruptly, glancing doubtfully at MacMaster, and indicating with his thumb the picture under the north light.

"Not very closely. I prefer to begin with something simpler; that's rather appalling, at first glance," replied MacMaster.

"Well may you say that, sir," said James warmly. "That one regular killed Sir 'Ugh; it regular broke 'im up, and nothink will ever convince me as 'ow it didn't bring on 'is second stroke."

When MacMaster walked back to High Street to take his bus his mind was divided between two exultant convictions. He felt that he had not only found Treffinger's greatest picture, but that, in James, he had discovered a kind of cryptic index to the painter's personality — a clue which, if tactfully followed, might lead to much.

Several days after his first visit to the studio, MacMaster wrote to Lady Mary Percy, telling her that he would be in London for some time and asking her if he might call. Lady Mary was an only sister of Lady Ellen Treffinger, the painter's widow, and MacMaster had known her during one winter he spent at Nice. He had known her, indeed, very well, and Lady Mary, who was astonishingly frank and communicative upon all subjects, had been no less so upon the matter of her sister's unfortunate marriage.

In her reply to his note Lady Mary named an

afternoon when she would be alone. She was as good as her word, and when MacMaster arrived he found the drawing room empty. Lady Mary entered shortly after he was announced. She was a tall woman, thin and stiffly jointed, and her body stood out under the folds of her gown with the rigor of cast iron. This rather metallic suggestion was further carried out in her heavily knuckled hands, her stiff gray hair, and her long, bold-featured face, which was saved from freakishness only by her alert eyes.

"Really," said Lady Mary, taking a seat beside him and giving him a sort of military inspection through her nose glasses, "really, I had begun to fear that I had lost you altogether. It's four years since I saw you at Nice, isn't it? I was in Paris last winter, but I heard nothing from you."

"I was in New York then."

"It occurred to me that you might be. And why are you in London?"

"Can you ask?" replied MacMaster gallantly.

Lady Mary smiled ironically. "But for what else, incidentally?"

"Well, incidentally, I came to see Treffinger's studio and his unfinished picture. Since I've been here, I've decided to stay the summer. I'm even thinking of attempting to do a biography of him."

"So that is what brought you to London?"

"Not exactly. I had really no intention of anything so serious when I came. It's his last picture, I fancy, that has rather thrust it upon me. The notion has settled down on me like a thing destined."

"You'll not be offended if I question the clemency of such a destiny," remarked Lady Mary dryly. "Isn't there rather a surplus of books on that subject already?"

"Such as they are. Oh, I've read them all" —
here MacMaster faced Lady Mary triumphantly.
"He has quite escaped your amiable critics," he
added, smiling.

"I know well enough what you think, and I daresay we are not much on art," said Lady Mary with
tolerant good humor. "We leave that to peoples
who have no physique. Treffinger made a stir for a
time, but it seems that we are not capable of a
sustained appreciation of such extraordinary
methods. In the end we go back to the pictures
we find agreeable and unperplexing. He was
regarded as an experiment, I fancy; and now it
seems that he was rather an unsuccessful one. If
you've come to us in a missionary spirit, we'll
tolerate you politely, but we'll laugh in our sleeve,
I warn you."

"That really doesn't daunt me, Lady Mary,"
declared MacMaster blandly. "As I told you, I'm
a man with a mission."

Lady Mary laughed her hoarse, baritone laugh.
"Bravo! And you've come to me for inspiration
for your panegyric?"

MacMaster smiled with some embarrassment.
"Not altogether for that purpose. But I want to
consult you, Lady Mary, about the advisability of
troubling Lady Ellen Treffinger in the matter. It
seems scarcely legitimate to go on without asking
her to give some sort of grace to my proceedings,
yet I feared the whole subject might be painful to
her. I shall rely wholly upon your discretion."

"I think she would prefer to be consulted,"
replied Lady Mary judicially. "I can't understand
how she endures to have the wretched affair
continually raked up, but she does. She seems to

feel a sort of moral responsibility. Ellen has always been singularly conscientious about this matter, insofar as her light goes, — which rather puzzles me, as hers is not exactly a magnanimous nature. She is certainly trying to do what she believes to be the right thing. I shall write to her, and you can see her when she returns from Italy."

"I want very much to meet her. She is, I hope, quite recovered in every way," queried MacMaster, hesitatingly.

"No, I can't say that she is. She has remained in much the same condition she sank to before his death. He trampled over pretty much whatever there was in her, I fancy. Women don't recover from wounds of that sort — at least, not women of Ellen's grain. They go on bleeding inwardly."

"You, at any rate, have not grown more reconciled," MacMaster ventured.

"Oh I give him his dues. He was a colorist, I grant you; but that is a vague and unsatisfactory quality to marry to; Lady Ellen Treffinger found it so."

"But, my dear Lady Mary," expostulated Mac-Master, "and just repress me if I'm becoming too personal — but it must, in the first place, have been a marriage of choice on her part as well as on his."

Lady Mary poised her glasses on her large forefinger and assumed an attitude suggestive of the clinical lecture room as she replied. "Ellen, my dear boy, is an essentially romantic person. She is quiet about it, but she runs deep. I never knew how deep until I came against her on the issue of that marriage. She was always discontented as a girl; she found things dull and prosaic, and the ardor of his courtship was agreeable to her.

124

He met her during her first season in town. She is handsome, and there were plenty of other men, but I grant you your scowling brigand was the most picturesque of the lot. In his courtship, as in everything else, he was theatrical to the point of being ridiculous, but Ellen's sense of humor is not her strongest quality. He had the charm of celebrity, the air of a man who could storm his way through anything to get what he wanted. That sort of vehemence is particularly effective with women like Ellen, who can be warmed only by reflected heat, and she couldn't at all stand out against it. He convinced her of his necessity; and that done, all's done."

"I can't help thinking that, even on such a basis, the marriage should have turned out better," Mac-Master remarked reflectively.

"The marriage," Lady Mary continued with a shrug, "was made on the basis of a mutual misunderstanding. Ellen, in the nature of the case, believed that she was doing something quite out of the ordinary in accepting him, and expected concessions which, apparently, it never occurred to him to make. After his marriage he relapsed into his old habits of incessant work, broken by violent and often brutal relaxations. He insulted her friends and foisted his own upon her — many of them well calculated to arouse aversion in any well-bred girl. He had Ghillini constantly at the house — a homeless vagabond, whose conversation was impossible. I don't say, mind you, that he had not grievances on his side. He had probably overrated the girl's possibilities, and he let her see that he was disappointed in her. Only a large and generous nature could have borne with him, and Ellen's is not that. She could not at all understand

125

that odious strain of plebeian pride which plumes itself upon not having risen above its sources."

As MacMaster drove back to his hotel he reflected that Lady Mary Percy had probably had good cause for dissatisfaction with her brother-in-law. Treffinger was, indeed, the last man who should have married into the Percy family. The son of a small tobacconist, he had grown up a sign-painter's apprentice; idle, lawless, and practically letterless until he had drifted into the night classes of the Albert League, where Ghillini sometimes lectured. From the moment he came under the eye and influence of that erratic Italian, then a political exile, his life had swerved sharply from its old channel. This man had been at once incentive and guide, friend and master, to his pupil. He had taken the raw clay out of the London streets and molded it anew. Seemingly he had divined at once where the boy's possibilities lay, and had thrown aside every canon of orthodox instruction in the training of him. Under him Treffinger acquired his superficial, yet facile, knowledge of the classics; had steeped himself in the monkish Latin and medieval romances which later gave his work so naive and remote a quality. That was the beginning of the wattle fences, the cobble pave, the brown roof beams, the cunningly wrought fabrics that gave to his pictures such a richness of decorative effect.

As he had told Lady Mary Percy, MacMaster had found the imperative inspiration of his purpose in Treffinger's unfinished picture, the *Marriage of Phaedra*. He had always believed that the key to Treffinger's individuality lay in his singular education; in the *Roman de la Rose,* in Boccaccio, and Amadis, those works which had literally transcribed themselves upon the blank soul of the London street boy, and through which he had been born into the world of spiritual things. Treffinger had been a man who lived after his imagination; and his mind, his ideals and, as MacMaster believed, even his personal ethics, had to the last been colored by the trend of his early training. There was in him alike the freshness and spontaneity, the frank brutality and the religious mysticism, which lay well back of the fifteenth century. In the *Marriage of Phaedra* MacMaster found the ultimate expression of this spirit, the final word as to Treffinger's point of view.

As in all Treffinger's classical subjects, the conception was wholly medieval. This Phaedra, just turning from her husband and maidens to greet her husband's son, giving him her first fearsome glance from under her half-lifted veil, was no daughter of Minos. The daughter of *heathenesse* and the early church she was; doomed to torturing visions and scourgings, and the wrangling of soul with flesh. The venerable Theseus might have been victorious Charlemagne, and Phaedra's maidens belonged rather in the train of Blanche of Castile than at the Cretan court. In the earlier studies Hippolytus had been done with a more pagan suggestion; but in each successive drawing the glorious figure bad been deflowered of something of its serene unconsciousness, until, in the canvas under the skylight, he appeared a very Christian knight. This male figure, and the face of Phaedra, painted with such magical preservation of tone under the heavy shadow of the veil, were plainly Treffinger's highest achievements of craftsmanship. By what labor he had reached the seemingly inevitable composition of the picture — with its twenty figures, its plenitude of light and air, its restful distances seen through white porticoes — countless studies bore witness.

From James's attitude toward the picture Mac-Master could well conjecture what the painter's had been. This picture was always uppermost in James's mind; its custodianship formed, in his eyes, his occupation. He was manifestly apprehensive when visitors — not many came nowadays — lingered near it. "It was the *Marriage* as killed 'im," he would often say, "and for the matter 'o that, it did like to 'av been the death of all of us."

By the end of his second week in London Mac-Master had begun the notes for his study of Hugh Treffinger and his work. When his researches led him occasionally to visit the studios of Treffinger's friends and erstwhile disciples, he found their Treffinger manner fading as the ring of Treffinger's personality died out in them. One by one they were stealing back into the fold of national British art; the hand that had wound them up was still. MacMaster despaired of them and confined himself more and more exclusively to the studio, to such of Treffinger's letters as were available — they were for the most part singularly negative and colorless — and to his interrogation of Treffinger's man.

He could not himself have traced the successive steps by which he was gradually admitted into James's confidence. Certainly most of his adroit strategies to that end failed humiliatingly, and whatever it was that built up an understanding between them must have been instinctive and intuitive on both sides. When at last James became anecdotal, personal, there was that in every word

128

he let fall which put breath and blood into Mac-Master's book. James had so long been steeped in that penetrating personality that he fairly exuded it. Many of his very phrases, mannerisms, and opinions were impressions that he had taken on like wet plaster in his daily contact with Treffinger. Inwardly he was lined with cast-off epitheliums, as outwardly he was clad in the painter's discarded coats. If the painter's letters were formal and perfunctory, if his expressions to his friends had been extravagant, contradictory, and often apparently insincere — still, MacMaster felt himself not entirely without authentic sources. It was James who possessed Treffinger's legend; it was with James that he had laid aside his pose. Only in his studio, alone, and face to face with his work, as it seemed, had the man invariably been himself. James had known him in the one attitude in which he was entirely honest; their relation had fallen well within the painter's only indubitable integrity. James's report of Treffinger was distorted by no hallucination of artistic insight, colored by no interpretation of his own. He merely held what he had heard and seen; his mind was a sort of camera obscura. His very limitations made him the more literal and minutely accurate.

One morning, when MacMaster was seated before the *Marriage of Phaedra,* James entered on his usual round of dusting.

"I've 'eard from Lydy Elling by the post, sir," he remarked, "an' she's give h'orders to 'ave the 'ouse put in readiness. I doubt she'll be 'ere by Thursday or Friday next."

"She spends most of her time abroad?" queried MacMaster; on the subject of Lady Treffinger

James consistently maintained a very delicate reserve.

"Well, you could 'ardly say she does that, sir. She finds the 'ouse a bit dull, I daresay, so durin' the season she stops mostly with Lydy Mary Percy, at Grosvenor Square. Lydy Mary's a h'only sister." After a few moments he continued, speaking in jerks governed by the rigor of his dusting: "H'only this morning I come upon this scarfpin," exhibiting a very striking instance of that article, "an' I recalled as 'ow Sir 'Ugh give it me when 'e was acourting of Lydy Elling. Blowed if I ever see a man go in for a 'oman like 'im! 'E was that gone, sir. 'E never went in on anythink so 'ard before nor since, till 'e went in on the *Marriage* there — though 'e mostly went in on things pretty keen; 'ad the measles when 'e was thirty, strong as cholera, an' come close to dyin' of 'em. 'E wasn't strong for Lydy Elling's set; they was a bit too stiff for 'im. A free an' easy gentleman, 'e was; 'e liked 'is dinner with a few friends an' them jolly, but 'e wasn't much on what you might call big affairs. But once 'e went in for Lydy Elling 'e broke 'imself to new paces; He give away 'is rings an' pins, an' the tylor's man an' the 'aberdasher's man was at 'is rooms continual. 'E got 'imself put up for a club in Piccadilly; 'e starved 'imself thin, an' worrited 'imself white, an' ironed 'imself out, an' drawed 'imself tight as a bow string. It was a good job 'e come a winner, or I don't know w'at'd 'a been to pay."

The next week, in consequence of an invitation from Lady Ellen Treffinger, MacMaster went one afternoon to take tea with her. He was shown into the garden that lay between the residence and the studio, where the tea table was set under a gnarled

130

pear tree. Lady Ellen rose as he approached — he was astonished to note how tall she was — and greeted him graciously, saying that she already knew him through her sister. MacMaster felt a certain satisfaction in her; in her reassuring poise and repose, in the charming modulations of her voice and the indolent reserve of her full, almond eyes. He was even delighted to find her face so inscrutable, though it chilled his own warmth and made the open frankness he had wished to permit himself impossible. It was a long face, narrow at the chin, very delicately featured, yet steeled by an impassive mask of self-control. It was behind just such finely cut, close-sealed faces, MacMaster reflected, that nature sometimes hid astonishing secrets. But in spite of this suggestion of hardness he felt that the unerring taste that Treffinger had always shown in larger matters had not deserted him when he came to the choosing of a wife, and he admitted that he could not himself have selected a woman who looked more as Treffinger's wife should look.

While he was explaining the purpose of his frequent visits to the studio she heard him with courteous interest. "I have read, I think, everything that has been published on Sir Hugh Treffinger's work, and it seems to me that there is much left to be said," he concluded.

"I believe they are rather inadequate," she remarked vaguely. She hesitated a moment, absently fingering the ribbons of her gown, then continued, without raising her eyes; "I hope you will not think me too exacting if I ask to see the proofs of such chapters of your work as have to do with Sir Hugh's personal life. I have always asked that privilege."

MacMaster hastily assured her as to this, adding, "I mean to touch on only such facts in his personal life as have to do directly with his work — such as his monkish education under Ghillini."

"I see your meaning, I think," said Lady Ellen, looking at him with wide, uncomprehending eyes.

When MacMaster stopped at the studio on leaving the house he stood for some time before Treffinger's one portrait of himself, that brigand of a picture, with its full throat and square head; the short upper lip blackened by the close-clipped mustache, the wiry hair tossed down over the forehead, the strong white teeth set hard on a short pipestem. He could well understand what manifold tortures the mere grain of the man's strong red and brown flesh might have inflicted upon a woman like Lady Ellen. He could conjecture, too, Treffinger's impotent revolt against that very repose which had so dazzled him when it first defied his daring; and how once possessed of it, his first instinct had been to crush it, since he could not melt it.

Toward the close of the season Lady Ellen Treffinger left town. MacMaster's work was progressing rapidly, and he and James wore away the days in their peculiar relation, which by this time had much of friendliness. Excepting for the regular visits of a Jewish picture dealer, there were few intrusions upon their solitude. Occasionally a party of Americans rang at the little door in the garden wall, but usually they departed speedily for the Moorish hall and tinkling fountain of the great show studio of London, not far away.

This Jew, an Austrian by birth, who had a large business in Melbourne, Australia, was a man of considerable discrimination, and at once selected the *Marriage of Phaedra* as the object of his especial interest. When, upon his first visit, Lichtenstein had declared the picture one of the things done for time, MacMaster had rather warmed toward him and had talked to him very freely. Later, however, the man's repulsive personality and innate vulgarity so wore upon him that, the more genuine the Jew's appreciation, the more he resented it and the more base he somehow felt it to be. It annoyed him to see Lichtenstein walking up and down before the picture, shaking his head and blinking his watery eyes over his nose glasses, ejaculating: "Dot is a chem, a chem! It is wordt to gome den dousant miles for such a bainting, eh? To make Eurobe abbreciate such a work of ardt it is necessary to take it away while she is napping. She has never abbreciated until she has lost, but," knowingly, "she will buy back."

James had, from the first, felt such a distrust of the man that he would never leave him alone in the studio for a moment. When Lichtenstein insisted upon having Lady Ellen Treffinger's address James rose to the point of insolence. "It ayn't no use to give it, noway. Lydy Treffinger never has nothink to do with dealers." MacMaster quietly repented his rash confidences, fearing that he might indirectly cause Lady Ellen annoyance from this merciless speculator, and he recalled with chagrin that Lichtenstein had extorted from him, little by little, pretty much the entire plan of his book, and especially the place in it which the *Marriage of Phaedra* was to occupy.

By this time the first chapters of MacMaster's book were in the hands of his publisher, and his visits to the studio were necessarily less frequent. The greater part of his time was now employed with the engravers who were to reproduce such of Treffinger's pictures as he intended to use as illustrations.

He returned to his hotel late one evening after a long and vexing day at the engravers to find James in his room, seated on his steamer trunk by the window, with the outline of a great square draped in sheets resting against his knee.

"Why, James, what's up?" he cried in astonishment, glancing inquiringly at the sheeted object.

"Ayn't you seen the pypers, sir?" jerked out the man.

"No, now I think of it, I haven't even looked at a paper. I've been at the engravers' plant all day. I haven't seen anything."

James drew a copy of the *Times* from his pocket and handed it to him, pointing with a tragic finger to a paragraph in the social column. It was merely the announcement of Lady Ellen Treffinger's engagement to Captain Alexander Gresham.

"Well, what of it, my man? That surely is her privilege."

James took the paper, turned to another page, and silently pointed to a paragraph in the art notes which stated that Lady Treffinger had presented to the X — gallery the entire collection of paintings and sketches now in her late husband's studio, with the exception of his unfinished picture, the *Marriage Of Phaedra,* which she had sold for a large sum to an Australian dealer who had come to London purposely to secure some of Treffinger's paintings.

MacMaster pursed up his lips and sat down, his overcoat still on. "Well, James, this is something of a — something of a jolt, eh? It never occurred to me she'd really do it."

"Lord, you don't know 'er, sir," said James bitterly, still staring at the floor in an attitude of abandoned dejection.

MacMaster started up in a flash of enlightenment, "What on earth have you got there, James? It's not — surely it's not —"

"Yes, it is, sir," broke in the man excitedly. "It's the *Marriage* itself. It ayn't agoing to H'Australia, no'ow!"

"But man, what are you going to do with it? It's Lichtenstein's property now, as it seems."

"It ayn't, sir, that it ayn't. No, by Gawd, it ayn't!" shouted James, breaking into a choking fury. He controlled himself with an effort and added supplicatingly: "Oh, sir, you ayn't a-going to see it go to H'Australia, w'ere they send convic's?" He unpinned and flung aside the sheets as though to let *Phaedra* plead for herself.

MacMaster sat down again and looked sadly at the doomed masterpiece. The notion of James having carried it across London that night rather appealed to his fancy. There was certainly a flavor about such a highhanded proceeding. "However did you get it here?" he queried.

"I got a four-wheeler and come over direct, sir. Good job I 'appened to 'ave the chaynge about me."

"You came up High Street, up Piccadilly, through the Haymarket and Trafalgar Square, and into the Strand?" queried MacMaster with a relish.

"Yes, sir. Of course, sir," assented James with surprise.

MacMaster laughed delightedly. "It was a beautiful idea, James, but I'm afraid we can't carry it any further."

"I was thinkin' as 'ow it would be a rare chance to take you to take the *Marriage* over to Paris for a year or two, sir, until the thing blows over?" suggested James blandly.

"I'm afraid that's out of the question, James. I haven't the right stuff in me for a pirate, or even a vulgar smuggler, I'm afraid." MacMaster found it surprisingly difficult to say this, and he busied himself with the lamp as he said it. He heard James's hand fall heavily on the trunk top, and he discovered that he very much disliked sinking in the man's estimation.

"Well, sir," remarked James in a more formal tone, after a protracted silence; "then there's nothink for it but as 'ow I'll 'ave to make way with it myself."

"And how about your character, James? The evidence would be heavy against you, and even if Lady Treffinger didn't prosecute you'd be done for."

"Blow my character! — your pardon, sir," cried James, starting to his feet. "W'at do I want of a character? I'll chuck the 'ole thing, and damned lively, too. The shop's to be sold out, an' my place is gone any'ow. I'm a-going to enlist, or try the gold fields. I've lived too long with h'artists; I'd never give satisfaction in livery now. You know 'ow it is yourself, sir; there ayn't no life like it, no'ow."

For a moment MacMaster was almost equal to abetting James in his theft. He reflected that pictures had been whitewashed, or hidden in the crypts of churches, or under the floors of palaces from meaner motives, and to save them from a fate less ignominious. But presently, with a sigh, he shook his head.

"No, James, it won't do at all. It has been tried

136

over and over again, ever since the world has been a-going and pictures a-making. It was tried in Florence and in Venice, but the pictures were always carried away in the end. You see, the difficulty is that although Treffinger told you what was not to be done with the picture, he did not say definitely what was to be done with it. Do you think Lady Treffinger really understands that he did not want it to be sold?"

"Well, sir, it was like this, sir," said James, resuming his seat on the trunk and again resting the picture against his knee. "My memory is as clear as glass about it. After Sir 'Ugh got up from 'is first stroke, 'e took a fresh start at the *Marriage*. Before that 'e 'ad been working at it only at night for a while back; the *Legend* was the big picture then, an' was under the north light w'ere 'e worked of a morning. But one day 'e bid me take the *Legend* down an' put the *Marriage* in its place, an' 'e says, dashin' on 'is jacket, 'Jymes, this is a start for the finish, this time.'

"From that on 'e worked at the night picture in the mornin' — a thing contrary to 'is custom. The *Marriage* went wrong, and wrong — an' Sir 'Ugh agettin' seedier an' seedier every day. 'E tried models an' models, an' smudged an' pynted out on account of 'er face goin' wrong in the shadow. Sometimes 'e layed it on the colors, an' swore at me an' things in general. He got that discouraged about 'imself that on 'is low days 'e used to say to me: 'Jymes, remember one thing; if anythink 'appens to me, the *Marriage* is not to go out of 'ere unfinished. It's worth the lot of 'em, my boy, an' it's not a-going to go shabby for lack of pains.' 'E said things to that effect repeated.

"He was workin' at the picture the last day,

before 'e went to 'is club. 'E kept the carriage waitin' near an hour while 'e put on a stroke an' then drawed back for to look at it, an' then put on another, careful like. After 'e 'ad 'is gloves on, 'e come back an' took away the brushes I was startin' to clean, an' put in another touch or two. 'It's a-comin', Jymes,' 'e says, 'by gad if it ayn't.' An' with that 'e goes out. It was cruel sudden, w'at come after.

"That night I was lookin' to 'is clothes at the 'ouse when they brought 'im 'ome. He was conscious, but w'en I ran downstairs for to 'elp lift 'im up, I knowed 'e was a finished man. After we got 'im into bed 'e kept lookin' restless at me and then at Lydy Elling and a-jerkin' of 'is 'and. Finally 'e quite raised it an' shot 'is thumb out toward the wall. 'He wants water; ring, Jymes,' says Lydy Elling, placid. But I knowed 'e was pointin' to the shop.

" 'Lydy Treffinger,' says I, bold, 'he's pointin' to the studio. He means about the *Marriage;* 'e told me today as 'ow 'e never wanted it sold unfinished. Is that it, Sir 'Ugh?'

"He smiled an' nodded slight an' closed 'is eyes. 'Thank you, Jymes,' says Lydy Elling, placid. Then 'e opened 'is eyes an' looked long and 'ard at Lydy Elling.

" 'Of course I'll try to do as you'd wish about the picture, 'Ugh, if that's w'at's troublin' you,' she says quiet. With that 'e closed 'is eyes and 'e never opened 'em. He died unconscious at four that mornin'.

"You see, sir, Lydy Elling was always cruel 'ard on the *Marriage.* From the first it went wrong, an' Sir 'Ugh was out of temper pretty constant. She came into the studio one day and looked at the

138

picture an 'asked 'im why 'e didn't throw it up an' quit a-worriting 'imself. He answered sharp, an' with that she said as 'ow she didn't see w'at there was to make such a row about, no'ow. She spoke 'er mind about that picture, free; an' Sir 'Ugh swore 'ot an' let a 'andful of brushes fly at 'is study, an' Lydy Elling picked up 'er skirts careful an' chill, an' drifted out of the studio with 'er eyes calm and 'er chin 'igh. If there was one thing Lydy Elling 'ad no comprehension of, it was the usefulness of swearin'. So the *Marriage* was a sore thing between 'em. She is uncommon calm, but uncommon bitter, is Lydy Elling. She's never come a-near the studio since that day she went out 'oldin' up of 'er skirts. W'en 'er friends goes over she excuses 'erself along o' the strain. Strain — Gawd!" James ground his wrath short in his teeth.

"I'll tell you what I'll do, James, and it's our only hope. I'll see Lady Ellen tomorrow. The *Times* says she returned today. You take the picture back to its place, and I'll do what I can for it. If anything is done to save it, it must be done through Lady Ellen Treffinger herself, that much is clear. I can't think that she fully understands the situation. If she did, you know, she really couldn't have any motive —" He stopped suddenly. Somehow, in the dusky lamplight, her small, close-sealed face came ominously back to him. He rubbed his forehead and knitted his brows thoughtfully. After a moment he shook his head and went on: "I am positive that nothing can be gained by highhanded methods, James. Captain Gresham is one of the most popular men in London, and his friends would tear up Treffinger's bones if he were annoyed by any scandal of

139

our making — and this scheme you propose would inevitably result in scandal. Lady Ellen has, of course, every legal right to sell the picture. Treffinger made considerable inroads upon her estate, and, as she is about to marry a man without income, she doubtless feels that she has a right to replenish her patrimony."

He found James amenable, though doggedly skeptical. He went down into the street, called a carriage, and saw James and his burden into it. Standing in the doorway, he watched the carriage roll away through the drizzling mist, weave in and out among the wet, black vehicles and darting cab lights, until it was swallowed up in the glare and confusion of the Strand. "It is rather a fine touch of irony," he reflected, "that he, who is so out of it, should be the one to really care. Poor Treffinger," he murmured as, with a rather spiritless smile, he turned back into his hotel. "Poor Treffinger; *sic transit gloria.*"

The next afternoon MacMaster kept his promise. When he arrived at Lady Mary Percy's house he saw preparations for a function of some sort, but he went resolutely up the steps, telling the footman that his business was urgent. Lady Ellen came down alone, excusing her sister. She was dressed for receiving, and MacMaster had never seen one so beautiful. The color in her cheeks sent a softening glow over her small, delicately cut features.

MacMaster apologized for his intrusion and came unflinchingly to the object of his call. He had come, he said, not only to offer her his warmest congratulations, but to express his regret that a great work of art was to leave England.

Lady Treffinger looked at him in wide-eyed

astonishment. Surely, she said, she had been careful to select the best of the pictures for the X—— gallery, in accordance with Sir Hugh Treffinger's wishes.

"And did he — pardon me, Lady Treffinger, but in mercy set my mind at rest — did he or did he not express any definite wish concerning this one picture, which to me seems worth all the others, unfinished as it is?"

Lady Treffinger paled perceptibly, but it was not the pallor of confusion. When she spoke there was a sharp tremor in her smooth voice, the edge of a resentment that tore her like pain. "I think his man has some such impression, but I believe it to be utterly unfounded. I cannot find that he ever expressed any wish concerning the disposition of the picture to any of his friends. Unfortunately, Sir Hugh was not always discreet in his remarks to his servants."

"Captain Gresham, Lady Ellingham, and Miss Ellingham," announced a servant, appearing at the door.

There was a murmur in the hall, and MacMaster greeted the smiling Captain and his aunt as he bowed himself out.

To all intents and purposes the *Marriage of Phaedra* was already entombed in a vague continent in the Pacific, somewhere on the other side of the world.

A Wagner Matinée

I received one morning a letter, written in pale ink on glassy, blue-lined notepaper, and bearing the postmark of a little Nebraska village. This communication, worn and rubbed, looking as though it had been carried for some days in a coat pocket that was none too clean, was from my Uncle Howard and informed me that his wife had been left a small legacy by a bachelor relative who had recently died, and that it would be necessary for her to go to Boston to attend to the settling of the estate. He requested me to meet her at the station and render her whatever services might be necessary. On examining the date indicated as that of her arrival I found it no later than tomorrow. He had characteristically delayed writing until, had I been away from home for a day, I must have missed the good woman altogether.

The name of my Aunt Georgiana called up not alone her own figure, at once pathetic and grotesque, but opened before my feet a gulf of recollection so wide and deep that, as the letter dropped from my hand, I felt suddenly a stranger to all the present conditions of my existence, wholly ill at ease and out of place amid the familiar surroundings of my study. I became, in short, the gangling farm boy my aunt had known,

142

scourged with chilblains and bashfulness, my hands cracked and sore from the corn husking. I felt the knuckles of my thumb tentatively, as though they were raw again. I sat again before her parlor organ, fumbling the scales with my stiff, red hands, while she, beside me, made canvas mittens for the huskers.

The next morning, after preparing my landlady somewhat, I set out for the station. When the train arrived I had some difficulty in finding my aunt. She was the last of the passengers to alight, and it was not until I got her into the carriage that she seemed really to recognize me. She had come all the way in a day coach; her linen duster had become black with soot, and her black bonnet gray with dust, during the journey. When we arrived at my boardinghouse the landlady put her to bed at once and I did not see her again until the next morning.

Whatever shock Mrs. Springer experienced at my aunt's appearance she considerately concealed. As for myself, I saw my aunt's misshapen figure with that feeling of awe and respect with which we behold explorers who have left their ears and fingers north of Franz-Josef-Land, or their health somewhere along the Upper Congo. My Aunt Georgiana had been a music teacher at the Boston Conservatory, somewhere back in the latter sixties. One summer, while visiting in the little village among the Green Mountains where her ancestors had dwelt for generations, she had kindled the callow fancy of the most idle and shiftless of all the village lads, and had conceived for this Howard Carpenter one of those extravagant passions which a handsome country boy of twenty-one sometimes inspires in an angular, spectacled

143

woman of thirty. When she returned to her duties in Boston, Howard followed her, and the upshot of this inexplicable infatuation was that she eloped with him, eluding the reproaches of her family and the criticisms of her friends by going with him to the Nebraska frontier. Carpenter, who, of course, had no money, had taken a homestead in Red Willow County, fifty miles from the railroad. There they had measured off their quarter section themselves by driving across the prairie in a wagon, to the wheel of which they had tied a red cotton handkerchief, and counting off its revolutions. They built a dugout in the red hillside, one of those cave dwellings whose inmates so often reverted to primitive conditions. Their water they got from the lagoons where the buffalo drank, and their slender stock of provisions was always at the mercy of bands of roving Indians. For thirty years my aunt had not been further than fifty miles from the homestead.

But Mrs. Springer knew nothing of all this, and must have been considerably shocked at what was left of my kinswoman. Beneath the soiled linen duster which, on her arrival, was the most conspicuous feature of her costume, she wore a black stuff dress, whose ornamentation showed that she had surrendered herself unquestioningly into the hands of a country dressmaker. My poor aunt's figure, however, would have presented astonishing difficulties to any dressmaker. Originally stooped, her shoulders were now almost bent together over her sunken chest. She wore no stays, and her gown, which trailed unevenly behind, rose in a sort of peak over her abdomen. She wore ill-fitting false teeth, and her skin was as yellow as a Mongolian's from constant exposure to a pitiless wind and to the alkaline water which hardens the most transparent cuticle into a sort of flexible leather.

I owed to this woman most of the good that ever came my way in my boyhood, and had a reverential affection for her. During the years when I was riding herd for my uncle, my aunt, after cooking the three meals — the first of which was ready at six o'clock in the morning — and putting the six children to bed, would often stand until midnight at her ironing board, with me at the kitchen table beside her, hearing me recite Latin declensions and conjugations, gently shaking me when my drowsy head sank down over a page of irregular verbs. It was to her, at her ironing or mending, that I read my first Shakespeare, and her old textbook on mythology was the first that ever came into my empty hands. She taught me my scales and exercises, too — on the little parlor organ, which her husband had bought her after fifteen years, during which she had not so much as seen any instrument, but an accordion that belonged to one of the Norwegian farmhands. She would sit beside me by the hour, darning and counting while I struggled with the "Joyous Farmer," but she seldom talked to me about music, and I understood why. She was a pious woman; she had the consolations of religion and, to her at least, her martyrdom was not wholly sordid. Once when I had been doggedly beating out some easy passages from an old score of *Euryanthe* I had found among her music books, she came up to me and, putting her hands over my eyes, gently drew my head back upon her shoulder, saying tremulously, "Don't love it so well, Clark, or it may be taken from you. Oh, dear boy, pray that whatever your sacrifice may be, it be not that."

When my aunt appeared on the morning after her arrival she was still in a semi-somnambulant state. She seemed not to realize that she was in the city where she had spent her youth, the place longed for hungrily half a lifetime. She had been so wretchedly train-sick throughout the journey that she had no recollection of anything but her discomfort, and, to all intents and purposes, there were but a few hours of nightmare between the farm in Red Willow County and my study on Newbury Street. I had planned a little pleasure for her that afternoon, to repay her for some of the glorious moments she had given me when we used to milk together in the straw-thatched cowshed and she, because I was more than usually tired, or because her husband had spoken sharply to me, would tell me of the splendid performance of the *Huguenots* she had seen in Paris, in her youth. At two o'clock the Symphony Orchestra was to give a Wagner program, and I intended to take my aunt; though, as I conversed with her I grew doubtful about her enjoyment of it. Indeed, for her own sake, I could only wish her taste for such things quite dead, and the long struggle mercifully ended at last. I suggested our visiting the Conservatory and the Common before lunch, but she seemed altogether too timid to wish to venture out. She questioned me absently about various changes in the city, but she was chiefly concerned that she had forgotten to leave instructions about feeding half-skimmed milk to a certain weakling calf, "old Maggie's calf, you know, Clark," she explained, evidently having forgotten how long I had been away. She was further troubled because she had neglected to tell her daughter about the freshly opened kit of mackerel in the cellar, which would spoil if it were not used directly.

I asked her whether she had ever heard any of the Wagnerian operas and found that she had not, though she was perfectly familiar with their respective situations, and had once possessed the piano score of *The Flying Dutchman.* I began to think it would have been best to get her back to Red Willow County without waking her, and regretted having suggested the concert.

From the time we entered the concert hall, however, she was a trifle less passive and inert, and for the first time seemed to perceive her surroundings. I had felt some trepidation lest she might become aware of the absurdities of her attire, or might experience some painful embarrassment at stepping suddenly into the world to which she had been dead for a quarter of a century. But, again, I found how superficially I had judged her. She sat looking about her with eyes as impersonal, almost as stony, as those with which the granite Rameses in a museum watches the froth and fret that ebbs and flows about his pedestal — separated from it by the lonely stretch of centuries. I have seen this same aloofness in old miners who drift into the Brown Hotel at Denver, their pockets full of bullion, their linen soiled, their haggard faces unshaven; standing in the thronged corridors as solitary as though they were still in a frozen camp on the Yukon, conscious that certain experiences have isolated them from their fellows by a gulf no haberdasher could bridge.

We sat at the extreme left of the first balcony, facing the arch of our own and the balcony above us, veritable hanging gardens, brilliant as tulip beds. The matinée audience was made up chiefly of women. One lost the contour of faces and figures — indeed, any effect of line whatever — and there was only the color of bodices past counting, the shimmer of fabrics soft and firm, silky and sheer: red, mauve, pink, blue, lilac, purple, ecru, rose, yellow, cream, and white, all the colors that an impressionist finds in a sunlit landscape, with here and there the dead shadow of a frock coat. My Aunt Georgiana regarded them as though they had been so many daubs of tube-paint on a palette.

When the musicians came out and took their places, she gave a little stir of anticipation and looked with quickening interest down over the rail at that invariable grouping, perhaps the first wholly familiar thing that had greeted her eye since she had left old Maggie and her weakling calf. I could feel how all those details sank into her soul, for I had not forgotten how they had sunk into mine when I came fresh from plowing forever and forever between green aisles of corn, where, as in a treadmill, one might walk from daybreak to dusk without perceiving a shadow of change. The clean profiles of the musicians, the gloss of their linen, the dull black of their coats, the beloved shapes of the instruments, the patches of yellow light thrown by the green-shaded lamps on the smooth, varnished bellies of the cellos and the bass viols in the rear, the restless, wind-tossed forest of fiddle necks and bows — I recalled how, in the first orchestra I had ever heard, those long bow strokes seemed to draw the heart out of me, as a conjurer's stick reels out yards of paper ribbon from a hat.

The first number was the *Tannhauser* overture. When the horns drew out the first strain of the Pilgrim's chorus my Aunt Georgiana clutched my coat sleeve. Then it was I first realized that for her this broke a silence of thirty years; the inconceivable silence of the plains. With the battle between the two motives, with the frenzy of the Venusberg theme and its ripping of strings, there came to me an overwhelming sense of the waste and wear we are so powerless to combat; and I saw again the tall, naked house on the prairie, black and grim as a wooden fortress; the black pond where I had learned to swim, its margin pitted with sun-dried cattle tracks; the rain-gullied clay banks about the naked house, the four dwarf ash seedlings where the dishcloths were always hung to dry before the kitchen door. The world there was the flat world of the ancients; to the east, a cornfield that stretched to daybreak; to the west, a corral that reached to sunset; between, the conquests of peace, dearer bought than those of war.

The overture closed; my aunt released my coat sleeve, but she said nothing. She sat staring at the orchestra through a dullness of thirty years, through the films made little by little by each of the three hundred and sixty-five days in every one of them. What, I wondered, did she get from it? She had been a good pianist in her day I knew, and her musical education had been broader than that of most music teachers of a quarter of a century ago. She had often told me of Mozart's operas and Meyerbeer's, and I could remember hearing her sing, years ago, certain melodies of Verdi's. When I had fallen ill with a fever in her house she used to sit by my cot in the evening — when the cool, night wind blew in through the faded mosquito netting tacked over the window, and I lay watching a certain bright star that burned red above the cornfield — and sing "Home to our mountains, O, let us return!" in a way fit to break the heart of a Vermont boy near dead of homesickness already.

I watched her closely through the prelude to *Tristan and Isolde,* trying vainly to conjecture what that seething turmoil of strings and winds might mean to her, but she sat mutely staring at the violin bows that drove obliquely downward, like the pelting streaks of rain in a summer shower. Had this music any message for her? Had she enough left to at all comprehend this power which had kindled the world since she had left it? I was in a fever of curiosity, but Aunt Georgiana sat silent upon her peak in Darien. She preserved this utter immobility throughout the number from *The Flying Dutchman,* though her fingers worked mechanically upon her black dress, as though, of themselves, they were recalling the piano score they had once played. Poor old hands! They had been stretched and twisted into mere tentacles to hold and lift and knead with; the palms unduly swollen, the fingers bent and knotted — on one of them a thin, worn band that had once been a wedding ring. As I pressed and gently quieted one of those groping hands I remembered with quivering eyelids their services for me in other days.

Soon after the tenor began the "Prize Song," I heard a quick drawn breath and turned to my aunt. Her eyes were closed, but the tears were glistening on her cheeks, and I think, in a moment more, they were in my eyes as well. It never really died, then — the soul that can suffer so excruciatingly and so interminably; it withers to the outward eye only; like that strange moss which can lie on a dusty shelf half a century and yet, if placed in water, grows green again. She wept so throughout the development and elaboration of the melody.

During the intermission before the second half of the concert, I questioned my aunt and found that the "Prize Song" was not new to her. Some years before there had drifted to the farm in Red Willow County a young German, a tramp cow-puncher, who had sung the chorus at Bayreuth, when he was a boy, along with the other peasant boys and girls. Of a Sunday morning he used to sit on his gingham-sheeted bed in the hands' bedroom which opened off the kitchen, cleaning the leather of his boots and saddle, singing the "Prize Song," while my aunt went about her work in the kitchen. She had hovered about him until she had prevailed upon him to join the country church, though his sole fitness for this step, insofar as I could gather, lay in his boyish face and his possession of this divine melody. Shortly afterward he had gone to town on the Fourth of July, been drunk for several days, lost his money at a faro table, ridden a saddled Texan steer on a bet, and disappeared with a fractured collarbone. All this my aunt told me huskily, wanderingly, as though she were talking in the weak lapses of illness.

"Well, we have come to better things than the old *Trovatore* at any rate, Aunt Georgie?" I queried, with a well-meant effort at jocularity.

Her lip quivered and she hastily put her hand-kerchief up to her mouth. From behind it she murmured, "And you have been hearing this ever since you left me, Clark?" Her question was the gentlest and saddest of reproaches.

151

The second half of the program consisted of four numbers from the *Ring,* and closed with Siegfried's funeral march. My aunt wept quietly, but almost continuously, as a shallow vessel overflows in a rainstorm. From time to time her dim eyes looked up at the lights which studded the ceiling, burning softly under their dull glass globes; doubtless they were stars in truth to her. I was still perplexed as to what measure of musical comprehension was left to her, she who had heard nothing but the singing of gospel hymns at Methodist services in the square frame schoolhouse on Section Thirteen for so many years. I was wholly unable to gauge how much of it had been dissolved in soapsuds, or worked into bread, or milked into the bottom of a pail.

The deluge of sound poured on and on; I never knew what she found in the shining current of it; I never knew how far it bore her, or past what happy islands. From the trembling of her face I could well believe that before the last numbers she had been carried out where the myriad graves are, into the gray, nameless burying grounds of the sea; or into some world of death vaster yet, where, from the beginning of the world, hope has lain down with hope and dream with dream and, renouncing, slept.

The concert was over; the people filed out of the hall chattering and laughing, glad to relax and find the living level again, but my kinswoman made no effort to rise. The harpist slipped its green felt cover over his instrument; the flute players shook the water from their mouthpieces; the men of the orchestra went out one by one, leaving the stage to the chairs and music stands, empty as a winter cornfield.

I spoke to my aunt. She burst into tears and sobbed pleadingly. "I don't want to go, Clark, I don't want to go!"

I understood. For her, just outside the door of the concert hall, lay the black pond with the cattle-tracked bluffs; the tall, unpainted house, with weather-curled boards; naked as a tower, the crook-backed ash seedlings where the dishcloths hung to dry; the gaunt, molting turkeys picking up refuse about the kitchen door.

PAUL'S CASE

A Study in Temperament

It was Paul's afternoon to appear before the
faculty of the Pittsburgh High School to account
for his various misdemeanors. He had been
suspended a week ago, and his father had called
at the Principal's office and confessed his perplexity about his son. Paul entered the faculty room
suave and smiling. His clothes were a trifle
outgrown, and the tan velvet on the collar of his
open overcoat was frayed and worn; but for all
that there was something of the dandy about him,
and he wore an opal pin in his neatly knotted
black four-in-hand, and a red carnation in his
buttonhole. This latter adornment the faculty
somehow felt was not properly significant of the
contrite spirit befitting a boy under the ban of
suspension.

Paul was tall for his age and very thin, with high,
cramped shoulders and a narrow chest. His eyes
were remarkable for a certain hysterical brilliancy,
and he continually used them in a conscious,
theatrical sort of way, peculiarly offensive in a
boy. The pupils were abnormally large, as though
he were addicted to belladonna, but there was a
glassy glitter about them which that drug does
not produce.

When questioned by the Principal as to why he

was there Paul stated, politely enough, that he wanted to come back to school. This was a lie, but Paul was quite accustomed to lying; found it, indeed, indispensable for overcoming friction. His teachers were asked to state their respective charges against him, which they did with such a rancor and aggrievedness as evinced that this was not a usual case. Disorder and impertinence were among the offenses named, yet each of his instructors felt that it was scarcely possible to put into words the real cause of the trouble, which lay in a sort of hysterically defiant manner of the boy's; in the contempt which they all knew he felt for them, and which he seemingly made not the least effort to conceal. Once, when he had been making a synopsis of a paragraph at the blackboard, his English teacher had stepped to his side and attempted to guide his hand. Paul had started back with a shudder and thrust his hands violently behind him. The astonished woman could scarcely have been more hurt and embarrassed had he struck at her. The insult was so involuntary and definitely personal as to be unforgettable. In one way and another he had made all his teachers, men and women alike, conscious of the same feeling of physical aversion. In one class he habitually sat with his hand shading his eyes; in another he always looked out of the window during the recitation; in another he made a running commentary on the lecture, with humorous intention.

His teachers felt this afternoon that his whole attitude was symbolized by his shrug and his flippantly red carnation flower, and they fell upon him without mercy, his English teacher leading the pack. He stood through it smiling, his pale lips parted over his white teeth. (His lips were continually twitching, and he had a habit of raising his eyebrows that was contemptuous and irritating to the last degree.) Older boys than Paul had broken down and shed tears under that baptism of fire, but his set smile did not once desert him, and his only sign of discomfort was the nervous trembling of the fingers that toyed with the buttons of his overcoat, and an occasional jerking of the other hand that held his hat. Paul was always smiling, always glancing about him, seeming to feel that people might be watching him and trying to detect something. This conscious expression, since it was as far as possible from boyish mirthfulness, was usually attributed to insolence or "smartness."

As the inquisition proceeded one of his instructors repeated an impertinent remark of the boy's, and the Principal asked him whether he thought that a courteous speech to have made a woman. Paul shrugged his shoulders slightly and his eyebrows twitched.

"I don't know," he replied. "I didn't mean to be polite or impolite, either. I guess it's a sort of way I have of saying things regardless."

The Principal, who was a sympathetic man, asked him whether he didn't think that a way it would be well to get rid of. Paul grinned and said he guessed so. When he was told that he could go he bowed gracefully and went out. His bow was but a repetition of the scandalous red carnation.

His teachers were in despair, and his drawing master voiced the feeling of them all when he declared there was something about the boy which none of them understood. He added: "I don't really believe that smile of his comes altogether from insolence; there's something sort of haunted

156

about it. The boy is not strong, for one thing. I happen to know that he was born in Colorado, only a few months before his mother died out there of a long illness. There is something wrong about the fellow."

The drawing master had come to realize that, in looking at Paul, one saw only his white teeth and the forced animation of his eyes. One warm afternoon the boy had gone to sleep at his drawing board, and his master had noted with amazement what a white, blue-veined face it was; drawn and wrinkled like an old man's about the eyes, the lips twitching even in his sleep, and stiff with a nervous tension that drew them back from his teeth.

His teachers left the building dissatisfied and unhappy; humiliated to have felt so vindictive toward a mere boy, to have uttered this feeling in cutting terms, and to have set each other on, as it were, in the gruesome game of intemperate reproach. Some of them remembered having seen a miserable street cat set at bay by a ring of tormentors.

As for Paul, he ran down the hill whistling the "Soldiers' Chorus" from *Faust,* looking wildly behind him now and then to see whether some of his teachers were not there to writhe under his lightheartedness. As it was now late in the afternoon and Paul was on duty that evening as usher at Carnegie Hall, he decided that he would not go home to supper. When he reached the concert hall the doors were not yet open and, as it was chilly outside, he decided to go up into the picture gallery — always deserted at this hour — where there were some of Raffelli's gay studies of Paris streets and an airy blue Venetian scene or two that

157

always exhilarated him. He was delighted to find no one in the gallery but the old guard, who sat in one corner, a newspaper on his knee, a black patch over one eye and the other closed. Paul possessed himself of the peace and walked confidently up and down, whistling under his breath. After a while he sat down before a blue Rico and lost himself. When he bethought him to look at his watch, it was after seven o'clock, and he rose with a start and ran downstairs, making a face at Augustus, peering out from the cast room, and an evil gesture at the Venus de Milo as he passed her on the stairway.

When Paul reached the ushers' dressing room half a dozen boys were there already, and he began excitedly to tumble into his uniform. It was one of the few that at all approached fitting, and Paul thought it very becoming — though he knew that the tight, straight coat accentuated his narrow chest, about which he was exceedingly sensitive. He was always considerably excited while he dressed, twanging all over to the tuning of the strings and the preliminary flourishes of the horns in the music room; but tonight he seemed quite beside himself, and he teased and plagued the boys until, telling him that he was crazy, they put him down on the floor and sat on him.

Somewhat calmed by his suppression, Paul dashed out to the front of the house to seat the early comers. He was a model usher; gracious and smiling he ran up and down the aisles; nothing was too much trouble for him; he carried messages and brought programs as though it were his greatest pleasure in life, and all the people in his section thought him a charming boy, feeling that he remembered and admired them. As the house filled, he grew more and more vivacious and animated, and the color came to his cheeks and lips. It was very much as though this were a great reception and Paul were the host. Just as the musicians came out to take their places, his English teacher arrived with checks for the seats which a prominent manufacturer had taken for the season. She betrayed some embarrassment when she handed Paul the tickets, and a hauteur which subsequently made her feel very foolish. Paul was startled for a moment, and had the feeling of wanting to put her out; what business had she here among all these fine people and gay colors? He looked her over and decided that she was not appropriately dressed and must be a fool to sit downstairs in such togs. The tickets had probably been sent her out of kindness, he reflected as he put down a seat for her, and she had about as much right to sit there as he had.

When the symphony began Paul sank into one of the rear seats with a long sigh of relief, and lost himself as he had done before the Rico. It was not that symphonies, as such, meant anything in particular to Paul, but the first sigh of the instruments seemed to free some hilarious and potent spirit within him; something that struggled there like the genie in the bottle found by the Arab fisherman. He felt a sudden zest of life; the lights danced before his eyes and the concert hall blazed into unimaginable splendor. When the soprano soloist came on Paul forgot even the nastiness of his teacher's being there and gave himself up to the peculiar stimulus such personages always had for him. The soloist chanced to be a German woman, by no means in her first youth, and the mother of many children; but she wore an elaborate gown and a tiara, and above all she had that indefinable air of achievement, that world-shine upon her, which, in Paul's eyes, made her a veritable queen of Romance.

After a concert was over Paul was always irritable and wretched until he got to sleep, and tonight he was even more than usually restless. He had the feeling of not being able to let down, of its being impossible to give up this delicious excitement which was the only thing that could be called living at all. During the last number he withdrew and, after hastily changing his clothes in the dressing room, slipped out to the side door where the soprano's carriage stood. Here he began pacing rapidly up and down the walk, waiting to see her come out.

Over yonder, the Schenley, in its vacant stretch, loomed big and square through the fine rain, the windows of its twelve stories glowing like those of a lighted cardboard house under a Christmas tree. All the actors and singers of the better class stayed there when they were in the city, and a number of the big manufacturers of the place lived there in the winter. Paul had often hung about the hotel, watching the people go in and out, longing to enter and leave schoolmasters and dull care behind him forever.

At last the singer came out, accompanied by the conductor, who helped her into her carriage and closed the door with a cordial *auf wiedersehen* which set Paul to wondering whether she were not an old sweetheart of his. Paul followed the carriage over to the hotel, walking so rapidly as not to be far from the entrance when the singer alighted, and disappeared behind the swinging glass doors that were opened by a Negro in a tall hat and a long coat. In the moment that the door was ajar it seemed to Paul that he, too, entered. He seemed to feel himself go after her up the steps, into the warm, lighted building, into an exotic, tropical world of shiny, glistening surfaces and basking ease. He reflected upon the mysterious dishes that were brought into the dining room, the green bottles in buckets of ice, as he had seen them in the supper party pictures of the *Sunday World* supplement. A quick gust of wind brought the rain down with sudden vehemence, and Paul was startled to find that he was still outside in the slush of the gravel driveway; that his boots were letting in the water and his scanty overcoat was clinging wet about him; that the lights in front of the concert hall were out and that the rain was driving in sheets between him and the orange glow of the windows above him. There it was, what he wanted — tangibly before him, like the fairy world of a Christmas pantomime — but mocking spirits stood guard at the doors, and, as the rain beat in his face, Paul wondered whether he were destined always to shiver in the black night outside, looking up at it.

He turned and walked reluctantly toward the car tracks. The end had to come sometime; his father in his nightclothes at the top of the stairs, explanations that did not explain, hastily improvised fictions that were forever tripping him up, his upstairs room and its horrible yellow wallpaper, the creaking bureau with the greasy plush collarbox, and over his painted wooden bed the pictures of George Washington and John Calvin, and the framed motto, "Feed my Lambs," which had been worked in red worsted by his mother.

Half an hour later Paul alighted from his car

and went slowly down one of the side streets off the main thoroughfare. It was a highly respectable street, where all the houses were exactly alike, and where businessmen of moderate means begot and reared large families of children, all of whom went to Sabbath school and learned the shorter catechism, and were interested in arithmetic; all of whom were as exactly alike as their homes, and of a piece with the monotony in which they lived. Paul never went up Cordelia Street without a shudder of loathing. His home was next to the house of the Cumberland minister. He approached it tonight with the nerveless sense of defeat, the hopeless feeling of sinking back forever into ugliness and commonness that he had always had when he came home. The moment he turned into Cordelia Street he felt the waters close above his head. After each of these orgies of living he experienced all the physical depression which follows a debauch; the loathing of respectable beds, of common food, of a house penetrated by kitchen odors; a shuddering repulsion for the flavorless, colorless mass of everyday existence; a morbid desire for cool things and soft lights and fresh flowers.

The nearer he approached the house, the more absolutely unequal Paul felt to the sight of it all: his ugly sleeping chamber; the cold bathroom with the grimy zinc tub, the cracked mirror, the dripping spiggots; his father, at the top of the stairs, his hairy legs sticking out from his nightshirt, his feet thrust into carpet slippers. He was so much later than usual that there would certainly be inquiries and reproaches. Paul stopped short before the door. He felt that he could not be accosted by his father tonight; that he could not toss again on that miserable bed. He would not go in. He would tell his father that he had no carfare and it was raining so hard he had gone home with one of the boys and stayed all night.

Meanwhile, he was wet and cold. He went around to the back of the house and tried one of the basement windows, found it open, raised it cautiously, and scrambled down the cellar wall to the floor. There he stood, holding his breath, terrified by the noise he had made, but the floor above him was silent, and there was no creak on the stairs. He found a soapbox, and carried it over to the soft ring of light that streamed from the furnace door, and sat down. He was horribly afraid of rats, so he did not try to sleep, but sat looking distrustfully at the dark, still terrified lest he might have awakened his father. In such reactions, after one of the experiences which made days and nights out of the dreary blanks of the calendar, when his senses were deadened, Paul's head was always singularly clear. Suppose his father had heard him getting in at the window and had come down and shot him for a burglar? Then, again, suppose his father had come down, pistol in hand, and he had cried out in time to save himself, and his father had been horrified to think how nearly he had killed him? Then, again, suppose a day should come when his father would remember that night, and wish there had been no warning cry to stay his hand? With this last supposition Paul entertained himself until daybreak.

The following Sunday was fine; the sodden November chill was broken by the last flash of autumnal summer. In the morning Paul had to go to church and Sabbath school, as always. On seasonable Sunday afternoons the burghers of

163

Cordelia Street always sat out on their front stoops and talked to their neighbors on the next stoop, or called to those across the street in neighborly fashion. The men usually sat on gay cushions placed upon the steps that led down to the sidewalk, while the women, in their Sunday "waists," sat in rockers on the cramped porches, pretending to be greatly at their ease. The children played in the streets; there were so many of them that the place resembled the recreation grounds of a kindergarten. The men on the steps — all in their shirt sleeves, their vests unbuttoned — sat with their legs well apart, their stomachs comfortably protruding, and talked of the prices of things, or told anecdotes of the sagacity of their various chiefs and overlords. They occasionally looked over the multitude of squabbling children, listened affectionately to their high-pitched, nasal voices, smiling to see their own proclivities reproduced in their offspring, and interspersed their legends of the iron kings with remarks about their sons' progress at school, their grades in arithmetic, and the amounts they had saved in their toy banks.

On this last Sunday of November Paul sat all the afternoon on the lowest step of his stoop, staring into the street, while his sisters, in their rockers, were talking to the minister's daughters next door about how many shirtwaists they had made in the last week, and bow many waffles someone had eaten at the last church supper. When the weather was warm, and his father was in a particularly jovial frame of mind, the girls made lemonade, which was always brought out in a red-glass pitcher, ornamented with forget-me-nots in blue enamel. This the girls thought very fine, and the neighbors always joked about the suspicious color of the pitcher.

Today Paul's father sat on the top step, talking to a young man who shifted a restless baby from knee to knee. He happened to be the young man who was daily held up to Paul as a model, and after whom it was his father's dearest hope that he would pattern. This young man was of a ruddy complexion, with a compressed, red mouth, and faded, nearsighted eyes, over which he wore thick spectacles, with gold bows that curved about his ears. He was clerk to one of the magnates of a great steel corporation, and was looked upon in Cordelia Street as a young man with a future. There was a story that, some five years ago — he was now barely twenty-six — he had been a trifle dissipated, but in order to curb his appetites and save the loss of time and strength that a sowing of wild oats might have entailed, he had taken his chief's advice, oft reiterated to his employees, and at twenty-one had married the first woman whom he could persuade to share his fortunes. She happened to be an angular schoolmistress, much older than he, who also wore thick glasses, and who had now borne him four children, all nearsighted, like herself.

The young man was relating how his chief, now cruising in the Mediterranean, kept in touch with all the details of the business, arranging his office hours on his yacht just as though he were at home, and "knocking off work enough to keep two stenographers busy." His father told, in turn, the plan his corporation was considering, of putting in an electric railway plant in Cairo. Paul snapped his teeth; he had an awful apprehension that they might spoil it all before he got there. Yet he rather liked to hear these legends of the iron kings that were told and retold on Sundays and holidays; these stories of palaces in Venice, yachts on the Mediterranean, and high play at Monte Carlo appealed to his fancy, and he was interested in the triumphs of these cash boys who had become famous, though he had no mind for the cash-boy stage.

After supper was over and he had helped to dry the dishes, Paul nervously asked his father whether he could go to George's to get some help in his geometry, and still more nervously asked for carfare. This latter request he had to repeat, as his father, on principle, did not like to hear requests for money, whether much or little. He asked Paul whether he could not go to some boy who lived nearer, and told him that he ought not to leave his schoolwork until Sunday; but he gave him the dime. He was not a poor man, but he had a worthy ambition to come up in the world. His only reason for allowing Paul to usher was that he thought a boy ought to be earning a little.

Paul bounded upstairs, scrubbed the greasy odor of the dishwater from his hands with the ill-smelling soap he hated, and then shook over his fingers a few drops of violet water from the bottle he kept hidden in his drawer. He left the house with his geometry conspicuously under his arm, and the moment he got out of Cordelia Street and boarded a downtown car, he shook off the lethargy of two deadening days and began to live again.

The leading juvenile of the permanent stock company which played at one of the downtown theaters was an acquaintance of Paul's, and the boy had been invited to drop in at the Sunday-night rehearsals whenever he could. For more than a year Paul had spent every available moment loitering about Charley Edwards's dressing room. He had won a place among Edwards's following not only because the young actor, who could not afford to employ a dresser, often found him useful, but because he recognized in Paul something akin to what churchmen term "vocation."

It was at the theater and at Carnegie Hall that Paul really lived; the rest was but a sleep and a forgetting. This was Paul's fairy tale, and it had for him all the allurement of a secret love. The moment he inhaled the gassy, painty, dusty odor behind the scenes, he breathed like a prisoner set free, and felt within him the possibility of doing or saying splendid, brilliant, poetic things. The moment the cracked orchestra beat out the overture from *Martha,* or jerked at the serenade from *Rigoletto,* all stupid and ugly things slid from him, and his senses were deliciously, yet delicately fired.

Perhaps it was because, in Paul's world, the natural nearly always wore the guise of ugliness, that a certain element of artificiality seemed to him necessary in beauty. Perhaps it was because his experience of life elsewhere was so full of Sabbath-school picnics, petty economies, wholesome advice as to how to succeed in life, and the inescapable odors of cooking, that he found this existence so alluring, these smartly clad men and women so attractive, that he was so moved by these starry apple orchards that bloomed perennially under the limelight.

It would be difficult to put it strongly enough how convincingly the stage entrance of that theater was for Paul the actual portal of Romance.

Certainly none of the company ever suspected it, least of all Charley Edwards. It was very like the old stories that used to float about London of fabulously rich Jews, who had subterranean halls there, with palms, and fountains, and soft lamps and richly appareled women who never saw the disenchanting light of London day. So, in the midst of that smoke-palled city, enamored of figures and grimy toil, Paul had his secret temple, his wishing carpet, his bit of blue-and-white Mediterranean shore bathed in perpetual sunshine.

Several of Paul's teachers had a theory that his imagination had been perverted by garish fiction, but the truth was that he scarcely ever read at all. The books at home were not such as would either tempt or corrupt a youthful mind, and as for reading the novels that some of his friends urged upon him — well, he got what he wanted much more quickly from music; any sort of music, from an orchestra to a barrel organ. He needed only the spark, the indescribable thrill that made his imagination master of his senses, and he could make plots and pictures enough of his own. It was equally true that he was not stagestruck — not, at any rate, in the usual acceptation of that expression. He had no desire to become an actor, any more than he had to become a musician. He felt no necessity to do any of these things; what he wanted was to see, to be in the atmosphere, float on the wave of it, to be carried out, blue league after blue league, away from everything.

After a night behind the scenes Paul found the schoolroom more than ever repulsive; the bare floors and naked walls; the prosy men who never wore frock coats, or violets in their buttonholes;

the women with their dull gowns, shrill voices, and pitiful seriousness about prepositions that govern the dative. He could not bear to have the other pupils think, for a moment, that he took these people seriously; he must convey to them that he considered it all trivial, and was there only by way of a jest, anyway. He had autographed pictures of all the members of the stock company which he showed his classmates, telling them the most incredible stories of his familiarity with these people, of his acquaintance with the soloists who came to Carnegie Hall, his suppers with them and the flowers he sent them. When these stories lost their effect, and his audience grew listless, he became desperate and would bid all the boys good-by, announcing that he was going to travel for a while; going to Naples, to Venice, to Egypt. Then, next Monday, he would slip back, conscious and nervously smiling; his sister was ill, and he should have to defer his voyage until spring.

Matters went steadily worse with Paul at school. In the itch to let his instructors know how heartily he despised them and their homilies, and how thoroughly he was appreciated elsewhere, he mentioned once or twice that he had no time to fool with theorems; adding — with a twitch of the eyebrows and a touch of that nervous bravado which so perplexed them — that he was helping the people down at the stock company; they were old friends of his.

The upshot of the matter was that the Principal went to Paul's father, and Paul was taken out of school and put to work. The manager at Carnegie Hall was told to get another usher in his stead; the doorkeeper at the theater was warned not to admit him to the house; and Charley Edwards remorsefully promised the boy's father not to see him again.

The members of the stock company were vastly amused when some of Paul's stories reached them — especially the women. They were hardworking women, most of them supporting indigent husbands or brothers, and they laughed rather bitterly at having stirred the boy to such fervid and florid inventions. They agreed with the faculty and with his father that Paul's was a bad case.

The eastbound train was plowing through a January snowstorm; the dull dawn was beginning to show gray when the engine whistled a mile out of Newark. Paul started up from the seat where he had lain curled in uneasy slumber, rubbed the breath-misted window glass with his hand, and peered out. The snow was whirling in curling eddies above the white bottom lands, and the drifts lay already deep in the fields and along the fences, while here and there the long dead grass and dried weed stalks protruded black above it. Lights shone from the scattered houses, and a gang of laborers who stood beside the track waved their lanterns.

Paul had slept very little, and he felt grimy and uncomfortable. He had made the all-night journey in a day coach, partly because he was ashamed, dressed as he was, to go into a Pullman, and partly because he was afraid of being seen there by some Pittsburgh businessman, who might have noticed him in Denny & Carson's office. When the whistle awoke him, he clutched quickly at his breast pocket, glancing about him with an uncertain smile. But the little, clay-bespattered Italians were still sleeping, the slatternly women across the aisle were in open-mouthed oblivion, and even the

170

crumby, crying babies were for the nonce stilled. Paul settled back to struggle with his impatience as best he could.

When he arrived at the Jersey City station he hurried through his breakfast, manifestly ill at ease and keeping a sharp eye about him. After he reached the Twenty-third Street station, he consulted a cabman and had himself driven to a men's-furnishings establishment that was just opening for the day. He spent upward of two hours there, buying with endless reconsidering and great care. His new street suit he put on in the fitting room; the frock coat and dress clothes he had bundled into the cab with his linen. Then he drove to a hatter's and a shoe house. His next errand was at Tiffany's, where he selected his silver and a new scarf pin. He would not wait to have his silver marked, he said. Lastly, he stopped at a trunk shop on Broadway and had his purchases packed into various traveling bags.

It was a little after one o'clock when he drove up to the Waldorf, and after settling with the cabman, went into the office. He registered from Washington; said his mother and father had been abroad, and that he had come down to await the arrival of their steamer. He told his story plausibly and had no trouble, since he volunteered to pay for them in advance, in engaging his rooms; a sleeping room, sitting room, and bath.

Not once, but a hundred times, Paul had planned this entry into New York. He had gone over every detail of it with Charley Edwards, and in his scrapbook at home there were pages of description about New York hotels, cut from the Sunday papers. When he was shown to his sitting room on the eighth floor he saw at a glance that everything was as it should be; there was but one detail in his mental picture that the place did not realize, so he rang for the bellboy and sent him down for flowers. He moved about nervously until the boy returned, putting away his new linen and fingering it delightedly as he did so. When the flowers came he put them hastily into water, and then tumbled into a hot bath. Presently he came out of his white bathroom, resplendent in his new silk underwear, and playing with the tassels of his red robe. The snow was whirling so fiercely outside his windows that he could scarcely see across the street, but within the air was deliciously soft and fragrant. He put the violets and jonquils on the taboret beside the couch, and threw himself down, with a long sigh, covering himself with a Roman blanket. He was thoroughly tired; he had been in such haste, he had stood up to such a strain, covered so much ground in the last twenty-four hours, that he wanted to think how it had all come about. Lulled by the sound of the wind, the warm air, and the cool fragrance of the flowers, he sank into deep, drowsy retrospection.

It had been wonderfully simple; when they had shut him out of the theater and concert hall, when they had taken away his bone, the whole thing was virtually determined. The rest was a mere matter of opportunity. The only thing that at all surprised him was his own courage — for he realized well enough that he had always been tormented by fear, a sort of apprehensive dread that, of late years, as the meshes of the lies he had told closed about him, had been pulling the muscles of his body tighter and tighter. Until now he could not remember the time when he had not been dreading something. Even when he was a little boy it was always there — behind him, or before, or on either side. There had always been the shadowed corner, the dark place into which he dared not look, but from which something seemed always to be watching him — and Paul had done things that were not pretty to watch, he knew.

But now he had a curious sense of relief, as though he had at last thrown down the gauntlet to the thing in the corner.

Yet it was but a day since he had been sulking in the traces; but yesterday afternoon that he had been sent to the bank with Denny & Carson's deposit, as usual — but this time he was instructed to leave the book to be balanced. There was above two thousand dollars in checks, and nearly a thousand in the bank notes which he had taken from the book and quietly transferred to his pocket. At the bank he had made out a new deposit slip. His nerves had been steady enough to permit of his returning to the office, where he had finished his work and asked for a full day's holiday tomorrow, Saturday, giving a perfectly reasonable pretext. The bankbook, he knew, would not be returned before Monday or Tuesday, and his father would be out of town for the next week. From the time he slipped the bank notes into his pocket until he boarded the night train for New York, he had not known a moment's hesitation. It was not the first time Paul had steered through treacherous waters.

How astonishingly easy it had all been; here he was, the thing done; and this time there would be no awakening, no figure at the top of the stairs. He watched the snowflakes whirling by his window until he fell asleep.

When he awoke, it was three o'clock in the afternoon. He bounded up with a start; half of one of his precious days gone already! He spent more than an hour in dressing, watching every stage of his toilet carefully in the mirror. Everything was quite perfect; he was exactly the kind of boy he had always wanted to be.

When he went downstairs Paul took a carriage and drove up Fifth Avenue toward the Park. The snow had somewhat abated; carriages and tradesmen's wagons were hurrying soundlessly to and fro in the winter twilight; boys in woolen mufflers were shoveling off the doorsteps; the avenue stages made fine spots of color against the white street. Here and there on the corners were stands, with whole flower gardens blooming under glass cases, against the sides of which the snowflakes stuck and melted; violets, roses, carnations, lilies of the valley — somehow vastly more lovely and alluring that they blossomed thus unnaturally in the snow. The Park itself was a wonderful stage winterpiece.

When he returned, the pause of the twilight had ceased and the tune of the streets had changed. The snow was falling faster, lights streamed from the hotels that reared their dozen stories fearlessly up into the storm, defying the raging Atlantic winds. A long, black stream of carriages poured down the avenue, intersected here and there by other streams, tending horizontally. There were a score of cabs about the entrance of his hotel, and his driver had to wait. Boys in livery were running in and out of the awning stretched across the sidewalk, up and down the red velvet carpet laid from the door to the street. Above, about, within it all was the rumble and roar, the hurry and toss of thousands of human beings as hot for pleasure as himself, and on every side of him towered the glaring affirmation of the omnipotence of wealth.

The boy set his teeth and drew his shoulders together in a spasm of realization; the plot of all dramas, the text of all romances, the nerve-stuff of all sensations was whirling about him like the snowflakes. He burnt like a faggot in a tempest.

When Paul went down to dinner the music of the orchestra came floating up the elevator shaft to greet him. His head whirled as he stepped into the thronged corridor, and he sank back into one of the chairs against the wall to get his breath. The lights, the chatter, the perfumes, the bewildering medley of color — he had, for a moment, the feeling of not being able to stand it. But only for a moment; these were his own people, he told himself. He went slowly about the corridors, through the writing rooms, smoking rooms, reception rooms, as though he were exploring the chambers of an enchanted palace, built and peopled for him alone.

When he reached the dining room he sat down at a table near a window. The flowers, the white linen, the many-colored wineglasses, the gay toilettes of the women, the low popping of corks, the undulating repetitions of the *Blue Danube* from the orchestra, all flooded Paul's dream with bewildering radiance. When the roseate tinge of his champagne was added — that cold, precious, bubbling stuff that creamed and foamed in his glass — Paul wondered that there were honest men in the world at all. This was what all the world was fighting for, he reflected; this was what all the struggle was about. He doubted the reality of his past. Had he ever known a place called Cordelia Street, a place where fagged-looking busi-

175

nessmen got on the early car; mere rivets in a machine they seemed to Paul, — sickening men, with combings of children's hair always hanging to their coats, and the smell of cooking in their clothes. Cordelia Street — Ah, that belonged to another time and country; had he not always been thus, had he not sat here night after night, from as far back as he could remember, looking pensively over just such shimmering textures and slowly twirling the stem of a glass like this one between his thumb and middle finger? He rather thought he had.

He was not in the least abashed or lonely. He had no especial desire to meet or to know any of these people; all he demanded was the right to look on and conjecture, to watch the pageant. The mere stage properties were all he contended for. Nor was he lonely later in the evening, in his lodge at the Metropolitan. He was now entirely rid of his nervous misgivings, of his forced aggressiveness, of the imperative desire to show himself different from his surroundings. He felt now that his surroundings explained him. Nobody questioned the purple; he had only to wear it passively. He had only to glance down at his attire to reassure himself that here it would be impossible for anyone to humiliate him.

He found it hard to leave his beautiful sitting room to go to bed that night, and sat long watching the raging storm from his turret window. When he went to sleep it was with the lights turned on in his bedroom; partly because of his old timidity, and partly so that, if he should wake in the night, there would be no wretched moment of doubt, no horrible suspicion of yellow wallpaper, or of Washington and Calvin above his bed.

Sunday morning the city was practically snow-bound. Paul breakfasted late, and in the afternoon he fell in with a wild San Francisco boy, a freshman at Yale, who said he had run down for a "little flyer" over Sunday. The young man offered to show Paul the night side of the town, and the two boys went out together after dinner, not returning to the hotel until seven o'clock the next morning. They had started out in the confiding warmth of a champagne friendship, but their parting in the elevator was singularly cool. The freshman pulled himself together to make his train, and Paul went to bed. He awoke at two o'clock in the afternoon, very thirsty and dizzy, and rang for icewater, coffee, and the Pittsburgh papers.

On the part of the hotel management, Paul excited no suspicion. There was this to be said for him, that he wore his spoils with dignity and in no way made himself conspicuous. Even under the glow of his wine he was never boisterous, though he found the stuff like a magician's wand for wonder-building. His chief greediness lay in his ears and eyes, and his excesses were not offensive ones. His dearest pleasures were the gray winter twilights in his sitting room; his quiet enjoyment of his flowers, his clothes, his wide divan, his cigarette, and his sense of power. He could not remember a time when he had felt so at peace with himself. The mere release from the necessity of petty lying, lying every day and every day, restored his self-respect. He had never lied for pleasure, even at school; but to be noticed and admired, to assert his difference from other Cordelia Street boys; and he felt a good deal more manly, more honest, even, now that he had no need for boastful pretensions, now that he could,

177

as his actor friends used to say, "dress the part." It was characteristic that remorse did not occur to him. His golden days went by without a shadow, and he made each as perfect as he could.

On the eighth day after his arrival in New York he found the whole affair exploited in the Pittsburgh papers, exploited with a wealth of detail which indicated that local news of a sensational nature was at a low ebb. The firm of Denny & Carson announced that the boy's father had refunded the full amount of the theft and that they had no intention of prosecuting. The Cumberland minister had been interviewed, and expressed his hope of yet reclaiming the motherless lad, and his Sabbath-school teacher declared that she would spare no effort to that end. The rumor had reached Pittsburgh that the boy had been seen in a New York hotel, and his father had gone East to find him and bring him home.

Paul had just come in to dress for dinner; he sank into a chair, weak to the knees, and clasped his head in his hands. It was to be worse than jail, even; the tepid waters of Cordelia Street were to close over him finally and forever. The gray monotony stretched before him in hopeless, unrelieved years; Sabbath school, Young People's Meeting, the yellow-papered room, the damp dishtowels; it all rushed back upon him with a sickening vividness. He had the old feeling that the orchestra had suddenly stopped, the sinking sensation that the play was over. The sweat broke out on his face, and he sprang to his feet, looked about him with his white, conscious smile, and winked at himself in the mirror. With something of the old childish belief in miracles with which he had so often gone to class, all his lessons unlearned, Paul dressed and dashed whistling down the corridor to the elevator.

He had no sooner entered the dining room and caught the measure of the music than his remembrance was lightened by his old elastic power of claiming the moment, mounting with it, and finding it all-sufficient. The glare and glitter about him, the mere scenic accessories had again, and for the last time, their old potency. He would show himself that he was game, he would finish the thing splendidly. He doubted, more than ever, the existence of Cordelia Street, and for the first time he drank his wine recklessly. Was he not, after all, one of those fortunate beings born to the purple, was he not still himself and in his own place? He drummed a nervous accompaniment to the Pagliacci music and looked about him, telling himself over and over that it had paid.

He reflected drowsily, to the swell of the music and the chill sweetness of his wine, that he might have done it more wisely. He might have caught an outbound steamer and been well out of their clutches before now. But the other side of the world had seemed too far away and too uncertain then; he could not have waited for it; his need had been too sharp. If he had to choose over again, he would do the same thing tomorrow. He looked affectionately about the dining room, now gilded with a soft mist. Ah, it had paid indeed!

Paul was awakened next morning by a painful throbbing in his head and feet. He had thrown himself across the bed without undressing, and had slept with his shoes on. His limbs and hands were lead heavy, and his tongue and throat were parched and burnt. There came upon him one of those fateful attacks of clearheadedness that never occurred except when he was physically exhausted and his nerves hung loose. He lay still, closed his eyes, and let the tide of things wash over him.

His father was in New York; "stopping at some joint or other," he told himself. The memory of successive summers on the front stoop fell upon him like a weight of black water. He had not a hundred dollars left; and he knew now, more than ever, that money was everything, the wall that stood between all he loathed and all he wanted. The thing was winding itself up; he had thought of that on his first glorious day in New York, and had even provided a way to snap the thread. It lay on his dressing table now; he had got it out last night when he came blindly up from dinner, but the shiny metal hurt his eyes, and he disliked the looks of it.

He rose and moved about with a painful effort, succumbing now and again to attacks of nausea. It was the old depression exaggerated; all the world had become Cordelia Street. Yet somehow he was not afraid of anything, was absolutely calm; perhaps because he had looked into the dark corner at last and knew. It was bad enough, what he saw there, but somehow not so bad as his long fear of it had been. He saw everything clearly now. He had a feeling that he had made the best of it, that he had lived the sort of life he was meant to live, and for half an hour he sat staring at the revolver. But he told himself that was not the way, so he went downstairs and took a cab to the ferry.

When Paul arrived in Newark he got off the train and took another cab, directing the driver to follow the Pennsylvania tracks out of the town. The snow lay heavy on the roadways and had drifted deep in the open fields. Only here and there the dead grass or dried weed stalks projected, singularly black, above it. Once well into the country, Paul dismissed the carriage and walked, floundering along the tracks, his mind a medley of irrelevant things. He seemed to hold in his brain an actual picture of everything he had seen that morning. He remembered every feature of both his drivers, of the toothless old woman from whom he had bought the red flowers in his coat, the agent from whom he had got his ticket, and all of his fellow passengers on the ferry. His mind, unable to cope with vital matters near at hand, worked feverishly and deftly at sorting and grouping these images. They made for him a part of the ugliness of the world, of the ache in his head, and the bitter burning on his tongue. He stooped and put a handful of snow into his mouth as he walked, but that, too, seemed hot. When he reached a little hillside, where the tracks ran through a cut some twenty feet below him, he stopped and sat down.

The carnations in his coat were drooping with the cold, he noticed, their red glory all over. It occurred to him that all the flowers he had seen in the glass cases that first night must have gone the same way, long before this. It was only one splendid breath they had, in spite of their brave mockery at the winter outside the glass; and it was a losing game in the end, it seemed, this revolt against the homilies by which the world is run. Paul took one of the blossoms carefully from his coat and scooped a little hole in the snow, where he covered it up. Then he dozed awhile, from his weak condition, seemingly insensible to the cold.

The sound of an approaching train awoke him, and he started to his feet, remembering only his resolution, and afraid lest he should be too late. He stood watching the approaching locomotive, his teeth chattering, his lips drawn away from them in a frightened smile; once or twice he glanced nervously sidewise, as though he were being watched. When the right moment came, he jumped. As he fell, the folly of his haste occurred to him with merciless clearness, the vastness of what he had left undone. There flashed through his brain, clearer than ever before, the blue of Adriatic water, the yellow of Algerian sands.

He felt something strike his chest, and that his body was being thrown swiftly through the air, on and on, immeasurably far and fast, while his limbs were gently relaxed. Then, because the picture-making mechanism was crushed, the disturbing visions flashed into black, and Paul dropped back into the immense design of things.

OTHER SHORT STORIES

COMING, APHRODITE!

I

Don Hedger had lived for four years on the top floor of an old house on the south side of Washington Square, and nobody had ever disturbed him. He occupied one big room with no outside exposure except on the north, where he had built in a many-paned studio window that looked upon a court and upon the roofs and walls of other buildings. His room was very cheerless, since he never got a ray of direct sunlight; the south corners were always in shadow. In one of the corners was a clothes closet, built against the partition, in another a wide divan, serving as a seat by day and a bed by night. In the front corner, the one farther from the window, was a sink, and a table with two gas burners where he sometimes cooked his food. There, too, in the perpetual dusk, was the dog's bed, and often a bone or two for his comfort.

The dog was a Boston bull terrier, and Hedger explained his surly disposition by the fact that he had been bred to the point where it told on his nerves. His name was Caesar III, and he had taken prizes at very exclusive dog shows. When he and his master went out to prowl about University

Place or to promenade along West Street, Caesar III was invariably fresh and shining. His pink skin showed through his mottled coat, which glistened as if it had just been rubbed with olive oil, and he wore a brass-studded collar, bought at the smartest saddler's. Hedger, as often as not, was hunched up in an old striped blanket coat, with a shapeless felt hat pulled over his bushy hair, wearing black shoes that had become grey, or brown ones that had become black, and he never put on gloves unless the day was biting cold.

Early in May, Hedger learned that he was to have a new neighbour in the rear apartment — two rooms, one large and one small, that faced the west. His studio was shut off from the larger of these rooms by double doors, which, though they were fairly tight, left him a good deal at the mercy of the occupant. The rooms had been leased, long before he came there, by a trained nurse who considered herself knowing in old furniture. She went to auction sales and bought up mahogany and dirty brass and stored it away here, where she meant to live when she retired from nursing. Meanwhile, she sub-let her rooms, with their precious furniture, to young people who came to New York to "write" or to "paint" — who proposed to live by the sweat of the brow rather than of the hand, and who desired artistic surroundings. When Hedger first moved in, these rooms were occupied by a young man who tried to write plays, — and who kept on trying until a week ago, when the nurse had put him out for unpaid rent.

A few days after the playwright left, Hedger heard an ominous murmur of voices through the bolted double doors: the lady-like intonation of the nurse — doubtless exhibiting her treasures — and another voice, also a woman's, but very different; young, fresh, unguarded, confident. All the same, it would be very annoying to have a woman in there. The only bath-room on the floor was at the top of the stairs in the front hall, and he would always be running into her as he came or went from his bath. He would have to be more careful to see that Caesar didn't leave bones about the hall, too; and she might object when he cooked steak and onions on his gas burner.

As soon as the talking ceased and the women left, he forgot them. He was absorbed in a study of paradise fish at the Aquarium, staring out at people through the glass and green water of their tank. It was a highly gratifying idea; the incommunicability of one stratum of animal life with another, — though Hedger pretended it was only an experiment in unusual lighting. When he heard trunks knocking against the sides of the narrow hall, then he realized that she was moving in at once. Toward noon, groans and deep gasps and the creaking of ropes, made him aware that a piano was arriving. After the tramp of the movers died away down the stairs, somebody touched off a few scales and chords on the instrument, and then there was peace. Presently he heard her lock her door and go down the hall humming something; going out to lunch, probably. He stuck his brushes in a can of turpentine and put on his hat, not stopping to wash his hands. Caesar was smelling along the crack under the bolted doors; his bony tail stuck out hard as a hickory withe, and the hair was standing up about his elegant collar.

Hedger encouraged him. "Come along, Caesar. You'll soon get used to a new smell."

In the hall stood an enormous trunk, behind the ladder that led to the roof, just opposite Hedger's door. The dog flew at it with a growl of hurt amazement. They went down three flights of stairs and out into the brilliant May afternoon.

Behind the Square, Hedger and his dog descended into a basement oyster house where there were no tablecloths on the tables and no handles on the coffee cups, and the floor was covered with sawdust, and Caesar was always welcome, — not that he needed any such precautionary flooring. All the carpets of Persia would have been safe for him. Hedger ordered steak and onions absent-mindedly, not realizing why he had an apprehension that this dish might be less readily at hand hereafter. While he ate, Caesar sat beside his chair, gravely disturbing the sawdust with his tail.

After lunch Hedger strolled about the Square for the dog's health and watched the stages pull out; — that was almost the very last summer of the old horse stages on Fifth Avenue. The fountain had but lately begun operations for the season and was throwing up a mist of rainbow water which now and then blew south and sprayed a bunch of Italian babies that were being supported on the outer rim by older, very little older, brothers and sisters. Plump robins were hopping about on the soil; the grass was newly cut and blindingly green. Looking up the Avenue through the Arch, one could see the young poplars with their bright, sticky leaves, and the Brevoort glistening in its spring coat of paint, and shining horses and carriages, — occasionally an automobile, misshapen and sullen, like an ugly threat in a stream of things that were bright and beautiful and alive.

While Caesar and his master were standing by

the fountain, a girl approached them, crossing the Square. Hedger noticed her because she wore a lavender cloth suit and carried in her arms a big bunch of fresh lilacs. He saw that she was young and handsome, — beautiful, in fact, with a splendid figure and good action. She, too, paused by the fountain and looked back through the Arch up the Avenue. She smiled rather patronizingly as she looked, and at the same time seemed delighted. Her slowly curving upper lip and half-closed eyes seemed to say: "You're gay, you're exciting, you are quite the right sort of thing; but you're none too fine for me!"

In the moment she tarried, Caesar stealthily approached her and sniffed at the hem of her lavender skirt, then, when she went south like an arrow, he ran back to his master and lifted a face full of emotion and alarm, his lower lip twitching under his sharp white teeth and his hazel eyes pointed with a very definite discovery. He stood thus, motionless, while Hedger watched the lavender girl go up the steps and through the door of the house in which he lived.

"You're right, my boy, it's she! She might be worse looking, you know."

When they mounted to the studio, the new lodger's door, at the back of the hall, was a little ajar, and Hedger caught the warm perfume of lilacs just brought in out of the sun. He was used to the musty smell of the old hall carpet. (The nurse-lessee had once knocked at his studio door and complained that Caesar must be somewhat responsible for the particular flavour of that mustiness, and Hedger had never spoken to her since.) He was used to the old smell, and he preferred it to that of the lilacs, and so did his companion, whose nose was so much more discriminating. Hedger shut his door vehemently, and fell to work.

Most young men who dwell in obscure studios in New York have had a beginning, come out of something, have somewhere a home town, a family, a paternal roof. But Don Hedger had no such background. He was a foundling, and had grown up in a school for homeless boys, where book-learning was a negligible part of the curriculum. When he was sixteen, a Catholic priest took him to Greensburg, Pennsylvania, to keep house for him. The priest did something to fill in the large gaps in the boy's education, — taught him to like "Don Quixote" and "The Golden Legend," and encouraged him to mess with paints and crayons in his room up under the slope of the mansard. When Don wanted to go to New York to study at the Art League, the priest got him a night job as packer in one of the big department stores. Since then, Hedger had taken care of himself; that was his only responsibility. He was singularly unencumbered; had no family duties, no social ties, no obligations toward any one but his landlord. Since he travelled light, he had travelled rather far. He had got over a good deal of the earth's surface, in spite of the fact that he never in his life had more than three hundred dollars ahead at any one time, and he had already outlived a succession of convictions and revelations about his art.

Though he was now but twenty-six years old, he had twice been on the verge of becoming a marketable product; once through some studies of New York streets he did for a magazine, and once through a collection of pastels he brought home from New Mexico, which Remington, then at the height of his popularity, happened to see, and generously tried to push. But on both occasions Hedger decided that this was something he didn't wish to carry further, — simply the old thing over again and got nowhere, — so he took enquiring dealers experiments in a "later manner," that made them put him out of the shop. When he ran short of money, he could always get any amount of commercial work; he was an expert draughtsman and worked with lightning speed. The rest of his time he spent in groping his way from one kind of painting into another, or travelling about without luggage, like a tramp, and he was chiefly occupied with getting rid of ideas he had once thought very fine.

Hedger's circumstances, since he had moved to Washington Square, were affluent compared to anything he had ever known before. He was now able to pay advance rent and turn the key on his studio when he went away for four months at a stretch. It didn't occur to him to wish to be richer than this. To be sure, he did without a great many things other people think necessary, but he didn't miss them, because he had never had them. He belonged to no clubs, visited no houses, had no studio friends, and he ate his dinner alone in some decent little restaurant, even on Christmas and New Year's. For days together he talked to nobody but his dog and the janitress and the lame oyster-man.

After he shut the door and settled down to his paradise fish on that first Tuesday in May, Hedger forgot all about his new neighbour. When the light failed, he took Caesar out for a walk. On the way home he did his marketing on West Houston Street, with a one-eyed Italian woman who always cheated him. After he had cooked his beans and scallopini, and drunk half a bottle of Chianti, he put his dishes in the sink and went up on the roof to smoke. He was the only person in the house who ever went to the roof, and he had a secret understanding with the janitress about it. He was to have "the privilege of the roof," as she said, if he opened the heavy trapdoor on sunny days to air out the upper hall, and was watchful to close it when rain threatened. Mrs. Foley was fat and dirty and hated to climb stairs, — besides, the roof was reached by a perpendicular iron ladder, definitely inaccessible to a woman of her bulk, and the iron door at the top of it was too heavy for any but Hedger's strong arm to lift. Hedger was not above medium height, but he practised with weights and dumb-bells, and in the shoulders he was as strong as a gorilla.

So Hedger had the roof to himself. He and Caesar often slept up there on hot nights, rolled in blankets he had brought home from Arizona. He mounted with Caesar under his left arm. The dog had never learned to climb a perpendicular ladder, and never did he feel so much his master's greatness and his own dependence upon him, as when he crept under his arm for this perilous ascent. Up there was even gravel to scratch in, and a dog could do whatever he liked, so long as he did not bark. It was a kind of Heaven, which no one was strong enough to reach but his great, paint-smelling master.

On this blue May night there was a slender, girl-ish looking young moon in the west, playing with a whole company of silver stars. Now and then one of them darted away from the group and shot off into the gauzy blue with a soft little trail of light, like laughter. Hedger and his dog were

192

delighted when a star did this. They were quite lost in watching the glittering game, when they were suddenly diverted by a sound, — not from the stars, though it was music. It was not the Prologue to Pagliacci, which rose ever and anon on hot evenings from an Italian tenement on Thompson Street, with the gasps of the corpulent baritone who got behind it; nor was it the hurdy-gurdy man, who often played at the corner in the balmy twilight. No, this was a woman's voice, singing the tempestuous, over-lapping phrases of Signor Puccini, then comparatively new in the world, but already so popular that even Hedger recognized his unmistakable gusts of breath. He looked about over the roofs; all was blue and still, with the well-built chimneys that were never used now standing up dark and mournful. He moved softly toward the yellow quadrangle where the gas from the hall shone up through the half-lifted trapdoor. Oh yes! It came up through the hole like a strong draught, a big, beautiful voice, and it sounded rather like a professional's. A piano had arrived in the morning, Hedger remembered. This might be a very great nuisance. It would be pleasant enough to listen to, if you could turn it on and off as you wished; but you couldn't. Caesar, with the gas light shining on his collar and his ugly but sensitive face, panted and looked up for information. Hedger put down a reassuring hand.

"I don't know. We can't tell yet. It may not be so bad."

He stayed on the roof until all was still below, and finally descended, with quite a new feeling about his neighbour. Her voice, like her figure, inspired respect, — if one did not choose to call it admiration. Her door was shut, the transom was dark; nothing remained of her but the obtrusive trunk, unrightfully taking up room in the narrow hall.

II

For two days Hedger didn't see her. He was painting eight hours a day just then, and only went out to hunt for food. He noticed that she practised scales and exercises for about an hour in the morning; then she locked her door, went humming down the hall, and left him in peace. He heard her getting her coffee ready at about the same time he got his. Earlier still, she passed his room on her way to her bath. In the evening she sometimes sang, but on the whole she didn't bother him. When he was working well he did not notice anything much. The morning paper lay before his door until he reached out for his milk bottle, then he kicked the sheet inside and it lay on the floor until evening. Sometimes he read it and sometimes he did not. He forgot there was anything of importance going on in the world outside of his third floor studio. Nobody had ever taught him that he ought to be interested in other people; in the Pittsburgh steel strike, in the Fresh Air Fund, in the scandal about the Babies' Hospital. A grey wolf, living in a Wyoming canyon, would hardly have been less concerned about these things than was Don Hedger.

One morning he was coming out of the bathroom at the front end of the hall, having just given Caesar his bath and rubbed him into a glow with a heavy towel. Before the door, lying in wait for him, as it were, stood a tall figure in a flowing blue silk dressing gown that fell away from her marble arms. In her hands she carried various ac-

194

cessories of the bath.

"I wish," she said distinctly, standing in his way, "I wish you wouldn't wash your dog in the tub. I never heard of such a thing! I've found his hair in the tub, and I've smelled a doggy smell, and now I've caught you at it. It's an outrage!"

Hedger was badly frightened. She was so tall and positive, and was fairly blazing with beauty and anger. He stood blinking, holding on to his sponge and dog-soap, feeling that he ought to bow very low to her. But what he actually said was:

"Nobody has ever objected before. I always wash the tub, — and, anyhow, he's cleaner than most people."

"Cleaner than me?" her eyebrows went up, her white arms and neck and her fragrant person seemed to scream at him like a band of outraged nymphs. Something flashed through his mind about a man who was turned into a dog, or was pursued by dogs, because he unwittingly intruded upon the bath of beauty.

"No, I didn't mean that," he muttered, turning scarlet under the bluish stubble of his muscular jaws. "But I know he's cleaner than I am."

"That I don't doubt!" Her voice sounded like a soft shivering of crystal, and with a smile of pity she drew the folds of her voluminous blue robe close about her and allowed the wretched man to pass. Even Caesar was frightened; he darted like a streak down the hall, through the door and to his own bed in the corner among the bones.

Hedger stood still in the doorway, listening to indignant sniffs and coughs and a great swishing of water about the sides of the tub. He had washed it; but as he had washed it with Caesar's sponge, it was quite possible that a few bristles remained;

195

the dog was shedding now. The playwright had never objected, nor had the jovial illustrator who occupied the front apartment, — but he, as he admitted, "was usually pye-eyed, when he wasn't in Buffalo." He went home to Buffalo sometimes to rest his nerves.

It had never occurred to Hedger that any one would mind using the tub after Caesar; — but then, he had never seen a beautiful girl caparisoned for the bath before. As soon as he beheld her standing there, he realized the unfitness of it. For that matter, she ought not to step into a tub that any other mortal had bathed in; the illustrator was sloppy and left cigarette ends on the moulding.

All morning as he worked he was gnawed by a spiteful desire to get back at her. It rankled that he had been so vanquished by her disdain. When he heard her locking her door to go out for lunch, he stepped quickly into the hall in his messy painting coat, and addressed her.

"I don't wish to be exigent, Miss," — he had certain grand words that he used upon occasion — "but if this is your trunk, it's rather in the way here."

"Oh, very well!" she exclaimed carelessly, dropping her keys into her handbag. "I'll have it moved when I can get a man to do it," and she went down the hall with her free, roving stride.

Her name, Hedger discovered from her letters, which the postman left on the table in the lower hall, was Eden Bower.

III

In the closet that was built against the partition separating his room from Miss Bower's, Hedger kept all his wearing apparel, some of it on hooks and hangers, some of it on the floor. When he opened his closet door now-a-days, little dust-coloured insects flew out on downy wing, and he suspected that a brood of moths were hatching in his winter overcoat. Mrs. Foley, the janitress, told him to bring down all his heavy clothes and she would give them a beating and hang them in the court. The closet was in such disorder that he shunned the encounter, but one hot afternoon he set himself to the task. First he threw out a pile of forgotten laundry and tied it up in a sheet. The bundle stood as high as his middle when he had knotted the corners. Then he got his shoes and overshoes together. When he took his overcoat from its place against the partition, a long ray of yellow light shot across the dark enclosure, — a knot hole, evidently, in the high wainscoating of the west room. He had never noticed it before, and without realizing what he was doing, he stooped and squinted through it.

Yonder, in a pool of sunlight, stood his new neighbour, wholly unclad, doing exercises of some sort before a long gilt mirror. Hedger did not happen to think how unpardonable it was of him to watch her. Nudity was not improper to any one who had worked so much from the figure, and he continued to look, simply because he had never seen a woman's body so beautiful as this one, — positively glorious in action. As she swung her arms and changed from one pivot of motion to another, muscular energy seemed to flow through her from her toes to her finger-tips. The soft flush of exercise and the gold of afternoon sun played over her flesh together, enveloped her in a luminous mist which, as she turned and twisted, made now an arm, now a shoulder, now a thigh, dissolve in pure light and instantly recover its outline with the next gesture. Hedger's fingers curved as if he were holding a crayon; mentally he was doing the whole figure in a single running line, and the charcoal seemed to explode in his hand at the point where the energy of each gesture was discharged into the whirling disc of light, from a foot or shoulder, from the up-thrust chin or the lifted breasts.

He could not have told whether he watched her for six minutes or sixteen. When her gymnastics were over, she paused to catch up a lock of hair that had come down, and examined with solicitude a little reddish mole that grew under her left arm-pit. Then, with her hand on her hip, she walked unconcernedly across the room and disappeared through the door into her bedchamber.

Disappeared — Don Hedger was crouching on his knees, staring at the golden shower which poured in through the west windows, at the lake of gold sleeping on the faded Turkish carpet. The spot was enchanted; a vision out of Alexandria, out of the remote pagan past, had bathed itself there in Helianthine fire.

When he crawled out of his closet, he stood blinking at the grey sheet stuffed with laundry, not knowing what had happened to him. He felt a little sick as he contemplated the bundle. Everything here was different; he hated the disorder of the place, the grey prison light, his old shoes and himself and all his slovenly habits. The black calico curtains that ran on wires over his big window were white with dust. There were three greasy frying pans in the sink, and the sink itself — He felt desperate. He couldn't stand this another minute.

He took up an armful of winter clothes and ran down four flights into the basement.

"Mrs. Foley," he began, "I want my room cleaned this afternoon, thoroughly cleaned. Can you get a woman for me right away?"

"Is it company you're having?" the fat, dirty janitress enquired. Mrs. Foley was the widow of a useful Tammany man, and she owned real estate in Flatbush. She was huge and soft as a feather bed. Her face and arms were permanently coated with dust, grained like wood where the sweat had trickled.

"Yes, company. That's it."

"Well, this is a queer time of the day to be asking for a cleaning woman. It's likely I can get you old Lizzie, if she's not drunk. I'll send Willy round to see."

Willy, the son of fourteen, roused from the stupor and stain of his fifth box of cigarettes by the gleam of a quarter, went out. In five minutes he returned with old Lizzie, — she smelling strong of spirits and wearing several jackets which she had put on one over the other, and a number of skirts, long and short, which made her resemble an animated dish-clout. She had, of course, to borrow her equipment from Mrs. Foley, and toiled up the long flights, dragging mop and pail and broom. She told Hedger to be of good cheer, for he had got the right woman for the job, and showed him a great leather strap she wore about her wrist to prevent dislocation of tendons. She swished about the place, scattering dust and splashing soapsuds, while he watched her in nervous despair. He stood over Lizzie and made her scour the sink, directing her roughly, then paid her and got rid of her. Shutting the door on his

199

failure, he hurried off with his dog to lose himself among the stevedores and dock labourers on West Street.

A strange chapter began for Don Hedger. Day after day, at that hour in the afternoon, the hour before his neighbour dressed for dinner, he crouched down in his closet to watch her go through her mysterious exercises. It did not occur to him that his conduct was detestable; there was nothing shy or retreating about this unclad girl, — a bold body, studying itself quite coolly and evidently well pleased with itself, doing all this for a purpose. Hedger scarcely regarded his action as conduct at all; it was something that had happened to him. More than once he went out and tried to stay away for the whole afternoon, but at about five o'clock he was sure to find himself among his old shoes in the dark. The pull of that aperture was stronger than his will, — and he had always considered his will the strongest thing about him. When she threw herself upon the divan and lay resting, he still stared, holding his breath. His nerves were so on edge that a sudden noise made him start and brought out the sweat on his forehead. The dog would come and tug at his sleeve, knowing that something was wrong with his master. If he attempted a mournful whine, those strong hands closed about his throat.

When Hedger came slinking out of his closet, he sat down on the edge of the couch, sat for hours without moving. He was not painting at all now. This thing, whatever it was, drank him up as ideas had sometimes done, and he sank into a stupor of idleness as deep and dark as the stupor of work. He could not understand it; he was no boy, he had worked from models for years, and a woman's body was no mystery to him. Yet now he did nothing but sit and think about one. He slept very little, and with the first light of morning he awoke as completely possessed by this woman as if he had been with her all the night before. The unconscious operations of life went on in him only to perpetuate this excitement. His brain held but one image now — vibrated, burned with it. It was a heathenish feeling; without friendliness, almost without tenderness.

Women had come and gone in Hedger's life. Not having had a mother to begin with, his relations with them, whether amorous or friendly, had been casual. He got on well with janitresses and wash-women, with Indians and with the peasant women of foreign countries. He had friends among the silk-skirt factory girls who came to eat their lunch in Washington Square, and he sometimes took a model for a day in the country. He felt an unreasoning antipathy toward the well-dressed women he saw coming out of big shops, or driving in the Park. If, on his way to the Art Museum, he noticed a pretty girl standing on the steps of one of the houses on upper Fifth Avenue, he frowned at her and went by with his shoulders hunched up as if he were cold. He had never known such girls, or heard them talk, or seen the inside of the houses in which they lived; but he believed them all to be artificial and, in an aesthetic sense, perverted. He saw them enslaved by desire of merchandise and manufactured articles, effective only in making life complicated and insincere and in embroidering it with ugly and meaningless trivialities. They were enough, he thought, to make one almost forget woman as she existed in art, in thought, and in the universe.

He had no desire to know the woman who had, for the time at least, so broken up his life, — no curiosity about her every-day personality. He shunned any revelation of it, and he listened for Miss Bower's coming and going, not to encounter, but to avoid her. He wished that the girl who wore shirt-waists and got letters from Chicago would keep out of his way, that she did not exist. With her he had naught to make. But in a room full of sun, before an old mirror, on a little enchanted rug of sleeping colours, he had seen a woman who emerged naked through a door, and disappeared naked. He thought of that body as never having been clad, or as having worn the stuffs and dyes of all the centuries but his own. And for him she had no geographical associations; unless with Crete, or Alexandria, or Veronese's Venice. She was the immortal conception, the perennial theme.

The first break in Hedger's lethargy occurred one afternoon when two young men came to take Eden Bower out to dine. They went into her music room, laughed and talked for a few minutes, and then took her away with them. They were gone a long while, but he did not go out for food himself; he waited for them to come back. At last he heard them coming down the hall, gayer and more talkative than when they left. One of them sat down at the piano, and they all began to sing. This Hedger found absolutely unendurable. He snatched up his hat and went running down the stairs. Caesar leaped beside him, hoping that old times were coming back. They had supper in the oysterman's basement and then sat down in front of their own doorway. The moon stood full over the Square, a thing of regal glory; but Hedger did not see the moon; he was looking, murderously, for men. Presently two, wearing straw hats and white trousers and carrying canes, came down the steps from his house. He rose and dogged them across the Square. They were laughing and seemed very much elated about something. As one stopped to light a cigarette, Hedger caught from the other:

"Don't you think she has a beautiful talent?"

His companion threw away his match. "She has a beautiful figure." They both ran to catch the stage.

Hedger went back to his studio. The light was shining from her transom. For the first time he violated her privacy at night, and peered through that fatal aperture. She was sitting, fully dressed, in the window, smoking a cigarette and looking out over the housetops. He watched her until she rose, looked about her with a disdainful, crafty smile, and turned out the light.

The next morning, when Miss Bower went out, Hedger followed her. Her white skirt gleamed ahead of him as she sauntered about the Square. She sat down behind the Garibaldi statue and opened a music book she carried. She turned the leaves carelessly, and several times glanced in his direction. He was on the point of going over to her, when she rose quickly and looked up at the sky. A flock of pigeons had risen from somewhere in the crowded Italian quarter to the south, and were wheeling rapidly up through the morning air, soaring and dropping, scattering and coming together, now grey, now white as silver, as they caught or intercepted the sunlight. She put up her hand to shade her eyes and followed them with a kind of defiant delight in her face.

Hedger came and stood beside her. "You've

surely seen them before?"

"Oh, yes," she replied, still looking up. "I see them every day from my windows. They always come home about five o'clock. Where do they live?"

"I don't know. Probably some Italian raises them for the market. They were here long before I came, and I've been here four years."

"In that same gloomy room? Why didn't you take mine when it was vacant?"

"It isn't gloomy. That's the best light for painting."

"Oh, is it? I don't know anything about painting. I'd like to see your pictures sometime. You have such a lot in there. Don't they get dusty, piled up against the wall like that?"

"Not very. I'd be glad to show them to you. Is your name really Eden Bower? I've seen your letters on the table."

"Well, it's the name I'm going to sing under. My father's name is Bowers, but my friend Mr. Jones, a Chicago newspaper man who writes about music, told me to drop the 's.' He's crazy about my voice."

Miss Bower didn't usually tell the whole story, — about anything. Her first name, when she lived in Huntington, Illinois, was Edna, but Mr. Jones had persuaded her to change it to one which he felt would be worthy of her future. She was quick to take suggestions, though she told him she "didn't see what was the matter with 'Edna.' "

She explained to Hedger that she was going to Paris to study. She was waiting in New York for Chicago friends who were to take her over, but who had been detained. "Did you study in Paris?" she asked.

"No, I've never been in Paris. But I was in the south of France all last summer, studying with C——. He's the biggest man among the moderns, — at least I think so."

Miss Bower sat down and made room for him on the bench. "Do tell me about it. I expected to be there by this time, and I can't wait to find out what it's like."

Hedger began to relate how he had seen some of this Frenchman's work in an exhibition, and deciding at once that this was the man for him, he had taken a boat for Marseilles the next week, going over steerage. He proceeded at once to the little town on the coast where his painter lived, and presented himself. The man never took pupils, but because Hedger had come so far, he let him stay. Hedger lived at the master's house and every day they went out together to paint, sometimes on the blazing rocks down by the sea. They wrapped themselves in light woollen blankets and didn't feel the heat. Being there and working with C—— was being in Paradise, Hedger concluded; he learned more in three months than in all his life before.

Eden Bower laughed. "You're a funny fellow. Didn't you do anything but work? Are the women very beautiful? Did you have awfully good things to eat and drink?"

Hedger said some of the women were fine looking, especially one girl who went about selling fish and lobsters. About the food there was nothing remarkable, — except the ripe figs, he liked those. They drank sour wine, and used goat-butter, which was strong and full of hair, as it was churned in a goat skin.

"But don't they have parties or banquets? Aren't

there any fine hotels down there?"

"Yes, but they are all closed in summer, and the country people are poor. It's a beautiful country, though."

"How, beautiful?" she persisted.

"If you want to go in, I'll show you some sketches, and you'll see."

Miss Bower rose. "All right. I won't go to my fencing lesson this morning. Do you fence? Here comes your dog. You can't move but he's after you. He always makes a face at me when I meet him in the hall, and shows his nasty little teeth as if he wanted to bite me."

In the studio Hedger got out his sketches, but to Miss Bower, whose favourite pictures were Christ Before Pilate and a redhaired Magdalen of Henner, these landscapes were not at all beautiful, and they gave her no idea of any country whatsoever. She was careful not to commit herself, however. Her vocal teacher had already convinced her that she had a great deal to learn about many things.

"Why don't we go out to lunch somewhere?" Hedger asked, and began to dust his fingers with a handkerchief — which he got out of sight as swiftly as possible.

"All right, the Brevoort," she said carelessly. "I think that's a good place, and they have good wine. I don't care for cocktails."

Hedger felt his chin uneasily. "I'm afraid I haven't shaved this morning. If you could wait for me in the Square? It won't take me ten minutes."

Left alone, he found a clean collar and handkerchief, brushed his coat and blacked his shoes, and last of all dug up ten dollars from the bottom of an old copper kettle he had brought from Spain.

His winter hat was of such a complexion that the Brevoort hall boy winked at the porter as he took it and placed it on the rack in a row of fresh straw ones.

IV

That afternoon Eden Bower was lying on the couch in her music room, her face turned to the window, watching the pigeons. Reclining thus she could see none of the neighbouring roofs, only the sky itself and the birds that crossed and recrossed her field of vision, white as scraps of paper blowing in the wind. She was thinking that she was young and handsome and had had a good lunch, that a very easy-going, light-hearted city lay in the streets below her; and she was wondering why she found this queer painter chap, with his lean, bluish cheeks and heavy black eyebrows, more interesting than the smart young men she met at her teacher's studio.

Eden Bower was, at twenty, very much the same person that we all know her to be at forty, except that she knew a great deal less. But one thing she knew: that she was to be Eden Bower. She was like some one standing before a great show window full of beautiful and costly things, deciding which she will order. She understands that they will not all be delivered immediately, but one by one they will arrive at her door. She already knew some of the many things that were to happen to her; for instance, that the Chicago millionaire who was going to take her abroad with his sister as chaperone, would eventually press his claim in quite another manner. He was the most circumspect of bachelors, afraid of everything obvious, even of women who were too flagrantly

207

handsome. He was a nervous collector of pictures and furniture, a nervous patron of music, and a nervous host; very cautious about his health, and about any course of conduct that might make him ridiculous. But she knew that he would at last throw all his precautions to the winds.

People like Eden Bower are inexplicable. Her father sold farming machinery in Huntington, Illinois, and she had grown up with no acquaintances or experiences outside of that prairie town. Yet from her earliest childhood she had not one conviction or opinion in common with the people about her, — the only people she knew. Before she was out of short dresses she had made up her mind that she was going to be an actress, that she would live far away in great cities, that she would be much admired by men and would have everything she wanted. When she was thirteen, and was already singing and reciting for church entertainments, she read in some illustrated magazine a long article about the late Czar of Russia, then just come to the throne or about to come to it. After that, lying in the hammock on the front porch on summer evenings, or sitting through a long sermon in the family pew, she amused herself by trying to make up her mind whether she would or would not be the Czar's mistress when she played in his Capital. Now Edna had met this fascinating word only in the novels of Ouida, — her hard-worked little mother kept a long row of them in the upstairs storeroom, behind the linen chest. In Huntington, women who bore that relation to men were called by a very different name, and their lot was not an enviable one; of all the shabby and poor, they were the shabbiest. But then, Edna had never lived in Huntington, not even before she began to find books like "Sapho" and "Mademoiselle de Maupin," secretly sold in paper covers throughout Illinois. It was as if she had come into Huntington, into the Bowers family, on one of the trains that puffed over the marshes behind their back fence all day long, and was waiting for another train to take her out.

As she grew older and handsomer, she had many beaux, but these small-town boys didn't interest her. If a lad kissed her when he brought her home from a dance, she was indulgent and she rather liked it. But if he pressed her further, she slipped away from him, laughing. After she began to sing in Chicago, she was consistently discreet. She stayed as a guest in rich people's houses, and she knew that she was being watched like a rabbit in a laboratory. Covered up in bed, with the lights out, she thought her own thoughts, and laughed.

This summer in New York was her first taste of freedom. The Chicago capitalist, after all his arrangements were made for sailing, had been compelled to go to Mexico to look after oil interests. His sister knew an excellent singing master in New York. Why should not a discreet, well-balanced girl like Miss Bower spend the summer there, studying quietly? The capitalist suggested that his sister might enjoy a summer on Long Island; he would rent the Griffiths' place for her, with all the servants, and Eden could stay there. But his sister met this proposal with a cold stare. So it fell out, that between selfishness and greed, Eden got a summer all her own, — which really did a great deal toward making her an artist and whatever else she was afterward to become. She had time to look about, to watch without being watched; to select diamonds in one window and furs in another, to select shoulders and moustaches in the big hotels where she went to lunch. She had the easy freedom of obscurity and the consciousness of power. She enjoyed both. She was in no hurry.

While Eden Bower watched the pigeons, Don Hedger sat on the other side of the bolted doors, looking into a pool of dark turpentine, at his idle brushes, wondering why a woman could do this to him. He, too, was sure of his future and knew that he was a chosen man. He could not know, of course, that he was merely the first to fall under a fascination which was to be disastrous to a few men and pleasantly stimulating to many thousands. Each of these two young people sensed the future, but not completely. Don Hedger knew that nothing much would ever happen to him. Eden Bower understood that to her a great deal would happen. But she did not guess that her neighbour would have more tempestuous adventures sitting in his dark studio than she would find in all the capitals of Europe, or in all the latitude of conduct she was prepared to permit herself.

V

One Sunday morning Eden was crossing the Square with a spruce young man in a white flannel suit and a panama hat. They had been breakfasting at the Brevoort and he was coaxing her to let him come up to her rooms and sing for an hour.

"No, I've got to write letters. You must run along now. I see a friend of mine over there, and I want to ask him about something before I go up."

"That fellow with the dog? Where did you pick him up?" the young man glanced toward the seat under a sycamore where Hedger was reading the morning paper.

"Oh, he's an old friend from the West," said Eden easily. "I won't introduce you, because he doesn't like people. He's a recluse. Good-bye. I can't be sure about Tuesday. I'll go with you if I have time after my lesson." She nodded, left him, and went over to the seat littered with newspapers. The young man went up the Avenue without looking back.

"Well, what are you going to do today? Shampoo this animal all morning?" Eden enquired teasingly.

Hedger made room for her on the seat. "No, at twelve o'clock I'm going out to Coney Island. One of my models is going up in a balloon this afternoon. I've often promised to go and see her, and now I'm going."

Eden asked if models usually did such stunts. No, Hedger told her, but Molly Welch added to her earnings in that way. "I believe," he added, "she likes the excitement of it. She's got a good deal of spirit. That's why I like to paint her. So many models have flaccid bodies."

"And she hasn't, eh? Is she the one who comes to see you? I can't help hearing her, she talks so loud."

"Yes, she has a rough voice, but she's a fine girl. I don't suppose you'd be interested in going?"

"I don't know," Eden sat tracing patterns on the asphalt with the end of her parasol. "Is it any fun? I got up feeling I'd like to do something different today. It's the first Sunday I've not had to sing in church. I had that engagement for breakfast at the Brevoort, but it wasn't very exciting. That chap can't talk about anything but himself."

Hedger warmed a little. "If you've never been to Coney Island, you ought to go. It's nice to see all the people; tailors and bar-tenders and prize-fighters with their best girls, and all sorts of folks taking a holiday."

Eden looked sidewise at him. So one ought to be interested in people of that kind, ought one? He was certainly a funny fellow. Yet he was never, somehow, tiresome. She had seen a good deal of him lately, but she kept wanting to know him better, to find out what made him different from men like the one she had just left — whether he really was as different as he seemed. "I'll go with you," she said at last, "if you'll leave that at home." She pointed to Caesar's flickering ears with her sunshade.

"But he's half the fun. You'd like to hear him bark at the waves when they come in."

"No, I wouldn't. He's jealous and disagreeable if he sees you talking to any one else. Look at him now."

"Of course, if you make a face at him. He knows what that means, and he makes a worse face. He likes Molly Welch, and she'll be disappointed if I don't bring him."

Eden said decidedly that he couldn't take both of them. So at twelve o'clock when she and Hedger got on the boat at Desbrosses street, Caesar was lying on his pallet, with a bone.

Eden enjoyed the boat-ride. It was the first time she had been on the water, and she felt as if she were embarking for France. The light warm breeze and the plunge of the waves made her very wide awake, and she liked crowds of any kind. They went to the balcony of a big, noisy restaurant and had a shore dinner, with tall steins of beer. Hedger

212

had got a big advance from his advertising firm since he first lunched with Miss Bower ten days ago, and he was ready for anything.

After dinner they went to the tent behind the bathing beach, where the tops of two balloons bulged out over the canvas. A red-faced man in a linen suit stood in front of the tent, shouting in a hoarse voice and telling the people that if the crowd was good for five dollars more, a beautiful young woman would risk her life for their entertainment. Four little boys in dirty red uniforms ran about taking contributions in their pillbox hats. One of the balloons was bobbing up and down in its tether and people were shoving forward to get nearer the tent.

"Is it dangerous, as he pretends?" Eden asked.

"Molly says it's simple enough if nothing goes wrong with the balloon. Then it would be all over, I suppose."

"Wouldn't you like to go up with her?"

"I? Of course not. I'm not fond of taking foolish risks."

Eden sniffed. "I shouldn't think sensible risks would be very much fun."

Hedger did not answer, for just then every one began to shove the other way and shout, "Look out. There she goes!" and a band of six pieces commenced playing furiously.

As the balloon rose from its tent enclosure, they saw a girl in green tights standing in the basket, holding carelessly to one of the ropes with one hand and with the other waving to the spectators. A long rope trailed behind to keep the balloon from blowing out to sea.

As it soared, the figure in green tights in the basket diminished to a mere spot, and the balloon itself, in the brilliant light, looked like a big silver-grey bat, with its wings folded. When it began to sink, the girl stepped through the hole in the basket to a trapeze that hung below, and gracefully descended through the air, holding to the rod with both hands, keeping her body taut and her feet close together. The crowd, which had grown very large by this time, cheered vociferously. The men took off their hats and waved, little boys shouted, and fat old women, shining with the heat and a beer lunch, murmured admiring comments upon the balloonist's figure. "Beautiful legs, she has!"

"That's so," Hedger whispered. "Not many girls would look well in that position." Then, for some reason, he blushed a slow, dark, painful crimson.

The balloon descended slowly, a little way from the tent, and the red-faced man in the linen suit caught Molly Welch before her feet touched the ground, and pulled her to one side. The band struck up "Blue Bell" by way of welcome, and one of the sweaty pages ran forward and presented the balloonist with a large bouquet of artificial flowers. She smiled and thanked him, and ran back across the sand to the tent.

"Can't we go inside and see her?" Eden asked. "You can explain to the door man. I want to meet her." Edging forward, she herself addressed the man in the linen suit and slipped something from her purse into his hand.

They found Molly seated before a trunk that had a mirror in the lid and a "make-up" outfit spread upon the tray. She was wiping the cold cream and powder from her neck with a discarded chemise.

"Hello, Don," she said cordially. "Brought a friend?"

Eden liked her. She had an easy, friendly manner, and there was something boyish and devil-may-care about her.

"Yes, it's fun. I'm mad about it," she said in reply to Eden's questions. "I always want to let go, when I come down on the bar. You don't feel your weight at all, as you would on a stationary trapeze."

The big drum boomed outside, and the publicity man began shouting to newly arrived boat-loads. Miss Welch took a last pull at her cigarette. "Now you'll have to get out, Don. I change for the next act. This time I go up in a black evening dress, and lose the skirt in the basket before I start down."

"Yes, go along," said Eden. "Wait for me outside the door. I'll stay and help her dress."

Hedger waited and waited, while women of every build bumped into him and begged his pardon, and the red pages ran about holding out their caps for coins, and the people ate and perspired and shifted parasols against the sun. When the band began to play a two-step, all the bathers ran up out of the surf to watch the ascent. The second balloon bumped and rose, and the crowd began shouting to the girl in a black evening dress who stood leaning against the ropes and smiling. "It's a new girl," they called. "It ain't the Countess this time. You're a peach, girlie!"

The balloonist acknowledged these compliments, bowing and looking down over the sea of upturned faces, — but Hedger was determined she should not see him, and he darted behind the tent-fly. He was suddenly dripping with cold sweat, his mouth was full of the bitter taste of anger and his tongue felt stiff behind his teeth. Molly Welch, in a shirt-waist and a white tam-o'-shanter cap, slipped out from the tent under his arm and laughed up in his face. "She's a crazy one you brought along. She'll get what she wants!"

"Oh, I'll settle with you, all right!" Hedger brought out with difficulty.

"It's not my fault, Donnie. I couldn't do anything with her. She bought me off. What's the matter with you? Are you soft on her? She's safe enough. It's as easy as rolling off a log, if you keep cool." Molly Welch was rather excited herself, and she was chewing gum at a high speed as she stood beside him, looking up at the floating silver cone. "Now watch," she exclaimed suddenly. "She's coming down on the bar. I advised her to cut that out, but you see she does it first-rate. And she got rid of the skirt, too. Those black tights show off her legs very well. She keeps her feet together like I told her, and makes a good line along the back. See the light on those silver slippers, — that was a good idea I had. Come along to meet her. Don't be a grouch; she's done it fine!"

Molly tweaked his elbow, and then left him standing like a stump, while she ran down the beach with the crowd.

Though Hedger was sulking, his eye could not help seeing the low blue welter of the sea, the arrested bathers, standing in the surf, their arms and legs stained red by the dropping sun, all shading their eyes and gazing upward at the slowly falling silver star.

Molly Welch and the manager caught Eden under the arms and lifted her aside, a red page dashed up with a bouquet, and the band struck

216

up "Blue Bell." Eden laughed and bowed, took Molly's arm, and ran up the sand in her black tights and silver slippers, dodging the friendly old women, and the gallant sports who wanted to offer their homage on the spot.

When she emerged from the tent, dressed in her own clothes, that part of the beach was almost deserted. She stepped to her companion's side and said carelessly: "Hadn't we better try to catch this boat? I hope you're not sore at me. Really, it was lots of fun."

Hedger looked at his watch. "Yes, we have fifteen minutes to get to the boat," he said politely.

As they walked toward the pier, one of the pages ran up panting. "Lady, you're carrying off the bouquet," he said, aggrievedly.

Eden stopped and looked at the bunch of spotty cotton roses in her hand. "Of course. I want them for a souvenir. You gave them to me yourself."

"I give 'em to you for looks, but you can't take 'em away. They belong to the show."

"Oh, you always use the same bunch?"

"Sure we do. There ain't too much money in this business."

She laughed and tossed them back to him. "Why are you angry?" she asked Hedger. "I wouldn't have done it if I'd been with some fellows, but I thought you were the sort who wouldn't mind. Molly didn't for a minute think you would."

"What possessed you to do such a fool thing?" he asked roughly.

"I don't know. When I saw her coming down, I wanted to try it. It looked exciting. Didn't I hold myself as well as she did?"

Hedger shrugged his shoulders, but in his heart he forgave her.

217

The return boat was not crowded, though the boats that passed them, going out, were packed to the rails. The sun was setting. Boys and girls sat on the long benches with their arms about each other, singing. Eden felt a strong wish to propitiate her companion, to be alone with him. She had been curiously wrought up by her balloon trip; it was a lark, but not very satisfying unless one came back to something after the flight. She wanted to be admired and adored. Though Eden said nothing, and sat with her arms limp on the rail in front of her, looking languidly at the rising silhouette of the city and the bright path of the sun, Hedger felt a strange drawing near to her. If he but brushed her white skirt with his knee, there was an instant communication between them, such as there had never been before. They did not talk at all, but when they went over the gang-plank she took his arm and kept her shoulder close to his. He felt as if they were enveloped in a highly charged atmosphere, an invisible network of subtle, almost painful sensibility. They had somehow taken hold of each other.

An hour later, they were dining in the back garden of a little French hotel on Ninth Street, long since passed away. It was cool and leafy there, and the mosquitoes were not very numerous. A party of South Americans at another table were drinking champagne, and Eden murmured that she thought she would like some, if it were not too expensive. "Perhaps it will make me think I am in the balloon again. That was a very nice feeling. You've forgiven me, haven't you?"

Hedger gave her a quick straight look from under his black eyebrows, and something went over her that was like a chill, except that it was

218

warm and feathery. She drank most of the wine; her companion was indifferent to it. He was talking more to her tonight than he had ever done before. She asked him about a new picture she had seen in his room; a queer thing full of stiff, supplicating female figures. "It's Indian, isn't it?"

"Yes. I call it Rain Spirits, or maybe, Indian Rain. In the Southwest, where I've been a good deal, the Indian traditions make women have to do with the rain-fall. They were supposed to control it, somehow, and to be able to find springs, and make moisture come out of the earth. You see I'm trying to learn to paint what people think and feel; to get away from all that photographic stuff. When I look at you, I don't see what a camera would see, do I?"

"How can I tell?"

"Well, if I should paint you, I could make you understand what I see." For the second time that day Hedger crimsoned unexpectedly, and his eyes fell and steadily contemplated a dish of little radishes. "That particular picture I got from a story a Mexican priest told me; he said he found it in an old manuscript book in a monastery down there, written by some Spanish Missionary, who got his stories from the Aztecs. This one he called 'The Forty Lovers of the Queen,' and it was more or less about rain-making."

"Aren't you going to tell it to me?" Eden asked.

Hedger fumbled among the radishes. "I don't know if it's the proper kind of story to tell a girl."

She smiled; "Oh, forget about that! I've been balloon riding today. I like to hear you talk."

Her low voice was flattering. She had seemed like clay in his hands ever since they got on the boat to come home. He leaned back in his chair, forgot his food, and, looking at her intently, began to tell his story, the theme of which he somehow felt was dangerous tonight.

The tale began, he said, somewhere in Ancient Mexico, and concerned the daughter of a king. The birth of this Princess was preceded by unusual portents. Three times her mother dreamed that she was delivered of serpents, which betokened that the child she carried would have power with the rain gods. The serpent was the symbol of water. The Princess grew up dedicated to the gods, and wise men taught her the rain-making mysteries. She was with difficulty re-strained from men and was guarded at all times, for it was the law of the Thunder that she be maiden until her marriage. In the years of her adolescence, rain was abundant with her people. The oldest man could not remember such fertil-ity. When the Princess had counted eighteen sum-mers, her father went to drive out a war party that harried his borders on the north and troubled his prosperity. The King destroyed the invaders and brought home many prisoners. Among the prison-ers was a young chief, taller than any of his cap-tors, of such strength and ferocity that the King's people came a day's journey to look at him. When the Princess beheld his great stature, and saw that his arms and breast were covered with the figures of wild animals, bitten into the skin and coloured, she begged his life from her father. She desired that he should practise his art upon her, and prick upon her skin the signs of Rain and Lightning and Thunder, and stain the wounds with herb-juices, as they were upon his own body. For many days, upon the roof of the King's house, the Princess submitted herself to the bone needle,

220

and the women with her marvelled at her fortitude. But the Princess was without shame before the Captive, and it came about that he threw from him his needles and his stains, and fell upon the Princess to violate her honour; and her women ran down from the roof screaming, to call the guard which stood at the gateway of the King's house, and none stayed to protect their mistress. When the guard came, the Captive was thrown into bonds, and he was gelded, and his tongue was torn out, and he was given for a slave to the Rain Princess.

The country of the Aztecs to the east was tormented by thirst, and their king, hearing much of the rain-making arts of the Princess, sent an embassy to her father, with presents and an offer of marriage. So the Princess went from her father to be the Queen of the Aztecs, and she took with her the Captive, who served her in everything with entire fidelity and slept upon a mat before her door.

The King gave his bride a fortress on the outskirts of the city, whither she retired to entreat the rain gods. This fortress was called the Queen's House, and on the night of the new moon the Queen came to it from the palace. But when the moon waxed and grew toward the round, because the god of Thunder had had his will of her, then the Queen returned to the King. Drought abated in the country and rain fell abundantly by reason of the Queen's power with the stars.

When the Queen went to her own house she took with her no servant but the Captive, and he slept outside her door and brought her food after she had fasted. The Queen had a jewel of great value, a turquoise that had fallen from the sun, and had the image of the sun upon it. And when she desired a young man whom she had seen in the army or among the slaves, she sent the Captive to him with the jewel, for a sign that he should come to her secretly at the Queen's House upon business concerning the welfare of all. And some, after she had talked with them, she sent away with rewards; and some she took into her chamber and kept them by her for one night or two. Afterward she called the Captive and bade him conduct the youth by the secret way he had come, underneath the chambers of the fortress. But for the going away of the Queen's lovers the Captive took out the bar that was beneath a stone in the floor of the passage, and put in its stead a rush-reed, and the youth stepped upon it and fell through into a cavern that was the bed of an underground river, and whatever was thrown into it was not seen again. In this service nor in any other did the Captive fail the Queen.

But when the Queen sent for the Captain of the Archers, she detained him four days in her chamber, calling often for food and wine, and was greatly content with him. On the fourth day she went to the Captive outside her door and said: "Tomorrow take this man up by the sure way, by which the King comes, and let him live."

In the Queen's door were arrows, purple and white. When she desired the King to come to her publicly, with his guard, she sent him a white arrow; but when she sent the purple, he came secretly, and covered himself with his mantle to be hidden from the stone gods at the gate. On the fifth night that the Queen was with her lover, the Captive took a purple arrow to the King, and the King came secretly and found them together. He killed the Captain with his own hand, but the Queen he brought to public trial. The Captive, when he was put to the question, told on his fingers forty men that he had let through the underground passage into the river. The Captive and the Queen were put to death by fire, both on the same day, and afterward there was scarcity of rain.

Eden Bower sat shivering a little as she listened. Hedger was not trying to please her, she thought, but to antagonize and frighten her by his brutal story. She had often told herself that his lean, big-boned lower jaw was like his bull-dog's, but tonight his face made Caesar's most savage and determined expression seem an affectation. Now she was looking at the man he really was. Nobody's eyes had ever defied her like this. They were searching her and seeing everything; all she had concealed from Livingston, and from the millionaire and his friends, and from the newspaper men. He was testing her, trying her out, and she was more ill at ease than she wished to show.

"That's quite a thrilling story," she said at last, rising and winding her scarf about her throat. "It must be getting late. Almost every one has gone."

They walked down the Avenue like people who have quarrelled, or who wish to get rid of each other. Hedger did not take her arm at the street crossings, and they did not linger in the Square. At her door he tried none of the old devices of the Livingston boys. He stood like a post, having forgotten to take off his hat, gave her a harsh, threatening glance, muttered "goodnight," and shut his own door noisily.

There was no question of sleep for Eden Bower.

Her brain was working like a machine that would never stop. After she undressed, she tried to calm her nerves by smoking a cigarette, lying on the divan by the open window. But she grew wider and wider awake, combating the challenge that had flamed all evening in Hedger's eyes. The balloon had been one kind of excitement, the wine another; but the thing that had roused her, as a blow rouses a proud man, was the doubt, the contempt, the sneering hostility with which the painter had looked at her when he told his savage story. Crowds and balloons were all very well, she reflected, but woman's chief adventure is man. With a mind over active and a sense of life over strong, she wanted to walk across the roofs in the starlight, to sail over the sea and face at once a world of which she had never been afraid.

Hedger must be asleep; his dog had stopped sniffing under the double doors. Eden put on her wrapper and slippers and stole softly down the hall over the old carpet; one loose board creaked just as she reached the ladder. The trap-door was open, as always on hot nights. When she stepped out on the roof she drew a long breath and walked across it, looking up at the sky. Her foot touched something soft; she heard a low growl, and on the instant Caesar's sharp little teeth caught her ankle and waited. His breath was like steam on her leg. Nobody had ever intruded upon his roof before, and he panted for the movement or the word that would let him spring his jaw. Instead, Hedger's hand seized his throat.

"Wait a minute. I'll settle with him," he said grimly. He dragged the dog toward the manhole and disappeared. When he came back, he found Eden standing over by the dark chimney, looking away in an offended attitude.

"I caned him unmercifully," he panted. "Of course you didn't hear anything; he never whines when I beat him. He didn't nip you, did he?"

"I don't know whether he broke the skin or not," she answered aggrievedly, still looking off into the west.

"If I were one of your friends in white pants, I'd strike a match to find whether you were hurt, though I know you are not, and then I'd see your ankle, wouldn't I?"

"I suppose so."

He shook his head and stood with his hands in the pockets of his old painting jacket. "I'm not up to such boy-tricks. If you want the place to yourself, I'll clear out. There are plenty of places where I can spend the night, what's left of it. But if you stay here and I stay here —" He shrugged his shoulders.

Eden did not stir, and she made no reply. Her head drooped slightly, as if she were considering. But the moment he put his arms about her they began to talk, both at once, as people do in an opera. The instant avowal brought out a flood of trivial admissions. Hedger confessed his crime, was reproached and forgiven, and now Eden knew what it was in his look that she had found so disturbing of late.

Standing against the black chimney, with the sky behind and blue shadows before, they looked like one of Hedger's own paintings of that period; two figures, one white and one dark, and nothing whatever distinguishable about them but that they were male and female. The faces were lost, the contours blurred in shadow, but the figures were a man and a woman, and that was their whole concern and their mysterious beauty, — it was the rhythm in which they moved, at last, along the roof and down into the dark hole; he first, drawing her gently after him. She came down very slowly. The excitement and bravado and uncertainty of that long day and night seemed all at once to tell upon her. When his feet were on the carpet and he reached up to lift her down, she twined her arms about his neck as after a long separation, and turned her face to him, and her lips, with their perfume of youth and passion.

One Saturday afternoon Hedger was sitting in the window of Eden's music room. They had been watching the pigeons come wheeling over the roofs from their unknown feeding grounds.

"Why," said Eden suddenly, "don't we fix those big doors into your studio so they will open? Then, if I want you, I won't have to go through the hall. That illustrator is loafing about a good deal of late."

"I'll open them, if you wish. The bolt is on your side."

"Isn't there one on yours, too?"

"No. I believe a man lived there for years before I came in, and the nurse used to have these rooms herself. Naturally, the lock was on the lady's side."

Eden laughed and began to examine the bolt. "It's all stuck up with paint." Looking about, her eye lighted upon a bronze Buddah which was one of the nurse's treasures. Taking him by his head, she struck the bolt a blow with his squatting posteriors. The two doors creaked, sagged, and swung weakly inward a little way, as if they were too old for such escapades. Eden tossed the heavy idol into a stuffed chair. "That's better," she

226

exclaimed exultantly. "So the bolts are always on the lady's side? What a lot society takes for granted!"

Hedger laughed, sprang up and caught her arms roughly. "Whoever takes you for granted — Did anybody, ever?"

"Everybody does. That's why I'm here. You are the only one who knows anything about me. Now I'll have to dress if we're going out for dinner."

He lingered, keeping his hold on her. "But I won't always be the only one, Eden Bower. I won't be the last."

"No, I suppose not," she said carelessly. "But what does that matter? You are the first."

As a long, despairing whine broke in the warm stillness, they drew apart. Caesar, lying on his bed in the dark corner, had lifted his head at this invasion of sunlight, and realized that the side of his room was broken open, and his whole world shattered by change. There stood his master and this woman, laughing at him! The woman was pulling the long black hair of this mightiest of men, who bowed his head and permitted it.

VI

In time they quarrelled, of course, and about an abstraction, — as young people often do, as mature people almost never do. Eden came in late one afternoon. She had been with some of her musical friends to lunch at Burton Ives' studio, and she began telling Hedger about its splendours. He listened a moment and then threw down his brushes. "I know exactly what it's like," he said impatiently. "A very good department-store conception of a studio. It's one of the show places."

"Well, it's gorgeous, and he said I could bring you to see him. The boys tell me he's awfully kind about giving people a lift, and you might get something out of it."

Hedger started up and pushed his canvas out of the way. "What could I possibly get from Burton Ives? He's almost the worst painter in the world; the stupidest, I mean."

Eden was annoyed. Burton Ives had been very nice to her and had begged her to sit for him. "You must admit that he's a very successful one," she said coldly.

"Of course he is! Anybody can be successful who will do that sort of thing. I wouldn't paint his pictures for all the money in New York."

"Well, I saw a lot of them, and I think they are beautiful."

Hedger bowed stiffly.

"What's the use of being a great painter if nobody knows about you?" Eden went on persuasively. "Why don't you paint the kind of pictures people can understand, and then, after you're successful, do whatever you like?"

"As I look at it," said Hedger brusquely, "I am successful."

Eden glanced about. "Well, I don't see any evidences of it," she said, biting her lip. "He has a Japanese servant and a wine cellar, and keeps a riding horse."

Hedger melted a little. "My dear, I have the most expensive luxury in the world, and I am much more extravagant than Burton Ives, for I work to please nobody but myself."

"You mean you could make money and don't? That you don't try to get a public?"

"Exactly. A public only wants what has been

done over and over. I'm painting for painters, — who haven't been born."

"What would you do if I brought Mr. Ives down here to see your things?"

"Well, for God's sake, don't! Before he left I'd probably tell him what I thought of him."

Eden rose. "I give you up. You know very well there's only one kind of success that's real."

"Yes, but it's not the kind you mean. So you've been thinking me a scrub painter, who needs a helping hand from some fashionable studio man? What the devil have you had anything to do with me for, then?"

"There's no use talking to you," said Eden walking slowly toward the door. "I've been trying to pull wires for you all afternoon, and this is what it comes to." She had expected that the tidings of a prospective call from the great man would be received very differently, and had been thinking as she came home in the stage how, as with a magic wand, she might gild Hedger's future, float him out of his dark hole on a tide of prosperity, see his name in the papers and his pictures in the windows on Fifth Avenue.

Hedger mechanically snapped the midsummer leash on Caesar's collar and they ran downstairs and hurried through Sullivan Street off toward the river. He wanted to be among rough, honest people, to get down where the big drays bumped over stone paving blocks and the men wore corduroy trowsers and kept their shirts open at the neck. He stopped for a drink in one of the sagging bar-rooms on the water front. He had never in his life been so deeply wounded; he did not know he could be so hurt. He had told this girl all his secrets. On the roof, in these warm, heavy summer nights, with her hands locked in his, he had been able to explain all his misty ideas about an unborn art the world was waiting for; had been able to explain them better than he had ever done to himself. And she had looked away to the chattels of this uptown studio and coveted them for him! To her he was only an unsuccessful Burton Ives.

Then why, as he had put it to her, did she take up with him? Young, beautiful, talented as she was, why had she wasted herself on a scrub? Pity? Hardly; she wasn't sentimental. There was no explaining her. But in this passion that had seemed so fearless and so fated to be, his own position now looked to him ridiculous; a poor dauber without money or fame, — it was her caprice to load him with favours. Hedger ground his teeth so loud that his dog, trotting beside him, heard him and looked up.

While they were having supper at the oyster-man's, he planned his escape. Whenever he saw her again, everything he had told her, that he should never have told any one, would come back to him; ideas he had never whispered even to the painter whom he worshipped and had gone all the way to France to see. To her they must seem his apology for not having horses and a valet, or merely the puerile boastfulness of a weak man. Yet if she slipped the bolt tonight and came through the doors and said, "Oh, weak man, I belong to you!" what could he do? That was the danger. He would catch the train out to Long Beach tonight, and tomorrow he would go on to the north end of Long Island, where an old friend of his had a summer studio among the sand dunes. He would stay until things came right in his mind. And she could find a smart painter, or take her punishment.

When he went home, Eden's room was dark; she was dining out somewhere. He threw his things into a hold-all he had carried about the world with him, strapped up some colours and canvases, and ran downstairs.

VII

Five days later Hedger was a restless passenger on a dirty, crowded Sunday train, coming back to town. Of course he saw now how unreasonable he had been in expecting a Huntington girl to know anything about pictures; here was a whole continent full of people who knew nothing about pictures and he didn't hold it against them. What had such things to do with him and Eden Bower? When he lay out on the dunes, watching the moon come up out of the sea, it had seemed to him that there was no wonder in the world like the wonder of Eden Bower. He was going back to her because she was older than art, because she was the most overwhelming thing that had ever come into his life.

He had written her yesterday, begging her to be at home this evening, telling her that he was contrite, and wretched enough.

Now that he was on his way to her, his stronger feeling unaccountably changed to a mood that was playful and tender. He wanted to share everything with her, even the most trivial things. He wanted to tell her about the people on the train, coming back tired from their holiday with bunches of wilted flowers and dirty daisies; to tell her that the fish-man, to whom she had often sent him for lobsters, was among the passengers, disguised in a silk shirt and a spotted tie, and how his wife looked exactly like a fish, even to her eyes, on which cataracts were forming. He could tell her, too, that he hadn't as much as unstrapped his canvases, — that ought to convince her.

In those days passengers from Long Island came into New York by ferry. Hedger had to be quick about getting his dog out of the express car in order to catch the first boat. The East River, and the bridges, and the city to the west, were burning in the conflagration of the sunset; there was that great home-coming reach of evening in the air.

The car changes from Thirty-fourth Street were too many and too perplexing; for the first time in his life Hedger took a hansom cab for Washington Square. Caesar sat bolt upright on the worn leather cushion beside him, and they jogged off, looking down on the rest of the world.

It was twilight when they drove down lower Fifth Avenue into the Square, and through the Arch behind them were the two long rows of pale violet lights that used to bloom so beautifully against the grey stone and asphalt. Here and yonder about the Square hung globes that shed a radiance not unlike the blue mists of evening, emerging softly when daylight died, as the stars emerged in the thin blue sky. Under them the sharp shadows of the trees fell on the cracked pavement and the sleeping grass. The first stars and the first lights were growing silver against the gradual darkening, when Hedger paid his driver and went into the house, — which, thank God, was still there! On the hall table lay his letter of yesterday, unopened.

He went upstairs with every sort of fear and every sort of hope clutching at his heart; it was as if tigers were tearing him. Why was there no gas burning in the top hall? He found matches and the gas bracket. He knocked, but got no answer; nobody was there. Before his own door were exactly five bottles of milk, standing in a row. The milk-boy had taken spiteful pleasure in thus reminding him that he forgot to stop his order.

Hedger went down to the basement; it, too, was dark. The janitress was taking her evening airing on the basement steps. She sat waving a palm-leaf fan majestically, her dirty calico dress open at the neck. She told him at once that there had been "changes." Miss Bower's room was to let again, and the piano would go tomorrow. Yes, she left yesterday, she sailed for Europe with friends from Chicago. They arrived on Friday, heralded by many telegrams. Very rich people they were said to be, though the man had refused to pay the nurse a month's rent in lieu of notice, — which would have been only right, as the young lady had agreed to take the rooms until October. Mrs. Foley had observed, too, that he didn't overpay her or Willy for their trouble, and a great deal of trouble they had been put to, certainly. Yes, the young lady was very pleasant, but the nurse said there were rings on the mahogany table where she had put tumblers and wine glasses. It was just as well she was gone. The Chicago man was uppish in his ways, but not much to look at. She supposed he had poor health, for there was nothing to him inside his clothes.

Hedger went slowly up the stairs — never had they seemed so long, or his legs so heavy. The upper floor was emptiness and silence. He unlocked his room, lit the gas, and opened the windows. When he went to put his coat in the closet, he found, hanging among his clothes, a pale, flesh-tinted dressing gown he had liked to see her wear, with a perfume — oh, a perfume that was still Eden Bower! He shut the door behind him and there, in the dark, for a moment he lost his manliness. It was when he held this garment to him that he found a letter in the pocket.

The note was written with a lead pencil, in haste: She was sorry that he was angry, but she still didn't know just what she had done. She had thought Mr. Ives would be useful to him; she guessed he was too proud. She wanted awfully to see him again, but Fate came knocking at her door after he had left her. She believed in Fate. She would never forget him, and she knew he would become the greatest painter in the world. Now she must pack. She hoped he wouldn't mind her leaving the dressing gown; somehow, she could never wear it again.

After Hedger read this, standing under the gas, he went back into the closet and knelt down before the wall; the knot hole had been plugged up with a ball of wet paper, — the same blue notepaper on which her letter was written.

He was hard hit. Tonight he had to bear the loneliness of a whole lifetime. Knowing himself so well, he could hardly believe that such a thing had ever happened to him, that such a woman had lain happy and contented in his arms. And now it was over. He turned out the light and sat down on his painter's stool before the big window. Caesar, on the floor beside him, rested his head on his master's knee. We must leave Hedger thus, sitting in his tank with his dog, looking up at the stars.

Coming, Aphrodite! This legend, in electric lights over the Lexington Opera House, had long announced the return of Eden Bower to New York after years of spectacular success in Paris. She came at last, under the management of an American Opera Company, but bringing her own *chef d'orchestre.*

One bright December afternoon Eden Bower was going down Fifth Avenue in her car, on the way to her broker, in Williams Street. Her thoughts were entirely upon stocks, — Cerro de Pasco, and how much she should buy of it, — when she suddenly looked up and realized that she was skirting Washington Square. She had not seen the place since she rolled out of it in an old-fashioned four-wheeler to seek her fortune, eighteen years ago.

"Arrêtez, Alphonse. Attendez moi," she called, and opened the door before he could reach it. The children who were streaking over the asphalt on roller skates saw a lady in a long fur coat, and short, high-heeled shoes, alight from a French car and pace slowly about the Square, holding her muff to her chin. This spot, at least, had changed very little, she reflected; the same trees, the same fountain, the white arch, and over yonder, Garibaldi, drawing the sword for freedom. There, just opposite her, was the old red brick house.

"Yes, that is the place," she was thinking. "I can smell the carpets now, and the dog, — what was his name? That grubby bathroom at the end of the hall, and that dreadful Hedger — still, there was something about him, you know —" She glanced up and blinked against the sun. From somewhere in the crowded quarter south of the Square a flock of pigeons rose, wheeling quickly upward into the brilliant blue sky. She threw back her head, pressed her muff closer to her chin, and watched them with a smile of amazement and

235

delight. So they still rose, out of all that dirt and noise and squalor, fleet and silvery, just as they used to rise that summer when she was twenty and went up in a balloon on Coney Island!

Alphonse opened the door and tucked her robes about her. All the way down town her mind wandered from Cerro de Pasco, and she kept smiling and looking up at the sky.

When she had finished her business with the broker, she asked him to look in the telephone book for the address of M. Gaston Jules, the picture dealer, and slipped the paper on which he wrote it into her glove. It was five o'clock when she reached the French Galleries, as they were called. On entering she gave the attendant her card, asking him to take it to M. Jules. The dealer appeared very promptly and begged her to come into his private office, where he pushed a great chair toward his desk for her and signalled his secretary to leave the room.

"How good your lighting is in here," she observed, glancing about. "I met you at Simon's studio, didn't I? Oh, no! I never forget anybody who interests me." She threw her muff on his writing table and sank into the deep chair. "I have come to you for some information that's not in my line. Do you know anything about an American painter named Hedger?"

He took the seat opposite her. "Don Hedger? But, certainly! There are some very interesting things of his in an exhibition at V——'s. If you would care to —"

She held up her hand. "No, no. I've no time to go to exhibitions. Is he a man of any importance?"

"Certainly. He is one of the first men among the moderns. That is to say, among the very moderns.

He is always coming up with something different. He often exhibits in Paris, you must have seen —"

"No, I tell you I don't go to exhibitions. Has he had great success? That is what I want to know."

M. Jules pulled at his short grey moustache. "But, Madame, there are many kinds of success," he began cautiously.

Madame gave a dry laugh. "Yes, so he used to say. We once quarrelled on that issue. And how would you define his particular kind?"

M. Jules grew thoughtful. "He is a great name with all the young men, and he is decidedly an influence in art. But one can't definitely place a man who is original, erratic, and who is changing all the time."

She cut him short. "Is he much talked about at home? In Paris, I mean? Thanks. That's all I want to know." She rose and began buttoning her coat. "One doesn't like to have been an utter fool, even at twenty."

"Mais, non!" M. Jules handed her her muff with a quick, sympathetic glance. He followed her out through the carpeted show-room, now closed to the public and draped in cheesecloth, and put her into her car with words appreciative of the honour she had done him in calling.

Leaning back in the cushions, Eden Bower closed her eyes, and her face, as the street lamps flashed their ugly orange light upon it, became hard and settled, like a plaster cast; so a sail, that has been filled by a strong breeze, behaves when the wind suddenly dies. Tomorrow night the wind would blow again, and this mask would be the golden face of Aphrodite. But a "big" career takes its toll, even with the best of luck.

THE DIAMOND MINE

I

I first became aware that Cressida Garnet was on board when I saw young men with cameras going up to the boat deck. In that exposed spot she was good-naturedly posing for them — amid fluttering lavender scarfs — wearing a most unseaworthy hat, her broad, vigorous face wreathed in smiles. She was too much an American not to believe in publicity. All advertising was good. If it was good for breakfast foods, it was good for prima donna, — especially for a prima donna who would never be any younger and who had just announced her intention of marrying a fourth time.

Only a few days before, when I was lunching with some friends at Sherry's, I had seen Jerome Brown come in with several younger men, looking so pleased and prosperous that I exclaimed upon it.

"His affairs," some one explained, "are looking up. He's going to marry Cressida Garnet. Nobody believed it at first, but since she confirms it he's getting all sorts of credit. That woman's a diamond mine."

If there was ever a man who needed a diamond mine at hand, immediately convenient, it was

238

Jerome Brown. But as an old friend of Cressida Garnet, I was sorry to hear that mining operations were to be begun again.

I had been away from New York and had not seen Cressida for a year; now I paused on the gangplank to note how very like herself she still was, and with what undiminished zeal she went about even the most trifling things that pertained to her profession. From that distance I could recognize her "carrying" smile, and even what, in Columbus, we used to call "the Garnet look."

At the foot of the stairway leading up to the boat deck stood two of the factors in Cressida's destiny. One of them was her sister, Miss Julia; a woman of fifty with a relaxed, mournful face, an ageing skin that browned slowly, like meerchaum, and the unmistakable "look" by which one knew a Garnet. Beside her, pointedly ignoring her, smoking a cigarette while he ran over the passenger list with supercilious almond eyes, stood a youth in a pink shirt and a green plush hat, holding a French bull-dog on the leash. This was "Horace," Cressida's only son. He, at any rate, had not the Garnet look. He was rich and ruddy, indolent and insolent, with soft oval cheeks and the blooming complexion of twenty-two. There was the beginning of a silky shadow on his upper lip. He seemed like a ripe fruit grown out of a rich soil; "oriental," his mother called his peculiar lusciousness. His aunt's restless and aggrieved glance kept flecking him from the side, but the two were as motionless as the *bouledogue,* standing there on his bench legs and surveying his travelling basket with loathing. They were waiting, in constrained immobility, for Cressida to descend and reanimate them, — will them to do or to be

239

something. Forward, by the rail, I saw the stooped, eager back for which I was unconsciously looking: Miletus Poppas, the Greek Jew, Cressida's accompanist and shadow. We were all there, I thought with a smile, except Jerome Brown.

The first member of Cressida's party with whom I had speech was Mr. Poppas. When we were two hours out I came upon him in the act of dropping overboard a steamer cushion made of American flags. Cressida never sailed, I think, that one of these vivid comforts of travel did not reach her at the dock. Poppas recognized me just as the striped object left his hand. He was standing with his arm still extended over the rail, his fingers contemptuously sprung back. "Lest we forget!" he said with a shrug. "Does Madame Cressida know we are to have the pleasure of your company for this voyage?" He spoke deliberate, grammatical English — he despised the American rendering of the language — but there was an indescribably foreign quality in his voice, — a something muted; and though he aspirated his "th's" with such conscientious thoroughness, there was always the thud of a "d" in them. Poppas stood before me in a short, tightly buttoned grey coat and cap, exactly the colour of his greyish skin and hair and waxed moustache; a monocle on a very wide black ribbon dangled over his chest. As to his age, I could not offer a conjecture. In the twelve years I had known his thin lupine face behind Cressida's shoulder, it had not changed. I was used to his cold, supercilious manner, to his alarming, deep-set eyes, — very close together, in colour a yellowish green, and always gleaming with something like defeated fury, as if he were actually on the point of having it out with you, or with the world, at last.

I asked him if Cressida had engagements in London.

"Quite so; the Manchester Festival, some concerts at Queen's Hall, and the Opera at Covent Garden; a rather special production of the operas of Mozart. That she can still do quite well, — which is not at all, of course, what we might have expected, and only goes to show that our Madame Cressida is now, as always, a charming exception to rules." Poppas' tone about his client was consistently patronizing, and he was always trying to draw one into a conspiracy of two, based on a mutual understanding of her shortcomings.

I approached him on the one subject I could think of which was more personal than his usefulness to Cressida, and asked him whether he still suffered from facial neuralgia as much as he had done in former years, and whether he was therefore dreading London, where the climate used to be so bad for him.

"And is still," he caught me up, "And is still! For me to go to London is martyrdom, _chère Madame._ In New York it is bad enough, but in London it is the _auto da fé,_ nothing less. My nervous system is exotic in any country washed by the Atlantic ocean, and it shivers like a little hairless dog from Mexico. It never relaxes. I think I have told you about my favourite city in the middle of Asia, _la sainte Asie,_ where the rainfall is absolutely nil, and you are protected on every side by hundreds of metres of warm, dry sand. I was there when I was a child once, and it is still my intention to retire there when I have finished with all this. I would be there now, n-ow-ow," his voice rose querulously, "if Madame Cressida did not imagine that she needs me, — and her fancies, you know," he flourished his hands, "one gives in to them. In humouring her caprices you and I have already played some together."

We were approaching Cressida's deck chairs, ranged under the open windows of her stateroom. She was already recumbent, swathed in lavender scarfs and wearing purple orchids — doubtless from Jerome Brown. At her left, Horace had settled down to a French novel, and Julia Garnet, at her right, was complainingly regarding the grey horizon. On seeing me, Cressida struggled under her fur-lined robes and got to her feet, — which was more than Horace or Miss Julia managed to do. Miss Julia, as I could have foretold, was not pleased. All the Garnets had an awkward manner with me. Whether it was that I reminded them of things they wished to forget, or whether they thought I esteemed Cressida too highly and the rest of them too lightly, I do not know; but my appearance upon their scene always put them greatly on their dignity. After Horace had offered me his chair and Miss Julia had said doubtfully that she thought I was looking rather better than when she last saw me, Cressida took my arm and walked me off toward the stern.

"Do you know, Carrie, I half wondered whether I shouldn't find you here, or in London, because you always turn up at critical moments in my life." She pressed my arm confidentially, and I felt that she was once more wrought up to a new purpose. I told her that I had heard some rumour of her engagement.

"It's quite true, and it's all that it should be," she reassured me. "I'll tell you about it later, and you'll see that it's a real solution. They are against me, of course, — all except Horace. He has been such a comfort."

Horace's support, such as it was, could always be had in exchange for his mother's signature, I suspected. The pale May day had turned bleak and chilly, and we sat down by an open hatchway which emitted warm air from somewhere below. At this close range I studied Cressida's face, and felt reassured of her unabated vitality; the old force of will was still there, and with it her characteristic optimism, the old hope of a "solution."

"You have been in Columbus lately?" she was saying. "No, you needn't tell me about it," with a sigh. "Why is it, Caroline, that there is so little of my life I would be willing to live over again? So little that I can even think of without depression. Yet I've really not such a bad conscience. It may mean that I still belong to the future more than to the past, do you think?"

My assent was not warm enough to fix her attention, and she went on thoughtfully: "Of course, it was a bleak country and a bleak period. But I've sometimes wondered whether the bleakness may not have been in me, too; for it has certainly followed me. There, that is no way to talk!" she drew herself up from a momentary attitude of dejection. "Sea air always lets me down at first. That's why it's so good for me in the end."

"I think Julia always lets you down, too," I said bluntly. "But perhaps that depression works out in the same way."

Cressida laughed. "Julia is rather more depressing than Georgie, isn't she? But it was Julia's turn. I can't come alone, and they've grown to expect

243

it. They haven't, either of them, much else to expect."

At this point the deck steward approached us with a blue envelope. "A wireless for you, Madame Garnet."

Cressida put out her hand with impatience, thanked him graciously, and with every indication of pleasure tore open the blue envelope. "It's from Jerome Brown," she said with some confusion, as she folded the paper small and tucked it between the buttons of her close-fitting gown, "something he forgot to tell me. How long shall you be in London? Good; I want you to meet him. We shall probably be married there as soon as my engagements are over." She rose. "Now I must write some letters. Keep two places at your table, so that I can slip away from my party and dine with you sometimes."

I walked with her toward her chair, in which Mr. Poppas was now reclining. He indicated his readiness to rise, but she shook her head and entered the door of her deck suite. As she passed him, his eye went over her with assurance until it rested upon the folded bit of blue paper in her corsage. He must have seen the original rectangle in the steward's hand; having found it again, he dropped back between Horace and Miss Julia, whom I think he disliked no more than he did the rest of the world. He liked Julia quite as well as he liked me, and he liked me quite as well as he liked any of the women to whom he would be fitfully agreeable upon the voyage. Once or twice, during each crossing, he did his best and made himself very charming indeed, to keep his hand in, — for the same reason that he kept a dummy keyboard in his stateroom, somewhere down in the bowels of the boat. He practised all the small economies; paid the minimum rate, and never took a deck chair, because, as Horace was usually in the card-room, he could sit in Horace's.

The three of them lay staring at the swell which was steadily growing heavier. Both men had covered themselves with rugs, after dutifully bundling up Miss Julia. As I walked back and forth on the deck, I was struck by their various degrees of in-expressiveness. Opaque brown eyes, almond-shaped and only half open; wolfish green eyes, close-set and always doing something, with a crooked gleam boring in this direction or in that; watery grey eyes, like the thick edges of broken skylight glass: I would have given a great deal to know what was going on behind each pair of them.

These three were sitting there in a row because they were all woven into the pattern of one large and rather splendid life. Each had a bond, and each had a grievance. If they could have their will, what would they do with the generous, credulous creature who nourished them, I wondered? How deep a humiliation would each egotism exact? They would scarcely have harmed her in fortune or in person (though I think Miss Julia looked forward to the day when Cressida would "break" and could be mourned over), — but the fire at which she warmed herself, the little secret hope, — the illusion, ridiculous or sublime, which kept her going, — that they would have stamped out on the instant, with the whole Garnet pack behind them to make extinction sure. All, except, perhaps, Miletus Poppas. He was a vulture of the vulture race, and he had the beak of one. But I always felt that if ever he had her thus at his mercy, — if ever he came upon the softness that was hidden under so much hardness, the warm credulity under a life so dated and scheduled and "reported" and generally exposed, — he would hold his hand and spare.

The weather grew steadily rougher. Miss Julia at last plucked Poppas by the sleeve and indicated that she wished to be released from her wrappings. When she disappeared, there seemed to be every reason to hope that she might be off the scene for awhile. As Cressida said, if she had not brought Julia, she would have had to bring Georgie, or some other Garnet. Cressida's family was like that of the unpopular Prince of Wales, of whom, when he died, some wag wrote:

If it had been his brother,
Better him than another.
If it had been his sister,
No one would have missed her.

Miss Julia was dampening enough, but Miss Georgie was aggressive and intrusive. She was out to prove to the world, and more especially to Ohio, that all the Garnets were as like Cressida as two peas. Both sisters were club-women, social service workers, and directors in musical societies, and they were continually travelling up and down the Middle West to preside at meetings or to deliver addresses. They reminded one of two sombre, bumping electrics, rolling about with no visible means of locomotion, always running out of power and lying beached in some inconvenient spot until they received a check or a suggestion from Cressy. I was only too well acquainted with the strained, anxious expression that the sight of their handwriting brought to Cressida's face when she ran over her morning mail at breakfast. She usually put their letters by to read "when she was feeling up to it" and hastened to open others which might possibly contain something gracious or pleasant. Sometimes these family unburdenings lay about unread for several days. Any other letters would have got themselves lost, but these bulky epistles, never properly fitted to their envelopes, seemed immune to mischance and unfailingly disgorged to Cressida long explanations as to why her sisters had to do and to have certain things precisely upon her account and because she was so much a public personage.

The truth was that all the Garnets, and particularly her two sisters, were consumed by an habitual, bilious, unenterprising envy of Cressy. They never forgot that, no matter what she did for them or how far she dragged them about the world with her, she would never take one of them to live with her in her Tenth Street house in New York. They thought that was the thing they most wanted. But what they wanted, in the last analysis, was to *be* Cressida. For twenty years she had been plunged in struggle; fighting for her life at first, then for a beginning, for growth, and at last for eminence and perfection; fighting in the dark, and afterward in the light, — which, with her bad preparation, and with her uninspired youth already behind her, took even more courage. During those twenty years the Garnets had been comfortable and indolent and vastly self-satisfied; and now they expected Cressida to make them equal sharers in the finer rewards of her struggle. When her brother Buchanan told me he thought Cressida ought "to make herself one of them," he stated the converse of what he meant. They coveted the qualities which had made her success, as well as the benefits which came from it. More than her furs or her fame or her fortune, they wanted her personal effectiveness, her brighter glow and stronger will to live.

"Sometimes," I have heard Cressida say, looking up from a bunch of those sloppily written letters, "sometimes I get discouraged."

For several days the rough weather kept Miss Julia cloistered in Cressida's deck suite with the maid, Luisa, who confided to me that the Signorina Garnet was *"dificile."* After dinner I usually found Cressida unincumbered, as Horace was always in the cardroom and Mr. Poppas either nursed his neuralgia or went through the exercise of making himself interesting to some one of the young women on board. One evening, the third night out, when the sea was comparatively quiet and the sky was full of broken black clouds, silvered by the moon at their ragged edges, Cressida talked to me about Jerome Brown.

I had known each of her former husbands. The first one, Charley Wilton, Horace's father, was my cousin. He was organist in a church in Columbus, and Cressida married him when she was nineteen. He died of tuberculosis two years after Horace was born. Cressida nursed him through a long illness and made the living besides. Her courage during the three years of her first marriage was fine enough to foreshadow her future to any discerning eye, and it had made me feel that she deserved any number of chances at marital happiness. There had, of course, been a particular reason for each subsequent experiment, and a sufficiently alluring promise of success. Her motives, in the case of Jerome Brown, seemed to me more vague and less convincing than those which she had explained to me on former occasions.

"It's nothing hasty," she assured me. "It's been coming on for several years. He has never pushed me, but he was always there — some one to count on. Even when I used to meet him at the Whitings, while I was still singing at the Metropolitan, I always felt that he was different from the others; that if I were in straits of any kind, I could call on him. You can't know what that feeling means to me, Carrie. If you look back, you'll see it's something I've never had."

I admitted that, in so far as I knew, she had never been much addicted to leaning on people.

"I've never had any one to lean on," she said with a short laugh. Then she went on, quite seriously: "Somehow, my relations with people always become business relations in the end. I suppose it's because, — except for a sort of professional personality, which I've had to get, just as I've had to get so many other things, — I've not very much that's personal to give people. I've had to give too much else. I've had to try too hard for people who wouldn't try at all."

"Which," I put in firmly, "has done them no good, and has robbed the people who really cared about you."

"By making me grubby, you mean?"

"By making you anxious and distracted so much of the time; empty."

She nodded mournfully. "Yes, I know. You used to warn me. Well, there's not one of my brothers and sisters who does not feel that I carried off the family success, just as I might have carried off the family silver, — if there'd been any! They take the view that there were just so many prizes in the bag; I reached in and took them, so there were

249

none left for the others. At my age, that's a dismal truth to waken up to." Cressida reached for my hand and held it a moment, as if she needed courage to face the facts in her case. "When one remembers one's first success; how one hoped to go home like a Christmas tree full of presents — How much one learns in a life-time! That year when Horace was a baby and Charley was dying, and I was touring the West with the Williams band, it was my feeling about my own people that made me go at all. Why I didn't drop myself into one of those muddy rivers, or turn on the gas in one of those dirty hotel rooms, I don't know to this day. At twenty-two you must hope for something more than to be able to bury your husband decently, and what I hoped for was to make my family happy. It was the same afterward in Germany. A young woman must live for human people. Horace wasn't enough. I might have had lovers, of course. I suppose you will say it would have been better if I had."

Though there seemed no need for me to say anything, I murmured that I thought there were more likely to be limits to the rapacity of a lover than to that of a discontented and envious family.

"Well," Cressida gathered herself up, "once I got out from under it all, didn't I? And perhaps, in a milder way, such a release can come again. You were the first person I told when I ran away with Charley, and for a long while you were the only one who knew about Blasius Bouchalka. That time, at least, I shook the Garnets. I wasn't distracted or empty. That time I was all there!"

"Yes," I echoed her, "that time you were all there. It's the greatest possible satisfaction to remember it."

"But even that," she sighed, "was nothing but lawyers and accounts in the end — and a hurt. A hurt that has lasted. I wonder what is the matter with me?"

The matter with Cressida was, that more than any woman I have ever known, she appealed to the acquisitive instinct in men; but this was not easily said, even in the brutal frankness of a long friendship.

We would probably have gone further into the Bouchalka chapter of her life, had not Horace appeared and nervously asked us if we did not wish to take a turn before we went inside. I pleaded indolence, but Cressida rose and disappeared with him. Later I came upon them, standing at the stern above the huddled steerage deck, which was by this time bathed in moonlight, under an almost clear sky. Down there on the silvery floor, little hillocks were scattered about under quilts and shawls; family units, presumably, — male, female, and young. Here and there a black shawl sat alone, nodding. They crouched submissively under the moonlight as if it were a spell. In one of those hillocks a baby was crying, but the sound was faint and thin, a slender protest which aroused no response. Everything was so still that I could hear snatches of the low talk between my friends. Cressida's voice was deep and entreating. She was remonstrating with Horace about his losses at bridge, begging him to keep away from the card-room.

"But what else is there to do on a trip like this, my Lady?" he expostulated, tossing his spark of a cigarette-end overboard. "What is there, now, to do?"

"Oh, Horace!" she murmured, "how can you be

251

so? If I were twenty-two, and a boy, with some one to back me —"

Horace drew his shoulders together and buttoned his top-coat. "Oh, I've not your energy, Mother dear. We make no secret of that. I am as I am. I didn't ask to be born into this charming world."

To this gallant speech Cressida made no answer. She stood with her hand on the rail and her head bent forward, as if she had lost herself in thought. The ends of her scarf, lifted by the breeze, fluttered upward, almost transparent in the argent light. Presently she turned away, — as if she had been alone and were leaving only the night sea behind her, — and walked slowly forward; a strong, solitary figure on the white deck, the smoke-like scarf twisting and climbing and falling back upon itself in the light over her head. She reached the door of her stateroom and disappeared. Yes, she was a Garnet, but she was also Cressida; and she had done what she had done.

II

My first recollections of Cressida Garnet have to do with the Columbus Public Schools; a little girl with sunny brown hair and eager bright eyes, looking anxiously at the teacher and reciting the names and dates of the Presidents: "James Buchanan, 1857–1861; Abraham Lincoln, 1861–1865"; etc. Her family came from North Carolina, and they had that to feel superior about before they had Cressy. The Garnet "look," indeed, though based upon a strong family resemblance, was nothing more than the restless, preoccupied expression of an inflamed sense of importance. The father was a Democrat, in the sense that other men were doctors or lawyers. He scratched up some sort of poor living for his family behind office windows inscribed with the words "Real Estate. Insurance. Investments." But it was his political faith that, in a Republican community, gave him his feeling of eminence and originality. The Garnet children were all in school then, scattered along from the first grade to the ninth. In almost any room of our school building you might chance to enter, you saw the self-conscious little face of one or another of them. They were restrained, uncomfortable children, not frankly boastful, but insinuating, and somehow forever demanding special consideration and holding grudges against teachers and classmates who did not show it them; all but Cressida, who was naturally as sunny and open as a May morning.

It was no wonder that Cressy ran away with young Charley Wilton, who hadn't a shabby thing about him except his health. He was her first music teacher, the choir-master of the church in which she sang. Charley was very handsome; the "romantic" son of an old, impoverished family. He had refused to go into a good business with his uncles and had gone abroad to study music when that was an extravagant and picturesque thing for an Ohio boy to do. His letters home were handed round among the members of his own family and of other families equally conservative. Indeed, Charley and what his mother called "his music" were the romantic expression of a considerable group of people; young cousins and old aunts and quiet-dwelling neighbours, allied by the amity of several generations. Nobody was properly married in our part of Columbus unless Charley Wilton, and no other, played the wedding march.

The old ladies of the First Church used to say that he "hovered over the keys like a spirit." At nineteen Cressida was beautiful enough to turn a much harder head than the pale, ethereal one Charley Wilton bent above the organ.

That the chapter which began so gracefully ran on into such a stretch of grim, hard prose, was simply Cressida's relentless bad luck. In her undertakings, in whatever she could lay hold of with her two hands, she was successful; but whatever happened to her was almost sure to be bad. Her family, her husbands, her son, would have crushed any other woman I have ever known. Cressida lived, more than most of us, "for others"; and what she seemed to promote among her beneficiaries was indolence and envy and discord — even dishonesty and turpitude.

Her sisters were fond of saying — at club luncheons — that Cressida had remained "untouched by the breath of scandal," which was not strictly true. There were captious people who objected to her long and close association with Miletus Poppas. Her second husband, Ransome McChord, the foreign representative of the great McChord Harvester Company, whom she married in Germany, had so persistently objected to Poppas that she was eventually forced to choose between them. Any one who knew her well could easily understand why she chose Poppas.

While her actual self was the least changed, the least modified by experience that it would be possible to imagine, there had been, professionally, two Cressida Garnets; the big handsome girl, already a "popular favourite" of the concert stage, who took with her to Germany the raw material of a great voice; — and the accomplished artist who came back. The singer that returned was largely the work of Miletus Poppas. Cressida had at least known what she needed, hunted for it, found it, and held fast to it. After experimenting with a score of teachers and accompanists, she settled down to work her problem out with Poppas. Other coaches came and went — she was always trying new ones — but Poppas survived them all. Cressida was not musically intelligent; she never became so. Who does not remember the countless rehearsals which were necessary before she first sang *Isolde* in Berlin; the disgust of the conductor, the sullenness of the tenor, the rages of the blonde *teufelin,* boiling with the impatience of youth and genius, who sang her *Brangaena?* Everything but her driving power Cressida had to get from the outside.

Poppas was, in his way, quite as incomplete as his pupil. He possessed a great many valuable things for which there is no market; intuitions, discrimination, imagination, a whole twilight world of intentions and shadowy beginnings which were dark to Cressida. I remember that when "Trilby" was published she fell into a fright and said such books ought to be prohibited by law; which gave me an intimation of what their relationship had actually become.

Poppas was indispensable to her. He was like a book in which she had written down more about herself than she could possibly remember — and it was information that she might need at any moment. He was the one person who knew her absolutely and who saw into the bottom of her grief. An artist's saddest secrets are those that have to do with his artistry. Poppas knew all the simple things that were so desperately hard for

255

Cressida, all the difficult things in which she could count on herself; her stupidities and inconsistencies, the chiaroscuro of the voice itself and what could be expected from the mind somewhat mismated with it. He knew where she was sound and where she was mended. With him she could share the depressing knowledge of what a wretchedly faulty thing any productive faculty is.

But if Poppas was necessary to her career, she was his career. By the time Cressida left the Metropolitan Opera Company, Poppas was a rich man. He had always received a retaining fee and a percentage of her salary, — and he was a man of simple habits. Her liberality with Poppas was one of the weapons that Horace and the Garnets used against Cressida, and it was a point in the argument by which they justified to themselves their rapacity. Whatever they didn't get, they told themselves, Poppas would. What they got, therefore, they were only saving from Poppas. The Greek ached a good deal at the general pillage, and Cressida's conciliatory methods with her family made him sarcastic and spiteful. But he had to make terms, somehow, with the Garnets and Horace, and with the husband, if there happened to be one. He sometimes reminded them, when they fell to wrangling, that they must not, after all, overturn the boat under them, and that it would be better to stop just before they drove her wild than just after. As he was the only one among them who understood the sources of her fortune, — and they knew it, — he was able, when it came to a general set-to, to proclaim sanctuary for the goose that laid the golden eggs.

That Poppas had caused the break between Cressida and McChord was another stick her sisters held over her. They pretended to understand perfectly, and were always explaining what they termed her "separation"; but they let Cressida know that it cast a shadow over her family and took a good deal of living down.

A beautiful soundness of body, a seemingly exhaustless vitality, and a certain "squareness" of character as well as of mind, gave Cressida Garnet earning powers that were exceptional even in her lavishly rewarded profession. Managers chose her over the heads of singers much more gifted, because she was so sane, so conscientious, and above all, because she was so sure. Her efficiency was like a beacon to lightly anchored men, and in the intervals between her marriages she had as many suitors as Penelope. Whatever else they saw in her at first, her competency so impressed and delighted them that they gradually lost sight of everything else. Her sterling character was the subject of her story. Once, as she said, she very nearly escaped her destiny. With Blasius Bouchalka she became almost another woman, but not quite. Her "principles," or his lack of them, drove those two apart in the end. It was of Bouchalka that we talked upon that last voyage I ever made with Cressida Garnet, and not of Jerome Brown. She remembered the Bohemian kindly, and since it was the passage in her life to which she most often reverted, it is the one I shall relate here.

III

Late one afternoon in the winter of 189–, Cressida and I were walking in Central Park after the first heavy storm of the year. The snow had been falling thickly all the night before, and all day, until about four o'clock. Then the air grew much

257

warmer and the sky cleared. Overhead it was a soft, rainy blue, and to the west a smoky gold. All around the horizon everything became misty and silvery; even the big, brutal buildings looked like pale violet water-colours on a silver ground. Under the elm trees along the Mall the air was purple as wisterias. The sheep-field, toward Broadway, was smooth and white, with a thin gold wash over it. At five o'clock the carriage came for us, but Cressida sent the driver home to the Tenth Street house with the message that she would dine uptown, and that Horace and Mr. Poppas were not to wait for her. As the horses trotted away we turned up the Mall.

"I won't go indoors this evening for any one," Cressida declared. "Not while the sky is like that. Now we will go back to the laurel wood. They are so black, over the snow, that I could cry for joy. I don't know when I've felt so care-free as I feel tonight. Country winter, country stars — they always make me think of Charley Wilton."

She was singing twice a week, sometimes oftener, at the Metropolitan that season, quite at the flood-tide of her powers, and so enmeshed in operatic routine that to be walking in the park at an unaccustomed hour, unattended by one of the men of her entourage, seemed adventurous. As we strolled along the little paths among the snow banks and the bronze laurel bushes, she kept going back to my poor young cousin, dead so long. "Things happen out of season. That's the worst of living. It was untimely for both of us, and yet," she sighed softly, "since he had to die, I'm not sorry. There was one beautifully happy year, though we were so poor, and it gave him — something! It would have been too hard if he'd had to miss everything." (I remember her simplicity, which never changed any more than winter or Ohio change.) "Yes," she went on, "I always feel very tenderly about Charley. I believe I'd do the same thing right over again, even knowing all that had to come after. If I were nineteen tonight, I'd rather go sleigh-riding with Charley Wilton than anything else I've ever done."

We walked until the procession of carriages on the driveway, getting people home to dinner, grew thin, and then we went slowly toward the Seventh Avenue gate, still talking of Charley Wilton. We decided to dine at a place not far away, where the only access from the street was a narrow door, like a hole in the wall, between a tobacconist's and a flower shop. Cressida deluded herself into believing that her incognito was more successful in such non-descript places. She was wearing a long sable coat, and a deep fur hat, hung with red cherries, which she had brought from Russia. Her walk had given her a fine colour, and she looked so much a personage that no disguise could have been wholly effective.

The dining-rooms, frescoed with conventional Italian scenes, were built round a court. The orchestra was playing as we entered and selected our table. It was not a bad orchestra, and we were no sooner seated than the first violin began to speak, to assert itself, as if it were suddenly done with mediocrity.

"We have been recognized," Cressida said complacently. "What a good tone he has, quite unusual. What does he look like?" She sat with her back to the musicians.

The violinist was standing, directing his men with his head and with the beak of his violin. He

259

was a tall, gaunt young man, big-boned and rugged, in skin-tight clothes. His high forehead had a kind of luminous pallour, and his hair was jet black and somewhat stringy. His manner was excited and dramatic. At the end of the number he acknowledged the applause, and Cressida looked at him graciously over her shoulder. He swept her with a brilliant glance and bowed again. Then I noticed his red lips and thick black eyebrows.

"He looks as if he were poor or in trouble," Cressida said. "See how short his sleeves are, and how he mops his face as if the least thing upset him. This is a hard winter for musicians."

The violinist rummaged among some music piled on a chair, turning over the sheets with flurried rapidity, as if he were searching for a lost article of which he was in desperate need. Presently he placed some sheets upon the piano and began vehemently to explain something to the pianist. The pianist stared at the music doubtfully — he was a plump old man with a rosy, bald crown, and his shiny linen and neat tie made him look as if he were on his way to a party. The violinist bent over him, suggesting rhythms with his shoulders and running his bony finger up and down the pages. When he stepped back to his place, I noticed that the other players sat at ease, without raising their instruments.

"He is going to try something unusual," I commented. "It looks as if it might be manuscript."

It was something, at all events, that neither of us had heard before, though it was very much in the manner of the later Russian composers who were just beginning to be heard in New York. The young man made a brilliant dash of it, despite a lagging, scrambling accompaniment by the conservative pianist. This time we both applauded him vigorously and again, as he bowed, he swept us with his eye.

The usual repertory of restaurant music followed, varied by a charming bit from Massenet's "Manon," then little known in this country. After we paid our check, Cressida took out one of her visiting cards and wrote across the top of it: *"We thank you for the unusual music and the pleasure your playing has given us."* She folded the card in the middle, and asked the waiter to give it to the director of the orchestra. Pausing at the door, while the porter dashed out to call a cab, we saw, in the wall mirror, a pair of wild black eyes following us quite despairingly from behind the palms at the other end of the room. Cressida observed as we went out that the young man was probably having a hard struggle. "He never got those clothes here, surely. They were probably made by a country tailor in some little town in Austria. He seemed wild enough to grab at anything, and was trying to make himself heard above the dishes, poor fellow. There are so many like him. I wish I could help them all! I didn't quite have the courage to send him money. His smile, when he bowed to us, was not that of one who would take it, do you think?"

"No," I admitted, "it wasn't. He seemed to be pleading for recognition. I don't think it was money he wanted."

A week later I came upon some curious-looking manuscript songs on the piano in Cressida's music room. The text was in some Slavic tongue with a French translation written underneath. Both the handwriting and the musical script were done in a manner experienced, even distinguished. I was looking at them when Cressida came in.

"Oh, yes!" she exclaimed. "I meant to ask you to try them over. Poppas thinks they are very interesting. They are from that young violinist, you remember, — the one we noticed in the restaurant that evening. He sent them with such a nice letter. His name is Blasius Bouchalka (Boúkal-ka), a Bohemian."

I sat down at the piano and busied myself with the manuscript, while Cressida dashed off necessary notes and wrote checks in a large square checkbook, six to a page. I supposed her immersed in sumptuary preoccupations when she suddenly looked over her shoulder and said, "Yes, that legend, *Sarka,* is the most interesting. Run it through a few times and I'll try it over with you."

There was another, *"Dans les ombres des fôrets tristess,"* which I thought quite as beautiful. They were fine songs; very individual, and each had that spontaneity which makes a song seem inevitable and, once for all, "done." The accompaniments were difficult, but not unnecessarily so; they were free from fatuous ingenuity and fine writing.

"I wish he'd indicated his tempi a little more clearly," I remarked as I finished *Sarka* for the third time. "It matters, because he really has something to say. An orchestral accompaniment would be better, I should think."

"Yes, he sent the orchestral arrangement. Poppas has it. It works out beautifully, — so much colour in the instrumentation. The English horn comes in so effectively there," she rose and indicated the passage, "just right with the voice. I've asked him to come next Sunday, so please be

here if you can. I want to know what you think of
him."

Cressida was always at home to her friends on
Sunday afternoon unless she was billed for the
evening concert at the Opera House, in which
case we were sufficiently advised by the daily
press. Bouchalka must have been told to come
early, for when I arrived on Sunday, at four, he
and Cressida had the music-room quite to themselves and were standing by the piano in earnest
conversation. In a few moments they were separated by other early comers, and I led Bouchalka
across the hall to the drawing-room. The guests,
as they came in, glanced at him curiously. He wore
a dark blue suit, soft and rather baggy, with a short
coat, and a high double-breasted vest with two
rows of buttons coming up to the loops of his
black tie. This costume was even more foreign-
looking than his skin-tight dress clothes, but it
was more becoming. He spoke hurried, elliptical
English, and very good French. All his sympathies
were French rather than German — the Czecks
lean to the one culture or to the other. I found
him a fierce, a transfixing talker. His brilliant eyes,
his gaunt hands, his white, deeply-lined forehead,
all entered into his speech.

I asked him whether he had not recognized
Madame Garnet at once when we entered the
restaurant that evening more than a week ago.

"*Mais, certainement!* I hear her twice when she
sings in the afternoon, and sometimes at night for
the last act. I have a friend who buys a ticket for
the first part, and he comes out and gives to me
his pass-back check, and I return for the last act.
That is convenient if I am broke." He explained
the trick with amusement but without embarrass-

ment, as if it were a shift that we might any of us be put to.

I told him that I admired his skill with the violin, but his songs much more.

He threw out his red under-lip and frowned. "Oh, I have no instrument! The violin I play from necessity; the flute, the piano, as it happens. For three years now I write all the time, and it spoils the hand for violin."

When the maid brought him his tea, he took both muffins and cakes and told me that he was very hungry. He had to lunch and dine at the place where he played, and he got very tired of the food. "But since," his black eyebrows nearly met in an acute angle, "but since, before, I eat at a bakery, with the slender brown roach on the pie, I guess I better let alone well enough." He paused to drink his tea; as he tasted one of the cakes his face lit with sudden animation and he gazed across the hall after the maid with the tray — she was now holding it before the aged and ossified 'cellist of the Hempfstangle Quartette. *"Des gâteaux,"* he murmured feelingly, *"ou est-ce qu'elle peut trouver de tels gâteaux ici à* New York?"

I explained to him that Madame Garnet had an accomplished cook who made them, — an Austrian, I thought.

He shook his head. *"Austrichienne? Je ne pense pas."*

Cressida was approaching with the new Spanish soprano, Mme. Bartolas, who was all black velvet and long black feathers, with a lace veil over her rich pallour and even a little black patch on her chin. I beckoned them. "Tell me, Cressida, isn't Ruzenka an Austrian?"

She looked surprised. "No, a Bohemian, though

I got her in Vienna." Bouchalka's expression, and the remnant of a cake in his long fingers, gave her the connection. She laughed. "You like them? Of course, they are of your own country. You shall have more of them." She nodded and went away to greet a guest who had just come in.

A few moments later, Horace, then a beautiful lad in Eton clothes, brought another cup of tea and a plate of cakes for Bouchalka. We sat down in a corner, and talked about his songs. He was neither boastful nor deprecatory. He knew exactly in what respects they were excellent. I decided as I watched his face, that he must be under thirty. The deep lines in his forehead probably came there from his habit of frowning densely when he struggled to express himself, and suddenly elevating his coal-black eyebrows when his ideas cleared. His teeth were white, very irregular and interesting. The corrective methods of modern dentistry would have taken away half his good looks. His mouth would have been much less attractive for any re-arranging of those long, narrow, over-crowded teeth. Along with his frown and his way of thrusting out his lip, they contributed, somehow, to the engaging impetuousness of his conversation. As we talked about his songs, his manner changed. Before that he had seemed responsive and easily pleased. Now he grew abstracted, as if I had taken away his pleasant afternoon and wakened him to his miseries. He moved restlessly in his clothes. When I mentioned Puccini, he held his head in his hands. "Why is it they like that always and always? A little, oh yes, very nice. But so much, always the same thing! Why?" He pierced me with the despairing glance which had followed us out of the restaurant.

I asked him whether he had sent any of his songs to the publishers and named one whom I knew to be discriminating. He shrugged his shoulders. "They not want Bohemian songs. They not want my music. Even the street cars will not stop for me here, like for other people. Every time, I wait on the corner until somebody else make a signal to the car, and then it stop, — but not for me."

Most people cannot become utterly poor; whatever happens, they can right themselves a little. But one felt that Bouchalka was the sort of person who might actually starve or blow his brains out. Something very important had been left out either of his make-up or of his education; something that we are not accustomed to miss in people.

Gradually the parlour was filled with little groups of friends, and I took Bouchalka back to the music-room where Cressida was surrounded by her guests; feathered women, with large sleeves and hats, young men of no importance, in frock coats, with shining hair, and the smile which is intended to say so many flattering things but which really expresses little more than a desire to get on. The older men were standing about waiting for a word *à deux* with the hostess. To these people Bouchalka had nothing to say. He stood stiffly at the outer edge of the circle, watching Cressida with intent, impatient eyes, until, under the pretext of showing him a score, she drew him into the alcove at the back end of the long room, where she kept her musical library. The bookcases ran from the floor to the ceiling. There was a table and a reading-lamp, and a window seat looking upon the little walled garden. Two persons could be quite withdrawn there, and yet be a part of the general friendly scene. Cressida took a score from the shelf, and sat down with Bouchalka upon the window seat, the book open between them, though neither of them looked at it again. They fell to talking with great earnestness. At last the Bohemian pulled out a large, yellowing silver watch, held it up before him, and stared at it a moment as if it were an object of horror. He sprang up, bent over Cressida's hand and murmured something, dashed into the hall and out of the front door without waiting for the maid to open it. He had worn no overcoat, apparently. It was then seven o'clock; he would surely be late at his post in the up-town restaurant. I hoped he would have wit enough to take the elevated.

After supper Cressida told me his story. His parents, both poor musicians, — the mother a singer — died while he was yet a baby, and he was left to the care of an arbitrary uncle who resolved to make a priest of him. He was put into a monastery school and kept there. The organist and choir-director, fortunately for Blasius, was an excellent musician, a man who had begun his career brilliantly, but who had met with crushing sorrows and disappointments in the world. He devoted himself to his talented pupil, and was the only teacher the young man ever had. At twenty-one, when he was ready for the novitiate, Blasius felt that the call of life was too strong for him, and he ran away out into a world of which he knew nothing. He tramped southward to Vienna, begging and playing his fiddle from town to town. In Vienna he fell in with a gipsy band which was being recruited for a Paris restaurant and went with them to Paris. He played in cafés and in cheap theatres, did transcribing for a music publisher, tried to get pupils. For four years he was the mouse, and hunger was the cat. She kept him on the jump. When he got work he did not understand why; when he lost a job he did not understand why. During the time when most of us acquire a practical sense, get a half-unconscious knowledge of hard facts and market values, he had been shut away from the world, fed like the pigeons in the bell-tower of his monastery. Bouchalka had now been in New York a year, and for all he knew about it, Cressida said, he might have landed the day before yesterday.

Several weeks went by, and as Bouchalka did not reappear on Tenth Street, Cressida and I went once more to the place where he had played, only to find another violinist leading the orchestra. We summoned the proprietor, a Swiss-Italian, polite and solicitous. He told us the gentleman was not playing there any more, — was playing somewhere else, but he had forgotten where. We insisted upon talking to the old pianist, who at last reluctantly admitted that the Bohemian had been dismissed. He had arrived very late one Sunday night three weeks ago, and had hot words with the proprietor. He had been late before, and had been warned. He was a very talented fellow, but wild and not to be depended upon. The old man gave us the address of a French boarding-house on Seventh Avenue where Bouchalka used to room. We drove there at once, but the woman who kept the place said that he had gone away two weeks before, leaving no address, as he never got letters. Another Bohemian, who did engraving on glass, had a room with her, and when he came home perhaps he could tell where Bouchalka was, for they were friends.

It took us several days to run Bouchalka down, but when we did find him Cressida promptly busied herself in his behalf. She sang his *"Sarka"* with the Metropolitan Opera orchestra at a Sunday night concert, she got him a position with the Symphony Orchestra, and persuaded the conservative Hempfstangle Quartette to play one of his chamber compositions from manuscript. She aroused the interest of a publisher in his work, and introduced him to people who were helpful to him.

By the new year Bouchalka was fairly on his feet. He had proper clothes now, and Cressida's friends found him attractive. He was usually at her house on Sunday afternoons; so usually, indeed, that Poppas began pointedly to absent himself. When other guests arrived, the Bohemian and his patroness were always found at the critical point of discussion, — at the piano, by the fire, in the alcove at the end of the room — both of them interested and animated. He was invariably respectful and admiring, deferring to her in every tone and gesture, and she was perceptibly pleased and flattered, — as if all this were new to her and she were tasting the sweetness of a first success.

One wild day in March Cressida burst tempestuously into my apartment and threw herself down, declaring that she had just come from the most trying rehearsal she had ever lived through. When I tried to question her about it, she replied absently and continued to shiver and crouch by the fire. Suddenly she rose, walked to the window, and stood looking out over the Square, glittering with ice and rain and strewn with the wrecks of umbrellas. When she turned again, she approached me with determination.

"I shall have to ask you to go with me," she said firmly. "That crazy Bouchalka has gone and got a pleurisy or something. It may be pneumonia; there is an epidemic of it just now. I've sent Dr. Brooks to him, but I can never tell anything from what a doctor says. I've got to see Bouchalka and his nurse, and what sort of place he's in. I've been rehearsing all day and I'm singing tomorrow night; I can't have so much on my mind. Can you come with me? It will save time in the end."

I put on my furs, and we went down to Cressida's carriage, waiting below. She gave the driver a number on Seventh Avenue, and then began feeling her throat with the alarmed expression which meant that she was not going to talk. We drove in silence to the address, and by this time it was growing dark. The French landlady was a cordial, comfortable person who took Cressida in at a glance and seemed much impressed. Cressida's incognito was never successful. Her black gown was inconspicuous enough, but over it she wore a dark purple velvet carriage coat, lined with fur and furred at the cuffs and collar. The Frenchwoman's eye ran over it delightedly and scrutinized the veil which only half-concealed the well-known face behind it. She insisted upon conducting us up to the fourth floor herself, running ahead of us and turning up the gas jets in the dark, musty-smelling halls. I suspect that she tarried outside the door after we sent the nurse for her walk.

We found the sick man in a great walnut bed, a relic of the better days which this lodging house must have seen. The grimy red plush carpet, the red velvet chairs with broken springs, the double gilt-framed mirror above the mantel, had all been

270

respectable, substantial contributions to comfort in their time. The fireplace was now empty and grateless, and an ill-smelling gas stove burned in its sooty recess under the cracked marble. The huge arched windows were hung with heavy red curtains, pinned together and lightly stirred by the wind which rattled the loose frames.

I was examining these things while Cressida bent over Bouchalka. Her carriage cloak she threw over the foot of his bed, either from a protective impulse, or because there was no place else to put it. After she had greeted him and seated herself, the sick man reached down and drew the cloak up over him, looking at it with weak, childish pleasure and stroking the velvet with his long fingers. *"Couleur de gloire, couleur des reines!"* I heard him murmur. He thrust the sleeve under his chin and closed his eyes. His loud, rapid breathing was the only sound in the room. If Cressida brushed back his hair or touched his hand, he looked up long enough to give her a smile of utter adoration, naive and uninquiring, as if he were smiling at a dream or a miracle.

The nurse was gone for an hour, and we sat quietly, Cressida with her eyes fixed on Bouchalka, and I absorbed in the strange atmosphere of the house, which seemed to seep in under the door and through the walls. Occasionally we heard a call for *"de l'eau chaude!"* and the heavy trot of a serving woman on the stairs. On the floor below somebody was struggling with Schubert's Marche Militaire on a coarse-toned upright piano. Sometimes, when a door was opened, one could hear a parrot screaming, *"Voilà, voilà, tonnerre!"* The house was built before 1870, as one could tell from windows and mouldings, and the walls were

271

thick. The sounds were not disturbing and Bouchalka was probably used to them.

When the nurse returned and we rose to go, Bouchalka still lay with his cheek on her cloak, and Cressida left it. "It seems to please him," she murmured as we went down the stairs. "I can go home without a wrap. It's not far." I had, of course, to give her my furs, as I was not singing *Donna Anna* tomorrow evening and she was.

After this I was not surprised by any devout attitude in which I happened to find the Bohemian when I entered Cressida's music-room unannounced, or by any radiance on her face when she rose from the window-seat in the alcove and came down the room to greet me.

Bouchalka was, of course, very often at the Opera now. On almost any night when Cressida sang, one could see his narrow black head — high above the temples and rather constrained behind the ears — peering from some part of the house. I used to wonder what he thought of Cressida as an artist, but probably he did not think seriously at all. A great voice, a handsome woman, a great prestige, all added together made a "great artist," the common synonym for success. Her success, and the material evidences of it, quite blinded him. I could never draw from him anything adequate about Anna Straka, Cressida's Slavic rival, and this perhaps meant that he considered comparison disloyal. All the while that Cressida was singing reliably, and satisfying the management, Straka was singing uncertainly and making history. Her voice was primarily defective, and her immediate vocal method was bad. Cressida was always living up to her contract, delivering the whole order in good condition; while the Slav was sometimes almost voiceless, sometimes inspired. She put you off with a hope, a promise, time after time. But she was quite as likely to put you off with a revelation, — with an interpretation that was inimitable, unrepeatable.

Bouchalka was not a reflective person. He had his own idea of what a great prima donna should be like, and he took it for granted that Mme. Garnet corresponded to his conception. The curious thing was that he managed to impress his idea upon Cressida herself. She began to see herself as he saw her, to try to be like the notion of her that he carried somewhere in that pointed head of his. She was exalted quite beyond herself. Things that had been chilled under the grind came to life in her that winter, with the breath of Bouchalka's adoration. Then, if ever in her life, she heard the bird sing on the branch outside her window; and she wished she were younger, lovelier, freer. She wished there were no Poppas, no Horace, no Garnets. She longed to be only the bewitching creature Bouchalka imagined her.

One April day when we were driving in the Park, Cressida, superb in a green-and-primrose costume hurried over from Paris, turned to me smiling and said: "Do you know, this is the first spring I haven't dreaded. It's the first one I've ever really had. Perhaps people never have more than one, whether it comes early or late." She told me that she was overwhelmingly in love.

Our visit to Bouchalka when he was ill had, of course, been reported, and the men about the Opera House had made of it the only story they have the wit to invent. They could no more change the pattern of that story than the spider could change the design of its web. But being, as she

273

said, "in love" suggested to Cressida only one plan of action; to have the Tenth Street house done over, to put more money into her brothers' business, send Horace to school, raise Poppas' percentage, and then with a clear conscience be married in the Church of the Ascension. She went through this program with her usual thoroughness. She was married in June and sailed immediately with her husband. Poppas was to join them in Vienna in August, when she would begin to work again. From her letters I gathered that all was going well, even beyond her hopes.

When they returned in October, both Cressida and Blasius seemed changed for the better. She was perceptibly freshened and renewed. She attacked her work at once with more vigour and more ease; did not drive herself so relentlessly. A little carelessness became her wonderfully. Bouchalka was less gaunt, and much less flighty and perverse. His frank pleasure in the comfort and order of his wife's establishment was ingratiating, even if it was a little amusing. Cressida had the sewing-room at the top of the house made over into a study for him. When I went up there to see him, I usually found him sitting before the fire or walking about with his hands in his coat pockets, admiring his new possessions. He explained the ingenious arrangement of his study to me a dozen times.

With Cressida's friends and guests, Bouchalka assumed nothing for himself. His deportment amounted to a quiet, unobtrusive appreciation of her and of his good fortune. He was proud to owe his wife so much. Cressida's Sunday afternoons were more popular than ever, since she herself had so much more heart for them. Bouchalka's picturesque presence stimulated her graciousness and charm. One still found them conversing together as eagerly as in the days when they saw each other but seldom. Consequently their guests were never bored. We felt as if the Tenth Street house had a pleasant climate quite its own. In the spring, when the Metropolitan company went on tour, Cressida's husband accompanied her, and afterward they again sailed for Genoa.

During the second winter people began to say that Bouchalka was becoming too thoroughly domesticated, and that since he was growing heavier in body he was less attractive. I noticed his increasing reluctance to stir abroad. Nobody could say that he was "wild" now. He seemed to dread leaving the house, even for an evening. Why should he go out, he said, when he had everything he wanted at home? He published very little. One was given to understand that he was writing an opera. He lived in the Tenth Street house like a tropical plant under glass. Nowhere in New York could he get such cookery as Ruzenka's. Ruzenka ("little Rose") had, like her mistress, bloomed afresh, now that she had a man and a compatriot to cook for. Her invention was tireless, and she took things with a high hand in the kitchen, confident of a perfect appreciation. She was a plump, fair, blue-eyed girl, giggly and easily flattered, with teeth like cream. She was passionately domestic, and her mind was full of homely stories and proverbs and superstitions which she somehow worked into her cookery. She and Bouchalka had between them a whole literature of traditions about sauces and fish and pastry. The cellar was full of the wines he liked, and Ruzenka always knew what wines to serve with the dinner. Blasius' monastery had been famous for good living.

That winter was a very cold one, and I think the even temperature of the house enslaved Bouchalka. "Imagine it," he once said to me when I dropped in during a blinding snowstorm and found him reading before the fire. "To be warm all the time, every day! It is like Aladdin. In Paris I have had weeks together when I was not warm once, when I did not have a bath once, like the cats in the street. The nights were a misery. People have terrible dreams when they are so cold. Here I waken up in the night so warm I do not know what it means. Her door is open, and I turn on my light. I cannot believe in myself until I see that she is there."

I began to think that Bouchalka's wildness had been the desperation which the tamest animals exhibit when they are tortured or terrorized. Naturally luxurious, he had suffered more than most men under the pinch of penury. Those first beautiful compositions, full of the folk-music of his own country, had been wrung out of him by home-sickness and heart-ache. I wondered whether he could compose only under the spur of hunger and loneliness, and whether his talent might not subside with his despair. Some such apprehension must have troubled Cressida, though his gratitude would have been propitiatory to a more exacting task-master. She had always liked to make people happy, and he was the first one who had accepted her bounty without sourness. When he did not accompany her upon her spring tour, Cressida said it was because travelling interfered with composition; but I felt that she was deeply disappointed. Blasius, or Blažej, as his wife had with difficulty learned to call him, was not showy or extravagant. He hated hotels, even the best of them. Cressida had always fought for the hearthstone and the fireside, and the humour of Destiny is sometimes to give us too much of what we desire. I believe she would have preferred even enthusiasm about other women to his utter *oisiveté*. It was his old fire, not his docility, that had won her.

During the third season after her marriage Cressida had only twenty-five performances at the Metropolitan, and she was singing out of town a great deal. Her husband did not bestir himself to accompany her, but he attended, very faithfully, to her correspondence and to her business at home. He had no ambitious schemes to increase her fortune, and he carried out her directions exactly. Nevertheless, Cressida faced her concert tours somewhat grimly, and she seldom talked now about their plans for the future.

The crisis in this growing estrangement came about by accident, — one of those chance occurrences that affect our lives more than years of ordered effort, — and it came in an inverted form of a situation old to comedy. Cressida had been on the road for several weeks; singing in Minneapolis, Cleveland, St. Paul, then up into Canada and back to Boston. From Boston she was to go directly to Chicago, coming down on the five o'clock train and taking the eleven, over the Lake Shore, for the West. By her schedule she would have time to change cars comfortably at the Grand Central station.

On the journey down from Boston she was seized with a great desire to see Blasius. She decided, against her custom, one might say against her principles, to risk a performance with the

Chicago orchestra without rehearsal, to stay the night in New York and go west by the afternoon train the next day. She telegraphed Chicago, but she did not telegraph Blasius, because she wished — the old fallacy of affection! — to "surprise" him. She could take it for granted that, at eleven on a cold winter night, he would be in the Tenth Street house and nowhere else in New York. She sent Poppas — paler than usual with accusing scorn — and her trunks on to Chicago, and with only her travelling bag and a sense of being very audacious in her behaviour and still very much in love, she took a cab for Tenth Street.

Since it was her intention to disturb Blasius as little as possible and to delight him as much as possible, she let herself in with her latch-key and went directly to his room. She did not find him there. Indeed, she found him where he should not have been at all. There must have been a trying scene.

Ruzenka was sent away in the morning, and the other two maids as well. By eight o'clock Cressida and Bouchalka had the house to themselves. Nobody had any breakfast. Cressida took the afternoon train to keep her engagement with Theodore Thomas, and to think over the situation. Blasius was left in the Tenth Street house with only the furnace man's wife to look after him. His explanation of his conduct was that he had been drinking too much. His digression, he swore, was casual. It had never occurred before, and he could only appeal to his wife's magnanimity. But it was, on the whole, easier for Cressida to be firm than to be yielding, and she knew herself too well to attempt a readjustment. She had never made shabby compromises, and it was too late for her to begin. When she returned to New York she went to a hotel, and she never saw Bouchalka alone again. Since he admitted her charge, the legal formalities were conducted so quietly that the granting of her divorce was announced in the morning papers before her friends knew that there was the least likelihood of one. Cressida's concert tours had interrupted the hospitalities of the house.

While the lawyers were arranging matters, Bouchalka came to see me. He was remorseful and miserable enough, and I think his perplexity was quite sincere. If there had been an intrigue with a woman of her own class, an infatuation, an affair, he said, he could understand. But anything so venial and accidental — He shook his head slowly back and forth. He assured me that he was not at all himself on that fateful evening, and that when he recovered himself he would have sent Ruzenka away, making proper provision for her, of course. It was an ugly thing, but ugly things sometimes happened in one's life, and one had to put them away and forget them. He could have overlooked any accident that might have occurred when his wife was on the road, with Poppas, for example. I cut him short, and he bent his head to my reproof.

"I know," he said, "such things are different with her. But when have I said that I am noble as she is? Never. But I have appreciated and I have adored. About me, say what you like. But if you say that in this there was any *méprise* to my wife, that is not true. I have lost all my place here. I came in from the streets; but I understand her, and all the fine things in her, better than any of you here. If that accident had not been, she would

279

have lived happy with me for years. As for me, I have never believed in this happiness. I was not born under a good star. How did it come? By accident. It goes by accident. She tried to give good fortune to an unfortunate man, *un miserable;* that was her mistake. It cannot be done in this world. The lucky should marry the lucky." Bouchalka stopped and lit a cigarette. He sat sunk in my chair as if he never meant to get up again. His large hands, now so much plumper than when I first knew him, hung limp. When he had consumed his cigarette he turned to me again.

"I, too, have tried. Have I so much as written one note to a lady since she first put out her hand to help me? Some of the artists who sing my compositions have been quite willing to plague my wife a little if I make the least sign. With the Española, for instance, I have had to be very stern, *farouche;* she is so very playful. I have never given my wife the slightest annoyance of this kind. Since I married her, I have not kissed the cheek of one lady! Then one night I am bored and drink too much champagne and I become a fool. What does it matter? Did my wife marry the fool of me? No, she married me, with my mind and my feelings all here, as I am today. But she is getting a divorce from the fool of me, which she would never see *anyhow!* The stupidity which excuse me is the thing she will not overlook. Even in her memory of me she will be harsh."

His view of his conduct and its consequences was fatalistic: he was meant to have just so much misery every day of his life; for three years it had been withheld, had been piling up somewhere, underground, overhead; now the accumulation burst over him. He had come to pay his respects to me, he said, to declare his undying gratitude to Madame Garnet, and to bid me farewell. He took up his hat and cane and kissed my hand. I have never seen him since. Cressida made a settlement upon him, but even Poppas, tortured by envy and curiosity, never discovered how much it was. It was very little, she told me. *"Pour des gâteaux,"* she added with a smile that was not unforgiving. She could not bear to think of his being in want when so little could make him comfortable.

He went back to his own village in Bohemia. He wrote her that the old monk, his teacher, was still alive, and that from the windows of his room in the town he could see the pigeons flying forth from and back to the monastery bell-tower all day long. He sent her a song, with his own words, about those pigeons, — quite a lovely thing. He was the bell tower, and *les colombes* were his memories of her.

IV

Jerome Brown proved, on the whole, the worst of Cressida's husbands, and, with the possible exception of her eldest brother, Buchanan Garnet, he was the most rapacious of the men with whom she had had to do. It was one thing to gratify every wish of a cake-loving fellow like Bouchalka, but quite another to stand behind a financier. And Brown would be a financier or nothing. After her marriage with him, Cressida grew rapidly older. For the first time in her life she wanted to go abroad and live — to get Jerome Brown away from the scene of his unsuccessful but undiscouraged activities. But Brown was not a man who could be amused and kept out of mischief in Continental hotels. He had to be a figure, if only a "mark," in

Wall street. Nothing else would gratify his peculiar vanity. The deeper he went in, the more affectionately he told Cressida that now all her cares and anxieties were over. To try to get related facts out of his optimism was like trying to find framework in a feather bed. All Cressida knew was that she was perpetually "investing" to save investments. When she told me she had put a mortgage on the Tenth Street house, her eyes filled with tears. "Why is it? I have never cared about money, except to make people happy with it, and it has been the curse of my life. It has spoiled all my relations with people. Fortunately," she added irrelevantly, drying her eyes, "Jerome and Poppas get along well." Jerome could have got along with anybody; that is a promoter's business. His warm hand, his flushed face, his bright eye, and his newest funny story, — Poppas had no weapons that could do execution with a man like that.

Though Brown's ventures never came home, there was nothing openly disastrous until the outbreak of the revolution in Mexico jeopardized his interests there. Then Cressida went to England — where she could always raise money from a faithful public — for a winter concert tour. When she sailed, her friends knew that her husband's affairs were in a bad way; but we did not know how bad until after Cressida's death.

Cressida Garnet, as all the world knows, was lost on the *Titanic*. Poppas and Horace, who had been travelling with her, were sent on a week earlier and came as safely to port as if they had never stepped out of their London hotel. But Cressida had waited for the first trip of the sea monster — she still believed that all advertising was good — and she went down on the road between the old world and the new. She had been ill, and when the collision occurred she was in her stateroom, a modest one somewhere down in the boat, for she was travelling economically. Apparently she never left her cabin. She was not seen on the decks, and none of the survivors brought any word of her.

On Monday, when the wireless messages were coming from the *Carpathia* with the names of the passengers who had been saved, I went, with so many hundred others, down to the White Star offices. There I saw Cressida's motor, her redoubtable initials on the door, with four men sitting in the limousine. Jerome Brown, stripped of the promoter's joviality and looking flabby and old, sat behind with Buchanan Garnet, who had come on from Ohio. I had not seen him for years. He was now an old man, but he was still conscious of being in the public eye, and sat turning a cigar about in his face with that foolish look of importance which Cressida's achievement had stamped upon all the Garnets. Poppas was in front, with Horace. He was gnawing the finger of his chamois glove as it rested on the top of his cane. His head was sunk, his shoulders drawn together; he looked as old as Jewry. I watched them, wondering whether Cressida would come back to them if she could. After the last names were posted, the four men settled back into the powerful car — one of the best made — and the chauffeur backed off. I saw him dash away the tears from his face with the back of his driving glove. He was an Irish boy, and had been devoted to Cressida.

When the will was read, Henry Gilbert, the lawyer, an old friend of her early youth, and I, were named executors. A nice job we had of it.

Most of her large fortune had been converted into stocks that were almost worthless. The marketable property realized only a hundred and fifty thousand dollars. To defeat the bequest of fifty thousand dollars to Poppas, Jerome Brown and her family contested the will. They brought Cressida's letters into court to prove that the will did not represent her intentions, often expressed in writing through many years, to "provide well" for them.

Such letters they were! The writing of a tired, overdriven woman; promising money, sending money herewith, asking for an acknowledgment of the draft sent last month, etc. In the letters to Jerome Brown she begged for information about his affairs and entreated him to go with her to some foreign city where they could live quietly and where she could rest; if they were careful, there would "be enough for all." Neither Brown nor her brothers and sisters had any sense of shame about these letters. It seemed never to occur to them that this golden stream, whether it rushed or whether it trickled, came out of the industry, out of the mortal body of a woman. They regarded her as a natural source of wealth; a copper vein, a diamond mine.

Henry Gilbert is a good lawyer himself, and he employed an able man to defend the will. We determined that in this crisis we would stand by Poppas, believing it would be Cressida's wish. Out of the lot of them, he was the only one who had helped her to make one penny of the money that had brought her so much misery. He was at least more deserving than the others. We saw to it that Poppas got his fifty thousand, and he actually departed, at last, for his city in *la sainte Asie*, where it never rains and where he will never again have to hold a hot water bottle to his face.

The rest of the property was fought for to a finish. Poppas out of the way, Horace and Brown and the Garnets quarrelled over her personal effects. They went from floor to floor of the Tenth Street house. The will provided that Cressida's jewels and furs and gowns were to go to her sisters. Georgie and Julia wrangled over them down to the last moleskin. They were deeply disappointed that some of the muffs and stoles which they remembered as very large, proved, when exhumed from storage and exhibited beside furs of a modern cut, to be ridiculously scant. A year ago the sisters were still reasoning with each other about pearls and opals and emeralds.

I wrote Poppas some account of these horrors, as during the court proceedings we had become rather better friends than of old. His reply arrived only a few days ago; a photograph of himself upon a camel, under which is written:

> Traulich und Treu
> ist's nur in der Tiefe:
> falsch und feig
> ist was dort oben sich freut!

His reply, and the memories it awakens — memories which have followed Poppas into the middle of Asia, seemingly, — prompted this informal narration.

A GOLD SLIPPER

Marshall McKann followed his wife and her friend Mrs. Post down the aisle and up the steps to the stage of the Carnegie Music Hall with an ill-concealed feeling of grievance. Heaven knew he never went to concerts, and to be mounted upon the stage in this fashion, as if he were a "highbrow" from Sewickley, or some unfortunate with a musical wife, was ludicrous. A man went to concerts when he was courting, while he was a junior partner. When he became a person of substance he stopped that sort of nonsense. His wife, too, was a sensible person, the daughter of an old Pittsburgh family as solid and well-rooted as the McKanns. She would never have bothered him about this concert had not the meddlesome Mrs. Post arrived to pay her a visit. Mrs. Post was an old school friend of Mrs. McKann, and because she lived in Cincinnati she was always keeping up with the world and talking about things in which no one else was interested, music among them. She was an aggressive lady, with weighty opinions, and a deep voice like a jovial bassoon. She had arrived only last night, and at dinner she brought it out that she could on no account miss Kitty Ayrshire's recital; it was, she said, the sort of thing no one could afford to miss.

When McKann went into town in the morning he found that every seat in the music-hall was sold. He telephoned his wife to that effect, and, thinking he had settled the matter, made his reservation on the 11.25 train for New York. He was unable to get a drawing-room because this same Kitty Ayrshire had taken the last one. He had not intended going to New York until the following week, but he preferred to be absent during Mrs. Post's incumbency.

In the middle of the morning, when he was deep in his correspondence, his wife called him up to say the enterprising Mrs. Post had telephoned some musical friends in Sewickley and had found that two hundred folding-chairs were to be placed on the stage of the concert-hall, behind the piano, and that they would be on sale at noon. Would he please get seats in the front row? McKann asked if they would not excuse him, since he was going over to New York on the late train, would be tired, and would not have time to dress, etc. No, not at all. It would be foolish for two women to trail up to the stage unattended. Mrs. Post's husband always accompanied her to concerts, and she expected that much attention from her host. He needn't dress, and he could take a taxi from the concert-hall to the East Liberty station.

The outcome of it all was that, though his bag was at the station, here was McKann, in the worst possible humour, facing the large audience to which he was well known, and sitting among a lot of music students and excitable old maids. Only the desperately zealous or the morbidly curious would endure two hours in those wooden chairs, and he sat in the front row of this hectic body, somehow made a party to a transaction for which he had the utmost contempt.

When McKann had been in Paris, Kitty Ayrshire was singing at the Comique, and he wouldn't go to hear her — even there, where one found so little that was better to do. She was too much talked about, too much advertised; always being thrust in an American's face as if she were something to be proud of. Perfumes and petticoats and cutlets were named for her. Some one had pointed Kitty out to him one afternoon when she was driving in the Bois with a French composer — old enough, he judged, to be her father — who was said to be infatuated, carried away by her. McKann was told that this was one of the historic passions of old age. He had looked at her on that occasion, but she was so befrilled and befeathered that he caught nothing but a graceful outline and a small, dark head above a white ostrich boa. He had noted with disgust, however, the stooped shoulders and white imperial of the silk-hatted man beside her, and the senescent line of his back. McKann described to his wife this unpleasing picture only last night, while he was undressing, when he was making every possible effort to avert this concert party. But Bessie only looked superior and said she wished to hear Kitty Ayrshire sing, and that her "private life" was something in which she had no interest.

Well, here he was; hot and uncomfortable, in a chair much too small for him, with a row of blinding footlights glaring in his eyes. Suddenly the door at his right elbow opened. Their seats were at one end of the front row; he had thought they would be less conspicuous there than in the centre, and he had not foreseen that the singer would walk over him every time she came upon the stage.

288

Her velvet train brushed against his trousers as she passed him. The applause which greeted her was neither overwhelming nor prolonged. Her conservative audience did not know exactly how to accept her toilette. They were accustomed to dignified concert gowns, like those which Pittsburgh matrons (in those days!) wore at their daughters' coming-out teas.

Kitty's gown that evening was really quite outrageous — the repartée of a conscienceless Parisian designer who took her hint that she wished something that would be entirely novel in the States. Today, after we have all of us, even in the uttermost provinces, been educated by Baskt and the various Ballets Russes, we would accept such a gown without distrust; but then it was a little disconcerting, even to the well-disposed. It was constructed of a yard or two of green velvet — a reviling, shrieking green which would have made a fright of any woman who had not inextinguishable beauty — and it was made without armholes, a device to which we were then so unaccustomed that it was nothing less than alarming. The velvet skirt split back from a transparent gold-lace petticoat, gold stockings, gold slippers. The narrow train was, apparently, looped to both ankles, and it kept curling about her feet like a serpent's tail, turning up its gold lining as if it were squirming over on its back. It was not, we felt, a costume in which to sing Mozart and Handel and Beethoven.

Kitty sensed the chill in the air, and it amused her. She liked to be thought a brilliant artist by other artists, but by the world at large she liked to be thought a daring creature. She had every reason to believe, from experience and from example, that to shock the great crowd was the

289

surest way to get its money and to make her name a household word. Nobody ever became a household word of being an artist, surely; and you were not a thoroughly paying proposition until your name meant something on the sidewalk and in the barber-shop. Kitty studied her audience with an appraising eye. She liked the stimulus of this disapprobation. As she faced this hard-shelled public she felt keen and interested; she knew that she would give such a recital as cannot often be heard for money. She nodded gaily to the young man at the piano, fell into an attitude of seriousness, and began the group of Beethoven and Mozart songs.

Though McKann would not have admitted it, there were really a great many people in the concert-hall who knew what the prodigal daughter of their country was singing, and how well she was doing it. They thawed gradually under the beauty of her voice and the subtlety of her interpretation. She had sung seldom in concert then, and they had supposed her very dependent upon the accessories of the opera. Clean singing, finished artistry, were not what they expected from her. They began to feel, even, the wayward charm of her personality.

McKann, who stared coldly up at the balconies during her first song, during the second glanced cautiously at the green apparition before him. He was vexed with her for having retained a débutante figure. He comfortably classed all singers — especially operatic singers — as "fat Dutchwomen" or "shifty Sadies," and Kitty would not fit into his clever generalization. She displayed, under his nose, the only kind of figure he considered worth looking at — that of a very young girl, supple and sinuous and quicksilverish; thin, eager shoulders, polished white arms that were nowhere too fat and nowhere too thin. McKann found it agreeable to look at Kitty, but when he saw that the authoritative Mrs. Post, red as a turkey-cock with opinions she was bursting to impart, was studying and appraising the singer through her lorgnette, he gazed indifferently out into the house again. He felt for his watch, but his wife touched him warningly with her elbow — which, he noticed, was not at all like Kitty's.

When Miss Ayrshire finished her first group of songs, her audience expressed its approval positively, but guardedly. She smiled bewitchingly upon the people in front, glanced up at the balconies, and then turned to the company huddled on the stage behind her. After her gay and careless bows, she retreated toward the stage door. As she passed McKann, she again brushed lightly against him, and this time she paused long enough to glance down at him and murmur, "Pardon!"

In the moment her bright, curious eyes rested upon him, McKann seemed to see himself as if she were holding a mirror up before him. He beheld himself a heavy, solid figure, unsuitably clad for the time and place, with a florid, square face, well-visored with good living and sane opinions — an inexpressive countenance. Not a rock face, exactly, but a kind of pressed-brick-and-cement face, a "business" face upon which years and feelings had made no mark — in which cocktails might eventually blast out a few hollows. He had never seen himself so distinctly in his shaving-glass as he did in that instant when Kitty Ayrshire's liquid eye held him, when her bright, inquiring glance roamed over his person. After her prehensile train curled over his boot and she was gone, his wife turned to him and said in the tone of approbation one uses when an infant manifests its groping intelligence, "Very gracious of her, I'm sure!" Mrs. Post nodded oracularly. McKann grunted.

Kitty began her second number, a group of romantic German songs which were altogether more her affair than her first number. When she turned once to acknowledge the applause behind her, she caught McKann in the act of yawning behind his hand — he of course wore no gloves — and he thought she frowned a little. This did not embarrass him; it somehow made him feel important. When she retired after the second part of the program, she again looked him over curiously as she passed, and she took marked precaution that her dress did not touch him. Mrs. Post and his wife again commented upon her consideration.

The final number was made up of modern French songs which Kitty sang enchantingly, and at last her frigid public was thoroughly aroused. While she was coming back again and again to smile and curtsy, McKann whispered to his wife that if there were to be encores he had better make a dash for his train.

"Not at all," put in Mrs. Post. "Kitty is going on the same train. She sings in *Faust* at the opera tomorrow night, so she'll take no chances."

McKann once more told himself how sorry he felt for Post. At last Miss Ayrshire returned, escorted by her accompanist, and gave the people what she of course knew they wanted: the most popular aria from the French opera of which the title-rôle had become synonymous with her name — an opera written for her and to her and round about her, by the veteran French composer who adored her, — the last and not the palest flash of his creative fire. This brought her audience all the way. They clamoured for more of it, but she was not to be coerced. She had been unyielding through storms to which this was a summer breeze. She came on once more, shrugged her shoulders, blew them a kiss, and was gone. Her last smile was for that uncomfortable part of her audience seated behind her, and she looked with recognition at McKann and his ladies as she nodded good night to the wooden chairs.

McKann hurried his charges into the foyer by the nearest exit and put them into his motor. Then he went over to the Schenley to have a glass of beer and a rarebit before train-time. He had not, he admitted to himself, been so much bored as he pretended. The minx herself was well enough, but it was absurd in his fellow-townsmen to look owlish and uplifted about her. He had no rooted dislike for pretty women; he even didn't deny that gay girls had their place in the world, but they ought to be kept in their place. He was born a Presbyterian, just as he was born a McKann. He sat in his pew in the First Church every Sunday, and he never missed a presbytery meeting when he was in town. His religion was not very spiritual, certainly, but it was substantial and concrete, made up of good, hard convictions and opinions. It had something to do with citizenship, with whom one ought to marry, with the coal business (in which his own name was powerful), with the Republican party, and with all majorities and established precedents. He was hostile to fads, to

293

enthusiasms, to individualism, to all changes except in mining machinery and in methods of transportation.

His equanimity restored by his lunch at the Schenley, McKann lit a big cigar, got into his taxi, and bowled off through the sleet.

There was not a sound to be heard or a light to be seen. The ice glittered on the pavement and on the naked trees. No restless feet were abroad. At eleven o'clock the rows of small, comfortable houses looked as empty of the troublesome bubble of life as the Allegheny cemetery itself. Suddenly the cab stopped, and McKann thrust his head out of the window. A woman was standing in the middle of the street addressing his driver in a tone of excitement. Over against the curb a lone electric stood despondent in the storm. The young woman, her cloak blowing about her, turned from the driver to McKann himself, speaking rapidly and somewhat incoherently.

"Could you not be so kind as to help us? It is Mees Ayrshire, the singer. The juice is gone out and we cannot move. We must get to the station. Mademoiselle cannot miss the train; she sings tomorrow night in New York. It is very important. Could you not take us to the station at East Liberty?"

McKann opened the door. "That's all right, but you'll have to hurry. It's eleven-ten now. You've only got fifteen minutes to make the train. Tell her to come along."

The maid drew back and looked up at him in amazement. "But, the hand-luggage to carry, and Mademoiselle to walk! The street is like glass!"

McKann threw away his cigar and followed her. He stood silent by the door of the derelict, while

294

the maid explained that she had found help. The driver had gone off somewhere to telephone for a car. Miss Ayrshire seemed not at all apprehensive; she had not doubted that a rescuer would be forthcoming. She moved deliberately; out of a whirl of skirts she thrust one fur-topped shoe — McKann saw the flash of the gold stocking above it — and alighted.

"So kind of you! So fortunate for us!" she murmured. One hand she placed upon his sleeve, and in the other she carried an armful of roses that had been sent up to the concert stage. The petals showered upon the sooty, sleety pavement as she picked her way along. They would be lying there tomorrow morning, and the children in those houses would wonder if there had been a funeral. The maid followed with two leather bags. As soon as he had lifted Kitty into his cab she exclaimed:

"My jewel-case! I have forgotten it. It is on the back seat, please. I am so careless!"

He dashed back, ran his hand along the cushions, and discovered a small leather bag. When he returned he found the maid and the luggage bestowed on the front seat, and a place left for him on the back seat beside Kitty and her flowers.

"Shall we be taking you far out of your way?" she asked sweetly. "I haven't an idea where the station is. I'm not even sure about the name. Céline thinks it is East Liberty, but I think it is West Liberty. An odd name, anyway. It is a Bohemian quarter, perhaps? A district where the law relaxes a trifle?"

McKann replied grimly that he didn't think the name referred to that kind of liberty.

"So much the better," sighed Kitty. "I am a

Californian; that's the only part of America I know very well, and out there, when we called a place Liberty Hill or Liberty Hollow — well, we meant it. You will excuse me if I'm uncommunicative, won't you? I must not talk in this raw air. My throat is sensitive after a long program." She lay back in her corner and closed her eyes.

When the cab rolled down the incline at East Liberty station, the New York express was whistling in. A porter opened the door. McKann sprang out, gave him a claim check and his Pullman ticket, and told him to get his bag at the check-stand and rush it on that train.

Miss Ayrshire, having gathered up her flowers, put out her hand to take his arm. "Why, it's you!" she exclaimed, as she saw his face in the light. "What a coincidence!" She made no further move to alight, but sat smiling as if she had just seated herself in a drawing-room and were ready for talk and a cup of tea.

McKann caught her arm. "You must hurry, Miss Ayrshire, if you mean to catch that train. It stops here only a moment. Can you run?"

"Can I run!" she laughed. "Try me!"

As they raced through the tunnel and up the inside stairway, McKann admitted that he had never before made a dash with feet so quick and sure stepping out beside him. The white-furred boots chased each other like lambs at play, the gold stockings flashed like the spokes of a bicycle wheel in the sun. They reached the door of Miss Ayrshire's state-room just as the train began to pull out. McKann was ashamed of the way he was panting, for Kitty's breathing was as soft and regular as when she was reclining on the back seat of his taxi. It had somehow run in his head that

296

all these stage women were a poor lot physically — unsound, overfed creatures, like canaries that are kept in a cage and stuffed with song-restorer. He retreated to escape her thanks. "Good night! Pleasant journey! Pleasant dreams!" With a friendly nod in Kitty's direction he closed the door behind him.

He was somewhat surprised to find his own bag, his Pullman ticket in the strap, on the seat just outside Kitty's door. But there was nothing strange about it. He had got the last section left on the train, No. 13, next the drawing-room. Every other berth in the car was made up. He was just starting to look for the porter when the door of the state-room opened and Kitty Ayrshire came out. She seated herself carelessly in the front seat beside his bag.

"Please talk to me a little," she said coaxingly. "I'm always wakeful after I sing, and I have to hunt some one to talk to. Céline and I get so tired of each other. We can speak very low, and we shall not disturb any one." She crossed her feet and rested her elbow on his Gladstone. Though she still wore her gold slippers and stockings, she did not, he thanked Heaven, have on her concert gown, but a very demure black velvet with some sort of pearl trimming about the neck. "Wasn't it funny," she proceeded, "that it happened to be you who picked me up? I wanted a word with you, anyway."

McKann smiled in a way that meant he wasn't being taken in. "Did you? We are not very old acquaintances."

"No, perhaps not. But you disapproved tonight, and I thought I was singing very well. You are very critical in such matters?"

He had been standing, but now he sat down. "My dear young lady, I am not critical at all. I know nothing about 'such matters.' "

"And care less?" she said for him, "Well, then we know where we are, in so far as that is concerned. What did displease you? My gown, perhaps? It may seem a little *outré* here, but it's the sort of thing all the imaginative designers abroad are doing. You like the English sort of concert gown better?"

"About gowns," said McKann, "I know even less than about music. If I looked uncomfortable, it was probably because I was uncomfortable. The seats were bad and the lights were annoying."

Kitty looked up with solicitude. "I was sorry they sold those seats. I don't like to make people uncomfortable in any way. Did the lights give you a headache? They are very trying. They burn one's eyes out in the end, I believe." She paused and waved the porter away with a smile as he came toward them. Half-clad Pittsburghers were tramping up and down the aisle, casting sidelong glances at McKann and his companion. "How much better they look with all their clothes on," she murmured. Then, turning directly to McKann again: "I saw you were not well seated, but I felt something quite hostile and personal. You were displeased with me. Doubtless many people are, but I seldom get an opportunity to question them. It would be nice if you took the trouble to tell me why you were displeased."

She spoke frankly, pleasantly, without a shadow of challenge or hauteur. She did not seem to be angling for compliments. McKann settled himself in his seat. He thought he would try her out. She had come for it, and he would let her have it. He

298

found, however, that it was harder to formulate the grounds of his disapproval than he would have supposed. Now that he sat face to face with her, now that she was leaning against his bag, he had no wish to hurt her.

"I'm a hard-headed business man," he said evasively, "and I don't much believe in any of you fluffy-ruffles people. I have a sort of natural distrust of them all, the men more than the women."

She looked thoughtful. "Artists, you mean?" drawing her words slowly. "What is your business?"

"Coal."

"I don't feel any natural distrust of business men, and I know ever so many. I don't know any coal-men, but I think I could become very much interested in coal. Am I larger-minded than you?"

McKann laughed. "I don't think you know when you are interested or when you are not. I don't believe you know what it feels like to be really interested. There is so much fake about your profession. It's an affectation on both sides. I know a great many of the people who went to hear you tonight, and I know that most of them neither know nor care anything about music. They imagine they do, because it's supposed to be the proper thing."

Kitty sat upright and looked interested. She was certainly a lovely creature — the only one of her tribe he had ever seen that he would cross the street to see again. Those were remarkable eyes she had — curious, penetrating, restless, somewhat impudent, but not at all dulled by self-conceit.

"But isn't that so in everything?" she cried. "How many of your clerks are honest because of a

299

fine, individual sense of honour? They are honest because it is the accepted rule of good conduct in business. Do you know" — she looked at him squarely — "I thought you would have something quite definite to say to me; but this is funny-paper stuff, the sort of objection I'd expect from your office-boy."

"Then you don't think it silly for a lot of people to get together and pretend to enjoy something they know nothing about?"

"Of course I think it silly, but that's the way God made audiences. Don't people go to church in exactly the same way? If there were a spiritual-pressure test-machine at the door, I suspect not many of you would get to your pews."

"How do you know I go to church?"

She shrugged her shoulders. "Oh, people with these old, ready-made opinions usually go to church. But you can't evade me like that." She tapped the edge of his seat with the toe of her gold slipper. "You sat there all evening, glaring at me as if you could eat me alive. Now I give you a chance to state your objections, and you merely criticize my audience. What is it? Is it merely that you happen to dislike my personality? In that case, of course, I won't press you."

"No," McKann frowned, "I perhaps dislike your professional personality. As I told you, I have a natural distrust of your variety."

"Natural, I wonder?" Kitty murmured. "I don't see why you should naturally dislike singers any more than I naturally dislike coal-men. I don't classify people by their occupations. Doubtless I should find some coal-men repulsive, and you may find some singers so. But I have reason to believe that, at least, I'm one of the less repellent."

"I don't doubt it," McKann laughed, "and you're a shrewd woman to boot. But you are, all of you, according to my standards, light people. You're brilliant, some of you, but you've no depth."

Kitty seemed to assent, with a dive of her girlish head. "Well, it's a merit in some things to be heavy, and in others to be light. Some things are meant to go deep, and others to go high. Do you want all the women in the world to be profound?"

"You are all," he went on steadily, watching her with indulgence, "fed on hectic emotions. You are pampered. You don't help to carry the burdens of the world. You are self-indulgent and appetent."

"Yes, I am," she assented, with a candour which he did not expect. "Not all artists are, but I am. Why not? If I could once get a convincing statement as to why I should not be self-indulgent, I might change my ways. As for the burdens of the world —" Kitty rested her chin on her clasped hands and looked thoughtful. "One should give pleasure to others. My dear sir, granting that the great majority of people can't enjoy anything very keenly, you'll admit that I give pleasure to many more people than you do. One should help others who are less fortunate; at present I am supporting just eight people, besides those I hire. There was never another family in California that had so many cripples and hard-luckers as that into which I had the honour to be born. The only ones who could take care of themselves were ruined by the San Francisco earthquake some time ago. One should make personal sacrifices. I do; I give money and time and effort to talented students. Oh, I give something much more than that! something that you probably have never given to any one. I give, to the really gifted ones, my *wish,* my desire, my light, if I have any; and that, Mr. Worldly Wiseman, is like giving one's blood! It's the kind of thing you prudent people never give. That is what was in the box of precious ointment." Kitty threw off her fervour with a slight gesture, as if it were a scarf, and leaned back, tucking her slipper up on the edge of his seat. "If you saw the houses I keep up," she sighed, "and the people I employ, and the motor-cars I run — And, after all, I've only this to do it with." She indicated her slender person, which Marshall could almost have broken in two with his bare hands.

She was, he thought, very much like any other charming woman, except that she was more so. Her familiarity was natural and simple. She was at ease because she was not afraid of him or of herself, or of certain half-clad acquaintances of his who had been wandering up and down the car oftener than was necessary. Well, he was not afraid, either.

Kitty put her arms over her head and sighed again, feeling the smooth part in her black hair. Her head was small — capable of great agitation, like a bird's; or of great resignation, like a nun's. "I can't see why I shouldn't be self-indulgent, when I indulge others. I can't understand your equivocal scheme of ethics. Now I can understand Count Tolstoy's, perfectly. I had a long talk with him once, about his book 'What is Art?' As nearly as I could get it, he believes that we are a race who can exist only by gratifying appetites; the appetites are evil, and the existence they carry on is evil. We were always sad, he says, without knowing why; even in the Stone Age. In some miraculous way a divine ideal was disclosed to us, directly at variance with our appetites. It gave us a new craving, which we could only satisfy by starving all the other hungers in us. Happiness lies in ceasing to be and to cause being, because the thing revealed to us is dearer than any existence our appetites can ever get for us. I can understand that. It's something one often feels in art. It is even the subject of the greatest of all operas, which, because I can never hope to sing it, I love more than all the others." Kitty pulled herself up. "Perhaps you agree with Tolstoy?" she added languidly.

"No; I think he's a crank," said McKann, cheerfully.

"What do you mean by a crank?"

"I mean an extremist."

Kitty laughed. "Weighty word! You'll always have a world full of people who keep to the golden mean. Why bother yourself about me and Tolstoy?"

"I don't, except when you bother me."

"Poor man! It's true this isn't your fault. Still, you did provoke it by glaring at me. Why did you go to the concert?"

"I was dragged."

"I might have known!" she chuckled, and shook her head. "No, you don't give me any good reasons. Your morality seems to me the compromise of cowardice, apologetic and sneaking. When righteousness becomes alive and burning, you hate it as much as you do beauty. You want a little of each in your life, perhaps — adulterated, sterilized, with the sting taken out. It's true enough they are both fearsome things when they get loose in the world; they don't, often."

McKann hated tall talk. "My views on women,"

he said slowly, "are simple."

"Doubtless," Kitty responded dryly, "but are they consistent? Do you apply them to your stenographers as well as to me? I take it for granted you have unmarried stenographers. Their position, economically, is the same as mine."

McKann studied the toe of her shoe. "With a woman, everything comes back to one thing." His manner was judicial.

She laughed indulgently. "So we are getting down to brass tacks, eh? I have beaten you in argument, and now you are leading trumps." She put her hands behind her head and her lips parted in a half-yawn. "Does everything come back to one thing? I wish I knew! It's more than likely that, under the same conditions, I should have been very like your stenographers — if they are good ones. Whatever I was, I would have been a good one. I think people are very much alike. You are more different than any one I have met for some time, but I know that there are a great many more at home like you. And even you — I believe there is a real creature down under these custom-made prejudices that save you the trouble of thinking. If you and I were shipwrecked on a desert island, I have no doubt that we would come to a simple and natural understanding. I'm neither a coward nor a shirk. You would find, if you had to undertake any enterprise of danger or difficulty with a woman, that there are several qualifications quite as important as the one to which you doubtless refer."

McKann felt nervously for his watch-chain. "Of course," he brought out, "I am not laying down any generalizations —" His brows wrinkled.

"Oh, aren't you?" murmured Kitty. "Then I

totally misunderstood. But remember" — holding up a finger — "it is you, not I, who are afraid to pursue this subject further. Now, I'll tell you something." She leaned forward and clasped her slim, white hands about her velvet knee. "I am as much a victim of these ineradicable prejudices as you. Your stenographer seems to you a better sort. Well, she does to me. Just because her life is, presumably, greyer than mine, she seems better. My mind tells me that dulness, and a mediocre order of ability, and poverty, are not in themselves admirable things. Yet in my heart I always feel that the sales-women in shops and the working girls in factories are more meritorious than I. Many of them, with my opportunities, would be more selfish than I am. Some of them, with their own opportunities, are more selfish. Yet I make this sentimental genuflection before the nun and the charwoman. Tell me, haven't you any weakness? Isn't there any foolish natural thing that unbends you a trifle and makes you feel gay?"

"I like to go fishing."

"To see how many fish you can catch?"

"No, I like the woods and the weather. I like to play a fish and work hard for him. I like the pussy-willows and the cold; and the sky, whether it's blue or grey — night coming on, every thing about it."

He spoke devoutly, and Kitty watched him through half-closed eyes. "And you like to feel that there are light-minded girls like me, who only care about the inside of shops and theatres and hotels, eh? You amuse me, you and your fish! But I mustn't keep you any longer. Haven't I given you every opportunity to state your case against me? I thought you would have more to say for yourself. Do you know, I believe it's not a case you have at all, but a grudge. I believe you are envious; that you'd like to be a tenor, and a perfect lady-killer!" She rose, smiling, and paused with her hand on the door of her stateroom. "Anyhow, thank you for a pleasant evening. And, by the way, dream of me tonight, and not of either of those ladies who sat beside you. It does not matter much whom we live with in this world, but it matters a great deal whom we dream of." She noticed his bricky flush. "You are very naive, after all, but, oh, so cautious! You are naturally afraid of everything new, just as I naturally want to try everything: new people, new religions — new miseries, even. If only there were more new things — If only you were really new! I might learn something. I'm like the Queen of Sheba — I'm not above learning. But you, my friend, would be afraid to try a new shaving soap. It isn't gravitation that holds the world in place; it's the lazy, obese cowardice of the people on it. All the same" — taking his hand and smiling encouragingly — "I'm going to haunt you a little. *Adios!*"

When Kitty entered her state-room, Céline, in her dressing-gown, was nodding by the window.

"Mademoiselle found the fat gentleman interesting?" she asked. "It is nearly one."

"Negatively interesting. His kind always say the same thing. If I could find one really intelligent man who held his views, I should adopt them."

"Monsieur did not look like an original," murmured Céline, as she began to take down her lady's hair.

McKann slept heavily, as usual, and the porter had to shake him in the morning. He sat up in his berth, and, after composing his hair with his fingers, began to hunt about for his clothes. As he put up the window-blind some bright object in the little hammock over his bed caught the sunlight and glittered. He stared and picked up a delicately turned gold slipper.

"Minx! hussy!" he ejaculated. "All that tall talk — ! Probably got it from some man who hangs about; learned it off like a parrot. Did she poke this in here herself last night, or did she send that sneak-faced Frenchwoman? I like her nerve!" He wondered whether he might have been breathing audibly when the intruder thrust her head between his curtains. He was conscious that he did not look a Prince Charming in his sleep. He dressed as fast as he could, and, when he was ready to go to the wash-room, glared at the slipper. If the porter should start to make up his berth in his absence — He caught the slipper, wrapped it in his pajama jacket, and thrust it into his bag. He escaped from the train without seeing his tormentor again.

Later McKann threw the slipper into the waste-basket in his room at the Knickerbocker, but the chambermaid, seeing that it was new and mate-less, thought there must be a mistake, and placed it in his clothes-closet. He found it there when he returned from the theatre that evening. Consider-ably mellowed by food and drink and cheerful company, he took the slipper in his hand and decided to keep it as a reminder that absurd things could happen to people of the most clocklike deportment. When he got back to Pittsburgh, he stuck it in a lock-box in his vault, safe from pry-ing clerks.

McKann has been ill for five years now, poor fellow! He still goes to the office, because it is the only place that interests him, but his partners do most of the work, and his clerks find him sadly changed — "morbid," they call his state of mind. He has had the pine-trees in his yard cut down because they remind him of cemeteries. On Sundays or holidays, when the office is empty, and he takes his will or his insurance-policies out of his lock-box, he often puts the tarnished gold slipper on his desk and looks at it. Somehow it suggests life to his tired mind, as his pine-trees suggested death — life and youth. When he drops over some day, his executors will be puzzled by the slipper.

As for Kitty Ayrshire, she has played so many jokes, practical and impractical, since then, that she has long ago forgotten the night when she threw away a slipper to be a thorn in the side of a just man.

SCANDAL

Kitty Ayrshire had a cold, a persistent inflamma-
tion of the vocal cords which defied the throat
specialist. Week after week her name was posted
at the Opera, and week after week it was canceled,
and the name of one of her rivals was substituted.
For nearly two months she had been deprived of
everything she liked, even of the people she liked,
and had been shut up until she had come to hate
the glass windows between her and the world, and
the wintry stretch of the Park they looked out
upon. She was losing a great deal of money, and,
what was worse, she was losing life; days of which
she wanted to make the utmost were slipping by,
and nights which were to have crowned the days,
nights of incalculable possibilities, were being
stolen from her by women for whom she had no
great affection. At first she had been courageous,
but the strain of prolonged uncertainty was telling
on her, and her nervous condition did not improve
her larynx. Every morning Miles Creedon looked
down her throat, only to put her off with evasions,
to pronounce improvement that apparently never
got her anywhere, to say that tomorrow he might
be able to promise something definite.

Her illness, of course, gave rise to rumours —
rumours that she had lost her voice, that at some

time last summer she must have lost her discretion. Kitty herself was frightened by the way in which this cold hung on. She had had many sharp illnesses in her life, but always, before this, she had rallied quickly. Was she beginning to lose her resiliency? Was she, by any cursed chance, facing a bleak time when she would have to cherish herself? She protested, as she wandered about her sunny, many-windowed rooms on the tenth floor, that if she was going to have to live frugally, she wouldn't live at all. She wouldn't live on any terms but the very generous ones she had always known. She wasn't going to hoard her vitality. It must be there when she wanted it, be ready for any strain she chose to put upon it, let her play fast and loose with it; and then, if necessary, she would be ill for a while and pay the piper. But be systematically prudent and parsimonious she would not.

When she attempted to deliver all this to Doctor Creedon, he merely put his finger on her lips and said they would discuss these things when she could talk without injuring her throat. He allowed her to see no one except the Director of the Opera, who did not shine in conversation and was not apt to set Kitty going. The Director was a glum fellow, indeed, but during this calamitous time he had tried to be soothing, and he agreed with Creedon that she must not risk a premature appearance. Kitty was tormented by a suspicion that he was secretly backing the little Spanish woman who had sung many of her parts since she had been ill. He furthered the girl's interests because his wife had a very special consideration for her, and Madame had that consideration because — But that was too long and too dreary a story to follow out in one's mind. Kitty felt a tonsilitis disgust for opera-house politics, which, when she was in health, she rather enjoyed, being no mean strategist herself. The worst of being ill was that it made so many things and people look base.

She was always afraid of being disillusioned. She wished to believe that everything for sale in Vanity Fair was worth the advertised price. When she ceased to believe in these delights, she told herself, her pulling power would decline and she would go to pieces. In some way the chill of her disillusionment would quiver through the long, black line which reached from the box-office down to Seventh Avenue on nights when she sang. They shivered there in the rain and cold, all those people, because they loved to believe in her inextinguishable zest. She was no prouder of what she drew in the boxes than she was of that long, oscillating tail; little fellows in thin coats, Italians, Frenchmen, South-Americans, Japanese.

When she had been cloistered like a Trappist for six weeks, with nothing from the outside world but notes and flowers and disquieting morning papers, Kitty told Miles Creedon that she could not endure complete isolation any longer.

"I simply cannot live through the evenings. They have become horrors to me. Every night is the last night of a condemned man. I do nothing but cry, and that makes my throat worse."

Miles Creedon, handsomest of his profession, was better looking with some invalids than with others. His athletic figure, his red cheeks, and splendid teeth always had a cheering effect upon this particular patient, who hated anything weak or broken.

"What can I do, my dear? What do you wish?

311

Shall I come and hold your lovely hand from eight to ten? You have only to suggest it."

"Would you do that, even? No, *caro mio,* I take far too much of your time as it is. For an age now you have been the only man in the world to me, and you have been charming! But the world is big, and I am missing it. Let some one come tonight, some one interesting, but not too interesting. Pierce Tevis, for instance. He is just back from Paris. Tell the nurse I may see him for an hour tonight," Kitty finished pleadingly, and put her fingers on the doctor's sleeve. He looked down at them and smiled whimsically.

Like other people, he was weak to Kitty Ayrshire. He would do for her things that he would do for no one else; would break any engagement, desert a dinner-table, leaving an empty place and an offended hostess, to sit all evening in Kitty's dressing-room, spraying her throat and calming her nerves, using every expedient to get her through a performance. He had studied her voice like a singing master; knew all of its idiosyncracies and the emotional and nervous perturbations which affected it. When it was permissible, sometimes when it was not permissible, he indulged her caprices. On this sunny morning her wan, disconsolate face moved him.

"Yes, you may see Tevis this evening if you will assure me that you will not shed one tear for twenty-four hours. I may depend on your word?" He rose, and stood before the deep couch on which his patient reclined. Her arch look seemed to say, "On what could you depend more?" Creedon smiled, and shook his head. "If I find you worse tomorrow —"

He crossed to the writing-table and began to

separate a bunch of tiny flame-coloured rosebuds. "May I?" Selecting one, he sat down on the chair from which he had lately risen, and leaned forward while Kitty pinched the thorns from the stem and arranged the flower in his buttonhole.

"Thank you. I like to wear one of yours. Now I must be off to the hospital. I've a nasty little operation to do this morning. I'm glad it's not you. Shall I telephone Tevis about this evening?"

Kitty hesitated. Her eyes ran rapidly about, seeking a likely pretext. Creedon laughed.

"Oh, I see. You've already asked him to come. You were so sure of me! Two hours in bed after lunch, with all the windows open, remember. Read something diverting, but not exciting; some homely British author; nothing *abandonné*. And don't make faces at me. Until to-morrow!"

When her charming doctor had disappeared through the doorway, Kitty fell back on her cushions and closed her eyes. Her mocking-bird, excited by the sunlight, was singing in his big gilt cage, and a white lilac-tree that had come that morning was giving out its faint sweetness in the warm room. But Kitty looked paler and wearier than when the doctor was with her. Even with him she rose to her part just a little; couldn't help it. And he took his share of her vivacity and sparkle, like every one else. He believed that his presence was soothing to her. But he admired; and whoever admired, blew on the flame, however lightly.

The mocking-bird was in great form this morning. He had the best bird-voice she had ever heard, and Kitty wished there were some way to note down his improvisations; but his intervals were not expressible in any scale she knew. Parker

White had brought him to her, from Ojo Caliente, in New Mexico, where he had been trained in the pine forests by an old Mexican and an ill-tempered, lame master-bird, half thrush, that taught young birds to sing. This morning, in his song there were flashes of silvery Southern springtime; they opened inviting roads of memory. In half an hour he had sung his disconsolate mistress to sleep.

That evening Kitty sat curled up on the deep couch before the fire, awaiting Pierce Tevis. Her costume was folds upon folds of diaphanous white over equally diaphanous rose, with a line of white fur about her neck. Her beautiful arms were bare. Her tiny Chinese slippers were embroidered so richly that they resembled the painted porcelain of old vases. She looked like a sultan's youngest, newest bride; a beautiful little toy-woman, sitting at one end of the long room which composed about her, — which, in the soft light, seemed happily arranged for her. There were flowers everywhere: rose-trees; camellia-bushes, red and white; the first forced hyacinths of the season; a feathery mimosa-tree, tall enough to stand under.

The long front of Kitty's study was all windows. At one end was the fireplace, before which she sat. At the other end, back in a lighted alcove, hung a big, warm, sympathetic interior by Lucien Simon, — a group of Kitty's friends having tea in the painter's salon in Paris. The room in the picture was flooded with early lamp-light, and one could feel the grey, chill winter twilight in the Paris streets outside. There stood the cavalier-like old composer, who had done much for Kitty, in his most characteristic attitude, before the hearth. Mme. Simon sat at the tea-table. B——, the historian, and H——, the philologist, stood in animated discussion behind the piano, while Mme. H—— was tying on the bonnet of her lovely little daughter. Marcel Durand, the physicist, sat alone in a corner, his startling black-and-white profile lowered broodingly, his cold hands locked over his sharp knee. A genial, red-bearded sculptor stood over him, about to touch him on the shoulder and waken him from his dream.

This painting made, as it were, another room; so that Kitty's study on Central Park West seemed to open into that charming French interior, into one of the most highly harmonized and richly associated rooms in Paris. There her friends sat or stood about, men distinguished, women at once plain and beautiful, with their furs and bonnets, their clothes that were so distinctly not smart — all held together by the warm lamp-light, by an indescribable atmosphere of graceful and gracious human living.

Pierce Tevis, after he had entered noiselessly and greeted Kitty, stood before her fire and looked over her shoulder at this picture.

"It's nice that you have them there together, now that they are scattered, God knows where, fighting to preserve just that. But your own room, too, is charming," he added at last, taking his eyes from the canvas.

Kitty shrugged her shoulders.

"Bah! I can help to feed the lamp, but I can't supply the dear things it shines upon."

"Well, tonight it shines upon you and me, and we aren't so bad." Tevis stepped forward and took her hand affectionately. "You've been over a rough bit of road. I'm so sorry. It's left you looking very lovely, though. Has it been very hard to get on?"

315

She brushed his hand gratefully against her cheek and nodded.

"Awfully dismal. Everything has been shut out from me but — gossip. That always gets in. Often I don't mind, but this time I have. People do tell such lies about me."

"Of course we do. That's part of our fun, one of the many pleasures you give us. It only shows how hard up we are for interesting public personages; for a royal family, for romantic fiction, if you will. But I never hear any stories that wound me, and I'm very sensitive about you."

"I'm gossiped about rather more than the others, am I not?"

"I believe! Heaven send that the day when you are not gossiped about is far distant! Do you want to bite off your nose to spite your pretty face? You are the sort of person who makes myths. You can't turn around without making one. That's your singular good luck. A whole staff of publicity men, working day and night, couldn't do for you what you do for yourself. There is an affinity between you and the popular imagination."

"I suppose so," said Kitty, and sighed. "All the same, I'm getting almost as tired of the person I'm supposed to be as of the person I really am. I wish you would invent a new Kitty Ayrshire for me, Pierce. Can't I do something revolutionary? Marry, for instance?"

Tevis rose in alarm.

"Whatever you do, don't try to change your legend. You have now the one that gives the greatest satisfaction to the greatest number of people. Don't disappoint your public. The popular imagination, to which you make such a direct appeal, for some reason wished you to have a son, so it

316

has given you one. I've heard a dozen versions of the story, but it is always a son, never by any chance a daughter. Your public gives you what is best for you. Let well enough alone."

Kitty yawned and dropped back on her cushions.

"He still persists, does he, in spite of never being visible?"

"Oh, but he has been seen by ever so many people. Let me think a moment." He sank into an attitude of meditative ease. "The best description I ever had of him was from a friend of my mother, an elderly woman, thoroughly truthful and matter-of-fact. She has seen him often. He is kept in Russia, in St. Petersburg, that was. He is about eight years old and of marvellous beauty. He is always that in every version. My old friend has seen him being driven in his sledge on the Nevskii Prospekt on winter afternoons; black horses with silver bells and a giant in uniform on the seat beside the driver. He is always attended by this giant, who is responsible to the Grand Duke Paul for the boy. This lady can produce no evidence beyond his beauty and his splendid furs and the fact that all the Americans in Petrograd know he is your son."

Kitty laughed mournfully.

"If the Grand Duke Paul had a son, any old rag of a son, the province of Moscow couldn't contain him! He may, for aught I know, actually pretend to have a son. It would be very like him." She looked at her finger-tips and her rings disapprovingly for a moment. "Do you know, I've been thinking that I would rather like to lay hands on that youngster. I believe he'd be interesting. I'm bored with the world."

Tevis looked up and said quickly:

"Would you like him, really?"

317

"Of course I should," she said indignantly. "But, then, I like other things, too; and one has to choose. When one has only two or three things to choose from, life is hard; when one has many, it is harder still. No, on the whole, I don't mind that story. It's rather pretty, except for the Grand Duke. But not all of them are pretty."

"Well, none of them are very ugly; at least I never heard but one that troubled me, and that was long ago."

She looked interested.

"That is what I want to know; how do the ugly ones get started? How did that one get going and what was it about? Is it too dreadful to repeat?"

"No, it's not especially dreadful; merely rather shabby. If you really wish to know, and won't be vexed, I can tell you exactly how it got going, for I took the trouble to find out. But it's a long story, and you really had nothing whatever to do with it."

"Then who did have to do with it? Tell me; I should like to know exactly how even one of them originated."

"Will you be comfortable and quiet and not get into a rage, and let me look at you as much as I please?"

Kitty nodded, and Tevis sat watching her indolently while he debated how much of his story he ought not to tell her. Kitty liked being looked at by intelligent persons. She knew exactly how good looking she was; and she knew, too, that, pretty as she was, some of those rather sallow women in the Simon painting had a kind of beauty which she would never have. This knowledge, Tevis was thinking, this important realization, contributed more to her loveliness than any other thing about

318

her; more than her smooth, ivory skin or her changing grey eyes, the delicate forehead above them, or even the dazzling smile, which was gradually becoming too bright and too intentional, — out in the world, at least. Here by her own fire she still had for her friends a smile less electric than the one she flashed from stages. She could still be, in short, *intime,* a quality which few artists keep, which few ever had.

Kitty broke in on her friend's meditations.

"You may smoke. I had rather you did. I hate to deprive people of things they like."

"No, thanks. May I have those chocolates on the tea-table? They are quite as bad for me. May you? No, I suppose not." He settled himself by the fire, with the candy beside him, and began in the agreeable voice which always soothed his listener.

"As I said, it was a long while ago, when you first came back to this country and were singing at the Manhattan. I dropped in at the Metropolitan one evening to hear something new they were trying out. It was an off night, no pullers in the cast, and nobody in the boxes but governesses and poor relations. At the end of the first act two people entered one of the boxes in the second tier. The man was Siegmund Stein, the department-store millionaire, and the girl, so the men about me in the omnibus box began to whisper, was Kitty Ayrshire. I didn't know you then, but I was unwilling to believe that you were with Stein. I could not contradict them at that time, however, for the resemblance, if it was merely a resemblance, was absolute, and all the world knew that you were not singing at the Manhattan that night. The girl's hair was dressed just as you then wore yours. Moreover, her head was small and restless like yours, and she had your colouring, your eyes, your chin. She carried herself with the critical indifference one might expect in an artist who had come for a look at a new production that was clearly doomed to failure. She applauded lightly. She made comments to Stein when comments were natural enough. I thought, as I studied her face with the glass, that her nose was a trifle thinner than yours, a prettier nose, my dear Kitty, but stupider and more inflexible. All the same, I was troubled until I saw her laugh, — and then I knew she was a counterfeit. I had never seen you laugh, but I knew that you would not laugh like that. It was not boisterous; indeed, it was consciously refined, — mirthless, meaningless. In short, it was not the laugh of one whom our friends in there" — pointing to the Simon painting — "would honour with their affection and admiration."

Kitty rose on her elbow and burst out indignantly:

"So you would really have been hood-winked except for that! You may be sure that no woman, no intelligent woman, would have been. Why do we ever take the trouble to look like anything for any of you? I could count on my four fingers" — she held them up and shook them at him — "the men I've known who had the least perception of what any woman really looked like, and they were all dressmakers. Even painters" — glancing back in the direction of the Simon picture — "never get more than one type through their thick heads; they try to make all women look like some wife or mistress. You are all the same; you never see our real faces. What you do see, is some cheap conception of prettiness you got from a coloured supplement when you were adolescents. It's too discouraging. I'd rather take vows and veil my face for ever from such abominable eyes. In the kingdom of the blind any petticoat is a queen." Kitty thumped the cushion with her elbow. "Well, I can't do anything about it. Go on with your story."

"Aren't you furious, Kitty! And I thought I was so shrewd. I've quite forgotten where I was. Anyhow, I was not the only man fooled. After the last curtain I met Villard, the press man of that management, in the lobby, and asked him whether Kitty Ayrshire was in the house. He said he thought so. Stein had telephoned for a box, and said he was bringing one of the artists from the other company. Villard had been too busy about the new production to go to the box, but he was quite sure the woman was Ayrshire, whom he had met in Paris.

"Not long after that I met Dan Leland, a classmate of mine, at the Harvard Club. He's a journalist, and he used to keep such eccentric hours that I had not run across him for a long time. We got to talking about modern French music, and discovered that we both had a very lively interest in Kitty Ayrshire.

" 'Could you tell me,' Dan asked abruptly, 'why, with pretty much all the known world to choose her friends from, this young woman should flit about with Siegmund Stein? It prejudices people against her. He's a most objectionable person.'

" 'Have you,' I asked, 'seen her with him, yourself?'

"Yes, he had seen her driving with Stein, and some of the men on his paper had seen her dining with him at rather queer places down town. Stein

321

was always hanging about the Manhattan on nights when Kitty sang. I told Dan that I suspected a masquerade. That interested him, and he said he thought he would look into the matter. In short, we both agreed to look into it. Finally, we got the story, though Dan could never use it, could never even hint at it, because Stein carries heavy advertising in his paper.

"To make you see the point, I must give you a little history of Siegmund Stein. Any one who has seen him never forgets him. He is one of the most hideous men in New York, but it's not at all the common sort of ugliness that comes from over-eating and automobiles. He isn't one of the fat horrors. He has one of those rigid, horselike faces that never tell anything; a long nose, flattened as if it had been tied down; a scornful chin; long, white teeth; flat cheeks, yellow as a Mongolian's; tiny, black eyes, with puffy lids and no lashes; dingy, dead-looking hair — looks as if it were glued on.

"Stein came here a beggar from somewhere in Austria. He began by working on the machines in old Rosenthal's garment factory. He became a speeder, a foreman, a salesman; worked his way ahead steadily until the hour when he rented an old dwelling-house on Seventh Avenue and began to make misses' and juniors' coats. I believe he was the first manufacturer to specialize in those particular articles. Dozens of garment manufacturers have come along the same road, but Stein is like none of the rest of them. He is, and always was, a personality. While he was still at the machine, a hideous, underfed little whippersnapper, he was already a youth of many-coloured ambitions, deeply concerned about his dress, his associates, his recreations. He haunted the old As-

322

tor Library and the Metropolitan Museum, learned something about pictures and porcelains, took singing lessons, though he had a voice like a crow's. When he sat down to his baked apple and doughnut in a basement lunch-room, he would prop a book up before him and address his food with as much leisure and ceremony as if he were dining at his club. He held himself at a distance from his fellow-workmen and somehow always managed to impress them with his superiority. He had inordinate vanity, and there are many stories about his foppishness. After his first promotion in Rosenthal's factory, he bought a new overcoat. A few days later, one of the men at the machines, which Stein had just quitted, appeared in a coat exactly like it. Stein could not discharge him, but he gave his own coat to a newly arrived Russian boy and got another. He was already magnificent.

"After he began to make headway with misses' and juniors' cloaks, he became a collector — etchings, china, old musical instruments. He had a dancing master, and engaged a beautiful Brazilian widow — she was said to be a secret agent for some South American republic — to teach him Spanish. He cultivated the society of the unknown great: poets, actors, musicians. He entertained them sumptuously, and they regarded him as a deep, mysterious Jew who had the secret of gold, which they had not. His business associates thought him a man of taste and culture, a patron of the arts, a credit to the garment trade.

"One of Stein's many ambitions was to be thought a success with women. He got considerable notoriety in the garment world by his attentions to an emotional actress who is now quite forgotten, but who had her little hour of expectation. Then there was a dancer; then, just after Gorky's visit here, a Russian anarchist woman. After that the coat-makers and shirtwaist-makers began to whisper that Stein's great success was with Kitty Ayrshire.

"It is the hardest thing in the world to disprove such a story, as Dan Leland and I discovered. We managed to worry down the girl's address through a taxi-cab driver who got next to Stein's chauffeur. She had an apartment in a decent-enough house on Waverly Place. Nobody ever came to see her but Stein, her sisters, and a little Italian girl from whom we got the story.

"The counterfeit's name was Ruby Mohr. She worked in a shirtwaist factory, and this Italian girl, Margarita, was her chum. Stein came to the factory when he was hunting for living models for his new department store. He looked the girls over, and picked Ruby out from several hundred. He had her call at his office after business hours, tried her out in cloaks and evening gowns, and offered her a position. She never, however, appeared as a model in the Sixth Avenue store. Her likeness to the newly arrived prima donna suggested to Stein another act in the play he was always putting on. He gave two of her sisters positions as saleswomen, but Ruby he established in an apartment on Waverly Place.

"To the outside world Stein became more mysterious in his behaviour than ever. He dropped his Bohemian friends. No more suppers and theatre-parties. Whenever Kitty sang, he was in his box at the Manhattan, usually alone, but not always. Sometimes he took two or three good customers, large buyers from St. Louis or Kansas City. His coat factory is still the biggest earner of his properties. I've seen him there with these buyers, and they carried themselves as if they were being let in on something; took possession of the box with a proprietory air, smiled and applauded and looked wise as if each and every one of them were friends of Kitty Ayrshire. While they buzzed and trained their field-glasses on the prima donna, Stein was impassive and silent. I don't imagine he even told many lies. He is the most insinuating cuss, anyhow. He probably dropped his voice or lifted his eyebrows when he invited them, and let their own eager imaginations do the rest. But what tales they took back to their provincial capitals!

"Sometimes, before they left New York, they were lucky enough to see Kitty dining with their clever garment man at some restaurant, her back to the curious crowd, her face half concealed by a veil or a fur collar. Those people are like children; nothing that is true or probable interests them. They want the old, gaudy lies, told always in the same way. Siegmund Stein and Kitty Ayrshire — a story like that, once launched, is repeated unchallenged for years among New York factory sports. In St. Paul, St. Jo, Sioux City, Council Bluffs, there used to be clothing stores where a photograph of Kitty Ayrshire hung in the fitting-room or over the proprietor's desk.

"This girl impersonated you successfully to the lower manufacturing world of New York for two seasons. I doubt if it could have been put across anywhere else in the world except in this city, which pays you so magnificently and believes of you what it likes. Then you went over to the Metropolitan, stopped living in hotels, took this apartment, and began to know people. Stein discontinued his pantomime at the right moment, withdrew his patronage. Ruby, of course, did not go back to shirtwaists. A business friend of Stein's took her over, and she dropped out of sight. Last winter, one cold, snowy night, I saw her once again. She was going into a saloon hotel with a tough-looking young fellow. She had been drinking, she was shabby, and her blue shoes left stains in the slush. But she still looked amazingly, convincingly like a battered, hardened Kitty Ayrshire. As I saw her going up the brass-edged stairs, I said to myself —"

"Never mind that." Kitty rose quickly, took an impatient step to the hearth, and thrust one shining porcelain slipper out to the fire. "The girl doesn't interest me. There is nothing I can do about her, and of course she never looked like me at all. But what did Stein do without me?"

"Stein? Oh, he chose a new rôle. He married with great magnificence — married a Miss Mandelbaum, a California heiress. Her people have a line of department stores along the Pacific Coast. The Steins now inhabit a great house on Fifth Avenue that used to belong to people of a very different sort. To old New-Yorkers, it's an historic house."

Kitty laughed, and sat down on the end of her couch nearest her guest; sat upright, without cushions.

"I imagine I know more about that house than you do. Let me tell you how I made the sequel to your story.

"It has to do with Peppo Amoretti. You may remember that I brought Peppo to this country, and brought him in, too, the year the war broke out, when it wasn't easy to get boys who hadn't done military service out of Italy. I had taken him

326

to Munich to have some singing lessons. After the war came on we had to get from Munich to Naples in order to sail at all. We were told that we could take only hand luggage on the railways, but I took nine trunks and Peppo. I dressed Peppo in knickerbockers, made him brush his curls down over his ears like doughnuts, and carry a little violin-case. It took us eleven days to reach Naples. I got my trunks through purely by personal persuasion. Once at Naples, I had a frightful time getting Peppo on the boat. I declared him as hand-luggage; he was so travel-worn and so crushed by his absurd appearance that he did not look like much else. One inspector had a sense of humour, and passed him at that, but the other was inflexible. I had to be very dramatic. Peppo was frightened, and there is no fight in him, anyhow.

" '*Per me tutto e indifferente, Signorina,*' he kept whimpering. 'Why should I go without it? I have lost it.'

" 'Which?' I screamed. '*Not* the hat-trunk?'

" '*No, no; mia voce.* It is gone since Ravenna.'

"He thought he had lost his voice somewhere along the way. At last I told the inspector that I couldn't live without Peppo, and that I would throw myself into the bay. I took him into my confidence. Of course, when I found I had to play on that string, I wished I hadn't made the boy such a spectacle. But ridiculous as he was, I managed to make the inspector believe that I had kidnapped him, and that he was indispensable to my happiness. I found that incorruptible official, like most people, willing to aid one so utterly depraved. I could never have got that boy out for any proper, reasonable purpose, such as giving him a job or sending him to school. Well, it's a

327

queer world! But I must cut all that and get to the Steins.

"That first winter Peppo had no chance at the Opera. There was an iron ring about him, and my interest in him only made it all the more difficult. We've become a nest of intrigues down there; worse than the Scala. Peppo had to scratch along just any way. One evening he came to me and said he could get an engagement to sing for the grand rich Steins, but the condition was that I should sing with him. They would pay, oh, anything! And the fact that I had sung a private engagement with him would give him other engagements of the same sort. As you know, I never sing private engagements; but to help the boy along, I consented.

"On the night of the party, Peppo and I went to the house together in a taxi. My car was ailing. At the hour when the music was about to begin, the host and hostess appeared at my dressing-room, up-stairs. Isn't he wonderful? Your description was most inadequate. I never encountered such restrained, frozen, sculptured vanity. My hostess struck me as extremely good natured and jolly, though somewhat intimate in her manner. Her reassuring pats and smiles puzzled me at the time, I remember, when I didn't know that she had anything in particular to be large-minded and charitable about. Her husband made known his willingness to conduct me to the music-room, and we ceremoniously descended a staircase blooming like the hanging-gardens of Babylon. From there I had my first glimpse of the company. They *were* strange people. The women glittered like Christmas-trees. When we were half-way down the stairs, the buzz of conversation stopped so suddenly that some foolish remark I happened to be making rang out like oratory. Every face was lifted toward us. My host and I completed our descent and went the length of the drawing-room through a silence which somewhat awed me. I couldn't help wishing that one could ever get that kind of attention in a concert-hall. In the music-room Stein insisted upon arranging things for me. I must say that he was neither awkward nor stupid, not so wooden as most rich men who rent singers. I was properly affable. One has, under such circumstances, to be either gracious or pouty. Either you have to stand and sulk, like an old-fashioned German singer who wants the piano moved about for her like a tea-wagon, and the lights turned up and the lights turned down, — or you have to be a trifle forced, like a débutante trying to make good. The fixed attention of my audience affected me. I was aware of unusual interest, of a thoroughly enlisted public. When, however, my host at last left me, I felt the tension relax to such an extent that I wondered whether by any chance he, and not I, was the object of so much curiosity. But, at any rate, their cordiality pleased me so well that after Peppo and I had finished our numbers I sang an encore or two, and I stayed through Peppo's performance because I felt that they liked to look at me.

"I had asked not to be presented to people, but Mrs. Stein, of course, brought up a few friends. The throng began closing in upon me, glowing faces bore down from every direction, and I realized that, among people of such unscrupulous cordiality, I must look out for myself. I ran through the drawing-room and fled up the stair-way, which was thronged with Old Testament characters. As I passed them, they all looked at me with delighted, cherishing eyes, as if I had at last come back to my native hamlet. At the top of the stairway a young man, who looked like a camel with its hair parted on the side, stopped me, seized my hands and said he must present himself, as he was such an old friend of Siegmund's bachelor days. I said, 'Yes, how interesting!' The atmosphere was somehow so thick and personal that I felt uncomfortable.

"When I reached my dressing-room Mrs. Stein followed me to say that I would, of course, come down to supper, as a special table had been prepared for me. I replied that it was not my custom.

" 'But here it is different. With us you must feel perfect freedom. Siegmund will never forgive me if you do not stay. After supper our car will take you home.' She was overpowering. She had the manner of an intimate and indulgent friend of long standing. She seemed to have come to make me a visit. I could only get rid of her by telling her that I must see Peppo at once, if she would be good enough to send him to me. She did not come back, and I began to fear that I would actually be dragged down to supper. It was as if I had been kidnapped. I felt like *Gulliver* among the giants. These people were all too — well, too much what they were. No chill of manner could hold them off. I was defenseless. I must get away. I ran to the top of the staircase and looked down. There was that fool Peppo, beleaguered by a bevy of fair women. They were simply looting him, and he was grinning like an idiot. I gathered up my train, ran down, and made a dash at him, yanked him out of that circle of rich contours, and dragged him by a limp cuff up the stairs after me. I told him that I must escape from that house at once. If he could get to the telephone, well and good; but if he couldn't get past so many deep-breathing ladies, then he must break out of the front door and hunt me a cab on foot. I felt as if I were about to be immured within a harem.

"He had scarcely dashed off when the host called my name several times outside the door. Then he knocked and walked in, uninvited. I told him that I would be inflexible about supper. He must make my excuses to his charming friends; any pretext he chose. He did not insist. He took up his stand by the fireplace and began to talk; said rather intelligent things. I did not drive him out; it was his own house, and he made himself agreeable. After a time a deputation of his friends came down the hall, somewhat boisterously, to say that supper could not be served until we came down. Stein was still standing by the mantel, I remember. He scattered them, without moving or speaking to them, by a portentous look. There is something hideously forceful about him. He took a very profound leave of me, and said he would order his car at once. In a moment Peppo arrived, splashed to the ankles, and we made our escape together.

"A week later Peppo came to me in a rage, with a paper called *The American Gentleman,* and showed me a page devoted to three photographs: Mr. and Mrs. Siegmund Stein, lately married in New York City, and Kitty Ayrshire, operatic soprano, who sang at their house-warming. Mrs. Stein and I were grinning our best, looked frantic with delight, and Siegmund frowned inscrutably between us. Poor Peppo wasn't mentioned. Stein has a publicity sense."

Tevis rose.

"And you have enormous publicity value and no discretion. It was just like you to fall for such a plot, Kitty. You'd be sure to."

"What's the use of discretion?" She murmured behind her hand. "If the Steins want to adopt you into their family circle, they'll get you in the end. That's why I don't feel compassionate about your Ruby. She and I are in the same boat. We are both the victims of circumstance, and in New York so many of the circumstances are Steins."

ALEXANDER'S BRIDGE

CHAPTER I

Late one brilliant April afternoon Professor Lucius Wilson stood at the head of Chestnut Street, looking about him with the pleased air of a man of taste who does not very often get to Boston. He had lived there as a student, but for twenty years and more, since he had been Professor of Philosophy in a Western university, he had seldom come East except to take a steamer for some foreign port. Wilson was standing quite still, contemplating with a whimsical smile the slanting street, with its worn paving, its irregular, gravely colored houses, and the row of naked trees on which the thin sunlight was still shining. The gleam of the river at the foot of the hill made him blink a little, not so much because it was too bright as because he found it so pleasant. The few passers-by glanced at him unconcernedly, and even the children who hurried along with their school-bags under their arms seemed to find it perfectly natural that a tall brown gentleman should be standing there, looking up through his glasses at the gray housetops.

The sun sank rapidly; the silvery light had faded from the bare boughs and the watery twilight was setting in when Wilson at last walked down the hill, descending into cooler and cooler depths of grayish shadow. His nostril, long unused to it, was quick to detect the smell of wood smoke in the air, blended with the odor of moist spring earth and the saltiness that came up the river with the tide. He crossed Charles Street between jangling street cars and shelving lumber drays, and after a moment of uncertainty wound into Brimmer Street. The street was quiet, deserted, and hung with a thin bluish haze. He had already fixed his sharp eye upon the house which he reasoned should be his objective point, when he noticed a woman approaching rapidly from the opposite direction. Always an interested observer of women, Wilson would have slackened his pace anywhere to follow this one with his impersonal, appreciative glance. She was a person of distinction he saw at once, and, moreover, very handsome. She was tall, carried her beautiful head proudly, and moved with ease and certainty. One immediately took for granted the costly privileges and fine spaces that must lie in the background from which such a figure could emerge with this rapid and elegant gait. Wilson noted her dress, too, — for, in his way, he had an eye for such things, — particularly her brown furs and her hat. He got a blurred impression of her fine color, the violets she wore, her white gloves, and, curiously enough, of her veil, as she turned up a flight of steps in front of him and disappeared.

Wilson was able to enjoy lovely things that passed him on the wing as completely and deliberately as if they had been dug-up marvels, long anticipated, and definitely fixed at the end of a railway journey. For a few pleasurable seconds he quite forgot where he was going, and only after the door had closed behind her did he realize that the young woman had entered the house to which he had directed his trunk from the South Station that morning. He hesitated a moment before mounting the steps. "Can that," he murmured in amazement, — "can that possibly have been Mrs. Alexander?"

When the servant admitted him, Mrs. Alexander was still standing in the hallway. She heard him give his name, and came forward holding out her hand.

"Is it you, indeed, Professor Wilson? I was afraid that you might get here before I did. I was detained at a concert, and Bartley telephoned that he would be late. Thomas will show you your room. Had you rather have your tea brought to you there, or will you have it down here with me, while we wait for Bartley?"

Wilson was pleased to find that he had been the cause of her rapid walk, and with her he was even more vastly pleased than before. He followed her through the drawing-room into the library, where the wide back windows looked out upon the garden and the sunset and a fine stretch of silver-colored river. A harp-shaped elm stood stripped against the pale-colored evening sky, with ragged last year's birds' nests in its forks, and through the bare branches the evening star quivered in the misty air. The long brown room breathed the peace of a rich and amply guarded quiet. Tea was brought in immediately and placed in front of the wood fire. Mrs. Alexander sat down in a high-backed chair and began to pour it, while Wilson sank into a low seat opposite her and took his cup

335

with a great sense of ease and harmony and comfort.

"You have had a long journey, haven't you?" Mrs. Alexander asked, after showing gracious concern about his tea. "And I am so sorry Bartley is late. He's often tired when he's late. He flatters himself that it is a little on his account that you have come to this Congress of Psychologists."

"It is," Wilson assented, selecting his muffin carefully; "and I hope he won't be tired tonight. But, on my own account, I'm glad to have a few moments alone with you, before Bartley comes. I was somehow afraid that my knowing him so well would not put me in the way of getting to know you."

"That's very nice of you." She nodded at him above her cup and smiled, but there was a little formal tightness in her tone which had not been there when she greeted him in the hall.

Wilson leaned forward. "Have I said something awkward? I live very far out of the world, you know. But I didn't mean that you would exactly fade dim, even if Bartley were here."

Mrs. Alexander laughed relentingly. "Oh, I'm not so vain! How terribly discerning you are."

She looked straight at Wilson, and he felt that this quick, frank glance brought about an understanding between them.

He liked everything about her, he told himself, but he particularly liked her eyes; when she looked at one directly for a moment they were like a glimpse of fine windy sky that may bring all sorts of weather.

"Since you noticed something," Mrs. Alexander went on, "it must have been a flash of the distrust I have come to feel whenever I meet any of the people who knew Bartley when he was a boy. It is always as if they were talking of someone I had never met. Really, Professor Wilson, it would seem that he grew up among the strangest people. They usually say that he has turned out very well, or remark that he always was a fine fellow. I never know what reply to make."

Wilson chuckled and leaned back in his chair, shaking his left foot gently. "I expect the fact is that we none of us knew him very well, Mrs. Alexander. Though I will say for myself that I was always confident he'd do something extraordinary."

Mrs. Alexander's shoulders gave a slight movement, suggestive of impatience. "Oh, I should think that might have been a safe prediction. Another cup, please?"

"Yes, thank you. But predicting, in the case of boys, is not so easy as you might imagine, Mrs. Alexander. Some get a bad hurt early and lose their courage; and some never get a fair wind. Bartley" — he dropped his chin on the back of his long hand and looked at her admiringly — "Bartley caught the wind early, and it has sung in his sails ever since."

Mrs. Alexander sat looking into the fire with intent preoccupation, and Wilson studied her half-averted face. He liked the suggestion of stormy possibilities in the proud curve of her lip and nostril. Without that, he reflected, she would be too cold.

"I should like to know what he was really like when he was a boy. I don't believe he remembers," she said suddenly. "Won't you smoke, Mr. Wilson?"

Wilson lit a cigarette. "No, I don't suppose he

does. He was never introspective. He was simply the most tremendous response to stimuli I have ever known. We didn't know exactly what to do with him."

A servant came in and noiselessly removed the tea-tray. Mrs. Alexander screened her face from the firelight, which was beginning to throw wavering bright spots on her dress and hair as the dusk deepened.

"Of course," she said, "I now and again hear stories about things that happened when he was in college."

"But that isn't what you want." Wilson wrinkled his brows and looked at her with the smiling familiarity that had come about so quickly. "What you want is a picture of him, standing back there at the other end of twenty years. You want to look down through my memory."

She dropped her hands in her lap. "Yes, yes; that's exactly what I want."

At this moment they heard the front door shut with a jar, and Wilson laughed as Mrs. Alexander rose quickly. "There he is. Away with perspective! No past, no future for Bartley; just the fiery moment. The only moment that ever was or will be in the world!"

The door from the hall opened, a voice called "Winifred?" hurriedly, and a big man came through the drawing-room with a quick, heavy tread, bringing with him a smell of cigar smoke and chill out-of-doors air. When Alexander reached the library door, he switched on the lights and stood six feet and more in the archway, glowing with strength and cordiality and rugged, blond good looks. There were other bridge-builders in the world, certainly, but it was always Alexander's

338

picture that the Sunday Supplement men wanted, because he looked as a tamer of rivers ought to look. Under his tumbled sandy hair his head seemed as hard and powerful as a catapult, and his shoulders looked strong enough in themselves to support a span of any one of his ten great bridges that cut the air above as many rivers.

After dinner Alexander took Wilson up to his study. It was a large room over the library, and looked out upon the black river and the row of white lights along the Cambridge Embankment. The room was not at all what one might expect of an engineer's study. Wilson felt at once the harmony of beautiful things that have lived long together without obtrusions of ugliness or change. It was none of Alexander's doing, of course; those warm consonances of color had been blending and mellowing before he was born. But the wonder was that he was not out of place there, — that it all seemed to glow like the inevitable background for his vigor and vehemence. He sat before the fire, his shoulders deep in the cushions of his chair, his powerful head upright, his hair rumpled above his broad forehead. He sat heavily, a cigar in his large, smooth hand, a flush of after-dinner color in his face, which wind and sun and exposure to all sorts of weather had left fair and clear-skinned.

"You are off for England on Saturday, Bartley, Mrs. Alexander tells me."

"Yes, for a few weeks only. There's a meeting of British engineers, and I'm doing another bridge in Canada, you know."

"Oh, every one knows about that. And it was in Canada that you met your wife, wasn't it?"

"Yes, at Allway. She was visiting her great-aunt there. A most remarkable old lady. I was working with MacKeller then, an old Scotch engineer who had picked me up in London and taken me back to Quebec with him. He had the contract for the Allway Bridge, but before he began work on it he found out that he was going to die, and he advised the committee to turn the job over to me. Otherwise I'd never have got anything good so early. MacKeller was an old friend of Mrs. Pemberton, Winifred's aunt. He had mentioned me to her, so when I went to Allway she asked me to come to see her. She was a wonderful old lady."

"Like her niece?" Wilson queried.

Bartley laughed. "She had been very handsome, but not in Winifred's way. When I knew her she was little and fragile, very pink and white, with a splendid head and a face like fine old lace, somehow, — but perhaps I always think of that because she wore a lace scarf on her hair. She had such a flavor of life about her. She had known Gordon and Livingstone and Beaconsfield when she was young, — every one. She was the first woman of that sort I'd ever known. You know how it is in the West, — old people are poked out of the way. Aunt Eleanor fascinated me as few young women have ever done. I used to go up from the works to have tea with her, and sit talking to her for hours. It was very stimulating, for she couldn't tolerate stupidity."

"It must have been then that your luck began, Bartley," said Wilson, flicking his cigar ash with his long finger. "It's curious, watching boys," he went on reflectively. "I'm sure I did you justice in the matter of ability. Yet I always used to feel that there was a weak spot where some day strain would tell. Even after you began to climb, I stood down in the crowd and watched you with — well, not with confidence. The more dazzling the front you presented, the higher your facade rose, the more I expected to see a big crack zigzagging from top to bottom," — he indicated its course in the air with his forefinger, — "then a crash and clouds of dust. It was curious. I had such a clear picture of it. And another curious thing, Bartley," Wilson spoke with deliberateness and settled deeper into his chair, "is that I don't feel it any longer. I am sure of you."

Alexander laughed. "Nonsense! It's not I you feel sure of; it's Winifred. People often make that mistake."

"No, I'm serious, Alexander. You've changed. You have decided to leave some birds in the bushes. You used to want them all."

Alexander's chair creaked. "I still want a good many," he said rather gloomily. "After all, life doesn't offer a man much. You work like the devil and think you're getting on, and suddenly you discover that you've only been getting yourself tied up. A million details drink you dry. Your life keeps going for things you don't want, and all the while you are being built alive into a social structure you don't care a rap about. I sometimes wonder what sort of chap I'd have been if I hadn't been this sort; I want to go and live out his potentialities, too. I haven't forgotten that there are birds in the bushes."

Bartley stopped and sat frowning into the fire, his shoulders thrust forward as if he were about to spring at something. Wilson watched him, wondering. His old pupil always stimulated him at first, and then vastly wearied him. The machin-

341

ery was always pounding away in this man, and Wilson preferred companions of a more reflective habit of mind. He could not help feeling that there were unreasoning and unreasonable activities going on in Alexander all the while; that even after dinner, when most men achieve a decent impersonality, Bartley had merely closed the door of the engine-room and come up for an airing. The machinery itself was still pounding on.

Bartley's abstraction and Wilson's reflections were cut short by a rustle at the door, and almost before they could rise Mrs. Alexander was standing by the hearth. Alexander brought a chair for her, but she shook her head.

"No, dear, thank you. I only came in to see whether you and Professor Wilson were quite comfortable. I am going down to the music-room."

"Why not practice here? Wilson and I are growing very dull. We are tired of talk."

"Yes, I beg you, Mrs. Alexander," Wilson began, but he got no further.

"Why, certainly, if you won't find me too noisy. I am working on the Schumann 'Carnival,' and, though I don't practice a great many hours, I am very methodical," Mrs. Alexander explained, as she crossed to an upright piano that stood at the back of the room, near the windows.

Wilson followed, and, having seen her seated, dropped into a chair behind her. She played brilliantly and with great musical feeling. Wilson could not imagine her permitting herself to do anything badly, but he was surprised at the cleanness of her execution. He wondered how a woman with so many duties had managed to keep herself up to a standard really professional. It must take a great deal of time, certainly, and Bartley must take a great deal of time. Wilson reflected that he had never before known a woman who had been able, for any considerable while, to support both a personal and an intellectual passion. Sitting behind her, he watched her with perplexed admiration, shading his eyes with his hand. In her dinner dress she looked even younger than in street clothes, and, for all her composure and self-sufficiency, she seemed to him strangely alert and vibrating, as if in her, too, there were something never altogether at rest. He felt that he knew pretty much what she demanded in people and what she demanded from life, and he wondered how she squared Bartley. After ten years she must know him; and however one took him, however much one admired him, one had to admit that he simply wouldn't square. He was a natural force, certainly, but beyond that, Wilson felt, he was not anything very really or for very long at a time.

Wilson glanced toward the fire, where Bartley's profile was still wreathed in cigar smoke that curled up more and more slowly. His shoulders were sunk deep in the cushions and one hand hung large and passive over the arm of his chair. He had slipped on a purple velvet smoking-coat. His wife, Wilson surmised, had chosen it. She was clearly very proud of his good looks and his fine color. But, with the glow of an immediate interest gone out of it, the engineer's face looked tired, even a little haggard. The three lines in his forehead, directly above the nose, deepened as he sat thinking, and his powerful head drooped forward heavily. Although Alexander was only forty-three, Wilson thought that beneath his vigorous color he detected the dulling weariness of on-coming middle age.

The next afternoon, at the hour when the river was beginning to redden under the declining sun, Wilson again found himself facing Mrs. Alexander at the tea-table in the library.

"Well," he remarked, when he was bidden to give an account of himself, "there was a long morning with the psychologists, luncheon with Bartley at his club, more psychologists, and here I am. I've looked forward to this hour all day."

Mrs. Alexander smiled at him across the vapor from the kettle. "And do you remember where we stopped yesterday?"

"Perfectly. I was going to show you a picture. But I doubt whether I have color enough in me. Bartley makes me feel a faded monochrome. You can't get at the young Bartley except by means of color." Wilson paused and deliberated. Suddenly he broke out: "He wasn't a remarkable student, you know, though he was always strong in higher mathematics. His work in my own department was quite ordinary. It was as a powerfully equipped nature that I found him interesting. That is the most interesting thing a teacher can find. It has the fascination of a scientific discovery. We come across other pleasing and endearing qualities so much oftener than we find force."

"And, after all," said Mrs. Alexander, "that is the thing we all live upon. It is the thing that takes us forward."

Wilson thought she spoke a little wistfully. "Exactly," he assented warmly. "It builds the bridges into the future, over which the feet of every one of us will go."

"How interested I am to hear you put it in that

344

way. The bridges into the future — I often say that to myself. Bartley's bridges always seem to me like that. Have you ever seen his first suspension bridge in Canada, the one he was doing when I first knew him? I hope you will see it sometime. We were married as soon as it was finished, and you will laugh when I tell you that it always has a rather bridal look to me. It is over the wildest river, with mists and clouds always battling about it, and it is as delicate as a cobweb hanging in the sky. It really was a bridge into the future. You have only to look at it to feel that it meant the beginning of a great career. But I have a photograph of it here." She drew a portfolio from behind a bookcase. "And there, you see, on the hill, is my aunt's house."

Wilson took up the photograph. "Bartley was telling me something about your aunt last night. She must have been a delightful person."

Winifred laughed. "The bridge, you see, was just at the foot of the hill, and the noise of the engines annoyed her very much at first. But after she met Bartley she pretended to like it, and said it was a good thing to be reminded that there were things going on in the world. She loved life, and Bartley brought a great deal of it in to her when he came to the house. Aunt Eleanor was very worldly in a frank, Early-Victorian manner. She liked men of action, and disliked young men who were careful of themselves and who, as she put it, were always trimming their wick as if they were afraid of their oil's giving out. MacKeller, Bartley's first chief, was an old friend of my aunt, and he told her that Bartley was a wild, ill-governed youth, which really pleased her very much. I remember we were sitting alone in the dusk after

345

Bartley had been there for the first time. I knew that Aunt Eleanor had found him much to her taste, but she hadn't said anything. Presently she came out, with a chuckle: 'MacKeller found him sowing wild oats in London, I believe. I hope he didn't stop him too soon. Life coquets with dashing fellows. The coming men are always like that. We must have him to dinner, my dear.' And we did. She grew much fonder of Bartley than she was of me. I had been studying in Vienna, and she thought that absurd. She was interested in the army and in politics, and she had a great contempt for music and art and philosophy. She used to declare that the Prince Consort had brought all that stuff over out of Germany. She always sniffed when Bartley asked me to play for him. She considered that a newfangled way of making a match of it."

When Alexander came in a few moments later, he found Wilson and his wife still confronting the photograph. "Oh, let us get that out of the way," he said, laughing. "Winifred, Thomas can bring my trunk down. I've decided to go over to New York to-morrow night and take a fast boat. I shall save two days."

CHAPTER II

On the night of his arrival in London, Alexander went immediately to the hotel on the Embankment at which he always stopped, and in the lobby he was accosted by an old acquaintance, Maurice Mainhall, who fell upon him with effusive cordiality and indicated a willingness to dine with him. Bartley never dined alone if he could help it, and Mainhall was a good gossip who always knew what had been going on in town; especially, he knew everything that was not printed in the newspapers. The nephew of one of the standard Victorian novelists, Mainhall bobbed about among the various literary cliques of London and its outlying suburbs, careful to lose touch with none of them. He had written a number of books himself; among them a "History of Dancing," a "History of Costume," a "Key to Shakespeare's Sonnets," a study of "The Poetry of Ernest Dowson," etc. Although Mainhall's enthusiasm was often tiresome, and although he was often unable to distinguish between facts and vivid figments of his imagination, his imperturbable good nature overcame even the people whom he bored most, so that they ended by becoming, in a reluctant manner, his friends. In appearance, Mainhall was astonishingly like the conventional stage-Englishman of American drama: tall and thin, with high, hitching shoulders and a small head glistening with closely brushed yellow hair. He spoke with an extreme Oxford accent, and when he was talking well, his face sometimes wore the rapt expression of a very emotional man listening to music. Mainhall liked Alexander because he was an engineer. He had preconceived ideas about everything, and his idea about Americans was that they should be engineers or mechanics. He hated them when they presumed to be anything else.

While they sat at dinner Mainhall acquainted Bartley with the fortunes of his old friends in London, and as they left the table he proposed that they should go to see Hugh MacConnell's new comedy, "Bog Lights."

"It's really quite the best thing MacConnell's done," he explained as they got into a hansom. "It's tremendously well put on, too. Florence Merrill and Cyril Henderson. But Hilda Burgoyne's the hit of the piece. Hugh's written a delightful part for her, and she's quite inexpressible. It's been on only two weeks, and I've been half a dozen times already. I happen to have MacConnell's box for tonight or there'd be no chance of our getting places. There's everything in seeing Hilda while she's fresh in a part. She's apt to grow a bit stale after a time. The ones who have any imagination do."

"Hilda Burgoyne!" Alexander exclaimed mildly. "Why, I haven't heard of her for — years."

Mainhall laughed. "Then you can't have heard much at all, my dear Alexander. It's only lately, since MacConnell and his set have got hold of her, that she's come up. Myself, I always knew she had it in her. If we had one real critic in London — but what can one expect? Do you know, Alexander," — Mainhall looked with perplexity up into the top of the hansom and rubbed his pink cheek with his gloved finger, — "do you know, I sometimes think of taking to criticism seriously myself. In a way, it would be a sacrifice; but, dear me, we do need some one."

Just then they drove up to the Duke of York's, so Alexander did not commit himself, but followed Mainhall into the theatre. When they entered the stage-box on the left the first act was well under way, the scene being the interior of a cabin in the south of Ireland. As they sat down, a burst of applause drew Alexander's attention to the stage. Miss Burgoyne and her donkey were thrusting their heads in at the half door. "After all," he reflected, "there's small probability of her recognizing me. She doubtless hasn't thought of me for years." He felt the enthusiasm of the house at once, and in a few moments he was caught up by the current of MacConnell's irresistible comedy. The audience had come forewarned, evidently, and whenever the ragged slip of a donkey-girl ran upon the stage there was a deep murmur of approbation, every one smiled and glowed, and Mainhall hitched his heavy chair a little nearer the brass railing.

"You see," he murmured in Alexander's ear, as the curtain fell on the first act, "one almost never sees a part like that done without smartness or mawkishness. Of course, Hilda is Irish, — the Burgoynes have been stage people for generations, — and she has the Irish voice. It's delightful to hear it in a London theatre. That laugh, now, when she doubles over at the hips — who ever heard it out of Galway? She saves her hand, too. She's at her best in the second act. She's really MacConnell's poetic motif, you see; makes the whole thing a fairy tale."

The second act opened before Philly Doyle's underground still, with Peggy and her battered donkey come in to smuggle a load of potheen across the bog, and to bring Philly word of what was doing in the world without, and of what was happening along the roadsides and ditches with the first gleam of fine weather. Alexander, annoyed by Mainhall's sighs and exclamations, watched her with keen, half-skeptical interest. As Mainhall had said, she was the second act; the plot and feeling alike depended upon her lightness of foot, her lightness of touch, upon the shrewdness and deft fancifulness that played alternately, and sometimes together, in her mirthful brown eyes. When she began to dance, by way of showing the gossoons what she had seen in the fairy rings at

349

night, the house broke into a prolonged uproar. After her dance she withdrew from the dialogue and retreated to the ditch wall back of Philly's burrow, where she sat singing "The Rising of the Moon" and making a wreath of primroses for her donkey.

When the act was over Alexander and Mainhall strolled out into the corridor. They met a good many acquaintances; Mainhall, indeed, knew almost every one, and he babbled on incontinently, screwing his small head about over his high collar. Presently he hailed a tall, bearded man, grim-browed and rather battered-looking, who had his opera cloak on his arm and his hat in his hand, and who seemed to be on the point of leaving the theatre.

"MacConnell, let me introduce Mr. Bartley Alexander. I say! It's going famously to-night, Mac. And what an audience! You'll never do anything like this again, mark me. A man writes to the top of his bent only once."

The playwright gave Mainhall a curious look out of his deep-set faded eyes and made a wry face. "And have I done anything so fool as that, now?" he asked.

"That's what I was saying," Mainhall lounged a little nearer and dropped into a tone even more conspicuously confidential. "And you'll never bring Hilda out like this again. Dear me, Mac, the girl couldn't possibly be better, you know."

MacConnell grunted. "She'll do well enough if she keeps her pace and doesn't go off on us in the middle of the season, as she's more than like to do."

He nodded curtly and made for the door, dodging acquaintances as he went.

"Poor old Hugh," Mainhall murmured. "He's hit terribly hard. He's been wanting to marry Hilda these three years and more. She doesn't take up with anybody, you know. Irene Burgoyne, one of her family, told me in confidence that there was a romance somewhere back in the beginning. One of your countrymen, Alexander, by the way; an American student whom she met in Paris, I believe. I dare say it's quite true that there's never been any one else." Mainhall vouched for her constancy with a loftiness that made Alexander smile, even while a kind of rapid excitement was tingling through him. Blinking up at the lights, Mainhall added in his luxurious, worldly way: "She's an elegant little person, and quite capable of an extravagant bit of sentiment like that. Here comes Sir Harry Towne. He's another who's awfully keen about her. Let me introduce you. Sir Harry Towne, Mr. Bartley Alexander, the American engineer."

Sir Harry Towne bowed and said that he had met Mr. Alexander and his wife in Tokyo.

Mainhall cut in impatiently.

"I say, Sir Harry, the little girl's going famously to-night, isn't she?"

Sir Harry wrinkled his brows judiciously. "Do you know, I thought the dance a bit conscious to-night, for the first time. The fact is, she's feeling rather seedy, poor child. Westmere and I were back after the first act, and we thought she seemed quite uncertain of herself. A little attack of nerves, possibly."

He bowed as the warning bell rang, and Mainhall whispered: "You know Lord Westmere, of course, — the stooped man with the long gray mustache, talking to Lady Dowle. Lady Westmere

351

is very fond of Hilda."

When they reached their box the house was darkened and the orchestra was playing "The Cloak of Old Gaul." In a moment Peggy was on the stage again, and Alexander applauded vigorously with the rest. He even leaned forward over the rail a little. For some reason he felt pleased and flattered by the enthusiasm of the audience. In the half-light he looked about at the stalls and boxes and smiled a little consciously, recalling with amusement Sir Harry's judicial frown. He was beginning to feel a keen interest in the slender, barefoot donkey-girl who slipped in and out of the play, singing, like some one winding through a hilly field. He leaned forward and beamed felicitations as warmly as Mainhall himself when, at the end of the play, she came again and again before the curtain, panting a little and flushed, her eyes dancing and her eager, nervous little mouth tremulous with excitement.

When Alexander returned to his hotel — he shook Mainhall at the door of the theatre — he had some supper brought up to his room, and it was late before he went to bed. He had not thought of Hilda Burgoyne for years; indeed, he had almost forgotten her. He had last written to her from Canada, after he first met Winifred, telling her that everything was changed with him — that he had met a woman whom he would marry if he could; if he could not, then all the more was everything changed for him. Hilda had never replied to his letter. He felt guilty and unhappy about her for a time, but after Winifred promised to marry him he really forgot Hilda altogether. When he wrote her that everything was changed for him, he was telling the truth. After he met

Winifred Pemberton he seemed to himself like a different man. One night when he and Winifred were sitting together on the bridge, he told her that things had happened while he was studying abroad that he was sorry for, — one thing in particular, — and he asked her whether she thought she ought to know about them. She considered a moment and then said "No, I think not, though I am glad you ask me. You see, one can't be jealous about things in general; but about particular, definite, personal things," — here she had thrown her hands up to his shoulders with a quick, impulsive gesture — "oh, about those I should be very jealous. I should torture myself — I couldn't help it." After that it was easy to forget, actually to forget. He wondered to-night, as he poured his wine, how many times he had thought of Hilda in the last ten years. He had been in London more or less, but he had never happened to hear of her. "All the same," he lifted his glass, "here's to you, little Hilda. You've made things come your way, and I never thought you'd do it.

"Of course," he reflected, "she always had that combination of something homely and sensible, and something utterly wild and daft. But I never thought she'd do anything. She hadn't much ambition then, and she was too fond of trifles. She must care about the theatre a great deal more than she used to. Perhaps she has me to thank for something, after all. Sometimes a little jolt like that does one good. She was a daft, generous little thing. I'm glad she's held her own since. After all, we were awfully young. It was youth and poverty and proximity, and everything was young and kindly. I shouldn't wonder if she could laugh about it with me now. I shouldn't wonder — But they've probably spoiled her, so that she'd be tiresome if one met her again."

Bartley smiled and yawned and went to bed.

CHAPTER III

The next evening Alexander dined alone at a club, and at about nine o'clock he dropped in at the Duke of York's. The house was sold out and he stood through the second act. When he returned to his hotel he examined the new directory, and found Miss Burgoyne's address still given as off Bedford Square, though at a new number. He remembered that, in so far as she had been brought up at all, she had been brought up in Bloomsbury. Her father and mother played in the provinces most of the year, and she was left a great deal in the care of an old aunt who was crippled by rheumatism and who had had to leave the stage altogether. In the days when Alexander knew her, Hilda always managed to have a lodging of some sort about Bedford Square, because she clung tenaciously to such scraps and shreds of memories as were connected with it. The mummy room of the British Museum had been one of the chief delights of her childhood. That forbidding pile was the goal of her truant fancy, and she was sometimes taken there for a treat, as other children are taken to the theatre. It was long since Alexander had thought of any of these things, but now they came back to him quite fresh, and had a significance they did not have when they were first told him in his restless twenties. So she was still in the old neighborhood, near Bedford Square. The new number probably meant increased prosperity. He hoped so. He would like to know that she was snugly settled. He looked at his watch. It was a quarter past ten; she would not be home for a good two hours yet, and he might as well walk over and have a look at the place. He remembered the shortest way.

It was a warm, smoky evening, and there was a grimy moon. He went through Covent Garden to Oxford Street, and as he turned into Museum Street he walked more slowly, smiling at his own nervousness as he approached the sullen gray mass at the end. He had not been inside the Museum, actually, since he and Hilda used to meet there; sometimes to set out for gay adventures at Twickenham or Richmond, sometimes to linger about the place for a while and to ponder by Lord Elgin's marbles upon the lastingness of some things, or, in the mummy room, upon the awful brevity of others. Since then Bartley had always thought of the British Museum as the ultimate repository of mortality, where all the dead things in the world were assembled to make one's hour of youth the more precious. One trembled lest before he got out it might somehow escape him, lest he might drop the glass from over-eagerness and see it shivered on the stone floor at his feet. How one hid his youth under his coat and hugged it! And how good it was to turn one's back upon all that vaulted cold, to take Hilda's arm and hurry out of the great door and down the steps into the sunlight among the pigeons — to know that the warm and vital thing within him was still there and had not been snatched away to flush Caesar's lean cheek or to feed the veins of some bearded Assyrian king. They in their day had carried the flaming liquor, but to-day was his! So the song used to run in his head those summer mornings a dozen years ago.

Alexander walked by the place very quietly, as if he were afraid of waking some one.

He crossed Bedford Square and found the number he was looking for. The house, a comfortable, well-kept place enough, was dark except for the four front windows on the second floor, where a low, even light was burning behind the white muslin sash curtains. Outside there were window boxes, painted white and full of flowers. Bartley was making a third round of the Square when he heard the far-flung hoof-beats of a hansom-cab horse, driven rapidly. He looked at his watch, and was astonished to find that it was a few minutes after twelve. He turned and walked back along the iron railing as the cab came up to Hilda's number and stopped. The hansom must have been one that she employed regularly, for she did not stop to pay the driver. She stepped out quickly and lightly. He heard her cheerful "Good-night, cabby," as she ran up the steps and opened the door with a latchkey. In a few moments the lights flared up brightly behind the white curtains, and as he walked away he heard a window raised. But he had gone too far to look up without turning round. He went back to his hotel, feeling that he had had a good evening, and he slept well.

For the next few days Alexander was very busy. He took a desk in the office of a Scotch engineering firm on Henrietta Street, and was at work almost constantly. He avoided the clubs and usually dined alone at his hotel. One afternoon, after he had tea, he started for a walk down the Embankment toward Westminster, intending to end his stroll at Bedford Square and to ask whether Miss Burgoyne would let him take her to the theatre. But he did not go so far. When he reached the Abbey, he turned back and crossed Westminster Bridge and sat down to watch the trails of smoke behind the Houses of Parliament catch fire with the sunset. The slender towers were washed by a rain of golden light and licked by little flickering flames; Somerset House and the bleached gray pinnacles about Whitehall were floated in a luminous haze. The yellow light poured through the trees and the leaves seemed to burn with soft fires. There was a smell of acacias in the air everywhere, and the laburnums were dripping gold over the walls of the gardens. It was a sweet, lonely kind of summer evening. Remembering Hilda as she used to be, was doubtless more satisfactory than seeing her as she must be now — and, after all, Alexander asked himself, what was it but his own young years that he was remembering?

He crossed back to Westminster, went up to the Temple, and sat down to smoke in the Middle Temple gardens, listening to the thin voice of the fountain and smelling the spice of the sycamores that came out heavily in the damp evening air. He thought, as he sat there, about a great many things: about his own youth and Hilda's; above all, he thought of how glorious it had been, and how quickly it had passed; and, when it had passed, how little worth while anything was. None of the things he had gained in the least compensated. In the last six years his reputation had become, as the saying is, popular. Four years ago he had been called to Japan to deliver, at the Emperor's request, a course of lectures at the Imperial University, and had instituted reforms throughout the islands, not only in the practice of bridge-building but in drainage and road-making.

357

On his return he had undertaken the bridge at Moorlock, in Canada, the most important piece of bridge-building going on in the world, — a test, indeed, of how far the latest practice in bridge structure could be carried. It was a spectacular undertaking by reason of its very size, and Bartley realized that, whatever else he might do, he would probably always be known as the engineer who designed the great Moorlock Bridge, the longest cantilever in existence. Yet it was to him the least satisfactory thing he had ever done. He was cramped in every way by a niggardly commission, and was using lighter structural material than he thought proper. He had vexations enough, too, with his work at home. He had several bridges under way in the United States, and they were always being held up by strikes and delays resulting from a general industrial unrest.

Though Alexander often told himself he had never put more into his work than he had done in the last few years, he had to admit that he had never got so little out of it. He was paying for success, too, in the demands made on his time by boards of civic enterprise and committees of public welfare. The obligations imposed by his wife's fortune and position were sometimes distracting to a man who followed his profession, and he was expected to be interested in a great many worthy endeavors on her account as well as on his own. His existence was becoming a network of great and little details. He had expected that success would bring him freedom and power; but it had brought only power that was in itself another kind of restraint. He had always meant to keep his personal liberty at all costs, as old Mac-Keller, his first chief, had done, and not, like so many American engineers, to become a part of a professional movement, a cautious board member, a Nestor *de pontibus*. He happened to be engaged in work of public utility, but he was not willing to become what is called a public man. He found himself living exactly the kind of life he had determined to escape. What, he asked himself, did he want with these genial honors and substantial comforts? Hardships and difficulties he had carried lightly; overwork had not exhausted him; but this dead calm of middle life which confronted him, — of that he was afraid. He was not ready for it. It was like being buried alive. In his youth he would not have believed such a thing possible. The one thing he had really wanted all his life was to be free; and there was still something unconquered in him, something besides the strong workhorse that his profession had made of him. He felt rich to-night in the possession of that unstultified survival; in the light of his experience, it was more precious than honors or achievement. In all those busy, successful years there had been nothing so good as this hour of wild light-heartedness. This feeling was the only happiness that was real to him, and such hours were the only ones in which he could feel his own continuous identity — feel the boy he had been in the rough days of the old West, feel the youth who had worked his way across the ocean on a cattle-ship and gone to study in Paris without a dollar in his pocket. The man who sat in his offices in Boston was only a powerful machine. Under the activities of that machine the person who, in such moments as this, he felt to be himself, was fading and dying. He remembered how, when he was a little boy and his father called him in the morning, he used to leap from his bed into the full consciousness of himself. That consciousness was Life itself. Whatever took its place, action, reflection, the power of concentrated thought, were only functions of a mechanism useful to society; things that could be bought in the market. There was only one thing that had an absolute value for each individual, and it was just that original impulse, that internal heat, that feeling of one's self in one's own breast.

When Alexander walked back to his hotel, the red and green lights were blinking along the docks on the farther shore, and the soft white stars were shining in the wide sky above the river.

The next night, and the next, Alexander repeated this same foolish performance. It was always Miss Burgoyne whom he started out to find, and he got no farther than the Temple gardens and the Embankment. It was a pleasant kind of loneliness. To a man who was so little given to reflection, whose dreams always took the form of definite ideas, reaching into the future, there was a seductive excitement in renewing old experiences in imagination. He started out upon these walks half guiltily, with a curious longing and expectancy which were wholly gratified by solitude. Solitude, but not solitariness; for he walked shoulder to shoulder with a shadowy companion — not little Hilda Burgoyne, by any means, but some one vastly dearer to him than she had ever been — his own young self, the youth who had waited for him upon the steps of the British Museum that night, and who, though he had tried to pass so quietly, had known him and come down and linked an arm in his.

It was not until long afterward that Alexander

learned that for him this youth was the most dangerous of companions.

One Sunday evening, at Lady Walford's, Alexander did at last meet Hilda Burgoyne. Mainhall had told him that she would probably be there. He looked about for her rather nervously, and finally found her at the farther end of the large drawing-room, the centre of a circle of men, young and old. She was apparently telling them a story. They were all laughing and bending toward her. When she saw Alexander, she rose quickly and put out her hand. The other men drew back a little to let him approach.

"Mr. Alexander! I am delighted. Have you been in London long?"

Bartley bowed, somewhat laboriously, over her hand. "Long enough to have seen you more than once. How fine it all is!"

She laughed as if she were pleased. "I'm glad you think so. I like it. Won't you join us here?"

"Miss Burgoyne was just telling us about a donkey-boy she had in Galway last summer," Sir Harry Towne explained as the circle closed up again. Lord Westmere stroked his long white mustache with his bloodless hand and looked at Alexander blankly. Hilda was a good story-teller. She was sitting on the edge of her chair, as if she had alighted there for a moment only. Her primrose satin gown seemed like a soft sheath for her slender, supple figure, and its delicate color suited her white Irish skin and brown hair. Whatever she wore, people felt the charm of her active, girlish body with its slender hips and quick, eager shoulders. Alexander heard little of the story, but he watched Hilda intently. She must certainly, he reflected, be thirty, and he was honestly delighted to see that the years had treated her so indulgently. If her face had changed at all, it was in a slight hardening of the mouth — still eager enough to be very disconcerting at times, he felt — and in an added air of self-possession and self-reliance. She carried her head, too, a little more resolutely.

When the story was finished, Miss Burgoyne turned pointedly to Alexander, and the other men drifted away.

"I thought I saw you in MacConnell's box with Mainhall one evening, but I supposed you had left town before this."

She looked at him frankly and cordially, as if he were indeed merely an old friend whom she was glad to meet again.

"No, I've been mooning about here."

Hilda laughed gayly. "Mooning! I see you mooning! You must be the busiest man in the world. Time and success have done well by you, you know. You're handsomer than ever and you've gained a grand manner."

Alexander blushed and bowed. "Time and success have been good friends to both of us. Aren't you tremendously pleased with yourself?"

She laughed again and shrugged her shoulders. "Oh, so-so. But I want to hear about you. Several years ago I read such a lot in the papers about the wonderful things you did in Japan, and how the Emperor decorated you. What was it, Commander of the Order of the Rising Sun? That sounds like 'The Mikado.' And what about your new bridge — in Canada, isn't it, and it's to be the longest one in the world and has some queer name I can't remember."

Bartley shook his head and smiled drolly. "Since

when have you been interested in bridges? Or have you learned to be interested in everything? And is that a part of success?"

"Why, how absurd! As if I were not always interested!" Hilda exclaimed.

"Well, I think we won't talk about bridges here, at any rate." Bartley looked down at the toe of her yellow slipper which was tapping the rug impatiently under the hem of her gown. "But I wonder whether you'd think me impertinent if I asked you to let me come to see you sometime and tell you about them?"

"Why should I? Ever so many people come on Sunday afternoons."

"I know. Mainhall offered to take me. But you must know that I've been in London several times within the last few years, and you might very well think that just now is a rather inopportune time —"

She cut him short. "Nonsense. One of the pleasantest things about success is that it makes people want to look one up, if that's what you mean. I'm like every one else — more agreeable to meet when things are going well with me. Don't you suppose it gives me any pleasure to do something that people like?"

"Does it? Oh, how fine it all is, your coming on like this! But I didn't want you to think it was because of that I wanted to see you." He spoke very seriously and looked down at the floor.

Hilda studied him in wide-eyed astonishment for a moment, and then broke into a low, amused laugh. "My dear Mr. Alexander, you have strange delicacies. If you please, that is exactly why you wish to see me. We understand that, do we not?"

Bartley looked ruffled and turned the seal ring

363

on his little finger about awkwardly.

Hilda leaned back in her chair, watching him indulgently out of her shrewd eyes. "Come, don't be angry, but don't try to pose for me, or to be anything but what you are. If you care to come, it's yourself I'll be glad to see, and you thinking well of yourself. Don't try to wear a cloak of humility; it doesn't become you. Stalk in as you are and don't make excuses. I'm not accustomed to inquiring into the motives of my guests. That would hardly be safe, even for Lady Walford, in a great house like this."

"Sunday afternoon, then," said Alexander, as she rose to join her hostess. "How early may I come?"

She gave him her hand and flushed and laughed. He bent over it a little stiffly. She went away on Lady Walford's arm, and as he stood watching her yellow train glide down the long floor he looked rather sullen. He felt that he had not come out of it very brilliantly.

CHAPTER IV

On Sunday afternoon Alexander remembered Miss Burgoyne's invitation and called at her apartment. He found it a delightful little place and he met charming people there. Hilda lived alone, attended by a very pretty and competent French servant who answered the door and brought in the tea. Alexander arrived early, and some twenty-odd people dropped in during the course of the afternoon. Hugh MacConnell came with his sister, and stood about, managing his tea-cup awkwardly and watching every one out of his deep-set, faded eyes. He seemed to have made a resolute effort at tidiness of attire, and his sister, a robust, florid

364

woman with a splendid joviality about her, kept eyeing his freshly creased clothes apprehensively. It was not very long, indeed, before his coat hung with a discouraged sag from his gaunt shoulders and his hair and beard were rumpled as if he had been out in a gale. His dry humor went under a cloud of absent-minded kindliness which, Mainhall explained, always overtook him here. He was never so witty or so sharp here as elsewhere, and Alexander thought he behaved as if he were an elderly relative come in to a young girl's party.

The editor of a monthly review came with his wife, and Lady Kildare, the Irish philanthropist, brought her young nephew, Robert Owen, who had come up from Oxford, and who was visibly excited and gratified by his first introduction to Miss Burgoyne. Hilda was very nice to him, and he sat on the edge of his chair, flushed with his conversational efforts and moving his chin about nervously over his high collar. Sarah Frost, the novelist, came with her husband, a very genial and placid old scholar who had become slightly deranged upon the subject of the fourth dimension. On other matters he was perfectly rational and he was easy and pleasing in conversation. He looked very much like Agassiz, and his wife, in her old-fashioned black silk dress, overskirted and tight-sleeved, reminded Alexander of the early pictures of Mrs. Browning. Hilda seemed particularly fond of this quaint couple, and Bartley himself was so pleased with their mild and thoughtful converse that he took his leave when they did, and walked with them over to Oxford Street, where they waited for their 'bus. They asked him to come to see them in Chelsea, and they spoke very tenderly of Hilda. "She's a dear, unworldly little thing," said the philosopher absently; "more like the stage people of my young days — folk of simple manners. There aren't many such left. American tours have spoiled them, I'm afraid. They have all grown very smart. Lamb wouldn't care a great deal about many of them, I fancy."

Alexander went back to Bedford Square a second Sunday afternoon. He had a long talk with MacConnell, but he got no word with Hilda alone, and he left in a discontented state of mind. For the rest of the week he was nervous and unsettled, and kept rushing his work as if he were preparing for immediate departure. On Thursday afternoon he cut short a committee meeting, jumped into a hansom, and drove to Bedford Square. He sent up his card, but it came back to him with a message scribbled across the front.

> So sorry I can't see you. Will you come and dine with me Sunday evening at half-past seven?
>
> H.B.

When Bartley arrived at Bedford Square on Sunday evening, Marie, the pretty little French girl, met him at the door and conducted him upstairs. Hilda was writing in her living-room, under the light of a tall desk lamp. Bartley recognized the primrose satin gown she had worn that first evening at Lady Walford's.

"I'm so pleased that you think me worth that yellow dress, you know," he said, taking her hand and looking her over admiringly from the toes of her canary slippers to her smoothly parted brown hair. "Yes, it's very, very pretty. Every one at Lady Walford's was looking at it."

Hilda curtsied. "Is that why you think it pretty? I've no need for fine clothes in Mac's play this time, so I can afford a few duddies for myself. It's owing to that same chance, by the way, that I am able to ask you to dinner. I don't need Marie to dress me this season, so she keeps house for me, and my little Galway girl has gone home for a visit. I should never have asked you if Molly had been here, for I remember you don't like English cookery."

Alexander walked about the room, looking at everything.

"I haven't had a chance yet to tell you what a jolly little place I think this is. Where did you get those etchings? They're quite unusual, aren't they?"

"Lady Westmere sent them to me from Rome last Christmas. She is very much interested in the American artist who did them. They are all sketches made about the Villa d'Este, you see. He painted that group of cypresses for the Salon, and it was bought for the Luxembourg."

Alexander walked over to the bookcases. "It's the air of the whole place here that I like. You haven't got anything that doesn't belong. Seems to me it looks particularly well to-night. And you have so many flowers. I like these little yellow irises."

"Rooms always look better by lamplight — in London, at least. Though Marie is clean — really clean, as the French are. Why do you look at the flowers so critically? Marie got them all fresh in Covent Garden market yesterday morning."

"I'm glad," said Alexander simply. "I can't tell you how glad I am to have you so pretty and comfortable here, and to hear every one saying such nice things about you. You've got awfully nice friends," he added humbly, picking up a little jade elephant from her desk. "Those fellows are all very loyal, even Mainhall. They don't talk of any one else as they do of you."

Hilda sat down on the couch and said seriously: "I've a neat little sum in the bank, too, now, and I own a mite of a hut in Galway. It's not worth much, but I love it. I've managed to save something every year, and that with helping my three sisters now and then, and tiding poor Cousin Mike over bad seasons. He's that gifted, you know, but he will drink and loses more good engagements than other fellows ever get. And I've traveled a bit, too."

Marie opened the door and smilingly announced that dinner was served.

"My dining-room," Hilda explained, as she led the way, "is the tiniest place you have ever seen."

It was a tiny room, hung all round with French prints, above which ran a shelf full of china. Hilda saw Alexander look up at it.

"It's not particularly rare," she said, "but some of it was my mother's. Heaven knows how she managed to keep it whole, through all our wanderings, or in what baskets and bundles and theatre trunks it hasn't been stowed away. We always had our tea out of those blue cups when I was a little girl, sometimes in the queerest lodgings, and sometimes on a trunk at the theatre — queer theatres, for that matter."

It was a wonderful little dinner. There was watercress soup, and sole, and a delightful omelette stuffed with mushrooms and truffles, and two small rare ducklings, and artichokes, and a dry yellow Rhone wine of which Bartley had always

368

been very fond. He drank it appreciatively and remarked that there was still no other he liked so well.

"I have some champagne for you, too. I don't drink it myself, but I like to see it behave when it's poured. There is nothing else that looks so jolly."

"Thank you. But I don't like it so well as this." Bartley held the yellow wine against the light and squinted into it as he turned the glass slowly about. "You have traveled, you say. Have you been in Paris much these late years?"

Hilda lowered one of the candle-shades carefully. "Oh, yes, I go over to Paris often. There are few changes in the old Quarter. Dear old Madame Anger is dead — but perhaps you don't remember her?"

"Don't I, though! I'm so sorry to hear it. How did her son turn out? I remember how she saved and scraped for him, and how he always lay abed till ten o'clock. He was the laziest fellow at the Beaux Arts; and that's saying a good deal."

"Well, he is still clever and lazy. They say he is a good architect when he will work. He's a big, handsome creature, and he hates Americans as much as ever. But Angel — do you remember Angel?"

"Perfectly. Did she ever get back to Brittany and her *bains de mer*?"

"Ah, no. Poor Angel! She got tired of cooking and scouring the coppers in Madame Anger's little kitchen, so she ran away with a soldier, and then with another soldier. Too bad! She still lives about the Quarter, and, though there is always a *soldat*, she has become a *blanchisseuse de fin*. She did my blouses beautifully the last time I was there,

369

and was so delighted to see me again. I gave her all my old clothes, even my old hats, though she always wears her Breton headdress. Her hair is still like flax, and her blue eyes are just like a baby's, and she has the same three freckles on her little nose, and talks about going back to her *bains de mer.*"

Bartley looked at Hilda across the yellow light of the candles and broke into a low, happy laugh. "How jolly it was being young, Hilda! Do you remember that first walk we took together in Paris? We walked down to the Place Saint-Michel to buy some lilacs. Do you remember how sweet they smelled?"

"Indeed I do. Come, we'll have our coffee in the other room, and you can smoke."

Hilda rose quickly, as if she wished to change the drift of their talk, but Bartley found it pleasant to continue it.

"What a warm, soft spring evening that was," he went on, as they sat down in the study with the coffee on a little table between them; "and the sky, over the bridges, was just the color of the lilacs. We walked on down by the river, didn't we?"

Hilda laughed and looked at him questioningly. He saw a gleam in her eyes that he remembered even better than the episode he was recalling.

"I think we did," she answered demurely. "It was on the Quai we met that woman who was crying so bitterly. I gave her a spray of lilac, I remember, and you gave her a franc. I was frightened at your prodigality."

"I expect it was the last franc I had. What a strong brown face she had, and very tragic. She looked at us with such despair and longing, out from under her black shawl. What she wanted from us was neither our flowers nor our francs, but just our youth. I remember it touched me so. I would have given her some of mine off my back, if I could. I had enough and to spare then," Bartley mused, and looked thoughtfully at his cigar.

They were both remembering what the woman had said when she took the money: "God give you a happy love!" It was not in the ingratiating tone of the habitual beggar: it had come out of the depths of the poor creature's sorrow, vibrating with pity for their youth and despair at the terribleness of human life; it had the anguish of a voice of prophecy. Until she spoke, Bartley had not realized that he was in love. The strange woman, and her passionate sentence that rang out so sharply, had frightened them both. They went home sadly with the lilacs, back to the Rue Saint-Jacques, walking very slowly, arm in arm. When they reached the house where Hilda lodged, Bartley went across the court with her, and up the dark old stairs to the third landing; and there he had kissed her for the first time. He had shut his eyes to give him the courage, he remembered, and she had trembled so —

Bartley started when Hilda rang the little bell beside her. "Dear me, why did you do that? I had quite forgotten — I was back there. It was very jolly," he murmured lazily, as Marie came in to take away the coffee.

Hilda laughed and went over to the piano. "Well, we are neither of us twenty now, you know. Have I told you about my new play? Mac is writing one; really for me this time. You see, I'm coming on."

"I've seen nothing else. What kind of a part is it? Shall you wear yellow gowns? I hope so."

He was looking at her round slender figure, as

371

she stood by the piano, turning over a pile of music, and he felt the energy in every line of it.

"No, it isn't a dress-up part. He doesn't seem to fancy me in fine feathers. He says I ought to be minding the pigs at home, and I suppose I ought. But he's given me some good Irish songs. Listen."

She sat down at the piano and sang. When she finished, Alexander shook himself out of a reverie.

"Sing 'The Harp That Once,' Hilda. You used to sing it so well."

"Nonsense. Of course I can't really sing, except the way my mother and grandmother did before me. Most actresses nowadays learn to sing properly, so I tried a master; but he confused me, just!"

Alexander laughed. "All the same, sing it, Hilda."

Hilda started up from the stool and moved restlessly toward the window. "It's really too warm in this room to sing. Don't you feel it?"

Alexander went over and opened the window for her. "Aren't you afraid to let the wind low like that on your neck? Can't I get a scarf or something?"

"Ask a theatre lady if she's afraid of drafts!" Hilda laughed. "But perhaps, as I'm so warm — give me your handkerchief. There, just in front." He slipped the corners carefully under her shoulder-straps. "There, that will do. It looks like a bib." She pushed his hand away quickly and stood looking out into the deserted square. "Isn't London a tomb on Sunday night?"

Alexander caught the agitation in her voice. He stood a little behind her, and tried to steady himself as he said: "It's soft and misty. See how white the stars are."

For a long time neither Hilda nor Bartley spoke.

They stood close together, looking out into the wan, watery sky, breathing always more quickly and lightly, and it seemed as if all the clocks in the world had stopped. Suddenly he moved the clenched hand he held behind him and dropped it violently at his side. He felt a tremor run through the slender yellow figure in front of him.

She caught his handkerchief from her throat and thrust it at him without turning round. "Here, take it. You must go now, Bartley. Good-night."

Bartley leaned over her shoulder, without touching her, and whispered in her ear: "You are giving me a chance?"

"Yes. Take it and go. This isn't fair, you know. Good-night."

Alexander unclenched the two hands at his sides. With one he threw down the window and with the other — still standing behind her — he drew her back against him.

She uttered a little cry, threw her arms over her head, and drew his face down to hers. "Are you going to let me love you a little, Bartley?" she whispered.

CHAPTER V

It was the afternoon of the day before Christmas. Mrs. Alexander had been driving about all the morning, leaving presents at the houses of her friends. She lunched alone, and as she rose from the table she spoke to the butler: "Thomas, I am going down to the kitchen now to see Norah. In half an hour you are to bring the greens up from the cellar and put them in the library. Mr. Alexander will be home at three to hang them himself. Don't forget the stepladder, and plenty of tacks and string. You may bring the azaleas upstairs.

Take the white one to Mr. Alexander's study. Put the two pink ones in this room, and the red one in the drawing-room."

A little before three o'clock Mrs. Alexander went into the library to see that everything was ready. She pulled the window shades high, for the weather was dark and stormy, and there was little light, even in the streets. A foot of snow had fallen during the morning, and the wide space over the river was thick with flying flakes that fell and wreathed the masses of floating ice. Winifred was standing by the window when she heard the front door open. She hurried to the hall as Alexander came stamping in, covered with snow. He kissed her joyfully and brushed away the snow that fell on her hair.

"I wish I had asked you to meet me at the office and walk home with me, Winifred. The Common is beautiful. The boys have swept the snow off the pond and are skating furiously. Did the cyclamens come?"

"An hour ago. What splendid ones! But aren't you frightfully extravagant?"

"Not for Christmas-time. I'll go upstairs and change my coat. I shall be down in a moment. Tell Thomas to get everything ready."

When Alexander reappeared, he took his wife's arm and went with her into the library. "When did the azaleas get here? Thomas has got the white one in my room."

"I told him to put it there."

"But, I say, it's much the finest of the lot!"

"That's why I had it put there. There is too much color in that room for a red one, you know."

Bartley began to sort the greens. "It looks very splendid there, but I feel piggish to have it.

374

However, we really spend more time there than anywhere else in the house. Will you hand me the holly?"

He climbed up the stepladder, which creaked under his weight, and began to twist the tough stems of the holly into the frame-work of the chandelier.

"I forgot to tell you that I had a letter from Wilson, this morning, explaining his telegram. He is coming on because an old uncle up in Vermont has conveniently died and left Wilson a little money — something like ten thousand. He's coming on to settle up the estate. Won't it be jolly to have him?"

"And how fine that he's come into a little money. I can see him posting down State Street to the steamship offices. He will get a good many trips out of that ten thousand. What can have detained him? I expected him here for luncheon."

"Those trains from Albany are always late. He'll be along sometime this afternoon. And now, don't you want to go upstairs and lie down for an hour? You've had a busy morning and I don't want you to be tired to-night."

After his wife went upstairs Alexander worked energetically at the greens for a few moments. Then, as he was cutting off a length of string, he sighed suddenly and sat down, staring out of the window at the snow. The animation died out of his face, but in his eyes there was a restless light, a look of apprehension and suspense. He kept clasping and unclasping his big hands as if he were trying to realize something. The clock ticked through the minutes of a half-hour and the afternoon outside began to thicken and darken turbidly. Alexander, since he first sat down, had not changed his position. He leaned forward, his hands between his knees, scarcely breathing, as if he were holding himself away from his surroundings, from the room, and from the very chair in which he sat, from everything except the wild eddies of snow above the river on which his eyes were fixed with feverish intentness, as if he were trying to project himself thither. When at last Lucius Wilson was announced, Alexander sprang eagerly to his feet and hurried to meet his old instructor.

"Hello, Wilson. What luck! Come into the library. We are to have a lot of people to dinner to-night, and Winifred's lying down. You will excuse her, won't you? And now what about yourself? Sit down and tell me everything."

"I think I'd rather move about, if you don't mind. I've been sitting in the train for a week, it seems to me." Wilson stood before the fire with his hands behind him and looked about the room. "You HAVE been busy. Bartley, if I'd had my choice of all possible places in which to spend Christmas, your house would certainly be the place I'd have chosen. Happy people do a great deal for their friends. A house like this throws its warmth out. I felt it distinctly as I was coming through the Berkshires. I could scarcely believe that I was to see Mrs. Bartley again so soon."

"Thank you, Wilson. She'll be as glad to see you. Shall we have tea now? I'll ring for Thomas to clear away this litter. Winifred says I always wreck the house when I try to do anything. Do you know, I am quite tired. Looks as if I were not used to work, doesn't it?" Alexander laughed and dropped into a chair. "You know, I'm sailing the day after New Year's."

"Again? Why, you've been over twice since I was here in the spring, haven't you?"

"Oh, I was in London about ten days in the summer. Went to escape the hot weather more than anything else. I shan't be gone more than a month this time. Winifred and I have been up in Canada for most of the autumn. That Moorlock Bridge is on my back all the time. I never had so much trouble with a job before." Alexander moved about restlessly and fell to poking the fire.

"Haven't I seen in the papers that there is some trouble about a tidewater bridge of yours in New Jersey?"

"Oh, that doesn't amount to anything. It's held up by a steel strike. A bother, of course, but the sort of thing one is always having to put up with. But the Moorlock Bridge is a continual anxiety. You see, the truth is, we are having to build pretty well to the strain limit up there. They've crowded me too much on the cost. It's all very well if everything goes well, but these estimates have never been used for anything of such length before. However, there's nothing to be done. They hold me to the scale I've used in shorter bridges. The last thing a bridge commission cares about is the kind of bridge you build."

When Bartley had finished dressing for dinner he went into his study, where he found his wife arranging flowers on his writing-table.

"These pink roses just came from Mrs. Hastings," she said, smiling, "and I am sure she meant them for you."

Bartley looked about with an air of satisfaction at the greens and the wreaths in the windows. "Have you a moment, Winifred? I have just now

377

been thinking that this is our twelfth Christmas. Can you realize it?" He went up to the table and took her hands away from the flowers, drying them with his pocket handkerchief. "They've been awfully happy ones, all of them, haven't they?" He took her in his arms and bent back, lifting her a little and giving her a long kiss. "You are happy, aren't you Winifred? More than anything else in the world, I want you to be happy. Sometimes, of late, I've thought you looked as if you were troubled."

"No; it's only when you are troubled and harassed that I feel worried, Bartley. I wish you always seemed as you do to-night. But you don't, always." She looked earnestly and inquiringly into his eyes.

Alexander took her two hands from his shoulders and swung them back and forth in his own, laughing his big blond laugh.

"I'm growing older, my dear; that's what you feel. Now, may I show you something? I meant to save them until to-morrow, but I want you to wear them to-night." He took a little leather box out of his pocket and opened it. On the white velvet lay two long pendants of curiously worked gold, set with pearls. Winifred looked from the box to Bartley and exclaimed: —

"Where did you ever find such gold work, Bartley?"

"It's old Flemish. Isn't it fine?"

"They are the most beautiful things, dear. But, you know, I never wear earrings."

"Yes, yes, I know. But I want you to wear them. I have always wanted you to. So few women can. There must be a good ear, to begin with, and a nose" — he waved his hand — "above reproach.

378

Most women look silly in them. They go only with faces like yours — very, very proud, and just a little hard."

Winifred laughed as she went over to the mirror and fitted the delicate springs to the lobes of her ears. "Oh, Bartley, that old foolishness about my being hard. It really hurts my feelings. But I must go down now. People are beginning to come."

Bartley drew her arm about his neck and went to the door with her. "Not hard to me, Winifred," he whispered. "Never, never hard to me."

Left alone, he paced up and down his study. He was at home again, among all the dear familiar things that spoke to him of so many happy years. His house to-night would be full of charming people, who liked and admired him. Yet all the time, underneath his pleasure and hopefulness and satisfaction, he was conscious of the vibration of an unnatural excitement. Amid this light and warmth and friendliness, he sometimes started and shuddered, as if some one had stepped on his grave. Something had broken loose in him of which he knew nothing except that it was sullen and powerful, and that it wrung and tortured him. Sometimes it came upon him softly, in enervating reveries. Sometimes it battered him like the cannon rolling in the hold of the vessel. Always, now, it brought with it a sense of quickened life, of stimulating danger. To-night it came upon him suddenly, as he was walking the floor, after his wife left him. It seemed impossible; he could not believe it. He glanced entreatingly at the door, as if to call her back. He heard voices in the hall below, and knew that he must go down. Going over to the window, he looked out at the lights across the river. How could this happen here, in his own house, among the things he loved? What was it that reached in out of the darkness and thrilled him? As he stood there he had a feeling that he would never escape. He shut his eyes and pressed his forehead against the cold window glass, breathing in the chill that came through it. "That this," he groaned, "that this should have happened to ME!"

On New Year's day a thaw set in, and during the night torrents of rain fell. In the morning, the morning of Alexander's departure for England, the river was streaked with fog and the rain drove hard against the windows of the breakfast-room. Alexander had finished his coffee and was pacing up and down. His wife sat at the table, watching him. She was pale and unnaturally calm. When Thomas brought the letters, Bartley sank into his chair and ran them over rapidly.

"Here's a note from old Wilson. He's safe back at his grind, and says he had a bully time. 'The memory of Mrs. Bartley will make my whole winter fragrant.' Just like him. He will go on getting measureless satisfaction out of you by his study fire. What a man he is for looking on at life!" Bartley sighed, pushed the letters back impatiently, and went over to the window. "This is a nasty sort of day to sail. I've a notion to call it off. Next week would be time enough."

"That would only mean starting twice. It wouldn't really help you out at all," Mrs. Alexander spoke soothingly. "And you'd come back late for all your engagements."

Bartley began jingling some loose coins in his pocket. "I wish things would let me rest. I'm tired of work, tired of people, tired of trailing about."

He looked out at the storm-beaten river.

Winifred came up behind him and put a hand on his shoulder. "That's what you always say, poor Bartley! At bottom you really like all these things. Can't you remember that?"

He put his arm about her. "All the same, life runs smoothly enough with some people, and with me it's always a messy sort of patchwork. It's like the song; peace is where I am not. How can you face it all with so much fortitude?"

She looked at him with that clear gaze which Wilson had so much admired, which he had felt implied such high confidence and fearless pride. "Oh, I faced that long ago, when you were on your first bridge, up at old Allway. I knew then that your paths were not to be paths of peace, but I decided that I wanted to follow them."

Bartley and his wife stood silent for a long time; the fire crackled in the grate, the rain beat insistently upon the windows, and the sleepy Angora looked up at them curiously.

Presently Thomas made a discreet sound at the door. "Shall Edward bring down your trunks, sir?"

"Yes; they are ready. Tell him not to forget the big portfolio on the study table."

Thomas withdrew, closing the door softly. Bartley turned away from his wife, still holding her hand. "It never gets any easier, Winifred."

They both started at the sound of the carriage on the pavement outside. Alexander sat down and leaned his head on his hand. His wife bent over him. "Courage," she said gayly. Bartley rose and rang the bell. Thomas brought him his hat and stick and ulster. At the sight of these, the supercilious Angora moved restlessly, quitted her red cushion by the fire, and came up, waving her tail in vexation at these ominous indications of change. Alexander stooped to stroke her, and then plunged into his coat and drew on his gloves. His wife held his stick, smiling. Bartley smiled too, and his eyes cleared. "I'll work like the devil, Winifred, and be home again before you realize I've gone." He kissed her quickly several times, hurried out of the front door into the rain, and waved to her from the carriage window as the driver was starting his melancholy, dripping black horses. Alexander sat with his hands clenched on his knees. As the carriage turned up the hill, he lifted one hand and brought it down violently. "This time" — he spoke aloud and through his set teeth — "this time I'm going to end it!"

On the afternoon of the third day out, Alexander was sitting well to the stern, on the windward side where the chairs were few, his rugs over him and the collar of his fur-lined coat turned up about his ears. The weather had so far been dark and raw. For two hours he had been watching the low, dirty sky and the beating of the heavy rain upon the iron-colored sea. There was a long, oily swell that made exercise laborious. The decks smelled of damp woolens, and the air was so humid that drops of moisture kept gathering upon his hair and mustache. He seldom moved except to brush them away. The great open spaces made him passive and the restlessness of the water quieted him. He intended during the voyage to decide upon a course of action, but he held all this away from him for the present and lay in a blessed gray oblivion. Deep down in him somewhere his resolution was weakening and strengthening, ebbing and flowing. The thing that perturbed him went on as steadily as his pulse, but he was almost unconscious of it. He was submerged in the vast impersonal grayness about him, and at intervals the sidelong roll of the boat measured off time like the ticking of a clock. He felt released from everything that troubled and perplexed him. It was as if he had tricked and outwitted torturing memories, had actually managed to get on board without them. He thought of nothing at all. If his mind now and again picked a face out of the grayness, it was Lucius Wilson's, or the face of an old schoolmate, forgotten for years; or it was the slim outline of a favorite greyhound he used to hunt jack-rabbits with when he was a boy.

Toward six o'clock the wind rose and tugged at the tarpaulin and brought the swell higher. After dinner Alexander came back to the wet deck, piled his damp rugs over him again, and sat smoking, losing himself in the obliterating blackness and drowsing in the rush of the gale. Before he went below a few bright stars were pricked off between heavily moving masses of cloud.

The next morning was bright and mild, with a fresh breeze. Alexander felt the need of exercise even before he came out of his cabin. When he went on deck the sky was blue and blinding, with heavy whiffs of white cloud, smoke-colored at the edges, moving rapidly across it. The water was roughish, a cold, clear indigo breaking into whitecaps. Bartley walked for two hours, and then stretched himself in the sun until lunch-time.

In the afternoon he wrote a long letter to Winifred. Later, as he walked the deck through a splendid golden sunset, his spirits rose continually. It was agreeable to come to himself again after several days of numbness and torpor. He stayed out until the last tinge of violet had faded from the water. There was literally a taste of life on his lips as he sat down to dinner and ordered a bottle of champagne. He was late in finishing his dinner, and drank rather more wine than he had meant to. When he went above, the wind had risen and the deck was almost deserted. As he stepped out of the door a gale lifted his heavy fur coat about his shoulders. He fought his way up the deck with keen exhilaration. The moment he stepped, almost out of breath, behind the shelter of the stern, the wind was cut off, and he felt, like a rush of warm air, a sense of close and intimate companionship. He started back and tore his coat open as if something warm were actually clinging to him beneath it. He hurried up the deck and went into the saloon parlor, full of women who had retreated thither from the sharp wind. He threw himself upon them. He talked delightfully to the older ones and played accompaniments for the younger ones until the last sleepy girl had followed her mother below. Then he went into the smoking-room. He played bridge until two o'clock in the morning, and managed to lose a considerable sum of money without really noticing that he was doing so.

After the break of one fine day the weather was pretty consistently dull. When the low sky thinned a trifle, the pale white spot of a sun did no more than throw a bluish lustre on the water, giving it the dark brightness of newly cut lead. Through one after another of those gray days Alexander drowsed and mused, drinking in the grateful moisture. But the complete peace of the first part of the voyage was over. Sometimes he rose suddenly from his chair as if driven out, and paced the deck for hours. People noticed his propensity for walking in rough weather, and watched him curiously as he did his rounds. From his abstraction and the determined set of his jaw, they fancied he must be thinking about his bridge. Every one had heard of the new cantilever bridge in Canada.

But Alexander was not thinking about his work. After the fourth night out, when his will suddenly softened under his hands, he had been continually hammering away at himself. More and more often, when he first wakened in the morning or when he stepped into a warm place after being chilled on the deck, he felt a sudden painful delight at being nearer another shore. Sometimes when he was most despondent, when he thought himself worn out with this struggle, in a flash he was free of it and leaped into an overwhelming consciousness of himself. On the instant he felt that marvelous return of the impetuousness, the intense excitement, the increasing expectancy of youth.

CHAPTER VI

The last two days of the voyage Bartley found almost intolerable. The stop at Queenstown, the tedious passage up the Mersey, were things that he noted dimly through his growing impatience. He had planned to stop in Liverpool; but, instead, he took the boat train for London.

Emerging at Euston at half-past three o'clock in the afternoon, Alexander had his luggage sent to the Savoy and drove at once to Bedford Square. When Marie met him at the door, even her strong sense of the proprieties could not restrain her surprise and delight. She blushed and smiled and fumbled his card in her confusion before she ran upstairs. Alexander paced up and down the hallway, buttoning and unbuttoning his overcoat, until she returned and took him up to Hilda's living-room. The room was empty when he entered. A coal fire was crackling in the grate and the lamps were lit, for it was already beginning to grow dark outside. Alexander did not sit down. He stood his ground over by the windows until Hilda came in. She called his name on the threshold, but in her swift flight across the room she felt a change in him and caught herself up so deftly that he could not tell just when she did it. She merely brushed his cheek with her lips and put a hand lightly and joyously on either shoulder.

"Oh, what a grand thing to happen on a raw day! I felt it in my bones when I woke this morning that something splendid was going to turn up. I thought it might be Sister Kate or Cousin Mike would be happening along. I never dreamed it would be you, Bartley. But why do you let me chatter on like this? Come over to the fire; you're chilled through."

She pushed him toward the big chair by the fire, and sat down on a stool at the opposite side of the hearth, her knees drawn up to her chin, laughing like a happy little girl.

"When did you come, Bartley, and how did it happen? You haven't spoken a word."

"I got in about ten minutes ago. I landed at Liverpool this morning and came down on the boat train."

Alexander leaned forward and warmed his hands before the blaze. Hilda watched him with perplexity.

386

"There's something troubling you, Bartley. What is it?"

Bartley bent lower over the fire. "It's the whole thing that troubles me, Hilda. You and I."

Hilda took a quick, soft breath. She looked at his heavy shoulders and big, determined head, thrust forward like a catapult in leash.

"What about us, Bartley?" she asked in a thin voice.

He locked and unlocked his hands over the grate and spread his fingers close to the bluish flame, while the coals crackled and the clock ticked and a street vendor began to call under the window. At last Alexander brought out one word: —

"Everything!"

Hilda was pale by this time, and her eyes were wide with fright. She looked about desperately from Bartley to the door, then to the windows, and back again to Bartley. She rose uncertainly, touched his hair with her hand, then sank back upon her stool.

"I'll do anything you wish me to, Bartley," she said tremulously. "I can't stand seeing you miserable."

"I can't live with myself any longer," he answered roughly.

He rose and pushed the chair behind him and began to walk miserably about the room, seeming to find it too small for him. He pulled up a window as if the air were heavy.

Hilda watched him from her corner, trembling and scarcely breathing, dark shadows growing about her eyes.

"It . . . it hasn't always made you miserable, has it?" Her eyelids fell and her lips quivered.

"Always. But it's worse now. It's unbearable. It

387

tortures me every minute."

"But why NOW?" she asked piteously, wringing her hands.

He ignored her question. "I am not a man who can live two lives," he went on feverishly. "Each life spoils the other. I get nothing but misery out of either. The world is all there, just as it used to be, but I can't get at it any more. There is this deception between me and everything."

At that word "deception," spoken with such self-contempt, the color flashed back into Hilda's face as suddenly as if she had been struck by a whiplash. She bit her lip and looked down at her hands, which were clasped tightly in front of her.

"Could you — could you sit down and talk about it quietly, Bartley, as if I were a friend, and not some one who had to be defied?"

He dropped back heavily into his chair by the fire. "It was myself I was defying, Hilda. I have thought about it until I am worn out."

He looked at her and his haggard face softened. He put out his hand toward her as he looked away again into the fire.

She crept across to him, drawing her stool after her. "When did you first begin to feel like this, Bartley?"

"After the very first. The first was — sort of in play, wasn't it?"

Hilda's face quivered, but she whispered: "Yes, I think it must have been. But why didn't you tell me when you were here in the summer?"

Alexander groaned. "I meant to, but somehow I couldn't. We had only a few days, and your new play was just on, and you were so happy."

"Yes, I was happy, wasn't I?" She pressed his hand gently in gratitude. "Weren't you happy then, at all?"

She closed her eyes and took a deep breath, as if to draw in again the fragrance of those days. Something of their troubling sweetness came back to Alexander, too. He moved uneasily and his chair creaked.

"Yes, I was then. You know. But afterward . . ."

"Yes, yes," she hurried, pulling her hand gently away from him. Presently it stole back to his coat sleeve. "Please tell me one thing, Bartley. At least, tell me that you believe I thought I was making you happy."

His hand shut down quickly over the questioning fingers on his sleeves. "Yes, Hilda; I know that," he said simply.

She leaned her head against his arm and spoke softly: —

"You see, my mistake was in wanting you to have everything. I wanted you to eat all the cakes and have them, too. I somehow believed that I could take all the bad consequences for you. I wanted you always to be happy and handsome and successful — to have all the things that a great man ought to have, and, once in a way, the careless holidays that great men are not permitted."

Bartley gave a bitter little laugh, and Hilda looked up and read in the deepening lines of his face that youth and Bartley would not much longer struggle together.

"I understand, Bartley. I was wrong. But I didn't know. You've only to tell me now. What must I do that I've not done, or what must I not do?" She listened intently, but she heard nothing but the creaking of his chair. "You want me to say it?" she whispered. "You want to tell me that you can only see me like this, as old friends do, or out in the

389

world among people? I can do that."

"I can't," he said heavily.

Hilda shivered and sat still. Bartley leaned his head in his hands and spoke through his teeth. "It's got to be a clean break, Hilda. I can't see you at all, anywhere. What I mean is that I want you to promise never to see me again, no matter how often I come, no matter how hard I beg."

Hilda sprang up like a flame. She stood over him with her hands clenched at her side, her body rigid.

"No!" she gasped. "It's too late to ask that. Do you hear me, Bartley? It's too late. I won't promise. It's abominable of you to ask me. Keep away if you wish; when have I ever followed you? But, if you come to me, I'll do as I see fit. The shamefulness of your asking me to do that! If you come to me, I'll do as I see fit. Do you understand? Bartley, you're cowardly!"

Alexander rose and shook himself angrily. "Yes, I know I'm cowardly. I'm afraid of myself. I don't trust myself any more. I carried it all lightly enough at first, but now I don't dare trifle with it. It's getting the better of me. It's different now. I'm growing older, and you've got my young self here with you. It's through him that I've come to wish for you all and all the time." He took her roughly in his arms. "Do you know what I mean?"

Hilda held her face back from him and began to cry bitterly. "Oh, Bartley, what am I to do? Why didn't you let me be angry with you? You ask me to stay away from you because you want me! And I've got nobody but you. I will do anything you say — but that! I will ask the least imaginable, but I must have SOMETHING!"

Bartley turned away and sank down in his chair

390

again. Hilda sat on the arm of it and put her hands lightly on his shoulders.

"Just something Bartley. I must have you to think of through the months and months of loneliness. I must see you. I must know about you. The sight of you, Bartley, to see you living and happy and successful — can I never make you understand what that means to me?" She pressed his shoulders gently. "You see, loving some one as I love you makes the whole world different. If I'd met you later, if I hadn't loved you so well — but that's all over, long ago. Then came all those years without you, lonely and hurt and discouraged; those decent young fellows and poor Mac, and me never heeding — hard as a steel spring. And then you came back, not caring very much, but it made no difference."

She slid to the floor beside him, as if she were too tired to sit up any longer. Bartley bent over and took her in his arms, kissing her mouth and her wet, tired eyes.

"Don't cry, don't cry," he whispered. "We've tortured each other enough for tonight. Forget everything except that I am here."

"I think I have forgotten everything but that already," she murmured. "Ah, your dear arms!"

CHAPTER VII

During the fortnight that Alexander was in London he drove himself hard. He got through a great deal of personal business and saw a great many men who were doing interesting things in his own profession. He disliked to think of his visits to London as holidays, and when he was there he worked even harder than he did at home.

The day before his departure for Liverpool was

a singularly fine one. The thick air had cleared overnight in a strong wind which brought in a golden dawn and then fell off to a fresh breeze. When Bartley looked out of his windows from the Savoy, the river was flashing silver and the gray stone along the Embankment was bathed in bright, clear sunshine. London had wakened to life after three weeks of cold and sodden rain. Bartley breakfasted hurriedly and went over his mail while the hotel valet packed his trunks. Then he paid his account and walked rapidly down the Strand past Charing Cross Station. His spirits rose with every step, and when he reached Trafalgar Square, blazing in the sun, with its fountains playing and its column reaching up into the bright air, he signaled to a hansom, and, before he knew what he was about, told the driver to go to Bedford Square by way of the British Museum.

When he reached Hilda's apartment she met him, fresh as the morning itself. Her rooms were flooded with sunshine and full of the flowers he had been sending her. She would never let him give her anything else.

"Are you busy this morning, Hilda?" he asked as he sat down, his hat and gloves in his hand.

"Very. I've been up and about three hours, working at my part. We open in February, you know."

"Well, then you've worked enough. And so have I. I've seen all my men, my packing is done, and I go up to Liverpool this evening. But this morning we are going to have a holiday. What do you say to a drive out to Kew and Richmond? You may not get another day like this all winter. It's like a fine April day at home. May I use your telephone? I want to order the carriage."

"Oh, how jolly! There, sit down at the desk. And

while you are telephoning I'll change my dress. I shan't be long. All the morning papers are on the table."

Hilda was back in a few moments wearing a long gray squirrel coat and a broad fur hat.

Bartley rose and inspected her. "Why don't you wear some of those pink roses?" he asked.

"But they came only this morning, and they have not even begun to open. I was saving them. I am so unconsciously thrifty!" She laughed as she looked about the room. "You've been sending me far too many flowers, Bartley. New ones every day. That's too often; though I do love to open the boxes, and I take good care of them."

"Why won't you let me send you any of those jade or ivory things you are so fond of? Or pictures? I know a good deal about pictures."

Hilda shook her large hat as she drew the roses out of the tall glass. "No, there are some things you can't do. There's the carriage. Will you button my gloves for me?"

Bartley took her wrist and began to button the long gray suede glove. "How gay your eyes are this morning, Hilda."

"That's because I've been studying. It always stirs me up a little."

He pushed the top of the glove up slowly. "When did you learn to take hold of your parts like that?"

"When I had nothing else to think of. Come, the carriage is waiting. What a shocking while you take."

"I'm in no hurry. We've plenty of time."

They found all London abroad. Piccadilly was a stream of rapidly moving carriages, from which flashed furs and flowers and bright winter costumes. The metal trappings of the harnesses shone

393

dazzlingly, and the wheels were revolving disks that threw off rays of light. The parks were full of children and nursemaids and joyful dogs that leaped and yelped and scratched up the brown earth with their paws.

"I'm not going until to-morrow, you know," Bartley announced suddenly. "I'll cut off a day in Liverpool. I haven't felt so jolly this long while."

Hilda looked up with a smile which she tried not to make too glad. "I think people were meant to be happy, a little," she said.

They had lunch at Richmond and then walked to Twickenham, where they had sent the carriage. They drove back, with a glorious sunset behind them, toward the distant gold-washed city. It was one of those rare afternoons when all the thickness and shadow of London are changed to a kind of shining, pulsing, special atmosphere; when the smoky vapors become fluttering golden clouds, nacreous veils of pink and amber; when all that bleakness of gray stone and dullness of dirty brick trembles in aureate light, and all the roofs and spires, and one great dome, are floated in golden haze. On such rare afternoons the ugliest of cities becomes the most poetic, and months of sodden days are offset by a moment of miracle.

"It's like that with us Londoners, too," Hilda was saying. "Everything is awfully grim and cheerless, our weather and our houses and our ways of amusing ourselves. But we can be happier than anybody. We can go mad with joy, as the people do out in the fields on a fine Whitsunday. We make the most of our moment."

She thrust her little chin out defiantly over her gray fur collar, and Bartley looked down at her and laughed.

"You are a plucky one, you." He patted her glove with his hand. "Yes, you are a plucky one."

Hilda sighed. "No, I'm not. Not about some things, at any rate. It doesn't take pluck to fight for one's moment, but it takes pluck to go without — a lot. More than I have. I can't help it," she added fiercely.

After miles of outlying streets and little gloomy houses, they reached London itself, red and roaring and murky, with a thick dampness coming up from the river, that betokened fog again to-morrow. The streets were full of people who had worked indoors all through the priceless day and had now come hungrily out to drink the muddy lees of it. They stood in long black lines, waiting before the pit entrances of the theatres — short-coated boys, and girls in sailor hats, all shivering and chatting gayly. There was a blurred rhythm in all the dull city noises — in the clatter of the cab horses and the rumbling of the busses, in the street calls, and in the undulating tramp, tramp of the crowd. It was like the deep vibration of some vast underground machinery, and like the muffled pulsations of millions of human hearts.

"Seems good to get back, doesn't it?" Bartley whispered, as they drove from Bayswater Road into Oxford Street. "London always makes me want to live more than any other city in the world. You remember our priestess mummy over in the mummy-room, and how we used to long to go and bring her out on nights like this? Three thousand years! Ugh!"

"All the same, I believe she used to feel it when we stood there and watched her and wished her well. I believe she used to remember," Hilda said thoughtfully.

"I hope so. Now let's go to some awfully jolly place for dinner before we go home. I could eat all the dinners there are in London to-night. Where shall I tell the driver? The Piccadilly Restaurant? The music's good there."

"There are too many people there whom one knows. Why not that little French place in Soho, where we went so often when you were here in the summer? I love it, and I've never been there with any one but you. Sometimes I go by myself, when I am particularly lonely."

"Very well, the sole's good there. How many street pianos there are about to-night! The fine weather must have thawed them out. We've had five miles of 'Il Trovatore' now. They always make me feel jaunty. Are you comfy, and not too tired?"

"I'm not tired at all. I was just wondering how people can ever die. Why did you remind me of the mummy? Life seems the strongest and most indestructible thing in the world. Do you really believe that all those people rushing about down there, going to good dinners and clubs and theatres, will be dead some day, and not care about anything? I don't believe it, and I know I shan't die, ever! You see, I feel too — too powerful!"

The carriage stopped. Bartley sprang out and swung her quickly to the pavement. As he lifted her in his two hands he whispered: "You are — powerful!"

CHAPTER VIII

The last rehearsal was over, a tedious dress rehearsal which had lasted all day and exhausted the patience of every one who had to do with it. When Hilda had dressed for the street and came out of her dressing-room, she found Hugh Mac-Connell waiting for her in the corridor.

"The fog's thicker than ever, Hilda. There have been a great many accidents to-day. It's positively unsafe for you to be out alone. Will you let me take you home?"

"How good of you, Mac. If you are going with me, I think I'd rather walk. I've had no exercise to-day, and all this has made me nervous."

"I shouldn't wonder," said MacConnell dryly. Hilda pulled down her veil and they stepped out into the thick brown wash that submerged St. Martin's Lane. MacConnell took her hand and tucked it snugly under his arm. "I'm sorry I was such a savage. I hope you didn't think I made an ass of myself."

"Not a bit of it. I don't wonder you were peppery. Those things are awfully trying. How do you think it's going?"

"Magnificently. That's why I got so stirred up. We are going to hear from this, both of us. And that reminds me; I've got news for you. They are going to begin repairs on the theatre about the middle of March, and we are to run over to New York for six weeks. Bennett told me yesterday that it was decided."

Hilda looked up delightedly at the tall gray figure beside her. He was the only thing she could see, for they were moving through a dense opaqueness, as if they were walking at the bottom of the ocean.

"Oh, Mac, how glad I am! And they love your things over there, don't they?"

"Shall you be glad for — any other reason, Hilda?"

MacConnell put his hand in front of her to ward

off some dark object. It proved to be only a lamp-post, and they beat in farther from the edge of the pavement.

"What do you mean, Mac?" Hilda asked nervously.

"I was just thinking there might be people over there you'd be glad to see," he brought out awkwardly. Hilda said nothing, and as they walked on MacConnell spoke again, apologetically: "I hope you don't mind my knowing about it, Hilda. Don't stiffen up like that. No one else knows, and I didn't try to find out anything. I felt it, even before I knew who he was. I knew there was somebody, and that it wasn't I."

They crossed Oxford Street in silence, feeling their way. The busses had stopped running and the cab-drivers were leading their horses. When they reached the other side, MacConnell said suddenly, "I hope you are happy."

"Terribly, dangerously happy, Mac," — Hilda spoke quietly, pressing the rough sleeve of his greatcoat with her gloved hand.

"You've always thought me too old for you, Hilda, — oh, of course you've never said just that, — and here this fellow is not more than eight years younger than I. I've always felt that if I could get out of my old case I might win you yet. It's a fine, brave youth I carry inside me, only he'll never be seen."

"Nonsense, Mac. That has nothing to do with it. It's because you seem too close to me, too much my own kind. It would be like marrying Cousin Mike, almost. I really tried to care as you wanted me to, away back in the beginning."

"Well, here we are, turning out of the Square. You are not angry with me, Hilda? Thank you for this walk, my dear. Go in and get dry things on at once. You'll be having a great night to-morrow."

She put out her hand. "Thank you, Mac, for everything. Good-night."

MacConnell trudged off through the fog, and she went slowly upstairs. Her slippers and dress-ing gown were waiting for her before the fire. "I shall certainly see him in New York. He will see by the papers that we are coming. Perhaps he knows it already," Hilda kept thinking as she undressed. "Perhaps he will be at the dock. No, scarcely that; but I may meet him in the street even before he comes to see me." Marie placed the tea-table by the fire and brought Hilda her letters. She looked them over, and started as she came to one in a handwriting that she did not often see; Alexander had written to her only twice before, and he did not allow her to write to him at all. "Thank you, Marie. You may go now."

Hilda sat down by the table with the letter in her hand, still unopened. She looked at it intently, turned it over, and felt its thickness with her fingers. She believed that she sometimes had a kind of second-sight about letters, and could tell before she read them whether they brought good or evil tidings. She put this one down on the table in front of her while she poured her tea. At last, with a little shiver of expectancy, she tore open the envelope and read: —

BOSTON, February —

MY DEAR HILDA: —

It is after twelve o'clock. Every one else is in bed and I am sitting alone in my study. I have

399

been happier in this room than anywhere else in the world. Happiness like that makes one insolent. I used to think these four walls could stand against anything. And now I scarcely know myself here. Now I know that no one can build his security upon the nobleness of another person. Two people, when they love each other, grow alike in their tastes and habits and pride, but their moral natures (whatever we may mean by that canting expression) are never welded. The base one goes on being base, and the noble one noble, to the end.

The last week has been a bad one; I have been realizing how things used to be with me. Sometimes I get used to being dead inside, but lately it has been as if a window beside me had suddenly opened, and as if all the smells of spring blew in to me. There is a garden out there, with stars overhead, where I used to walk at night when I had a single purpose and a single heart. I can remember how I used to feel there, how beautiful everything about me was, and what life and power and freedom I felt in myself. When the window opens I know exactly how it would feel to be out there. But that garden is closed to me. How is it, I ask myself, that everything can be so different with me when nothing here has changed? I am in my own house, in my own study, in the midst of all these quiet streets where my friends live. They are all safe and at peace with themselves. But I am never at peace. I feel always on the edge of danger and change.

I keep remembering locoed horses I used to see on the range when I was a boy. They changed like that. We used to catch them and put them up in the corral, and they developed great cunning.

They would pretend to eat their oats like the other horses, but we knew they were always scheming to get back at the loco.

It seems that a man is meant to live only one life in this world. When he tries to live a second, he develops another nature. I feel as if a second man had been grafted into me. At first he seemed only a pleasure-loving simpleton, of whose company I was rather ashamed, and whom I used to hide under my coat when I walked the Embankment, in London. But now he is strong and sullen, and he is fighting for his life at the cost of mine. That is his one activity: to grow strong. No creature ever wanted so much to live. Eventually, I suppose, he will absorb me altogether. Believe me, you will hate me then.

And what have you to do, Hilda, with this ugly story? Nothing at all. The little boy drank of the prettiest brook in the forest and he became a stag. I write all this because I can never tell it to you, and because it seems as if I could not keep silent any longer. And because I suffer, Hilda. If any one I loved suffered like this, I'd want to know it. Help me, Hilda!

B.A.

CHAPTER IX

On the last Saturday in April, the New York "Times" published an account of the strike complications which were delaying Alexander's New Jersey bridge, and stated that the engineer himself was in town and at his office on West Tenth Street.

On Sunday, the day after this notice appeared, Alexander worked all day at his Tenth Street rooms. His business often called him to New York, and he had kept an apartment there for years, subletting it when he went abroad for any length of time. Besides his sleeping-room and bath, there was a large room, formerly a painter's studio, which he used as a study and office. It was furnished with the cast-off possessions of his bachelor days and with odd things which he sheltered for friends of his who followed itinerant and more or less artistic callings. Over the fireplace there was a large old-fashioned gilt mirror. Alexander's big work-table stood in front of one of the three windows, and above the couch hung the one picture in the room, a big canvas of charming color and spirit, a study of the Luxembourg Gardens in early spring, painted in his youth by a man who had since become a portrait-painter of international renown. He had done it for Alexander when they were students together in Paris.

Sunday was a cold, raw day and a fine rain fell continuously. When Alexander came back from dinner he put more wood on his fire, made himself comfortable, and settled down at his desk, where he began checking over estimate sheets. It was after nine o'clock and he was lighting a second pipe, when he thought he heard a sound at his door. He started and listened, holding the burning match in his hand; again he heard the same sound, like a firm, light tap. He rose and crossed the room quickly. When he threw open the door he recognized the figure that shrank back into the bare, dimly lit hallway. He stood for a moment in awkward constraint, his pipe in his hand.

"Come in," he said to Hilda at last, and closed the door behind her. He pointed to a chair by the fire and went back to his worktable. "Won't you sit down?"

He was standing behind the table, turning over a pile of blueprints nervously. The yellow light from the student's lamp fell on his hands and the purple sleeves of his velvet smoking-jacket, but his flushed face and big, hard head were in the shadow. There was something about him that made Hilda wish herself at her hotel again, in the street below, anywhere but where she was.

"Of course I know, Bartley," she said at last, "that after this you won't owe me the least consideration. But we sail on Tuesday. I saw that interview in the paper yesterday, telling where you were, and I thought I had to see you. That's all. Good-night; I'm going now." She turned and her hand closed on the door-knob.

Alexander hurried toward her and took her gently by the arm. "Sit down, Hilda; you're wet through. Let me take off your coat — and your boots; they're oozing water." He knelt down and began to unlace her shoes, while Hilda shrank into the chair. "Here, put your feet on this stool. You don't mean to say you walked down — and without overshoes!"

Hilda hid her face in her hands. "I was afraid to take a cab. Can't you see, Bartley, that I'm terribly frightened? I've been through this a hundred times to-day. Don't be any more angry than you can help. I was all right until I knew you were in town. If you'd sent me a note, or telephoned me, or anything! But you won't let me write to you, and I had to see you after that letter, that terrible letter you wrote me when you got home."

Alexander faced her, resting his arm on the mantel behind him, and began to brush the sleeve

403

of his jacket. "Is this the way you mean to answer it, Hilda?" he asked unsteadily.

She was afraid to look up at him. "Didn't — didn't you mean even to say goodby to me, Bartley? Did you mean just to — quit me?" she asked. "I came to tell you that I'm willing to do as you asked me. But it's no use talking about that now. Give me my things, please." She put her hand out toward the fender.

Alexander sat down on the arm of her chair. "Did you think I had forgotten you were in town, Hilda? Do you think I kept away by accident? Did you suppose I didn't know you were sailing on Tuesday? There is a letter for you there, in my desk drawer. It was to have reached you on the steamer. I was all the morning writing it. I told myself that if I were really thinking of you, and not of myself, a letter would be better than nothing. Marks on paper mean something to you." He paused. "They never did to me."

Hilda smiled up at him beautifully and put her hand on his sleeve. "Oh, Bartley! Did you write to me? Why didn't you telephone me to let me know that you had? Then I wouldn't have come."

Alexander slipped his arm about her. "I didn't know it before, Hilda, on my honor I didn't, but I believe it was because, deep down in me somewhere, I was hoping I might drive you to do just this. I've watched that door all day. I've jumped up if the fire crackled. I think I have felt that you were coming." He bent his face over her hair.

"And I," she whispered, — "I felt that you were feeling that. But when I came, I thought I had been mistaken."

Alexander started up and began to walk up and down the room.

404

"No, you weren't mistaken. I've been up in Canada with my bridge, and I arranged not to come to New York until after you had gone. Then, when your manager added two more weeks, I was already committed." He dropped upon the stool in front of her and sat with his hands hanging between his knees. "What am I to do, Hilda?"

"That's what I wanted to see you about, Bartley. I'm going to do what you asked me to do when you were in London. Only I'll do it more completely. I'm going to marry."

"Who?"

"Oh, it doesn't matter much! One of them. Only not Mac. I'm too fond of him."

Alexander moved restlessly. "Are you joking, Hilda?"

"Indeed I'm not."

"Then you don't know what you're talking about."

"Yes, I know very well. I've thought about it a great deal, and I've quite decided. I never used to understand how women did things like that, but I know now. It's because they can't be at the mercy of the man they love any longer."

Alexander flushed angrily. "So it's better to be at the mercy of a man you don't love?"

"Under such circumstances, infinitely!"

There was a flash in her eyes that made Alexander's fall. He got up and went over to the window, threw it open, and leaned out. He heard Hilda moving about behind him. When he looked over his shoulder she was lacing her boots. He went back and stood over her.

"Hilda you'd better think a while longer before you do that. I don't know what I ought to say, but I don't believe you'd be happy; truly I don't.

405

Aren't you trying to frighten me?"

She tied the knot of the last lacing and put her boot-heel down firmly. "No; I'm telling you what I've made up my mind to do. I suppose I would better do it without telling you. But afterward I shan't have an opportunity to explain, for I shan't be seeing you again."

Alexander started to speak, but caught himself. When Hilda rose he sat down on the arm of her chair and drew her back into it.

"I wouldn't be so much alarmed if I didn't know how utterly reckless you CAN be. Don't do anything like that rashly." His face grew troubled. "You wouldn't be happy. You are not that kind of woman. I'd never have another hour's peace if I helped to make you do a thing like that." He took her face between his hands and looked down into it. "You see, you are different, Hilda. Don't you know you are?" His voice grew softer, his touch more and more tender. "Some women can do that sort of thing, but you — you can love as queens did, in the old time."

Hilda had heard that soft, deep tone in his voice only once before. She closed her eyes; her lips and eyelids trembled. "Only one, Bartley. Only one. And he threw it back at me a second time."

She felt the strength leap in the arms that held her so lightly.

"Try him again, Hilda. Try him once again."

She looked up into his eyes, and hid her face in her hands.

CHAPTER X

On Tuesday afternoon a Boston lawyer, who had been trying a case in Vermont, was standing on the siding at White River Junction when the

Canadian Express pulled by on its northward journey. As the day-coaches at the rear end of the long train swept by him, the lawyer noticed at one of the windows a man's head, with thick rumpled hair. "Curious," he thought; "that looked like Alexander, but what would he be doing back there in the daycoaches?"

It was, indeed, Alexander.

That morning a telegram from Moorlock had reached him, telling him that there was serious trouble with the bridge and that he was needed there at once, so he had caught the first train out of New York. He had taken a seat in a day-coach to avoid the risk of meeting any one he knew, and because he did not wish to be comfortable. When the telegram arrived, Alexander was at his rooms on Tenth Street, packing his bag to go to Boston. On Monday night he had written a long letter to his wife, but when morning came he was afraid to send it, and the letter was still in his pocket. Winifred was not a woman who could bear disappointment. She demanded a great deal of herself and of the people she loved; and she never failed herself. If he told her now, he knew, it would be irretrievable. There would be no going back. He would lose the thing he valued most in the world; he would be destroying himself and his own happiness. There would be nothing for him afterward. He seemed to see himself dragging out a restless existence on the Continent — Cannes, Hyeres, Algiers, Cairo — among smartly dressed, disabled men of every nationality; forever going on journeys that led nowhere; hurrying to catch trains that he might just as well miss; getting up in the morning with a great bustle and splashing of water, to begin a day that had no purpose and no meaning; dining late to shorten the night, sleeping late to shorten the day.

And for what? For a mere folly, a masquerade, a little thing that he could not let go. AND HE COULD EVEN LET IT GO, he told himself. But he had promised to be in London at midsummer, and he knew that he would go. . . . It was impossible to live like this any longer.

And this, then, was to be the disaster that his old professor had foreseen for him: the crack in the wall, the crash, the cloud of dust. And he could not understand how it had come about. He felt that he himself was unchanged, that he was still there, the same man he had been five years ago, and that he was sitting stupidly by and letting some resolute offshoot of himself spoil his life for him. This new force was not he, it was but a part of him. He would not even admit that it was stronger than he; but it was more active. It was by its energy that this new feeling got the better of him. His wife was the woman who had made his life, gratified his pride, given direction to his tastes and habits. The life they led together seemed to him beautiful. Winifred still was, as she had always been, Romance for him, and whenever he was deeply stirred he turned to her. When the grandeur and beauty of the world challenged him — as it challenges even the most self-absorbed people — he always answered with her name. That was his reply to the question put by the mountains and the stars; to all the spiritual aspects of life. In his feeling for his wife there was all the tenderness, all the pride, all the devotion of which he was capable. There was everything but energy; the energy of youth which must register itself and cut its name before it passes. This new feeling was so fresh, so unsatisfied and light of foot. It ran and was not wearied, anticipated him everywhere. It put a girdle round the earth while he was going from New York to Moorlock. At this moment, it was tingling through him, exultant, and live as quicksilver, whispering, "In July you will be in England."

Already he dreaded the long, empty days at sea, the monotonous Irish coast, the sluggish passage up the Mersey, the flash of the boat train through the summer country. He closed his eyes and gave himself up to the feeling of rapid motion and to swift, terrifying thoughts. He was sitting so, his face shaded by his hand, when the Boston lawyer saw him from the siding at White River Junction.

When at last Alexander roused himself, the afternoon had waned to sunset. The train was passing through a gray country and the sky overhead was flushed with a wide flood of clear color. There was a rose-colored light over the gray rocks and hills and meadows. Off to the left, under the approach of a weather-stained wooden bridge, a group of boys were sitting around a little fire. The smell of the wood smoke blew in at the window. Except for an old farmer, jogging along the highroad in his box-wagon, there was not another living creature to be seen. Alexander looked back wistfully at the boys, camped on the edge of a little marsh, crouching under their shelter and looking gravely at their fire. They took his mind back a long way, to a campfire on a sandbar in a Western river, and he wished he could go back and sit down with them. He could remember exactly how the world had looked then.

It was quite dark and Alexander was still thinking of the boys, when it occurred to him that the train must be nearing Allway. In going to his new bridge at Moorlock he had always to pass through Allway. The train stopped at Allway Mills, then wound two miles up the river, and then the hollow sound under his feet told Bartley that he was on his first bridge again. The bridge seemed longer than it had ever seemed before, and he was glad when he felt the beat of the wheels on the solid roadbed again. He did not like coming and going across that bridge, or remembering the man who built it. And was he, indeed, the same man who used to walk that bridge at night, promising such things to himself and to the stars? And yet, he could remember it all so well: the quiet hills sleeping in the moonlight, the slender skeleton of the bridge reaching out into the river, and up yonder, alone on the hill, the big white house; upstairs, in Winifred's window, the light that told him she was still awake and still thinking of him. And after the light went out he walked alone, taking the heavens into his confidence, unable to tear himself away from the white magic of the night, unwilling to sleep because longing was so sweet to him, and because, for the first time since first the hills were hung with moonlight, there was a lover in the world. And always there was the sound of the rushing water underneath, the sound which, more than anything else, meant death; the wearing away of things under the impact of physical forces which men could direct but never circumvent or diminish. Then, in the exaltation of love, more than ever it seemed to him to mean death, the only other thing as strong as love. Under the moon, under the cold, splendid stars, there were only those two things awake and sleepless;

death and love, the rushing river and his burning heart.

Alexander sat up and looked about him. The train was tearing on through the darkness. All his companions in the day-coach were either dozing or sleeping heavily, and the murky lamps were turned low. How came he here among all these dirty people? Why was he going to London? What did it mean — what was the answer? How could this happen to a man who had lived through that magical spring and summer, and who had felt that the stars themselves were but flaming particles in the far-away infinitudes of his love?

What had he done to lose it? How could he endure the baseness of life without it? And with every revolution of the wheels beneath him, the unquiet quicksilver in his breast told him that at midsummer he would be in London. He remembered his last night there: the red foggy darkness, the hungry crowds before the theatres, the hand-organs, the feverish rhythm of the blurred, crowded streets, and the feeling of letting himself go with the crowd. He shuddered and looked about him at the poor unconscious companions of his journey, unkempt and travel-stained, now doubled in unlovely attitudes, who had come to stand to him for the ugliness he had brought into the world.

And those boys back there, beginning it all just as he had begun it; he wished he could promise them better luck. Ah, if one could promise any one better luck, if one could assure a single human being of happiness! He had thought he could do so, once; and it was thinking of that that he at last fell asleep. In his sleep, as if it had nothing fresher to work upon, his mind went back and tortured itself with something years and years away, an old, long-forgotten sorrow of his childhood.

When Alexander awoke in the morning, the sun was just rising through pale golden ripples of cloud, and the fresh yellow light was vibrating through the pine woods. The white birches, with their little unfolding leaves, gleamed in the lowlands, and the marsh meadows were already coming to life with their first green, a thin, bright color which had run over them like fire. As the train rushed along the trestles, thousands of wild birds rose screaming into the light. The sky was already a pale blue and of the clearness of crystal. Bartley caught up his bag and hurried through the Pullman coaches until he found the conductor. There was a stateroom unoccupied, and he took it and set about changing his clothes. Last night he would not have believed that anything could be so pleasant as the cold water he dashed over his head and shoulders and the freshness of clean linen on his body.

After he had dressed, Alexander sat down at the window and drew into his lungs deep breaths of the pine-scented air. He had awakened with all his old sense of power. He could not believe that things were as bad with him as they had seemed last night, that there was no way to set them entirely right. Even if he went to London at midsummer, what would that mean except that he was a fool? And he had been a fool before. That was not the reality of his life. Yet he knew that he would go to London.

Half an hour later the train stopped at Moorlock. Alexander sprang to the platform and hurried up the siding, waving to Philip Horton, one of his assistants, who was anxiously looking up at the windows of the coaches. Bartley took his arm and they went together into the station buffet.

"I'll have my coffee first, Philip. Have you had yours? And now, what seems to be the matter up here?"

The young man, in a hurried, nervous way, began his explanation.

But Alexander cut him short. "When did you stop work?" he asked sharply.

The young engineer looked confused. "I haven't stopped work yet, Mr. Alexander. I didn't feel that I could go so far without definite authorization from you."

"Then why didn't you say in your telegram exactly what you thought, and ask for your authorization? You'd have got it quick enough."

"Well, really, Mr. Alexander, I couldn't be absolutely sure, you know, and I didn't like to take the responsibility of making it public."

Alexander pushed back his chair and rose. "Anything I do can be made public, Phil. You say that you believe the lower chords are showing strain, and that even the workmen have been talking about it, and yet you've gone on adding weight."

"I'm sorry, Mr. Alexander, but I had counted on your getting here yesterday. My first telegram missed you somehow. I sent one Sunday evening, to the same address, but it was returned to me."

"Have you a carriage out there? I must stop to send a wire."

Alexander went up to the telegraph-desk and penciled the following message to his wife: —

I may have to be here for some time. Can you come up at once? Urgent.

BARTLEY.

The Moorlock Bridge lay three miles above the town. When they were seated in the carriage, Alexander began to question his assistant further. If it were true that the compression members showed strain, with the bridge only two thirds done, then there was nothing to do but pull the whole structure down and begin over again. Horton kept repeating that he was sure there could be nothing wrong with the estimates.

Alexander grew impatient. "That's all true, Phil, but we never were justified in assuming that a scale that was perfectly safe for an ordinary bridge would work with anything of such length. It's all very well on paper, but it remains to be seen whether it can be done in practice. I should have thrown up the job when they crowded me. It's all nonsense to try to do what other engineers are doing when you know they're not sound."

"But just now, when there is such competition," the younger man demurred. "And certainly that's the new line of development."

Alexander shrugged his shoulders and made no reply.

When they reached the bridge works, Alexander began his examination immediately. An hour later he sent for the superintendent. "I think you had better stop work out there at once, Dan. I should say that the lower chord here might buckle at any moment. I told the Commission that we were using higher unit stresses than any practice has established, and we've put the dead load at a low estimate. Theoretically it worked out well enough,

414

but it had never actually been tried." Alexander put on his overcoat and took the superintendent by the arm. "Don't look so chopfallen, Dan. It's a jolt, but we've got to face it. It isn't the end of the world, you know. Now we'll go out and call the men off quietly. They're already nervous, Horton tells me, and there's no use alarming them. I'll go with you, and we'll send the end riveters in first."

Alexander and the superintendent picked their way out slowly over the long span. They went deliberately, stopping to see what each gang was doing, as if they were on an ordinary round of inspection. When they reached the end of the river span, Alexander nodded to the superintendent, who quietly gave an order to the foreman. The men in the end gang picked up their tools and, glancing curiously at each other, started back across the bridge toward the river-bank. Alexander himself remained standing where they had been working, looking about him. It was hard to believe, as he looked back over it, that the whole great span was incurably disabled, was already as good as condemned, because something was out of line in the lower chord of the cantilever arm.

The end riveters had reached the bank and were dispersing among the tool-houses, and the second gang had picked up their tools and were starting toward the shore. Alexander, still standing at the end of the river span, saw the lower chord of the cantilever arm give a little, like an elbow bending. He shouted and ran after the second gang, but by this time every one knew that the big river span was slowly settling. There was a burst of shouting that was immediately drowned by the scream and cracking of tearing iron, as all the tension work began to pull asunder. Once the chords began to

415

buckle, there were thousands of tons of ironwork, all riveted together and lying in midair without support. It tore itself to pieces with roaring and grinding and noises that were like the shrieks of a steam whistle. There was no shock of any kind; the bridge had no impetus except from its own weight. It lurched neither to right nor left, but sank almost in a vertical line, snapping and breaking and tearing as it went, because no integral part could bear for an instant the enormous strain loosed upon it. Some of the men jumped and some ran, trying to make the shore.

At the first shriek of the tearing iron, Alexander jumped from the downstream side of the bridge. He struck the water without injury and disappeared. He was under the river a long time and had great difficulty in holding his breath. When it seemed impossible, and his chest was about to heave, he thought he heard his wife telling him that he could hold out a little longer. An instant later his face cleared the water. For a moment, in the depths of the river, he had realized what it would mean to die a hypocrite, and to lie dead under the last abandonment of her tenderness. But once in the light and air, he knew he should live to tell her and to recover all he had lost. Now, at last, he felt sure of himself. He was not startled. It seemed to him that he had been through something of this sort before. There was nothing horrible about it. This, too, was life, and life was activity, just as it was in Boston or in London. He was himself, and there was something to be done; everything seemed perfectly natural. Alexander was a strong swimmer, but he had gone scarcely a dozen strokes when the bridge itself, which had been settling faster and faster, crashed into the water behind him. Immediately the river was full of drowning men. A gang of French Canadians fell almost on top of him. He thought he had cleared them, when they began coming up all around him, clutching at him and at each other. Some of them could swim, but they were either hurt or crazed with fright. Alexander tried to beat them off, but there were too many of them. One caught him about the neck, another gripped him about the middle, and they went down together. When he sank, his wife seemed to be there in the water beside him, telling him to keep his head, that if he could hold out the men would drown and release him. There was something he wanted to tell his wife, but he could not think clearly for the roaring in his ears. Suddenly he remembered what it was. He caught his breath, and then she let him go.

The work of recovering the dead went on all day and all the following night. By the next morning forty-eight bodies had been taken out of the river, but there were still twenty missing. Many of the men had fallen with the bridge and were held down under the debris. Early on the morning of the second day a closed carriage was driven slowly along the river-bank and stopped a little below the works, where the river boiled and churned about the great iron carcass which lay in a straight line two thirds across it. The carriage stood there hour after hour, and word soon spread among the crowds on the shore that its occupant was the wife of the Chief Engineer; his body had not yet been found. The widows of the lost workmen, moving up and down the bank with shawls over their heads, some of them carrying babies, looked

417

at the rusty hired hack many times that morning. They drew near it and walked about it, but none of them ventured to peer within. Even half-indifferent sightseers dropped their voices as they told a newcomer: "You see that carriage over there? That's Mrs. Alexander. They haven't found him yet. She got off the train this morning. Horton met her. She heard it in Boston yesterday — heard the newsboys crying it in the street."

At noon Philip Horton made his way through the crowd with a tray and a tin coffee-pot from the camp kitchen. When he reached the carriage he found Mrs. Alexander just as he had left her in the early morning, leaning forward a little, with her hand on the lowered window, looking at the river. Hour after hour she had been watching the water, the lonely, useless stone towers, and the convulsed mass of iron wreckage over which the angry river continually spat up its yellow foam.

"Those poor women out there, do they blame him very much?" she asked, as she handed the coffee-cup back to Horton.

"Nobody blames him, Mrs. Alexander. If any one is to blame, I'm afraid it's I. I should have stopped work before he came. He said so as soon as I met him. I tried to get him here a day earlier, but my telegram missed him, somehow. He didn't have time really to explain to me. If he'd got here Monday, he'd have had all the men off at once. But, you see, Mrs. Alexander, such a thing never happened before. According to all human calculations, it simply couldn't happen."

Horton leaned wearily against the front wheel of the cab. He had not had his clothes off for thirty hours, and the stimulus of violent excitement was beginning to wear off.

"Don't be afraid to tell me the worst, Mr. Horton. Don't leave me to the dread of finding out things that people may be saying. If he is blamed, if he needs any one to speak for him," — for the first time her voice broke and a flush of life, tearful, painful, and confused, swept over her rigid pallor, — "if he needs any one, tell me, show me what to do." She began to sob, and Horton hurried away.

When he came back at four o'clock in the afternoon he was carrying his hat in his hand, and Winifred knew as soon as she saw him that they had found Bartley. She opened the carriage door before he reached her and stepped to the ground.

Horton put out his hand as if to hold her back and spoke pleadingly: "Won't you drive up to my house, Mrs. Alexander? They will take him up there."

"Take me to him now, please. I shall not make any trouble."

The group of men down under the riverbank fell back when they saw a woman coming, and one of them threw a tarpaulin over the stretcher. They took off their hats and caps as Winifred approached, and although she had pulled her veil down over her face they did not look up at her. She was taller than Horton, and some of the men thought she was the tallest woman they had ever seen. "As tall as himself," some one whispered. Horton motioned to the men, and six of them lifted the stretcher and began to carry it up the embankment. Winifred followed them the half-mile to Horton's house. She walked quietly, without once breaking or stumbling. When the bearers put the stretcher down in Horton's spare bedroom, she thanked them and gave her hand to

419

each in turn. The men went out of the house and through the yard with their caps in their hands. They were too much confused to say anything as they went down the hill.

Horton himself was almost as deeply perplexed. "Mamie," he said to his wife, when he came out of the spare room half an hour later, "will you take Mrs. Alexander the things she needs? She is going to do everything herself. Just stay about where you can hear her and go in if she wants you."

Everything happened as Alexander had foreseen in that moment of prescience under the river. With her own hands she washed him clean of every mark of disaster. All night he was alone with her in the still house, his great head lying deep in the pillow. In the pocket of his coat Winifred found the letter that he had written her the night before he left New York, water-soaked and illegible, but because of its length, she knew it had been meant for her.

For Alexander death was an easy creditor. Fortune, which had smiled upon him consistently all his life, did not desert him in the end. His harshest critics did not doubt that, had he lived, he would have retrieved himself. Even Lucius Wilson did not see in this accident the disaster he had once foretold.

When a great man dies in his prime there is no surgeon who can say whether he did well; whether or not the future was his, as it seemed to be. The mind that society had come to regard as a powerful and reliable machine, dedicated to its service, may for a long time have been sick within itself and bent upon its own destruction.

Professor Wilson had been living in London for six years and he was just back from a visit to America. One afternoon, soon after his return, he put on his frock-coat and drove in a hansom to pay a call upon Hilda Burgoyne, who still lived at her old number, off Bedford Square. He and Miss Burgoyne had been fast friends for a long time. He had first noticed her about the corridors of the British Museum, where he read constantly. Her being there so often had made him feel that he would like to know her, and as she was not an inaccessible person, an introduction was not difficult. The preliminaries once over, they came to depend a great deal upon each other, and Wilson, after his day's reading, often went round to Bedford Square for his tea. They had much more in common than their memories of a common friend. Indeed, they seldom spoke of him. They saved that for the deep moments which do not come often, and then their talk of him was mostly silence. Wilson knew that Hilda had loved him; more than this he had not tried to know.

It was late when Wilson reached Hilda's apartment on this particular December afternoon, and he found her alone. She sent for fresh tea and made him comfortable, as she had such a knack of making people comfortable.

"How good you were to come back before Christmas! I quite dreaded the Holidays without you. You've helped me over a good many Christmases." She smiled at him gayly.

"As if you needed me for that! But, at any rate, I needed YOU. How well you are looking, my dear, and how rested."

He peered up at her from his low chair, balancing the tips of his long fingers together in a judicial manner which had grown on him with years.

Hilda laughed as she carefully poured his cream. "That means that I was looking very seedy at the end of the season, doesn't it? Well, we must show wear at last, you know."

Wilson took the cup gratefully. "Ah, no need to remind a man of seventy, who has just been home to find that he has survived all his contemporaries. I was most gently treated — as a sort of precious relic. But, do you know, it made me feel awkward to be hanging about still."

"Seventy? Never mention it to me." Hilda looked appreciatively at the Professor's alert face, with so many kindly lines about the mouth and so many quizzical ones about the eyes. "You've got to hang about for me, you know. I can't even let you go home again. You must stay put, now that I have you back. You're the realest thing I have."

Wilson chuckled. "Dear me, am I? Out of so many conquests and the spoils of conquered cities! You've really missed me? Well, then, I shall hang. Even if you have at last to put ME in the mummy-room with the others. You'll visit me often, won't you?"

"Every day in the calendar. Here, your cigarettes are in this drawer, where you left them." She struck a match and lit one for him. "But you did, after all, enjoy being at home again?"

"Oh, yes. I found the long railway journeys trying. People live a thousand miles apart. But I did it thoroughly; I was all over the place. It was in Boston I lingered longest."

"Ah, you saw Mrs. Alexander?"

"Often. I dined with her, and had tea there a

422

dozen different times, I should think. Indeed, it was to see her that I lingered on and on. I found that I still loved to go to the house. It always seemed as if Bartley were there, somehow, and that at any moment one might hear his heavy tramp on the stairs. Do you know, I kept feeling that he must be up in his study." The Professor looked reflectively into the grate. "I should really have liked to go up there. That was where I had my last long talk with him. But Mrs. Alexander never suggested it."

"Why?"

Wilson was a little startled by her tone, and he turned his head so quickly that his cuff-link caught the string of his nose-glasses and pulled them awry. "Why? Why, dear me, I don't know. She probably never thought of it."

Hilda bit her lip. "I don't know what made me say that. I didn't mean to interrupt. Go on please, and tell me how it was."

"Well, it was like that. Almost as if he were there. In a way, he really is there. She never lets him go. It's the most beautiful and dignified sorrow I've ever known. It's so beautiful that it has its compensations, I should think. Its very completeness is a compensation. It gives her a fixed star to steer by. She doesn't drift. We sat there evening after evening in the quiet of that magically haunted room, and watched the sunset burn on the river, and felt him. Felt him with a difference, of course."

Hilda leaned forward, her elbow on her knee, her chin on her hand. "With a difference? Because of her, you mean?"

Wilson's brow wrinkled. "Something like that, yes. Of course, as time goes on, to her he becomes

423

more and more their simple personal relation."

Hilda studied the droop of the Professor's head intently. "You didn't altogether like that? You felt it wasn't wholly fair to him?"

Wilson shook himself and readjusted his glasses. "Oh, fair enough. More than fair. Of course, I always felt that my image of him was just a little different from hers. No relation is so complete that it can hold absolutely all of a person. And I liked him just as he was; his deviations, too; the places where he didn't square."

Hilda considered vaguely. "Has she grown much older?" she asked at last.

"Yes, and no. In a tragic way she is even handsomer. But colder. Cold for everything but him. 'Forget thyself to marble'; I kept thinking of that. Her happiness was a happiness *à deux*, not apart from the world, but actually against it. And now her grief is like that. She saves herself for it and doesn't even go through the form of seeing people much. I'm sorry. It would be better for her, and might be so good for them, if she could let other people in."

"Perhaps she's afraid of letting him out a little, of sharing him with somebody."

Wilson put down his cup and looked up with vague alarm. "Dear me, it takes a woman to think of that, now! I don't, you know, think we ought to be hard on her. More, even, than the rest of us she didn't choose her destiny. She underwent it. And it has left her chilled. As to her not wishing to take the world into her confidence — well, it is a pretty brutal and stupid world, after all, you know."

Hilda leaned forward. "Yes, I know, I know. Only I can't help being glad that there was something for him even in stupid and vulgar people. My little Marie worshiped him. When she is dusting I always know when she has come to his picture."

Wilson nodded. "Oh, yes! He left an echo. The ripples go on in all of us. He belonged to the people who make the play, and most of us are only onlookers at the best. We shouldn't wonder too much at Mrs. Alexander. She must feel how useless it would be to stir about, that she may as well sit still; that nothing can happen to her after Bartley."

"Yes," said Hilda softly, "nothing can happen to one after Bartley."

They both sat looking into the fire.

PETER

"No, Antone, I have told thee many times, no, thou shalt not sell it until I am gone."

"But I need money; what good is that old fiddle to thee? The very crows laugh at thee when thou art trying to play. Thy hand trembles so thou canst scarce hold the bow. Thou shalt go with me to the Blue to cut wood to-morrow. See to it thou art up early."

"What, on the Sabbath, Antone, when it is so cold? I get so very cold, my son, let us not go to-morrow."

"Yes, to-morrow, thou lazy old man. Do not I cut wood upon the Sabbath? Care I how cold it is? Wood thou shalt cut, and haul it too, and as for the fiddle, I tell thee I will sell it yet." Antone pulled his ragged cap down over his low heavy brow, and went out. The old man drew his stool up nearer the fire, and sat stroking his violin with trembling fingers and muttering, "Not while I live, not while I live."

Five years ago they had come here, Peter Sadelack, and his wife, and oldest son Antone, and countless smaller Sadelacks, here to the dreariest part of south-western Nebraska, and had taken up a homestead. Antone was the acknowledged master of the premises, and people said he

426

was a likely youth, and would do well. That he was mean and untrustworthy every one knew, but that made little difference. His corn was better tended than any in the county, and his wheat always yielded more than other men's.

Of Peter no one knew much, nor had any one a good word to say for him. He drank whenever he could get out of Antone's sight long enough to pawn his hat or coat for whiskey. Indeed there were but two things he would not pawn, his pipe and his violin. He was a lazy, absent minded old fellow, who liked to fiddle better than to plow, though Antone surely got work enough out of them all, for that matter. In the house of which Antone was master there was no one, from the little boy three years old, to the old man of sixty, who did not earn his bread. Still people said that Peter was worthless, and was a great drag on Antone, his son, who never drank, and was a much better man than his father had ever been. Peter did not care what people said. He did not like the country, nor the people, least of all he liked the plowing. He was very homesick for Bohemia. Long ago, only eight years ago by the calendar, but it seemed eight centuries to Peter, he had been a second violinist in the great theatre at Prague. He had gone into the theatre very young, and had been there all his life, until he had a stroke of paralysis, which made his arm so weak that his bowing was uncertain. Then they told him he could go. Those were great days at the theatre. He had plenty to drink then, and wore a dress coat every evening, and there were always parties after the play. He could play in those days, ay, that he could! He could never read the notes well, so he did not play first; but his touch, he had a touch indeed, so Herr Mikilsdoff, who led the orchestra, had said. Sometimes now Peter thought he could plow better if he could only bow as he used to. He had seen all the lovely women in the world there, all the great singers and the great players. He was in the orchestra when Rachel played, and he heard Liszt play when the Countess d'Agoult sat in the stage box and threw the master white lilies. Once, a French woman came and played for weeks, he did not remember her name now. He did not remember her face very well either, for it changed so, it was never twice the same. But the beauty of it, and the great hunger men felt at the sight of it, that he remembered. Most of all he remembered her voice. He did not know French, and could not understand a word she said, but it seemed to him that she must be talking the music of Chopin. And her voice, he thought he should know that in the other world. The last night she played a play in which a man touched her arm, and she stabbed him. As Peter sat among the smoking gas jets down below the footlights with his fiddle on his knee, and looked up at her, he thought he would like to die too, if he could touch her arm once, and have her stab him so. Peter went home to his wife very drunk that night. Even in those days he was a foolish fellow, who cared for nothing but music and pretty faces.

It was all different now. He had nothing to drink and little to eat, and here, there was nothing but sun, and grass, and sky. He had forgotten almost everything, but some things he remembered well enough. He loved his violin and the holy Mary, and above all else he feared the Evil One, and his son Antone.

The fire was low, and it grew cold. Still Peter sat

by the fire remembering. He dared not throw more cobs on the fire; Antone would be angry. He did not want to cut wood tomorrow, it would be Sunday, and he wanted to go to mass. Antone might let him do that. He held his violin under his wrinkled chin, his white hair fell over it, and he began to play "Ave Maria." His hand shook more than ever before, and at last refused to work the bow at all. He sat stupefied for a while, then arose, and taking his violin with him, stole out into the old sod stable. He took Antone's shotgun down from its peg, and loaded it by the moonlight which streamed in through the door. He sat down on the dirt floor, and leaned back against the dirt wall. He heard the wolves howling in the distance, and the night wind screaming as it swept over the snow. Near him he heard the regular breathing of the horses in the dark. He put his crucifix above his heart, and folding his hands said brokenly all the Latin he had ever known, *"Pater noster, qui in cælum est."* Then he raised his head and sighed, "Not one kreutzer will Antone pay them to pray for my soul, not one kreutzer, he is so careful of his money, is Antone, he does not waste it in drink, he is a better man than I, but hard sometimes. He works the girls too hard, women were not made to work so. But he shall not sell thee, my fiddle, I can play thee no more, but they shall not part us. We have seen it all together, and we will forget it together, the French woman and all." He held his fiddle under his chin a moment, where it had lain so often, then put it across his knee and broke it through the middle. He pulled off his old boot, held the gun between his knees with the muzzle against his forehead, and pressed the trigger with his toe.

In the morning Antone found him stiff, frozen fast in a pool of blood. They could not straighten him out enough to fit a coffin, so they buried him in a pine box. Before the funeral Antone carried to town the fiddle-bow which Peter had forgotten to break. Antone was very thrifty, and a better man than his father had been.

ON THE DIVIDE

Near Rattlesnake Creek, on the side of a little draw stood Canute's shanty. North, east, south, stretched the level Nebraska plain of long rust-red grass that undulated constantly in the wind. To the west the ground was broken and rough, and a narrow strip of timber wound along the turbid, muddy little stream that had scarcely ambition enough to crawl over its black bottom. If it had not been for the few stunted cottonwoods and elms that grew along its banks, Canute would have shot himself years ago. The Norwegians are a timber-loving people, and if there is even a turtle pond with a few plum bushes around it they seem irresistibly drawn toward it.

As to the shanty itself, Canute had built it without aid of any kind, for when he first squatted along the banks of Rattlesnake Creek there was not a human being within twenty miles. It was built of logs split in halves, the chinks stopped with mud and plaster. The roof was covered with earth and was supported by one gigantic beam curved in the shape of a round arch. It was almost impossible that any tree had ever grown in that shape. The Norwegians used to say that Canute had taken the log across his knee and bent it into the shape he wished. There were two rooms, or

431

rather there was one room with a partition made of ash saplings interwoven and bound together like big straw basket work. In one corner there was a cook stove, rusted and broken. In the other a bed made of unplaned planks and poles. It was fully eight feet long, and upon it was a heap of dark bed clothing. There was a chair and a bench of colossal proportions. There was an ordinary kitchen cupboard with a few cracked dirty dishes in it, and beside it on a tall box a tin wash-basin. Under the bed was a pile of pint flasks, some broken, some whole, all empty. On the wood box lay a pair of shoes of almost incredible dimensions. On the wall hung a saddle, a gun, and some ragged clothing, conspicuous among which was a suit of dark cloth, apparently new, with a paper collar carefully wrapped in a red silk handkerchief and pinned to the sleeve. Over the door hung a wolf and a badger skin, and on the door itself a brace of thirty or forty snake skins whose noisy tails rattled ominously every time it opened. The strangest things in the shanty were the wide window-sills. At first glance they looked as though they had been ruthlessly hacked and mutilated with a hatchet, but on closer inspection all the notches and holes in the wood took form and shape. There seemed to be a series of pictures. They were, in a rough way, artistic, but the figures were heavy and labored, as though they had been cut very slowly and with very awkward instruments. There were men plowing with little horned imps sitting on their shoulders and on their horses' heads. There were men praying with a skull hanging over their heads and little demons behind them mocking their attitudes. There were men fighting with big serpents, and skeletons

432

dancing together. All about these pictures were blooming vines and foliage such as never grew in this world, and coiled among the branches of the vines there was always the scaly body of a serpent, and behind every flower there was a serpent's head. It was a veritable Dance of Death by one who had felt its sting. In the wood box lay some boards, and every inch of them was cut up in the same manner. Sometimes the work was very rude and careless, and looked as though the hand of the workman had trembled. It would sometimes have been hard to distinguish the men from their evil geniuses but for one fact, the men were always grave and were either toiling or praying, while the devils were always smiling and dancing. Several of these boards had been split for kindling and it was evident that the artist did not value his work highly.

It was the first day of winter on the Divide. Canute stumbled into his shanty carrying a basket of cobs, and after filling the stove, sat down on a stool and crouched his seven foot frame over the fire, staring drearily out of the window at the wide gray sky. He knew by heart every individual clump of bunch grass in the miles of red shaggy prairie that stretched before his cabin. He knew it in all the deceitful loveliness of its early summer, in all the bitter barrenness of its autumn. He had seen it smitten by all the plagues of Egypt. He had seen it parched by drought, and sogged by rain, beaten by hail, and swept by fire, and in the grasshopper years he had seen it eaten as bare and clean as bones that the vultures have left. After the great fires he had seen it stretch for miles and miles, black and smoking as the floor of hell.

He rose slowly and crossed the room, dragging

his big feet heavily as though they were burdens to him. He looked out of the window into the hog corral and saw the pigs burying themselves in the straw before the shed. The leaden gray clouds were beginning to spill themselves, and the snowflakes were settling down over the white leprous patches of frozen earth where the hogs had gnawed even the sod away. He shuddered and began to walk, tramping heavily with his ungainly feet. He was the wreck of ten winters on the Divide and he knew what they meant. Men fear the winters of the Divide as a child fears night or as men in the North Seas fear the still dark cold of the polar twilight.

His eyes fell upon his gun, and he took it down from the wall and looked it over. He sat down on the edge of his bed and held the barrel towards his face, letting his forehead rest upon it, and laid his finger on the trigger. He was perfectly calm, there was neither passion nor despair in his face, but the thoughtful look of a man who is considering. Presently he laid down the gun, and reaching into the cupboard, drew out a pint bottle of raw white alcohol. Lifting it to his lips, he drank greedily. He washed his face in the tin basin and combed his rough hair and shaggy blond beard. Then he stood in uncertainty before the suit of dark clothes that hung on the wall. For the fiftieth time he took them in his hands and tried to summon courage to put them on. He took the paper collar that was pinned to the sleeve of the coat and cautiously slipped it under his rough beard, looking with timid expectancy into the cracked, splashed glass that hung over the bench. With a short laugh he threw it down on the bed, and pulling on his old black hat, he went out, striking off

434

across the level.

It was a physical necessity for him to get away from his cabin once in a while. He had been there for ten years, digging and plowing and sowing, and reaping what little the hail and the hot winds and the frosts left him to reap. Insanity and suicide are very common things on the Divide. They come on like an epidemic in the hot wind season. Those scorching dusty winds that blow up over the bluffs from Kansas seem to dry up the blood in men's veins as they do the sap in the corn leaves. Whenever the yellow scorch creeps down over the tender inside leaves about the ear, then the coroners prepare for active duty; for the oil of the country is burned out and it does not take long for the flame to eat up the wick. It causes no great sensation there when a Dane is found swinging to his own windmill tower, and most of the Poles after they have become too careless and discouraged to shave themselves keep their razors to cut their throats with.

It may be that the next generation on the Divide will be very happy, but the present one came too late in life. It is useless for men that have cut hemlocks among the mountains of Sweden for forty years to try to be happy in a country as flat and gray and as naked as the sea. It is not easy for men that have spent their youths fishing in the Northern seas to be content with following a plow, and men that have served in the Austrian army hate hard work and coarse clothing and the loneliness of the plains, and long for marches and excitement and tavern company and pretty barmaids. After a man has passed his fortieth birthday it is not easy for him to change the habits and conditions of his life. Most men bring with them

435

to the Divide only the dregs of the lives that they have squandered in other lands and among other peoples.

Canute Canuteson was as mad as any of them, but his madness did not take the form of suicide or religion but of alcohol. He had always taken liquor when he wanted it, as all Norwegians do, but after his first year of solitary life he settled down to it steadily. He exhausted whisky after a while, and went to alcohol, because its effects were speedier and surer. He was a big man with a terrible amount of resistant force, and it took a great deal of alcohol even to move him. After nine years of drinking, the quantities he could take would seem fabulous to an ordinary drinking man. He never let it interfere with his work, he generally drank at night and on Sundays. Every night, as soon as his chores were done, he began to drink. While he was able to sit up he would play on his mouth harp or hack away at his window sills with his jack knife. When the liquor went to his head he would lie down on his bed and stare out of the window until he went to sleep. He drank alone and in solitude not for pleasure or good cheer, but to forget the awful loneliness and level of the Divide. Milton made a sad blunder when he put mountains in hell. Mountains postulate faith and aspiration. All mountain peoples are religious. It was the cities of the plains that, because of their utter lack of spirituality and the mad caprice of their vice, were cursed of God.

Alcohol is perfectly consistent in its effects upon man. Drunkenness is merely an exaggeration. A foolish man drunk becomes maudlin; a bloody man, vicious; a coarse man, vulgar. Canute was none of these, but he was morose and gloomy, and liquor took him through all the hells of Dante. As he lay on his giant's bed all the horrors of this world and every other were laid bare to his chilled senses. He was a man who knew no joy, a man who toiled in silence and bitterness. The skull and the serpent were always before him, the symbols of eternal futileness and of eternal hate.

When the first Norwegians near enough to be called neighbors came, Canute rejoiced, and planned to escape from his bosom vice. But he was not a social man by nature and had not the power of drawing out the social side of other people. His new neighbors rather feared him because of his great strength and size, his silence and his lowering brows. Perhaps, too, they knew that he was mad, mad from the eternal treachery of the plains, which every spring stretch green and rustle with the promises of Eden, showing long grassy lagoons full of clear water and cattle whose hoofs are stained with wild roses. Before autumn the lagoons are dried up, and the ground is burnt dry and hard until it blisters and cracks open.

So instead of becoming a friend and neighbor to the men that settled about him, Canute became a mystery and a terror. They told awful stories of his size and strength and of the alcohol he drank. They said that one night, when he went out to see to his horses just before he went to bed, his steps were unsteady and the rotten planks of the floor gave way and threw him behind the feet of a fiery young stallion. His foot was caught fast in the floor, and the nervous horse began kicking frantically. When Canute felt the blood trickling down in his eyes from a scalp wound in his head, he roused himself from his kingly indifference, and with the quiet stoical courage of a drunken man leaned forward and wound his arms about the horse's hind legs and held them against his breast with crushing embrace. All through the darkness and cold of the night he lay there, matching strength against strength. When little Jim Peterson went over the next morning at four o'clock to go with him to the Blue to cut wood, he found him so, and the horse was on its fore knees, trembling and whinnying with fear. This is the story the Norwegians tell of him, and if it is true it is no wonder that they feared and hated this Holder of the Heels of Horses.

One spring there moved to the next "eighty" a family that made a great change in Canute's life. Ole Yensen was too drunk most of the time to be afraid of any one, and his wife Mary was too garrulous to be afraid of any one who listened to her talk, and Lena, their pretty daughter, was not afraid of man nor devil. So it came about that Canute went over to take his alcohol with Ole oftener than he took it alone. After a while the report spread that he was going to marry Yensen's daughter, and the Norwegian girls began to tease Lena about the great bear she was going to keep house for. No one could quite see how the affair had come about, for Canute's tactics of courtship were somewhat peculiar. He apparently never spoke to her at all: he would sit for hours with Mary chattering on one side of him and Ole drinking on the other and watch Lena at her work. She teased him, and threw flour in his face and put vinegar in his coffee, but he took her rough jokes with silent wonder, never even smiling. He took her to church occasionally, but the most watchful and curious people never saw him speak

438

to her. He would sit staring at her while she giggled and flirted with the other men.

Next spring Mary Lee went to town to work in a steam laundry. She came home every Sunday, and always ran across to Yensens to startle Lena with stories of ten cent theaters, firemen's dances, and all the other esthetic delights of metropolitan life. In a few weeks Lena's head was completely turned, and she gave her father no rest until he let her go to town to seek her fortune at the ironing board. From the time she came home on her first visit she began to treat Canute with contempt. She had bought a plush cloak and kid gloves, had her clothes made by the dress-maker, and assumed airs and graces that made the other women of the neighborhood cordially detest her. She generally brought with her a young man from town who waxed his mustache and wore a red necktie, and she did not even introduce him to Canute.

The neighbors teased Canute a good deal until he knocked one of them down. He gave no sign of suffering from her neglect except that he drank more and avoided the other Norwegians more carefully than ever. He lay around in his den and no one knew what he felt or thought, but little Jim Peterson, who had seen him glowering at Lena in church one Sunday when she was there with the town man, said that he would not give an acre of his wheat for Lena's life or the town chap's either; and Jim's wheat was so wondrously worthless that the statement was an exceedingly strong one.

Canute had bought a new suit of clothes that looked as nearly like the town man's as possible. They had cost him half a millet crop; for tailors are not accustomed to fitting giants and they charge for it. He had hung those clothes in his shanty two months ago and had never put them on, partly from fear of ridicule, partly from discouragement, and partly because there was something in his own soul that revolted at the littleness of the device.

Lena was at home just at this time. Work was slack in the laundry and Mary had not been well, so Lena stayed at home, glad enough to get an opportunity to torment Canute once more.

She was washing in the side kitchen, singing loudly as she worked. Mary was on her knees, blacking the stove and scolding violently about the young man who was coming out from town that night. The young man had committed the fatal error of laughing at Mary's ceaseless babble and had never been forgiven.

"He is no good, and you will come to a bad end by running with him! I do not see why a daughter of mine should act so. I do not see why the Lord should visit such a punishment upon me as to give me such a daughter. There are plenty of good men you can marry."

Lena tossed her head and answered curtly, "I don't happen to want to marry any man right away, and so long as Dick dresses nice and has plenty of money to spend, there is no harm in my going with him."

"Money to spend? Yes, and that is all he does with it I'll be bound. You think it very fine now, but you will change your tune when you have been married five years and see your children running naked and your cupboard empty. Did Anne Hermanson come to any good end by marrying a town man?"

"I don't know anything about Anne Herman-son, but I know any of the laundry girls would have Dick quick enough if they could get him."

"Yes, and a nice lot of store clothes huzzies you are too. Now there is Canuteson who has an 'eighty' proved up and fifty head of cattle and ———"

"And hair that ain't been cut since he was a baby, and a big dirty beard, and he wears overalls on Sundays, and drinks like a pig. Besides he will keep. I can have all the fun I want, and when I am old and ugly like you he can have me and take care of me. The Lord knows there ain't nobody else going to marry him."

Canute drew his hand back from the latch as though it were red hot. He was not the kind of a man to make a good eavesdropper, and he wished he had knocked sooner. He pulled himself together and struck the door like a battering ram. Mary jumped and opened it with a screech.

"God! Canute, how you scared us! I thought it was crazy Lou, — he has been tearing around the neighborhood trying to convert folks. I am afraid as death of him. He ought to be sent off, I think. He is just as liable as not to kill us all, or burn the barn, or poison the dogs. He has been worrying even the poor minister to death, and he laid up with the rheumatism, too! Did you notice that he was too sick to preach last Sunday? But don't stand there in the cold, — come in. Yensen isn't here, but he just went over to Sorenson's for the mail; he won't be gone long. Walk right in the other room and sit down."

Canute followed her, looking steadily in front of him and not noticing Lena as he passed her. But Lena's vanity would not allow him to pass unmolested. She took the wet sheet she was wringing out and cracked him across the face with it, and ran giggling to the other side of the room. The blow stung his cheeks and the soapy water flew in his eyes, and he involuntarily began rubbing them with his hands. Lena giggled with delight at his discomfiture, and the wrath in Canute's face grew blacker than ever. A big man humiliated is vastly more undignified than a little one. He forgot the sting of his face in the bitter consciousness that he had made a fool of himself. He stumbled blindly into the living room, knocking his head against the door jamb because he forgot to stoop. He dropped into a chair behind the stove, thrusting his big feet back helplessly on either side of him.

Ole was a long time in coming, and Canute sat there, still and silent, with his hands clenched on his knees, and the skin of his face seemed to have shriveled up into little wrinkles that trembled when he lowered his brows. His life had been one long lethargy of solitude and alcohol, but now he was awakening, and it was as when the dumb stagnant heat of summer breaks out into thunder.

When Ole came staggering in, heavy with liquor, Canute rose at once.

"Yensen," he said quietly, "I have come to see if you will let me marry your daughter today."

"Today!" gasped Ole.

"Yes, I will not wait until tomorrow. I am tired of living alone."

Ole braced his staggering knees against the bedstead, and stammered eloquently: "Do you think I will marry my daughter to a drunkard? a man who drinks raw alcohol? a man who sleeps with rattle snakes? Get out of my house or I will kick you out for your impudence." And Ole began

442

looking anxiously for his feet.

Canute answered not a word, but he put on his hat and went out into the kitchen. He went up to Lena and said without looking at her, "Get your things on and come with me!"

The tones of his voice startled her, and she said angrily, dropping the soap, "Are you drunk?"

"If you do not come with me, I will take you, — you had better come," said Canute quietly.

She lifted a sheet to strike him, but he caught her arm roughly and wrenched the sheet from her. He turned to the wall and took down a hood and shawl that hung there, and began wrapping her up. Lena scratched and fought like a wild thing. Ole stood in the door, cursing, and Mary howled and screeched at the top of her voice. As for Canute, he lifted the girl in his arms and went out of the house. She kicked and struggled, but the helpless wailing of Mary and Ole soon died away in the distance, and her face was held down tightly on Canute's shoulder so that she could not see whither he was taking her. She was conscious only of the north wind whistling in her ears, and of rapid steady motion and of a great breast that heaved beneath her in quick, irregular breaths. The harder she struggled the tighter those iron arms that had held the heels of horses crushed about her, until she felt as if they would crush the breath from her, and lay still with fear. Canute was striding across the level fields at a pace at which man never went before, drawing the stinging north wind into his lungs in great gulps. He walked with his eyes half closed and looking straight in front of him, only lowering them when he bent his head to blow away the snow flakes that settled on her hair. So it was that Canute took her to his home, even as his bearded barbarian ancestors took the fair frivolous women of the South in their hairy arms and bore them down to their war ships. For ever and anon the soul becomes weary of the conventions that are not of it, and with a single stroke shatters the civilized lies with which it is unable to cope, and the strong arm reaches out and takes by force what it cannot win by cunning.

When Canute reached his shanty he placed the girl upon a chair, where she sat sobbing. He stayed only a few minutes. He filled the stove with wood and lit the lamp, drank a huge swallow of alcohol and put the bottle in his pocket. He paused a moment, staring heavily at the weeping girl, then he went off and locked the door and disappeared in the gathering gloom of the night.

Wrapped in flannels and soaked with turpentine, the little Norwegian preacher sat reading his Bible, when he heard a thundering knock at his door, and Canute entered, covered with snow and with his beard frozen fast to his coat.

"Come in, Canute, you must be frozen," said the little man, shoving a chair towards his visitor.

Canute remained standing with his hat on and said quietly, "I want you to come over to my house tonight to marry me to Lena Yensen."

"Have you got a license, Canute?"

"No, I don't want a license. I want to be married."

"But I can't marry you without a license, man. It would not be legal."

A dangerous light came in the big Norwegian's eye. "I want you to come over to my house to marry me to Lena Yensen."

"No, I can't, it would kill an ox to go out in a

444

storm like this, and my rheumatism is bad to-night."

"Then if you will not go I must take you," said Canute with a sigh.

He took down the preacher's bearskin coat and bade him put it on while he hitched up his buggy. He went out and closed the door softly after him. Presently he returned and found the frightened minister crouching before the fire with his coat lying beside him. Canute helped him put it on and gently wrapped his head in his big muffler. Then he picked him up and carried him out and placed him in his buggy. As he tucked the buffalo robes around him he said: "Your horse is old, he might flounder or lose his way in this storm. I will lead him."

The minister took the reins feebly in his hands and sat shivering with the cold. Sometimes when there was a lull in the wind, he could see the horse struggling through the snow with the man plodding steadily beside him. Again the blowing snow would hide them from him altogether. He had no idea where they were or what direction they were going. He felt as though he were being whirled away in the heart of the storm, and he said all the prayers he knew. But at last the long four miles were over, and Canute set him down in the snow while he unlocked the door. He saw the bride sitting by the fire with her eyes red and swollen as though she had been weeping. Canute placed a huge chair for him, and said roughly, —

"Warm yourself."

Lena began to cry and moan afresh, begging the minister to take her home. He looked helplessly at Canute. Canute said simply, —

"If you are warm now, you can marry us."

445

"My daughter, do you take this step of your own free will?" asked the minister in a trembling voice.

"No sir, I don't, and it is disgraceful he should force me into it! I won't marry him."

"Then, Canute, I cannot marry you," said the minister, standing as straight as his rheumatic limbs would let him.

"Are you ready to marry us now, sir?" said Canute, laying one iron hand on his stooped shoulder. The little preacher was a good man, but like most men of weak body he was a coward and had a horror of physical suffering, although he had known so much of it. So with many qualms of conscience he began to repeat the marriage service. Lena sat sullenly in her chair, staring at the fire. Canute stood beside her, listening with his head bent reverently and his hands folded on his breast. When the little man had prayed and said amen, Canute began bundling him up again.

"I will take you home, now," he said as he carried him out and placed him in his buggy, and started off with him through the fury of the storm, floundering among the snow drifts that brought even the giant himself to his knees.

After she was left alone, Lena soon ceased weeping. She was not of a particularly sensitive temperament, and had little pride beyond that of vanity. After the first bitter anger wore itself out, she felt nothing more than a healthy sense of humiliation and defeat. She had no inclination to run away, for she was married now, and in her eyes that was final and all rebellion was useless. She knew nothing about a license, but she knew that a preacher married folks. She consoled herself by thinking that she had always intended to marry Canute some day, any way.

She grew tired of crying and looking into the fire, so she got up and began to look about her. She had heard queer tales about the inside of Canute's shanty, and her curiosity soon got the better of her rage. One of the first things she noticed was the new black suit of clothes hanging on the wall. She was dull, but it did not take a vain woman long to interpret anything so decidedly flattering, and she was pleased in spite of herself. As she looked through the cupboard, the general air of neglect and discomfort made her pity the man who lived there.

"Poor fellow, no wonder he wants to get married to get somebody to wash up his dishes. Batchin's pretty hard on a man."

It is easy to pity when once one's vanity has been tickled. She looked at the window sill and gave a little shudder and wondered if the man were crazy. Then she sat down again and sat a long time wondering what her Dick and Ole would do.

"It is queer Dick didn't come right over after me. He surely came, for he would have left town before the storm began and he might just as well come right on as go back. If he'd hurried he would have gotten here before the preacher came. I suppose he was afraid to come, for he knew Canuteson could pound him to jelly, the coward!" Her eyes flashed angrily.

The weary hours wore on and Lena began to grow horribly lonesome. It was an uncanny night and this was an uncanny place to be in. She could hear the coyotes howling hungrily a little way from the cabin, and more terrible still were all the unknown noises of the storm. She remembered the tales they told of the big log overhead and she was afraid of those snaky things on the window sills. She remembered the man who had been killed in the draw, and she wondered what she would do if she saw crazy Lou's white face glaring into the window. The rattling of the door became unbearable, she thought the latch must be loose and took the lamp to look at it. Then for the first time she saw the ugly brown snake skins whose death rattle sounded every time the wind jarred the door.

"Canute, Canute!" she screamed in terror.

Outside the door she heard a heavy sound as of a big dog getting up and shaking himself. The door opened and Canute stood before her, white as a snow drift.

"What is it?" he asked kindly.

"I am cold," she faltered.

He went out and got an armful of wood and a basket of cobs and filled the stove. Then he went out and lay in the snow before the door. Presently he heard her calling again.

"What is it?" he said, sitting up.

"I'm so lonesome, I'm afraid to stay in here all alone."

"I will go over and get your mother." And he got up.

"She won't come."

"I'll bring her," said Canute grimly.

"No, no. I don't want her, she will scold all the time."

"Well, I will bring your father."

She spoke again and it seemed as though her mouth was close up to the key-hole. She spoke lower than he had ever heard her speak before, so low that he had to put his ear up to the lock to hear her.

"I don't want him either, Canute, — I'd rather have you."

For a moment she heard no noise at all, then something like a groan. With a cry of fear she opened the door, and saw Canute stretched in the snow at her feet, his face in his hands, sobbing on the door step.

ERIC HERMANNSON'S SOUL

I.

It was a great night at the Lone Star schoolhouse — a night when the Spirit was present with power and when God was very near to man. So it seemed to Asa Skinner, servant of God and Free Gospeller. The schoolhouse was crowded with the saved and sanctified, robust men and women, trembling and quailing before the power of some mysterious psychic force. Here and there among this cowering, sweating multitude crouched some poor wretch who had felt the pangs of an awakened conscience, but had not yet experienced that complete divestment of reason, that frenzy born of a convulsion of the mind, which, in the parlance of the Free Gospellers, is termed "the Light." On the floor, before the mourners' bench, lay the unconscious figure of a man in whom outraged nature had sought her last resort. This "trance" state is the highest evidence of grace among the Free Gospellers, and indicates a close walking with God.

Before the desk stood Asa Skinner, shouting of the mercy and vengeance of God, and in his eyes shone a terrible earnestness, an almost prophetic flame. Asa was a converted train gambler who used to run between Omaha and Denver. He was a man made for the extremes of life; from the most debauched of men he had become the most ascetic. His was a bestial face, a face that bore the stamp of Nature's eternal injustice. The forehead was low, projecting over the eyes, and the sandy hair was plastered down over it and then brushed back at an abrupt right angle. The chin was heavy, the nostrils were low and wide, and the lower lip hung loosely except in his moments of spasmodic earnestness, when it shut like a steel trap. Yet about those coarse features there were deep, rugged furrows, the scars of many a hand-to-hand struggle with the weakness of the flesh, and about that drooping lip were sharp, strenuous lines that had conquered it and taught it to pray. Over those seamed cheeks there was a certain pallor, a grayness caught from many a vigil. It was as though, after Nature had done her worst with that face, some fine chisel had gone over it, chastening and almost transfiguring it. To-night, as his muscles twitched with emotion, and the perspiration dropped from his hair and chin, there was a certain convincing power in the man. For Asa Skinner was a man possessed of a belief, of that sentiment of the sublime before which all inequalities are leveled, that transport of conviction which seems superior to all laws of condition, under which debauchees have become martyrs; which made a tinker an artist and a camel-driver the founder of an empire. This was with Asa Skinner to-night, as he stood proclaiming the vengeance of God.

It might have occurred to an impartial observer that Asa Skinner's God was indeed a vengeful God if he could reserve vengeance for those of his creatures who were packed into the Lone Star schoolhouse that night. Poor exiles of all nations; men from the south and the north, peasants from almost every country of Europe, most of them from the mountainous, night-bound coast of Norway. Honest men for the most part, but men with whom the world had dealt hardly; the failures of all countries, men sobered by toil and saddened by exile, who had been driven to fight for the dominion of an untoward soil, to sow where others should gather, the advance-guard of a mighty civilization to be.

Never had Asa Skinner spoken more earnestly than now. He felt that the Lord had this night a special work for him to do. To-night Eric Hermannson, the wildest lad on all the Divide, sat in his audience with a fiddle on his knee, just as he had dropped in on his way to play for some dance. The violin is an object of particular abhorrence to the Free Gospellers. Their antagonism to the church organ is bitter enough, but the fiddle they regard as a very incarnation of evil desires, singing forever of worldly pleasures and inseparably associated with all forbidden things.

Eric Hermannson had long been the object of the prayers of the revivalists. His mother had felt the power of the Spirit weeks ago, and special prayer-meetings had been held at her house for her son. But Eric had only gone his ways laughing, the ways of youth, which are short enough at best, and none too flowery on the Divide. He slipped away from the prayer-meetings to meet the Campbell boys in Genereau's saloon, or hug the plump little French girls at Chevalier's dances, and sometimes, of a summer night, he even went across the dewy cornfields and through the wild-plum thicket to play the fiddle for Lena Hanson, whose name was a reproach through all the Divide country, where the women are usually too plain and too busy and too tired to depart from the ways of virtue. On such occasions Lena, attired in a pink wrapper and silk stockings and tiny pink slippers, would sing to him, accompanying herself on a battered guitar. It gave him a delicious sense of freedom and experience to be with a woman who, no matter how, had lived in big cities and knew the ways of town-folk, who had never worked in the fields and had kept her hands white and soft, her throat fair and tender, who had heard great singers in Denver and Salt Lake, and who knew the strange language of flattery and idleness and mirth.

Yet, careless as he seemed, the frantic prayers of his mother were not altogether without their effect upon Eric. For days he had been fleeing before them as a criminal from his pursuers, and over his pleasures had fallen the shadow of something dark and terrible that dogged his steps. The harder he danced, the louder he sang, the more was he conscious that this phantom was gaining upon him, that in time it would track him down. One Sunday afternoon, late in the fall, when he had been drinking beer with Lena Hanson and listening to a song which made his cheeks burn, a rattlesnake had crawled out of the side of the sod house and thrust its ugly head in under the screen door. He was not afraid of snakes, but he knew enough of Gospellism to feel the significance of the reptile lying coiled there upon her doorstep. His lips were cold when he kissed Lena good-by, and he went there no more.

The final barrier between Eric and his mother's

faith was his violin, and to that he clung as a man sometimes will cling to his dearest sin, to the weakness more precious to him than all his strength. In the great world beauty comes to men in many guises, and art in a hundred forms, but for Eric there was only his violin. It stood, to him, for all the manifestations of art; it was his only bridge into the kingdom of the soul.

It was to Eric Hermannson that the evangelist directed his impassioned pleading that night.

"Saul, Saul, why persecutest thou me? Is there a Saul here to-night who has stopped his ears to that gentle pleading, who has thrust a spear into that bleeding side? Think of it, my brother; you are offered this wonderful love and you prefer the worm that dieth not and the fire which will not be quenched. What right have you to lose one of God's precious souls? *Saul, Saul, why persecutest thou me?"*

A great joy dawned in Asa Skinner's pale face, for he saw that Eric Hermannson was swaying to and fro in his seat. The minister fell upon his knees and threw his long arms up over his head.

"O my brothers! I feel it coming, the blessing we have prayed for. I tell you the Spirit is coming! Just a little more prayer, brothers, a little more zeal, and he will be here. I can feel his cooling wing upon my brow. Glory be to God forever and ever, amen!"

The whole congregation groaned under the pressure of this spiritual panic. Shouts and hallelujahs went up from every lip. Another figure fell prostrate upon the floor. From the mourners' bench rose a chant of terror and rapture:

"Eating honey and drinking wine,

454

 Glory to the bleeding Lamb!
I am my Lord's and he is mine,
 Glory to the bleeding Lamb!"

The hymn was sung in a dozen dialects and voiced all the vague yearning of these hungry lives, of these people who had starved all the passions so long, only to fall victims to the basest of them all, fear.

A groan of ultimate anguish rose from Eric Hermannson's bowed head, and the sound was like the groan of a great tree when it falls in the forest.

The minister rose suddenly to his feet and threw back his head, crying in a loud voice:

"*Lazarus, come forth!* Eric Hermannson, you are lost, going down at sea. In the name of God, and Jesus Christ his Son, I throw you the life-line. Take hold! Almighty God, my soul for his!" The minister threw his arms out and lifted his quivering face.

Eric Hermannson rose to his feet; his lips were set and the lightning was in his eyes. He took his violin by the neck and crushed it to splinters across his knee, and to Asa Skinner the sound was like the shackles of sin broken audibly asunder.

II

For more than two years Eric Hermannson kept the austere faith to which he had sworn himself, kept it until a girl from the East came to spend a week on the Nebraska Divide. She was a girl of other manners and conditions, and there were greater distances between her life and Eric's than all the miles which separated Rattlesnake Creek from New York city. Indeed, she had no business to be in the West at all; but ah! across what leagues

455

of land and sea, by what improbable chances, do the unrelenting gods bring to us our fate!

It was in a year of financial depression that Wyllis Elliot came to Nebraska to buy cheap land and revisit the country where he had spent a year of his youth. When he had graduated from Harvard it was still customary for moneyed gentlemen to send their scapegrace sons to rough it on ranches in the wilds of Nebraska or Dakota, or to consign them to a living death in the sage-brush of the Black Hills. These young men did not always return to the ways of civilized life. But Wyllis Elliot had not married a half-breed, nor been shot in a cow-punchers' brawl, nor wrecked by bad whisky, nor appropriated by a smirched adventuress. He had been saved from these things by a girl, his sister, who had been very near to his life ever since the days when they read fairy tales together and dreamed the dreams that never come true. On this, his first visit to his father's ranch since he left it six years before, he brought her with him. She had been laid up half the winter from a sprain received while skating, and had had too much time for reflection during those months. She was restless and filled with a desire to see something of the wild country of which her brother had told her so much. She was to be married the next winter, and Wyllis understood her when she begged him to take her with him on this long, aimless jaunt across the continent, to taste the last of their freedom together. It comes to all women of her type — that desire to taste the unknown which allures and terrifies, to run one's whole soul's length out to the wind — just once.

It had been an eventful journey. Wyllis somehow understood that strain of gypsy blood in his sister, and he knew where to take her. They had slept in sod houses on the Platte River, made the acquaintance of the personnel of a third-rate opera company on the train to Deadwood, dined in a camp of railroad constructors at the world's end beyond New Castle, gone through the Black Hills on horseback, fished for trout in Dome Lake, watched a dance at Cripple Creek, where the lost souls who hide in the hills gathered for their besotted revelry. And now, last of all, before the return to thraldom, there was this little shack, anchored on the windy crest of the Divide, a little black dot against the flaming sunsets, a scented sea of cornland bathed in opalescent air and blinding sunlight.

Margaret Elliot was one of those women of whom there are so many in this day, when old order, passing, giveth place to new; beautiful, talented, critical, unsatisfied, tired of the world at twenty-four. For the moment the life and people of the Divide interested her. She was there but a week; perhaps had she stayed longer, that inexorable ennui which travels faster even than the Vestibule Limited would have overtaken her. The week she tarried there was the week that Eric Hermannson was helping Jerry Lockhart thresh; a week earlier or a week later, and there would have been no story to write.

It was on Thursday and they were to leave on Saturday. Wyllis and his sister were sitting on the wide piazza of the ranchhouse, staring out into the afternoon sunlight and protesting against the gusts of hot wind that blew up from the sandy river-bottom twenty miles to the southward.

The young man pulled his cap lower over his eyes and remarked:

"This wind is the real thing; you don't strike it anywhere else. You remember we had a touch of it in Algiers and I told you it came from Kansas. It's the key-note of this country."

Wyllis touched her hand that lay on the hammock and continued gently:

"I hope it's paid you, Sis. Roughing it's dangerous business; it takes the taste out of things."

She shut her fingers firmly over the brown hand that was so like her own.

"Paid? Why, Wyllis, I haven't been so happy since we were children and were going to discover the ruins of Troy together some day. Do you know, I believe I could just stay on here forever and let the world go on its own gait. It seems as though the tension and strain we used to talk of last winter were gone for good, as though one could never give one's strength out to such petty things any more."

Wyllis brushed the ashes of his pipe away from the silk handkerchief that was knotted about his neck and stared moodily off at the sky-line.

"No, you're mistaken. This would bore you after a while. You can't shake the fever of the other life. I've tried it. There was a time when the gay fellows of Rome could trot down into the Thebaid and burrow into the sandhills and get rid of it. But it's all too complex now. You see we've made our dissipations so dainty and respectable that they've gone further in than the flesh, and taken hold of the ego proper. You couldn't rest, even here. The war-cry would follow you."

"You don't waste words, Wyllis, but you never miss fire. I talk more than you do, without saying half so much. You must have learned the art of silence from these taciturn Norwegians. I think I like silent men."

"Naturally," said Wyllis, "since you have decided to marry the most brilliant talker you know."

Both were silent for a time, listening to the sighing of the hot wind through the parched morning-glory vines. Margaret spoke first.

"Tell me, Wyllis, were many of the Norwegians you used to know as interesting as Eric Hermannson?"

"Who, Siegfried? Well, no. He used to be the flower of the Norwegian youth in my day, and he's rather an exception, even now. He has retrograded, though. The bonds of the soil have tightened on him, I fancy."

"Siegfried? Come, that's rather good, Wyllis. He looks like a dragon-slayer. What is it that makes him so different from the others? I can talk to him; he seems quite like a human being."

"Well," said Wyllis, meditatively, "I don't read Bourget as much as my cultured sister, and I'm not so well up in analysis, but I fancy it's because one keeps cherishing a perfectly unwarranted suspicion that under that big, hulking anatomy of his, he may conceal a soul somewhere. Nicht wahr?"

"Something like that," said Margaret, thoughtfully, "except that it's more than a suspicion, and it isn't groundless. He has one, and he makes it known, somehow, without speaking."

"I always have my doubts about loquacious souls," Wyllis remarked, with the unbelieving smile that had grown habitual with him.

Margaret went on, not heeding the interruption. "I knew it from the first, when he told me about the suicide of his cousin, the Bernstein boy. That kind of blunt pathos can't be summoned at will in anybody. The earlier novelists rose to it, sometimes, unconsciously. But last night when I sang for him I was doubly sure. Oh, I haven't told you about that yet! Better light your pipe again. You see, he stumbled in on me in the dark when I was pumping away at that old parlor organ to please Mrs. Lockhart. It's her household fetish and I've forgotten how many pounds of butter she made and sold to buy it. Well, Eric stumbled in, and in some inarticulate manner made me understand that he wanted me to sing for him. I sang just the old things, of course. It's queer to sing familiar things here at the world's end. It makes one think how the hearts of men have carried them around the world, into the wastes of Iceland and the jungles of Africa and the islands of the Pacific. I think if one lived here long enough one would quite forget how to be trivial, and would read only the great books that we never get time to read in the world, and would remember only the great music, and the things that are really worth while would stand out clearly against that horizon over there. And of course I played the intermezzo from 'Cavalleria Rusticana' for him; it goes rather better on an organ than most things do. He shuffled his feet and twisted his big hands up into knots and blurted out that he didn't know there was any music like that in the world. Why, there were tears in his voice, Wyllis! Yes, like Rossetti, I *heard* his tears. Then it dawned upon me that it was probably the first good music he had ever heard in all his life. Think of it, to care for music as he does and never to hear it, never to know that it exists on earth! To long for it as we long for other perfect experiences that never come. I can't tell you what music means to that man. I never saw any one so susceptible to it. It gave him speech, he became alive. When I had finished the intermezzo, he began telling me about a little crippled brother who died and whom he loved and used to carry everywhere in his arms. He did not wait for encouragement. He took up the story and told it slowly, as if to himself, just sort of rose up and told his own woe to answer Mascagni's. It overcame me."

"Poor devil," said Wyllis, looking at her with mysterious eyes, "and so you've given him a new woe. Now he'll go on wanting Grieg and Schubert the rest of his days and never getting them. That's a girl's philanthropy for you!"

Jerry Lockhart came out of the house screwing his chin over the unusual luxury of a stiff white collar, which his wife insisted upon as a necessary article of toilet while Miss Elliot was at the house. Jerry sat down on the step and smiled his broad, red smile at Margaret.

"Well, I've got the music for your dance, Miss Elliot. Olaf Oleson will bring his accordion and Mollie will play the organ, when she isn't lookin' after the grub, and a little chap from Frenchtown will bring his fiddle — though the French don't mix with the Norwegians much."

"Delightful! Mr. Lockhart, that dance will be the feature of our trip, and it's so nice of you to get it up for us. We'll see the Norwegians in character at last," cried Margaret, cordially.

"See here, Lockhart, I'll settle with you for backing her in this scheme," said Wyllis, sitting up and knocking the ashes out of his pipe. "She's done crazy things enough on this trip, but to talk of dancing all night with a gang of half-mad Norwegians and taking the carriage at four to catch the six o'clock train out of Riverton — well, it's tommy-rot, that's what it is!"

"Wyllis, I leave it to your sovereign power of reason to decide whether it isn't easier to stay up all night than to get up at three in the morning. To get up at three, think what that means! No, sir, I prefer to keep my vigil and then get into a sleeper."

"But what do you want with the Norwegians? I thought you were tired of dancing."

"So I am, with some people. But I want to see a Norwegian dance, and I intend to. Come, Wyllis, you know how seldom it is that one really wants to do anything nowadays. I wonder when I have really wanted to go to a party before. It will be something to remember next month at Newport, when we have to and don't want to. Remember your own theory that contrast is about the only thing that makes life endurable. This is my party and Mr. Lockhart's; your whole duty to-morrow night will consist in being nice to the Norwegian girls. I'll warrant you were adept enough at it once. And you'd better be very nice indeed, for if there are many such young valkyrs as Eric's sister among them, they would simply tie you up in a knot if they suspected you were guying them."

Wyllis groaned and sank back into the hammock to consider his fate, while his sister went on.

"And the guests, Mr. Lockhart, did they accept?"

Lockhart took out his knife and began sharpening it on the sole of his plowshoe.

"Well, I guess we'll have a couple dozen. You see it's pretty hard to get a crowd together here any more. Most of 'em have gone over to the Free Gospellers, and they'd rather put their feet in the fire than shake 'em to a fiddle."

Margaret made a gesture of impatience.

"Those Free Gospellers have just cast an evil spell over this country, haven't they?"

"Well," said Lockhart, cautiously, "I don't just like to pass judgment on any Christian sect, but if you're to know the chosen by their works, the Gospellers can't make a very proud showin', an' that's a fact. They're responsible for a few suicides, and they've sent a good-sized delegation to the state insane asylum, an' I don't see as they've made the rest of us much better than we were before. I had a little herdboy last spring, as square a little Dane as I want to work for me, but after the Gospellers got hold of him and sanctified him, the little beggar used to get down on his knees out on the prairie and pray by the hour and let the cattle get into the corn, an' I had to fire him. That's about the way it goes. Now there's Eric; that chap used to be a hustler and the spryest dancer in all this section — called all the dances. Now he's got no ambition and he's glum as a preacher. I don't suppose we can even get him to come in to-morrow night."

"Eric? Why, he must dance, we can't let him off," said Margaret, quickly. "Why, I intend to dance with him myself!"

"I'm afraid he won't dance. I asked him this morning if he'd help us out and he said, 'I don't dance now, any more,' " said Lockhart, imitating the labored English of the Norwegian.

" 'The Miller of Hoffbau, the Miller of Hoffbau, O my Princess!' " chirped Wyllis, cheerfully, from his hammock.

The red on his sister's cheek deepened a little, and she laughed mischievously. "We'll see about that, sir. I'll not admit that I am beaten until I have asked him myself."

Every night Eric rode over to St. Anne, a little village in the heart of the French settlement, for the mail. As the road lay through the most attractive part of the Divide country, on several occasions Margaret Elliot and her brother had accompanied him. To-night Wyllis had business with Lockhart, and Margaret rode with Eric, mounted on a frisky little mustang that Mrs. Lockhart had broken to the side-saddle. Margaret regarded her escort very much as she did the servant who always accompanied her on long rides at home, and the ride to the village was a silent one. She was occupied with thoughts of another world, and Eric was wrestling with more thoughts than had ever been crowded into his head before. He rode with his eyes riveted on that slight figure before him, as though he wished to absorb it through the optic nerves and hold it in his brain forever. He understood the situation perfectly. His brain worked slowly, but he had a keen sense of the values of things. This girl represented an entirely new species of humanity to him, but he knew where to place her. The prophets of old, when an angel first appeared unto them, never doubted its high origin.

Eric was patient under the adverse conditions of his life, but he was not servile. The Norse blood in him had not entirely lost its self-reliance. He came of a proud fisher line, men who were not afraid of anything but the ice and the devil, and he had prospects before him when his father went down off the North Cape in the long Arctic night, and his mother, seized by a violent horror of seafaring life, had followed her brother to America.

Eric was eighteen then, handsome as young Siegfried, a giant in stature, with a skin singularly pure and delicate, like a Swede's; hair as yellow as the locks of Tennyson's amorous Prince, and eyes of a fierce, burning blue, whose flash was most dangerous to women. He had in those days a certain pride of bearing, a certain confidence of approach, that usually accompanies physical perfection. It was even said of him then that he was in love with life, and inclined to levity, a vice most unusual on the Divide. But the sad history of those Norwegian exiles, transplanted in an arid soil and under a scorching sun, had repeated itself in his case. Toil and isolation had sobered him, and he grew more and more like the clods among which he labored. It was as though some red-hot instrument had touched for a moment those delicate fibers of the brain which respond to acute pain or pleasure, in which lies the power of exquisite sensation, and had seared them quite away. It is a painful thing to watch the light die out of the eyes of those Norsemen, leaving an expression of impenetrable sadness, quite passive, quite hopeless, a shadow that is never lifted. With some this change comes almost at once, in the first bitterness of homesickness, with others it comes more slowly, according to the time it takes each man's heart to die.

Oh, those poor Northmen of the Divide! They are dead many a year before they are put to rest in the little graveyard on the windy hill where exiles of all nations grow akin.

The peculiar species of hypochondria to which the exiles of his people sooner or later succumb had not developed in Eric until that night at the Lone Star schoolhouse, when he had broken his

465

violin across his knee. After that, the gloom of his people settled down upon him, and the gospel of maceration began its work. *"If thine eye offend thee, pluck it out,"* et cetera. The pagan smile that once hovered about his lips was gone, and he was one with sorrow. Religion heals a hundred hearts for one that it embitters, but when it destroys, its work is quick and deadly, and where the agony of the cross has been, joy will not come again. This man understood things literally: one must live without pleasure to die without fear; to save the soul it was necessary to starve the soul.

The sun hung low above the cornfields when Margaret and her cavalier left St. Anne. South of the town there is a stretch of road that runs for some three miles through the French settlement, where the prairie is as level as the surface of a lake. There the fields of flax and wheat and rye are bordered by precise rows of slender, tapering Lombard poplars. It was a yellow world that Margaret Elliot saw under the wide light of the setting sun.

The girl gathered up her reins and called back to Eric, "It will be safe to run the horses here, won't it?"

"Yes, I think so, now," he answered, touching his spur to his pony's flank. They were off like the wind. It is an old saying in the West that newcomers always ride a horse or two to death before they get broken in to the country. They are tempted by the great open spaces and try to outride the horizon, to get to the end of something. Margaret galloped over the level road, and Eric, from behind, saw her long veil fluttering in the wind. It had fluttered just so in his dreams last night and the night before. With a sudden inspiration of courage he overtook her and rode beside her, looking intently at her half-averted face. Before, he had only stolen occasional glances at it, seen it in blinding flashes, always with more or less embarrassment, but now he determined to let every line of it sink into his memory. Men of the world would have said that it was an unusual face, nervous, finely cut, with clear, elegant lines that betokened ancestry. Men of letters would have called it a historic face, and would have conjectured at what old passions, long asleep, what old sorrows forgotten time out of mind, doing battle together in ages gone, had curved those delicate nostrils, left their unconscious memory in those eyes. But Eric read no meaning in these details. To him this beauty was something more than color and line; it was as a flash of white light, in which one cannot distinguish color because all colors are there. To him it was a complete revelation, an embodiment of those dreams of impossible loveliness that linger by a young man's pillow on midsummer nights; yet, because it held something more than the attraction of health and youth and shapeliness, it troubled him, and in its presence he felt as the Goths before the white marbles in the Roman Capitol, not knowing whether they were men or gods. At times he felt like uncovering his head before it, again the fury seized him to break and despoil, to find the clay in this spirit-thing and stamp upon it. Away from her, he longed to strike out with his arms, and take and hold; it maddened him that this woman whom he could break in his hands should be so much stronger than he. But near her, he never questioned this strength; he admitted its potentiality as he admitted the miracles of the Bible; it enervated and conquered him. To-night, when he rode so close to her that he could have touched her, he knew that he might as well reach out his hand to take a star.

Margaret stirred uneasily under his gaze and turned questioningly in her saddle.

"This wind puts me a little out of breath when we ride fast," she said.

Eric turned his eyes away.

"I want to ask you if I go to New York to work, if I maybe hear music like you sang last night? I been a purty good hand to work," he asked, timidly.

Margaret looked at him with surprise, and then, as she studied the outline of his face, pityingly.

"Well, you might — but you'd lose a good deal else. I shouldn't like you to go to New York — and be poor, you'd be out of atmosphere, some way," she said, slowly. Inwardly she was thinking: "There he would be altogether sordid, impossible — a machine who would carry one's trunks upstairs, perhaps. Here he is every inch a man, rather picturesque; why is it?" "No," she added aloud, "I shouldn't like that."

"Then I not go," said Eric, decidedly.

Margaret turned her face to hide a smile. She was a trifle amused and a trifle annoyed. Suddenly she spoke again.

"But I'll tell you what I do want you to do, Eric. I want you to dance with us to-morrow night and teach me some of the Norwegian dances; they say you know them all. Won't you?"

Eric straightened himself in his saddle and his eyes flashed as they had done in the Lone Star schoolhouse when he broke his violin across his knee.

"Yes, I will," he said, quietly, and he believed that he delivered his soul to hell as he said it.

They had reached the rougher country now, where the road wound through a narrow cut in one of the bluffs along the creek, when a beat of hoofs ahead and the sharp neighing of horses made the ponies start and Eric rose in his stirrups. Then down the gulch in front of them and over the steep clay banks thundered a herd of wild ponies, nimble as monkeys and wild as rabbits, such as horse-traders drive east from the plains of Montana to sell in the farming country. Margaret's pony made a shrill sound, a neigh that was almost a scream, and started up the clay bank to meet them, all the wild blood of the range breaking out in an instant. Margaret called to Eric just as he threw himself out of the saddle and caught her pony's bit. But the wiry little animal had gone mad and was kicking and biting like a devil. Her wild brothers of the range were all about her, neighing, and pawing the earth, and striking her with their fore feet and snapping at her flanks. It was the old liberty of the range that the little beast fought for.

"Drop the reins and hold tight, tight!" Eric called, throwing all his weight upon the bit, struggling under those frantic fore feet that now beat at his breast, and now kicked at the wild mustangs that surged and tossed about him. He succeeded in wrenching the pony's head toward him and crowding her withers against the clay bank, so that she could not roll.

"Hold tight, tight!" he shouted again, launching a kick at a snorting animal that reared back against Margaret's saddle. If she should lose her courage and fall now, under those hoofs —— He struck out again and again, kicking right and left with all his might. Already the negligent drivers had galloped into the cut, and their long quirts were whistling over the heads of the herd. As suddenly as it had come, the struggling, frantic wave of wild life swept up out of the gulch and on across the open prairie, and with a long despairing whinny of farewell the pony dropped her head and stood trembling in her sweat, shaking the foam and blood from her bit.

Eric stepped close to Margaret's side and laid his hand on her saddle. "You are not hurt?" he asked, hoarsely. As he raised his face in the soft starlight she saw that it was white and drawn and that his lips were working nervously.

"No, no, not at all. But you, you are suffering; they struck you!" she cried in sharp alarm.

He stepped back and drew his hand across his brow.

"No, it is not that," he spoke rapidly now, with his hands clenched at his side. "But if they had hurt you, I would beat their brains out with my hands, I would kill them all. I was never afraid before. You are the only beautiful thing that has ever come close to me. You came like an angel out of the sky. You are like the music you sing, you are like the stars and the snow on the mountains where I played when I was a little boy. You are like all that I wanted once and never had, you are all that they have killed in me. I die for you to-night, to-morrow, for all eternity. I am not a coward; I was afraid because I love you more than Christ who died for me, more than I am afraid of hell, or hope for heaven. I was never afraid before. If you had fallen — oh, my God!" he threw his arms out blindly and dropped his head upon the pony's mane, leaning limply against the animal like a man struck by some sickness. His shoulders rose and fell perceptibly with his labored breathing. The horse stood cowed with exhaustion and fear. Presently Margaret laid her hand on Eric's head and said gently:

"You are better now, shall we go on? Can you get your horse?"

"No, he has gone with the herd. I will lead yours, she is not safe. I will not frighten you again." His voice was still husky, but it was steady now. He took hold of the bit and tramped home in silence.

When they reached the house, Eric stood stolidly by the pony's head until Wyllis came to lift his sister from the saddle.

"The horses were badly frightened, Wyllis. I think I was pretty thoroughly scared myself," she said as she took her brother's arm and went slowly up the hill toward the house. "No, I'm not hurt, thanks to Eric. You must thank him for taking such good care of me. He's a mighty fine fellow. I'll tell you all about it in the morning, dear. I was pretty well shaken up and I'm going right to bed now. Good-night."

When she reached the low room in which she slept, she sank upon the bed in her riding-dress face downward.

"Oh, I pity him! I pity him!" she murmured, with a long sigh of exhaustion. She must have slept a little. When she rose again, she took from her dress a letter that had been waiting for her at the village post-office. It was closely written in a long, angular hand, covering a dozen pages of foreign note-paper, and began: —

"My Dearest Margaret: If I should attempt to

471

say *how like a winter hath thine absence been,* I should incur the risk of being tedious. Really, it takes the sparkle out of everything. Having nothing better to do, and not caring to go anywhere in particular without you, I remained in the city until Jack Courtwell noted my general despondency and brought me down here to his place on the sound to manage some open-air theatricals he is getting up. 'As You Like It' is of course the piece selected. Miss Harrison plays Rosalind. I wish you had been here to take the part. Miss Harrison reads her lines well, but she is either a maiden-all-forlorn or a tomboy; insists on reading into the part all sorts of deeper meanings and highly colored suggestions wholly out of harmony with the pastoral setting. Like most of the professionals, she exaggerates the emotional element and quite fails to do justice to Rosalind's facile wit and really brilliant mental qualities. Gerard will do Orlando, but rumor says he is épris of your sometime friend, Miss Meredith, and his memory is treacherous and his interest fitful.

"My new pictures arrived last week on the 'Gascogne.' The Puvis de Chavannes is even more beautiful than I thought it in Paris. A pale dream-maiden sits by a pale dream-cow, and a stream of anemic water flows at her feet. The Constant, you will remember, I got because you admired it. It is here in all its florid splendor, the whole dominated by a glowing sensuosity. The drapery of the female figure is as wonderful as you said; the fabric all barbaric pearl and gold, painted with an easy, effortless voluptuousness, and that white, gleaming line of African coast in the background recalls memories of you very precious to me. But it is useless to deny that Constant irritates me. Though

472

I cannot prove the charge against him, his brilliancy always makes me suspect him of cheapness."

Here Margaret stopped and glanced at the remaining pages of this strange love-letter. They seemed to be filled chiefly with discussions of pictures and books, and with a slow smile she laid them by.

She rose and began undressing. Before she lay down she went to open the window. With her hand on the sill, she hesitated, feeling suddenly as though some danger were lurking outside, some inordinate desire waiting to spring upon her in the darkness. She stood there for a long time, gazing at the infinite sweep of the sky.

"Oh, it is all so little, so little there," she murmured. "When everything else is so dwarfed, why should one expect love to be great? Why should one try to read highly colored suggestions into a life like that? If only I could find one thing in it all that mattered greatly, one thing that would warm me when I am alone! Will life never give me that one great moment?"

As she raised the window, she heard a sound in the plum-bushes outside. It was only the house-dog roused from his sleep, but Margaret started violently and trembled so that she caught the foot of the bed for support. Again she felt herself pursued by some overwhelming longing, some desperate necessity for herself, like the outstretching of helpless, unseen arms in the darkness, and the air seemed heavy with sighs of yearning. She fled to her bed with the words, "I love you more than Christ, who died for me!" ringing in her ears.

III.

About midnight the dance at Lockhart's was at its
height. Even the old men who had come to "look
on" caught the spirit of revelry and stamped the
floor with the vigor of old Silenus. Eric took the
violin from the Frenchman, and Minna Oleson
sat at the organ, and the music grew more and
more characteristic — rude, half-mournful music,
made up of the folk-songs of the North, that the
villagers sing through the long night in hamlets by
the sea, when they are thinking of the sun, and
the spring, and the fishermen so long away. To
Margaret some of it sounded like Grieg's Peer
Gynt music. She found something irresistibly
infectious in the mirth of these people who were
so seldom merry, and she felt almost one of them.
Something seemed struggling for freedom in them
to-night, something of the joyous childhood of the
nations which exile had not killed. The girls were
all boisterous with delight. Pleasure came to them
but rarely, and when it came, they caught at it
wildly and crushed its fluttering wings in their
strong brown fingers. They had a hard life enough,
most of them. Torrid summers and freezing
winters, labor and drudgery and ignorance, were
the portion of their girlhood; a short wooing, a
hasty, loveless marriage, unlimited maternity,
thankless sons, premature age and ugliness, were
the dower of their womanhood. But what matter?
To-night there was hot liquor in the glass and hot
blood in the heart; to-night they danced.

To-night Eric Hermannson had renewed his
youth. He was no longer the big, silent Norwegian
who had sat at Margaret's feet and looked hope-
lessly into her eyes. To-night he was a man, with a

474

man's rights and a man's power. To-night he was Siegfried indeed. His hair was yellow as the heavy wheat in the ripe of summer, and his eyes flashed like the blue water between the ice-packs in the North Seas. He was not afraid of Margaret to-night, and when he danced with her he held her firmly. She was tired and dragged on his arm a little, but the strength of the man was like an all-pervading fluid, stealing through her veins, awakening under her heart some nameless, unsuspected existence that had slumbered there all these years and that went out through her throbbing fingertips to his that answered. She wondered if the hoydenish blood of some lawless ancestor, long asleep, were calling out in her to-night, some drop of a hotter fluid that the centuries had failed to cool, and why, if this curse were in her, it had not spoken before. But was it a curse, this awakening, this wealth before undiscovered, this music set free? For the first time in her life her heart held something stronger than herself, was not this worth while? Then she ceased to wonder. She lost sight of the lights and the faces, and the music was drowned by the beating of her own arteries. She saw only the blue eyes that flashed above her, felt only the warmth of that throbbing hand which held hers and which the blood of his heart fed. Dimly, as in a dream, she saw the drooping shoulders, high white forehead and tight, cynical mouth of the man she was to marry in December. For an hour she had been crowding back the memory of that face with all her strength.

"Let us stop, this is enough," she whispered. His only answer was to tighten the arm behind her. She sighed and let that masterful strength bear her where it would. She forgot that this man was little more than a savage, that they would part at dawn. The blood has no memories, no reflections, no regrets for the past, no consideration of the future.

"Let us go out where it is cooler," she said when the music stopped; thinking, "I am growing faint here, I shall be all right in the open air." They stepped out into the cool, blue air of the night.

Since the older folk had begun dancing, the young Norwegians had been slipping out in couples to climb the windmill tower into the cooler atmosphere, as is their custom.

"You like to go up?" asked Eric, close to her ear.

She turned and looked at him with suppressed amusement. "How high is it?"

"Forty feet, about. I not let you fall." There was a note of irresistible pleading in his voice, and she felt that he tremendously wished her to go. Well, why not? This was a night of the unusual, when she was not herself at all, but was living an unreality. To-morrow, yes, in a few hours, there would be the Vestibule Limited and the world.

"Well, if you'll take good care of me. I used to be able to climb, when I was a little girl."

Once at the top and seated on the platform, they were silent. Margaret wondered if she would not hunger for that scene all her life, through all the routine of the days to come. Above them stretched the great Western sky, serenely blue, even in the night, with its big, burning stars, never so cold and dead and far away as in denser atmospheres. The moon would not be up for twenty minutes yet, and all about the horizon, that wide horizon, which seemed to reach around the world, lingered a pale, white light, as of a universal dawn. The weary wind brought up to them the heavy odors

476

of the cornfields. The music of the dance sounded faintly from below. Eric leaned on his elbow beside her, his legs swinging down on the ladder. His great shoulders looked more than ever like those of the stone Doryphorus, who stands in his perfect, reposeful strength in the Louvre, and had often made her wonder if such men died forever with the youth of Greece.

"How sweet the corn smells at night," said Margaret nervously.

"Yes, like the flowers that grow in paradise, I think."

She was somewhat startled by this reply, and more startled when this taciturn man spoke again.

"You go away to-morrow?"

"Yes, we have stayed longer than we thought to now."

"You not come back any more?"

"No, I expect not. You see, it is a long trip; half-way across the continent."

"You soon forget about this country, I guess." It seemed to him now a little thing to lose his soul for this woman, but that she should utterly forget this night into which he threw all his life and all his eternity, that was a bitter thought.

"No, Eric, I will not forget. You have all been too kind to me for that. And you won't be sorry you danced this one night, will you?"

"I never be sorry. I have not been so happy before. I not be so happy again, ever. You will be happy many nights yet, I only this one. I will dream sometimes, maybe."

The mighty resignation of his tone alarmed and touched her. It was as when some great animal composes itself for death, as when a great ship goes down at sea.

She sighed, but did not answer him. He drew a little closer and looked into her eyes.

"You are not always happy, too?" he asked.

"No, not always, Eric; not very often, I think."

"You have a trouble?"

"Yes, but I cannot put it into words. Perhaps if I could do that, I could cure it."

He clasped his hands together over his heart, as children do when they pray, and said falteringly, "If I own all the world, I give him you."

Margaret felt a sudden moisture in her eyes, and laid her hand on his.

"Thank you, Eric; I believe you would. But perhaps even then I should not be happy. Perhaps I have too much of it already."

She did not take her hand away from him; she did not dare. She sat still and waited for the traditions in which she had always believed to speak and save her. But they were dumb. She belonged to an ultra-refined civilization which tries to cheat nature with elegant sophistries. Cheat nature? Bah! One generation may do it, perhaps two, but the third —— Can we ever rise above nature or sink below her? Did she not turn on Jerusalem as upon Sodom, upon St. Anthony in his desert as upon Nero in his seraglio? Does she not always cry in brutal triumph: "I am here still, at the bottom of things, warming the roots of life; you cannot starve me nor tame me nor thwart me; I made the world, I rule it, and I am its destiny."

This woman, on a windmill tower at the world's end with a giant barbarian, heard that cry tonight, and she was afraid! Ah! the terror and the delight of that moment when first we fear ourselves! Until then we have not lived.

"Come, Eric, let us go down; the moon is up

478

and the music has begun again," she said.

He rose silently and stepped down upon the ladder, putting his arm about her to help her. That arm could have thrown Thor's hammer out in the cornfields yonder, yet it scarcely touched her, and his hand trembled as it had done in the dance. His face was level with hers now and the moonlight fell sharply upon it. All her life she had searched the faces of men for the look that lay in his eyes. She knew that that look had never shone for her before, would never shine for her on earth again, that such love comes to one only in dreams or in impossible places like this, unattainable always. This was Love's self, in a moment it would die. Stung by the agonized appeal that emanated from the man's whole being, she leaned forward and laid her lips on his. Once, twice and again she heard the deep respirations rattle in his throat while she held them there, and the riotous force under her heart became an engulfing weakness. He drew her up to him until he felt all the resistance go out of her body, until every nerve relaxed and yielded. When she drew her face back from his, it was white with fear.

"Let us go down, oh, my God! let us go down!" she muttered. And the drunken stars up yonder seemed reeling to some appointed doom as she clung to the rounds of the ladder. All that she was to know of love she had left upon his lips.

"The devil is loose again," whispered Olaf Oleson, as he saw Eric dancing a moment later, his eyes blazing.

But Eric was thinking with an almost savage exultation of the time when he should pay for this. Ah, there would be no quailing then! If ever a soul went fearlessly, proudly down to the gates infernal, his should go. For a moment he fancied he was there already, treading down the tempest of flame, hugging the fiery hurricane to his breast. He wondered whether in ages gone, all the countless years of sinning in which men had sold and lost and flung their souls away, any man had ever so cheated Satan, had ever bartered his soul for so great a price.

It seemed but a little while till dawn.

The carriage was brought to the door and Wyllis Elliot and his sister said good-by. She could not meet Eric's eyes as she gave him her hand, but as he stood by the horse's head, just as the carriage moved off, she gave him one swift glance that said, "I will not forget." In a moment the carriage was gone.

Eric changed his coat and plunged his head into the watertank and went to the barn to hook up his team. As he led his horses to the door, a shadow fell across his path, and he saw Skinner rising in his stirrups. His rugged face was pale and worn with looking after his wayward flock, with dragging men into the way of salvation.

"Good-morning, Eric. There was a dance here last night?" he asked, sternly.

"A dance? Oh, yes, a dance," replied Eric, cheerfully.

"Certainly you did not dance, Eric?"

"Yes, I danced. I danced all the time."

The minister's shoulders drooped, and an expression of profound discouragement settled over his haggard face. There was almost anguish in the yearning he felt for this soul.

"Eric, I didn't look for this from you. I thought God had set his mark on you if he ever had on any man. And it is for things like this that you set

480

your soul back a thousand years from God. O foolish and perverse generation!"

Eric drew himself up to his full height and looked off to where the new day was gilding the corn-tassels and flooding the uplands with light. As his nostrils drew in the breath of the dew and the morning, something from the only poetry he had ever read flashed across his mind, and he murmured, half to himself, with dreamy exultation:

" 'And a day shall be as a thousand years, and a thousand years as a day.' "

The Sentimentality of William Tavener

It takes a strong woman to make any sort of success of living in the West, and Hester undoubtedly was that. When people spoke of William Tavener as the most prosperous farmer in McPherson County, they usually added that his wife was a "good manager." She was an executive woman, quick of tongue and something of an imperatrix. The only reason her husband did not consult her about his business was that she did not wait to be consulted.

It would have been quite impossible for one man, within the limited sphere of human action, to follow all Hester's advice, but in the end William usually acted upon some of her suggestions. When she incessantly denounced the "shiftlessness" of letting a new threshing machine stand unprotected in the open, he eventually built a shed for it. When she sniffed contemptuously at his notion of fencing a hog corral with sod walls, he made a spiritless beginning on the structure — merely to "show his temper," as she put it — but in the end he went off quietly to town and bought enough barbed wire to complete the fence. When the first heavy rains came on, and the pigs rooted down the sod wall and made little paths all over it to facilitate their ascent, he heard his wife relate

482

with relish the story of the little pig that built a mud house, to the minister at the dinner table, and William's gravity never relaxed for an instant. Silence, indeed, was William's refuge and his strength.

William set his boys a wholesome example to respect their mother. People who knew him very well suspected that he even admired her. He was a hard man towards his neighbors, and even towards his sons; grasping, determined and ambitious.

There was an occasional blue day about the house when William went over the store bills, but he never objected to items relating to his wife's gowns or bonnets. So it came about that many of the foolish, unnecessary little things that Hester bought for boys, she had charged to her personal account.

One spring night Hester sat in a rocking chair by the sitting room window, darning socks. She rocked violently and sent her long needle vigorously back and forth over her gourd, and it took only a very casual glance to see that she was wrought up over something. William sat on the other side of the table reading his farm paper. If he had noticed his wife's agitation, his calm, clean-shaven face betrayed no sign of concern. He must have noticed the sarcastic turn of her remarks at the supper table, and he must have noticed the moody silence of the older boys as they ate. When supper was but half over little Billy, the youngest, had suddenly pushed back his plate and slipped away from the table, manfully trying to swallow a sob. But William Tavener never heeded ominous forecasts in the domestic horizon, and he never looked for a storm until it broke.

After supper the boys had gone to the pond under the willows in the big cattle corral, to get rid of the dust of plowing. Hester could hear an occasional splash and a laugh ringing clear through the stillness of the night, as she sat by the open window. She sat silent for almost an hour reviewing in her mind many plans of attack. But she was too vigorous a woman to be much of a strategist, and she usually came to her point with directness. At last she cut her thread and suddenly put her darning down, saying emphatically:

"William, I don't think it would hurt you to let the boys go to that circus in town to-morrow."

William continued to read his farm paper, but it was not Hester's custom to wait for an answer. She usually divined his arguments and assailed them one by one before he uttered them.

"You've been short of hands all summer, and you've worked the boys hard, and a man ought use his own flesh and blood as well as he does his hired hands. We're plenty able to afford it, and it's little enough our boys ever spend. I don't see how you can expect 'em to be steady and hard workin', unless you encourage 'em a little. I never could see much harm in circuses, and our boys have never been to one. Oh, I know Jim Howley's boys get drunk an' carry on when they go, but our boys ain't that sort, an' you know it, William. The animals are real instructive, an' our boys don't get to see much out here on the prairie. It was different where we were raised, but the boys have got no advantages here, an' if you don't take care, they'll grow up to be greenhorns."

Hester paused a moment, and William folded up his paper, but vouchsafed no remark. His sisters in Virginia had often said that only a quiet

484

man like William could ever have lived with Hester Perkins. Secretly, William was rather proud of his wife's "gift of speech," and of the fact that she could talk in prayer meeting as fluently as a man. He confined his own efforts in that line to a brief prayer at Covenant meetings.

Hester shook out another sock and went on.

"Nobody was ever hurt by goin' to a circus. Why, law me! I remember I went to one myself once, when I was little. I had most forgot about it. It was over at Pewtown, an' I remember how I had set my heart on going. I don't think I'd ever forgiven my father if he hadn't taken me, though that red clay road was in a frightful way after the rain. I mind they had an elephant and six poll parrots, an' a Rocky Mountain lion, an' a cage of monkeys, an' two camels. My! but they were a sight to me then!"

Hester dropped the black sock and shook her head and smiled at the recollection. She was not expecting anything from William yet, and she was fairly startled when he said gravely, in much the same tone in which he announced the hymns in prayer meeting:

"No, there was only one camel. The other was a dromedary."

She peered around the lamp and looked at him keenly.

"Why, William, how come you to know?"

William folded his paper and answered with some hesitation, "I was there, too."

Hester's interest flashed up. — "Well, I never, William! To think of my finding it out after all these years! Why, you couldn't have been much bigger'n our Billy then. It seems queer I never saw you when you was little, to remember about

485

you. But then you Back Creek folks never have anything to do with us Gap people. But how come you to go? Your father was stricter with you than you are with your boys."

"I reckon I shouldn't 'a gone," he said slowly, "but boys will do foolish things. I had done a good deal of fox hunting the winter before, and father let me keep the bounty money. I hired Tom Smith's Tap to weed the corn for me, an' I slipped off unbeknownst to father an' went to the show."

Hester spoke up warmly: "Nonsense, William! It didn't do you no harm, I guess. You was always worked hard enough. It must have been a big sight for a little fellow. That clown must have just tickled you to death."

William crossed his knees and leaned back in his chair.

"I reckon I could tell all that fool's jokes now. Sometimes I can't help thinkin' about 'em in meetin' when the sermon's long. I mind I had on a pair of new boots that hurt me like the mischief, but I forgot all about 'em when that fellow rode the donkey. I recall I had to take them boots off as soon as I got out of sight o' town, and walked home in the mud barefoot."

"O poor little fellow!" Hester ejaculated, drawing her chair nearer and leaning her elbows on the table. "What cruel shoes they did use to make for children. I remember I went up to Back Creek to see the circus wagons go by. They came down from Romney, you know. The circus men stopped at the creek to water the animals, an' the elephant got stubborn an' broke a big limb off the yellow willow tree that grew there by the toll house porch, an' the Scribners were 'fraid as death he'd pull the house down. But this much I saw him do;

he waded in the creek an' filled his trunk with water, and squirted it in at the window and nearly ruined Ellen Scribner's pink lawn dress that she had just ironed an' laid out on the bed ready to wear to the circus."

"I reckon that must have been a trial to Ellen," chuckled William, "for she was mighty prim in them days."

Hester drew her chair still nearer William's. Since the children had begun growing up, her conversation with her husband had been almost wholly confined to questions of economy and expense. Their relationship had become purely a business one, like that between landlord and tenant. In her desire to indulge her boys she had unconsciously assumed a defensive and almost hostile attitude towards her husband. No debtor ever haggled with his usurer more doggedly than did Hester with her husband in behalf of her sons. The strategic contest had gone on so long that it had almost crowded out the memory of a closer relationship. This exchange of confidences tonight, when common recollections took them unawares and opened their hearts, had all the miracle of romance. They talked on and on; of old neighbors, of old familiar faces in the valley where they had grown up, of long forgotten incidents of their youth — weddings, picnics, sleighing parties and baptizings. For years they had talked of nothing else but butter and eggs and the prices of things, and now they had as much to say to each other as people who meet after a long separation.

When the clock struck ten, William rose and went over to his walnut secretary and unlocked it. From his red leather wallet he took out a ten dollar bill and laid it on the table beside Hester.

487

"Tell the boys not to stay late, an' not to drive the horses hard," he said quietly, and went off to bed.

Hester blew out the lamp and sat still in the dark a long time. She left the bill lying on the table where William had placed it. She had a painful sense of having missed something, or lost something; she felt that somehow the years had cheated her.

The little locust trees that grew by the fence were white with blossoms. Their heavy odor floated in to her on the night wind and recalled a night long ago, when the first whip-poor-Will of the Spring was heard, and the rough, buxom girls of Hawkins Gap had held her laughing and struggling under the locust trees, and searched in her bosom for a lock of her sweetheart's hair, which is supposed to be on every girl's breast when the first whip-poor-Will sings. Two of those same girls had been her bridesmaids. Hester had been a very happy bride. She rose and went softly into the room where William lay. He was sleeping heavily, but occasionally moved his hand before his face to ward off the flies. Hester went into the parlor and took the piece of mosquito net from the basket of wax apples and pears that her sister had made before she died. One of the boys had brought it all the way from Virginia, packed in a tin pail, since Hester would not risk shipping so precious an ornament by freight. She went back to the bed room and spread the net over William's head. Then she sat down by the bed and listened to his deep, regular breathing until she heard the boys returning. She went out to meet them and warn them not to waken their father.

"I'll be up early to get your breakfast, boys. Your

488

father says you can go to the show." As she handed the money to the eldest, she felt a sudden throb of allegiance to her husband and said sharply, "And you be careful of that, an' don't waste it. Your father works hard for his money."

The boys looked at each other in astonishment and felt that they had lost a powerful ally.

THE NAMESAKE

Seven of us, students, sat one evening in Hartwell's studio on the Boulevard St. Michel. We were all fellow-countrymen; one from New Hampshire, one from Colorado, another from Nevada, several from the farm lands of the Middle West, and I myself from California. Lyon Hartwell, though born abroad, was simply, as every one knew, "from America." He seemed, almost more than any other one living man, to mean all of it — from ocean to ocean. When he was in Paris, his studio was always open to the seven of us who were there that evening, and we intruded upon his leisure as often as we thought permissible.

Although we were within the terms of the easiest of all intimacies, and although the great sculptor, even when he was more than usually silent, was at all times the most gravely cordial of hosts, yet, on that long remembered evening, as the sunlight died on the burnished brown of the horse-chestnuts below the windows, a perceptible dullness yawned through our conversation.

We were, indeed, somewhat low in spirit, for one of our number, Charley Bentley, was leaving us indefinitely, in response to an imperative summons from home. To-morrow his studio, just across the hall from Hartwell's, was to pass into other hands, and Bentley's luggage was even now piled in discouraged resignation before his door. The various bales and boxes seemed literally to weigh upon us as we sat in his neighbor's hospitable rooms, drearily putting in the time until he should leave us to catch the ten o'clock express for Dieppe.

The day we had got through very comfortably, for Bentley made it the occasion of a somewhat pretentious luncheon at Maxim's. There had been twelve of us at table, and the two young Poles were thirsty, the Gascon so fabulously entertaining, that it was near upon five o'clock when we put down our liqueur glasses for the last time, and the red, perspiring waiter, having pocketed the reward of his arduous and protracted services, bowed us affably to the door, flourishing his napkin and brushing back the streaks of wet, black hair from his rosy forehead. Our guests having betaken themselves belated to their respective engagements, the rest of us returned with Bentley — only to be confronted by the depressing array before his door. A glance about his denuded rooms had sufficed to chill the glow of the afternoon, and we fled across the hall in a body and begged Lyon Hartwell to take us in.

Bentley had said very little about it, but we all knew what it meant to him to be called home. Each of us knew what it would mean to himself, and each had felt something of that quickened sense of opportunity which comes at seeing another man in any way counted out of the race. Never had the game seemed so enchanting, the chance to play it such a piece of unmerited, unbelievable good fortune.

It must have been, I think, about the middle of

October, for I remember that the sycamores were almost bare in the Luxembourg Gardens that morning, and the terrace about the queens of France were strewn with crackling brown leaves. The fat red roses, out the summer long on the stand of the old flower woman at the corner, had given place to dahlias and purple asters. First glimpses of autumn toilettes flashed from the carriages; wonderful little bonnets nodded at one along the Champs-Elysées; and in the Quarter an occasional feather boa, red or black or white, brushed one's coat sleeve in the gay twilight of the early evening. The crisp, sunny autumn air was all day full of the stir of people and carriages and of the cheer of salutations; greetings of the students, returned brown and bearded from their holiday, gossip of people come back from Trouville, from St. Valery, from Dieppe, from all over Brittany and the Norman coast. Everywhere was the joyousness of return, the taking up again of life and work and play.

I had felt ever since early morning that this was the saddest of all possible seasons for saying good-by to that old, old city of youth, and to that little corner of it on the south shore which since the Dark Ages themselves — yes, and before — has been so peculiarly the land of the young.

I can recall our very postures as we lounged about Hartwell's rooms that evening, with Bentley making occasional hurried trips to his desolated workrooms across the hall — as if haunted by a feeling of having forgotten something — or stopping to poke nervously at his *perroquets,* which he had bequeathed to Hartwell, gilt cage and all. Our host himself sat on the couch, his big, bronze-like shoulders backed up against the window, his shaggy head, beaked nose, and long chin cut clean against the gray light.

Our drowsing interest, in so far as it could be said to be fixed upon anything, was centered upon Hartwell's new figure, which stood on the block ready to be cast in bronze, intended as a monument for some American battlefield. He called it "The Color Sergeant." It was the figure of a young soldier running, clutching the folds of a flag, the staff of which had been shot away. We had known it in all the stages of its growth, and the splendid action and feeling of the thing had come to have a kind of special significance for the half dozen of us who often gathered at Hartwell's rooms — though, in truth, there was as much to dishearten one as to inflame, in the case of a man who had done so much in a field so amazingly difficult; who had thrown up in bronze all the restless, teeming force of that adventurous wave still climbing westward in our own land across the waters. We recalled his "Scout," his "Pioneer," his "Gold Seekers," and those monuments in which he had invested one and another of the heroes of the Civil War with such convincing dignity and power.

"Where in the world does he get the heat to make an idea like that carry?" Bentley remarked morosely, scowling at the clay figure. "Hang me, Hartwell, if I don't think it's just because you're not really an American at all, that you can look at it like that."

The big man shifted uneasily against the window. "Yes," he replied smiling, "perhaps there is something in that. My citizenship was somewhat belated and emotional in its flowering. I've half a mind to tell you about it, Bentley." He rose uncertainly, and, after hesitating a moment, went back into his workroom, where he began fumbling among the litter in the corners.

At the prospect of any sort of personal expression from Hartwell, we glanced questioningly at one another; for although he made us feel that he liked to have us about, we were always held at a distance by a certain diffidence of his. There were rare occasions — when he was in the heat of work or of ideas — when he forgot to be shy, but they were so exceptional that no flattery was quite so seductive as being taken for a moment into Hartwell's confidence. Even in the matter of opinions — the commonest of currency in our circle — he was niggardly and prone to qualify. No man ever guarded his mystery more effectually. There was a singular, intense spell, therefore, about those few evenings when he had broken through this excessive modesty, or shyness, or melancholy, and had, as it were, committed himself.

When Hartwell returned from the back room, he brought with him an unframed canvas which he put on an easel near his clay figure. We drew close about it, for the darkness was rapidly coming on. Despite the dullness of the light, we instantly recognized the boy of Hartwell's "Color Sergeant." It was the portrait of a very handsome lad in uniform, standing beside a charger impossibly rearing. Not only in his radiant countenance and flashing eyes, but in every line of his young body there was an energy, a gallantry, a joy of life, that arrested and challenged one.

"Yes, that's where I got the notion," Hartwell remarked, wandering back to his seat in the window. "I've wanted to do it for years, but I've never felt quite sure of myself. I was afraid of missing it. He was an uncle of mine, my father's half-brother, and I was named for him. He was killed in one of the big battles of Sixty-four, when I was a child. I never saw him — never knew him until he had been dead for twenty years. And then, one night, I came to know him as we sometimes do living persons — intimately, in a single moment."

He paused to knock the ashes out of his short pipe, refilled it, and puffed at it thoughtfully for a few moments with his hands on his knees. Then, settling back heavily among the cushions and looking absently out of the window, he began his story. As he proceeded further and further into the experience which he was trying to convey to us, his voice sank so low and was sometimes so charged with feeling, that I almost thought he had forgotten our presence and was remembering aloud. Even Bentley forgot his nervousness in astonishment and sat breathless under the spell of the man's thus breathing his memories out into the dusk.

"It was just fifteen years ago this last spring that I first went home, and Bentley's having to cut away like this brings it all back to me.

"I was born, you know, in Italy. My father was a sculptor, though I dare say you've not heard of him. He was one of those first fellows who went over after Story and Powers, — went to Italy for 'Art,' quite simply; to lift from its native bough the willing, iridescent bird. Their story is told, informingly enough, by some of those ingenuous marble things at the Metropolitan. My father came over some time before the outbreak of the Civil War, and was regarded as a renegade by his family because he did not go home to enter the army. His half-brother, the only child of my grandfather's second marriage, enlisted at fifteen and was killed the next year. I was ten years old when the news of his death reached us. My mother died the following winter, and I was sent away to a Jesuit school, while my father, already ill himself, stayed on at Rome, chipping away at his Indian maidens and marble goddesses, still gloomily seeking the thing for which he had made himself the most unhappy of exiles.

"He died when I was fourteen, but even before that I had been put to work under an Italian sculptor. He had an almost morbid desire that I should carry on his work, under, as he often pointed out to me, conditions so much more auspicious. He left me in the charge of his one intimate friend, an American gentleman in the consulate at Rome, and his instructions were that I was to be educated there and to live there until I was twenty-one. After I was of age, I came to Paris and studied under one master after another until I was nearly thirty. Then, almost for the first time, I was confronted by a duty which was not my pleasure.

"My grandfather's death, at an advanced age, left an invalid maiden sister of my father's quite alone in the world. She had suffered for years from a cerebral disease, a slow decay of the faculties which rendered her almost helpless. I decided to go to America and, if possible, bring her back to Paris, where I seemed on my way toward what my poor father had wished for me.

"On my arrival at my father's birthplace, however, I found that this was not to be thought of. To tear this timid, feeble, shrinking creature, doubly aged by years and illness, from the spot where she had been rooted for a lifetime, would have been little short of brutality. To leave her to

496

the care of strangers seemed equally heartless. There was clearly nothing for me to do but to remain and wait for that slow and painless malady to run its course. I was there something over two years.

"My grandfather's home, his father's homestead before him, lay on the high banks of a river in Western Pennsylvania. The little town twelve miles down the stream, whither my great-grandfather used to drive his ox-wagon on market days, had become, in two generations, one of the largest manufacturing cities in the world. For hundreds of miles about us the gentle hill slopes were honeycombed with gas wells and coal shafts; oil derricks creaked in every valley and meadow; the brooks were sluggish and discolored with crude petroleum, and the air was impregnated by its searching odor. The great glass and iron manufactories had come up and up the river almost to our very door; their smoky exhalations brooded over us, and their crashing was always in our ears. I was plunged into the very incandescence of human energy. But, though my nerves tingled with the feverish, passionate endeavor which snapped in the very air about me, none of these great arteries seemed to feed me; this tumultuous life did not warm me. On every side were the great muddy rivers, the ragged mountains from which the timber was being ruthlessly torn away, the vast tracts of wild country, and the gulches that were like wounds in the earth; everywhere the glare of that relentless energy which followed me like a searchlight and seemed to scorch and consume me. I could only hide myself in the tangled garden, where the dropping of a leaf or the whistle of a bird was the only incident.

"The Hartwell homestead had been sold away little by little, until all that remained of it was garden and orchard. The house, a square brick structure, stood in the midst of a great garden which sloped toward the river, ending in a grassy bank which fell some forty feet to the water's edge. The garden was now little more than a tangle of neglected shrubbery; damp, rank, and of that intense blue-green peculiar to vegetation in smoky places where the sun shines but rarely, and the mists form early in the evening and hang late in the morning.

"I shall never forget it as I saw it first, when I arrived there in the chill of a backward June. The long, rank grass, thick and soft and falling in billows, was always wet until midday. The gravel walks were bordered with great lilac-bushes, mock-orange, and bridal-wreath. Back of the house was a neglected rose garden, surrounded by a low stone wall over which the long suckers trailed and matted. They had wound their pink, thorny tentacles, layer upon layer, about the lock and the hinges of the rusty iron gate. Even the porches of the house, and the very windows, were damp and heavy with growth: wistaria, clematis, honeysuckle, and trumpet vine. The garden was grown up with trees, especially that part of it which lay above the river. The bark of the old locusts was blackened by the smoke that crept continually up the valley, and their feathery foliage, so merry in its movement and so yellow and joyous in its color, seemed peculiarly precious under that somber sky. There were sycamores and copper beeches; gnarled apple-trees, too old to bear; and fall pear-trees, hung with a sharp, hard fruit in October; all with a leafage singularly rich

498

and luxuriant, and peculiarly vivid in color. The oaks about the house had been old trees when my great-grandfather built his cabin there, more than a century before, and this garden was almost the only spot for miles along the river where any of the original forest growth still survived. The smoke from the mills was fatal to trees of the larger sort, and even these had the look of doomed things — bent a little toward the town and seemed to wait with head inclined before that on-coming, shrieking force.

"About the river, too, there was a strange hush, a tragic submission — it was so leaden and sullen in its color, and it flowed so soundlessly forever past our door.

"I sat there every evening, on the high veranda overlooking it, watching the dim outlines of the steep hills on the other shore, the flicker of the lights on the island, where there was a boat-house, and listening to the call of the boatmen through the mist. The mist came as certainly as night, whitened by moonshine or starshine. The tin water-pipes went splash, splash, with it all evening, and the wind, when it rose at all, was little more than a sighing of the old boughs and a troubled breath in the heavy grasses.

"At first it was to think of my distant friends and my old life that I used to sit there; but after awhile it was simply to watch the days and weeks go by, like the river which seemed to carry them away.

"Within the house I was never at home. Month followed month, and yet I could feel no sense of kinship with anything there. Under the roof where my father and grandfather were born, I remained utterly detached. The somber rooms never spoke

499

to me, the old furniture never seemed tinctured with race. This portrait of my boy uncle was the only thing to which I could draw near, the only link with anything I had ever known before.

"There is a good deal of my father in the face, but it is my father transformed and glorified; his hesitating discontent drowned in a kind of triumph. From my first day in that house, I continually turned to this handsome kinsman of mine, wondering in what terms he had lived and had his hope; what he had found there to look like that, to bound at one, after all those years, so joyously out of the canvas.

"From the timid, clouded old woman over whose life I had come to watch, I learned that in the backyard, near the old rose garden, there was a locust-tree which my uncle had planted. After his death, while it was still a slender sapling, his mother had a seat built round it, and she used to sit there on summer evenings. His grave was under the apple-trees in the old orchard.

"My aunt could tell me little more than this. There were days when she seemed not to remember him at all.

"It was from an old soldier in the village that I learned the boy's story. Lyon was, the old man told me, but fourteen when the first enlistment occurred, but was even then eager to go. He was in the court-house square every evening to watch the recruits at their drill, and when the home company was ordered off he rode into the city on his pony to see the men board the train and to wave them good-by. The next year he spent at home with a tutor, but when he was fifteen he held his parents to their promise and went into the army. He was color sergeant of his regiment and fell in a charge upon the breastworks of a fort about a year after his enlistment.

"The veteran showed me an account of this charge which had been written for the village paper by one of my uncle's comrades who had seen his part in the engagement. It seems that as his company were running at full speed across the bottom lands toward the fortified hill, a shell burst over them. This comrade, running beside my uncle, saw the colors waver and sink as if falling, and looked to see that the boy's hand and forearm had been torn away by the exploding shrapnel. The boy, he thought, did not realize the extent of his injury, for he laughed, shouted something which his comrade did not catch, caught the flag in his left hand, and ran on up the hill. They went splendidly up over the breastworks, but just as my uncle, his colors flying, reached the top of the embankment, a second shell carried away his left arm at the arm-pit, and he fell over the wall with the flag settling about him.

"It was because this story was ever present with me, because I was unable to shake it off, that I began to read such books as my grandfather had collected upon the Civil War. I found that this war was fought largely by boys, that more men enlisted at eighteen than at any other age. When I thought of those battlefields — and I thought of them much in those days — there was always that glory of youth above them, that impetuous, generous passion stirring the long lines on the march, the blue battalions in the plain. The bugle, whenever I have heard it since, has always seemed to me the very golden throat of that boyhood which spent itself so gaily, so incredibly.

"I used often to wonder how it was that this

uncle of mine, who seemed to have possessed all the charm and brilliancy allotted to his family and to have lived up its vitality in one splendid hour, had left so little trace in the house where he was born and where he had awaited his destiny. Look as I would, I could find no letters from him, no clothing or books that might have been his. He had been dead but twenty years, and yet nothing seemed to have survived except the tree he had planted. It seemed incredible and cruel that no physical memory of him should linger to be cherished among his kindred, — nothing but the dull image in the brain of that aged sister. I used to pace the garden walks in the evening, wondering that no breath of his, no echo of his laugh, of his call to his pony or his whistle to his dogs, should linger about those shaded paths where the pale roses exhaled their dewy, country smell. Sometimes, in the dim starlight, I have thought that I heard on the grasses beside me the stir of a footfall lighter than my own, and under the black arch of the lilacs I have fancied that he bore me company.

"There was, I found, one day in the year for which my old aunt waited, and which stood out from the months that were all of a sameness to her. On the thirtieth of May she insisted that I should bring down the big flag from the attic and run it up upon the tall flagstaff beside Lyon's tree in the garden. Later in the morning she went with me to carry some of the garden flowers to the grave in the orchard, — a grave scarcely larger than a child's.

"I had noticed, when I was hunting for the flag in the attic, a leather trunk with my own name stamped upon it, but was unable to find the key.

My aunt was all day less apathetic than usual; she seemed to realize more clearly who I was, and to wish me to be with her. I did not have an opportunity to return to the attic until after dinner that evening, when I carried a lamp up-stairs and easily forced the lock of the trunk. I found all the things that I had looked for; put away, doubtless, by his mother, and still smelling faintly of lavender and rose leaves; his clothes, his exercise books, his letters from the army, his first boots, his riding-whip, some of his toys, even. I took them out and replaced them gently. As I was about to shut the lid, I picked up a copy of the Æneid, on the fly-leaf of which was written in a slanting, boyish hand,

Lyon Hartwell, January, 1862.

He had gone to the wars in Sixty-three, I remembered.

"My uncle, I gathered, was none too apt at his Latin, for the pages were dog-eared and rubbed and interlined, the margins mottled with pencil sketches — bugles, stacked bayonets, and artillery carriages. In the act of putting the book down, I happened to run over the pages to the end, and on the fly-leaf at the back I saw his name again, and a drawing — with his initials and a date — of the Federal flag; above it, written in a kind of arch and in the same unformed hand:

'Oh, say, can you see by the dawn's early light
What so proudly we hailed at the twilight's last gleaming?'

It was a stiff, wooden sketch, not unlike a detail from some Egyptian inscription, but, the moment

I saw it, wind and color seemed to touch it. I caught up the book, blew out the lamp, and rushed down into the garden.

"I seemed, somehow, at last to have known him; to have been with him in that careless, unconscious moment and to have known him as he was then.

"As I sat there in the rush of this realization, the wind began to rise, stirring the light foliage of the locust over my head and bringing, fresher than before, the woody odor of the pale roses that overran the little neglected garden. Then, as it grew stronger, it brought the sound of something sighing and stirring over my head in the perfumed darkness.

"I thought of that sad one of the Destinies who, as the Greeks believed, watched from birth over those marked for a violent or untimely death. Oh, I could see him, there in the shine of the morning, his book idly on his knee, his flashing eyes looking straight before him, and at his side that grave figure, hidden in her draperies, her eyes following his, but seeing so much farther — seeing what he never saw, that great moment at the end, when he swayed above his comrades on the earthen wall.

"All the while, the bunting I had run up in the morning flapped fold against fold, heaving and tossing softly in the dark — against a sky so black with rain clouds that I could see above me only the blur of something in soft, troubled motion.

"The experience of that night, coming so overwhelmingly to a man so dead, almost rent me in pieces. It was the same feeling that artists know when we, rarely, achieve truth in our work; the feeling of union with some great force, of purpose and security, of being glad that we have lived. For the first time I felt the pull of race and blood and kindred, and felt beating within me things that had not begun with me. It was as if the earth under my feet had grasped and rooted me, and were pouring its essence into me. I sat there until the dawn of morning, and all night long my life seemed to be pouring out of me and running into the ground."

Hartwell drew a long breath that lifted his heavy shoulders, and then let them fall again. He shifted a little and faced more squarely the scattered, silent company before him. The darkness had made us almost invisible to each other, and, except for the occasional red circuit of a cigarette end traveling upward from the arm of a chair, he might have supposed us all asleep.

"And so," Hartwell added thoughtfully, "I naturally feel an interest in fellows who are going home. It's always an experience."

No one said anything, and in a moment there was a loud rap at the door, — the concierge, come to take down Bentley's luggage and to announce that the cab was below. Bentley got his hat and coat, enjoined Hartwell to take good care of his *perroquets,* gave each of us a grip of the hand, and went briskly down the long flights of stairs. We followed him into the street, calling our good wishes, and saw him start on his drive across the lighted city to the Gare St. Lazare.

The Enchanted Bluff

Harper's, April 1909
We had our swim before sundown, and while we were cooking our supper the oblique rays of light made a dazzling glare on the white sand about us. The translucent red ball itself sank behind the brown stretches of corn field as we sat down to eat, and the warm layer of air that had rested over the water and our clean sand-bar grew fresher and smelled of the rank ironweed and sunflowers growing on the flatter shore. The river was brown and sluggish, like any other of the half-dozen streams that water the Nebraska corn lands. On one shore was an irregular line of bald clay bluffs where a few scrub-oaks with thick trunks and flat, twisted tops threw light shadows on the long grass. The western shore was low and level, with corn fields that stretched to the sky-line, and all along the water's edge were little sandy coves and beaches where slim cottonwoods and willow saplings flickered.

The turbulence of the river in spring-time discouraged milling, and, beyond keeping the old red bridge in repair, the busy farmers did not concern themselves with the stream; so the Sandtown boys were left in undisputed possession. In the autumn we hunted quail through the miles of stubble and fodder land along the flat shore, and, after the winter skating season was over and the ice had gone out, the spring freshets and flooded bottoms gave us our great excitement of the year. The channel was never the same for two successive seasons. Every spring the swollen stream undermined a bluff to the east, or bit out a few acres of corn field to the west and whirled the soil away to deposit it in spumy mud banks somewhere else. When the water fell low in midsummer, new sand-bars were thus exposed to dry and whiten in the August sun. Sometimes these were banked so firmly that the fury of the next freshet failed to unseat them; the little willow seedlings emerged triumphantly from the yellow froth, broke into spring leaf, shot up into summer growth, and with their mesh of roots bound together the moist sand beneath them against the batterings of another April. Here and there a cottonwood soon glittered among them, quivering in the low current of air that, even on breathless days when the dust hung like smoke above the wagon road, trembled along the face of the water.

It was on such an island, in the third summer of its yellow green, that we built our watch-fire; not in the thicket of dancing willow wands, but on the level terrace of fine sand which had been added that spring; a little new bit of world, beautifully ridged with ripple marks, and strewn with the tiny skeletons of turtles and fish, all as white and dry as if they had been expertly cured. We had been careful not to mar the freshness of the place, although we often swam out to it on summer evenings and lay on the sand to rest.

This was our last watch-fire of the year, and

there were reasons why I should remember it better than any of the others. Next week the other boys were to file back to their old places in the Sandtown High School, but I was to go up to the Divide to teach my first country school in the Norwegian district. I was already homesick at the thought of quitting the boys with whom I had always played; of leaving the river, and going up into a windy plain that was all windmills and corn fields and big pastures; where there was nothing wilful or unmanageable in the landscape, no new islands, and no chance of unfamiliar birds — such as often followed the watercourses.

Other boys came and went and used the river for fishing or skating, but we six were sworn to the spirit of the stream, and we were friends mainly because of the river. There were the two Hassler boys, Fritz and Otto, sons of the little German tailor. They were the youngest of us; ragged boys of ten and twelve, with sunburned hair, weather-stained faces, and pale blue eyes. Otto, the elder, was the best mathematician in school, and clever at his books, but he always dropped out in the spring term as if the river could not get on without him. He and Fritz caught the fat, horned catfish and sold them about the town, and they lived so much in the water that they were as brown and sandy as the river itself.

There was Percy Pound, a fat, freckled boy with chubby cheeks, who took half a dozen boys' story-papers and was always being kept in for reading detective stories behind his desk. There was Tip Smith, destined by his freckles and red hair to be the buffoon in all our games, though he walked like a timid little old man and had a funny, cracked laugh. Tip worked hard in his father's grocery store every afternoon, and swept it out before school in the morning. Even his recreations were laborious. He collected cigarette cards and tin tobacco-tags indefatigably, and would sit for hours humped up over a snarling little scroll-saw which he kept in his attic. His dearest possessions were some little pill-bottles that purported to contain grains of wheat from the Holy Land, water from the Jordan and the Dead Sea, and earth from the Mount of Olives. His father had bought these dull things from a Baptist missionary who peddled them, and Tip seemed to derive great satisfaction from their remote origin.

The tall boy was Arthur Adams. He had fine hazel eyes that were almost too reflective and sympathetic for a boy, and such a pleasant voice that we all loved to hear him read aloud. Even when he had to read poetry aloud at school, no one ever thought of laughing. To be sure, he was not at school very much of the time. He was seventeen and should have finished the High School the year before, but he was always off somewhere with his gun. Arthur's mother was dead, and his father, who was feverishly absorbed in promoting schemes, wanted to send the boy away to school and get him off his hands; but Arthur always begged off for another year and promised to study. I remember him as a tall, brown boy with an intelligent face, always lounging among a lot of us little fellows, laughing at us oftener than with us, but such a soft, satisfied laugh that we felt rather flattered when we provoked it. In after-years people said that Arthur had been given to evil ways even as a lad, and it is true that we often saw him with the gambler's sons and with old Spanish Fanny's boy, but if he learned anything ugly in their company he never betrayed it to us. We would have followed Arthur anywhere, and I am bound to say that he led us into no worse places than the cattail marshes and the stubble fields. These, then, were the boys who camped with me that summer night upon the sand-bar.

After we finished our supper we beat the willow thicket for driftwood. By the time we had collected enough, night had fallen, and the pungent, weedy smell from the shore increased with the coolness. We threw ourselves down about the fire and made another futile effort to show Percy Pound the Little Dipper. We had tried it often before, but he could never be got past the big one.

"You see those three big stars just below the handle, with the bright one in the middle?" said Otto Hassler; "that's Orion's belt, and the bright one is the clasp." I crawled behind Otto's shoulder and sighted up his arm to the star that seemed perched upon the tip of his steady forefinger. The Hassler boys did seine-fishing at night, and they knew a good many stars.

Percy gave up the Little Dipper and lay back on the sand, his hands clasped under his head. "I can see the North Star," he announced, contentedly, pointing toward it with his big toe. "Any one might get lost and need to know that."

We all looked up at it.

"How do you suppose Columbus felt when his compass didn't point north any more?" Tip asked.

Otto shook his head. "My father says that there was another North Star once, and that maybe this one won't last always. I wonder what would happen to us down here if anything went wrong with it?"

Arthur chuckled. "I wouldn't worry, Ott. Nothing's apt to happen to it in your time. Look at the Milky Way! There must be lots of good dead Indians."

We lay back and looked, meditating, at the dark cover of the world. The gurgle of the water had become heavier. We had often noticed a mutinous, complaining note in it at night, quite different from its cheerful daytime chuckle, and seeming like the voice of a much deeper and more powerful stream. Our water had always these two moods: the one of sunny complaisance, the other of inconsolable, passionate regret.

"Queer how the stars are all in sort of diagrams," remarked Otto. "You could do most any proposition in geometry with 'em. They always look as if they meant something. Some folks say everybody's fortune is all written out in the stars, don't they?"

"They believe so in the old country," Fritz affirmed.

But Arthur only laughed at him. "You're thinking of Napoleon, Fritzey. He had a star that went out when he began to lose battles. I guess the stars don't keep any close tally on Sandtown folks."

We were speculating on how many times we could count a hundred before the evening star went down behind the corn fields, when some one cried, "There comes the moon, and it's as big as a cart wheel!"

We all jumped up to greet it as it swam over the bluffs behind us. It came up like a galleon in full sail; an enormous, barbaric thing, red as an angry heathen god.

"When the moon came up red like that, the Aztecs used to sacrifice their prisoners on the temple top," Percy announced.

"Go on, Perce. You got that out of *Golden Days.* Do you believe that, Arthur?" I appealed.

Arthur answered, quite seriously: "Like as not. The moon was one of their gods. When my father was in Mexico City he saw the stone where they used to sacrifice their prisoners."

As we dropped down by the fire again some one asked whether the Mound-Builders were older than the Aztecs. When we once got upon the Mound-Builders we never willingly got away from them, and we were still conjecturing when we heard a loud splash in the water.

"Must have been a big cat jumping," said Fritz. "They do sometimes. They must see bugs in the dark. Look what a track the moon makes!"

There was a long, silvery streak on the water, and where the current fretted over a big log it boiled up like gold pieces.

"Suppose there ever *was* any gold hid away in this old river?" Fritz asked. He lay like a little brown Indian, close to the fire, his chin on his hand and his bare feet in the air. His brother laughed at him, but Arthur took his suggestion seriously.

"Some of the Spaniards thought there was gold up here somewhere. Seven cities chuck full of gold, they had it, and Coronado and his men came up to hunt it. The Spaniards were all over this country once."

Percy looked interested. "Was that before the Mormons went through?"

We all laughed at this.

"Long enough before. Before the Pilgrim Fathers, Perce. Maybe they came along this very river. They always followed the watercourses."

"I wonder where this river really does begin?"

Tip mused. That was an old and a favorite mystery which the map did not clearly explain. On the map the little black line stopped somewhere in western Kansas; but since rivers generally rose in mountains, it was only reasonable to suppose that ours came from the Rockies. Its destination, we knew, was the Missouri, and the Hassler boys always maintained that we could embark at Sandtown in flood-time, follow our noses, and eventually arrive at New Orleans. Now they took up their old argument. "If us boys had grit enough to try it, it wouldn't take no time to get to Kansas City and St. Joe."

We began to talk about the places we wanted to go to. The Hassler boys wanted to see the stockyards in Kansas City, and Percy wanted to see a big store in Chicago. Arthur was interlocutor and did not betray himself.

"Now it's your turn, Tip."

Tip rolled over on his elbow and poked the fire, and his eyes looked shyly out of his queer, tight little face. "My place is awful far away. My uncle Bill told me about it."

Tip's Uncle Bill was a wanderer, bitten with mining fever, who had drifted into Sandtown with a broken arm, and when it was well had drifted out again.

"Where is it?"

"Aw, it's down in New Mexico somewheres. There aren't no railroads or anything. You have to go on mules, and you run out of water before you get there and have to drink canned tomatoes."

"Well, go on, kid. What's it like when you do get there?"

Tip sat up and excitedly began his story.

"There's a big red rock there that goes right up

513

out of the sand for about nine hundred feet. The country's flat all around it, and this here rock goes up all by itself, like a monument. They call it the Enchanted Bluff down there, because no white man has ever been on top of it. The sides are smooth rock, and straight up, like a wall. The Indians say that hundreds of years ago, before the Spaniards came, there was a village away up there in the air. The tribe that lived there had some sort of steps, made out of wood and bark, hung down over the face of the bluff, and the braves went down to hunt and carried water up in big jars swung on their backs. They kept a big supply of water and dried meat up there, and never went down except to hunt. They were a peaceful tribe that made cloth and pottery, and they went up there to get out of the wars. You see, they could pick off any war party that tried to get up their little steps. The Indians say they were a handsome people, and they had some sort of a queer religion. Uncle Bill thinks they were Cliff-Dwellers who had got into trouble and left home. They weren't fighters, anyhow.

"One time the braves were down hunting and an awful storm came up — a kind of waterspout — and when they got back to their rock they found their little staircase had been all broken to pieces, and only a few steps were left hanging away up in the air. While they were camped at the foot of the rock, wondering what to do, a war party from the north came along and massacred 'em to a man, with all the old folks and women looking on from the rock. Then the war party went on south and left the village to get down the best way they could. Of course they never got down. They starved to death up there, and when the war party came back on their way north, they could hear the children crying from the edge of the bluff where they had crawled out, but they didn't see a sign of a grown Indian, and nobody has ever been up there since."

We exclaimed at this dolorous legend and sat up.

"There couldn't have been many people up there," Percy demurred. "How big is the top, Tip?"

"Oh, pretty big. Big enough so that the rock doesn't look nearly as tall as it is. The top's bigger than the base. The bluff is sort of worn away for several hundred feet up. That's one reason it's so hard to climb."

I asked how the Indians got up, in the first place.

"Nobody knows how they got up or when. A hunting party came along once and saw that there was a town up there, and that was all."

Otto rubbed his chin and looked thoughtful. "Of course there must be some way to get up there. Couldn't people get a rope over someway and pull a ladder up?"

Tip's little eyes were shining with excitement. "I know a way. Me and Uncle Bill talked it all over. There's a kind of rocket that would take a rope over — life-savers use 'em — and then you could hoist a rope-ladder and peg it down at the bottom and make it tight with guy-ropes on the other side. I'm going to climb that there bluff, and I've got it all planned out."

Fritz asked what he expected to find when he got up there.

"Bones, maybe, or the ruins of their town, or pottery, or some of their idols. There might be 'most anything up there. Anyhow, I want to see."

"Sure nobody else has been up there, Tip?" Ar-

515

thur asked.

"Dead sure. Hardly anybody ever goes down there. Some hunters tried to cut steps in the rock once, but they didn't get higher than a man can reach. The Bluff's all red granite, and Uncle Bill thinks it's a boulder the glaciers left. It's a queer place, anyhow. Nothing but cactus and desert for hundreds of miles, and yet right under the bluff there's good water and plenty of grass. That's why the bison used to go down there."

Suddenly we heard a scream above our fire, and jumped up to see a dark, slim bird floating southward far above us — a whooping-crane, we knew by her cry and her long neck. We ran to the edge of the island, hoping we might see her alight, but she wavered southward along the rivercourse until we lost her. The Hassler boys declared that by the look of the heavens it must be after midnight, so we threw more wood on our fire, put on our jackets, and curled down in the warm sand. Several of us pretended to doze, but I fancy we were really thinking about Tip's Bluff and the extinct people. Over in the wood the ring-doves were calling mournfully to one another, and once we heard a dog bark, far away. "Somebody getting into old Tommy's melon patch," Fritz murmured, sleepily, but nobody answered him. By and by Percy spoke out of the shadow.

"Say, Tip, when you go down there will you take me with you?"

"Maybe."

"Suppose one of us beats you down there, Tip?"

"Whoever gets to the Bluff first has got to promise to tell the rest of us exactly what he finds," remarked one of the Hassler boys, and to this we all readily assented.

Somewhat reassured, I dropped off to sleep. I must have dreamed about a race for the Bluff, for I awoke in a kind of fear that other people were getting ahead of me and that I was losing my chance. I sat up in my damp clothes and looked at the other boys, who lay tumbled in uneasy attitudes about the dead fire. It was still dark, but the sky was blue with the last wonderful azure of night. The stars glistened like crystal globes, and trembled as if they shone through a depth of clear water. Even as I watched, they began to pale and the sky brightened. Day came suddenly, almost instantaneously. I turned for another look at the blue night, and it was gone. Everywhere the birds began to call, and all manner of little insects began to chirp and hop about in the willows. A breeze sprang up from the west and brought the heavy smell of ripened corn. The boys rolled over and shook themselves. We stripped and plunged into the river just as the sun came up over the windy bluffs.

When I came home to Sandtown at Christmas time, we skated out to our island and talked over the whole project of the Enchanted Bluff, renewing our resolution to find it.

Although that was twenty years ago, none of us have ever climbed the Enchanted Bluff. Percy Pound is a stockbroker in Kansas City and will go nowhere that his red touring-car cannot carry him. Otto Hassler went on the railroad and lost his foot braking; after which he and Fritz succeeded their father as the town tailors.

Arthur sat about the sleepy little town all his life — he died before he was twenty-five. The last time I saw him, when I was home on one of my college vacations, he was sitting in a steamer-chair under a cottonwood tree in the little yard behind one of the two Sandtown saloons. He was very untidy and his hand was not steady, but when he rose, unabashed, to greet me, his eyes were as clear and warm as ever. When I had talked with him for an hour and heard him laugh again, I wondered how it was that when Nature had taken such pains with a man, from his hands to the arch of his long foot, she had ever lost him in Sandtown. He joked about Tip Smith's Bluff, and declared he was going down there just as soon as the weather got cooler; he thought the Grand Cañon might be worth while, too.

I was perfectly sure when I left him that he would never get beyond the high plank fence and the comfortable shade of the cottonwood. And, indeed, it was under that very tree that he died one summer morning.

Tip Smith still talks about going to New Mexico. He married a slatternly, unthrifty country girl, has been much tied to a perambulator, and has grown stooped and gray from irregular meals and broken sleep. But the worst of his difficulties are now over, and he has, as he says, come into easy water. When I was last in Sandtown I walked home with him late one moonlight night, after he had balanced his cash and shut up his store. We took the long way around and sat down on the schoolhouse steps, and between us we quite revived the romance of the lone red rock and the extinct people. Tip insists that he still means to go down there, but he thinks now he will wait until his boy, Bert, is old enough to go with him. Bert has been let into the story, and thinks of nothing but the Enchanted Bluff.

THE JOY OF NELLY
DEANE

Nell and I were almost ready to go on for the last act of "Queen Esther," and we had for the moment got rid of our three patient dressers, Mrs. Dow, Mrs. Freeze, and Mrs. Spinny. Nell was peering over my shoulder into the little cracked looking-glass that Mrs. Dow had taken from its nail on her kitchen wall and brought down to the church under her shawl that morning. When she realized that we were alone, Nell whispered to me in the quick, fierce way she had:

"Say, Peggy, won't you go up and stay with me to-night? Scott Spinny's asked to take me home, and I don't want to walk up with him alone."

"I guess so, if you'll ask my mother."

"Oh, I'll fix her!" Nell laughed, with a toss of her head which meant that she usually got what she wanted, even from people much less tractable than my mother.

In a moment our tiring-women were back again. The three old ladies — at least they seemed old to us — fluttered about us, more agitated than we were ourselves. It seemed as though they would never leave off patting Nell and touching her up. They kept trying things this way and that, never able in the end to decide which way was best. They wouldn't hear to her using rouge, and as they powdered her neck and arms, Mrs. Freeze murmured that she hoped we wouldn't get into the habit of using such things. Mrs. Spinny divided her time between pulling up and tucking down the "illusion" that filled in the square neck of Nelly's dress. She didn't like things much low, she said; but after she had pulled it up, she stood back and looked at Nell thoughtfully through her glasses. While the excited girl was reaching for this and that, buttoning a slipper, pinning down a curl, Mrs. Spinny's smile softened more and more until, just before *Esther* made her entrance, the old lady tiptoed up to her and softly tucked the illusion down as far as it would go.

"She's so pink; it seems a pity not," she whispered apologetically to Mrs. Dow.

Every one admitted that Nelly was the prettiest girl in Riverbend, and the gayest — oh, the gayest! When she was not singing, she was laughing. When she was not laid up with a broken arm, the outcome of a foolhardy coasting feat, or suspended from school because she ran away at recess to go buggy-riding with Guy Franklin, she was sure to be up to mischief of some sort. Twice she broke through the ice and got soused in the river because she never looked where she skated or cared what happened so long as she went fast enough. After the second of these duckings our three dressers declared that she was trying to be a Baptist despite herself.

Mrs. Spinny and Mrs. Freeze and Mrs. Dow, who were always hovering about Nelly, often whispered to me their hope that she would eventually come into our church and not "go with the Methodists"; her family were Wesleyans. But to me these artless plans of theirs never wholly

520

explained their watchful affection. They had good daughters themselves, — except Mrs. Spinny, who had only the sullen Scott, — and they loved their plain girls and thanked God for them. But they loved Nelly differently. They were proud of her pretty figure and yellow-brown eyes, which dilated so easily and sparkled with a kind of golden effervescence. They were always making pretty things for her, always coaxing her to come to the sewing-circle, where she knotted her thread, and put in the wrong sleeve, and laughed and chattered and said a great many things that she should not have said, and somehow always warmed their hearts. I think they loved her for her unquenchable joy.

All the Baptist ladies liked Nell, even those who criticized her most severely, but the three who were first in fighting the battles of our little church, who held it together by their prayers and the labor of their hands, watched over her as they did over Mrs. Dow's century-plant before it blossomed. They looked for her on Sunday morning and smiled at her as she hurried, always a little late, up to the choir. When she rose and stood behind the organ and sang "There Is a Green Hill," one could see Mrs. Dow and Mrs. Freeze settle back in their accustomed seats and look up at her as if she had just come from that hill and had brought them glad tidings.

It was because I sang contralto, or, as we said, alto, in the Baptist choir that Nell and I became friends. She was so gay and grown up, so busy with parties and dances and picnics, that I would scarcely have seen much of her had we not sung together. She liked me better than she did any of the older girls, who tried clumsily to be like her, and I felt almost as solicitous and admiring as did Mrs. Dow and Mrs. Spinny. I think even then I must have loved to see her bloom and glow, and I loved to hear her sing, in "The Ninety and Nine,"

But one was out on the hills away

in her sweet, strong voice. Nell had never had a singing lesson, but she had sung from the time she could talk, and Mrs. Dow used fondly to say that it was singing so much that made her figure so pretty.

After I went into the choir it was found to be easier to get Nelly to choir practice. If I stopped outside her gate on my way to church and coaxed her, she usually laughed, ran in for her hat and jacket, and went along with me. The three old ladies fostered our friendship, and because I was "quiet," they esteemed me a good influence for Nelly. This view was propounded in a sewing-circle discussion and, leaking down to us through our mothers, greatly amused us. Dear old ladies! It was so manifestly for what Nell was that they loved her, and yet they were always looking for "influences" to change her.

The "Queen Esther" performance had cost us three months of hard practice, and it was not easy to keep Nell up to attending the tedious rehearsals. Some of the boys we knew were in the chorus of Assyrian youths, but the solo cast was made up of older people, and Nell found them very poky. We gave the cantata in the Baptist church on Christmas eve, "to a crowded house," as the Riverbend "Messenger" truly chronicled. The country folk for miles about had come in through a deep snow, and their teams and wagons stood in a long row at the hitch-bars on each side of the church door. It was certainly Nelly's night, for however much the tenor — he was her schoolmaster, and naturally thought poorly of her — might try to eclipse her in his dolorous solos about the rivers of Babylon, there could be no doubt as to whom the people had come to hear — and to see.

After the performance was over, our fathers and mothers came back to the dressing-rooms — the little rooms behind the baptistry where the candidates for baptism were robed — to congratulate us, and Nell persuaded my mother to let me go home with her. This arrangement may not have been wholly agreeable to Scott Spinny, who stood glumly waiting at the baptistry door; though I used to think he dogged Nell's steps not so much for any pleasure he got from being with her as for the pleasure of keeping other people away. Dear little Mrs. Spinny was perpetually in a state of humiliation on account of his bad manners, and she tried by a very special tenderness to make up to Nelly for the remissness of her ungracious son.

Scott was a spare, muscular fellow, good-looking, but with a face so set and dark that I used to think it very like the castings he sold. He was taciturn and domineering, and Nell rather liked to provoke him. Her father was so easy with her that she seemed to enjoy being ordered about now and then. That night, when every one was praising her and telling her how well she sang and how pretty she looked, Scott only said, as we came out of the dressing-room:

"Have you got your high shoes on?"

"No; but I've got rubbers on over my low ones. Mother doesn't care."

"Well, you just go back and put 'em on as fast

523

as you can."

Nell made a face at him and ran back, laughing. Her mother, fat, comfortable Mrs. Deane, was immensely amused at this.

"That's right, Scott," she chuckled. "You can do enough more with her than I can. She walks right over me an' Jud."

Scott grinned. If he was proud of Nelly, the last thing he wished to do was to show it. When she came back he began to nag again. "What are you going to do with all those flowers? They'll freeze stiff as pokers."

"Well, there won't none of *your* flowers freeze, Scott Spinny, so there!" Nell snapped. She had the best of him that time, and the Assyrian youths rejoiced. They were most of them high-school boys, and the poorest of them had "chipped in" and sent all the way to Denver for *Queen Esther*'s flowers. There were bouquets from half a dozen townspeople, too, but none from Scott. Scott was a prosperous hardware merchant and notoriously penurious, though he saved his face, as the boys said, by giving liberally to the church.

"There's no use freezing the fool things, anyhow. You get me some newspapers, and I'll wrap 'em up." Scott took from his pocket a folded copy of the Riverbend "Messenger" and began laboriously to wrap up one of the bouquets. When we left the church door he bore three large newspaper bundles, carrying them as carefully as if they had been so many newly frosted wedding-cakes, and left Nell and me to shift for ourselves as we floundered along the snow-burdened sidewalk.

Although it was after midnight, lights were shining from many of the little wooden houses, and the roofs and shrubbery were so deep in snow

524

that Riverbend looked as if it had been tucked down into a warm bed. The companies of people, all coming from church, tramping this way and that toward their homes and calling "Good night" and "Merry Christmas" as they parted company, all seemed to us very unusual and exciting.

When we got home, Mrs. Deane had a cold supper ready, and Jud Deane had already taken off his shoes and fallen to on his fried chicken and pie. He was so proud of his pretty daughter that he must give her her Christmas presents then and there, and he went into the sleeping-chamber behind the dining-room and from the depths of his wife's closet brought out a short sealskin jacket and a round cap and made Nelly put them on.

Mrs. Deane, who sat busy between a plate of spice cake and a tray piled with her famous whipped-cream tarts, laughed inordinately at his behavior.

"Ain't he worse than any kid you ever see? He's been running to that closet like a cat shut away from her kittens. I wonder Nell ain't caught on before this. I did think he'd make out now to keep 'em till Christmas morning; but he's never made out to keep anything yet."

That was true enough, and fortunately Jud's inability to keep anything seemed always to present a highly humorous aspect to his wife. Mrs. Deane put her heart into her cooking, and said that so long as a man was a good provider she had no cause to complain. Other people were not so charitable toward Jud's failing. I remember how many strictures were passed upon that little sealskin and how he was censured for his extravagance. But what a public-spirited thing, after all, it was for him to do! How, the winter through, we all enjoyed seeing Nell skating on the river or running about the town with the brown collar turned up about her bright cheeks and her hair blowing out from under the round cap! "No seal," Mrs. Dow said, "would have begrudged it to her. Why should we?" This was at the sewing-circle, when the new coat was under grave discussion.

At last Nelly and I got up-stairs and undressed, and the pad of Jud's slippered feet about the kitchen premises — where he was carrying up from the cellar things that might freeze — ceased. He called "Good night, daughter," from the foot of the stairs, and the house grew quiet. But one is not a prima donna the first time for nothing, and it seemed as if we could not go to bed. Our light must have burned long after every other in Riverbend was out. The muslin curtains of Nell's bed were drawn back; Mrs. Deane had turned down the white counterpane and taken off the shams and smoothed the pillows for us. But their fair plumpness offered no temptation to two such hot young heads. We could not let go of life even for a little while. We sat and talked in Nell's cozy room, where there was a tiny, white fur rug — the only one in Riverbend — before the bed; and there were white sash curtains, and the prettiest little desk and dressing-table I had ever seen. It was a warm, gay little room, flooded all day long with sunlight from east and south windows that had climbing-roses all about them in summer. About the dresser were photographs of adoring high-school boys; and one of Guy Franklin, much groomed and barbered, in a dress-coat and a boutonnière. I never liked to see that photograph there. The home boys looked properly modest and bashful on the dresser, but he seemed to be staring impudently all the time.

I knew nothing definite against Guy, but in Riverbend all "traveling-men" were considered worldly and wicked. He traveled for a Chicago dry-goods firm, and our fathers didn't like him because he put extravagant ideas into our mothers' heads. He had very smooth and nattering ways, and he introduced into our simple community a great variety of perfumes and scented soaps, and he always reminded me of the merchants in Cæsar, who brought into Gaul "those things which effeminate the mind," as we translated that delightfully easy passage.

Nell was silting before the dressing-table in her nightgown, holding the new fur coat and rubbing her cheek against it, when I saw a sudden gleam of tears in her eyes. "You know, Peggy," she said in her quick, impetuous way, "this makes me feel bad. I've got a secret from my daddy."

I can see her now, so pink and eager, her brown hair in two springy braids down her back, and her eyes shining with tears and with something even softer and more tremulous.

"I'm engaged, Peggy," she whispered, "really and truly."

She leaned forward, unbuttoning her nightgown, and there on her breast, hung by a little gold chain about her neck, was a diamond ring — Guy Franklin's solitaire; every one in Riverbend knew it well.

"I'm going to live in Chicago, and take singing lessons, and go to operas, and do all those nice things — oh, everything! I know you don't like him, Peggy, but you know you *are* a kid. You'll see how it is yourself when you grow up. He's so *different* from our boys, and he's just terribly in love

527

with me. And then, Peggy," — flushing all down over her soft shoulders, — "I'm awfully fond of him, too. Awfully."

"Are you, Nell, truly?" I whispered. She seemed so changed to me by the warm light in her eyes and that delicate suffusion of color. I felt as I did when I got up early on picnic mornings in summer, and saw the dawn come up in the breathless sky above the river meadows and make all the cornfields golden.

"Sure I do, Peggy; don't look so solemn. It's nothing to look that way about, kid. It's nice." She threw her arms about me suddenly and hugged me.

"I hate to think about your going so far away from us all, Nell."

"Oh, you'll love to come and visit me. Just you wait."

She began breathlessly to go over things Guy Franklin had told her about Chicago, until I seemed to see it all looming up out there under the stars that kept watch over our little sleeping town. We had neither of us ever been to a city, but we knew what it would be like. We heard it throbbing like great engines, and calling to us, that faraway world. Even after we had opened the windows and scurried into bed, we seemed to feel a pulsation across all the miles of snow. The winter silence trembled with it, and the air was full of something new that seemed to break over us in soft waves. In that snug, warm little bed I had a sense of imminent change and danger. I was somehow afraid for Nelly when I heard her breathing so quickly beside me, and I put my arm about her protectingly as we drifted toward sleep.

■ ■ ■ ■

In the following spring we were both graduated from the Riverbend high school, and I went away to college. My family moved to Denver, and during the next four years I heard very little of Nelly Deane. My life was crowded with new people and new experiences, and I am afraid I held her little in mind. I heard indirectly that Jud Deane had lost what little property he owned in a luckless venture in Cripple Creek, and that he had been able to keep his house in Riverbend only through the clemency of his creditors. Guy Franklin had his route changed and did not go to Riverbend any more. He married the daughter of a rich cattle-man out near Long Pine, and ran a dry-goods store of his own. Mrs. Dow wrote me a long letter about once a year, and in one of these she told me that Nelly was teaching in the sixth grade in the Riverbend school.

"Dear Nelly does not like teaching very well. The children try her, and she is so pretty it seems a pity for her to be tied down to uncongenial employment. Scott is still very attentive, and I have noticed him look up at the window of Nelly's room in a very determined way as he goes home to dinner. Scott continues prosperous; he has made money during these hard times and now owns both our hardware stores. He is close, but a very honorable fellow. Nelly seems to hold off, but I think Mrs. Spinny has hopes. Nothing would please her more. If Scott were more careful about his appearance, it would help. He of course gets black about his business, and Nelly, you know, is very dainty. People do say his mother does his courting for him, she is so eager. If only Scott does not turn out hard and penurious like his father! We must all have our schooling in this life, but I don't want Nelly's to be too severe. She is a dear girl, and keeps her color."

Mrs. Dow's own schooling had been none too easy. Her husband had long been crippled with rheumatism, and was bitter and faultfinding. Her daughters had married poorly, and one of her sons had fallen into evil ways. But her letters were always cheerful, and in one of them she gently remonstrated with me because I "seemed inclined to take a sad view of life."

In the winter vacation of my senior year I stopped on my way home to visit Mrs. Dow. The first thing she told me when I got into her old buckboard at the station was that "Scott had at last prevailed," and that Nelly was to marry him in the spring. As a preliminary step, Nelly was about to join the Baptist church. "Just think, you will be here for her baptizing! How that will please Nelly! She is to be immersed to-morrow night."

I met Scott Spinny in the post-office that morning, and he gave me a hard grip with one black hand. There was something grim and saturnine about his powerful body and bearded face and his strong, cold hands. I wondered what perverse fate had driven him for eight years to dog the footsteps of a girl whose charm was due to qualities naturally distasteful to him. It still seems strange to me that in easy-going Riverbend, where there were so many boys who could have lived contentedly enough with my little grasshopper, it was the pushing ant who must have her and all her careless ways.

By a kind of unformulated etiquette one did not

530

call upon candidates for baptism on the day of the ceremony, so I had my first glimpse of Nelly that evening. The baptistry was a cemented pit directly under the pulpit rostrum, over which we had our stage when we sang "Queen Esther." I sat through the sermon somewhat nervously. After the minister, in his long, black gown, had gone down into the water and the choir had finished singing, the door from the dressing-room opened, and, led by one of the deacons, Nelly came down the steps into the pool. Oh, she looked so little and meek and chastened! Her white cashmere robe clung about her, and her brown hair was brushed straight back and hung in two soft braids from a little head bent humbly. As she stepped down into the water I shivered with the cold of it, and I remembered sharply how much I had loved her. She went down until the water was well above her waist, and stood white and small, with her hands crossed on her breast, while the minister said the words about being buried with Christ in baptism. Then, lying in his arm, she disappeared under the dark water. "It will be like that when she dies," I thought, and a quick pain caught my heart. The choir began to sing "Washed in the Blood of the Lamb" as she rose again, the door behind the baptistry opened, revealing those three dear guardians, Mrs. Dow, Mrs. Freeze, and Mrs. Spinny, and she went up into their arms.

I went to see Nell next day, up in the little room of many memories. Such a sad, sad visit! She seemed changed — a little embarrassed and quietly despairing. We talked of many of the old Riverbend girls and boys, but she did not mention Guy Franklin or Scott Spinny, except to say that her father had got work in Scott's hardware store.

531

She begged me, putting her hands on my shoulders with something of her old impulsiveness, to come and stay a few days with her. But I was afraid — afraid of what she might tell me and of what I might say. When I sat in that room with all her trinkets, the foolish harvest of her girlhood, lying about, and the white curtains and the little white rug, I thought of Scott Spinny with positive terror and could feel his hard grip on my hand again. I made the best excuse I could about having to hurry on to Denver; but she gave me one quick look, and her eyes ceased to plead. I saw that she understood me perfectly. We had known each other so well. Just once, when I got up to go and had trouble with my veil, she laughed her old merry laugh and told me there were some things I would never learn, for all my schooling.

The next day, when Mrs. Dow drove me down to the station to catch the morning train for Denver, I saw Nelly hurrying to school with several books under her arm. She had been working up her lessons at home, I thought. She was never quick at her books, dear Nell.

It was ten years before I again visited Riverbend. I had been in Rome for a long time, and had fallen into bitter homesickness. One morning, sitting among the dahlias and asters that bloom so bravely upon those gigantic heaps of earth-red ruins that were once the palaces of the Cæsars, I broke the seal of one of Mrs. Dow's long yearly letters. It brought so much sad news that I resolved then and there to go home to Riverbend, the only place that had ever really been home to me. Mrs. Dow wrote me that her husband, after years of illness, had died in the cold spell last

March. "So good and patient toward the last," she wrote, "and so afraid of giving extra trouble." There was another thing she saved until the last. She wrote on and on, dear woman, about new babies and village improvements, as if she could not bear to tell me; and then it came:

"You will be sad to hear that two months ago our dear Nelly left us. It was a terrible blow to us all. I cannot write about it yet, I fear. I wake up every morning feeling that I ought to go to her. She went three days after her little boy was born. The baby is a fine child and will live, I think, in spite of everything. He and her little girl, now eight years old, whom she named Margaret, after you, have gone to Mrs. Spinny's. She loves them more than if they were her own. It seems as if already they had made her quite young again. I wish you could see Nelly's children."

Ah, that was what I wanted, to see Nelly's children! The wish came aching from my heart along with the bitter homesick tears; along with a quick, torturing recollection that flashed upon me, as I looked about and tried to collect myself, of how we two had sat in our sunny seat in the corner of the old bare school-room one September afternoon and learned the names of the seven hills together. In that place, at that moment, after so many years, how it all came back to me — the warm sun on my back, the chattering girl beside me, the curly hair, the laughing yellow eyes, the stubby little finger on the page! I felt as if even then, when we sat in the sun with our heads together, it was all arranged, written out like a story, that at this moment I should be sitting among the crumbling bricks and drying grass, and she should be lying in the place I knew so well, on that green hill far away.

Mrs. Dow sat with her Christmas sewing in the
familiar sitting-room, where the carpet and the
wall-paper and the table-cover had all faded into
soft, dull colors, and even the chromo of Hagar
and Ishmael had been toned to the sobriety of
age. In the bay-window the tall wire flower-stand
still bore its little terraces of potted plants, and
the big fuchsia and the Martha Washington
geranium had blossomed for Christmas-tide. Mrs.
Dow herself did not look greatly changed to me.
Her hair, thin ever since I could remember it, was
now quite white, but her spare, wiry little person
had all its old activity, and her eyes gleamed with
the old friendliness behind her silver-bowed
glasses. Her gray house-dress seemed just like
those she used to wear when I ran in after school
to take her angel-food cake down to the church
supper.

The house sat on a hill, and from behind the
geraniums I could see pretty much all of Riverbend, tucked down in the soft snow, and the air
above was full of big, loose flakes, falling from a
gray sky which betokened settled weather. Indoors
the hard-coal burner made a tropical temperature,
and glowed a warm orange from its isinglass sides.
We sat and visited, the two of us, with a great
sense of comfort and completeness. I had reached
Riverbend only that morning, and Mrs. Dow, who
had been haunted by thoughts of shipwreck and
suffering upon wintry seas, kept urging me to
draw nearer to the fire and suggesting incidental
refreshment. We had chattered all through the
winter morning and most of the afternoon, taking
up one after another of the Riverbend girls and

boys, and agreeing that we had reason to be well satisfied with most of them. Finally, after a long pause in which I had listened to the contented ticking of the clock and the crackle of the coal, I put the question I had until then held back:

"And now, Mrs. Dow, tell me about the one we loved best of all. Since I got your letter I've thought of her every day. Tell me all about Scott and Nelly."

The tears flashed behind her glasses, and she smoothed the little pink bag on her knee.

"Well, dear, I'm afraid Scott proved to be a hard man, like his father. But we must remember that Nelly always had Mrs. Spinny. I never saw anything like the love there was between those two. After Nelly lost her own father and mother, she looked to Mrs. Spinny for everything. When Scott was too unreasonable, his mother could 'most always prevail upon him. She never lifted a hand to fight her own battles with Scott's father, but she was never afraid to speak up for Nelly. And then Nelly took great comfort of her little girl. Such a lovely child!"

"Had she been very ill before the little baby came?"

"No, Margaret; I'm afraid 't was all because they had the wrong doctor. I feel confident that either Doctor Tom or Doctor Jones could have brought her through. But, you see, Scott had offended them both, and they'd stopped trading at his store, so he would have young Doctor Fox, a boy just out of college and a stranger. He got scared and didn't know what to do. Mrs. Spinny felt he wasn't doing right, so she sent for Mrs. Freeze and me. It seemed like Nelly had got discouraged. Scott would move into their big new house before the plastering was dry, and though 't was summer, she had taken a terrible cold that seemed to have drained her, and she took no interest in fixing the place up. Mrs. Spinny had been down with her back again and wasn't able to help, and things was just anyway. We won't talk about that, Margaret; I think 't would hurt Mrs. Spinny to have you know. She nearly died of mortification when she sent for us, and blamed her poor back. We did get Nelly fixed up nicely before she died. I prevailed upon Doctor Tom to come in at the last, and it 'most broke his heart. 'Why, Mis' Dow,' he said, 'if you'd only have come and told me how 't was, I'd have come and carried her right off in my arms.' "

"Oh, Mrs. Dow," I cried, "then it needn't have been?"

Mrs. Dow dropped her needle and clasped her hands quickly. "We mustn't look at it that way, dear," she said tremulously and a little sternly; "we mustn't let ourselves. We must just feel that our Lord wanted her *then,* and took her to Himself. When it was all over, she did look so like a child of God, young and trusting, like she did on her baptizing night, you remember?"

I felt that Mrs. Dow did not want to talk any more about Nelly then, and, indeed, I had little heart to listen; so I told her I would go for a walk, and suggested that I might stop at Mrs. Spinny's to see the children.

Mrs. Dow looked up thoughtfully at the clock. "I doubt if you'll find little Margaret there now. It's half-past four, and she'll have been out of school an hour and more. She'll be most likely coasting on Lupton's Hill. She usually makes for it with her sled the minute she is out of the schoolhouse door. You know, it's the old hill where you all used to slide. If you stop in at the church about six o'clock, you'll likely find Mrs. Spinny there with the baby. I promised to go down and help Mrs. Freeze finish up the tree, and Mrs. Spinny said she'd run in with the baby, if 't wasn't too bitter. She won't leave him alone with the Swede girl. She's like a young woman with her first."

Lupton's Hill was at the other end of town, and when I got there the dusk was thickening, drawing blue shadows over the snowy fields. There were perhaps twenty children creeping up the hill or whizzing down the packed sled-track. When I had been watching them for some minutes, I heard a lusty shout, and a little red sled shot past me into the deep snow-drift beyond. The child was quite buried for a moment, then she struggled out and stood dusting the snow from her short coat and red woolen comforter. She wore a brown fur cap, which was too big for her and of an old-fashioned shape, such as girls wore long ago, but I would have known her without the cap. Mrs. Dow had said a beautiful child, and there would not be two like this in Riverbend. She was off before I had time to speak to her, going up the hill at a trot, her sturdy little legs plowing through the trampled snow. When she reached the top she never paused to take breath, but threw herself upon her sled and came down with a whoop that was quenched only by the deep drift at the end.

"Are you Margaret Spinny?" I asked as she struggled out in a cloud of snow.

"Yes, 'm." She approached me with frank curiosity, pulling her little sled behind her. "Are you the strange lady staying at Mrs. Dow's?" I nodded, and she began to look my clothes over with

537

respectful interest.

"Your grandmother is to be at the church at six o'clock, isn't she?"

"Yes, 'm."

"Well, suppose we walk up there now. It's nearly six, and all the other children are going home." She hesitated, and looked up at the faintly gleaming track on the hill-slope. "Do you want another slide? Is that it?" I asked.

"Do you mind?" she asked shyly.

"No. I'll wait for you. Take your time; don't run."

Two little boys were still hanging about the slide, and they cheered her as she came down, her comforter streaming in the wind.

"Now," she announced, getting up out of the drift, "I'll show you where the church is."

"Shall I tie your comforter again?"

"No, 'm, thanks. I'm plenty warm." She put her mittened hand confidingly in mine and trudged along beside me.

Mrs. Dow must have heard us tramping up the snowy steps of the church, for she met us at the door. Every one had gone except the old ladies. A kerosene lamp flickered over the Sunday-school chart, with the lesson-picture of the Wise Men, and the little barrel-stove threw out a deep glow over the three white heads that bent above the baby. There the three friends sat, patting him, and smoothing his dress, and playing with his hands, which made theirs look so brown.

"You ain't seen nothing finer in all your travels," said Mrs. Spinny, and they all laughed.

They showed me his full chest and how strong his back was; had me feel the golden fuzz on his head, and made him look at me with his round, bright eyes. He laughed and reared himself in my arms as I took him up and held him close to me. He was so warm and tingling with life, and he had the flush of new beginnings, of the new morning and the new rose. He seemed to have come so lately from his mother's heart! It was as if I held her youth and all her young joy. As I put my cheek down against his, he spied a pink flower in my hat, and making a gleeful sound, he lunged at it with both fists.

"Don't let him spoil it," murmured Mrs. Spinny. "He loves color so — like Nelly."

The Bohemian Girl

I

The Trans-continental Express swung along the windings of the Sand River Valley, and in the rear seat of the observation car a young man sat greatly at his ease, not in the least discomfited by the fierce sunlight which beat in upon his brown face and neck and strong back. There was a look of relaxation and of great passivity about his broad shoulders, which seemed almost too heavy until he stood up and squared them. He wore a pale flannel shirt and a blue silk necktie with loose ends. His trousers were wide and belted at the waist, and his short sack-coat hung open. His heavy shoes had seen good service. His reddish-brown hair, like his clothes, had a foreign cut. He had deep-set, dark blue eyes under heavy reddish eyebrows. His face was kept clean only by close shaving, and even the sharpest razor left a glint of yellow in the smooth brown of his skin. His teeth and the palms of his hands were very white. His head, which looked hard and stubborn, lay indolently in the green cushion of the wicker chair, and as he looked out at the ripe summer country a teasing, not unkindly smile played over his lips. Once, as he basked thus comfortably, a

540

quick light flashed in his eyes, curiously dilating the pupils, and his mouth became a hard, straight line, gradually relaxing into its former smile of rather kindly mockery. He told himself, apparently, that there was no point in getting excited; and he seemed a master hand at taking his ease when he could. Neither the sharp whistle of the locomotive nor the brakeman's call disturbed him. It was not until after the train had stopped that he rose, put on a Panama hat, took from the rack a small valise and a flute-case, and stepped deliberately to the station platform. The baggage was already unloaded, and the stranger presented a check for a battered sole-leather steamer-trunk.

"Can you keep it here for a day or two?" he asked the agent. "I may send for it, and I may not."

"Depends on whether you like the country, I suppose?" demanded the agent in a challenging tone.

"Just so."

The agent shrugged his shoulders, looked scornfully at the small trunk, which was marked "N.E.," and handed out a claim check without further comment. The stranger watched him as he caught one end of the trunk and dragged it into the express room. The agent's manner seemed to remind him of something amusing. "Doesn't seem to be a very big place," he remarked, looking about.

"It's big enough for us," snapped the agent, as he banged the trunk into a corner.

That remark, apparently, was what Nils Ericson had wanted. He chuckled quietly as he took a leather strap from his pocket and swung his valise around his shoulder. Then he settled his Panama securely on his head, turned up his trousers, tucked the flute-case under his arm, and started off across the fields. He gave the town, as he would have said, a wide berth, and cut through a great fenced pasture, emerging, when he rolled under the barbed wire at the farther corner, upon a white dusty road which ran straight up from the river valley to the high prairies, where the ripe wheat stood yellow and the tin roofs and weather-cocks were twinkling in the fierce sunlight. By the time Nils had done three miles, the sun was sinking and the farm-wagons on their way home from town came rattling by, covering him with dust and making him sneeze. When one of the farmers pulled up and offered to give him a lift, he clambered in willingly. The driver was a thin, grizzled old man with a long lean neck and a foolish sort of beard, like a goat's. "How fur ye goin'?" he asked, as he clucked to his horses and started off.

"Do you go by the Ericson place?"

"Which Ericson?" The old man drew in his reins as if he expected to stop again.

"Preacher Ericson's."

"Oh, the Old Lady Ericson's!" He turned and looked at Nils. "La, me! If you're goin' out there you might 'a' rid out in the automobile. That's a pity, now. The Old Lady Ericson was in town with her auto. You might 'a' heard it snortin' anywhere about the post-office er the butcher-shop."

"Has she a motor?" asked the stranger absently.

" 'Deed an' she has! She runs into town every night about this time for her mail and meat for supper. Some folks say she's afraid her auto won't get exercise enough, but I say that's jealousy."

"Aren't there any other motors about here?"

542

"Oh, yes! we have fourteen in all. But nobody else gets around like the Old Lady Ericson. She's out, rain er shine, over the whole county, chargin' into town and out amongst her farms, an' up to her sons' places. Sure you ain't goin' to the wrong place?" He craned his neck and looked at Nils' flute-case with eager curiosity. "The old woman ain't got any piany that I knows on. Olaf, he has a grand. His wife's musical; took lessons in Chicago."

"I'm going up there to-morrow," said Nils imperturbably. He saw that the driver took him for a piano-tuner.

"Oh, I see!" The old man screwed up his eyes mysteriously. He was a little dashed by the stranger's non-communicativeness, but he soon broke out again.

"I'm one o' Mis' Ericson's tenants. Look after one of her places. I did own the place myself oncet, but I lost it a while back, in the bad years just after the World's Fair. Just as well, too, I say. Lets you out o' payin' taxes. The Ericsons do own most of the county now. I remember the old preacher's fav'rite text used to be, 'To them that hath shall be given.' They've spread something wonderful — run over this here country like bindweed. But I ain't one that begretches it to 'em. Folks is entitled to what they kin git; and they're hustlers. Olaf, he's in the Legislature now, and a likely man fur Congress. Listen, if that ain't the old woman comin' now. Want I should stop her?"

Nils shook his head. He heard the deep chug-chug of a motor vibrating steadily in the clear twilight behind them. The pale lights of the car swam over the hill, and the old man slapped his reins and turned clear out of the road, ducking his head at the first of three angry snorts from behind. The motor was running at a hot, even speed, and passed without turning an inch from its course. The driver was a stalwart woman who sat at ease in the front seat and drove her car bareheaded. She left a cloud of dust and a trail of gasoline behind her. Her tenant threw back his head and sneezed.

"Whew! I sometimes say I'd as lief be *before* Mrs. Ericson as behind her. She does beat all! Nearly seventy, and never lets another soul touch that car. Puts it into commission herself every morning, and keeps it tuned up by the hitch-bar all day. I never stop work for a drink o' water that I don't hear her a-churnin' up the road. I reckon her darter-in-laws never sets down easy nowadays. Never know when she'll pop in. Mis' Otto, she says to me: 'We're so afraid that thing'll blow up and do Ma some injury yet, she's so turrible venturesome.' Says I: 'I wouldn't stew, Mis' Otto; the old lady'll drive that car to the funeral of every darter-in-law she's got.' That was after the old woman had jumped a turrible bad culvert."

The stranger heard vaguely what the old man was saying. Just now he was experiencing something very much like homesickness, and he was wondering what had brought it about. The mention of a name or two, perhaps; the rattle of a wagon along a dusty road; the rank, resinous smell of sunflowers and ironweed, which the night damp brought up from the draws and low places; perhaps, more than all, the dancing lights of the motor that had plunged by. He squared his shoulders with a comfortable sense of strength.

The wagon, as it jolted westward, climbed a

pretty steady upgrade. The country, receding from the rough river valley, swelled more and more gently, as if it had been smoothed out by the wind. On one of the last of the rugged ridges, at the end of a branch road, stood a grim square house with a tin roof and double porches. Behind the house stretched a row of broken, wind-racked poplars, and down the hill-slope to the left straggled the sheds and stables. The old man stopped his horses where the Ericsons' road branched across a dry sand creek that wound about the foot of the hill.

"That's the old lady's place. Want I should drive in?"

"No, thank you. I'll roll out here. Much obliged to you. Good night."

His passenger stepped down over the front wheel, and the old man drove on reluctantly, looking back as if he would like to see how the stranger would be received.

As Nils was crossing the dry creek he heard the restive tramp of a horse coming toward him down the hill. Instantly he flashed out of the road and stood behind a thicket of wild plum bushes that grew in the sandy bed. Peering through the dusk, he saw a light horse, under tight rein, descending the hill at a sharp walk. The rider was a slender woman — barely visible against the dark hillside — wearing an old-fashioned derby hat and a long riding-skirt. She sat lightly in the saddle, with her chin high, and seemed to be looking into the distance. As she passed the plum thicket her horse snuffed the air and shied. She struck him, pulling him in sharply, with an angry exclamation, *"Blázne!"* in Bohemian. Once in the main road, she let him out into a lope, and they soon emerged upon the crest of high land, where they moved along the skyline, silhouetted against the band of faint color that lingered in the west. This horse and rider, with their free, rhythmical gallop, were the only moving things to be seen on the face of the flat country. They seemed, in the last sad light of evening, not to be there accidentally, but as an inevitable detail of the landscape.

Nils watched them until they had shrunk to a mere moving speck against the sky, then he crossed the sand creek and climbed the hill. When he reached the gate the front of the house was dark, but a light was shining from the side windows. The pigs were squealing in the hog corral, and Nils could see a tall boy, who carried two big wooden buckets, moving about among them. Half way between the barn and the house, the windmill wheezed lazily. Following the path that ran around to the back porch, Nils stopped to look through the screen door into the lamp-lit kitchen. The kitchen was the largest room in the house; Nils remembered that his older brothers used to give dances there when he was a boy. Beside the stove stood a little girl with two light yellow braids and a broad, flushed face, peering anxiously into a frying-pan. In the dining-room beyond, a large, broad-shouldered woman was moving about the table. She walked with an active, springy step. Her face was heavy and florid, almost without wrinkles, and her hair was black at seventy. Nils felt proud of her as he watched her deliberate activity; never a momentary hesitation, or a movement that did not tell. He waited until she came out into the kitchen and, brushing the child aside, took her place at the stove. Then he tapped on the screen door and entered.

"It's nobody but Nils, Mother. I expect you

weren't looking for me."

Mrs. Ericson turned away from the stove and stood staring at him. "Bring the lamp, Hilda, and let me look."

Nils laughed and unslung his valise. "What's the matter, Mother? Don't you know me?"

Mrs. Ericson put down the lamp. "You must be Nils. You don't look very different, anyway."

"Nor you, Mother. You hold your own. Don't you wear glasses yet?"

"Only to read by. Where's your trunk, Nils?"

"Oh, I left that in town. I thought it might not be convenient for you to have company so near threshing-time."

"Don't be foolish, Nils." Mrs. Ericson turned back to the stove. "I don't thresh now. I hitched the wheat land onto the next farm and have a tenant. Hilda, take some hot water up to the company room, and go call little Eric."

The tow-haired child, who had been standing in mute amazement, took up the tea-kettle and withdrew, giving Nils a long, admiring look from the door of the kitchen stairs.

"Who's the youngster?" Nils asked, dropping down on the bench behind the kitchen stove.

"One of your Cousin Henrik's."

"How long has Cousin Henrik been dead?"

"Six years. There are two boys. One stays with Peter and one with Anders. Olaf is their guardeen."

There was a clatter of pails on the porch, and a tall, lanky boy peered wonderingly in through the screen door. He had a fair, gentle face and big gray eyes, and wisps of soft yellow hair hung down under his cap. Nils sprang up and pulled him into the kitchen, hugging him and slapping him on the shoulders. "Well, if it isn't my kid! Look at the size of him! Don't you know me, Eric?"

The boy reddened under his sunburn and freckles, and hung his head. "I guess it's Nils," he said shyly.

"You're a good guesser," laughed Nils, giving the lad's hand a swing. To himself he was thinking: "That's why the little girl looked so friendly. He's taught her to like me. He was only six when I went away, and he's remembered for twelve years."

Eric stood fumbling with his cap and smiling. "You look just like I thought you would," he ventured.

"Go wash your hands, Eric," called Mrs. Ericson. "I've got cob corn for supper, Nils. You used to like it. I guess you don't get much of that in the old country. Here's Hilda; she'll take you up to your room. You'll want to get the dust off you before you eat."

Mrs. Ericson went into the dining-room to lay another plate, and the little girl came up and nodded to Nils as if to let him know that his room was ready. He put out his hand and she took it, with a startled glance up at his face. Little Eric dropped his towel, threw an arm about Nils and one about Hilda, gave them a clumsy squeeze, and then stumbled out to the porch.

During supper Nils heard exactly how much land each of his eight grown brothers farmed, how their crops were coming on, and how much live stock they were feeding. His mother watched him narrowly as she talked. "You've got better looking, Nils," she remarked abruptly, whereupon he grinned and the children giggled. Eric, although he was eighteen and as tall as Nils, was always accounted a child, being the last of so many sons. His face seemed childlike, too, Nils thought, and he had the open, wandering eyes of a little boy. All the others had been men at his age.

After supper Nils went out to the front porch and sat down on the step to smoke a pipe. Mrs. Ericson drew a rocking-chair up near him and began to knit busily. It was one of the few old-world customs she had kept up, for she could not bear to sit with idle hands.

"Where's little Eric, Mother?"

"He's helping Hilda with the dishes. He does it of his own will; I don't like a boy to be too handy about the house."

"He seems like a nice kid."

"He's very obedient."

Nils smiled a little in the dark. It was just as well to shift the line of conversation. "What are you knitting there, Mother?"

"Baby stockings. The boys keep me busy." Mrs. Ericson chuckled and clicked her needles.

"How many grandchildren have you?"

"Only thirty-one now. Olaf lost his three. They were sickly, like their mother."

"I supposed he had a second crop by this time!"

"His second wife has no children. She's too proud. She tears about on horseback all the time. But she'll get caught up with, yet. She sets herself very high, though nobody knows what for. They were low enough Bohemians she came of. I never thought much of Bohemians; always drinking."

Nils puffed away at his pipe in silence, and Mrs. Ericson knitted on. In a few moments she added grimly: "She was down here to-night, just before you came. She'd like to quarrel with me and come between me and Olaf, but I don't give her the chance. I suppose you'll be bringing a wife home some day."

"I don't know. I've never thought much about it."

"Well, perhaps it's best as it is," suggested Mrs. Ericson hopefully. "You'd never be contented tied down to the land. There was roving blood in your father's family, and it's come out in you. I expect your own way of life suits you best." Mrs. Ericson had dropped into a blandly agreeable tone which Nils well remembered. It seemed to amuse him a good deal and his white teeth flashed behind his pipe. His mother's strategies had always diverted him, even when he was a boy — they were so flimsy and patent, so illy proportioned to her vigor and force. "They've been waiting to see which way I'd jump," he reflected. He felt that Mrs. Ericson was pondering his case deeply as she sat clicking her needles.

"I don't suppose you've ever got used to steady work," she went on presently. "Men ain't apt to if they roam around too long. It's a pity you didn't come back the year after the World's Fair. Your father picked up a good bit of land cheap then, in the hard times, and I expect maybe he'd have give you a farm. It's too bad you put off comin' back so long, for I always thought he meant to do something by you."

Nils laughed and shook the ashes out of his pipe. "I'd have missed a lot if I had come back then. But I'm sorry I didn't get back to see father."

"Well, I suppose we have to miss things at one end or the other. Perhaps you are as well satisfied with your own doings, now, as you'd have been with a farm," said Mrs. Ericson reassuringly.

"Land's a good thing to have," Nils commented,

as he lit another match and sheltered it with his hand.

His mother looked sharply at his face until the match burned out. "Only when you stay on it!" she hastened to say.

Eric came round the house by the path just then, and Nils rose, with a yawn. "Mother, if you don't mind, Eric and I will take a little tramp before bed-time. It will make me sleep."

"Very well; only don't stay long. I'll sit up and wait for you. I like to lock up myself."

Nils put his hand on Eric's shoulder, and the two tramped down the hill and across the sand creek into the dusty highroad beyond. Neither spoke. They swung along at an even gait, Nils puffing at his pipe. There was no moon, and the white road and the wide fields lay faint in the starlight. Over everything was darkness and thick silence, and the smell of dust and sunflowers. The brothers followed the road for a mile or more without finding a place to sit down. Finally Nils perched on a stile over the wire fence, and Eric sat on the lower step.

"I began to think you never would come back, Nils," said the boy softly.

"Didn't I promise you I would?"

"Yes; but people don't bother about promises they make to babies. Did you really know you were going away for good when you went to Chicago with the cattle that time?"

"I thought it very likely, if I could make my way."

"I don't see how you did it, Nils. Not many fellows could." Eric rubbed his shoulder against his brother's knee.

"The hard thing was leaving home — you and father. It was easy enough, once I got beyond

Chicago. Of course I got awful homesick; used to cry myself to sleep. But I'd burned my bridges."

"You had always wanted to go, hadn't you?"

"Always. Do you still sleep in our little room? Is that cottonwood still by the window?"

Eric nodded eagerly and smiled up at his brother in the gray darkness.

"You remember how we always said the leaves were whispering when they rustled at night? Well, they always whispered to me about the sea. Sometimes they said names out of the geography books. In a high wind they had a desperate sound, like something trying to tear loose."

"How funny, Nils," said Eric dreamily, resting his chin on his hand. "That tree still talks like that, and 'most always it talks to me about you."

They sat a while longer, watching the stars. At last Eric whispered anxiously: "Hadn't we better go back now? Mother will get tired waiting for us." They rose and took a short cut home, through the pasture.

II

The next morning Nils woke with the first flood of light that came with dawn. The white-plastered walls of his room reflected the glare that shone through the thin window-shades, and he found it impossible to sleep. He dressed hurriedly and slipped down the hall and up the back stairs to the half-story room which he used to share with his little brother. Eric, in a skimpy night-shirt, was sitting on the edge of the bed, rubbing his eyes, his pale yellow hair standing up in tufts all over his head. When he saw Nils, he murmured something confusedly and hustled his long legs into his trousers. "I didn't expect you'd be up so early,

552

Nils," he said, as his head emerged from his blue shirt.

"Oh, you thought I was a dude, did you?" Nils gave him a playful tap which bent the tall boy up like a clasp-knife. "See here; I must teach you to box." Nils thrust his hands into his pockets and walked about. "You haven't changed things much up here. Got most of my old traps, haven't you?"

He took down a bent, withered piece of sapling that hung over the dresser. "If this isn't the stick Lou Sandberg killed himself with!"

The boy looked up from his shoe-lacing.

"Yes; you never used to let me play with that. Just how did he do it, Nils? You were with father when he found Lou, weren't you?"

"Yes. Father was going off to preach somewhere, and, as we drove along, Lou's place looked sort of forlorn, and we thought we'd stop and cheer him up. When we found him father said he'd been dead a couple days. He'd tied a piece of binding twine round his neck, made a noose in each end, fixed the nooses over the ends of a bent stick, and let the stick spring straight; strangled himself."

"What made him kill himself such a silly way?"

The simplicity of the boy's question set Nils laughing. He clapped little Eric on the shoulder. "What made him such a silly as to kill himself at all, I should say!"

"Oh, well! But his hogs had the cholera, and all up and died on him, didn't they?"

"Sure they did; but he didn't have cholera; and there were plenty of hogs left in the world, weren't there?"

"Well, but, if they weren't his, how could they do him any good?" Eric asked, in astonishment.

"Oh, scat! He could have had lots of fun with

other people's hogs. He was a chump, Lou Sandberg. To kill yourself for a pig — think of that,
now!" Nils laughed all the way downstairs, and
quite embarrassed little Eric, who fell to scrub-
bing his face and hands at the tin basin. While he
was patting his wet hair at the kitchen looking-
glass, a heavy tread sounded on the stairs. The
boy dropped his comb. "Gracious, there's Mother.
We must have talked too long." He hurried out to
the shed, slipped on his overalls, and disappeared
with the milking-pails.

Mrs. Ericson came in, wearing a clean white
apron, her black hair shining from the application
of a wet brush.

"Good morning, Mother. Can't I make the fire
for you?"

"No, thank you, Nils. It's no trouble to make a
cob fire, and I like to manage the kitchen stove
myself." Mrs. Ericson paused with a shovel full of
ashes in her hand. "I expect you will be wanting
to see your brothers as soon as possible. I'll take
you up to Anders' place this morning. He's
threshing, and most of our boys are over there."

"Will Olaf be there?"

Mrs. Ericson went on taking out the ashes, and
spoke between shovels. "No; Olaf's wheat is all in,
put away in his new barn. He got six thousand
bushel this year. He's going to town to-day to get
men to finish roofing his barn."

"So Olaf is building a new barn?" Nils asked
absently.

"Biggest one in the county, and almost done.
You'll likely be here for the barn-raising. He's going to have a supper and a dance as soon as
everybody's done threshing. Says it keeps the vot-
ers in a good humor. I tell him that's all nonsense;

but Olaf has a long head for politics."

"Does Olaf farm all Cousin Henrik's land?"

Mrs. Ericson frowned as she blew into the faint smoke curling up about the cobs. "Yes; he holds it in trust for the children, Hilda and her brothers. He keeps strict account of everything he raises on it, and puts the proceeds out at compound interest for them."

Nils smiled as he watched the little flames shoot up. The door of the back stairs opened, and Hilda emerged, her arms behind her, buttoning up her long gingham apron as she came. He nodded to her gaily, and she twinkled at him out of her little blue eyes, set far apart over her wide cheek-bones.

"There, Hilda, you grind the coffee — and just put in an extra handful; I expect your Cousin Nils likes his strong," said Mrs. Ericson, as she went out to the shed.

Nils turned to look at the little girl, who gripped the coffee-grinder between her knees and ground so hard that her two braids bobbed and her face flushed under its broad spattering of freckles. He noticed on her middle finger something that had not been there last night, and that had evidently been put on for company: a tiny gold ring with a clumsily set garnet stone. As her hand went round and round he touched the ring with the tip of his finger, smiling.

Hilda glanced toward the shed door through which Mrs. Ericson had disappeared. "My Cousin Clara gave me that," she whispered bashfully. "She's Cousin Olaf's wife."

III

Mrs. Olaf Ericson — Clara Vavrika, as many people still called her — was moving restlessly

555

about her big bare house that morning. Her husband had left for the county town before his wife was out of bed — her lateness in rising was one of the many things the Ericson family had against her. Clara seldom came downstairs before eight o'clock, and this morning she was even later, for she had dressed with unusual care. She put on, however, only a tight-fitting black dress, which people thereabouts thought very plain. She was a tall, dark woman of thirty, with a rather sallow complexion and a touch of dull salmon red in her cheeks, where the blood seemed to burn under her brown skin. Her hair, parted evenly above her low forehead, was so black that there were distinctly blue lights in it. Her black eyebrows were delicate half-moons and her lashes were long and heavy. Her eyes slanted a little, as if she had a strain of Tartar or gypsy blood, and were sometimes full of fiery determination and sometimes dull and opaque. Her expression was never altogether amiable; was often, indeed, distinctly sullen, or, when she was animated, sarcastic. She was most attractive in profile, for then one saw to advantage her small, well-shaped head and delicate ears, and felt at once that here was a very positive, if not an altogether pleasing, personality.

The entire management of Mrs. Olaf's household devolved upon her aunt, Johanna Vavrika, a superstitious, doting woman of fifty. When Clara was a little girl her mother died, and Johanna's life had been spent in ungrudging service to her niece. Clara, like many self-willed and discontented persons, was really very apt, without knowing it, to do as other people told her, and to let her destiny be decided for her by intelligences much below her own. It was her Aunt Johanna who had humored and spoiled her in her girlhood, who had got her off to Chicago to study piano, and who had finally persuaded her to marry Olaf Ericson as the best match she would be likely to make in that part of the country. Johanna Vavrika had been deeply scarred by smallpox in the old country. She was short and fat, homely and jolly and sentimental. She was so broad, and took such short steps when she walked, that her brother, Joe Vavrika, always called her his duck. She adored her niece because of her talent, because of her good looks and masterful ways, but most of all because of her selfishness.

Clara's marriage with Olaf Ericson was Johanna's particular triumph. She was inordinately proud of Olaf's position, and she found a sufficiently exciting career in managing Clara's house, in keeping it above the criticism of the Ericsons, in pampering Olaf to keep him from finding fault with his wife, and in concealing from every one Clara's domestic infelicities. While Clara slept of a morning, Johanna Vavrika was bustling about, seeing that Olaf and the men had their breakfast, and that the cleaning or the butter-making or the washing was properly begun by the two girls in the kitchen. Then, at about eight o'clock, she would take Clara's coffee up to her, and chat with her while she drank it, telling her what was going on in the house. Old Mrs. Ericson frequently said that her daughter-in-law would not know what day of the week it was if Johanna did not tell her every morning. Mrs. Ericson despised and pitied Johanna, but did not wholly dislike her. The one thing she hated in her daughter-in-law above everything else was the way in which Clara could come it over people. It enraged her that the affairs of her son's big, barn-like house went on as well as they did, and she used to feel that in this world we have to wait over-long to see the guilty punished. "Suppose Johanna Vavrika died or got sick?" the old lady used to say to Olaf. "Your wife wouldn't know where to look for her own dish-cloth." Olaf only shrugged his shoulders. The fact remained that Johanna did not die, and, although Mrs. Ericson often told her she was looking poorly, she was never ill. She seldom left the house, and she slept in a little room off the kitchen. No Ericson, by night or day, could come prying about there to find fault without her knowing it. Her one weakness was that she was an incurable talker, and she sometimes made trouble without meaning to.

This morning Clara was tying a wine-colored ribbon about her throat when Johanna appeared with her coffee. After putting the tray on a sewing-table, she began to make Clara's bed, chattering the while in Bohemian.

"Well, Olaf got off early, and the girls are baking. I'm going down presently to make some poppy-seed bread for Olaf. He asked for prune preserves at breakfast, and I told him I was out of them, and to bring some prunes and honey and cloves from town."

Clara poured her coffee. "Ugh! I don't see how men can eat so much sweet stuff. In the morning, too!"

Her aunt chuckled knowingly. "Bait a bear with honey, as we say in the old country."

"Was he cross?" her niece asked indifferently.

"Olaf? Oh, no! He was in fine spirits. He's never cross if you know how to take him. I never knew a man to make so little fuss about bills. I gave him a list of things to get a yard long, and he didn't say a word; just folded it up and put it in his pocket."

"I can well believe he didn't say a word," Clara remarked with a shrug. "Some day he'll forget how to talk."

"Oh, but they say he's a grand speaker in the Legislature. He knows when to keep quiet. That's why he's got such influence in politics. The people have confidence in him." Johanna beat up a pillow and held it under her fat chin while she slipped on the case. Her niece laughed.

"Maybe we could make people believe we were wise, Aunty, if we held our tongues. Why did you tell Mrs. Ericson that Norman threw me again last Saturday and turned my foot? She's been talking to Olaf."

Johanna fell into great confusion. "Oh, but, my precious, the old lady asked for you, and she's always so angry if I can't give an excuse. Anyhow, she needn't talk; she's always tearing up something with that motor of hers."

When her aunt clattered down to the kitchen, Clara went to dust the parlor. Since there was not much there to dust, this did not take very long. Olaf had built the house new for her before their marriage, but her interest in furnishing it had been short-lived. It went, indeed, little beyond a bathtub and her piano. They had disagreed about almost every other article of furniture, and Clara had said she would rather have her house empty than full of things she didn't want. The house was set in a hillside, and the west windows of the parlor looked out above the kitchen yard thirty feet below. The east windows opened directly into the front yard. At one of the latter, Clara, while she was dusting, heard a low whistle. She did not

559

turn at once, but listened intently as she drew her cloth slowly along the round of a chair. Yes, there it was:

"I dreamt that I dwelt in ma-a-arble halls."

She turned and saw Nils Ericson laughing in the sunlight, his hat in his hand, just outside the window. As she crossed the room he leaned against the wire screen. "Aren't you at all surprised to see me, Clara Vavrika?"

"No; I was expecting to see you. Mother Ericson telephoned Olaf last night that you were here."

Nils squinted and gave a long whistle. "Telephoned? That must have been while Eric and I were out walking. Isn't she enterprising? Lift this screen, won't you?"

Clara lifted the screen, and Nils swung his leg across the window-sill. As he stepped into the room she said: "You didn't think you were going to get ahead of your mother, did you?"

He threw his hat on the piano. "Oh, I do sometimes. You see, I'm ahead of her now. I'm supposed to be in Anders' wheat-field. But, as we were leaving, Mother ran her car into a soft place beside the road and sank up to the hubs. While they were going for horses to pull her out, I cut away behind the stacks and escaped." Nils chuckled. Clara's dull eyes lit up as she looked at him admiringly.

"You've got them guessing already. I don't know what your mother said to Olaf over the telephone, but he came back looking as if he'd seen a ghost, and he didn't go to bed until a dreadful hour — ten o'clock, I should think. He sat out on the porch in the dark like a graven image. It had been

560

one of his talkative days, too." They both laughed, easily and lightly, like people who have laughed a great deal together; but they remained standing.

"Anders and Otto and Peter looked as if they had seen ghosts, too, over in the threshing-field. What's the matter with them all?"

Clara gave him a quick, searching look. "Well, for one thing, they've always been afraid you have the other will."

Nils looked interested. "The other will?"

"Yes. A later one. They knew your father made another, but they never knew what he did with it. They almost tore the old house to pieces looking for it. They always suspected that he carried on a clandestine correspondence with you, for the one thing he would do was to get his own mail himself. So they thought he might have sent the new will to you for safekeeping. The old one, leaving everything to your mother, was made long before you went away, and it's understood among them that it cuts you out — that she will leave all the property to the others. Your father made the second will to prevent that. I've been hoping you had it. It would be such fun to spring it on them." Clara laughed mirthfully, a thing she did not often do now.

Nils shook his head reprovingly. "Come, now, you're malicious."

"No, I'm not. But I'd like something to happen to stir them all up, just for once. There never was such a family for having nothing ever happen to them but dinner and threshing. I'd almost be willing to die, just to have a funeral. *You* wouldn't stand it for three weeks."

Nils bent over the piano and began pecking at the keys with the finger of one hand. "I wouldn't?

561

My dear young lady, how do you know what I can stand? *You* wouldn't wait to find out."

Clara flushed darkly and frowned. "I didn't believe you would ever come back —" she said defiantly.

"Eric believed I would, and he was only a baby when I went away. However, all's well that ends well, and I haven't come back to be a skeleton at the feast. We mustn't quarrel. Mother will be here with a search-warrant pretty soon." He swung round and faced her, thrusting his hands into his coat pockets. "Come, you ought to be glad to see me, if you want something to happen. I'm something, even without a will. We can have a little fun, can't we? I think we can!"

She echoed him, "I think we can!" They both laughed and their eyes sparkled. Clara Vavrika looked ten years younger than when she had put the velvet ribbon about her throat that morning.

"You know, I'm so tickled to see mother," Nils went on. "I didn't know I was so proud of her. A regular pile-driver. How about little pigtails, down at the house? Is Olaf doing the square thing by those children?"

Clara frowned pensively. "Olaf has to do something that looks like the square thing, now that he's a public man!" She glanced drolly at Nils. "But he makes a good commission out of it. On Sundays they all get together here and figure. He lets Peter and Anders put in big bills for the keep of the two boys, and he pays them out of the estate. They are always having what they call accountings. Olaf gets something out of it, too. I don't know just how they do it, but it's entirely a family matter, as they say. And when the Ericsons say that —" Clara lifted her eyebrows.

Just then the angry *honk-honk* of an approaching motor sounded from down the road. Their eyes met and they began to laugh. They laughed as children do when they can not contain themselves, and can not explain the cause of their mirth to grown people, but share it perfectly together. When Clara Vavrika sat down at the piano after he was gone, she felt that she had laughed away a dozen years. She practised as if the house were burning over her head.

When Nils greeted his mother and climbed into the front seat of the motor beside her, Mrs. Ericson looked grim, but she made no comment upon his truancy until she had turned her car and was retracing her revolutions along the road that ran by Olaf's big pasture. Then she remarked dryly:

"If I were you I wouldn't see too much of Olaf's wife while you are here. She's the kind of woman who can't see much of men without getting herself talked about. She was a good deal talked about before he married her."

"Hasn't Olaf tamed her?" Nils asked indifferently.

Mrs. Ericson shrugged her massive shoulders. "Olaf don't seem to have much luck, when it comes to wives. The first one was meek enough, but she was always ailing. And this one has her own way. He says if he quarreled with her she'd go back to her father, and then he'd lose the Bohemian vote. There are a great many Bohunks in this district. But when you find a man under his wife's thumb you can always be sure there's a soft spot in him somewhere."

Nils thought of his own father, and smiled. "She brought him a good deal of money, didn't she, besides the Bohemian vote?"

Mrs. Ericson sniffed. "Well, she has a fair half section in her own name, but I can't see as that does Olaf much good. She will have a good deal of property some day, if old Vavrika don't marry again. But I don't consider a saloonkeeper's money as good as other people's money."

Nils laughed outright. "Come, Mother, don't let your prejudices carry you that far. Money's money. Old Vavrika's a mighty decent sort of saloonkeeper. Nothing rowdy about him."

Mrs. Ericson spoke up angrily: "Oh, I know you always stood up for them! But hanging around there when you were a boy never did you any good, Nils, nor any of the other boys who went there. There weren't so many after her when she married Olaf, let me tell you. She knew enough to grab her chance."

Nils settled back in his seat. "Of course I liked to go there, Mother, and you were always cross about it. You never took the trouble to find out that it was the one jolly house in this country for a boy to go to. All the rest of you were working yourselves to death, and the houses were mostly a mess, full of babies and washing and flies. Oh, it was all right — I understand that; but you are young only once, and I happened to be young then. Now, Vavrika's was always jolly. He played the violin, and I used to take my flute, and Clara played the piano, and Johanna used to sing Bohemian songs. She always had a big supper for us — herrings and pickles and poppyseed bread, and lots of cake and preserves. Old Joe had been in the army in the old country, and he could tell lots of good stories. I can see him cutting bread, at the head of the table, now. I don't know what I'd have done when I was a kid if it hadn't been for the Vavrikas, really."

"And all the time he was taking money that other people had worked hard in the fields for," Mrs. Ericson observed.

"So do the circuses, Mother, and they're a good thing. People ought to get fun for some of their money. Even father liked old Joe."

"Your father," Mrs. Ericson said grimly, "liked everybody."

As they crossed the sand creek and turned into her own place, Mrs. Ericson observed, "There's Olaf's buggy. He's stopped on his way from town." Nils shook himself and prepared to greet his brother, who was waiting on the porch.

Olaf was a big, heavy Norwegian, slow of speech and movement. His head was large and square, like a block of wood. When Nils, at a distance, tried to remember what his brother looked like, he could recall only his heavy head, high forehead, large nostrils, and pale-blue eyes, set far apart. Olaf's features were rudimentary: the thing one noticed was the face itself, wide and flat and pale, devoid of any expression, betraying his fifty years as little as it betrayed anything else, and powerful by reason of its very stolidness. When Olaf shook hands with Nils he looked at him from under his light eyebrows, but Nils felt that no one could ever say what that pale look might mean. The one thing he had always felt in Olaf was a heavy stubbornness, like the unyielding stickiness of wet loam against the plow. He had always found Olaf the most difficult of his brothers.

"How do you do, Nils? Expect to stay with us long?"

"Oh, I may stay forever," Nils answered gaily. "I like this country better than I used to."

"There's been some work put into it since you left," Olaf remarked.

"Exactly. I think it's about ready to live in now — and I'm about ready to settle down." Nils saw his brother lower his big head. ("Exactly like a bull," he thought.) "Mother's been persuading me to slow down now, and go in for farming," he went on lightly.

Olaf made a deep sound in his throat. "Farming ain't learned in a day," he brought out, still looking at the ground.

"Oh, I know! But I pick things up quickly." Nils had not meant to antagonize his brother, and he did not know now why he was doing it. "Of course," he went on, "I shouldn't expect to make a big success, as you fellows have done. But then, I'm not ambitious. I won't want much. A little land, and some cattle, maybe."

Olaf still stared at the ground, his head down. He wanted to ask Nils what he had been doing all these years, that he didn't have a business somewhere he couldn't afford to leave; why he hadn't more pride than to come back with only a little sole-leather trunk to show for himself, and to present himself as the only failure in the family. He did not ask one of these questions, but he made them all felt distinctly.

"Humph!" Nils thought. "No wonder the man never talks, when he can butt his ideas into you like that without ever saying a word. I suppose he uses that kind of smokeless powder on his wife all the time. But I guess she has her innings." He chuckled, and Olaf looked up. "Never mind me, Olaf. I laugh without knowing why, like little Eric. He's another cheerful dog."

"Eric," said Olaf slowly, "is a spoiled kid. He's

566

just let his mother's best cow go dry because he don't milk her right. I was hoping you'd take him away somewhere and put him into business. If he don't do any good among strangers, he never will." This was a long speech for Olaf, and as he finished it he climbed into his buggy.

Nils shrugged his shoulders. "Same old tricks," he thought. "Hits from behind you every time. What a whale of a man!" He turned and went round to the kitchen, where his mother was scolding little Eric for letting the gasoline get low.

IV

Joe Vavrika's saloon was not in the county-seat, where Olaf and Mrs. Ericson did their trading, but in a cheerfuller place, a little Bohemian settlement which lay at the other end of the county, ten level miles north of Olaf's farm. Clara rode up to see her father almost every day. Vavrika's house was, so to speak, in the back yard of his saloon. The garden between the two buildings was inclosed by a high board fence as tight as a partition, and in summer Joe kept beer-tables and wooden benches among the gooseberry bushes under his little cherry tree. At one of these tables Nils Ericson was seated in the late afternoon, three days after his return home. Joe had gone in to serve a customer, and Nils was lounging on his elbows, looking rather mournfully into his half-emptied pitcher, when he heard a laugh across the little garden. Clara, in her riding-habit, was standing at the back door of the house, under the grapevine trellis that old Joe had grown there long ago. Nils rose.

"Come out and keep your father and me company. We've been gossiping all afternoon. Nobody

567

to bother us but the flies."

She shook her head. "No, I never come out here any more. Olaf doesn't like it. I must live up to my position, you know."

"You mean to tell me you never come out and chat with the boys, as you used to? He *has* tamed you! Who keeps up these flower-beds?"

"I come out on Sundays, when father is alone, and read the Bohemian papers to him. But I am never here when the bar is open. What have you two been doing?"

"Talking, as I told you. I've been telling him about my travels. I find I can't talk much at home, not even to Eric."

Clara reached up and poked with her riding-whip at a white moth that was fluttering in the sunlight among the vine leaves. "I suppose you will never tell me about all those things."

"Where can I tell them? Not in Olaf's house, certainly. What's the matter with our talking here?" He pointed persuasively with his hat to the bushes and the green table, where the flies were singing lazily above the empty beer-glasses.

Clara shook her head weakly. "No, it wouldn't do. Besides, I am going now."

"I'm on Eric's mare. Would you be angry if I overtook you?"

Clara looked back and laughed. "You might try and see. I can leave you if I don't want you. Eric's mare can't keep up with Norman."

Nils went into the bar and attempted to pay his score. Big Joe, six feet four, with curly yellow hair and mustache, clapped him on the shoulder. "Not a God-damn a your money go in my drawer, you hear? Only next time you bring your flute, te-te-te-te-te-ty." Joe wagged his fingers in imitation of

568

the flute-player's position. "My Clara, she come all-a-time Sundays an' play for me. She not like to play at Ericson's place." He shook his yellow curls and laughed. "Not a God-damn a fun at Ericson's. You come a Sunday. You like-a fun. No forget de flute." Joe talked very rapidly and always tumbled over his English. He seldom spoke it to his customers, and had never learned much.

Nils swung himself into the saddle and trotted to the west end of the village, where the houses and gardens scattered into prairie-land and the road turned south. Far ahead of him, in the declining light, he saw Clara Vavrika's slender figure, loitering on horseback. He touched his mare with the whip, and shot along the white, level road, under the reddening sky. When he overtook Olaf's wife he saw that she had been crying. "What's the matter, Clara Vavrika?" he asked kindly.

"Oh, I get blue sometimes. It was awfully jolly living there with father. I wonder why I ever went away."

Nils spoke in a low, kind tone that he sometimes used with women: "That's what I've been wondering these many years. You were the last girl in the country I'd have picked for a wife for Olaf. What made you do it, Clara?"

"I suppose I really did it to oblige the neighbors" — Clara tossed her head. "People were beginning to wonder."

"To wonder?"

"Yes — why I didn't get married. I suppose I didn't like to keep them in suspense. I've discovered that most girls marry out of consideration for the neighborhood."

Nils bent his head toward her and his white

569

teeth flashed. "I'd have gambled that one girl I knew would say, 'Let the neighborhood be damned.' "

Clara shook her head mournfully. "You see, they have it on you, Nils; that is, if you're a woman. They say you're beginning to go off. That's what makes us get married: we can't stand the laugh."

Nils looked sidewise at her. He had never seen her head droop before. Resignation was the last thing he would have expected of her. "In your case, there wasn't something else?"

"Something else?"

"I mean, you didn't do it to spite somebody? Somebody who didn't come back?"

Clara drew herself up. "Oh, I never thought you'd come back. Not after I stopped writing to you, at least. *That* was all over, long before I married Olaf."

"It never occurred to you, then, that the meanest thing you could do to me was to marry Olaf?"

Clara laughed. "No; I didn't know you were so fond of Olaf."

Nils smoothed his horse's mane with his glove. "You know, Clara Vavrika, you are never going to stick it out. You'll cut away some day, and I've been thinking you might as well cut away with me."

Clara threw up her chin. "Oh, you don't know me as well as you think. I won't cut away. Sometimes, when I'm with father, I feel like it. But I can hold out as long as the Ericsons can. They've never got the best of me yet, and one can live, so long as one isn't beaten. If I go back to father, it's all up with Olaf in politics. He knows that, and he never goes much beyond sulking. I've as much wit as the Ericsons. I'll never leave them unless I can show them a thing or two."

"You mean unless you can come it over them?"

"Yes — unless I go away with a man who is cleverer than they are, and who has more money."

Nils whistled. "Dear me, you are demanding a good deal. The Ericsons, take the lot of them, are a bunch to beat. But I should think the excitement of tormenting them would have worn off by this time."

"It has, I'm afraid," Clara admitted mournfully.

"Then why don't you cut away? There are more amusing games than this in the world. When I came home I thought it might amuse me to bully a few quarter sections out of the Ericsons; but I've almost decided I can get more fun for my money somewhere else."

Clara took in her breath sharply. "Ah, you have got the other will! That was why you came home!"

"No, it wasn't. I came home to see how you were getting on with Olaf."

Clara struck her horse with the whip, and in a bound she was far ahead of him. Nils dropped one word, "Damn!" and whipped after her; but she leaned forward in her saddle and fairly cut the wind. Her long riding-skirt rippled in the still air behind her. The sun was just sinking behind the stubble in a vast, clear sky, and the shadows drew across the fields so rapidly that Nils could scarcely keep in sight the dark figure on the road. When he overtook her he caught her horse by the bridle. Norman reared, and Nils was frightened for her; but Clara kept her seat.

"Let me go, Nils Ericson!" she cried. "I hate you more than any of them. You were created to torture me, the whole tribe of you — to make me suffer in every possible way."

She struck her horse again and galloped away from him. Nils set his teeth and looked thoughtful. He rode slowly home along the deserted road, watching the stars come out in the clear violet sky. They flashed softly into the limpid heavens, like jewels let fall into clear water. They were a reproach, he felt, to a sordid world. As he turned across the sand creek, he looked up at the North Star and smiled, as if there were an understanding between them. His mother scolded him for being late for supper.

V

On Sunday afternoon Joe Vavrika, in his shirt-sleeves and carpet-slippers, was sitting in his garden, smoking a long-tasseled porcelain pipe with a hunting scene painted on the bowl. Clara sat under the cherry tree, reading aloud to him from the weekly Bohemian papers. She had worn a white muslin dress under her riding-habit, and the leaves of the cherry tree threw a pattern of sharp shadows over her skirt. The black cat was dozing in the sunlight at her feet, and Joe's dachshund was scratching a hole under the scarlet geraniums and dreaming of badgers. Joe was filling his pipe for the third time since dinner, when he heard a knocking on the fence. He broke into a loud guffaw and unlatched the little door that led into the street. He did not call Nils by name, but caught him by the hand and dragged him in. Clara stiffened and the color deepened under her dark skin. Nils, too, felt a little awkward. He had not seen her since the night when she rode away from him and left him alone on the level road between the fields. Joe dragged him to the wooden bench beside the green table.

"You bring de flute," he cried, tapping the leather case under Nils' arm. "Ah, das-a good! Now we have some liddle fun like old times. I got somet'ing good for you." Joe shook his finger at Nils and winked his blue eyes, a bright clear eye, full of fire, though the tiny blood-vessels on the ball were always a little distended. "I got somet'ing for you from" — he paused and waved his hand — "Hongarie. You know Hongarie? You wait!" He pushed Nils down on the bench, and went through the back door of his saloon.

Nils looked at Clara, who sat frigidly with her white skirts drawn tight about her. "He didn't tell you he had asked me to come, did he? He wanted a party and proceeded to arrange it. Isn't he fun? Don't be cross; let's give him a good time."

Clara smiled and shook out her skirt. "Isn't that like father? And he has sat here so meekly all day. Well, I won't pout. I'm glad you came. He doesn't have very many good times now any more. There are so few of his kind left. The second generation are a tame lot."

Joe came back with a flask in one hand and three wine-glasses caught by the stems between the fingers of the other. These he placed on the table with an air of ceremony, and, going behind Nils, held the flask between him and the sun, squinting into it admiringly. "You know dis, Tokai? A great friend of mine, he bring dis to me, a present out of Hongarie. You know how much it cost, dis wine? Chust so much what it weigh in gold. Nobody but de nobles drink him in Bohemie. Many, many years I save him up, dis Tokai." Joe whipped out his official cork-screw and delicately removed the cork. "De old man die what bring him to me, an' dis wine he lay on his belly in my

573

cellar an' sleep. An' now," carefully pouring out the heavy yellow wine, "an' now he wake up; and maybe he wake us up, too!" He carried one of the glasses to his daughter and presented it with great gallantry.

Clara shook her head, but, seeing her father's disappointment, relented. "You taste it first. I don't want so much."

Joe sampled it with a beatific expression, and turned to Nils. "You drink him slow, dis wine. He very soft, but he go down hot. You see!"

After a second glass Nils declared that he couldn't take any more without getting sleepy. "Now get your fiddle, Vavrika," he said as he opened his flute-case.

But Joe settled back in his wooden rocker and wagged his big carpet-slipper. "No-no-no-no-no-no-no! No play fiddle now any more: too much ache in de finger," waving them, "all-a-time rheumatiz. You play de flute, te-tety-te-tety-te. Bohemie songs."

"I've forgotten all the Bohemian songs I used to play with you and Johanna. But here's one that will make Clara pout. You remember how her eyes used to snap when we called her the Bohemian Girl?" Nils lifted his flute and began "When Other Lips and Other Hearts," and Joe hummed the air in a husky baritone, waving his carpet-slipper. "Oh-h-h, das-a fine music," he cried, clapping his hands as Nils finished. "Now 'Marble Halls, Marble Halls'! Clara, you sing him."

Clara smiled and leaned back in her chair, beginning softly:

"I dreamt that I dwelt in ma-a-arble halls,
With vassals and serfs at my knee,"

574

and Joe hummed like a big bumble-bee.

"There's one more you always played," Clara said quietly; "I remember that best." She locked her hands over her knee and began "The Heart Bowed Down," and sang it through without groping for the words. She was singing with a good deal of warmth when she came to the end of the old song:

> "For memory is the only friend
> That grief can call its own."

Joe flashed out his red silk handkerchief and blew his nose, shaking his head. "No-no-no-no-no-no-no! Too sad, too sad! I not like-a dat. Play quick somet'ing gay now."

Nils put his lips to the instrument, and Joe lay back in his chair, laughing and singing, "Oh, Evelina, Sweet Evelina!" Clara laughed, too. Long ago, when she and Nils went to high school, the model student of their class was a very homely girl in thick spectacles. Her name was Evelina Oleson; she had a long, swinging walk which somehow suggested the measure of that song, and they used mercilessly to sing it at her.

"Dat ugly Oleson girl, she teach in de school," Joe gasped, "an' she still walk chust like dat, yup-a, yup-a, yup-a, chust like a camel she go! Now, Nils, we have some more li'l drink. Oh, yes-yes-yes-yes-yes-yes-*yes!* Dis time you haf to drink, and Clara she haf to, so she show she not jealous. So, we all drink to your girl. You not tell her name, eh? No-no-no, I no make you tell. She pretty, eh? She make good sweetheart? I bet!" Joe winked and lifted his glass. "How soon you get married?"

Nils screwed up his eyes. "That I don't know.

When she says."

Joe threw out his chest. "Das-a way boys talks. No way for mans. Mans say, 'You come to de church, an' get a hurry on you.' Das-a way mans talks."

"Maybe Nils hasn't got enough to keep a wife," put in Clara ironically. "How about that, Nils?" she asked him frankly, as if she wanted to know.

Nils looked at her coolly, raising one eyebrow. "Oh, I can keep her, all right."

"The way she wants to be kept?"

"With my wife, I'll decide that," replied Nils calmly. "I'll give her what's good for her."

Clara made a wry face. "You'll give her the strap, I expect, like old Peter Oleson gave his wife."

"When she needs it," said Nils lazily, locking his hands behind his head and squinting up through the leaves of the cherry tree. "Do you remember the time I squeezed the cherries all over your clean dress, and Aunt Johanna boxed my ears for me? My gracious, weren't you mad! You had both hands full of cherries, and I squeezed 'em and made the juice fly all over you. I liked to have fun with you; you'd get so mad."

"We *did* have fun, didn't we? None of the other kids ever had so much fun. We knew how to play."

Nils dropped his elbows on the table and looked steadily across at her. "I've played with lots of girls since, but I haven't found one who was such good fun."

Clara laughed. The late afternoon sun was shining full in her face, and deep in the back of her eyes there shone something fiery, like the yellow drops of Tokai in the brown glass bottle. "Can you still play, or are you only pretending?"

"I can play better than I used to, and harder."

"Don't you ever work, then?" She had not intended to say it. It slipped out because she was confused enough to say just the wrong thing.

"I work between times." Nils' steady gaze still beat upon her. "Don't you worry about my working, Mrs. Ericson. You're getting like all the rest of them." He reached his brown, warm hand across the table and dropped it on Clara's, which was cold as an icicle. "Last call for play, Mrs. Ericson!" Clara shivered, and suddenly her hands and cheeks grew warm. Her fingers lingered in his a moment, and they looked at each other earnestly. Joe Vavrika had put the mouth of the bottle to his lips and was swallowing the last drops of the Tokai, standing. The sun, just about to sink behind his shop, glistened on the bright glass, on his flushed face and curly yellow hair. "Look," Clara whispered; "that's the way I want to grow old."

VI

On the day of Olaf Ericson's barn-raising, his wife, for once in a way, rose early. Johanna Vavrika had been baking cakes and frying and boiling and spicing meats for a week beforehand, but it was not until the day before the party was to take place that Clara showed any interest in it. Then she was seized with one of her fitful spasms of energy, and took the wagon and little Eric and spent the day on Plum Creek, gathering vines and swamp goldenrod to decorate the barn.

By four o'clock in the afternoon buggies and wagons began to arrive at the big unpainted building in front of Olaf's house. When Nils and his mother came at five, there were more than fifty people in the barn, and a great drove of children. On the ground floor stood six long tables, set with

577

the crockery of seven flourishing Ericson families, lent for the occasion. In the middle of each table was a big yellow pumpkin, hollowed out and filled with woodbine. In one corner of the barn, behind a pile of green-and-white-striped watermelons, was a circle of chairs for the old people; the younger guests sat on bushel measures or barbed-wire spools, and the children tumbled about in the haymow. The box-stalls Clara had converted into booths. The framework was hidden by goldenrod and sheaves of wheat, and the partitions were covered with wild grapevines full of fruit. At one of these Johanna Vavrika watched over her cooked meats, enough to provision an army; and at the next her kitchen girls had ranged the ice-cream freezers, and Clara was already cutting pies and cakes against the hour of serving. At the third stall, little Hilda, in a bright pink lawn dress, dispensed lemonade throughout the afternoon. Olaf, as a public man, had thought it inadvisable to serve beer in his barn; but Joe Vavrika had come over with two demijohns concealed in his buggy, and after his arrival the wagon-shed was much frequented by the men.

"Hasn't Cousin Clara fixed things lovely?" little Hilda whispered, when Nils went up to her stall and asked for lemonade.

Nils leaned against the booth, talking to the excited little girl and watching the people. The barn faced the west, and the sun, pouring in at the big doors, filled the whole interior with a golden light, through which filtered fine particles of dust from the haymow, where the children were romping. There was a great chattering from the stall where Johanna Vavrika exhibited to the admiring women her platters heaped with fried chicken, her roasts of beef, boiled tongues, and baked hams with cloves stuck in the crisp brown fat and garnished with tansy and parsley. The older women, having assured themselves that there were twenty kinds of cake, not counting cookies, and three dozen fat pies, repaired to the corner behind the pile of watermelons, put on their white aprons, and fell to their knitting and fancy-work. They were a fine company of old women, and a Dutch painter would have loved to find them there together, where the sun made bright patches on the floor and sent long, quivering shafts of gold through the dusky shade up among the rafters. There were fat, rosy old women who looked hot in their best black dresses; spare, alert old women with brown, dark-veined hands; and several of almost heroic frame, not less massive than old Mrs. Ericson herself. Few of them wore glasses, and old Mrs. Svendsen, a Danish woman, who was quite bald, wore the only cap among them. Mrs. Oleson, who had twelve big grandchildren, could still show two braids of yellow hair as thick as her own wrists. Among all these grandmothers there were more brown heads than white. They all had a pleased, prosperous air, as if they were more than satisfied with themselves and with life. Nils, leaning against Hilda's lemonade-stand, watched them as they sat chattering in four languages, their fingers never lagging behind their tongues.

"Look at them over there," he whispered, detaining Clara as she passed him. "Aren't they the Old Guard? I've just counted thirty hands. I guess they've wrung many a chicken's neck and warmed many a boy's jacket for him in their time."

In reality he fell into amazement when he thought of the Herculean labors those fifteen pairs of hands had performed: of the cows they had milked, the butter they had made, the gardens they had planted, the children and grandchildren they had tended, the brooms they had worn out, the mountains of food they had cooked. It made him dizzy. Clara Vavrika smiled a hard, enigmatical smile at him and walked rapidly away. Nils' eyes followed her white figure as she went toward the house. He watched her walking alone in the sunlight, looked at her slender, defiant shoulders and her little hard-set head with its coils of blue-black hair. "No," he reflected; "she'd never be like them, not if she lived here a hundred years. She'd only grow more bitter. You can't tame a wild thing; you can only chain it. People aren't all alike. I mustn't lose my nerve." He gave Hilda's pigtail a parting tweak and set out after Clara. "Where to?" he asked, as he came upon her in the kitchen.

"I'm going to the cellar for preserves."

"Let me go with you. I never get a moment alone with you. Why do you keep out of my way?"

Clara laughed. "I don't usually get in anybody's way."

Nils followed her down the stairs and to the far corner of the cellar, where a basement window let in a stream of light. From a swinging shelf Clara selected several glass jars, each labeled in Johanna's careful hand. Nils took up a brown flask. "What's this? It looks good."

"It is. It's some French brandy father gave me when I was married. Would you like some? Have you a corkscrew? I'll get glasses."

When she brought them, Nils took them from her and put them down on the window-sill. "Clara Vavrika, do you remember how crazy I used to be about you?"

Clara shrugged her shoulders. "Boys are always crazy about somebody or other. I dare say some silly has been crazy about Evelina Oleson. You got over it in a hurry."

"Because I didn't come back, you mean? I had to get on, you know, and it was hard sledding at first. Then I heard you'd married Olaf."

"And then you stayed away from a broken heart," Clara laughed.

"And then I began to think about you more than I had since I first went away. I began to wonder if you were really as you had seemed to me when I was a boy. I thought I'd like to see. I've had lots of girls, but no one ever pulled me the same way. The more I thought about you, the more I remembered how it used to be — like hearing a wild tune you can't resist, calling you out at night. It had been a long while since anything had pulled me out of my boots, and I wondered whether anything ever could again." Nils thrust his hands into his coat pockets and squared his shoulders, as his mother sometimes squared hers, as Olaf, in a clumsier manner, squared his. "So I thought I'd come back and see. Of course the family have tried to do me, and I rather thought I'd bring out father's will and make a fuss. But they can have their old land; they've put enough sweat into it." He took the flask and filled the two glasses carefully to the brim. "I've found out what I want from the Ericsons. Drink *skoal,* Clara." He lifted his glass, and Clara took hers with downcast eyes. "Look at me, Clara Vavrika. *Skoal!*"

She raised her burning eyes and answered fiercely: *"Skoal!"*

The barn supper began at six o'clock and lasted

581

for two hilarious hours. Yense Nelson had made a wager that he could eat two whole fried chickens, and he did. Eli Swanson stowed away two whole custard pies, and Nick Hermanson ate a chocolate layer cake to the last crumb. There was even a cooky contest among the children, and one thin, slablike Bohemian boy consumed sixteen and won the prize, a ginger-bread pig which Johanna Vavrika had carefully decorated with red candies and burnt sugar. Fritz Sweiheart, the German carpenter, won in the pickle contest, but he disappeared soon after supper and was not seen for the rest of the evening. Joe Vavrika said that Fritz could have managed the pickles all right, but he had sampled the demijohn in his buggy too often before sitting down to the table.

While the supper was being cleared away the two fiddlers began to tune up for the dance. Clara was to accompany them on her old upright piano, which had been brought down from her father's. By this time Nils had renewed old acquaintances. Since his interview with Clara in the cellar, he had been busy telling all the old women how young they looked, and all the young ones how pretty they were, and assuring the men that they had here the best farm-land in the world. He had made himself so agreeable that old Mrs. Ericson's friends began to come up to her and tell how lucky she was to get her smart son back again, and please to get him to play his flute. Joe Vavrika, who could still play very well when he forgot that he had rheumatism, caught up a fiddle from Johnny Oleson and played a crazy Bohemian dance tune that set the wheels going. When he dropped the bow every one was ready to dance.

Olaf, in a frock-coat and a solemn made-up

necktie, led the grand march with his mother. Clara had kept well out of *that* by sticking to the piano. She played the march with a pompous solemnity which greatly amused the prodigal son, who went over and stood behind her.

"Oh, aren't you rubbing it into them, Clara Vavrika? And aren't you lucky to have me here, or all your wit would be thrown away."

"I'm used to being witty for myself. It saves my life."

The fiddles struck up a polka, and Nils convulsed Joe Vavrika by leading out Evelina Oleson, the homely school-teacher. His next partner was a very fat Swedish girl, who, although she was an heiress, had not been asked for the first dance, but had stood against the wall in her tight, high-heeled shoes, nervously fingering a lace handkerchief. She was soon out of breath, so Nils led her, pleased and panting, to her seat, and went over to the piano, from which Clara had been watching his gallantry. "Ask Olena Yenson," she whispered. "She waltzes beautifully."

Olena, too, was rather inconveniently plump, handsome in a smooth, heavy way, with a fine color and good-natured, sleepy eyes. She was redolent of violet sachet powder, and had warm, soft, white hands, but she danced divinely, moving as smoothly as the tide coming in. "There, that's something like," Nils said as he released her. "You'll give me the next waltz, won't you? Now I must go and dance with my little cousin."

Hilda was greatly excited when Nils went up to her stall and held out his arm. Her little eyes sparkled, but she declared that she could not leave her lemonade. Old Mrs. Ericson, who happened along at this moment, said she would attend to

583

that, and Hilda came out, as pink as her pink dress. The dance was a schottische, and in a moment her yellow braids were fairly standing on end. "Bravo!" Nils cried encouragingly. "Where did you learn to dance so nicely?"

"My Cousin Clara taught me," the little girl panted.

Nils found Eric sitting with a group of boys who were too awkward or too shy to dance, and told him that he must dance the next waltz with Hilda.

The boy screwed up his shoulders. "Aw, Nils, I can't dance. My feet are too big; I look silly."

"Don't be thinking about yourself. It doesn't matter how boys look."

Nils had never spoken to him so sharply before, and Eric made haste to scramble out of his corner and brush the straw from his coat.

Clara nodded approvingly. "Good for you, Nils. I've been trying to get hold of him. They dance very nicely together; I sometimes play for them."

"I'm obliged to you for teaching him. There's no reason why he should grow up to be a lout."

"He'll never be that. He's more like you than any of them. Only he hasn't your courage." From her slanting eyes Clara shot forth one of those keen glances, admiring and at the same time challenging, which she seldom bestowed on any one, and which seemed to say, "Yes, I admire you, but I am your equal."

Clara was proving a much better host than Olaf, who, once the supper was over, seemed to feel no interest in anything but the lanterns. He had brought a locomotive headlight from town to light the revels, and he kept skulking about it as if he feared the mere light from it might set his new barn on fire. His wife, on the contrary, was cordial to every one, was animated and even gay. The deep salmon color in her cheeks burned vividly, and her eyes were full of life. She gave the piano over to the fat Swedish heiress, pulled her father away from the corner where he sat gossiping with his cronies, and made him dance a Bohemian dance with her. In his youth Joe had been a famous dancer, and his daughter got him so limbered up that every one sat round and applauded them. The old ladies were particularly delighted, and made them go through the dance again. From their corner where they watched and commented, the old women kept time with their feet and hands, and whenever the fiddles struck up a new air old Mrs. Svendsen's white cap would begin to bob.

Clara was waltzing with little Eric when Nils came up to them, brushed his brother aside, and swung her out among the dancers. "Remember how we used to waltz on rollers at the old skating-rink in town? I suppose people don't do that any more. We used to keep it up for hours. You know, we never did moon around as other boys and girls did. It was dead serious with us from the beginning. When we were most in love with each other, we used to fight. You were always pinching people; your fingers were like little nippers. A regular snapping-turtle, you were. Lord, how you'd like Stockholm! Sit out in the streets in front of cafés and talk all night in summer. Just like a reception — officers and ladies and funny English people. Jolliest people in the world, the Swedes, once you get them going. Always drinking things — champagne and stout mixed, half-and-half; serve it out of big pitchers, and serve plenty. Slow pulse, you know; they can stand a lot. Once they light up, they're glow-worms, I can tell you."

"All the same, you don't really like gay people."

"*I* don't?"

"No; I could see that when you were looking at the old women there this afternoon. They're the kind you really admire, after all; women like your mother. And that's the kind you'll marry."

"Is it, Miss Wisdom? You'll see who I'll marry, and she won't have a domestic virtue to bless herself with. She'll be a snapping-turtle, and she'll be a match for me. All the same, they're a fine bunch of old dames over there. You admire them yourself."

"No, I don't; I detest them."

"You won't, when you look back on them from Stockholm or Budapest. Freedom settles all that. Oh, but you're the real Bohemian Girl, Clara Vavrika!" Nils laughed down at her sullen frown and began mockingly to sing:

"Oh, how could a poor gypsy maiden like me
Expect the proud bride of a baron to be?"

Clara clutched his shoulder. "Hush, Nils; every one is looking at you."

"I don't care. They can't gossip. It's all in the family, as the Ericsons say when they divide up little Hilda's patrimony amongst them. Besides, we'll give them something to talk about when we hit the trail. Lord, it will be a godsend to them! They haven't had anything so interesting to chatter about since the grasshopper year. It'll give them a new lease of life. And Olaf won't lose the Bohemian vote, either. They'll have the laugh on him so that they'll vote two apiece. They'll send him to Congress. They'll never forget his barn party, or us. They'll always remember us as we're dancing together now. We're making a legend. Where's my waltz, boys?" he called as they whirled past the fiddlers.

The musicians grinned, looked at each other, hesitated, and began a new air; and Nils sang with them, as the couples fell from a quick waltz to a long, slow glide:

"When other lips and other hearts
  Their tale of love shall tell,
In language whose excess imparts
  The power they feel so well."

The old women applauded vigorously. "What a gay one he is, that Nils!" And old Mrs. Svendsen's cap lurched dreamily from side to side to the flowing measure of the dance.

"Of days that have as ha-a-p-py been,
  And you'll remember me."

VII

The moonlight flooded that great, silent land. The reaped fields lay yellow in it. The straw stacks and poplar windbreaks threw sharp black shadows. The roads were white rivers of dust. The sky was a deep, crystalline blue, and the stars were few and faint. Everything seemed to have succumbed, to have sunk to sleep, under the great, golden, tender, midsummer moon. The splendor of it seemed to transcend human life and human fate. The senses were too feeble to take it in, and every time one looked up at the sky one felt unequal to it, as if one were sitting deaf under the waves of a great river of melody. Near the road, Nils Ericson

587

was lying against a straw stack in Olaf's wheat-field. His own life seemed strange and unfamiliar to him, as if it were something he had read about, or dreamed, and forgotten. He lay very still, watching the white road that ran in front of him, lost itself among the fields, and then, at a distance, reappeared over a little hill. At last, against this white band he saw something moving rapidly, and he got up and walked to the edge of the field. "She is passing the row of poplars now," he thought. He heard the padded beat of hoofs along the dusty road, and as she came into sight he stepped out and waved his arms. Then, for fear of frightening the horse, he drew back and waited. Clara had seen him, and she came up at a walk. Nils took the horse by the bit and stroked his neck.

"What are you doing out so late, Clara Vavrika? I went to the house, but Johanna told me you had gone to your father's."

"Who can stay in the house on a night like this? Aren't you out yourself?"

"Ah, but that's another matter."

Nils turned the horse into the field.

"What are you doing? Where are you taking Norman?"

"Not far, but I want to talk to you to-night; I have something to say to you. I can't talk to you at the house, with Olaf sitting there on the porch, weighing a thousand tons."

Clara laughed. "He won't be sitting there now. He's in bed by this time, and asleep — weighing a thousand tons."

Nils plodded on across the stubble. "Are you really going to spend the rest of your life like this, night after night, summer after summer? Haven't you anything better to do on a night like this than

588

to wear yourself and Norman out tearing across the country to your father's and back? Besides, your father won't live forever, you know. His little place will be shut up or sold, and then you'll have nobody but the Ericsons. You'll have to fasten down the hatches for the winter then."

Clara moved her head restlessly. "Don't talk about that. I try never to think of it. If I lost father I'd lose everything, even my hold over the Ericsons."

"Bah! You'd lose a good deal more than that. You'd lose your race, everything that makes you yourself. You've lost a good deal of it now."

"Of what?"

"Of your love of life, your capacity for delight."

Clara put her hands up to her face. "I haven't, Nils Ericson, I haven't! Say anything to me but that. I won't have it!" she declared vehemently.

Nils led the horse up to a straw stack, and turned to Clara, looking at her intently, as he had looked at her that Sunday afternoon at Vavrika's. "But why do you fight for that so? What good is the power to enjoy, if you never enjoy? Your hands are cold again; what are you afraid of all the time? Ah, you're afraid of losing it; that's what's the matter with you! And you will, Clara Vavrika, you will! When I used to know you — listen; you've caught a wild bird in your hand, haven't you, and felt its heart beat so hard that you were afraid it would shatter its little body to pieces? Well, you used to be just like that, a slender, eager thing with a wild delight inside you. That is how I remembered you. And I come back and find you — a bitter woman. This is a perfect ferret fight here; you live by biting and being bitten. Can't you remember what life used to be? Can't you

589

remember that old delight? I've never forgotten it, or known its like, on land or sea."

He drew the horse under the shadow of the straw stack. Clara felt him take her foot out of the stirrup, and she slid softly down into his arms. He kissed her slowly. He was a deliberate man, but his nerves were steel when he wanted anything. Something flashed out from him like a knife out of a sheath. Clara felt everything slipping away from her; she was flooded by the summer night. He thrust his hand into his pocket, and then held it out at arm's length. "Look," he said. The shadow of the straw stack fell sharp across his wrist, and in the palm of his hand she saw a silver dollar shining. "That's my pile," he muttered; "will you go with me?"

Clara nodded, and dropped her forehead on his shoulder.

Nils took a deep breath. "Will you go with me to-night?"

"Where?" she whispered softly.

"To town, to catch the midnight flyer."

Clara lifted her head and pulled herself together. "Are you crazy, Nils? We couldn't go away like that."

"That's the only way we ever will go. You can't sit on the bank and think about it. You have to plunge. That's the way I've always done, and it's the right way for people like you and me. There's nothing so dangerous as sitting still. You've only got one life, one youth, and you can let it slip through your fingers if you want to; nothing easier. Most people do that. You'd be better off tramping the roads with me than you are here." Nils held back her head and looked into her eyes. "But I'm not that kind of a tramp, Clara. You won't have to

590

take in sewing. I'm with a Norwegian shipping line; came over on business with the New York offices, but now I'm going straight back to Bergen. I expect I've got as much money as the Ericsons. Father sent me a little to get started. They never knew about that. There, I hadn't meant to tell you; I wanted you to come on your own nerve."

Clara looked off across the fields. "It isn't that, Nils, but something seems to hold me. I'm afraid to pull against it. It comes out of the ground, I think."

"I know all about that. One has to tear loose. You're not needed here. Your father will understand; he's made like us. As for Olaf, Johanna will take better care of him than ever you could. It's now or never, Clara Vavrika. My bag's at the station; I smuggled it there yesterday."

Clara clung to him and hid her face against his shoulder. "Not to-night," she whispered. "Sit here and talk to me to-night. I don't want to go anywhere to-night. I may never love you like this again."

Nils laughed through his teeth. "You can't come that on me. That's not my way, Clara Vavrika. Eric's mare is over there behind the stacks, and I'm off on the midnight. It's good-by, or off across the world with me. My carriage won't wait. I've written a letter to Olaf; I'll mail it in town. When he reads it he won't bother us — not if I know him. He'd rather have the land. Besides, I could demand an investigation of his administration of Cousin Henrik's estate, and that would be bad for a public man. You've no clothes, I know; but you can sit up to-night, and we can get everything on the way. Where's your old dash, Clara Vavrika? What's become of your Bohemian blood? I used

591

to think you had courage enough for anything. Where's your nerve — what are you waiting for?"

Clara drew back her head, and he saw the slumberous fire in her eyes. "For you to say one thing, Nils Ericson."

"I never say that thing to any woman, Clara Vavrika." He leaned back, lifted her gently from the ground, and whispered through his teeth: "But I'll never, never let you go, not to any man on earth but me! Do you understand me? Now, wait here."

Clara sank down on a sheaf of wheat and covered her face with her hands. She did not know what she was going to do — whether she would go or stay. The great, silent country seemed to lay a spell upon her. The ground seemed to hold her as if by roots. Her knees were soft under her. She felt as if she could not bear separation from her old sorrows, from her old discontent. They were dear to her, they had kept her alive, they were a part of her. There would be nothing left of her if she were wrenched away from them. Never could she pass beyond that sky-line against which her restlessness had beat so many times. She felt as if her soul had built itself a nest there on that horizon at which she looked every morning and every evening, and it was dear to her, inexpressibly dear. She pressed her fingers against her eyeballs to shut it out. Beside her she heard the tramping of horses in the soft earth. Nils said nothing to her. He put his hands under her arms and lifted her lightly to her saddle. Then he swung himself into his own.

"We shall have to ride fast to catch the midnight train. A last gallop, Clara Vavrika. Forward!"

There was a start, a thud of hoofs along the

moonlit road, two dark shadows going over the hill; and then the great, still land stretched untroubled under the azure night. Two shadows had passed.

VIII

A year after the flight of Olaf Ericson's wife, the night train was steaming across the plains of Iowa. The conductor was hurrying through one of the day-coaches, his lantern on his arm, when a lank, fair-haired boy sat up in one of the plush seats and tweaked him by the coat.

"What is the next stop, please, sir?"

"Red Oak, Iowa. But you go through to Chicago, don't you?" He looked down, and noticed that the boy's eyes were red and his face was drawn, as if he were in trouble.

"Yes. But I was wondering whether I could get off at the next place and get a train back to Omaha."

"Well, I suppose you could. Live in Omaha?"

"No. In the western part of the State. How soon do we get to Red Oak?"

"Forty minutes. You'd better make up your mind, so I can tell the baggageman to put your trunk off."

"Oh, never mind about that! I mean, I haven't got any," the boy added, blushing.

"Run away," the conductor thought, as he slammed the coach door behind him.

Eric Ericson crumpled down in his seat and put his brown hand to his forehead. He had been crying, and he had had no supper, and his head was aching violently. "Oh, what shall I do?" he thought, as he looked dully down at his big shoes.

"Nils will be ashamed of me; I haven't got any spunk."

Ever since Nils had run away with his brother's wife, life at home had been hard for little Eric. His mother and Olaf both suspected him of complicity. Mrs. Ericson was harsh and fault-finding, constantly wounding the boy's pride; and Olaf was always getting her against him.

Joe Vavrika heard often from his daughter. Clara had always been fond of her father, and happiness made her kinder. She wrote him long accounts of the voyage to Bergen, and of the trip she and Nils took through Bohemia to the little town where her father had grown up and where she herself was born. She visited all her kinsmen there, and sent her father news of his brother, who was a priest; of his sister, who had married a horse-breeder — of their big farm and their many children. These letters Joe always managed to read to little Eric. They contained messages for Eric and Hilda. Clara sent presents, too, which Eric never dared to take home and which poor little Hilda never even saw, though she loved to hear Eric tell about them when they were out getting the eggs together. But Olaf once saw Eric coming out of Vavrika's house, — the old man had never asked the boy to come into his saloon, — and Olaf went straight to his mother and told her. That night Mrs. Ericson came to Eric's room after he was in bed and made a terrible scene. She could be very terrifying when she was really angry. She forbade him ever to speak to Vavrika again, and after that night she would not allow him to go to town alone. So it was a long while before Eric got any more news of his brother. But old Joe suspected what was going on, and he carried Clara's letters about in his pocket. One Sunday he drove out to see a German friend of his, and chanced to catch sight of Eric, sitting by the cattle-pond in the big pasture. They went together into Fritz Oberlies' barn, and read the letters and talked things over. Eric admitted that things were getting hard for him at home. That very night old Joe sat down and laboriously penned a statement of the case to his daughter.

Things got no better for Eric. His mother and Olaf felt that, however closely he was watched, he still, as they said, "heard." Mrs. Ericson could not admit neutrality. She had sent Johanna Vavrika packing back to her brother's, though Olaf would much rather have kept her than Anders' eldest daughter, whom Mrs. Ericson installed in her place. He was not so high-handed as his mother, and he once sulkily told her that she might better have taught her granddaughter to cook before she sent Johanna away. Olaf could have borne a good deal for the sake of prunes spiced in honey, the secret of which Johanna had taken away with her.

At last two letters came to Joe Vavrika: one from Nils, inclosing a postal order for money to pay Eric's passage to Bergen, and one from Clara, saying that Nils had a place for Eric in the offices of his company, that he was to live with them, and that they were only waiting for him to come. He was to leave New York on one of the boats of Nils' own line; the captain was one of their friends, and Eric was to make himself known at once.

Nils' directions were so explicit that a baby could have followed them, Eric felt. And here he was, nearing Red Oak, Iowa, and rocking backward and forward in despair. Never had he loved his brother so much, and never had the big world

595

called to him so hard. But there was a lump in his throat which would not go down. Ever since nightfall he had been tormented by the thought of his mother, alone in that big house that had sent forth so many men. Her unkindness now seemed so little, and her loneliness so great. He remembered everything she had ever done for him: how frightened she had been when he tore his hand in the corn-sheller, and how she wouldn't let Olaf scold him. When Nils went away he didn't leave his mother all alone, or he would never have gone. Eric felt sure of that.

The train whistled. The conductor came in, smiling not unkindly. "Well, young man, what are you going to do? We stop at Red Oak in three minutes."

"Yes, thank you. I'll let you know." The conductor went out, and the boy doubled up with misery. He couldn't let his one chance go like this. He felt for his breast pocket and crackled Nils' kind letter to give him courage. He didn't want Nils to be ashamed of him. The train stopped. Suddenly he remembered his brother's kind, twinkling eyes, that always looked at you as if from far away. The lump in his throat softened. "Ah, but Nils, Nils would *understand!*" he thought. "That's just it about Nils; he always understands."

A lank, pale boy with a canvas telescope stumbled off the train to the Red Oak siding, just as the conductor called, "All aboard!"

The next night Mrs. Ericson was sitting alone in her wooden rocking-chair on the front porch. Little Hilda had been sent to bed and had cried herself to sleep. The old woman's knitting was in her lap, but her hands lay motionless on top of it. For more than an hour she had not moved a muscle. She simply sat, as only the Ericsons and the mountains can sit. The house was dark, and there was no sound but the croaking of the frogs down in the pond of the little pasture.

Eric did not come home by the road, but across the fields, where no one could see him. He set his telescope down softly in the kitchen shed, and slipped noiselessly along the path to the front porch. He sat down on the step without saying anything. Mrs. Ericson made no sign, and the frogs croaked on. At last the boy spoke timidly.

"I've come back, Mother."

"Very well," said Mrs. Ericson.

Eric leaned over and picked up a little stick out of the grass.

"How about the milking?" he faltered.

"That's been done, hours ago."

"Who did you get?"

"Get? I did it myself. I can milk as good as any of you."

Eric slid along the step nearer to her. "Oh, Mother, why did you?" he asked sorrowfully. "Why didn't you get one of Otto's boys?"

"I didn't want anybody to know I was in need of a boy," said Mrs. Ericson bitterly. She looked straight in front of her and her mouth tightened. "I always meant to give you the home farm," she added.

The boy started and slid closer. "Oh, Mother," he faltered, "I don't care about the farm. I came back because I thought you might be needing me, maybe." He hung his head and got no further.

"Very well," said Mrs. Ericson. Her hand went out from her suddenly and rested on his head. Her fingers twined themselves in his soft, pale

597

hair. His tears splashed down on the boards; happiness filled his heart.

CONSEQUENCES

Henry Eastman, a lawyer, aged forty, was standing beside the Flatiron building in a driving November rainstorm, signaling frantically for a taxi. It was six-thirty, and everything on wheels was engaged. The streets were in confusion about him, the sky was in turmoil above him, and the Flatiron building, which seemed about to blow down, threw water like a mill-shoot. Suddenly, out of the brutal struggle of men and cars and machines and people tilting at each other with umbrellas, a quiet, well-mannered limousine paused before him, at the curb, and an agreeable, ruddy countenance confronted him through the open window of the car.

"Don't you want me to pick you up, Mr. Eastman? I'm running directly home now."

Eastman recognized Kier Cavenaugh, a young man of pleasure, who lived in the house on Central Park South, where he himself had an apartment.

"Don't I?" he exclaimed, bolting into the car. "I'll risk getting your cushions wet without compunction. I came up in a taxi, but I didn't hold it. Bad economy. I thought I saw your car down on Fourteenth Street about half an hour ago."

The owner of the car smiled. He had a pleasant, round face and round eyes, and a fringe of smooth, yellow hair showed under the rim of his soft felt hat. "With a lot of little broilers fluttering into it? You did. I know some girls who work in the cheap shops down there. I happened to be down-town and I stopped and took a load of them home. I do sometimes. Saves their poor little clothes, you know. Their shoes are never any good."

Eastman looked at his rescuer. "Aren't they notoriously afraid of cars and smooth young men?" he inquired.

Cavenaugh shook his head. "They know which cars are safe and which are chancy. They put each other wise. You have to take a bunch at a time, of course. The Italian girls can never come along; their men shoot. The girls understand, all right; but their fathers don't. One gets to see queer places, sometimes, taking them home."

Eastman laughed drily. "Every time I touch the circle of your acquaintance, Cavenaugh, it's a little wider. You must know New York pretty well by this time."

"Yes, but I'm on my good behavior below Twenty-third Street," the young man replied with simplicity. "My little friends down there would give me a good character. They're wise little girls. They have grand ways with each other, a romantic code of loyalty. You can find a good many of the lost virtues among them."

The car was standing still in a traffic block at Fortieth Street, when Cavenaugh suddenly drew his face away from the window and touched Eastman's arm. "Look, please. You see that hansom with the bony gray horse — driver has a

600

broken hat and red flannel around his throat. Can you see who is inside?"

Eastman peered out. The hansom was just cutting across the line, and the driver was making a great fuss about it, bobbing his head and waving his whip. He jerked his dripping old horse into Fortieth Street and clattered off past the Public Library grounds toward Sixth Avenue. "No, I couldn't see the passenger. Someone you know?"

"Could you see whether there was a passenger?" Cavenaugh asked.

"Why, yes. A man, I think. I saw his elbow on the apron. No driver ever behaves like that unless he has a passenger."

"Yes, I may have been mistaken," Cavenaugh murmured absent-mindedly. Ten minutes or so later, after Cavenaugh's car had turned off Fifth Avenue into Fifty-eighth Street, Eastman exclaimed, "There's your same cabby, and his cart's empty. He's headed for a drink now, I suppose." The driver in the broken hat and the red flannel neck cloth was still brandishing the whip over his old gray. He was coming from the west now, and turned down Sixth Avenue, under the elevated.

Cavenaugh's car stopped at the bachelor apartment house between Sixth and Seventh Avenues where he and Eastman lived, and they went up in the elevator together. They were still talking when the lift stopped at Cavenaugh's floor, and Eastman stepped out with him and walked down the hall, finishing his sentence while Cavenaugh found his latch-key. When he opened the door, a wave of fresh cigarette smoke greeted them. Cavenaugh stopped short and stared into his hallway. "Now how in the devil — !" he exclaimed angrily.

"Someone waiting for you? Oh, no, thanks. I

wasn't coming in. I have to work to-night. Thank you, but I couldn't." Eastman nodded and went up the two flights to his own rooms.

Though Eastman did not customarily keep a servant he had this winter a man who had been lent to him by a friend who was abroad. Rollins met him at the door and took his coat and hat.

"Put out my dinner clothes, Rollins, and then get out of here until ten o'clock. I've promised to go to a supper to-night. I shan't be dining. I've had a late tea and I'm going to work until ten. You may put out some kumiss and biscuit for me."

Rollins took himself off, and Eastman settled down at the big table in his sitting-room. He had to read a lot of letters submitted as evidence in a breach of contract case, and before he got very far he found that long paragraphs in some of the letters were written in German. He had a German dictionary at his office, but none here. Rollins had gone, and anyhow, the bookstores would be closed. He remembered having seen a row of dictionaries on the lower shelf of one of Cavenaugh's bookcases. Cavenaugh had a lot of books, though he never read anything but new stuff. Eastman prudently turned down his student's lamp very low — the thing had an evil habit of smoking — and went down two flights to Cavenaugh's door.

The young man himself answered Eastman's ring. He was freshly dressed for the evening, except for a brown smoking jacket, and his yellow hair had been brushed until it shone. He hesitated as he confronted his caller, still holding the door knob, and his round eyes and smooth forehead made their best imitation of a frown. When Eastman began to apologize, Cavenaugh's manner suddenly changed. He caught his arm and jerked him into the narrow hall. "Come in, come in. Right along!" he said excitedly. "Right along," he repeated as he pushed Eastman before him into his sitting-room. "Well I'll —" he stopped short at the door and looked about his own room with an air of complete mystification. The back window was wide open and a strong wind was blowing in. Cavenaugh walked over to the window and stuck out his head, looking up and down the fire escape. When he pulled his head in, he drew down the sash.

"I had a visitor I wanted you to see," he explained with a nervous smile. "At least I thought I had. He must have gone out that way," nodding toward the window.

"Call him back. I only came to borrow a German dictionary, if you have one. Can't stay. Call him back."

Cavenaugh shook his head despondently. "No use. He's beat it. Nowhere in sight."

"He must be active. Has he left something?" Eastman pointed to a very dirty white glove that lay on the floor under the window.

"Yes, that's his." Cavenaugh reached for his tongs, picked up the glove, and tossed it into the grate, where it quickly shriveled on the coals. Eastman felt that he had happened in upon something disagreeable, possibly something shady, and he wanted to get away at once. Cavenaugh stood staring at the fire and seemed stupid and dazed; so he repeated his request rather sternly, "I think I've seen a German dictionary down there among your books. May I have it?"

Cavenaugh blinked at him. "A German dictionary? Oh, possibly! Those were my father's. I scarcely know what there is." He put down the tongs and began to wipe his hands nervously with his handkerchief.

Eastman went over to the bookcase behind the Chesterfield, opened the door, swooped upon the book he wanted and stuck it under his arm. He felt perfectly certain now that something shady had been going on in Cavenaugh's rooms, and he saw no reason why he should come in for any hang-over. "Thanks. I'll send it back to-morrow," he said curtly as he made for the door.

Cavenaugh followed him. "Wait a moment. I wanted you to see him. You did see his glove," glancing at the grate.

Eastman laughed disagreeably. "I saw a glove. That's not evidence. Do your friends often use that means of exit? Somewhat inconvenient."

Cavenaugh gave him a startled glance. "Wouldn't you think so? For an old man, a very rickety old party? The ladders are steep, you know, and rusty." He approached the window again and put it up softly. In a moment he drew his head back with a jerk. He caught Eastman's arm and shoved him toward the window. "Hurry, please. Look! Down there." He pointed to the little patch of paved court four flights down.

The square of pavement was so small and the walls about it were so high, that it was a good deal like looking down a well. Four tall buildings backed upon the same court and made a kind of shaft, with flagstones at the bottom, and at the top a square of dark blue with some stars in it. At the bottom of the shaft Eastman saw a black figure, a man in a caped coat and a tall hat stealing cautiously around, not across the square of pavement, keeping close to the dark wall and

604

avoiding the streak of light that fell on the flagstones from a window in the opposite house. Seen from that height he was of course foreshortened and probably looked more shambling and decrepit than he was. He picked his way along with exaggerated care and looked like a silly old cat crossing a wet street. When he reached the gate that led into an alley way between two buildings, he felt about for the latch, opened the door a mere crack, and then shot out under the feeble lamp that burned in the brick arch over the gateway. The door closed after him.

"He'll get run in," Eastman remarked curtly, turning away from the window. "That door shouldn't be left unlocked. Any crook could come in. I'll speak to the janitor about it, if you don't mind," he added sarcastically.

"Wish you would." Cavenaugh stood brushing down the front of his jacket, first with his right hand and then with his left. "You saw him, didn't you?"

"Enough of him. Seems eccentric. I have to see a lot of buggy people. They don't take me in any more. But I'm keeping you and I'm in a hurry myself. Good night."

Cavenaugh put out his hand detainingly and started to say something; but Eastman rudely turned his back and went down the hall and out of the door. He had never felt anything shady about Cavenaugh before, and he was sorry he had gone down for the dictionary. In five minutes he was deep in his papers; but in the half hour when he was loafing before he dressed to go out, the young man's curious behavior came into his mind again.

Eastman had merely a neighborly acquaintance

605

with Cavenaugh. He had been to a supper at the young man's rooms once, but he didn't particularly like Cavenaugh's friends; so the next time he was asked, he had another engagement. He liked Cavenaugh himself, if for nothing else than because he was so cheerful and trim and ruddy. A good complexion is always at a premium in New York, especially when it shines reassuringly on a man who does everything in the world to lose it. It encourages fellow mortals as to the inherent vigor of the human organism and the amount of bad treatment it will stand for. "Footprints that perhaps another," etc.

Cavenaugh, he knew, had plenty of money. He was the son of a Pennsylvania preacher, who died soon after he discovered that his ancestral acres were full of petroleum, and Kier had come to New York to burn some of the oil. He was thirty-two and was still at it; spent his life, literally, among the breakers. His motor hit the Park every morning as if it were the first time ever. He took people out to supper every night. He went from restaurant to restaurant, sometimes to half-a-dozen in an evening. The head waiters were his hosts and their cordiality made him happy. They made a life-line for him up Broadway and down Fifth Avenue. Cavenaugh was still fresh and smooth, round and plump, with a lustre to his hair and white teeth and a clear look in his round eyes. He seemed absolutely unwearied and unimpaired; never bored and never carried away.

Eastman always smiled when he met Cavenaugh in the entrance hall, serenely going forth to or returning from gladiatorial combats with joy, or when he saw him rolling smoothly up to the door in his car in the morning after a restful night in one of the remarkable new roadhouses he was always finding. Eastman had seen a good many young men disappear on Cavenaugh's route, and he admired this young man's endurance.

To-night, for the first time, he had got a whiff of something unwholesome about the fellow — bad nerves, bad company, something on hand that he was ashamed of, a visitor old and vicious, who must have had a key to Cavenaugh's apartment, for he was evidently there when Cavenaugh returned at seven o'clock. Probably it was the same man Cavenaugh had seen in the hansom. He must have been able to let himself in, for Cavenaugh kept no man but his chauffeur; or perhaps the janitor had been instructed to let him in. In either case, and whoever he was, it was clear enough that Cavenaugh was ashamed of him and was mixing up in questionable business of some kind.

Eastman sent Cavenaugh's book back by Rollins, and for the next few weeks he had no word with him beyond a casual greeting when they happened to meet in the hall or the elevator. One Sunday morning Cavenaugh telephoned up to him to ask if he could motor out to a roadhouse in Connecticut that afternoon and have supper; but when Eastman found there were to be other guests he declined.

On New Year's eve Eastman dined at the University Club at six o'clock and hurried home before the usual manifestations of insanity had begun in the streets. When Rollins brought his smoking coat, he asked him whether he wouldn't like to get off early.

"Yes, sir. But won't you be dressing, Mr. Eastman?" he inquired.

"Not to-night." Eastman handed him a bill. "Bring some change in the morning. There'll be fees."

Rollins lost no time in putting everything to rights for the night, and Eastman couldn't help wishing that he were in such a hurry to be off somewhere himself. When he heard the hall door close softly, he wondered if there were any place, after all, that he wanted to go. From his window he looked down at the long lines of motors and taxis waiting for a signal to cross Broadway. He thought of some of their probable destinations and decided that none of those places pulled him very hard. The night was warm and wet, the air was drizzly. Vapor hung in clouds about the *Times* Building, half hid the top of it, and made a luminous haze along Broadway. While he was looking down at the army of wet, black carriage-tops and their reflected headlights and tail-lights, Eastman heard a ring at his door. He deliberated. If it were a caller, the hall porter would have telephoned up. It must be the janitor. When he opened the door, there stood a rosy young man in a tuxedo, without a coat or hat.

"Pardon. Should I have telephoned? I half thought you wouldn't be in."

Eastman laughed. "Come in, Cavenaugh. You weren't sure whether you wanted company or not, eh, and you were trying to let chance decide it? That was exactly my state of mind. Let's accept the verdict." When they emerged from the narrow hall into his sitting-room, he pointed out a seat by the fire to his guest. He brought a tray of decanters and soda bottles and placed it on his writing table.

Cavenaugh hesitated, standing by the fire. "Sure you weren't starting for somewhere?"

"Do I look it? No, I was just making up my mind to stick it out alone when you rang. Have one?" he picked up a tall tumbler.

"Yes, thank you. I always do."

Eastman chuckled. "Lucky boy! So will I. I had a very early dinner. New York is the most arid place on holidays," he continued as he rattled the ice in the glasses. "When one gets too old to hit the rapids down there, and tired of gobbling food to heathenish dance music, there is absolutely no place where you can get a chop and some milk toast in peace, unless you have strong ties of blood brotherhood on upper Fifth Avenue. But you, why aren't you starting for somewhere?"

The young man sipped his soda and shook his head as he replied:

"Oh, I couldn't get a chop, either. I know only flashy people, of course." He looked up at his host with such a grave and candid expression that Eastman decided there couldn't be anything very crooked about the fellow. His smooth cheeks were positively cherubic.

"Well, what's the matter with them? Aren't they flashing to-night?"

"Only the very new ones seem to flash on New Year's eve. The older ones fade away. Maybe they are hunting a chop, too."

"Well" — Eastman sat down — "holidays do dash one. I was just about to write a letter to a pair of maiden aunts in my old home town, up-state; old coasting hill, snow-covered pines, lights in the church windows. That's what you've saved me from."

Cavenaugh shook himself. "Oh, I'm sure that

wouldn't have been good for you. Pardon me," he rose and took a photograph from the bookcase, a handsome man in shooting clothes. "Dudley, isn't it? Did you know him well?"

"Yes. An old friend. Terrible thing, wasn't it? I haven't got over the jolt yet."

"His suicide? Yes, terrible! Did you know his wife?"

"Slightly. Well enough to admire her very much. She must be terribly broken up. I wonder Dudley didn't think of that."

Cavenaugh replaced the photograph carefully, lit a cigarette, and standing before the fire began to smoke. "Would you mind telling me about him? I never met him, but of course I'd read a lot about him, and I can't help feeling interested. It was a queer thing."

Eastman took out his cigar case and leaned back in his deep chair. "In the days when I knew him best he hadn't any story, like the happy nations. Everything was properly arranged for him before he was born. He came into the world happy, healthy, clever, straight, with the right sort of connections and the right kind of fortune, neither too large nor too small. He helped to make the world an agreeable place to live in until he was twenty-six. Then he married as he should have married. His wife was a Californian, educated abroad. Beautiful. You have seen her picture?"

Cavenaugh nodded. "Oh, many of them."

"She was interesting, too. Though she was distinctly a person of the world, she had retained something, just enough of the large Western manner. She had the habit of authority, of calling out a special train if she needed it, of using all our ingenious mechanical contrivances lightly and easily, without over-rating them. She and Dudley knew how to live better than most people. Their house was the most charming one I have ever known in New York. You felt freedom there, and a zest of life, and safety — absolute sanctuary — from everything sordid or petty. A whole society like that would justify the creation of man and would make our planet shine with a soft, peculiar radiance among the constellations. You think I'm putting it on thick?"

The young man sighed gently. "Oh, no! One has always felt there must be people like that. I've never known any."

"They had two children, beautiful ones. After they had been married for eight years, Rosina met this Spaniard. He must have amounted to something. She wasn't a flighty woman. She came home and told Dudley how matters stood. He persuaded her to stay at home for six months and try to pull up. They were both fair-minded people, and I'm as sure as if I were the Almighty, that she did try. But at the end of the time, Rosina went quietly off to Spain, and Dudley went to hunt in the Canadian Rockies. I met his party out there. I didn't know his wife had left him and talked about her a good deal. I noticed that he never drank anything, and his light used to shine through the log chinks of his room until all hours, even after a hard day's hunting. When I got back to New York, rumors were creeping about. Dudley did not come back. He bought a ranch in Wyoming, built a big log house and kept splendid dogs and horses. One of his sisters went out to keep house for him, and the children were there when they were not in school. He had a great many visitors, and everyone who came back talked about how well Dudley

611

kept things going.

"He put in two years out there. Then, last month, he had to come back on business. A trust fund had to be settled up, and he was administrator. I saw him at the club; same light, quick step, same gracious handshake. He was getting gray, and there was something softer in his manner; but he had a fine red tan on his face and said he found it delightful to be here in the season when everything is going hard. The Madison Avenue house had been closed since Rosina left it. He went there to get some things his sister wanted. That, of course, was the mistake. He went alone, in the afternoon, and didn't go out for dinner — found some sherry and tins of biscuit in the sideboard. He shot himself sometime that night. There were pistols in his smoking-room. They found burnt out candles beside him in the morning. The gas and electricity were shut off. I suppose there, in his own house, among his own things, it was too much for him. He left no letters."

Cavenaugh blinked and brushed the lapel of his coat. "I suppose," he said slowly, "that every suicide is logical and reasonable, if one knew all the facts."

Eastman roused himself. "No, I don't think so. I've known too many fellows who went off like that — more than I deserve, I think — and some of them were absolutely inexplicable. I can understand Dudley; but I can't see why healthy bachelors, with money enough, like ourselves, need such a device. It reminds me of what Dr. Johnson said, that the most discouraging thing about life is the number of fads and hobbies and fake religions it takes to put people through a few years of it."

"Dr. Johnson? The specialist? Oh, the old fellow!" said Cavenaugh imperturbably. "Yes, that's interesting. Still, I fancy if one knew the facts — Did you know about Wyatt?"

"I don't think so."

"You wouldn't, probably. He was just a fellow about town who spent money. He wasn't one of the *forestieri,* though. Had connections here and owned a fine old place over on Staten Island. He went in for botany, and had been all over, hunting things; rusts, I believe. He had a yacht and used to take a gay crowd down about the South Seas, botanizing. He really did botanize, I believe. I never knew such a spender — only not flashy. He helped a lot of fellows and he was awfully good to girls, the kind who come down here to get a little fun, who don't like to work and still aren't really tough, the kind you see talking hard for their dinner. Nobody knows what becomes of them, or what they get out of it, and there are hundreds of new ones every year. He helped dozens of 'em; it was he who got me curious about the little shop girls. Well, one afternoon when his tea was brought, he took prussic acid instead. He didn't leave any letters, either; people of any taste don't. They wouldn't leave any material reminder if they could help it. His lawyers found that he had just $314.72 above his debts when he died. He had planned to spend all his money, and then take his tea; he had worked it out carefully."

Eastman reached for his pipe and pushed his chair away from the fire. "That looks like a considered case, but I don't think philosophical suicides like that are common. I think they usually come from stress of feeling and are really, as

613

the newspapers call them, desperate acts; done without a motive. You remember when Anna Karenina was under the wheels, she kept saying, 'Why am I here?' "

Cavenaugh rubbed his upper lip with his pink finger and made an effort to wrinkle his brows. "May I, please?" reaching for the whiskey. "But have you," he asked, blinking as the soda flew at him, "have you ever known, yourself, cases that were really inexplicable?"

"A few too many. I was in Washington just before Captain Jack Purden was married and I saw a good deal of him. Popular army man, fine record in the Philippines, married a charming girl with lots of money; mutual devotion. It was the gayest wedding of the winter, and they started for Japan. They stopped in San Francisco for a week and missed their boat because, as the bride wrote back to Washington, they were too happy to move. They took the next boat, were both good sailors, had exceptional weather. After they had been out for two weeks, Jack got up from his deck chair one afternoon, yawned, put down his book, and stood before his wife. 'Stop reading for a moment and look at me.' She laughed and asked him why. 'Because you happen to be good to look at.' He nodded to her, went back to the stern and was never seen again. Must have gone down to the lower deck and slipped overboard, behind the machinery. It was the luncheon hour, not many people about; steamer cutting through a soft green sea. That's one of the most baffling cases I know. His friends raked up his past, and it was as trim as a cottage garden. If he'd so much as dropped an ink spot on his fatigue uniform, they'd have found it. He wasn't emotional or moody; wasn't,

614

indeed, very interesting; simply a good soldier, fond of all the pompous little formalities that make up a military man's life. What do you make of that, my boy?"

Cavenaugh stroked his chin. "It's very puzzling, I admit. Still, if one knew everything ———"

"But we do know everything. His friends wanted to find something to help them out, to help the girl out, to help the case of the human creature."

"Oh, I don't mean things that people could unearth," said Cavenaugh uneasily. "But possibly there were things that couldn't be found out."

Eastman shrugged his shoulders. "It's my experience that when there are 'things' as you call them, they're very apt to be found. There is no such thing as a secret. To make any move at all one has to employ human agencies, employ at least one human agent. Even when the pirates killed the men who buried their gold for them, the bones told the story."

Cavenaugh rubbed his hands together and smiled his sunny smile.

"I like that idea. It's reassuring. If we can have no secrets, it means that we can't, after all, go so far afield as we might," he hesitated, "yes, as we might."

Eastman looked at him sourly. "Cavenaugh, when you've practised law in New York for twelve years, you find that people can't go far in any direction, except ——" He thrust his forefinger sharply at the floor. "Even in that direction, few people can do anything out of the ordinary. Our range is limited. Skip a few baths, and we become personally objectionable. The slightest careless-ness can rot a man's integrity or give him pto-maine poisoning. We keep up only by incessant cleansing operations, of mind and body. What we call character, is held together by all sorts of tacks and strings and glue."

Cavenaugh looked startled. "Come now, it's not so bad as that, is it? I've always thought that a serious man, like you, must know a lot of Lancelots." When Eastman only laughed, the younger man squirmed about in his chair. He spoke again hastily, as if he were embarrassed. "Your military friend may have had personal experiences, however, that his friends couldn't possibly get a line on. He may accidentally have come to a place where he saw himself in too unpleasant a light. I believe people can be chilled by a draft from outside, somewhere."

"Outside?" Eastman echoed. "Ah, you mean the far outside! Ghosts, delusions, eh?"

Cavenaugh winced. "That's putting it strong. Why not say tips from the outside? Delusions belong to a diseased mind, don't they? There are some of us who have no minds to speak of, who yet have had experiences. I've had a little something in that line myself and I don't look it, do I?"

Eastman looked at the bland countenance turned toward him. "Not exactly. What's your delusion?"

"It's not a delusion. It's a haunt."

The lawyer chuckled. "Soul of a lost Casino girl?"

"No; an old gentleman. A most unattractive old gentleman, who follows me about."

"Does he want money?"

Cavenaugh sat up straight. "No. I wish to God he wanted anything — but the pleasure of my society! I'd let him clean me out to be rid of him. He's a real article. You saw him yourself that night when you came to my rooms to borrow a dictionary, and he went down the fire-escape. You saw him down in the court."

"Well, I saw somebody down in the court, but I'm too cautious to take it for granted that I saw what you saw. Why, anyhow, should I see your haunt? If it was your friend I saw, he impressed me disagreeably. How did you pick him up?"

Cavenaugh looked gloomy. "That was queer, too. Charley Burke and I had motored out to Long Beach, about a year ago, sometime in October, I think. We had supper and stayed until late. When we were coming home, my car broke down. We had a lot of girls along who had to get back for morning rehearsals and things; so I sent them all into town in Charley's car, and he was to send a man back to tow me home. I was driving myself, and didn't want to leave my machine. We had not taken a direct road back; so I was stuck in a lonesome, woody place, no houses about. I got chilly and made a fire, and was putting in the time comfortably enough, when this old party steps up. He was in shabby evening clothes and a top hat, and had on his usual white gloves. How he got there, at three o'clock in the morning, miles from any town or railway, I'll leave it to you to figure out. *He* surely had no car. When I saw him coming up to the fire, I disliked him. He had a silly, apologetic walk. His teeth were chattering, and I asked him to sit down. He got down like a clothes-horse folding up. I offered him a cigarette, and when he took off his gloves I couldn't help noticing how knotted and spotty his hands were. He was asthmatic, and took his breath with a wheeze. 'Haven't you got anything — refreshing in there?' he asked, nodding at the car. When I

617

told him I hadn't, he sighed. 'Ah, you young fellows are greedy. You drink it all up. You drink it all up, all up — up!' he kept chewing it over."

Cavenaugh paused and looked embarrassed again. "The thing that was most unpleasant is difficult to explain. The old man sat there by the fire and leered at me with a silly sort of admiration that was — well, more than humiliating. 'Gay boy, gay dog!' he would mutter, and when he grinned he showed his teeth, worn and yellow — shells. I remembered that it was better to talk casually to insane people; so I remarked carelessly that I had been out with a party and got stuck.

" 'Oh yes, I remember,' he said, 'Flora and Lottie and Maybelle and Marcelline, and poor Kate.'

"He had named them correctly; so I began to think I had been hitting the bright waters too hard.

"Things I drank never had seemed to make me woody; but you can never tell when trouble is going to hit you. I pulled my hat down and tried to look as uncommunicative as possible; but he kept croaking on from time to time, like this: 'Poor Kate! Splendid arms, but dope got her. She took up with Eastern religions after she had her hair dyed. Got to going to a Swami's joint, and smoking opium. Temple of the Lotus, it was called, and the police raided it.'

"This was nonsense, of course; the young woman was in the pink of condition. I let him rave, but I decided that if something didn't come out for me pretty soon, I'd foot it across Long Island. There wasn't room enough for the two of us. I got up and took another try at my car. He hopped right after me.

" 'Good car,' he wheezed, 'better than the little Ford.'

"I'd had a Ford before, but so has everybody; that was a safe guess.

" 'Still,' he went on, 'that run in from Huntington Bay in the rain wasn't bad. Arrested for speeding, he-he.'

"It was true I had made such a run, under rather unusual circumstances, and had been arrested. When at last I heard my life-boat snorting up the road, my visitor got up, sighed, and stepped back into the shadow of the trees. I didn't wait to see what became of him, you may believe. That was visitation number one. What do you think of it?"

Cavenaugh looked at his host defiantly. Eastman smiled.

"I think you'd better change your mode of life, Cavenaugh. Had many returns?" he inquired.

"Too many, by far." The young man took a turn about the room and came back to the fire. Standing by the mantel he lit another cigarette before going on with his story:

"The second visitation happened in the street, early in the evening, about eight o'clock. I was held up in a traffic block before the Plaza. My chauffeur was driving. Old Nibbs steps up out of the crowd, opens the door of my car, gets in and sits down beside me. He had on wilted evening clothes, same as before, and there was some sort of heavy scent about him. Such an unpleasant old party! A thorough-going rotter; you knew it at once. This time he wasn't talkative, as he had been when I first saw him. He leaned back in the car as if he owned it, crossed his hands on his stick and looked out at the crowd — sort of hungrily.

"I own I really felt a loathing compassion for

619

him. We got down the avenue slowly. I kept looking out at the mounted police. But what could I do? Have him pulled? I was afraid to. I was awfully afraid of getting him into the papers.

" 'I'm going to the New Astor,' I said at last. 'Can I take you anywhere?'

" 'No, thank you,' says he. 'I get out when you do. I'm due on West 44th. I'm dining to-night with Marcelline — all that is left of her!'

"He put his hand to his hat brim with a gruesome salute. Such a scandalous, foolish old face as he had! When we pulled up at the Astor, I stuck my hand in my pocket and asked him if he'd like a little loan.

" 'No, thank you, but' — he leaned over and whispered, ugh! — 'but save a little, save a little. Forty years from now — a little — comes in handy. Save a little.'

"His eyes fairly glittered as he made his remark. I jumped out. I'd have jumped into the North River. When he tripped off, I asked my chauffeur if he'd noticed the man who got into the car with me. He said he knew someone was with me, but he hadn't noticed just when he got in. Want to hear any more?"

Cavenaugh dropped into his chair again. His plump cheeks were a trifle more flushed than usual, but he was perfectly calm. Eastman felt that the young man believed what he was telling him.

"Of course I do. It's very interesting. I don't see quite where you are coming out though."

Cavenaugh sniffed. "No more do I. I really feel that I've been put upon. I haven't deserved it any more than any other fellow of my kind. Doesn't it impress you disagreeably?"

"Well, rather so. Has anyone else seen your friend?"

"You saw him."

"We won't count that. As I said, there's no certainty that you and I saw the same person in the court that night. Has anyone else had a look in?"

"People sense him rather than see him. He usually crops up when I'm alone or in a crowd on the street. He never approaches me when I'm with people I know, though I've seen him hanging about the doors of theatres when I come out with a party; loafing around the stage exit, under a wall; or across the street, in a doorway. To be frank, I'm not anxious to introduce him. The third time, it was I who came upon him. In November my driver, Harry, had a sudden attack of appendicitis. I took him to the Presbyterian Hospital in the car, early in the evening. When I came home, I found the old villain in my rooms. I offered him a drink, and he sat down. It was the first time I had seen him in a steady light, with his hat off.

"His face is lined like a railway map, and as to color — Lord, what a liver! His scalp grows tight to his skull, and his hair is dyed until it's perfectly dead, like a piece of black cloth."

Cavenaugh ran his fingers through his own neatly trimmed thatch, and seemed to forget where he was for a moment.

"I had a twin brother, Brian, who died when we were sixteen. I have a photograph of him on my wall, an enlargement from a kodak of him, doing a high jump, rather good thing, full of action. It seemed to annoy the old gentleman. He kept looking at it and lifting his eyebrows, and finally he got up, tip-toed across the room, and turned the picture to the wall.

" 'Poor Brian! Fine fellow, but died young,' says he.

"Next morning, there was the picture, still reversed."

"Did he stay long?" Eastman asked interestedly.

"Half an hour, by the clock."

"Did he talk?"

"Well, he rambled."

"What about?"

Cavenaugh rubbed his pale eyebrows before answering.

"About things that an old man ought to want to forget. His conversation is highly objectionable. Of course he knows me like a book; everything I've ever done or thought. But when he recalls them, he throws a bad light on them, somehow. Things that weren't much off color, look rotten. He doesn't leave one a shred of self-respect, he really doesn't. That's the amount of it." The young man whipped out his handkerchief and wiped his face.

"You mean he really talks about things that none of your friends know?"

"Oh, dear, yes! Recalls things that happened in school. Anything disagreeable. Funny thing, he always turns Brian's picture to the wall."

"Does he come often?"

"Yes, oftener, now. Of course I don't know how he gets in down-stairs. The hall boys never see him. But he has a key to my door. I don't know how he got it, but I can hear him turn it in the lock."

"Why don't you keep your driver with you, or telephone for me to come down?"

"He'd only grin and go down the fire escape as

622

he did before. He's often done it when Harry's come in suddenly. Everybody has to be alone sometimes, you know. Besides, I don't want anybody to see him. He has me there."

"But why not? Why do you feel responsible for him?"

Cavenaugh smiled wearily. "That's rather the point, isn't it? Why do I? But I absolutely do. That identifies him, more than his knowing all about my life and my affairs."

Eastman looked at Cavenaugh thoughtfully. "Well, I should advise you to go in for something altogether different and new, and go in for it hard; business, engineering, metallurgy, something this old fellow wouldn't be interested in. See if you can make him remember logarithms."

Cavenaugh sighed. "No, he has me there, too. People never really change; they go on being themselves. But I would never make much trouble. Why can't they let me alone, damn it! I'd never hurt anybody, except, perhaps ———"

"Except your old gentleman, eh?" Eastman laughed. "Seriously, Cavenaugh, if you want to shake him, I think a year on a ranch would do it. He would never be coaxed far from his favorite haunts. He would dread Montana."

Cavenaugh pursed up his lips. "So do I!"

"Oh, you think you do. Try it, and you'll find out. A gun and a horse beats all this sort of thing. Besides losing your haunt, you'd be putting ten years in the bank for yourself. I know a good ranch where they take people, if you want to try it."

"Thank you. I'll consider. Do you think I'm batty?"

"No, but I think you've been doing one sort of

thing too long. You need big horizons. Get out of this."

Cavenaugh smiled meekly. He rose lazily and yawned behind his hand. "It's late, and I've taken your whole evening." He strolled over to the window and looked out. "Queer place, New York; rough on the little fellows. Don't you feel sorry for them, the girls especially? I do. What a fight they put up for a little fun! Why, even that old goat is sorry for them, the only decent thing he kept."

Eastman followed him to the door and stood in the hall, while Cavenaugh waited for the elevator. When the car came up Cavenaugh extended his pink, warm hand. "Good night."

The cage sank and his rosy countenance disappeared, his round-eyed smile being the last thing to go.

Weeks passed before Eastman saw Cavenaugh again. One morning, just as he was starting for Washington to argue a case before the Supreme Court, Cavenaugh telephoned him at his office to ask him about the Montana ranch he had recommended; said he meant to take his advice and go out there for the spring and summer.

When Eastman got back from Washington, he saw dusty trunks, just up from the trunk room, before Cavenaugh's door. Next morning, when he stopped to see what the young man was about, he found Cavenaugh in his shirt sleeves, packing.

"I'm really going; off to-morrow night. You didn't think it of me, did you?" he asked gaily.

"Oh, I've always had hopes of you!" Eastman declared. "But you are in a hurry, it seems to me."

"Yes, I am in a hurry." Cavenaugh shot a pair of

624

leggings into one of the open trunks. "I telegraphed your ranch people, used your name, and they said it would be all right. By the way, some of my crowd are giving a little dinner for me at Rector's to-night. Couldn't you be persuaded, as it's a farewell occasion?" Cavenaugh looked at him hopefully.

Eastman laughed and shook his head. "Sorry, Cavenaugh, but that's too gay a world for me. I've got too much work lined up before me. I wish I had time to stop and look at your guns, though. You seem to know something about guns. You've more than you'll need, but nobody can have too many good ones." He put down one of the revolvers regretfully. "I'll drop in to see you in the morning, if you're up."

"I shall be up, all right. I've warned my crowd that I'll cut away before midnight."

"You won't, though," Eastman called back over his shoulder as he hurried down-stairs.

The next morning, while Eastman was dressing, Rollins came in greatly excited.

"I'm a little late, sir. I was stopped by Harry, Mr. Cavenaugh's driver. Mr. Cavenaugh shot himself last night, sir."

Eastman dropped his vest and sat down on his shoe-box. "You're drunk, Rollins," he shouted. "He's going away to-day!"

"Yes, sir. Harry found him this morning. Ah, he's quite dead, sir. Harry's telephoned for the coroner. Harry don't know what to do with the ticket."

Eastman pulled on his coat and ran down the stairway. Cavenaugh's trunks were strapped and piled before the door. Harry was walking up and down the hall with a long green railroad ticket in

625

his hand and a look of complete stupidity on his face.

"What shall I do about this ticket, Mr. Eastman?" he whispered. "And what about his trunks? He had me tell the transfer people to come early. They may be here any minute. Yes, sir. I brought him home in the car last night, before twelve, as cheerful as could be."

"Be quiet, Harry. Where is he?"

"In his bed, sir."

Eastman went into Cavenaugh's sleeping-room. When he came back to the sitting-room, he looked over the writing table; railway folders, time-tables, receipted bills, nothing else. He looked up for the photograph of Cavenaugh's twin brother. There it was, turned to the wall. Eastman took it down and looked at it; a boy in track clothes, half lying in the air, going over the string shoulders first, above the heads of a crowd of lads who were running and cheering. The face was somewhat blurred by the motion and the bright sunlight. Eastman put the picture back, as he found it. Had Cavenaugh entertained his visitor last night, and had the old man been more convincing than usual? "Well, at any rate, he's seen to it that the old man can't establish identity. What a soft lot they are, fellows like poor Cavenaugh!" Eastman thought of his office as a delightful place.

THE BOOKKEEPER'S WIFE

Nobody but the janitor was stirring about the offices of the Remsen Paper Company, and still Percy Bixby sat at his desk, crouched on his high stool and staring out at the tops of the tall buildings flushed with the winter sunset, at the hundreds of windows, so many rectangles of white electric light, flashing against the broad waves of violet that ebbed across the sky. His ledgers were all in their places, his desk was in order, his office coat on its peg, and yet Percy's smooth, thin face wore the look of anxiety and strain which usually meant that he was behind in his work. He was trying to persuade himself to accept a loan from the company without the company's knowledge. As a matter of fact, he had already accepted it. His books were fixed, the money, in a black-leather bill-book, was already inside his waistcoat pocket.

He had still time to change his mind, to rectify the false figures in his ledger, and to tell Stella Brown that they couldn't possibly get married next month. There he always halted in his reasoning, and went back to the beginning.

The Remsen Paper Company was a very wealthy concern, with easy, old-fashioned working methods. They did a longtime credit business with safe customers, who never thought of paying up very close on their large indebtedness. From the payments on these large accounts Percy had taken a hundred dollars here and two hundred there until he had made up the thousand he needed. So long as he stayed by the books himself and attended to the mail-orders he couldn't possibly be found out. He could move these little shortages about from account to account indefinitely. He could have all the time he needed to pay back the deficit, and more time than he needed.

Although he was so far along in one course of action, his mind still clung resolutely to the other. He did not believe he was going to do it. He was the least of a sharper in the world. Being scrupulously honest even in the most trifling matters was a pleasure to him. He was the sort of young man that Socialists hate more than they hate capitalists. He loved his desk, he loved his books, which had no handwriting in them but his own. He never thought of resenting the fact that he had written away in those books the good red years between twenty-one and twenty-seven. He would have hated to let any one else put so much as a pen-scratch in them. He liked all the boys about the office; his desk, worn smooth by the sleeves of his alpaca coat; his rulers and inks and pens and calendars. He had a great pride in working economics, and he always got so far ahead when supplies were distributed that he had drawers full of pencils and pens and rubber bands against a rainy day.

Percy liked regularity: to get his work done on time, to have his half-day off every Saturday, to go to the theater Saturday night, to buy a new necktie twice a month, to appear in a new straw hat on the right day in May, and to know what was going on in New York. He read the morning and evening papers coming and going on the elevated, and preferred journals of approximate reliability. He got excited about ballgames and elections and business failures, was not above an interest in murders and divorce scandals, and he checked the news off as neatly as he checked his mail-orders. In short, Percy Bixby was like the model pupil who is satisfied with his lessons and his teachers and his holidays, and who would gladly go to school all his life. He had never wanted anything outside his routine until he wanted Stella Brown to marry him, and that had upset everything.

It wasn't, he told himself for the hundredth time, that she was extravagant. Not a bit of it. She was like all girls. Moreover, she made good money, and why should she marry unless she could better herself? The trouble was that he had lied to her about his salary. There were a lot of fellows rushing Mrs. Brown's five daughters, and they all seemed to have fixed on Stella as first choice and this or that one of the sisters as second. Mrs. Brown thought it proper to drop an occasional hint in the presence of these young men to the effect that she expected Stella to "do well." It went without saying that hair and complexion like Stella's could scarcely be expected to do poorly. Most of the boys who went to the house and took the girls out in a bunch to dances and movies seemed to realize this. They merely wanted a whirl with Stella before they settled down to one of her sisters. It was tacitly understood that she came too high for them. Percy had sensed all this through those slumbering instincts which awake in us all to befriend us in love or in danger.

But there was one of his rivals, he knew, who was a man to be reckoned with. Charley Greengay was a young salesman who wore tailor-made clothes and spotted waistcoats, and had a necktie for every day in the month. His air was that of a young man who is out for things that come high and who is going to get them. Mrs. Brown was ever and again dropping a word before Percy about how the girl that took Charley would have her flat furnished by the best furniture people, and her china-closet stocked with the best ware, and would have nothing to worry about but nicks and scratches. It was because he felt himself pitted against this pulling power of Greengay's that Percy had brazenly lied to Mrs. Brown, and told her that his salary had been raised to fifty a week, and that now he wanted to get married.

When he threw out this challenge to Mother Brown, Percy was getting thirty-five dollars a week, and he knew well enough that there were several hundred thousand young men in New York who would do his work as well as he did for thirty.

These were the factors in Percy's present situation. He went over them again and again as he sat stooping on his tall stool. He had quite lost track of time when he heard the janitor call good night to the watchman. Without thinking what he was doing, he slid into his overcoat, caught his hat, and rushed out to the elevator, which was waiting for the janitor. The moment the car dropped, it occurred to him that the thing was decided without his having made up his mind at all. The familiar floors passed him, ten, nine, eight, seven. By the time he reached the fifth, there was no possibility of going back; the click of the drop-lever seemed to settle that. The money was in his pocket. Now, he told himself as he hurried out into the exciting clamor of the street, he was not going to worry about it any more.

When Percy reached the Browns' flat on 123d Street that evening he felt just the slightest chill in Stella's greeting. He could make that all right, he told himself, as he kissed her lightly in the dark three-by-four entrance-hall. Percy's courting had been prosecuted mainly in the Bronx or in winged pursuit of a Broadway car. When he entered the crowded sitting-room he greeted Mrs. Brown respectfully and the four girls playfully. They were all piled on one couch, reading the continued story in the evening paper, and they didn't think it necessary to assume more formal attitudes for Percy. They looked up over the smeary pink sheets of paper, and handed him, as Percy said, the same old jolly:

"Hullo, Perc'! Come to see me, ain't you? So flattered!"

"Any sweet goods on you, Perc'? Anything doing in the bong-bong line to-night?"

"Look at his new neckwear! Say, Perc', remember me. That tie would go lovely with my new tailored waist."

"Quit your kiddin', girls!" called Mrs. Brown, who was drying shirt-waists on the dining-room radiator. "And, Percy, mind the rugs when you're steppin' round among them gum-drops."

Percy fired his last shot at the recumbent figures, and followed Stella into the dining-room, where the table and two large easy-chairs formed, in Mrs. Brown's estimation, a proper background for a serious suitor.

"I say, Stell'," he began as he walked about the table with his hands in his pockets, "seems to me we ought to begin buying our stuff." She brightened perceptibly. "Ah," Percy thought, "so that *was* the trouble!" "To-morrow's Saturday; why can't we make an afternoon of it?" he went on cheerfully. "Shop till we're tired, then go to Houtin's for dinner, and end up at the theater."

As they bent over the lists she had made of things needed, Percy glanced at her face. She was very much out of her sisters' class and out of his, and he kept congratulating himself on his nerve. He was going in for something much too handsome and expensive and distinguished for him, he felt, and it took courage to be a plunger. To begin with, Stella was the sort of girl who had to be well dressed. She had pale primrose hair, with bluish tones in it, very soft and fine, so that it lay smooth however she dressed it, and pale-blue eyes, with blond eyebrows and long, dark lashes. She would have been a little too remote and languid even for the fastidious Percy had it not been for her hard, practical mouth, with lips that always kept their pink even when the rest of her face was pale. Her employers, who at first might be struck by her indifference, understood that anybody with that sort of mouth would get through the work.

After the shopping-lists had been gone over, Percy took up the question of the honeymoon. Stella said she had been thinking of Atlantic City. Percy met her with firmness. Whatever happened, he couldn't leave his books now.

"I want to do my traveling right here on Forty-second Street, with a high-price show every night," he declared. He made out an itinerary, punctuated by theaters and restaurants, which

Stella consented to accept as a substitute for Atlantic City.

"They give your fellows a week off when they're married, don't they?" she asked.

"Yes, but I'll want to drop into the office every morning to look after my mail. That's only businesslike."

"I'd like to have you treated as well as the others, though." Stella turned the rings about on her pale hand and looked at her polished finger-tips.

"I'll look out for that. What do you say to a little walk, Stell'?" Percy put the question coaxingly. When Stella was pleased with him she went to walk with him, since that was the only way in which Percy could ever see her alone. When she was displeased, she said she was too tired to go out. To-night she smiled at him incredulously, and went to put on her hat and gray fur piece.

Once they were outside, Percy turned into a shadowy side street that was only partly built up, a dreary waste of derricks and foundation holes, but comparatively solitary. Stella liked Percy's steady, sympathetic silences; she was not a chatterbox herself. She often wondered why she was going to marry Bixby instead of Charley Greengay. She knew that Charley would go further in the world. Indeed, she had often coolly told herself that Percy would never go very far. But, as she admitted with a shrug, she was "weak to Percy." In the capable New York stenographer, who estimated values coldly and got the most for the least outlay, there was something left that belonged to another kind of woman — something that liked the very things in Percy that were not good business assets. However much she dwelt upon the effectiveness of Greengay's dash and color and assurance, her mind always came back to Percy's neat little head, his clean-cut face, and warm, clear, gray eyes, and she liked them better than Charley's fullness and blurred floridness. Having reckoned up their respective chances with no doubtful result, she opposed a mild obstinacy to her own good sense. "I guess I'll take Percy, *anyway,*" she said simply, and that was all the good her clever business brain did her.

Percy spent a night of torment, lying tense on his bed in the dark, and figuring out how long it would take him to pay back the money he was advancing to himself. Any fool could do it in five years, he reasoned, but he was going to do it in three. The trouble was that his expensive courtship had taken every penny of his salary. With competitors like Charley Greengay, you had to spend money or drop out. Certain birds, he reflected ruefully, are supplied with more attractive plumage when they are courting, but nature hadn't been so thoughtful for men. When Percy reached the office in the morning he climbed on his tall stool and leaned his arms on his ledger. He was so glad to feel it there that he was faint and weak-kneed.

Oliver Remsen, Junior, had brought new blood into the Remsen Paper Company. He married shortly after Percy Bixby did, and in the five succeeding years he had considerably enlarged the company's business and profits. He had been particularly successful in encouraging efficiency and loyalty in the employees. From the time he came into the office he had stood for shorter hours, longer holidays, and a generous consideration of men's necessities. He came out of college on the wave of economic reform, and he continued to read and think a good deal about how the machinery of labor is operated. He knew more about the men who worked for him than their mere office records.

Young Remsen was troubled about Percy Bixby because he took no summer vacations — always asked for the two weeks' extra pay instead. Other men in the office had skipped a vacation now and then, but Percy had stuck to his desk for five years, had tottered to his stool through attacks of grippe and tonsilitis. He seemed to have grown fast to his ledger, and it was to this that Oliver objected. He liked his men to stay men, to look like men and live like men. He remembered how alert and wide-awake Bixby had seemed to him when he himself first came into the office. He had picked Bixby out as the most intelligent and interested of his father's employees, and since then had often wondered why he never seemed to see chances to forge ahead. Promotions, of course, went to the men who went after them. When Percy's baby died, he went to the funeral, and asked Percy to call on him if he needed money. Once when he chanced to sit down by Bixby on the elevated and found him reading Bryce's "American Commonwealth," he asked him to make use of his own large office library. Percy thanked him, but he never came for any books. Oliver wondered whether his bookkeeper really tried to avoid him.

One evening Oliver met the Bixbys in the lobby of a theater. He introduced Mrs. Remsen to them, and held them for some moments in conversation. When they got into their motor, Mrs. Remsen said:

635

"Is that little man afraid of you, Oliver? He looked like a scared rabbit."

Oliver snapped the door, and said with a shade of irritation:

"I don't know what's the matter with him. He's the fellow I've told you about who never takes a vacation. I half believe it's his wife. She looks pitiless enough for anything."

"She's very pretty of her kind," mused Mrs. Remsen, "but rather chilling. One can see that she has ideas about elegance."

"Rather unfortunate ones for a bookkeeper's wife. I surmise that Percy felt she was overdressed, and that made him awkward with me. I've always suspected that fellow of good taste."

After that, when Remsen passed the counting-room and saw Percy screwed up over his ledger, he often remembered Mrs. Bixby, with her cold, pale eyes and long lashes, and her expression that was something between indifference and discontent. She rose behind Percy's bent shoulders like an apparition.

One spring afternoon Remsen was closeted in his private office with his lawyer until a late hour. As he came down the long hall in the dusk he glanced through the glass partition into the counting-room, and saw Percy Bixby huddled up on his tall stool, though it was too dark to work. Indeed, Bixby's ledger was closed, and he sat with his two arms resting on the brown cover. He did not move a muscle when young Remsen entered.

"You are late, Bixby, and so am I," Oliver began genially as he crossed to the front of the room and looked out at the lighted windows of other tall buildings. "The fact is, I've been doing something that men have a foolish way of putting off. I've been making my will."

"Yes, sir." Percy brought it out with a deep breath.

"Glad to be through with it," Oliver went on. "Mr. Melton will bring the paper back to-morrow, and I'd like to ask you to be one of the witnesses."

"I'd be very proud, Mr. Remsen."

"Thank you, Bixby. Good night." Remsen took up his hat just as Percy slid down from his stool.

"Mr. Remsen, I'm told you're going to have the books gone over."

"Why, yes, Bixby. Don't let that trouble you. I'm taking in a new partner, you know, an old college friend. Just because he is a friend, I insist upon all the usual formalities. But it is a formality, and I'll guarantee the expert won't make a scratch on your books. Good night. You'd better be coming, too." Remsen had reached the door when he heard "Mr. Remsen!" in a desperate voice behind him. He turned, and saw Bixby standing uncertainly at one end of the desk, his hand still on his ledger, his uneven shoulders drooping forward and his head hanging as if he were seasick. Remsen came back and stood at the other end of the long desk. It was too dark to see Bixby's face clearly.

"What is it, Bixby?"

"Mr. Remsen, five years ago, just before I was married, I falsified the books a thousand dollars, and I used the money." Percy leaned forward against his desk, which took him just across the chest.

"What's that, Bixby?" Young Remsen spoke in a tone of polite surprise. He felt painfully embarrassed.

"Yes, sir. I thought I'd get it all paid back before

637

this. I've put back three hundred, but the books are still seven hundred out of true. I've played the shortages about from account to account these five years, but an expert would find 'em in twenty-four hours."

"I don't just understand how —" Oliver stopped and shook his head.

"I held it out of the Western remittances, Mr. Remsen. They were coming in heavy just then. I was up against it. I hadn't saved anything to marry on, and my wife thought I was getting more money than I was. Since we've been married, I've never had the nerve to tell her. I could have paid it all back if it hadn't been for the unforeseen expenses."

Remsen sighed.

"Being married is largely unforeseen expenses, Percy. There's only one way to fix this up: I'll give you seven hundred dollars in cash to-morrow, and you can give me your personal note, with the understanding that I hold ten dollars a week out of your pay-check until it is paid. I think you ought to tell your wife exactly how you are fixed, though. You can't expect her to help you much when she doesn't know."

That night Mrs. Bixby was sitting in their flat, waiting for her husband. She was dressed for a bridge party, and often looked with impatience from her paper to the Mission clock, as big as a coffin and with nothing but two weights dangling in its hollow framework. Percy had been loath to buy the clock when they got their furniture, and he had hated it ever since. Stella had changed very little since she came into the flat a bride. Then she wore her hair in a Floradora pompadour; now she wore it hooded close about her head like a scarf, in a rather smeary manner, like an Impressionist's brush-work. She heard her husband come in and close the door softly. While he was taking off his hat in the narrow tunnel of a hall, she called to him:

"I hope you've had something to eat down-town. You'll have to dress right away." Percy came in and sat down. She looked up from the evening paper she was reading. "You've no time to sit down. We must start in fifteen minutes."

He shaded his eyes from the glaring overhead light.

"I'm afraid I can't go anywhere to-night. I'm all in."

Mrs. Bixby rattled her paper, and turned from the theatrical page to the fashions.

"You'll feel better after you dress. We won't stay late."

Her even persistence usually conquered her husband. She never forgot anything she had once decided to do. Her manner of following it up grew more chilly, but never weaker. To-night there was no spring in Percy. He closed his eyes and replied without moving:

"I can't go. You had better telephone the Burks we aren't coming. I have to tell you something disagreeable."

Stella rose.

"I certainly am not going to disappoint the Burks and stay at home to talk about anything disagreeable."

"You're not very sympathetic, Stella."

She turned away.

"If I were, you'd soon settle down into a pretty dull proposition. We'd have no social life now if I didn't keep at you."

Percy roused himself a little.

"Social life? Well, we'll have to trim that pretty close for a while. I'm in debt to the company. We've been living beyond our means ever since we were married."

"We can't live on less than we do," Stella said quietly. "No use in taking that up again."

Percy sat up, clutching the arms of his chair.

"We'll have to take it up. I'm seven hundred dollars short, and the books are to be audited to-morrow. I told young Remsen and he's going to take my note and hold the money out of my pay-checks. He could send me to jail, of course."

Stella turned and looked down at him with a gleam of interest.

"Oh, you've been playing solitaire with the books, have you? And he's found you out! I hope I'll never see that man again. Sugar face!" She said this with intense acrimony. Her forehead flushed delicately, and her eyes were full of hate. Young Remsen was not her idea of a "business man."

Stella went into the other room. When she came back she wore her evening coat and carried long gloves and a black scarf. This she began to arrange over her hair before the mirror above the false fireplace. Percy lay inert in the Morris chair and watched her. Yes, he understood; it was very difficult for a woman with hair like that to be shabby and to go without things. Her hair made her conspicuous, and it had to be lived up to. It had been the deciding factor in his fate.

Stella caught the lace over one ear with a large gold hairpin. She repeated this until she got a good effect. Then turning to Percy, she began to draw on her gloves.

"I'm not worrying any, because I'm going back into business," she said firmly. "I meant to, anyway, if you didn't get a raise the first of the year. I have the offer of a good position, and we can live in an apartment hotel."

Percy was on his feet in an instant.

"I won't have you grinding in any office. That's flat."

Stella's lower lip quivered in a commiserating smile. "Oh, I won't lose my health. Charley Greengay's a partner in his concern now, and he wants a private secretary."

Percy drew back.

"You can't work for Greengay. He's got too bad a reputation. You've more pride than that, Stella."

The thin sweep of color he knew so well went over Stella's face.

"His business reputation seems to be all right," she commented, working the kid on with her left hand.

"What if it is?" Percy broke out. "He's the cheapest kind of a skate. He gets into scrapes with the girls in his own office. The last one got into the newspapers, and he had to pay the girl a wad."

"He don't get into scrapes with his books, anyway, and he seems to be able to stand getting into the papers. I excuse Charley. His wife's a pill."

"I suppose you think he'd have been all right if he'd married you," said Percy, bitterly.

"Yes, I do." Stella buttoned her glove with an air of finishing something, and then looked at Percy without animosity. "Charley and I both have sporty tastes, and we like excitement. You might as well live in Newark if you're going to sit at home in the evening. You oughtn't to have married a business woman; you need somebody domestic. There's nothing in this sort of life for either of us."

"That means, I suppose, that you're going around with Greengay and his crowd?"

"Yes, that's my sort of crowd, and you never did fit into it. You're too intellectual. I've always been proud of you, Percy. You're better style than Charley, but that gets tiresome. You will never burn much red fire in New York, now, will you?"

Percy did not reply. He sat looking at the minute-hand of the eviscerated Mission clock. His wife almost never took the trouble to argue with him.

"You're old style, Percy," she went on. "Of course everybody marries and wishes they hadn't, but nowadays people get over it. Some women go ahead on the quiet, but I'm giving it to you straight. I'm going to work for Greengay. I like his line of business, and I meet people well. Now I'm going to the Burks'."

Percy dropped his hands limply between his knees.

"I suppose," he brought out, "the real trouble is that you've decided my earning power is not very great."

"That's part of it, and part of it is you're old-fashioned." Stella paused at the door and looked back. "What made you rush me, anyway, Percy?" she asked indulgently. "What did you go and pretend to be a spender and get tied up with me for?"

"I guess everybody wants to be a spender when he's in love," Percy replied.

Stella shook her head mournfully.

"No, you're a spender or you're not. Greengay has been broke three times, fired, down and out, black-listed. But he's always come back, and he always will. You will never be fired, but you'll always be poor." She turned and looked back again before she went out.

Six months later Bixby came to young Oliver Remsen one afternoon and said he would like to have twenty dollars a week held out of his pay until his debt was cleared off.

Oliver looked up at his sallow employee and asked him how he could spare as much as that.

"My expenses are lighter," Bixby replied. "My wife has gone into business with a ready-to-wear firm. She is not living with me any more."

Oliver looked annoyed, and asked him if nothing could be done to readjust his domestic affairs. Bixby said no; they would probably remain as they were.

"But where are you living, Bixby? How have you arranged things?" the young man asked impatiently.

"I'm very comfortable. I live in a boarding-house and have my own furniture. There are several fellows there who are fixed the same way. Their wives went back into business, and they drifted apart."

With a baffled expression Remsen stared at the uneven shoulders under the skin-fitting alpaca desk coat as his bookkeeper went out. He had meant to do something for Percy, but somehow, he reflected, one never did do anything for a fellow who had been stung as hard as that.

ARDESSA

The grand-mannered old man who sat at a desk in the reception-room of "The Outcry" offices to receive visitors and incidentally to keep the time-book of the employees, looked up as Miss Devine entered at ten minutes past ten and condescendingly wished him good morning. He bowed profoundly as she minced past his desk, and with an indifferent air took her course down the corridor that led to the editorial offices. Mechanically he opened the flat, black book at his elbow and placed his finger on D, running his eye along the line of figures after the name Devine. "It's banker's hours she keeps, indeed," he muttered. What was the use of entering so capricious a record? Nevertheless, with his usual preliminary flourish he wrote 10:10 under this, the fourth day of May.

The employee who kept banker's hours rustled on down the corridor to her private room, hung up her lavender jacket and her trim spring hat, and readjusted her side combs by the mirror inside her closet door. Glancing at her desk, she rang for an office boy, and reproved him because he had not dusted more carefully and because there were lumps in her paste. When he disappeared with the paste-jar, she sat down to decide which of her employer's letters he should see and which he should not.

Ardessa was not young and she was certainly not handsome. The coquettish angle at which she carried her head was a mannerism surviving from a time when it was more becoming. She shuddered at the cold candor of the new business woman, and was insinuatingly feminine.

Ardessa's employer, like young Lochinvar, had come out of the West, and he had done a great many contradictory things before he became proprietor and editor of "The Outcry." Before he decided to go to New York and make the East take notice of him, O'Mally had acquired a punctual, reliable silver-mine in South Dakota. This silent friend in the background made his journalistic success comparatively easy. He had figured out, when he was a rich nobody in Nevada, that the quickest way to cut into the known world was through the printing-press. He arrived in New York, bought a highly respectable publication, and turned it into a red-hot magazine of protest, which he called "The Outcry." He knew what the West wanted, and it proved to be what everybody secretly wanted. In six years he had done the thing that had hitherto seemed impossible: built up a national weekly, out on the news-stands the same day in New York and San Francisco; a magazine the people howled for, a moving-picture film of their real tastes and interests.

O'Mally bought "The Outcry" to make a stir, not to make a career, but he had got built into the thing more than he ever intended. It had made him a public man and put him into politics. He found the publicity game diverting, and it held him longer than any other game had ever done. He had built up about him an organization of which he was somewhat afraid and with which he was vastly bored. On his staff there were five famous men, and he had made every one of them. At first it amused him to manufacture celebrities. He found he could take an average reporter from the daily press, give him a "line" to follow, a trust to fight, a vice to expose, — this was all in that good time when people were eager to read about their own wickedness, — and in two years the reporter would be recognized as an authority. Other people — Napoleon, Disraeli, Sarah Bernhardt — had discovered that advertising would go a long way; but Marcus O'Mally discovered that in America it would go all the way — as far as you wished to pay its passage. Any human countenance, plastered in three-sheet posters from sea to sea, would be revered by the American people. The strangest thing was that the owners of these grave countenances, staring at their own faces on newsstands and billboards, fell to venerating themselves; and even he, O'Mally, was more or less constrained by these reputations that he had created out of cheap paper and cheap ink.

Constraint was the last thing O'Mally liked. The most engaging and unusual thing about the man was that he couldn't be fooled by the success of his own methods, and no amount of "recognition" could make a stuffed shirt of him. No matter how much he was advertised as a great medicine-man in the councils of the nation, he knew that he was a born gambler and a soldier of fortune. He left his dignified office to take care of itself for a good many months of the year while he played about on the outskirts of social order. He liked being a great man from the East in rough-and-tumble Western cities where he had once been merely an unconsidered spender.

O'Mally's long absences constituted one of the supreme advantages of Ardessa Devine's position. When he was at his post her duties were not heavy, but when he was giving balls in Goldfield, Nevada, she lived an ideal life. She came to the office every day, indeed, to forward such of O'Mally's letters as she thought best, to attend to his club notices and tradesmen's bills, and to taste the sense of her high connections. The great men of the staff were all about her, as contemplative as Buddhas in their private offices, each meditating upon the particular trust or form of vice confided to his care. Thus surrounded, Ardessa had a pleasant sense of being at the heart of things. It was like a mental massage, exercise without exertion. She read and she embroidered. Her room was pleasant, and she liked to be seen at ladylike tasks and to feel herself a graceful contrast to the crude girls in the advertising and circulation departments across the hall. The younger stenographers, who had to get through with the enormous office correspondence, and who rushed about from one editor to another with wire baskets full of letters, made faces as they passed Ardessa's door and saw her cool and cloistered, daintily plying her needle. But no matter how hard the other stenographers were driven, no one, not even one of the five oracles of the staff, dared dictate so much as a letter to Ardessa. Like a sultan's bride, she was inviolate in her lord's absence; she had to be kept for him.

Naturally the other young women employed in "The Outcry" offices disliked Miss Devine. They were all competent girls, trained in the exacting methods of modern business, and they had to make good every day in the week, had to get through with a great deal of work or lose their position. O'Mally's private secretary was a mystery to them. Her exemptions and privileges, her patronizing remarks, formed an exhaustless subject of conversation at the lunch-hour. Ardessa had, indeed, as they knew she must have, a kind of "purchase" on her employer.

When O'Mally first came to New York to break into publicity, he engaged Miss Devine upon the recommendation of the editor whose ailing publication he bought and rechristened. That editor was a conservative, scholarly gentleman of the old school, who was retiring because he felt out of place in the world of brighter, breezier magazines that had been flowering since the new century came in. He believed that in this vehement world young O'Mally would make himself heard and that Miss Devine's training in an editorial office would be of use to him.

When O'Mally first sat down at a desk to be an editor, all the cards that were brought in looked pretty much alike to him. Ardessa was at his elbow. She had long been steeped in literary distinctions and in the social distinctions which used to count for much more than they do now. She knew all the great men, all the nephews and clients of great men. She knew which must be seen, which must be made welcome, and which could safely be sent away. She could give O'Mally on the instant the former rating in magazine offices of nearly every name that was brought in to him. She could give him an idea of the man's connections, of the price his work commanded, and insinuate whether he ought to be met with the old punctiliousness or with the new joviality. She was useful in explaining to her employer the significance of various invitations, and the standing of clubs and associations. At first she was virtually the social mentor of the bullet-headed young Westerner who wanted to break into everything, the solitary person about the office of the humming new magazine who knew anything about the editorial traditions of the eighties and nineties which, antiquated as they now were, gave an editor, as O'Mally said, a background.

Despite her indolence, Ardessa was useful to O'Mally as a social reminder. She was the card catalogue of his ever-changing personal relations. O'Mally went in for everything and got tired of everything; that was why he made a good editor. After he was through with people, Ardessa was very skilful in covering his retreat. She read and answered the letters of admirers who had begun to bore him. When great authors, who had been dined and fêted the month before, were suddenly left to cool their heels in the reception-room, thrown upon the suave hospitality of the grand old man at the desk, it was Ardessa who went out and made soothing and plausible explanations as to why the editor could not see them. She was the brake that checked the too-eager neophyte, the emollient that eased the severing of relationships, the gentle extinguisher of the lights that failed. When there were no longer messages of hope and cheer to be sent to ardent young writers and reformers, Ardessa delivered, as sweetly as possible, whatever messages were left.

In handling these people with whom O'Mally was quite through, Ardessa had gradually developed an industry which was immensely gratifying to her own vanity. Not only did she not crush them; she even fostered them a little. She continued to advise them in the reception-room and "personally" received their manuscripts long after O'Mally had declared that he would never read another line they wrote. She let them outline their plans for stories and articles to her, promising to bring these suggestions to the editor's attention. She denied herself to nobody, was gracious even to the Shakspere-Bacon man, the perpetual-motion man, the travel-article man, the ghosts which haunt every magazine office. The writers who had had their happy hour of O'Mally's favor kept feeling that Ardessa might reinstate them. She answered their letters of inquiry in her most polished and elegant style, and even gave them hints as to the subjects in which the restless editor was or was not interested at the moment: she feared it would be useless to send him an article on "How to Trap Lions," because he had just bought an article on "Elephant-Shooting in Majuba Land," etc.

So when O'Mally plunged into his office at 11:30 on this, the fourth day of May, having just got back from three-days' fishing, he found Ardessa in the reception-room, surrounded by a little court of discards. This was annoying, for he always wanted his stenographer at once. Telling the office boy to give her a hint that she was needed, he threw off his hat and topcoat and began to race through the pile of letters Ardessa had put on his desk. When she entered, he did not wait for her polite inquiries about his trip, but broke in at once.

"What is that fellow who writes about phossy jaw still hanging round here for? I don't want any articles on phossy jaw, and if I did, I wouldn't want his."

650

"He has just sold an article on the match industry to 'The New Age,' Mr. O'Mally," Ardessa replied as she took her seat at the editor's right.

"Why does he have to come and tell us about it? We've nothing to do with 'The New Age.' And that prison-reform guy, what's he loafing about for?"

Ardessa bridled.

"You remember, Mr. O'Mally, he brought letters of introduction from Governor Harper, the reform Governor of Mississippi."

O'Mally jumped up, kicking over his waste-basket in his impatience.

"That was months ago. I went through his letters and went through him, too. He hasn't got anything we want. I've been through with Governor Harper a long while. We're asleep at the switch in here. And let me tell you, if I catch sight of that causes-of-blindness-in-babies woman around here again, I'll do something violent. Clear them out, Miss Devine! Clear them out! We need a traffic policeman in this office. Have you got that article on 'Stealing Our National Water Power' ready for me?"

"Mr. Gerrard took it back to make modifications. He gave it to me at noon on Saturday, just before the office closed. I will have it ready for you to-morrow morning, Mr. O'Mally, if you have not too many letters for me this afternoon," Ardessa replied pointedly.

"Holy Mike!" muttered O'Mally, "we need a traffic policeman for the staff, too. Gerrard's modified that thing half a dozen times already. Why don't they get accurate information in the first place?"

He began to dictate his morning mail, walking briskly up and down the floor by way of giving his stenographer an energetic example. Her indolence and her ladylike deportment weighed on him. He wanted to take her by the elbows and run her around the block. He didn't mind that she loafed when he was away, but it was becoming harder and harder to speed her up when he was on the spot. He knew his correspondence was not enough to keep her busy, so when he was in town he made her type his own breezy editorials and various articles by members of his staff.

Transcribing editorial copy is always laborious, and the only way to make it easy is to farm it out. This Ardessa was usually clever enough to do. When she returned to her own room after O'Mally had gone out to lunch, Ardessa rang for an office boy and said languidly, "James, call Becky, please."

In a moment a thin, tense-faced Hebrew girl of eighteen or nineteen came rushing in, carrying a wire basket full of typewritten sheets. She was as gaunt as a plucked spring chicken, and her cheap, gaudy clothes might have been thrown on her. She looked as if she were running to catch a train and in mortal dread of missing it. While Miss Devine examined the pages in the basket, Becky stood with her shoulders drawn up and her elbows drawn in, apparently trying to hide herself in her insufficient open-work waist. Her wild, black eyes followed Miss Devine's hands desperately. Ardessa sighed.

"This seems to be very smeary copy again, Becky. You don't keep your mind on your work, and so you have to erase continually."

Becky spoke up in wailing self-vindication.

"It ain't that, Miss Devine. It's so many hard

652

words he uses that I have to be at the dictionary all the time. Look! Look!" She produced a bunch of manuscript faintly scrawled in pencil, and thrust it under Ardessa's eyes. "He don't write out the words at all. He just begins a word, and then makes waves for you to guess."

"I see you haven't always guessed correctly, Becky," said Ardessa, with a weary smile. "There are a great many words here that would surprise Mr. Gerrard, I am afraid."

"And the inserts," Becky persisted. "How is anybody to tell where they go, Miss Devine? It's mostly inserts; see, all over the top and sides and back."

Ardessa turned her head away.

"Don't claw the pages like that, Becky. You make me nervous. Mr. Gerrard has not time to dot his i's and cross his t's. That is what we keep copyists for. I will correct these sheets for you, — it would be terrible if Mr. O'Mally saw them, — and then you can copy them over again. It must be done by to-morrow morning, so you may have to work late. See that your hands are clean and dry, and then you will not smear it."

"Yes, ma'am. Thank you, Miss Devine. Will you tell the janitor, please, it's all right if I have to stay? He was cross because I was here Saturday afternoon doing this. He said it was a holiday, and when everybody else was gone I ought to —"

"That will do, Becky. Yes, I will speak to the janitor for you. You may go to lunch now."

Becky turned on one heel and then swung back.

"Miss Devine," she said anxiously, "will it be all right if I get white shoes for now?"

Ardessa gave her kind consideration.

"For office wear, you mean? No, Becky. With

only one pair, you could not keep them properly clean; and black shoes are much less conspicuous. Tan, if you prefer."

Becky looked down at her feet. They were too large, and her skirt was as much too short as her legs were too long.

"Nearly all the girls I know wear white shoes to business," she pleaded.

"They are probably little girls who work in factories or department stores, and that is quite another matter. Since you raise the question, Becky, I ought to speak to you about your new waist. Don't wear it to the office again, please. Those cheap open-work waists are not appropriate in an office like this. They are all very well for little chorus girls."

"But Miss Kalski wears expensive waists to business more open than this, and jewelry —"

Ardessa interrupted. Her face grew hard.

"Miss Kalski," she said coldly, "works for the business department. You are employed in the editorial offices. There is a great difference. You see, Becky, I might have to call you in here at any time when a scientist or a great writer or the president of a university is here talking over editorial matters, and such clothes as you have on to-day would make a bad impression. Nearly all our connections are with important people of that kind, and we ought to be well, but quietly, dressed."

"Yes, Miss Devine. Thank you," Becky gasped and disappeared. Heaven knew she had no need to be further impressed with the greatness of "The Outcry" office. During the year and a half she had been there she had never ceased to tremble. She knew the prices all the authors got as well as Miss

654

Devine did, and everything seemed to her to be done on a magnificent scale. She hadn't a good memory for long technical words, but she never forgot dates or prices or initials or telephone numbers.

Becky felt that her job depended on Miss Devine, and she was so glad to have it that she scarcely realized she was being bullied. Besides, she was grateful for all that she had learned from Ardessa; Ardessa had taught her to do most of the things that she was supposed to do herself. Becky wanted to learn, she had to learn; that was the train she was always running for. Her father, Isaac Tietelbaum, the tailor, who pressed Miss Devine's skirts and kept her ladylike suits in order, had come to his client two years ago and told her he had a bright girl just out of a commercial high school. He implored Ardessa to find some office position for his daughter. Ardessa told an appealing story to O'Mally, and brought Becky into the office, at a salary of six dollars a week, to help with the copying and to learn business routine. When Becky first came she was as ignorant as a young savage. She was rapid at her shorthand and typing, but a Kafir girl would have known as much about the English language. Nobody ever wanted to learn more than Becky. She fairly wore the dictionary out. She dug up her old school grammar and worked over it at night. She faithfully mastered Miss Devine's fussy system of punctuation.

There were eight children at home, younger than Becky, and they were all eager to learn. They wanted to get their mother out of the three dark rooms behind the tailor shop and to move into a flat up-stairs, where they could, as Becky said, "live private." The young Tietelbaums doubted their father's ability to bring this change about, for the more things he declared himself ready to do in his window placards, the fewer were brought to him to be done. "Dyeing, Cleaning, Ladies' Furs Remodeled" — it did no good.

Rebecca was out to "improve herself," as her father had told her she must. Ardessa had easy way with her. It was one of those rare relationships from which both persons profit. The more Becky could learn from Ardessa, the happier she was; and the more Ardessa could unload on Becky, the greater was her contentment. She easily broke Becky of the gum-chewing habit, taught her to walk quietly, to efface herself at the proper moment, and to hold her tongue. Becky had been raised to eight dollars a week; but she didn't care half so much about that as she did about her own increasing efficiency. The more work Miss Devine handed over to her the happier she was, and the faster she was able to eat it up. She tested and tried herself in every possible way. She now had full confidence that she would surely one day be a high-priced stenographer, a real "business woman."

Becky would have corrupted a really industrious person, but a bilious temperament like Ardessa's couldn't make even a feeble stand against such willingness. Ardessa had grown soft and had lost the knack of turning out work. Sometimes, in her importance and serenity, she shivered. What if O'Mally should die, and she were thrust out into the world to work in competition with the brazen, competent young women she saw about her everywhere? She believed herself indispensable, but she knew that in such a mischanceful world as

656

this the very powers of darkness might rise to separate her from this pearl among jobs.

When Becky came in from lunch she went down the long hall to the wash-room, where all the little girls who worked in the advertising and circulation departments kept their hats and jackets. There were shelves and shelves of bright spring hats, piled on top of one another, all as stiff as sheet-iron and trimmed with gay flowers. At the marble wash-stand stood Rena Kalski, the right bower of the business manager, polishing her diamond rings with a nail-brush.

"Hullo, kid," she called over her shoulder to Becky. "I've got a ticket for you for Thursday afternoon."

Becky's black eyes glowed, but the strained look on her face drew tighter than ever.

"I'll never ask her, Miss Kalski," she said rapidly. "I don't dare. I have to stay late to-night again; and I know she'd be hard to please after, if I was to try to get off on a week-day. I thank you, Miss Kalski, but I'd better not."

Miss Kalski laughed. She was a slender young Hebrew, handsome in an impudent, Tenderloin sort of way, with a small head, reddish-brown almond eyes, a trifle tilted, a rapacious mouth, and a beautiful chin.

"Ain't you under that woman's thumb, though! Call her bluff. She isn't half the prima donna she thinks she is. On my side of the hall we know who's who about this place."

The business and editorial departments of "The Outcry" were separated by a long corridor and a great contempt. Miss Kalski dried her rings with tissue-paper and studied them with an appraising eye.

657

"Well, since you're such a 'fraidy-calf,' " she went on, "maybe I can get a rise out of her myself. Now I've got you a ticket out of that shirt-front, I want you to go. I'll drop in on Devine this afternoon."

When Miss Kalski went back to her desk in the business manager's private office, she turned to him familiarly, but not impertinently.

"Mr. Henderson, I want to send a kid over in the editorial stenographers' to the Palace Thursday afternoon. She's a nice kid, only she's scared out of her skin all the time. Miss Devine's her boss, and she'll be just mean enough not to let the young one off. Would you say a word to her?"

The business manager lit a cigar.

"I'm not saying words to any of the high-brows over there. Try it out with Devine yourself. You're not bashful."

Miss Kalski shrugged her shoulders and smiled.

"Oh, very well." She serpentined out of the room and crossed the Rubicon into the editorial offices. She found Ardessa typing O'Mally's letters and wearing a pained expression.

"Good afternoon, Miss Devine," she said carelessly. "Can we borrow Becky over there for Thursday afternoon? We're short."

Miss Devine looked piqued and tilted her head.

"I don't think it's customary, Miss Kalski, for the business department to use our people. We never have girls enough here to do the work. Of course if Mr. Henderson feels justified —"

"Thanks awfully, Miss Devine," — Miss Kalski interrupted her with the perfectly smooth, good-natured tone which never betrayed a hint of the scorn every line of her sinuous figure expressed, — "I will tell Mr. Henderson. Perhaps we can do something for you some day." Whether this was a threat, a kind wish, or an insinuation, no mortal could have told. Miss Kalski's face was always suggesting insolence without being quite insolent. As she returned to her own domain she met the cashier's head clerk in the hall. "That Devine woman's a crime," she murmured. The head clerk laughed tolerantly.

That afternoon as Miss Kalski was leaving the office at 5:15, on her way down the corridor she heard a typewriter clicking away in the empty, echoing editorial offices. She looked in, and found Becky bending forward over the machine as if she were about to swallow it.

"Hello, kid. Do you sleep with that?" she called. She walked up to Becky and glanced at her copy. "What do you let 'em keep you up nights over that stuff for?" she asked contemptuously. "The world wouldn't suffer if that stuff never got printed."

Rebecca looked up wildly. Not even Miss Kalski's French pansy hat or her ear-rings and landscape veil could loosen Becky's tenacious mind from Mr. Gerrard's article on water power. She scarcely knew what Miss Kalski had said to her, certainly not what she meant.

"But I must make progress already, Miss Kalski," she panted.

Miss Kalski gave her low, siren laugh.

"I should say you must!" she ejaculated.

Ardessa decided to take her vacation in June, and she arranged that Miss Milligan should do O'Mally's work while she was away. Miss Milligan was blunt and noisy, rapid and inaccurate. It would be just as well for O'Mally to work with a coarse instrument for a time; he would be more appreciative, perhaps, of certain qualities to which he had seemed insensible of late. Ardessa was to leave for East Hampton on Sunday, and she spent Saturday morning instructing her substitute as to the state of the correspondence. At noon O'Mally burst into her room. All the morning he had been closeted with a new writer of mystery-stories just over from England.

"Can you stay and take my letters this afternoon, Miss Devine? You're not leaving until to-morrow."

Ardessa pouted, and tilted her head at the angle he was tired of.

"I'm sorry, Mr. O'Mally, but I've left all my shopping for this afternoon. I think Becky Tietelbaum could do them for you. I will tell her to be careful."

"Oh, all right." O'Mally bounced out with a reflection of Ardessa's disdainful expression on his face. Saturday afternoon was always a half-holiday, to be sure, but since she had weeks of freedom when he was away — However —

At two o'clock Becky Tietelbaum appeared at his door, clad in the sober office suit which Miss Devine insisted she should wear, her note-book in her hand, and so frightened that her fingers were cold and her lips were pale. She had never taken dictation from the editor before. It was a great and terrifying occasion.

"Sit down," he said encouragingly. He began dictating while he shook from his bag the manuscripts he had snatched away from the amazed English author that morning. Presently he looked up.

"Do I go too fast?"

"No, sir," Becky found strength to say.

At the end of an hour he told her to go and type as many of the letters as she could while he went over the bunch of stuff he had torn from the Englishman. He was with the Hindu detective in an opium den in Shanghai when Becky returned and placed a pile of papers on his desk.

"How many?" he asked, without looking up.

"All you gave me, sir."

"All, so soon? Wait a minute and let me see how many mistakes." He went over the letters rapidly, signing them as he read. "They seem to be all right. I thought you were the girl that made so many mistakes."

Rebecca was never too frightened to vindicate herself.

"Mr. O'Mally, sir, I don't make mistakes with letters. It's only copying the articles that have so many long words, and when the writing isn't plain, like Mr. Gerrard's. I never make many mistakes with Mr. Johnson's articles, or with yours I don't."

O'Mally wheeled round in his chair, looked with curiosity at her long, tense face, her black eyes, and straight brows.

"Oh, so you sometimes copy articles, do you? How does that happen?"

"Yes, sir. Always Miss Devine gives me the articles to do. It's good practice for me."

"I see." O'Mally shrugged his shoulders. He was thinking that he could get a rise out of the whole American public any day easier than he could get a rise out of Ardessa. "What editorials of mine have you copied lately, for instance?"

Rebecca blazed out at him, reciting rapidly:

"Oh, 'A Word about the Rosenbaums,' 'Useless Navy-Yards,' 'Who Killed Cock Robin' —"

"Wait a minute." O'Mally checked her flow. "What was that one about — Cock Robin?"

"It was all about why the secretary of the interior dismissed —"

"All right, all right. Copy those letters, and put them down the chute as you go out. Come in here for a minute on Monday morning."

Becky hurried home to tell her father that she had taken the editor's letters and had made no mistakes. On Monday she learned that she was to do O'Mally's work for a few days. He disliked Miss Milligan, and he was annoyed with Ardessa for trying to put her over on him when there was better material at hand. With Rebecca he got on very well; she was impersonal, unreproachful, and she fairly panted for work. Everything was done almost before he told her what he wanted. She raced ahead with him; it was like riding a good modern bicycle after pumping along on an old hard tire.

On the day before Miss Devine's return O'Mally strolled over for a chat with the business office.

"Henderson, your people are taking vacations now, I suppose? Could you use an extra girl?"

"If it's that thin black one, I can."

O'Mally gave him a wise smile.

"It isn't. To be honest, I want to put one over on you. I want you to take Miss Devine over here for a while and speed her up. I can't do anything. She's got the upper hand of me. I don't want to fire her, you understand, but she makes my life too difficult. It's my fault, of course. I've pampered her. Give her a chance over here; maybe she'll come back. You can be firm with 'em, can't you?"

Henderson glanced toward the desk where Miss Kalski's lightning eye was skimming over the printing-house bills that he was supposed to verify himself.

"Well, if I can't, I know who can," he replied, with a chuckle.

"Exactly," O'Mally agreed. "I'm counting on the force of Miss Kalski's example. Miss Devine's all right, Miss Kalski, but she needs regular exercise. She owes it to her complexion. I can't discipline people."

Miss Kalski's only reply was a low, indulgent laugh.

O'Mally braced himself on the morning of Ardessa's return. He told the waiter at his club to bring him a second pot of coffee and to bring it hot. He was really afraid of her. When she presented herself at his office at 10:30 he complimented her upon her tan and asked about her vacation. Then he broke the news to her.

"We want to make a few temporary changes about here, Miss Devine, for the summer months. The business department is short of help. Henderson is going to put Miss Kalski on the books for a while to figure out some economies for him, and he is going to take you over. Meantime I'll get Becky broken in so that she could take your work if you were sick or anything."

Ardessa drew herself up.

"I've not been accustomed to commercial work, Mr. O'Mally. I've no interest in it, and I don't care to brush up in it."

"Brushing up is just what we need, Miss Devine." O'Mally began tramping about his room expansively. "I'm going to brush everybody up. I'm going to brush a few people out; but I want you to stay with us, of course. You belong here.

663

Don't be hasty now. Go to your room and think it over."

Ardessa was beginning to cry, and O'Mally was afraid he would lose his nerve. He looked out of the window at a new sky-scraper that was building, while she retired without a word.

At her own desk Ardessa sat down breathless and trembling. The one thing she had never doubted was her unique value to O'Mally. She had, as she told herself, taught him everything. She would say a few things to Becky Tietelbaum, and to that pigeon-breasted tailor, her father, too! The worst of it was that Ardessa had herself brought it all about; she could see that clearly now. She had carefully trained and qualified her successor. Why had she ever civilized Becky? Why had she taught her manners and deportment, broken her of the gum-chewing habit, and made her presentable? In her original state O'Mally would never have put up with her, no matter what her ability.

Ardessa told herself that O'Mally was notoriously fickle; Becky amused him, but he would soon find out her limitations. The wise thing, she knew, was to humor him; but it seemed to her that she could not swallow her pride. Ardessa grew yellower within the hour. Over and over in her mind she bade O'Mally a cold adieu and minced out past the grand old man at the desk for the last time. But each exit she rehearsed made her feel sorrier for herself. She thought over all the offices she knew, but she realized that she could never meet their inexorable standards of efficiency.

While she was bitterly deliberating, O'Mally himself wandered in, rattling his keys nervously in his pocket. He shut the door behind him.

"Now, you're going to come through with this all right, aren't you, Miss Devine? I want Henderson to get over the notion that my people over here are stuck up and think the business department are old shoes. That's where we get our money from, as he often reminds me. You'll be the best-paid girl over there; no reduction, of course. You don't want to go wandering off to some new office where personality doesn't count for anything." He sat down confidentially on the edge of her desk. "Do you, now, Miss Devine?"

Ardessa simpered tearfully as she replied.

"Mr. O'Mally," she brought out, "you'll soon find that Becky is not the sort of girl to meet people for you when you are away. I don't see how you can think of letting her."

"That's one thing I want to change, Miss Devine. You're too soft-handed with the has-beens and the never-was-ers. You're too much of a lady for this rough game. Nearly everybody who comes in here wants to sell us a gold-brick, and you treat them as if they were bringing in wedding presents. Becky is as rough as sandpaper, and she'll clear out a lot of dead wood." O'Mally rose, and tapped Ardessa's shrinking shoulder. "Now, be a sport and go through with it, Miss Devine. I'll see that you don't lose. Henderson thinks you'll refuse to do his work, so I want you to get moved in there before he comes back from lunch. I've had a desk put in his office for you. Miss Kalski is in the bookkeeper's room half the time now."

Rena Kalski was amazed that afternoon when a line of office boys entered, carrying Miss Devine's effects, and when Ardessa herself coldly followed them. After Ardessa had arranged her desk, Miss Kalski went over to her and told her about some matters of routine very good-naturedly. Ardessa looked pretty badly shaken up, and Rena bore no grudges.

"When you want the dope on the correspondence with the paper men, don't bother to look it up. I've got it all in my head, and I can save time for you. If he wants you to go over the printing bills every week, you'd better let me help you with that for a while. I can stay almost any afternoon. It's quite a trick to figure out the plates and over-time charges till you get used to it. I've worked out a quick method that saves trouble."

When Henderson came in at three he found Ardessa, chilly, but civil, awaiting his instructions. He knew she disapproved of his tastes and his manners, but he didn't mind. What interested and amused him was that Rena Kalski, whom he had always thought as cold-blooded as an adding-machine, seemed to be making a hair-mattress of herself to break Ardessa's fall.

At five o'clock, when Ardessa rose to go, the business manager said breezily:

"See you at nine in the morning, Miss Devine. We begin on the stroke."

Ardessa faded out of the door, and Miss Kalski's slender back squirmed with amusement.

"I never thought to hear such words spoken," she admitted; "but I guess she'll limber up all right. The atmosphere is bad over there. They get moldy."

After the next monthly luncheon of the heads of departments, O'Mally said to Henderson, as he feed the coat-boy:

"By the way, how are you making it with the bartered bride?"

Henderson smashed on his Panama as he said: "Any time you want her back, don't be delicate." But O'Mally shook his red head and laughed. "Oh, I'm no Indian giver!"

Her Boss

I

Paul Wanning opened the front door of his house in Orange, closed it softly behind him, and stood looking about the hall as he drew off his gloves.

Nothing was changed there since last night, and yet he stood gazing about him with an interest which a long-married man does not often feel in his own reception hall. The rugs, the two pillars, the Spanish tapestry chairs, were all the same. The Venus di Medici stood on her column as usual and there, at the end of the hall (opposite the front door), was the full-length portrait of Mrs. Wanning, maturely blooming forth in an evening gown, signed with the name of a French painter who seemed purposely to have made his signature indistinct. Though the signature was largely what one paid for, one couldn't ask him to do it over.

In the dining room the colored man was moving about the table set for dinner, under the electric cluster. The candles had not yet been lighted. Wanning watched him with a homesick feeling in his heart. They had had Sam a long while, twelve years, now. His warm hall, the lighted dining-room, the drawing room where only the flicker of the wood fire played upon the shining surfaces of many objects — they seemed to Wanning like a haven of refuge. It had never occurred to him that his house was too full of things. He often said, and he believed, that the women of his household had "perfect taste." He had paid for these objects, sometimes with difficulty, but always with pride. He carried a heavy life-insurance and permitted himself to spend most of the income from a good law practise. He wished, during his life-time, to enjoy the benefits of his wife's discriminating extravagance.

Yesterday Wanning's doctor had sent him to a specialist. Today the specialist, after various laboratory tests, had told him most disconcerting things about the state of very necessary, but hitherto wholly uninteresting, organs of his body.

The information pointed to something incredible; insinuated that his residence in this house was only temporary; that he, whose time was so full, might have to leave not only his house and his office and his club, but a world with which he was extremely well satisfied — the only world he knew anything about.

Wanning unbuttoned his overcoat, but did not take it off. He stood folding his muffler slowly and carefully. What he did not understand was, how he could go while other people stayed. Sam would be moving about the table like this, Mrs. Wanning and her daughters would be dressing upstairs, when he would not be coming home to dinner any more; when he would not, indeed, be dining anywhere.

Sam, coming to turn on the parlor lights, saw Wanning and stepped behind him to take his coat.

"Good evening, Mr. Wanning, sah, excuse me.

You entahed so quietly, sah, I didn't heah you."

The master of the house slipped out of his coat and went languidly upstairs.

He tapped at the door of his wife's room, which stood ajar.

"Come in, Paul," she called from her dressing table.

She was seated, in a violet dressing gown, giving the last touches to her coiffure, both arms lifted. They were firm and white, like her neck and shoulders. She was a handsome woman of fifty-five, — still a woman, not an old person, Wanning told himself, as he kissed her cheek. She was heavy in figure, to be sure, but she had kept, on the whole, presentable outlines. Her complexion was good, and she wore less false hair than either of her daughters.

Wanning himself was five years older, but his sandy hair did not show the gray in it, and since his mustache had begun to grow white he kept it clipped so short that it was unobtrusive. His fresh skin made him look younger than he was. Not long ago he had overheard the stenographers in his law office discussing the ages of their employers. They had put him down at fifty, agreeing that his two partners must be considerably older than he — which was not the case. Wanning had an especially kindly feeling for the little new girl, a copyist, who had exclaimed that "Mr. Wanning couldn't be fifty; he seemed so boyish!"

Wanning lingered behind his wife, looking at her in the mirror.

"Well, did you tell the girls, Julia?" he asked, trying to speak casually.

Mrs. Wanning looked up and met his eyes in the glass. "The girls?"

She noticed a strange expression come over his face.

"About your health, you mean? Yes, dear, but I tried not to alarm them. They feel dreadfully. I'm going to have a talk with Dr. Seares myself. These specialists are all alarmists, and I've often heard of his frightening people."

She rose and took her husband's arm, drawing him toward the fireplace.

"You are not going to let this upset you, Paul? If you take care of yourself, everything will come out all right. You have always been so strong. One has only to look at you."

"Did you," Wanning asked, "say anything to Harold?"

"Yes, of course. I saw him in town today, and he agrees with me that Seares draws the worst conclusions possible. He says even the young men are always being told the most terrifying things. Usually they laugh at the doctors and do as they please. You certainly don't look like a sick man, and you don't feel like one, do you?"

She patted his shoulder, smiled at him encouragingly, and rang for the maid to come and hook her dress.

When the maid appeared at the door, Wanning went out through the bathroom to his own sleeping chamber. He was too much dispirited to put on a dinner coat, though such remissness was always noticed. He sat down and waited for the sound of the gong, leaving his door open, on the chance that perhaps one of his daughters would come in.

When Wanning went down to dinner he found his wife already at her chair, and the table laid for four.

"Harold," she explained, "is not coming home. He has to attend a first night in town."

A moment later their two daughters entered, obviously "dressed." They both wore earrings and masses of hair. The daughters' names were Roma and Florence, — Roma, Firenze, one of the young men who came to the house often, but not often enough, had called them. Tonight they were going to a rehearsal of "The Dances of the Nations," — a benefit performance in which Miss Roma was to lead the Spanish dances, her sister the Grecian.

The elder daughter had often been told that her name suited her admirably. She looked, indeed, as we are apt to think the unrestrained beauties of later Rome must have looked, — but as their portrait busts emphatically declare they did not. Her head was massive, her lips full and crimson, her eyes large and heavy-lidded, her forehead low. At costume balls and in living pictures she was always Semiramis, or Poppea, or Theodora. Barbaric accessories brought out something cruel and even rather brutal in her handsome face. The men who were attracted to her were somehow afraid of her.

Florence was slender, with a long, graceful neck, a restless head, and a flexible mouth — discontent lurked about the corners of it. Her shoulders were pretty, but her neck and arms were too thin. Roma was always struggling to keep within a certain weight — her chin and upper arms grew persistently more solid — and Florence was always striving to attain a certain weight. Wanning used sometimes to wonder why these disconcerting fluctuations could not go the other way; why Roma could not melt away as easily as did her sister, who had to be sent to Palm Beach to save

672

the precious pounds.

"I don't see why you ever put Rickie Allen in charge of the English country dances," Florence said to her sister, as they sat down. "He knows the figures, of course, but he has no real style."

Roma looked annoyed. Rickie Allen was one of the men who came to the house almost often enough.

"He is absolutely to be depended upon, that's why," she said firmly.

"I think he is just right for it, Florence," put in Mrs. Wanning. "It's remarkable he should feel that he can give up the time; such a busy man. He must be very much interested in the movement."

Florence's lip curled drolly under her soup spoon. She shot an amused glance at her mother's dignity.

"Nothing doing," her keen eyes seemed to say.

Though Florence was nearly thirty and her sister a little beyond, there was, seriously, nothing doing. With so many charms and so much preparation, they never, as Florence vulgarly said, quite pulled it off. They had been rushed, time and again, and Mrs. Wanning had repeatedly steeled herself to bear the blow. But the young men went to follow a career in Mexico or the Philippines, or moved to Yonkers, and escaped without a mortal wound.

Roma turned graciously to her father.

"I met Mr. Lane at the Holland House today, where I was lunching with the Burtons, father. He asked about you, and when I told him you were not so well as usual, he said he would call you up. He wants to tell you about some doctor he discovered in Iowa, who cures everything with massage and hot water. It sounds freakish, but

Mr. Lane is a very clever man, isn't he?"

"Very," assented Wanning.

"I should think he must be!" sighed Mrs. Wanning. "How in the world did he make all that money, Paul? He didn't seem especially promising years ago, when we used to see so much of them."

"Corporation business. He's attorney for the P. L. and G.," murmured her husband.

"What a pile he must have!" Florence watched the old negro's slow movements with restless eyes. "Here is Jenny, a Contessa, with a glorious palace in Genoa that her father must have bought her. Surely Aldrini had nothing. Have you seen the baby count's pictures, Roma? They're very cunning. I should think you'd go to Genoa and visit Jenny."

"We must arrange that, Roma. It's such an opportunity." Though Mrs. Wanning addressed her daughter, she looked at her husband. "You would get on so well among their friends. When Count Aldrini was here you spoke Italian much better than poor Jenny. I remember when we entertained him, he could scarcely say anything to her at all."

Florence tried to call up an answering flicker of amusement upon her sister's calm, well-bred face. She thought her mother was rather outdoing herself tonight, — since Aldrini had at least managed to say the one important thing to Jenny, somehow, somewhere. Jenny Lane had been Roma's friend and schoolmate, and the Count was an ephemeral hope in Orange. Mrs. Wanning was one of the first matrons to declare that she had no prejudices against foreigners, and at the dinners that were given for the Count, Roma was always put next him to act as interpreter.

Roma again turned to her father.

674

"If I were you, dear, I would let Mr. Lane tell me about his doctor. New discoveries are often made by queer people."

Roma's voice was low and sympathetic; she never lost her dignity.

Florence asked if she might have her coffee in her room, while she dashed off a note, and she ran upstairs humming "Bright Lights" and wondering how she was going to stand her family until the summer scattering. Why could Roma never throw off her elegant reserve and call things by their names? She sometimes thought she might like her sister, if she would only come out in the open and howl about her disappointments.

Roma, drinking her coffee deliberately, asked her father if they might have the car early, as they wanted to pick up Mr. Allen and Mr. Rydberg on their way to rehearsal.

Wanning said certainly. Heaven knew he was not stingy about his car, though he could never quite forget that in his day it was the young men who used to call for the girls when they went to rehearsals.

"You are going with us, Mother?" Roma asked as they rose.

"I think so dear. Your father will want to go to bed early, and I shall sleep better if I go out. I am going to town tomorrow to pour tea for Harold. We must get him some new silver, Paul. I am quite ashamed of his spoons."

Harold, the only son, was a playwright — as yet "unproduced" — and he had a studio in Washington Square.

A half-hour later, Wanning was alone in his library. He would not permit himself to feel aggrieved. What was more commendable than a mother's interest in her children's pleasures? Moreover, it was his wife's way of following things up, of never letting die grass grow under her feet, that had helped to push him along in the world. She was more ambitious than he, — that had been good for him. He was naturally indolent, and Julia's childlike desire to possess material objects, to buy what other people were buying, had been the spur that made him go after business. It had, moreover, made his house the attractive place he believed it to be.

"Suppose," his wife sometimes said to him when the bills came in from Céleste or Mme. Blanche, "suppose you had homely daughters; how would you like that?"

He wouldn't have liked it. When he went anywhere with his three ladies, Wanning always felt very well done by. He had no complaint to make about them, or about anything. That was why it seemed so unreasonable — He felt along his back incredulously with his hand. Harold, of course, was a trial; but among all his business friends, he knew scarcely one who had a promising boy.

The house was so still that Wanning could hear a faint, metallic tinkle from the butler's pantry. Old Sam was washing up the silver, which he put away himself every night.

Wanning rose and walked aimlessly down the hall and out through the dining-room.

"Any Apollinaris on ice, Sam? I'm not feeling very well tonight."

The old colored man dried his hands.

"Yessah, Mistah Wanning. Have a little rye with it, sah?"

"No, thank you, Sam. That's one of the things I can't do any more. I've been to see a big doctor in

676

the city, and he tells me there's something seri-ously wrong with me. My kidneys have sort of gone back on me."

It was a satisfaction to Wanning to name the organ that had betrayed him, while all the rest of him was so sound.

Sam was immediately interested. He shook his grizzled head and looked full of wisdom.

"Don't seem like a gen'leman of such a temper-ate life ought to have anything wrong thar, sah."

"No, it doesn't, does it?"

Wanning leaned against the china closet and talked to Sam for nearly half an hour. The special-ist who condemned him hadn't seemed half so much interested. There was not a detail about the examination and the laboratory tests in which Sam did not show the deepest concern. He kept asking Wanning if he could remember "straining himself" when he was a young man.

"I've knowed a strain like that to sleep in a man for yeahs and yeahs, and then come back on him, 'deed I have," he said, mysteriously. "An' again, it might be you got a floatin' kidney, sah. Aftah dey once teah loose, dey sometimes don't make no trouble for quite a while."

When Wanning went to his room he did not go to bed. He sat up until he heard the voices of his wife and daughters in the hall below. His own bed somehow frightened him. In all the years he had lived in this house he had never before looked about his room, at that bed, with the thought that he might one day be trapped there, and might not get out again. He had been ill, of course, but his room had seemed a particularly pleasant place for a sick man; sunlight, flowers, — agreeable, well-dressed women coming in and out.

Now there was something sinister about the bed itself, about its position, and its relation to the rest of the furniture.

II

The next morning, on his way downtown, Wanning got off the subway train at Astor Place and walked over to Washington Square. He climbed three flights of stairs and knocked at his son's studio. Harold, dressed, with his stick and gloves in his hand, opened the door. He was just going over to the Brevoort for breakfast. He greeted his father with the cordial familiarity practised by all the "boys" of his set, clapped him on the shoulder and said in his light, tonsilitis voice:

"Come in, Governor, how delightful! I haven't had a call from you in a long time."

He threw his hat and gloves on the writing table. He was a perfect gentleman, even with his father.

Florence said the matter with Harold was that he had heard people say he looked like Byron, and stood for it.

What Harold would stand for in such matters was, indeed, the best definition of him. When he read his play "The Street Walker" in drawing rooms and one lady told him it had the poetic symbolism of Tchekhov, and another said that it suggested the biting realism of Brieux, he never, in his most secret thoughts, questioned the acumen of either lady. Harold's speech, even if you heard it in the next room and could not see him, told you that he had no sense of the absurd, — a throaty staccato, with never a downward inflection, trustfully striving to please.

"Just going out?" his father asked. "I won't keep you. Your mother told you I had a discouraging

678

session with Seares?"

"So awfully sorry you've had this bother, Governor; just as sorry as I can be. No question about it's coming out all right, but it's a downright nuisance, your having to diet and that sort of thing. And I suppose you ought to follow directions, just to make us all feel comfortable, oughtn't you?" Harold spoke with fluent sympathy.

Wanning sat down on the arm of a chair and shook his head. "Yes, they do recommend a diet, but they don't promise much from it."

Harold laughed precipitately. "Delicious! All doctors are, aren't they? So profound and oracular! The medicine-man; it's quite the same idea, you see; with tom-toms."

Wanning knew that Harold meant something subtle, — one of the subtleties which he said were only spoiled by being explained — so he came bluntly to one of the issues he had in mind.

"I would like to see you settled before I quit the harness, Harold."

Harold was absolutely tolerant.

He took out his cigarette case and burnished it with his handkerchief.

"I perfectly understand your point of view, dear Governor, but perhaps you don't altogether get mine. Isn't it so? I am settled. What you mean by being settled, would unsettle me, completely. I'm cut out for just such an existence as this; to live four floors up in an attic, get my own breakfast, and have a charwoman to do for me. I should be awfully bored with an establishment. I'm quite content with a little diggings like this."

Wanning's eyes fell. Somebody had to pay the rent of even such modest quarters as contented Harold, but to say so would be rude, and Harold himself was never rude. Wanning did not, this morning, feel equal to hearing a statement of his son's uncommercial ideals.

"I know," he said hastily. "But now we're up against hard facts, my boy. I did not want to alarm your mother, but I've had a time limit put on me, and it's not a very long one."

Harold threw away the cigarette he had just lighted in a burst of indignation.

"That's the sort of thing I consider criminal, Father, absolutely criminal! What doctor has a right to suggest such a thing? Seares himself may be knocked out tomorrow. What have laboratory tests got to do with a man's will to live? The force of that depends upon his entire personality, not on any organ or pair of organs."

Harold thrust his hands in his pockets and walked up and down, very much stirred. "Really, I have a very poor opinion of scientists. They ought to be made serve an apprenticeship in art, to get some conception of the power of human motives. Such brutality!"

Harold's plays dealt with the grimmest and most depressing matters, but he himself was always agreeable, and he insisted upon high cheerfulness as the correct tone of human intercourse.

Wanning rose and turned to go. There was, in Harold, simply no reality, to which one could break through. The young man took up his hat and gloves.

"Must you go? Let me step along with you to the sub. The walk will do me good."

Harold talked agreeably all the way to Astor Place. His father heard little of what he said, but he rather liked his company and his wish to be pleasant.

Wanning went to his club for luncheon, meaning to spend the afternoon with some of his friends who had retired from business and who read the papers there in the empty hours between two and seven. He got no satisfaction, however. When he tried to tell these men of his present predicament, they began to describe ills of their own in which he could not feel interested. Each one of them had a treacherous organ of which he spoke with animation, almost with pride, as if it were a crafty business competitor whom he was constantly outwitting. Each had a doctor, too, for whom he was ardently soliciting business. They wanted either to telephone their doctor and make an appointment for Wanning, or to take him then and there to the consulting room. When he did not accept these invitations, they lost interest in him and remembered engagements. He called a taxi and returned to the offices of McQuiston, Wade, and Wanning.

Settled at his desk, Wanning decided that he would not go home to dinner, but would stay at the office and dictate a long letter to an old college friend who lived in Wyoming. He could tell Douglas Brown things that he had not succeeded in getting to any one else. Brown, out in the Wind River mountains, couldn't defend himself, couldn't slap Wanning on the back and tell him to gather up the sunbeams.

He called up his house in Orange to say that he would not be home until late. Roma answered the telephone. He spoke mournfully, but she was not disturbed by it.

"Very well, Father. Don't get too tired," she said in her well modulated voice.

When Wanning was ready to dictate his letter,

he looked out from his private office into the reception room and saw that his stenographer in her hat and gloves, and furs of the newest cut, was just leaving.

"Goodnight, Mr. Wanning," she said, drawing down her dotted veil.

Had there been important business letters to be got off on the night mail, he would have felt that he could detain her, but not for anything personal. Miss Doane was an expert legal stenographer, and she knew her value. The slightest delay in dispatching office business annoyed her. Letters that were not signed until the next morning awoke her deepest contempt. She was scrupulous in professional etiquette, and Wanning felt that their relations, though pleasant, were scarcely cordial.

As Miss Doane's trim figure disappeared through the outer door, little Annie Wooley, the copyist, came in from the stenographers' room. Her hat was pinned over one ear, and she was scrambling into her coat as she came, holding her gloves in her teeth and her battered handbag in the fist that was already through a sleeve.

"Annie, I wanted to dictate a letter. You were just leaving, weren't you?"

"Oh, I don't mind!" she answered cheerfully, and pulling off her old coat, threw it on a chair. "I'll get my book."

She followed him into his room and sat down by a table, — though she wrote with her book on her knee.

Wanning had several times kept her after office hours to take his private letters for him, and she had always been good-natured about it. On each occasion, when he gave her a dollar to get her dinner, she protested, laughing, and saying that

682

she could never eat so much as that.

She seemed a happy sort of little creature, didn't pout when she was scolded, and giggled about her own mistakes in spelling. She was plump and undersized, always dodging under the elbows of taller people and clattering about on high heels, much run over. She had bright black eyes and fuzzy black hair in which, despite Miss Doane's reprimands, she often stuck her pencil. She was the girl who couldn't believe that Wanning was fifty, and he had liked her ever since he overheard that conversation.

Tilting back his chair — he never assumed this position when he dictated to Miss Doane — Wanning began: "To Mr. D. E. Brown, South Forks, Wyoming."

He shaded his eyes with his hand and talked off a long letter to this man who would be sorry that his mortal frame was breaking up. He recalled to him certain fine months they had spent together on the Wind River when they were young men, and said he sometimes wished that like D. E. Brown, he had claimed his freedom in a big country where the wheels did not grind a man as hard as they did in New York. He had spent all these years hustling about and getting ready to live the way he wanted to live, and now he had a puncture the doctors couldn't mend. What was the use of it?

Wanning's thoughts were fixed on the trout streams and the great silver-firs in the canyons of the Wind River Mountains, when he was disturbed by a soft, repeated sniffling. He looked out between his fingers. Little Annie, carried away by his eloquence, was fairly panting to make dots and dashes fast enough, and she was sopping her

683

eyes with an unpresentable, end-of-the-day hand-kerchief.

Wanning rambled on in his dictation. Why was she crying? What did it matter to her? He was a man who said good-morning to her, who some-times took an hour of the precious few she had left at the end of the day and then complained about her bad spelling. When the letter was finished, he handed her a new two dollar bill.

"I haven't got any change tonight; and anyhow, I'd like you to eat a whole lot. I'm on a diet, and I want to see everybody else eat."

Annie tucked her notebook under her arm and stood looking at the bill which she had not taken up from the table.

"I don't like to be paid for taking letters to your friends, Mr. Wanning," she said impulsively. "I can run personal letters off between times. It ain't as if I needed the money," she added carelessly.

"Get along with you! Anybody who is eighteen years old and has a sweet tooth needs money, all they can get."

Annie giggled and darted out with the bill in her hand.

Wanning strolled aimlessly after her into the reception room.

"Let me have that letter before lunch tomorrow, please, and be sure that nobody sees it." He stopped and frowned. "I don't look very sick, do I?"

"I should say you don't!" Annie got her coat on after considerable tugging. "Why don't you call in a specialist? My mother called a specialist for my father before he died."

"Oh, is your father dead?"

"I should say he is! He was a painter by trade,

684

and he fell off a seventy-foot stack into the East River. Mother couldn't get anything out of the company, because he wasn't buckled. He lingered for four months, so I know all about taking care of sick people. I was attending business college then, and sick as he was, he used to give me dictation for practise. He made us all go into professions; the girls, too. He didn't like us to just run."

Wanning would have liked to keep Annie and hear more about her family, but it was nearly seven o'clock, and he knew he ought, in mercy, to let her go. She was the only person to whom he had talked about his illness who had been frank and honest with him, who had looked at him with eyes that concealed nothing. When he broke the news of his condition to his partners that morning, they shut him off as if he were uttering indecent ravings. All day they had met him with a hurried, abstracted manner. McQuiston and Wade went out to lunch together, and he knew what they were thinking, perhaps talking, about. Wanning had brought into the firm valuable business, but he was less enterprising than either of his partners.

III

In the early summer Wanning's family scattered. Roma swallowed her pride and sailed for Genoa to visit the Contessa Jenny. Harold went to Cornish to be in an artistic atmosphere. Mrs. Wanning and Florence took a cottage at York Harbor where Wanning was supposed to join them whenever he could get away from town. He did not often get away. He felt most at ease among his accustomed surroundings. He kept his car in the city and went back and forth from his office to

685

the club where he was living. Old Sam, his butler, came in from Orange every night to put his clothes in order and make him comfortable.

Wanning began to feel that he would not tire of his office in a hundred years. Although he did very little work, it was pleasant to go down town every morning when the streets were crowded, the sky clear, and the sunshine bright. From the windows of his private office he could see the harbor and watch the ocean liners come down the North River and go out to sea.

While he read his mail, he often looked out and wondered why he had been so long indifferent to that extraordinary scene of human activity and hopefulness. How had a short-lived race of beings the energy and courage valiantly to begin enterprises which they could follow for only a few years; to throw up towers and build sea-monsters and found great businesses, when the frailest of the materials with which they worked, the paper upon which they wrote, the ink upon their pens, had more permanence in this world than they? All this material rubbish lasted. The linen clothing and cosmetics of the Egyptians had lasted. It was only the human flame that certainly, certainly went out. Other things had a fighting chance; they might meet with mishap and be destroyed, they might not. But the human creature who gathered and shaped and hoarded and foolishly loved these things, he had no chance — absolutely none. Wanning's cane, his hat, his topcoat, might go from beggar to beggar and knock about in this world for another fifty years or so; but not he.

In the late afternoon he never hurried to leave his office now. Wonderful sunsets burned over the North River, wonderful stars trembled up among

686

the towers; more wonderful than anything he could hurry away to. One of his windows looked directly down upon the spire of Old Trinity, with the green churchyard and the pale sycamores far below. Wanning often dropped into the church when he was going out to lunch; not because he was trying to make his peace with Heaven, but because the church was old and restful and familiar, because it and its gravestones had sat in the same place for a long while. He bought flowers from the street boys and kept them on his desk, which his partners thought strange behavior, and which Miss Doane considered a sign that he was failing.

But there were graver things than bouquets for Miss Doane and the senior partner to ponder over.

The senior partner, McQuiston, in spite of his silvery hair and mustache and his important church connections, had rich natural taste for scandal. — After Mr. Wade went away for his vacation, in May, Wanning took Annie Wooley out of the copying room, put her at a desk in his private office, and raised her pay to eighteen dollars a week, explaining to McQuiston that for the summer months he would need a secretary. This explanation satisfied neither McQuiston nor Miss Doane.

Annie was also paid for overtime, and although Wanning attended to very little of the office business now, there was a great deal of overtime. Miss Doane was, of course, "above" questioning a chit like Annie; but what was he doing with his time and his new secretary, she wanted to know?

If anyone had told her that Wanning was writing a book, she would have said bitterly that it was just like him. In his youth Wanning had hankered for the pen. When he studied law, he had intended to combine that profession with some tempting form of authorship. Had he remained a bachelor, he would have been an unenterprising literary lawyer to the end of his days. It was his wife's restlessness and her practical turn of mind that had made him a money-getter. His illness seemed to bring back to him the illusions with which he left college.

As soon as his family were out of the way and he shut up the Orange house, he began to dictate his autobiography to Annie Wooley. It was not only the story of his life, but an expression of all his theories and opinions, and a commentary on the fifty years of events which he could remember.

Fortunately, he was able to take great interest in this undertaking. He had the happiest convictions about the clear-cut style he was developing and his increasing felicity in phrasing. He meant to publish the work handsomely, at his own expense and under his own name. He rather enjoyed the thought of how greatly disturbed Harold would be. He and Harold differed in their estimates of books. All the solid works which made up Wanning's library, Harold considered beneath contempt. Anybody, he said, could do that sort of thing.

When Wanning could not sleep at night, he turned on the light beside his bed and made notes on the chapter he meant to dictate the next day.

When he returned to the office after lunch, he gave instructions that he was not to be interrupted by telephone calls, and shut himself up with his secretary.

After he had opened all the windows and taken off his coat, he fell to dictating. He found it a delightful occupation, the solace of each day. Often he had sudden fits of tiredness; then he would lie down on the leather sofa and drop asleep, while Annie read "The Leopard's Spots" until he awoke.

Like many another business man Wanning had relied so long on stenographers that the operation of writing with a pen had become laborious to him. When he undertook it, he wanted to cut everything short. But walking up and down his private office, with the strong afternoon sun pouring in at his windows, a fresh air stirring, all the people and boats moving restlessly down there, he could say things he wanted to say. It was like living his life over again.

He did not miss his wife or his daughters. He had become again the mild, contemplative youth he was in college, before he had a profession and a family to grind for, before the two needs which shape our destiny had made of him pretty much what they make of every man.

At five o'clock Wanning sometimes went out for a cup of tea and took Annie along. He felt dull and discouraged as soon as he was alone. So long as Annie was with him, he could keep a grip on his own thoughts. They talked about what he had just been dictating to her. She found that he liked to be questioned, and she tried to be greatly interested in it all.

After tea, they went back to the office. Occasionally Wanning lost track of time and kept Annie until it grew dark. He knew he had old McQuiston guessing, but he didn't care. One day the senior partner came to him with a reproving air.

"I am afraid Miss Doane is leaving us, Paul. She feels that Miss Wooley's promotion is irregular."

"How is that any business of hers, I'd like to know? She has all my legal work. She is always disagreeable enough about doing anything else."

McQuiston's puffy red face went a shade darker.

"Miss Doane has a certain professional pride; a strong feeling for office organization. She doesn't care to fill an equivocal position. I don't know that I blame her. She feels that there is something not quite regular about the confidence you seem to place in this inexperienced young woman."

Wanning pushed back his chair.

"I don't care a hang about Miss Doane's sense of propriety. I need a stenographer who will carry out my instructions. I've carried out Miss Doane's long enough. I've let that schoolma'am hector me for years. She can go when she pleases."

That night McQuiston wrote to his partner that things were in a bad way, and they would have to keep an eye on Wanning. He had been seen at the theatre with his new stenographer.

That was true. Wanning had several times taken Annie to the Palace on Saturday afternoon. When all his acquaintances were off motoring or playing golf, when the down-town offices and even the streets were deserted, it amused him to watch a foolish show with a delighted, cheerful little person beside him.

Beyond her generosity, Annie had no shining merits of character, but she had the gift of thinking well of everything, and wishing well. When she was there Wanning felt as if there were someone who cared whether this was a good or a bad day with him. Old Sam, too, was like that. While the old black man put him to bed and made him comfortable, Wanning could talk to him as he talked to little Annie. Even if he dwelt upon his

690

illness, in plain terms, in detail, he did not feel as if he were imposing on them.

People like Sam and Annie admitted misfortune, — admitted it almost cheerfully. Annie and her family did not consider illness or any of its hard facts vulgar or indecent. It had its place in their scheme of life, as it had not in that of Wanning's friends.

Annie came out of a typical poor family of New York. Of eight children, only four lived to grow up. In such families the stream of life is broad enough, but runs shallow. In the children, vitality is exhausted early. The roots do not go down into anything very strong. Illness and deaths and funerals, in her own family and in those of her friends, had come at frequent intervals in Annie's life. Since they had to be, she and her sisters made the best of them. There was something to be got out of funerals, even, if they were managed right. They kept people in touch with old friends who had moved uptown, and revived kindly feelings.

Annie had often given up things she wanted because there was sickness at home, and now she was patient with her boss. What he paid her for overtime work by no means made up to her what she lost.

Annie was not in the least thrifty, nor were any of her sisters. She had to make a living, but she was not interested in getting all she could for her time, or in laying up for the future. Girls like Annie know that the future is a very uncertain thing, and they feel no responsibility about it. The present is what they have — and it is all they have. If Annie missed a chance to go sailing with the plumber's son on Saturday afternoon, why, she missed it. As for the two dollars her boss gave her, she handed them over to her mother. Now that Annie was getting more money, one of her sisters quit a job she didn't like and was staying at home for a rest. That was all promotion meant to Annie.

The first time Annie's boss asked her to work on Saturday afternoon, she could not hide her disappointment. He suggested that they might knock off early and go to a show, or take a run in his car, but she grew tearful and said it would be hard to make her family understand. Wanning thought perhaps he could explain to her mother. He called his motor and took Annie home.

When his car stopped in front of the tenement house on Eighth Avenue, heads came popping out of the windows for six storys up, and all the neighbor women, in dressing sacks and wrappers, gazed down at the machine and at the couple alighting from it. A motor meant a wedding or the hospital.

The plumber's son, Willy Steen, came over from the corner saloon to see what was going on, and Annie introduced him at the doorstep.

Mrs. Wooley asked Wanning to come into the parlor and invited him to have a chair of ceremony between the folding bed and the piano.

Annie, nervous and tearful, escaped to the dining-room — the cheerful spot where the daughters visited with each other and with their friends. The parlor was a masked sleeping chamber and store room.

The plumber's son sat down on the sofa beside Mrs. Wooley, as if he were accustomed to share in the family councils. Mrs. Wooley waited expectant and kindly. She looked the sensible, hard-working woman that she was, and one could see she hadn't lived all her life on Eighth Avenue without learning a great deal.

Wanning explained to her that he was writing a book which he wanted to finish during the summer months when business was not so heavy. He was ill and could not work regularly. His secretary would have to take his dictation when he felt able to give it; must, in short, be a sort of companion to him. He would like to feel that she could go out in his car with him, or even to the theater, when he felt like it. It might have been better if he had engaged a young man for this work, but since he had begun it with Annie, he would like to keep her if her mother was willing.

Mrs. Wooley watched him with friendly, searching eyes. She glanced at Willy Steen, who, wise in such distinctions, had decided that there was nothing shady about Annie's boss. He nodded his sanction.

"I don't want my girl to conduct herself in any such way as will prejudice her, Mr. Wanning," she said thoughtfully. "If you've got daughters, you know how that is. You've been liberal with Annie, and it's a good position for her. It's right she should go to business every day, and I want her to do her work right, but I like to have her home after working hours. I always think a young girl's time is her own after business hours, and I try not to burden them when they come home. I'm willing she should do your work as suits you, if it's her wish; but I don't like to press her. The good times she misses now, it's not you nor me, sir, that can make them up to her. These young things has their feelings."

"Oh, I don't want to press her, either," Wanning said hastily. "I simply want to know that you understand the situation. I've made her a little present in my will as a recognition that she is doing more for me than she is paid for."

"That's something above me, sir. We'll hope there won't be no question of wills for many years yet," Mrs. Wooley spoke heartily. "I'm glad if my girl can be of any use to you, just so she don't prejudice herself."

The plumber's son rose as if the interview were over.

"It's all right, Mama Wooley, don't you worry," he said.

He picked up his canvas cap and turned to Wanning. "You see, Annie ain't the sort of girl that would want to be spotted circulating around with a monied party her folks didn't know all about. She'd lose friends by it."

After this conversation Annie felt a great deal happier. She was still shy and a trifle awkward with poor Wanning when they were outside the office building, and she missed the old freedom of her Saturday afternoons. But she did the best she could, and Willy Steen tried to make it up to her.

In Annie's absence he often came in of an afternoon to have a cup of tea and a sugar-bun with Mrs. Wooley and the daughter who was "resting." As they sat at the dining-room table, they discussed Annie's employer, his peculiarities, his health, and what he had told Mrs. Wooley about his will.

Mrs. Wooley said she sometimes felt afraid he might disinherit his children, as rich people often did, and make talk; but she hoped for the best. Whatever came to Annie, she prayed it might not be in the form of taxable property.

IV

Late in September Wanning grew suddenly worse. His family hurried home, and he was put to bed in his house in Orange. He kept asking the doctors when he could get back to the office, but he lived only eight days.

The morning after his father's funeral, Harold went to the office to consult Wanning's partners and to read the will. Everything in the will was as it should be. There were no surprises except a codicil in the form of a letter to Mrs. Wanning, dated July 8th, requesting that out of the estate she should pay the sum of one thousand dollars to his stenographer, Annie Wooley, "in recognition of her faithful services."

"I thought Miss Doane was my father's stenographer," Harold exclaimed.

Alec McQuiston looked embarrassed and spoke in a low, guarded tone.

"She was, for years. But this spring, —" he hesitated.

McQuiston loved a scandal. He leaned across his desk toward Harold.

"This spring your father put this little girl, Miss Wooley, a copyist, utterly inexperienced, in Miss Doane's place. Miss Doane was indignant and left us. The change made comment here in the office. It was slightly — No, I will be frank with you, Harold, it was very irregular."

Harold also looked grave. "What could my father have meant by such a request as this to my mother?"

The silver haired senior partner flushed and spoke as if he were trying to break something gently.

"I don't understand it, my boy. But I think, indeed I prefer to think, that your father was not quite himself all this summer. A man like your father does not, in his right senses, find pleasure in the society of an ignorant, common little girl. He does not make a practise of keeping her at the office after hours, often until eight o'clock, or take her to restaurants and to the theater with him; not, at least, in a slanderous city like New York."

Harold flinched before McQuiston's meaning gaze and turned aside in pained silence. He knew, as a dramatist, that there are dark chapters in all men's lives, and this but too clearly explained why his father had stayed in town all summer instead of joining his family.

McQuiston asked if he should ring for Annie Wooley.

Harold drew himself up. "No. Why should I see her? I prefer not to. But with your permission, Mr. McQuiston, I will take charge of this request to my mother. It could only give her pain, and might awaken doubts in her mind."

"We hardly know," murmured the senior partner, "where an investigation would lead us. Technically, of course, I cannot agree with you. But if, as one of the executors of the will, you wish to assume personal responsibility for this bequest, under the circumstances — irregularities beget irregularities."

"My first duty to my father," said Harold, "is to protect my mother."

That afternoon McQuiston called Annie Wooley into his private office and told her that her services would not be needed any longer, and that in lieu of notice the clerk would give her two weeks' salary.

"Can I call up here for references?" Annie asked.

"Certainly. But you had better ask for me, personally. You must know there has been some criticism of you here in the office, Miss Wooley."

"What about?" Annie asked boldly.

"Well, a young girl like you cannot render so much personal service to her employer as you did to Mr. Wanning without causing unfavorable comment. To be blunt with you, for your own good, my dear young lady, your services to your employer should terminate in the office, and at the close of office hours. Mr. Wanning was a very sick man and his judgment was at fault, but you should have known what a girl in your station can do and what she cannot do."

The vague discomfort of months flashed up in little Annie. She had no mind to stand by and be lectured without having a word to say for herself.

"Of course he was sick, poor man!" she burst out. "Not as anybody seemed much upset about it. I wouldn't have given up my half-holidays for anybody if they hadn't been sick, no matter what they paid me. There wasn't anything in it for me."

McQuiston raised his hand warningly.

"That will do, young lady. But when you get another place, remember this: it is never your duty to entertain or to provide amusement for your employer."

He gave Annie a look which she did not clearly understand, although she pronounced him a nasty old man as she hustled on her hat and jacket.

When Annie reached home she found Willy Steen sitting with her mother and sister at the dining-room table. This was the first day that Annie had gone to the office since Wanning's death, and her family awaited her return with suspense.

"Hello yourself," Annie called as she came in and threw her handbag into an empty armchair.

"You're off early, Annie," said her mother gravely. "Has the will been read?"

"I guess so. Yes, I know it has. Miss Wilson got it out of the safe for them. The son came in. He's a pill."

"Was nothing said to you, daughter?"

"Yes, a lot. Please give me some tea, mother." Annie felt that her swagger was failing.

"Don't tantalize us, Ann," her sister broke in. "Didn't you get anything?"

"I got the mit, all right. And some back talk from the old man that I'm awful sore about."

Annie dashed away the tears and gulped her tea.

Gradually her mother and Willy drew the story from her. Willy offered at once to go to the office building and take his stand outside the door and never leave it until he had punched old Mr. Mc-Quiston's face. He rose as if to attend to it at once, but Mrs. Wooley drew him to his chair again and patted his arm.

"It would only start talk and get the girl in trouble, Willy. When it's lawyers, folks in our station is helpless. I certainly believed that man when he sat here; you heard him yourself. Such a gentleman as he looked."

Willy thumped his great fist, still in punching position, down on his knee.

"Never you be fooled again, Mama Wooley. You'll never get anything out of a rich guy that he ain't signed up in the courts for. Rich is tight. There's no exceptions."

Annie shook her head.

"I didn't want anything out of him. He was a nice, kind man, and he had his troubles, I guess.

He wasn't tight."

"Still," said Mrs. Wooley sadly, "Mr. Wanning had no call to hold out promises. I hate to be disappointed in a gentleman. You've had confining work for some time, daughter; a rest will do you good."